The

ENTIRELY
TRUE STORY
of the

FANTASTICAL
MESMERIST
NORA GREY

The
ENTIRELY
TRUE STORY
of the
FANTASTICAL
MESMERIST
NORA GREY

KATHLEEN KAUFMAN

KENSINGTON
PUBLISHING CORP.
kensingtonbooks.com

KENSINGTON BOOKS are published by

Kensington Publishing Corp.
900 Third Avenue
New York, NY 10022

All Kensington titles, imprints, and distributed lines are available at special quantity discounts for bulk purchases for sales promotion, premiums, fundraising, educational or institutional use. Special book excerpts or customized printings can also be created to fit specific needs. For details, write or phone the office of the Kensington Special Sales Manager: Kensington Publishing Corp., 900 Third Avenue, New York, NY 10022. Attn. Special Sales Department. Phone: 1-800-221-2647.

KENSINGTON and the K with book logo Reg. US Pat & TM Off.

Library of Congress Control Number: 2025934264

ISBN: 978-1-4967-5390-8

First Kensington Hardcover Edition: August 2025

ISBN: 978-1-4967-5392-2 (ebook)

10 9 8 7 6 5 4 3 2 1

Printed in the United States of America

The authorized representative in the EU for product safety and compliance
is eucomply OU, Parnu mnt 139b-14, Apt 123
Tallinn, Berlin 11317, hello@eucompliancepartner.com

To J.H. and Effie, please don't haunt me.

Part I

Nairna
Kirkcaldy
1900

Excerpt from A Scottish Girl—A Life in Spirit
by biographer Floradine Masters

Little is known of the early life of the great mesmerist and psychic Nora Grey beyond the basic reports of birth and stories told by those who claim to have known her as a girl. As with most that go on to greatness, the stories of Nora Grey's childhood have become the stuff of myth. A girl who was largely overlooked and by all accounts greatly neglected in her early years is suddenly remembered by all who ever saw her face and, in the true manner of legends, many who never did.

What we do know about Nora Grey's early years was that they were difficult and not atypical for many at this time in the Scottish countryside. Poverty was rampant, and her father, Tavish Grey, worked odd jobs, moving the pair from town to town. If it had not been for Nora Grey's extraordinary talents, the pair of them would have been lost in the collective history of the poor that is the landscape of all countries, in all times.

What is left is stories, from which we can hope to glean a bit of the truth.

Nairna

"Come, beloveds. Come and join us, come and join us." Tavish Liath's voice echoed off the corners of the cottage as the fire in the hearth crackled in defiance. "The spirits are waiting to be invited in, they watch through the glass windowpane, they scratch at the door. They are waiting for your word."

Silence filled the room. Lord Lennox sat closest to the hearth, his wife to his side, a stricken look on her face. The children huddled in the corner; in the dim light their wide eyes reflected the firelight in such a way they looked like a parliament of owls.

"Grady Lennox, do you invite the spirits into your house?" Tavish asked in a low voice, his eyes closed and arms skyward.

Lennox nodded stiffly. This hadn't been his idea. His wife, Elspeth, had taken ill last season and never quite recovered. And then little Maggie had died of the consumption in the spring, leaving one fewer set of owl eyes to watch the séance from the corner of the great room. Lennox had relented out of grief and fear, but it was clear to Nairna that he would rather not have eyes at the windowpane and scratching at the door. Her father had been paid five shillings already with a promise of five more plus the handful of coppers Lady Lennox had slipped into the pocket of Nairna's skirt when they entered the cottage. The Lennoxes weren't wealthy by Edinburgh standards, but here in the outlying villages they lived well enough. Lord Lennox had inherited his title from his father, along with a pile of debts and land that wouldn't grow a thistle in June. But still they kept up the appearance of prosperity, the cottage was well maintained, and it looked to be a real silver platter that sat over the hearth.

Tavish cast his daughter a look only she would discern and then began to chant in a low voice.

"*Teacht chun solais shìn.*"

Nairna knew that her father's grasp of the old language was limited; she only hoped it exceeded the Lennoxes'. She flinched to hear her father's rough words. She had studied the old ways with her Nań before they left for the road, but her father had always called it hogwash; English was the new way, he'd always said. That was until he realized a sprinkling of Gaelic added just the right authenticity and, for those who didn't know better, an air of mystery.

Lady Lennox looked as though she might pass clean out on the smooth dark wood table. Lord Lennox shifted uncomfortably and glanced at his children, who huddled in the corner, silent as mice. Nairna took a deep breath and shifted her leg in preparation.

"Come inside, *shìn*! Come in from the cold!" Her father began to shake from his feet to the top of his head, his midnight hair vibrating with his efforts. Nairna let out a deep sigh designed to draw the Lennoxes' attention away from her father. Then Nairna allowed her eyes to roll back so only the whites showed. It was a cheap parlor trick she'd learned in Aberdeen from the carnie folk but effective, nonetheless. Lady Lennox gasped as Tavish shook his leg with enough force to ring the tiny bells he had sewed into the inside pocket. The table jostled and shook as Lord Lennox began to rise either in fear or protest; Nairna took the cue and popped her knee joint out and in. The sound was faint but persistent, and it drove Lord Lennox back into his seat.

Tavish stopped his shaking and motioned to the door.

"She has arrived; your child is here. Oh *shìn*! What do you wish to say to your loving parents?"

Nairna stopped the knocking, her hands reaching in front of her and her eyes rolling back to their normal position. It hurt something terrible to do, and she feared one day she'd be stuck with her eyes clear in the back of her head. But it was easily the most effective bit of fright she had to employ.

"What is it, child? What do you wish to say to your loving parents?" Tavish whispered, forcing Lady Elspeth to lean forward, straining to hear. "The slate and chalk! Hurry before the message flies away!"

Tavish pushed a child's slate and a rough piece of chalk into her hand. Nairna kept her eyes straight ahead as she scrawled the words the grieving mother was paying to hear.

"Oh we have been blessed. Your child has spoken." Tavish's voice was filled with a practiced wonder. Nairna readied herself for the finale. As Lady and Lord Lennox stared wide-eyed at the chalk words on the slate, Nairna curled her toes under her feet and ignoring the pain pushed herself upward. It was a particularly athletic move that had taken a full year to perfect, but the end result was the illusion that she levitated from her seat for a moment. Lady Elspeth fell backward out of her chair in a full faint, and the mad scramble to aid her gave Nairna a chance to grimace in pain as she fell to the side. She stood and surveyed the room as though she had never seen the space before.

"What happened, Father? Did the spirits answer your call?" she asked innocently, pitching her voice to sound as childlike as possible. Though she was only sixteen, she was so slightly built that she often passed for younger. Her father said this was to her advantage, as a child wonder was far more fantastical than a young woman.

Lady Elspeth was coming to with the aid of her husband. The owls in the corner had all fled. Lord Lennox thrust a coin purse into her father's hand.

"Tavish Liath, your daughter's talents have been proven to be true. I saw the spirit of my Maggie standing behind her, I did." The man's face was pale, but his eyes were filled with fervor. Lady Elspeth reached into the pantry and pulled out a cloth sack, handing it to Nairna.

"I wish we could offer more," she said apologetically.

Nairna curtsied, her strained leg muscles screaming in protest, and offered a small smile.

"My gift is a blessing from the fae folk," she said in her best little girl voice.

"Come, my girl." Tavish ushered her to the door. "Let's leave these good people. *Slán.*"

"*Slán.*" Lord Lennox replied as he shut the door behind them.

Nairna

The pair walked in silence until they were a safe distance from the Lennoxes' cottage. The night was cold, and there was frost in the air. Nairna shivered under her wool cloak. Her father indicated for her to stop while he stomped around the area, looking for any indication that they were not alone.

"Here will do." They set out to start a small fire, and Nairna pulled a rough wool blanket from her rucksack. It was only then that her father poured the coins from the purse into his hand and counted.

"Four shillings, the cheap bastard. He promised five before and five after. Should've told 'em a demon was setting a curse upon their house. That'd keep 'em up at night; serve 'em right, I say. Let's have those coppers the good lady slipped you as well."

Nairna swallowed a complaint as she pulled the ha'pennies from her pocket and placed them in her father's waiting hand.

"Cheap bastards," he muttered.

"They gave us food, Da," Nairna said softly. Her stomach contracted in its emptiness. They'd last eaten the night before, when the butcher had thrown out a tray of burnt meat pies. She hadn't liked the idea of fighting off the rats in the bin for the last of them, but it had been better than nothing.

"Let's have at it then," Tavish said with resignation.

The sack did not disappoint. It held a loaf of freshly baked bread, salt crystals embedded in the golden crust. It also housed a hunk of goat's cheese wrapped in cloth and two apples, hard and bitter but still quite edible. Her father tore a wedge of bread from the loaf, smeared the goat cheese on it with his small knife and handed it to Nairna. She fought the urge to devour it whole and instead nibbled at the corner, savoring the flavors.

"You need to watch it with that fae talk," her father said between bites. "The closer we get to Edinburgh, the more that will only bring you trouble. It's only the country people who believe such rubbish. The city folk will run you out for paganism with that mouth."

Nairna nodded. She knew better than to argue with Tavish, especially when he was in a foul temper, as he was tonight.

"There's a harvest fair north of here, outside of Kirkcaldy. I could read cards. It would be good for a few shillings, and there's always plenty to eat; the food stalls throw out the leavings every night." Nairna spoke softly, hoping he'd agree. It would give them a rest, and she could fill her belly without breaking her toes in half or battling a starved rat in a rubbish bin.

Tavish nodded, thinking. "That'd be a fine idea, daughter. Lots of farms up in Kirkcaldy."

Nairna felt a pinprick of dread even though she was relieved they would be allowed to rest. Tavish sold himself as a water diviner to the country farmers, a scheme that had found themselves run out of Peterhead with an angry lot at their tails. Word spread fast. Nairna knew the farmers in Peterhead had likely spread their grievances about the charlatan who had taken their pence and not found a drop of fresh well water through the taverns from Peterhead to Edinburgh by now. She'd told Tavish then that he needed to abandon the trick. Stick to the cards and the occasional ghostly writing, and while she was sure she'd go straight to hell for it, she knew how to make a mother believe her beloved was nearby.

Nairna curled as close to the fire as she dared and tried to sleep. Deep in the woods surrounding her, she could hear the stir of creatures watching them from the periphery of the trees. She had sprinkled a bit of black salt in a circle around them when her father had gone off into the trees to relieve himself. He would have cursed her for superstition, but Nairna knew that neither the badgers and martens nor the fae folk would dare cross it while they slept. Nań had shown her the way to seal a circle back in their cottage in Inverness when she was just a child. Every night they had gone out to sprinkle the black salt that kept the voles and black rats from burrowing their way through the thatch roof. Da had been gone during those years, off to the factories in Glasgow for a spell, and then the harbor at Aberdeen. She sometimes wished he'd stayed gone and she'd been left to the peace of the little cottage and stone hearth where the great *coire* hung over the fire. Nairna drifted into a restless sleep while the forest fae kept watch.

Nairna

A farmer hauling beets and potatoes to the harvest fair let Tavish and Nairna ride in the back of his cart among the baskets and burlap sacks. The road was washed out in places by the late summer rains, and Tavish had to get out and help the farmer steady the horses and dig the wooden wheels out of the mud. Nairna had kept a still face but secretly enjoyed her father's discomfort. Nań used to curse him and say he was not meant for manual labor. He considered himself above getting calluses on his hands and dirt on his pretty face, she would sneer as she stoked the hearth. Nań hadn't been wrong. Tavish had been let go from the factories in Glasgow for sloth, and the ports had soon learned he was more use as an anchor than a shipyard man. So the grimace of disgust on his face as he stepped in a pile of fresh horse dung made it hard for Nairna not to laugh aloud. Tavish didn't dare complain, though. The farmer was doing them a good turn by offering a ride; it would have taken three days or more on foot.

Back on the road, Tavish muttered low enough the farmer couldn't hear. "Damned peasants. I tell you, daughter, our line comes from Robert the Bruce himself. We weren't meant for digging in the mud like a commoner."

Nairna closed her eyes and curled against a burlap sack of neeps. Their "line" changed with her father's fancy. Now they were descended from Robert the Bruce. If you'd asked him a month ago, he'd have sung the praises of Colin Campbell and claimed that they were in line to receive the riches of the East India Trading Company. Nairna suspected that they were more Sawney Bean than Robert the Bruce or Henry Bell, or any of the other noblemen who her father claimed lineage to. Tavish had a speckled history, and none of it was entangled with Robert the Bruce or Colin Campbell. The only records that existed stated that his father, Elis Liath, had been killed in a tunnel in Cwmaman Colliery in the same year that Tavish was born. The only mention of his mother, Lottie Liath, was a court record from 1866, when she'd been seen by a judge regarding a disturbance listed as a fit of "grief-induced mania." But there was nothing that followed it, no mention of what had become of her. There were no records of Tavish's birth or Lottie's death. Nothing at all to indicate why the infant Tavish had arrived at Smyllum Park Orphanage in Lanarkshire, Scotland, with only a small parcel of his mother's surviving possessions.

Tavish had survived the orphanage, but on an autumn night in his eleventh year he'd climbed out a dormitory window and burrowed like a jackrabbit under the imposing stone wall to the woods beyond. He'd made it all the way to Linthouse by the River Clyde, where he forged a labour card and found work in a brick factory. This history was courtesy of Nań, who had been against her daughter marrying Tavish Liath, a Welshman with a Scottish name who'd been born to a madwoman with a court record and had spent his youth running the streets like a common criminal.

Tavish didn't speak of his past much—his real past, that was. He would talk of Bonnie Prince Charlie and Rob Roy and all

the great men he wished he was descended from until your ears
were weary from the hearing. That was Tavish's way, lost in a
pretend world peopled by those he admired most. The reality
of daily life, the constant hunger that followed him and Nairna,
the impermanence they had known since Nań passed and they
headed to the road—all these things were an illusion to him. To
Nairna, however, they gnawed at her, and she longed for the
simple life she had known with Nań. Their hearth and the thick
stews Nań would make from barley and mutton. The stillness
of the woods at night, the sound of rain on the thatch. She'd
take it back in a heartbeat. Now, when she dreamt at night, she
allowed herself to fantasize about the little comforts she saw in
others, especially the city folk as they traveled from there to
here. Clean linens to sleep on, real soap to wash the dirt from
her face and hands, meats roasted in rich gravies and green vegetables.

By the time a young Tavish Liath had found his way to Inverness and Anne Bhasa's door, he'd long given up factory
work. He was selling his skills as a land prospector, skilled in
finding just the right spot to dig the well. He told Anne he was
twenty-five and a success, with a big manor back in Glasgow
on Cathedral Hill. She'd only been seventeen and by Nań's de-
scription utterly besotted. It was a matter of weeks before a
farmer outside of Inverness dug straight into a wall of rock instead of water, then traded his story with others. They pulled
Tavish out of his rented bed at the local inn and threatened to
tar and feather him if he didn't return their pence and leave
town. It was only after he'd been gone for several months and
Nairna was growing fast in her mother's belly that Anne found
out the grand manor, Cathedral Hill, and even his age were a
lie. He was a nineteen-year-old nomad who scraped a living
from cheating farmers and slept in barns and rafters when he
wasn't on the street.

Tavish promised to turn it around when he heard of the baby, though, and a local pastor ignored Anne's swollen belly and quietly married the pair in a ceremony that only Nań attended. Nań had been forced to admit that, liar as he was, Tavish was a sight with his dark eyes and coal black hair falling just so over his forehead. Anne matched his beauty, her skin pale and smooth, and her eyes containing the night sky in summer. Or so it had been told to Nairna all her childhood. She had only seen her father sporadically, as he returned from there and here with a little money from this job and that. He had tried his hand at honest labour for a spell, but finding that the Scottish wind added lines to his pretty face and calluses to his hands, he had gone back to his scams.

The seer cards had been brought to the family by Tavish. His story went that they'd belonged to his mother and hers before that, but there was no evidence to support the claim. Nań taught her to read the cards, but Nairna learned to see past the seeker's pride and confidence, their anger and sugary kindness. She was granted a glimpse of that which few dared to show the world. It made it hard to offer readings that successfully walked the line between truth and the desired result. She rarely gave an entirely honest reading at fairs and carnivals. She'd learned people hardly sought the truth, and when it was told to them, they reacted with anger or fear.

Two years she had traveled with Tavish. Two years since Nań had passed in her sleep, her breathing slowing and quieting until it left this world altogether. Nairna hadn't written her father; she had hoped he wouldn't hear the news and she could continue to live in the cottage in Inverness, reading the cards for coins and selling cheese from the goat in the small shed that served as a barn. But he had turned up, nonetheless. Someone from town had written him, or perhaps he'd seen the small notice in the local paper. Tavish Liath had arrived on a summer evening, walking through the door of the cottage without bothering to knock, something he never would have

done when Nań was alive. They'd stayed for a month or so before Tavish had seen her read the cards for a local woman
whose daughter was expecting. He'd been quiet as the tomb
during the reading, watching Nairna work, watching the coins
that exchanged hands.

They had left the next week, all of Nairna's belongings in a
rucksack, the cottage and the goat sold to a neighbor. *We'll
make a bloody fortune we will*, Tavish had said. *We'll buy that
manor house on Cathedral Hill or maybe even Edinburgh*. For
all his grand talk, they were still living off scraps two years
later, scamming wealthy families with lies and trickery. The
séances paid more than a simple card reading, but the dead did
not speak to Nairna; the only voice she heard was the pain of
the one who asked for contact with the other side. Tavish continued his claims as a water diviner and mesmerist even though
it typically got them run out of town after a matter of weeks.

The cart hit another ditch, and Tavish grunted as he climbed
down to dig the rear wheel from the muck. The farmer smiled
at Nairna as he walked back to help.

"Good thing you and yer Da needed a lift. I wouldn't have
made it past Berry Hill on me own."

The cart unlocked from the mud and the horses refreshed,
they set off again to Kirkcaldy. Nairna tilted her head back and
watched the clouds in the sky. She whispered a silent prayer for
the lies to stop, for her truth to be enough, a prayer for an end
to their inconstant existence.

Nairna

Kirkcaldy proper was a winding collection of stone and brick shop fronts and cobblestone streets. A cable car ran down High Street along the Causeway, and the market sold fresh strawberries from the fields in Fife. The harvest festival was along the southern wall, overlooking the waters of the North Sea. Nairna and Tavish thanked the farmer, who refused their ha'pennies, saying they had dug him out of enough ditches to more than pay their way.

Nairna breathed in the salt-tinged air as she and Tavish approached the festival grounds. As Tavish went to pay the fees and see about renting a cloth tent, Nairna wandered the grassy patch watching the farmers and shopkeepers set up their stalls. A woman with deep amber hair and freckles across her nose gave Nairna a fresh spun honey stick. The woman smiled at her and folded the sweet in her hand before Nairna could object. She realized that it had been a long stretch, since before the Lennox house, that she had found the chance to wash, and she could feel the sharp outline of her bones against her skin. The farmer had given them boiled potatoes, and Nairna had found some sweet pea root, but it was a meager ration, and her hunger had given up its screaming pains and retreated to a dull ache some time ago. She looked a sight, and as the kind-eyed woman pressed the treat into her hands, Nairna knew she looked like a lost and starving child.

"We're set!" Tavish walked up behind her, his face red from sun and exertion. "They had a vendor cancel, but the fees had already been paid, so we can have his tent, and they'll even throw in a table and a couple of chairs. Only cost me a pence, and we'll make that back in an hour." He paused, looking down at Nairna. "What's wrong, girl? I thought you'd be pleased. We have a bit of shelter, and as you yourself said, the food stalls throw out the leavings nightly. I bet I could even find us a pint here somewhere . . ."

Nairna shook her head. "I am glad, Da', I am. But promise me you'll not start in with the divining again. We could stay here a spell, even after the festival, maybe work High Street, rent a room?"

Tavish considered her words. His dark eyes scanned her face, and she saw a twitch in his normally unreadable expression. "P'r'aps that's not such a terrible idea. Winter comin' on and whatnot. You're lookin' a bit ragged; suppose I am, too. Come, girl, let's go get ourselves settled. We can go down to the water and wash up a bit, find a bite to eat, how's that sound?" His eyes held concern, and Nairna felt her guard go down. He was looking out for her in his own way. Soon she'd be old enough to do as she pleased, and she might even miss his company at that.

Later, after they had washed their faces and hands in the cold North Sea water and wrung out their clothes as best could be, the pair settled into the battered cloth tent where Nairna would read cards and palms for the crowds. Tavish would work the crowd, direct the passersby her way. Nairna was determined to prove to Tavish that they could make enough here to stay for a spell. Her bones were weary to the very core of her being, and she feared her father's actions if they ventured into the country-side. His stubbornness refused to let him give up on the con; every time he assured her he knew a new trick, a new method. Sometimes Nairna thought he actually believed he could divine water, even though it had been proven so many times that he had no talent for that or anything except for his uncanny ability to make nearly every man and woman he met trust his words.

As her father's snores rose up, Nairna snuck out the front of the tent. A few figures moved here and there. Most lived locally and would arrive in the early morning before the crowds.

"Girl! Come over here. Join us for a bite."

Nairna turned her head to see the amber-headed woman sitting by a circle of crackling logs with a man and two little boys who shared their mother's hair and freckles. The man smiled, and the woman waved her over, indicating a flat stone set over the fire where a bit of bread was heating.

"We've enough to share," the man said reassuringly.

Nairna cast a doubtful look at the tent behind her. Tavish would have her hide if he woke and discovered her gone. But the odor of the warm bread was more compelling than her fear.

"That's it, love," the woman said as Nairna crossed to them and sat by the fire, offering a smile. "I'm Wynfreyda. Call me Wyn. This is my husband, Ian, and these two little ones are Gavin and Kyle. Say hi, boys." The two small faces nodded, their eyes wide and staring.

"I'm Nairna. I came with my father. He's asleep now." Nairna's voice was barely more than a whisper, and her hands shook as the smell of the bread filled her senses.

Wyn nodded. "I saw you a bit earlier, looked a bit peaked. Long journey here, I expect. Have a bit of supper, perk yerself a bit." Wyn ladled a thin soup from a pot into an earthenware bowl and balanced a chunk of warm bread on the top.

Nairna nodded and tried to thank her, but her senses were

overwhelmed by her ravenous stomach. She greedily drank the soup straight from the bowl. The simple cabbage broth was better than the finest partan bree. She wiped the bowl clean with the bread and nearly choked as she practically inhaled it. A shameful awareness came over her, and she looked up at the stunned faces of the family sheepishly.

"I'm sorry . . . my manners . . . ," Nairna began.

"Are nothing to apologize for." Wyn smiled and took the bowl, refilling it with broth and adding another corner of bread. "Let's try that again, but p'r'aps a bit slower this time."

Nairna breathed a relieved sigh and allowed herself to enjoy the warm broth this time around, her stomach calming and her hands and feet regaining some warmth.

"You've been on the road a spell?" Ian asked gently.

"My Da and I came from outside Edinburgh. We travel quite a lot, never settle in one place. I hope we can stay here a bit longer with winter on its way," Nairna said softly, her voice gaining a bit of strength.

"Aye, it is at that." Wyn nodded. "And a fury it's setting to be. Already there's frost on the ground. We keep bees, hence the honey sweets like the one I gave yeh earlier. The night air's near froze our hive clean through, and it's not even the dark days yet. You'd do well to get off the road and find a place to rest. There's a boarding house up near Bute Wynd; we stayed there back when we were newlyweds, didn't we, love?" She winked at Ian, who smiled and nodded.

"That'd be nice," Nairna said.

"What's yer ware?" Wyn asked, nodding to the tent where Tavish slept on, oblivious to the world.

Nairna hesitated. "I . . . I read cards and palms, runes sometimes." She searched their faces for signs of shock. If they were religious, she'd be run off from the fire quick as anything.

Instead of shock, Wyn laughed. "Well, I guessed it, didn't I?" She looked to the two little boys, who nodded. "I said I bet she's a fortune teller when I saw yeh earlier. You have an air about yeh, like you can see the things we can't. Yeh any good?" she asked, her voice teasing.

Nairna smiled. "I try to be."

"Well that's all we can do, isn't it?" Wyn struggled to her feet. "Would yeh like a bit more? We should turn in; they'll be comin' early tomorrow."

Nairna shook her head and handed the bowl to Wyn's waiting hands. "Thank you. It had been a spell since I last ate."

"I suspected that, too," Wyn replied, her face filled with a mother's concern.

With a nod to the little family, Nairna made her way back to her tent, where Tavish still snored, utterly unaware that she had left at all. As she closed her eyes, Nairna tried to imagine the little boarding house in Bute Wynd, clean sheets, and a window that looked out to the sea.

Nairna

The first visitors to the festival started ambling through while the sun was still new to the sky. By mid-morning the stalls and tents were set, and the sound of children giggling and running underfoot filled the air. Nairna and Tavish had a small wooden table they'd covered with a gauzy cloth Nań had woven years back. A small glass orb sat in the center of the table. It wasn't crystal, and it held no power beyond the ache it put in Nairna's back to carry it in her rucksack, but it was a nice prop, nonetheless. Tavish was good at his task, and he sent Nairna a young woman wearing a silver luckenbooth pinned to her wool scarf, two hearts intricately carved in an intertwining pattern with an apple green stone embedded in the center that matched the young woman's eyes.

She didn't have to tell Nairna the truth she sought; her heart was full of equal measures of hope and fear, and the way she unconsciously rubbed the luckenbooth told Nairna that she had little experience in love. Nairna shuffled her worn tarot deck until she felt the energy biting at her fingers. When she did a serious reading, it was near enough to cause her to see stars flash before her eyes. This was not too serious. The young woman had paid her a handful of coppers, and Tavish had growled that anything lower than a thruppenny bit was to last no more than ten minutes.

"Yer engaged to be married." Nairna spoke softly but clearly, nodding to the luckenbooth.

The woman nodded. "I am. We're set to be married before the snow falls. I suppose I want to know . . . to know . . ."

"If he's true?" Nairna said with a smile. "If that were yer query, I could answer that by that fine token he's given you, silver and a bit of jade it looks to be. Oh, I'd say his heart is yers."

The woman smiled. "I suppose it is. What I really want to know is . . ." A shadow crossed her face, and she leaned forward. "Am I doing the right thing? Will I be happy?"

Nairna nodded and shuffled the deck a bit more until she felt the pleasant tingle of energy in her fingertips. She cut the deck and stacked the bottom cut on top. As the young woman's eyes grew wide as saucers, she drew three cards, placing them face up as she went.

Nairna looked up and smiled. "The King of Pentacles. That's yer love, I'd bet. Strong masculine energy—is he a bit older than you?" The woman nodded, her face pale. Nairna continued. "And the Page of Wands, there's you. A strong woman, coming into her own self. You've a mind for ambition, don't yeh?"

The young woman stared at Nairna as though she was revealed the secret to life and what lay after. "How do you know . . . ?"

Nairna nodded, keeping her face serene. "The cards tell the lot. The Hierophant, the minotaur. Your marriage will bring great blessing to yer community, yer family. Yer intended, he's well off, yes?"

The woman nodded. "After we're married, he's promised to

bind my father's farm to his and give lodging to my brothers and their wives."

Nairna nodded. "You'll be quite happy, yer family will be warm and well fed in the winter, yer crops will grow, and yer children will have round cheeks."

The young woman nodded; she looked satisfied but resigned. As she rose to go, Nairna drew the next card, curious as to what the outcome of this union would be. She said nothing as the young woman exited the tent but stared down at the Queen of Pentacles. The image on the card was a beautiful but stone-faced woman. A woman of business, an equal to her king. But this was not a card of love and passion; it told a future secured in landholdings and crop sales. The romance the young woman wished for was absent from this future.

The day continued in this way. As the afternoon carried on, Tavish brought Nairna an apple and a bit of hard cheese from a neighboring stall. He was pleased: they had a bag full of coins already, and it was only the first day. By the time the sun started to dip, Nairna's hands felt raw from the cards. She was about to pack them away when a woman wearing a finely woven blouse and intricately patterned skirt stood in the entryway, the setting sun behind her creating the illusion of a halo.

"I imagine you're quite finished for the day, but I wonder if there is time for one more?" she asked, her voice cultivated— her words held none of the country and all of the city. Nairna made a note to tone back the affectation she had spoken with for the sake of her customers all day. She had learned early that a bit of the local accent earned her trust from those that sat across from her.

"I'm happy to." Nairna nodded to the chair. "Please."

"Is that your father I saw out there?" the woman asked, a smile on her lips. Her golden hair was pulled into an impossible configuration on top of her head, and her skin seemed to almost glow.

"He is. Did he send you my way?" Nairna asked.

"No. I think he was on a bit of a break. I took it on myself to make my own appointment." She offered a smile which Nairna returned. Her words were liquid, her style effortless.

"What would you like to ask the cards?" Nairna held the deck in her hands. Already they were buzzing with an energy she'd not felt yet today.

"It's not me I'd like to inquire about. It's you," the woman said, her dark blue eyes locked on Nairna. "I'd like to know what our connection is. I felt drawn here, and I'd like to know why."

Nairna tilted her head, taking in the words. "I can ask, but the cards don't always give a clear answer."

"Perhaps this will help." The woman placed a gold sovereign on the table and nodded to the cards. "I accept whatever wisdom they might provide."

"Miss, that's far too much. I can't . . . ," Nairna started to object.

"Oh, but you can," the woman said, pushing the coin toward Nairna.

Nairna stared at the mysterious woman for a moment and then started shuffling the cards. They sent shocks of invisible energy though her fingers that radiated into her wrist and arm. She cut the deck and drew the three cards, placing them face up on the table. She stared at them for a moment, her heart beating fast.

"I . . . ," she started.

"Let me," the woman said softly, reaching across and taking Nairna's hand in hers. The soft skin of the lady's fingers felt like silk.

"The Ten of Pentacles: a painful passage in your life is coming to an end soon, very soon perhaps." The woman looked down at the cards, her blue-black eyes searching the images. "Judgement." She looked up at Nairna, studying her intently. Nairna could feel her hands shaking, and her throat was suddenly bone dry. "Judgement," the woman said again, "is a card of transformation. You are waking up, little one; your talent and your spirit are starting to show themselves. You are on the journey now, whether you feel it or not, and I believe I might be the one to guide you. The Chariot is a card of power and determination, a path you must follow."

Nairna nodded, her voice small and uncertain when she spoke. "I don't understand."

The woman smiled and squeezed Nairna's hand. "Oh, but you will. You will. It's no accident that you and I met. Now hide that sovereign before your father sees it. He has a nose for your earnings, doesn't he?" Nairna nodded and tucked the coin in her pocket. "I'll see you soon, very soon." With that she stood, turned and walked to the door. Tavish threw back the curtain and offered her his most agreeable smile.

"Well, pardon me, my girl, I didn't know you had a customer. Isn't she just wonderful?" Tavish said in his best showman voice, offering the lady his hand.

"She is indeed. Here, for your fine work." She placed a shilling in Tavish's hand and Nairna could see the excitement behind his tightly controlled expression.

"Well, thank you," Tavish drawled, holding the curtain for the lady's exit.

"My name is Rona Connell. I will be back. This young woman has an extraordinary gift." She nodded to Nairna and Tavish, then walked into the ever-dimming light.

Tavish waited a moment to make sure she was out of hearing before he fell into the seat across from Nairna.

"Well, how's that for a fine end to the night? We made a killing already, and that's a sweet on top, isn't it? Come." He smacked the table with the flat of his hand and grinned at Nairna. "Let's to the tavern. I'll buy you a proper dinner and a pint. No need to dig through the leavings tonight, my girl."

Nairna carefully tucked her cards in their wooden box into

her deep pocket alongside the sovereign. As she followed Tavish through the maze of tents and stalls, she thought about the last card drawn. The Chariot. Rona Connell had been right: it was a card of power and determination but also loneliness. It was power gained at the expense of others, the price of the voyage.

Nairna

The ruins of Ravenscraig looked to be aflame as the sun set behind them. The carriage pulled around the castle to the far more modernly styled carriage house that lay on the other side of the hill. Tavish stared out the window, making small humming sounds occasionally. He had been awoken from his drink-induced sleep to an invitation from Rona Connell. Her gentleman friend had recently lost his wife, and wouldn't Nairna join them this evening for a spirit session? The note had contained five crowns and a promise of much more, including a carriage ride to the house and dinner. Nairna hadn't seen him this animated for months.

Nairna found his enthusiasm frustrating, but she kept her feelings locked away. She had the sovereign hidden, and there would be more pay for tonight's work, but this was far more than money. Nairna could feel in her fingertips it was a chance, although at what she had no idea. Tavish didn't dare speak of their work with the driver in listening distance. But Nairna knew he expected quite a show tonight. She hadn't had to really work at the illusion for quite a time. Even at the Lennoxes' a few simple tricks and they were convinced they'd seen Hekate herself sitting at the hearth. But this would require more skill than Nairna had been made to employ for some time.

Her stomach growled. It was better not to be hungry, but this was one time when she needed her head clear. If she fainted, all the better; she could blame the spirits. Tavish shook his head slowly as they rounded the turn and the carriage house came into view. Gas lamps lit the walk, and the grounds were immaculate. The house itself was rather plain. Nairna couldn't help but feel surprised that such a grand lady would live in the solid but simply built stone house at the base of Ravenscraig.

Once they climbed from the carriage and the front door opened, Nairna's opinion, however, was entirely changed. Dark wood floors reflected the lamplight; gold candlesticks sat on the mantle. Rona Connell smiled, her face serene and expectant, as she waved them inside. A man in a black butler's coat took their wraps, and Nairna couldn't stop herself from turning in a circle as she admired the marble end tables and rich velvet sofa. Tavish glowered and tapped her arm, but Rona took Nairna's hand in hers and pulled her away from her father.

"Come, love. No need to hide your reaction. It is a grand place filled with grand things. See this?" She pointed to a painting on the wall of a gentle landscape, the colours melting into each other. Nairna felt a calm wash over her as she stared at the intentional effortlessness of the lines. "It's by a man named Camille Pissarro," Rona added. "He's quite the rage in Paris right now. Imagine my shock to find it hanging in this little nook."

Nairna looked to her in surprise. "You don't live here?" It was more statement than question, and suddenly she felt quite foolish. This grand lady was far too towny for Fife, and especially Kirkcaldy.

Rona smiled. "No. I live in Edinburgh, in New Town. Are you familiar with it?"

"A bit," Nairna said softly. She and Tavish had spent most of the past two years in the outlying villages around Edinburgh, but they'd spent a few weeks in Haymarket some months ago. Nairna had been entirely overwhelmed with the size and noise of the place.

"Well, let's get started, shall we?" Rona took Nairna's hand again and motioned for Tavish to follow as they passed through the great room to a small library in the rear of the cottage. Several figures milled about, crystal glasses of red wine in their hands. Nairna and Tavish stood together as Rona cleared her throat and the occupants of the room turned to face them. A tall, dignified gentleman in a dark suit nodded to Nairna from the back of the room.

"Hello, friends. I had the opportunity to meet this extraordinary girl at the festival yesterday, and she and her father have agreed to help us bridge the divide between this world and that. Frederick?" The gentleman nodded. "Allison was beloved by not only Frederick but all of us. We hope to say our last goodbyes tonight."

Tavish took his cue, his face becoming a showman's mask of practiced charm. "Welcome all! We would like to spend a few moments alone in the space, if that pleases you."

Rona motioned to the others, and they filed out to the great room. Tavish flashed a smile and closed the stained-glass doors behind him. Then he turned to Nairna.

"Are we ready?" he asked simply, his voice expectant.

Nairna nodded. "I need to be as close to this door as possible. The sound will echo best here. You are set as well?"

Tavish nodded. "I don't know how you landed this catch,

daughter, but these fish will set us right for the winter entire. Perhaps we will take a room in Kirkcaldy, if only till the winter passes."

Nairna smiled and nodded. A winter in a warm room—maybe she could take in sewing, do some honest work. Not that the cards weren't honest, but if the authorities ever got wind of it, she could find herself tried as a witch—plus no one save Rona Connell was willing to pay more than threepence for her services.

"Let's get started," Nairna said softly.

She sat in the chair closest to the door, her back to the finely dressed women and men as they reentered the space, her eyes closed, trying to feel the energy and emotion of her audience. There was something off here. Usually the grief was as thick as butter; she could feel it rolling off the bereaved in waves. This group was . . . different, particularly Frederick, the widower. He was too calm, as though he were going to a theatre show instead of a séance. Nairna felt nerves rise in her gut, and she quickly patted them back down.

Tavish stood to her right. The candles in the center of the dark wood table had been lit as they entered, but Tavish had turned the gas lamp sconces so low they were only good for casting shadow. The less they could see, the better: imagination filled in the gaps that reality left behind.

"Let us take a moment to close our eyes and breathe in deeply." Tavish's voice was rich and soothing. "We are gathered in this place to contact the soul of Allison. Allison, do you hear us call to you? Do you hear us call you?"

Nairna let her head loll forward, feeling the expectant hum of the others as they sat silently in the darkened room. She slipped her toes from the false bottom of her shoes. The leather had been cut along the soles, allowing her to fold it behind and prop her toes on their ends in the blackness under the table. She began to move her big toe back and forth until the clicking of the bones became a consistent and undeniable sound. Nairna was able to do this while barely moving her leg, and the clicking sounded like a faint rap at the stained-glass doors Tavish had closed behind them.

"Allison," Tavish said. "I hear you scratching at the door to be let in. I hear you reaching to the ones who loved you in life, the ones who love you still. *Teacht chun solais bean!*"

As always, Nairna internally cringed at his rough pronunciation, but a posh crowd from New Town were less likely to know the language.

"Frederick, what do you want to say to your lost love?" Tavish's voice was like a dark smoke; it wrapped its way around the room, whispered in ears, made especially the women feel as though what he said was for their minds only. He had his charm especially high that night; Nairna knew he would laugh about it later, how they folded to the mere sound of the words.

Nairna readied herself. She increased the rapidity of the clicking and began popping her right shoulder blade in and out— under her heavy shawl, the action was imperceptible, and it was the reason that Tavish always stayed to her right, to mask any movement that might be seen. Nairna heard a perceptible gasp from one of the women, and the nerves that had been eating her insides subsided. Richies were the same as the rest; they wanted to believe what they had lost could be found.

"Allison, my love, are you with us?" Frederick's low voice echoed in the small space. Nairna shook off the uneasiness again. He sounded rehearsed, practiced.

"Let her in, oh let her in!" Tavish's voice rose and fell as Nairna continued her bone clatter. On the count of ten, she threw her head back so her long thin neck was exposed. She forced her eyes to the back of her skull and emitted a long, low rasping sound that made her throat ache with the effort. As she righted her head, her eyes on fire and the world black before her, she heard the scrape of chairs as the women and men started and more gasps of shock.

"Allison! You have joined us! *Oh croi' daor!* Come inside!" Tavish's voice rose to a roar as Nairna added her knee joint to the cacophony of clicks and pops. It was just as the tension in the room reached a peak too intense to ignore that Nairna slipped her toes back into her shoes and readied herself to lean her weight onto her feet, completing the illusion of levitation. As she rose, her calves and thighs screaming with pain, Tavish shifted forward as though moved by the energy of the spirits. Even blind as she was, Nairna knew the faces that lined the table were fixed on her, not him; thus they didn't see the invisible thread he had secured to the bottom of the stained-glass door. His small movement caused the doors to fly open as though of their own accord. As she heard the clatter and a stifled scream from a woman's throat, Nairna allowed herself to drop and her eyes to roll back to their natural position. Her head hit the table hard, and she saw stars for a moment. It was likely to leave a bruise, but the impact of the move was worth it.

"My god." Frederick's voice was soft and tense from the other side of the table.

Nairna raised her head and arms with a dancer's grace as Tavish feigned concern.

"Oh my daughter, the spirits take too much. My dear one, are you well?" he pleaded in a voice that almost made Nairna believe him.

She opened her eyes and stared straight ahead where Frederick sat across from her, his eyes wide and perhaps a little frightened. As Nairna opened her mouth to deliver her next line, the words caught in her throat.

Behind Frederick was a slightly built woman wearing a loose cotton frock. Her long, black hair matched her eyes, and her skin was so pale it was translucent. She stared at Nairna with a sadness in her gaze that made tears rise to Nairna's eyes. She whispered a single word that filled Nairna's head so entirely it was as though all other sound had been removed.

"Enough."

Nairna

Nairna sat in the kitchen at the rough table, sipping a mug of cider. In the next room she could hear Tavish speaking low and urgently to Rona and Rona's calm and soothing replies. She could not make out the words, but she knew the gist. After the woman had appeared, Nairna had felt a blackness overcome her. She had awakened on the velvet sofa where Rona held a small vial of smelling salts under her nose. The finely dressed women and men had shuffled off to the parlour for more wine and brandy. Nairna had been given a mug of cider and a thick slab of black bread by the butler and left to her peace, but not before the old man leaned in and whispered, "They weren't expecting that."

He had sounded a bit delighted, and Nairna couldn't tell how to read the comment. Was it a good thing she had ended the séance with such dramatics? Had she simply proven herself to be a child and a fraud full of cheap parlour tricks who had finally managed to scare the wits out of herself? She was guessing by the tone of Tavish's voice the latter was closer than the former.

Rona entered the kitchen and sat across from Nairna. Nairna had started to stutter an apology when Rona shook her head and reached across the space to squeeze Nairna's hand.

"No. Eat. One thing I know for sure is your father is not taking adequate care of you. You are half-starved; anyone can see that. But I think I can help." Rona smiled.

"I . . . ," Nairna started, but again Rona cut her off.

"You should know a few things going forward. Frederick is my husband; there is no Allison, never was. The others are our friends from New Town; we are part of a club of sorts. A society if you will. I apologize for the trickery. We needed to vet your talents, and it goes without saying that you are very impressive."

Nairna felt her gut drop out from under her. She could only hope Rona and her friends did not call the authorities. The Witchcraft Act was as good a reason as any to lock her away on a work farm.

"Please do not fret so, *leann'an*," Rona said, smiling at Nairna's surprise. "We all speak the old language; it is part of our studies. We are members of the Edinburgh Spiritualists. We're a theosophical society, and we study under the great Madam Blavatsky. I found you quite by accident. We were coming back from St. Andrews and stopped for the festival. I heard a girl talking to her mates, quite shaken by the card reading she had just received. *She looked clear through to my soul*, she kept saying, so I knew I had to have a look." Rona paused, closely examining Nairna's face.

"You read the cards as well, though," Nairna said, her voice barely a whisper.

"I do. But you had such an Atma about you. Do you know what Atma is, *shìn*?" Rona asked gently.

Nairna shook her head and took a sip of the cider.

"You will. I've asked your father for the pair of you to accompany us back to Edinburgh. Join us, Nairna. Let me teach you about life and spirit and matter. You saw something or someone tonight you weren't expecting to see, did you not?"

Nairna nodded. Her head felt numb as though she were floating a distance above her body. "A woman. I've seen her before."

Rona nodded. "Your guide, perhaps. We can teach you to speak to her, let her lead you to the next world without dislocating every bone in your poor body."

Nairna stuttered, and Rona smiled gently and laid a soft finger on her lips. "No fear, *shìn*, we knew we were here for a show tonight, and we know your father, while perhaps a good man, is about as spiritual as that bread. It is you we want, but I have the feeling you are kindhearted enough that the idea of leaving your father to his own is not quite an option, at least yet."

Nairna shook her head. "He means well; he can be quite kind."

"I'm sure that is true. Come with us, *shìn*, learn from us, become what you are meant to be." Rona's voice was soft and warm, and in her smoky blue eyes, Naira could see the Chariot shining back at her.

Lottie
Cwmaman
1866

Cardiff Ledger, *June 1907*

It seems that the fae stories that brew about the old Argoll Downs may be more than imagination. For more years than this reporter has counted, the tales have swirled about the strange sights and sounds on Argoll Downs and its former inhabitant, Llywelyn ap Gruffydd. For years children have scared themselves silly with tales of the wailing woman who wanders the grounds of what used to be the Argoll Sanitorium, and as tales go, it was said that this woman was a scorned lover of old Llywelyn himself. A recent appraisal of sanitorium records, however, may have illuminated this mystery and exonerated Llywelyn ap Gruffydd once and for all. The truth may prove to be stranger than fiction in this case, as we unwind the story of a woman who had reason enough to wail, and whose story is more wrenching than that of a scorned lover.

Lottie Liath's true story sounds more fiction than fact and would leave the fae themselves gobsmacked by the winding tale of a young woman and how she came to wander the Argoll Downs.

Lottie

Lottie nodded to the other women and then looked down at her thin hands. Her fingers looked more bone than flesh, the nails tinged blue from the cold. Her expression held more confidence than her heart. She had told the women they would win, that Mr. Glasscock would see them, that he would listen, that he was a reasonable man and would listen to a reasonable case for the justice they had been denied. But as the minutes stretched to an hour and still they all waited on the bench outside the mine office, Lottie was beginning to doubt that Mr. Glasscock was even going to acknowledge their petition. It had been eighteen days since the tunnel collapsed, eighteen days since the message boy had brought that note, scrawled in ink and hardly readable. Lottie had stared at the words. Her reading was strong, but it took her a moment to understand what it had said.

Accident in the Cwmaman Colliery — come to
workman's reach

It had been eighteen days since Lottie had wrapped herself in her mum's black wool cloak and walked the distance to the

Cwmaman Colliery workman's reach, where she had found the others. Some of the women couldn't read at all and had had to find a neighbor or have the messenger boy read the note aloud; they all refused to believe the implication of the words. They had wrapped their arms around Lottie, nodded to her rounding belly, and smiled. *It's a'right*, they had said; *bein' cautious*, they had said. But Lottie had known. The colliery never sent for the family unless something terrible had happened; the others knew it, too.

Eighteen days since a red-cheeked foreman had stood in the door of the colliery office and told the group of women that a tunnel in Morris's Pit had collapsed and their men had been lost. Lottie had gasped. Elis was a hewer; he worked with his hands and a sharp pick right at the coal seam. He would be trapped for sure. *No survivors*, the red-cheeked foreman had said and closed the door as the women began to look to each other for assurance, before they could start to ask questions.

Lottie had taken the shock of the moment and sewn it away, not allowing it to turn to grief, not yet. She had a child on the way, she owed the landlord for the rent, and winter was deep upon them all. The other women had children of their own, landlords, and empty cupboards as well. They had no time for grief even as the loss and the savage abruptness of the news sat before them. Eighteen days had passed since that bitter afternoon, and still Lottie had not allowed herself to mourn; it wasn't real to her yet, not yet. Not even when the bodies were taken from the frozen dark of the mine, their faces twisted and their limbs in an awkward stillness. Lottie had not shed a single tear, not yet, not even when the priest had blessed the men and said the prayers as they were laid in the winter-crusted earth in the parish cemetery. All seven of the men were laid side by side, sharing a long stretch of ground. The wood carver's son, a lad of thirteen, made small crosses from the black poplar. He hadn't been asked, and no one had even a ha'penny to spare for his labour; the kindness nearly broke Lottie's frozen heart, but her eyes stayed dry while the boy quietly hammered them into the ground. Her Elis lost to the earth. A thousand never-agains marching across her brain. But still she did not indulge the grief that sat like a weight on her shoulders. She had a job to be done before she could collapse.

The women trusted her, they looked to her, always had. When the merchant raised the price of onions and radishes or refused to sell the Irish woman's son eggs, telling him he wasn't welcome, it was Lottie they came to. She had a presence, they said; she could convince anyone of anything, or so they thought. So when the insurance money owed by the mine didn't arrive, they came to Lottie; when the landlords, with no regard to their losses, came looking for the rent, they came to her for help. They needed her to be strong now, so Lottie's grief would have to wait until she forced Mr. Glasscock at the Cwmaman Colliery central office to hold their audience, to read the petition that Lottie had painstakingly and with great care written up and had the women sign. They were due their husbands' wages for the month as well as the insurance money promised upon injury or death. Without it, they would all be turned out in the street.

Eighteen days that felt like a lifetime had passed. Lottie was at least four months along, perhaps closer to five, and she felt nausea taking a constant seat at the back of her throat. She hadn't been sure, not really. Her cycle had a habit of not making a regular appearance, especially with the winter thick in the air and meals more porridge than meat. But this had been different. Elis had known, too; he had lain next to her in their cottage with the Enchanter's Nightshade that grew outside the windows and kissed her forehead. He had known. They hadn't discussed it much, not really. Elis was more superstitious than he would ever have admitted, and Lottie, while not one for fairy stories, believed in the power of bad luck to find you, especially when you went about bragging about the good you'd been dealt. Lottie supposed that was true even with grief. If she refused to acknowledge her loss, maybe it wouldn't stay real in the world, maybe Elis would walk back through the door, and she'd wake as though from a dream. Lottie was far too practical to truly believe it, but she kept her stoic front. Even the realization that Elis would never see their child couldn't force the tears from their holding spot. Not until she had finished her job would she allow the creeping rot of grief to overcome her. The insurance money would keep her in the cottage as long as she needed to formulate a plan for what came next. She had to survive first, then she could allow herself to feel.

The door opened, and a round-faced man with wooly sideburns and a nose that looked like a wad of unformed dough stepped onto the stoop and looked at the row of women shivering in the cold.

"Well, come in. Won't do to have you all freeze to death." He didn't wait for an answer but instead turned and stomped back into the office. Lottie nodded at the women, and they all rose, joints and muscles stiff from the frost, and made their way into the office.

"Tea?" the man asked as he sat behind a large wooden desk.

"Please," Lottie replied. "It's bitter out there, sir."

"Aye, it is. You know what they say about a bitter winter? It brings about a sweet spring." He nodded to a kettle with a stack of cheap porcelain cups stacked next to it. "Help yerselves, no need to stand at attention for my sake."

Hesitantly, the others went and poured the hot water, hoping to thaw their fingertips. Lottie stood firm before the great wooden desk. "Mr. Glasscock, you've read our petition. We've come here for what was promised us."

Mr. Glasscock adjusted the round spectacles that balanced on his unformed nose. "My dear girl, what was promised you? Did you work the mines, my dear? If you did, that would certainly be a promise that needs to be held, but did you go down in the carts every day, breathe in the dust and fire, and work ten hours at a stretch? Tell me, girl, did you?"

Lottie looked at the others who were starting to shift in fear and awkwardness. "No sir, you know right well none of us did. Our husbands had a month's wages due to them when they were lost in your mine, and they were promised insurance wages for injury or death . . ." The word caught in her throat and nearly choked her, but Lottie forced herself to continue. "We are the legal spouses of those men; there are children, sir, and rent is due. We are owed that money, and we have not been paid."

"I grieve for your loss, ladies, I do, but to take such a heartache and turn it to profit shudders me to my very core." Mr. Glasscock stared at Lottie, his beady eyes calculating and cold. "It makes me wonder what your men would think of you now, not going on into the world to earn yer way but instead here, begging for what was not rightly yers."

Lottie felt a white hot flash of rage fill her chest. "Mr. Glasscock, those are the devil's words. You know full well we are rightly entitled to what was our husbands' earnings, and we are here not out of greed but because we have mouths to feed, and we'll all be out on the street before long without it."

"I'd ask you to watch yer tone, young lady." Mr. Glasscock spoke each word carefully, over-enunciating each syllable. "I won't be spoken to by the likes of a woman on how to run my business. The truth is, we don't have the money to pay the lot of yeh. The mines have lost money for years; the insurance promise was made in loftier times. I'll see that you are given a week's wages from yer late husbands' earnings, and that will be it. I expect you can see yerself out?"

The other women set their empty teacups on the side table and looked to Lottie, their faces lost.

"No. We will not see ourselves out, Mr. Glasscock, not until we are paid what we are owed. A week's wages are not a month's, and the insurance money was promised. You have no right to deny a promise no matter how lofty the time was when it was made. We'll not leave until we have what we came fer." Lottie steadied herself, her feet planted, her voice strong.

Mr. Glasscock stood and walked to the door, which he opened to the outside and motioned to two men who stood by the landing. "If you'll not show yerselves out, I'll have you shown. I consider this conversation closed. Thank you so very much for coming to see me. It's not often I have the company of women in my office, and I declare the winter is a bit less bitter already. Please leave, Mrs. Liath."

The men entered the room and stood looking at the group of women. Lottie knew they had no choice, at least not right now. These men weren't the law, but the polis would show soon enough if Mr. Glasscock had a mind to call for them.

"Ladies, we will go for now, but Mr. Glasscock, we are not done discussing this. I shall be contacting the commissioner, and we will see what is owed us," Lottie said as she ushered the others out the door.

"By all means, my dear, contact whoever you like; my offer will not change." Mr. Glasscock nodded to the two men, who herded the group out into the cold. Lottie heard the click of the door lock as the winter air once again hit their senses. They'd taken a hired cart to Aberdare that morning, and Lottie hoped it was still at the station. Otherwise it would be a long walk home to Cwmaman.

"Ladies, this isn't over. Let's get home before the sun escapes, and we will decide what to do once we're out of the cold."

Lottie led her group of ragged warriors through the streets. She would write another petition; she had time.

Lottie

Twenty days. It had now been twenty days since that terrible knock on the door, since Lottie had felt her heart leave her body entire. The others were looking to her for help, and she was paralyzed with indecision. She had struggled through the writing of another petition, her hand unsteady and gaps in her memory where the spelling of words should be. She had attended school, but her mum had pulled her early; she needed the help at home, and there was little use for an educated girl. Lottie had been about ten, if her memory was reliable. She knew her letters and could read well enough if given the time to do it, but her handwriting was childish and blocky. She looked at the paper before her in frustration. No wonder Mr. Glass-cock saw no urgency in her situation—the petition looked to have been written by a child, the wording was simplistic, and some of the other women couldn't even sign their names properly. The lot of them did not inspire action or pity. Lottie stared at the hateful letter before her and wondered if she should just accept that wretched man's offer—a week's salary. The landlord had tacked the overdue notice to her door that morning, not respecting her loss, and she knew he had no mind for the other women either. Her cottage was on the outskirts of the mine compound, and she knew the colliery had a mind to rent it out for far more than she could pay if she were to fall behind. She'd be on the streets, or at a workhouse in Aberdare—with a baby, no less. Suddenly Lottie felt overwhelmed with nausea and bent over the wooden bucket she kept at her side more and more often, expelling her simple breakfast of oats.

No, a week's salary wouldn't even pay her way to Aberdare. She needed to ensure her and the baby's survival until spring, until she could formulate a better plan. With a sigh, Lottie wiped her mouth and took a sip of water. The sound of raised voices outside drew her attention, and she pulled herself to her feet, wondering how she would feel in a few months' time if it were this difficult to move now. Outside the window, Bryn, the youngest of the wives at only sixteen, was arguing with a man who was attempting to pin an eviction notice to her front door. It would only get worse; Lottie was one note away from eviction herself. With new resolve, Lottie sat down at the table and set to recopying the petition. She would beg a ride to Aberdare and not leave until Mr. Glasscock had heard her voice.

Lottie

Lottie settled into the stiff seat of the omnibus and wrapped her winter shawl around her shoulders. The sun had made an appearance for a moment that morning as she waited at the station but quickly retreated into the gloom. She hadn't had enough for the ticket, not entirely, but the carriage man had a sympathetic eye, he knew, as everyone did, about the collapse at Morris's Pit, and after all the paying customers were settled, he'd waved her into an empty seat.

"I'm headin' that direction anyhow," he'd whispered with a wink.

Her stomach felt as though she'd swallowed daggers, she'd not been able to eat this morning, and her coal ration had run out, so the cottage had been ice when she woke. Still, she had forced herself to wash her face and pull her nicest housedress from the cedar chest. She had people depending on her, and she intended to wait as long as she needed for Mr. Glasscock's attention. He would hear her. She'd freeze to death in front of his office before he turned her away again.

Careful what you wish fer, a voice whispered in her head.

Lottie batted it away and pulled her scarf over her ears. It was a three-hour trip to Aberdare in this weather, and she allowed herself to close her eyes as the horses pulled the omnibus over the uneven roads. Elis would have been turning twenty-three this coming week. They wouldn't have had money for a proper celebration, but Lottie would've bought some dried apples for a makeshift *pwdin eva*. It was just one of many things she'd had to learn when she'd followed Elis to Wales. Her home, Glasgow, felt like an entirely different universe, worlds apart from this remote place. It'd been pure chance they'd even met, no reason in the known world why she should have crossed paths with Elis Liath. He'd been in Glasgow on a holiday of sorts, twenty years old and his skin kissed with the summer sun. He was working a porter ship up from Pembrokeshire. He was under orders not to leave the Glasgow port, but he and his mates had, of course, left the port the first chance they had. They found themselves at Saracen's Head in Gollowgate, full of beer and utterly baffled as to the direction back to port. Lottie had been newly sixteen and working nights in the laundry at the Cathedral House, on her way home from her shift when she'd seen Elis standing in front of the pub, right in the middle of the lane, a look of pure frustration on his face. She'd stopped and watched him for a minute. She'd find out later that his mates had left him there, sure they knew the way, but Elis hadn't followed, not trusting their memory of the twisting path that had led them to the pub.

"Do yeh need help?" Lottie had called across the street, and as Elis had turned, she'd felt her heart drop straight from her chest to her stomach. He had dark eyes and a bronze to his skin that was clearly from out of town. His dark hair fell over his eyes, and as he identified who was speaking to him, he smiled. Lottie felt as though the full weight of the sun had shone on her in that moment. She stood, stunned, watching him watch her.

"Yeh, I think I do," he called back. "I think I'm lost."

"Are yeh?" Lottie replied. "Why'd yeh get yerself lost?"

"Can't say . . ." Elis took a step closer to her and stopped. "Maybe not so lost but rather maybe I'm in the right place after all . . . It's awful late, Miss. What're you doing out at this hour?"

"Not that if it's what yer implyin'," Lottie snapped, but she hadn't been able to feel fully angry or even annoyed. She was too fixated on his muscular form silhouetted beneath his simple workman's clothes.

"Not implyin' a thing, Miss . . . Miss, yeh do have a name, I assume . . . ," he asked with a grin.

"I do. Not sure yeh need to know it, though," Lottie said teasingly. "I could help yeh, if yer lost. I know this town quite well."

"I'd appreciate it, Miss. I think I'll call you Miss Coeth," he said, taking another step toward her.

"Why are yeh set to callin' me that?" Lottie asked curiously, enjoying this game immensely.

"I'll never tell. Stop asking," Elis replied, with a grin on his lips. "Maybe I can buy yeh a pint before yeh help."

Lottie scoffed at the offer. "You saw an old man in there behind the bar? Scar on the side of his face?"

Elis nodded.

"That's Cullen Sheffren, and he'll tell my Da I was out drinking in pubs instead of going straight home from work faster than you can say *Amen*." Lottie took another step toward Elis. "So if I am to help yeh, I best get to it, before my family wakes up and realizes I'm not back."

"What an offer." Elis never took his eyes from hers. He held out a hand. "I'm Elis Liath."

Lottie had walked him the long way back to the port, intentionally extending their path. She knew she should practice more caution, but something about Elis Liath—the light behind his eyes, the way he carried himself, like he hadn't a care in the world—something about him felt familiar and also brand-new. She told him about her job at the Cathedral House, how she'd left school to help her family, how her da had taken ill, couldn't work anymore. Elis had listened and watched her lips move as she talked. In turn he told her how he was done with the shipping freights. This was his last run; he was taking a job in the mines back home in Wales after this run.

"Why would yeh give this up to be in a hole all day?" Lottie wrinkled her nose.

"They pay more, and in just a few years, I can take myself to Swansea or even London itself and make a real life." Elis looked up at the stars. "So much out there I've never seen. Even with a thousand ports and a thousand port pubs, I've seen but a piece of it all. I want to travel far from this place. Did you know there's a mosque in Constantinople that was built in 537 A.D.? It's survived wars and fires, and still it's there, older than the world around it. They say when the sun sets and catches it just right, it shines as though it were built from pure gold."

"You're learned. Why are you running port freighters and dreamin' of mines? Why aren't yeh at university?" Lottie asked curiously. They'd reached the port and were sitting on a low stone wall as the dark waves rolled in and out.

"School—eh, well, that's a rich man's game. Any learnin' I've acquired has been on my own. I left school for the same reason you did. My family's from Cardiff. My own da ran off early enough I've no memory of him, then my mother signed me to my first job at the ports to keep coal in the stove and food in my younger brothers' bellies."

"It seems we have a bit in common," Lottie said softly.

Elis turned to her, the light from the port catching his eyes. "What do you want in this world, Miss Coeth? Where is it you want to find yerself?"

Lottie stuttered, the full attention, the fire in his eyes nearly overwhelming her. "I—I don't think much of it. Mostly, I know where I don't want to find myself. And the laundry at the Cathedral House is one place I don't want to be for much longer. Glasgow entire I could leave behind. What's the name of the place in Constantinople?"

"Hagia Sophia. It's called the Hagia Sophia," Elis said softly.

"I think I'd like to see an ancient place built from pure gold," Lottie said, breaking her gaze from Elis and looking out over the sea.

"I'm glad I was lost," Elis said, and his hand moved over hers. Lottie felt a static charge surge though her body at the slight touch.

"I'm glad yeh were, too," she said. "I have to go, I've been gone far too long; they'll know my shift was long over by now."

"Can I write yeh?" Elis asked. "I can send letters to the Cathedral House. Yeh can read well enough, yes?"

"I can, and I'd like that," Lottie said softly. "Maybe you can tell me about all the places you'll visit when yer rich from the mines."

"Maybe I can." Elis pulled Lottie to her feet. "Thank you, Miss Coeth."

"It's Lottie, Lottie Carlisle," she said softly, transfixed by his voice.

"Exquisite." Elis's eyes were locked on hers. "That's what *Coeth* means in Welsh. You are exquisite."

Lottie received a letter a week from Elis from that point on. The girls at the Cathedral House giggled when handing her the mail and crowded around until she shooed them away while she read. Elis wrote his whole heart on those pages. He told her of temples in Egypt that were built for ancient pharaohs and places in Brazil where the trees were so thick daylight never reached the jungle floor. He promised to take her; he promised so many things. So when, three months later, he asked her to join him in Aberdare and marry him, Lottie hadn't hesitated. Her mum and da had screamed murder about it, but she was grown in the eyes of the law and free to marry who she wanted. She'd felt like a traitor looking at the small flat where they all lived, but Lottie knew she was meant for more than this. If she stayed in Glasgow, she'd be tied to the laundry or cleaning houses for the rest of her life, taking care of her da who drank away any money she brought home. If she didn't leave, she'd be stuck here in this dank hole of a city till the drink took her da and her mum both.

She and Elis had married at the courthouse in Aberdare and stayed in Glamorgan on their wedding night. Lottie hadn't known much of what went on between men and women, just what the night girls showed to the men outside the pubs and the whispers from the girls at the laundry. Elis had been gentle and slow, taking his time, kissing her softly. He'd had her whole heart with his letters, but from that night on she was his entire. They stayed up all night whispering all their grand plans, all the places they would see, the things they would do. It was exquisite.

Even once in Cwmaman, those dreams didn't fade, not really. Elis came home covered in thick dust and tired to his bones, but Lottie knew his dreams were still alive, somewhere beneath the dirt and grime of the mines. They would leave this place eventually, and make it to London and the rest of the world after that.

The omnibus hit a hole in the path and jerked Lottie out of her dreams. She clung to the dreams, the sweet memories of Elis that remained around the edges of her consciousness, but it was gone, and she was back in the Welsh cold, alone. Twenty-one days gone.

Lottie

"Ye'd do well to step inside," the old woman barked at Lottie from the doorway across from the colliery central office. "The boss isn't in, not now, and ye'll freeze to death standing there."

Lottie turned to see the origin of the sound. The cold had made her movements slow and cautious, the wind cutting through all her layers of wool. The old woman gestured her inside her shop, and Lottie hobbled toward her, her legs wary of obeying her command. She had been waiting outside the colliery office for an hour now, and no one had appeared. The old woman was right—she could wait hours more and die in the cold or wait in what looked to be a yarn merchant's shop.

"I thank yeh," Lottie said, her voice unsteady as she breathed in the relief of the wood stove in the middle of the shop.

The woman regarded her for a long moment as Lottie stood as close to the stove as she dared and stretched her fingers toward the heat. "Not that it's any of my say, but ye'd be well advised to take whatever the son of a goat offers yeh and leave it be."

"I don't have a choice," Lottie said, steeling herself. "I'll be in the workhouse if I don't figure a way through this."

"I'd take the workhouse to what that *pric pwdin* is known to do to those that look to call him out. Trust me on this, girl." The woman looked to the window. "Looks like the bastard's returned. Take my advice, love, settle for what he's offerin' yeh, and get as far from this place as yeh can. Morris's Pit was an embarrassment for the good Mr. Glasscock, and he's lookin' to forget it, not answer fer it."

Lottie looked out the window to see Mr. Glasscock unlocking and entering the colliery office. "I thank yeh, I do."

"*Mae chwarae'n troin chwerw wrth chwarae hefo-tân,*" the woman said with a nod.

"What does it mean?" Lottie asked, shaking her head.

"Things turn sour when yeh play with fire," the woman said. "Ye'd best be off."

Lottie nodded a final thank you and left through the shop door, the bitter winter wind hitting her with spiteful force.

Lottie

"Mrs. Liath, that is your name? Mrs. Liath?" Mr. Glasscock motioned to the chair opposite him, his great oak desk between them.

"Yes, Mr. Glasscock. I'm glad you remember me." Lottie took care to articulate her words. She wanted to sound townie, as a country girl was unlikely to be given a minute's consideration by a man like Glasscock.

"Yer not from here, are you, Mrs. Liath?" he said, leaning back and lighting a wooden pipe. A puff of smoke rose from the tobacco, and he looked at Lottie, his small eyes assessing her silently.

"From Wales, sir?" Lottie said, trying to keep her voice steady. "No, I grew up in Glasgow."

"Yeh have that Scottish brogue, I can hear yeh trying to hide it, but it's clear as *disgleirio fel ceilliau ci* that yer not Welsh."

Lottie stared at him uncomfortably, his beady eyes full of mockery. "My husband was Welsh through and through, as our child will be."

"Yeh don't know what that means, do you?" Glasscock

asked, never breaking eye contact with her as he puffed at his pipe. "*Disgleirio fel ceilliau ci* . . . do yeh know?"

Lottie shook her head.

"A dog's bollocks. It's as clear as a dog's bollocks that yer not Welsh." Glasscock set the pipe down and leaned forward, his eyes boring into her.

Lottie's hands were shaking in her lap, but she forced out the words. "I do not appreciate the vulgarity, Mr. Glasscock. I'm here to discuss . . ."

"Because if yeh were Welsh, ye'd understand that it's considered rude, unspeakably rude, to demand that which is not yers to demand." Mr. Glasscock's voice was crisp and even, his words as sharp as the winter wind outside the door. "And ye'd understand that a woman who seeks to profit from her husband's death is nothing but a *wrach*, but I'd suppose that not being Welsh, yeh don't know what that is either?" He tilted his head and stared at Lottie, his words hanging in the air between them.

"Mr. Glasscock, I am not asking for anything that is not due my husband and, by merit of being his lawful wife, due me . . ." Lottie felt a rush of anger race up her spine, and her words flew from her mouth. "The only witch in this room is you, Mr. Glasscock. Yer the devil's man, and denying a widow what's rightfully hers is the devil's own work if I've ever seen it. I'm not Welsh, but in Glasgow we know how to settle our affairs, and the honor is keepin' yer word. And in my home yer nothin' but a goat's *bawbag*, but I'm guessin' yeh don't know what that is." Lottie rose to her feet, her face and throat burning.

Mr. Glasscock's face darkened to a shade that looked fit to burst. "Our business is done, Mrs. Liath." He hissed the sound of her name, his voice contained but deadly quiet. "You can see yerself out. My previous offer stands, but it won't fer long—a week's wages, and that's that."

"Piss on yer offer." Lottie slammed her hand on the oak desk, sending papers flying to the floor.

"Yer tryin' my patience, girl," Mr. Glasscock growled, a vein beginning to pulse in his temple.

"I happen to know that Morris's Pit is a blight on yer good reputation." Lottie leaned forward, both hands on the desk, her anger a wave ready to break. "If I leave here without a month's wages and the insurance pay, I'll head straight to the *Aberdare Times* office. If yeh won't listen to me, I'll tell them my story. And after that, I'll tell the *Aberdare Leader*, and then maybe I'll tell the *Cardiff Ledger* and I'll keep on tellin' until the world entire knows just what a *wrach* yeh really are."

"Yeh try that, girl, and yeh see exactly how far yeh get. Yer nothing, a crazy little girl, driven mad by grief. Melancholia is known to cause delusions. Yeh think the papers are interested in a fairy story told by a mad girl?" Glasscock stood to meet her eyes.

Lottie's entire body was shaking, her voice rising in pitch with her anger. "The only one who's mad here is you. I'm as sane as they come, and I'm right, they'll see that I'm right." She laid her hand on the dark wood desk to steady herself and found her fingers wrapping themselves around the heavy glass ashtray that held Mr. Glasscock's pipe. A wave of rage flashed through her, and she felt her fist closing around the cool, rounded edges. The image of Mr. Glasscock's brains splattered against the wall behind her filled her mind. A tiny voice in the very back of her head tried to cry out, but her arm was already in motion. The glass ashtray and the lit pipe flew at Mr. Glasscock's face with the full force of her rage. He ducked, but his bloated frame was too slow. He cried out as he clutched at his eye, and Lottie stumbled back at the sight of bright red blood dripping down his mottled face.

"Damn you! Yeh damn idgit! Yer no woman, yer a petulant child!" Mr. Glasscock reached behind him with his free hand

and pulled a bellrope, the sound echoing in a room beyond the wall of his office. Lottie could hear the echo of the bell. He pulled a handkerchief from his pocket and held it to his face. All Lottie could see was blood, the extent of the injury hidden by the thick red stain.

"Yer a pig." Lottie spat the words at him, the blood only stoking her rage further. "I don't know why I ever expected yeh to be fair. Yer like all the *olphéist* in all the stories, yer a—"

Lottie was cut off by a hand that reeked of dirt and soot covering her mouth. She choked on the words that stuck in her tongue and felt her body being pulled backward. Mr. Glasscock nodded to the figure who was holding her.

"Thank god. Get this child out of my office, and call the doctor. This damnable girl is suffering from an episode, damn near took my eye! Get the polis. Maybe they can settle her."

"I understand, sir," the man holding Lottie said, and she felt her hands being wrenched behind her back by another, a rope wrapped around her wrists. She pulled out of their grip and landed an elbow squarely in one of the men's guts. She heard a grunt and a temporary reprieve from the pain of their grip.

"Here, give her a draught of this. She's hysterical; this will knock her down a bit." Mr. Glasscock pulled a glass bottle from his desk drawer, Lottie struggled against the men that held her as she saw the opium label flash before her.

"Of course," the voice behind her said.

The hand left her mouth but before she could scream, her lips were pried open with the filthy finger, and the bitter liquid was poured down her throat. She spat it back up, and it dribbled down her chin, but the fingers increased their grip on her mouth. She tasted blood as her lips were sliced by her teeth. She began to feel dizzy; enough of the opium had found its way down her throat. She staggered and was steadied by the hands that held her. Lottie felt the strength drain from her legs, and she dropped abruptly to the floor, her knees hitting the hard wood with brutal force. The pain felt a thousand yards away, as though it belonged to someone else entirely. She struggled to move her tongue, but the words clotted at her bruised and swollen lips. As blackness overtook her entirely, Lottie's last sight of the free world was Mr. Glasscock's bloated face and the satisfying drip of fresh blood.

Part II

Nairna
New Town, Edinburgh
1901

Excerpt from the Speech Given by Fredmont Rogers of the London Society for Psychical Research at the 1972 International Convention for Esoteric Studies in Vienna, Austria

Nora Grey is often overlooked in the annals of medium study. She is not the Fox Sisters or Daniel Dunglas Home. She did not have the mystique of Dorothy Kellings or the fantastical cult following of the great Madame Blavatsky. Nora Grey was just a girl, a country girl who was well trained in all the deception and thievery that accompanied spiritualism and continues to blacken its name. We should revile her; instead, she has become one of the most elusive figures in modern spiritualism, and we cannot turn away. She is at the center of the events that changed the way we define the physical medium and how we view the veil that divides our worlds.

You are all well versed in the events that have firmly placed Nora Grey in our collective pursuits, as we commence the twentieth year of the International Convention for Esoteric Studies, here in Vienna, a city that the subject of tonight's talk never stepped foot in. It seems a strange way to begin, but without the contributions of Nora Grey to the Spiritualist movement, we very likely would not be here ourselves.

Let us begin . . .

Nairna

"You've been betrayed," Nairna said quietly, staring at the Eight of Cups before her, the card reversed; next to it the Ace of Swords, also inverse; and on the end of the spread, the Eight of Pentacles, a mule with a flowered ring around its long ears, the sun shining overhead. The three sisters were friends of Rona and had heard of the young wunderkind that she was fostering. Rona had allowed Nairna to do the reading, but Nairna had seen a heavy bag of coins change hands first. It wasn't unlike what Tavish used to broker for Nairna's talents, but at least here in the grand town house on Princes Street in New Town, Edinburgh, she was fed better than she'd been her entire life and her closet was filled with dresses the like of which she'd never seen, fine leather boots and delicate slippers that looked as though they'd break in two with the weight of her foot. The staff called her Miss, and her bed was meticulously made with sheets of the finest cloth. Nairna did not mind being brokered nearly so much if she didn't have to starve and sleep in the cold to do it.

Miss Leticia Fairwright shook her head theatrically and looked to her sisters, who had leaned in, their mouths slightly agape. "It's Miriam's son, it is. He's stolen from us, he's taken the money from the estate, moved it all to Cornwall, and left us here living on practically nothing, starving. We'll be on charity before long."

Nairna fought to keep her reaction from showing on her face. The three sisters were far from destitute. It was true Miriam's grown son controlled the bulk of the family money from his estate in England, but Nairna was not seeing him in the cards.

"No, not him. I am seeing this betrayal did not come from your nephew, your son." Nairna nodded to Miriam, who shot a coal-fire look at her sister. "It comes from you, all three of you. You trusted someone outside your circle and that someone has betrayed you. I am seeing a man . . ." Nairna closed her eyes, and the frantic energy of the three sisters swirled up behind her lids like a storm. "I am seeing a man who promised you health, youth, someone who flattered you." Nairna was hit with the smell of manure and the fresh rot of hay left in the stall past its time. "You had a herd of something, a farm somewhere . . ."

"The horses!" the third sister cried. "They sold the Clydesdales to the man; he said he could double our earnings, and instead he disappeared with the lot!"

"Oh, and that was all our doing, was it?" Miriam barked at her sister.

"And you had nothing at all to do with it, then?" Leticia growled at her sister.

"Stop," Nairna said firmly. In her old life she would never have told the grown women surrounding her to be quiet, as her tiny, newly seventeen-year-old frame hardly commanded that sort of authority, but now that Rona had sowed tales of her visions, it seemed Nairna's voice had gained strength.

The old women were immediately silent. Even the men's voices on the other side of the parlor door were hushed.

"You asked for my sight, so you must allow me to tell you what I see," Nairna said firmly. Her eyes still shut, the image of a tall man with a dark beard and a moth-eaten coat appeared before her. "He took the money you gave him, and you will not see it again. The horses are gone as well."

Leticia drew in a sharp breath, and Nairna held up one hand as a warning against any further talk.

"The Eight of Pentacles speaks of redemption, of a renewal. From this loss comes greater gain. There is something still on this farm. You still have the land, and something is still there that was meant to be hidden and will bring more attention to your family name than the horses or even the coins you gave this man. I'm seeing a division, a place where one splits into two, a forked tree reaching high into the sky. I see night owls and voles. Send your son to this place, tell him to search; he will find something that others are seeking."

Nairna opened her eyes to see three stunned faces staring back at her.

"Do you have such a place on this farm?" Nairna asked.

"We do. I'll call Colin right away, or maybe there's a local boy who can go investigate . . . the village nearby—" Miriam was speaking low and rapidly.

"No." Nairna cut her off. "It must be your own blood. Do not trust others; you already lost enough to your misplaced trust. Send your son. What he seeks is buried deep beneath the dead roots of the tree."

"How can you possibly see all this?" Leticia whispered.

"Do you doubt me?" Nairna asked, staring into the old woman's eyes.

Leticia Fairwright shook her head. Nairna took a breath, feeling the exhaustion that followed her visions coming over her.

"Pardon me," she said and reached for the small bell next to her, which would call Rona from the next room to politely usher the three old women out. As Rona was showing the Fairwright sisters out, Tavish came bursting into the space.

"I don't like this business, girl, not a bit," he blustered, his breath reeking of whiskey. "I need to see what it is you're doing, and they're taking more money than they're ever going to be splitting with us. I won't have you worked for free."

"Calm down, Da." Nairna rested her head on her hands, her eyes heavy. "You've been at the drink."

"So what if I have been? Doesn't make me wrong." Tavish fell back into the chair previously occupied by Leticia Fairwright.

"It does, Da, it does. You're wrong. No one is cheating us. You're being rude." Nairna massaged her temples, which were beginning to pound.

"Rude? Yer my daughter, no one else's, and I manage yer affairs," Tavish growled.

"And you nearly starved the poor girl while you did it." Rona spoke from the doorway.

Tavish started and lurched to his feet. "You've nothing to say about how I take care of my own daughter."

"I think I do." Rona motioned for Tavish to sit, which he did. "Calm yourself, sir. We only have Nairna's best interests at heart. When we found you both, she was half-starved. Now, after all these months in our fine house, she has roses in her cheeks. She looks as she should, a fine young lady with the world at her fingertips." Rona smiled gently at Nairna, who felt a tug toward the woman who had been her savior. Truth was, she didn't care if she ever received a penny of the money Rona collected from those who wanted Nairna to read for them. Living in this grand house, walking Princes Street every day, strolling through the garden at the portrait gallery—that was enough for any life. The first week she'd spent in the town house, she'd been sick every night from the rich flavors and full plates. But as her body learned to reset its expectations, she reveled in the fresh vegetables, fine cuts of meat, rich soups, and freshly baked bread that the cook and her assistants prepared daily. Even Tavish had an unlimited supply of fine liquor, which he indulged in to the point of passing out more often than not.

"Da, stop yer fussing," Nairna said softly. "What is it that's got you so upset? You wanted to sit in on the reading? You never wanted to before."

Tavish stood and stalked out of the room. Nairna felt a sliver of fear shoot down her spine. His behavior would have them booted out before too long; there was only so much Rona and Frederick would put up with, and Tavish didn't seem to have a care in the world that he and Nairna could end up on the street again fast as anything.

Rona cast an unreadable glance at the door that Tavish had exited through and sat next to Nairna. "Never mind him, dear. You are not responsible for his actions. He is scared of losing control of you, of you outgrowing him, not needing him."

"I don't need him now." Nairna sighed. "Even out on the road, all that time, I felt as though I was the parent and he the child most times. He'd drink or gamble our earnings away lest I hid them, then he'd beat me for hiding coins from him."

"Let's not pollute our minds with Tavish Liath. I want to know what you told the Fairwright sisters that had them so shaken." Rona stood to pour two cups of tea from the delicate porcelain pot that sat on the sideboard behind them.

"I saw they had lost their livelihood, and they were blaming the wrong person," Nairna said, accepting the tea.

"That's been the gossip around Edinburgh, but not common enough that you'd have known it," Rona replied, her blue eyes darkening as she took a sip of tea. "Miriam's son sends them an allowance, but they scream to the heavens that he's starving them. Starving them." Rona let out an exasperated sigh. "The three old bats still had the deed to the family horse farm down near Leeds, but they sold it last I heard, lost their shirts."

"I saw that, too. They gave their money and the horses to a man who said he would double the profits. Instead he's gone;

so are the horses and all the money." Nairna sipped her tea. "I saw something else, though—a forked tree, a dead tree, at night, and something buried beneath it. I told them to send their son to dig."

Rona watched her carefully. "What did you see beneath the tree?"

"I don't know. I just know it's there, and it doesn't want to be any longer," Nairna said.

"Then it should be found," Rona said. "Are you ready for tonight, love?"

Nairna smiled. "I have some nerves, and you're sure you have Tavish occupied?"

Rona smiled back. "Frederick and his colleagues have invited your father to their card game. He won't interrupt."

Nairna nodded. She was accompanying Rona to a scrying session that evening, to be held in the darkly furnished back parlour of the town house. Rona was also a guest at the session, the woman who would be practicing the art of catoptromancy was a mysterious figure from across the sea on the American shore. Dorothy Kellings claimed to see the future by staring into a small mirror. She had made quite a name for herself among the Rochester psychic circle in America and was here in Edinburgh as part of a tour courtesy of London's Society for Psychical Research. Nairna had met her only once since she'd arrived the week before. Tall and full of fire, she'd been known as the Scarlet Sunbird in her youth, and she dressed in a style just different enough from the conservative Edinburgh ladies to make her stand out no matter her actions. And tonight, she was attending a grand dinner at the Connells' town house and would be demonstrating her special skill. Nairna was buzzing with excitement.

"She's heard of you." Rona refilled Nairna's tea.

"Me?" Nairna said with surprise.

"Yes, dear, you've made quite a wave since your arrival. I

fear your reputation precedes you," Rona said with a smile, and she headed to the door of the parlor.

Nairna closed her eyes and enjoyed the stillness of the parlor. Behind her lids, she saw the cards she had drawn this morning: the King of Wands, inverse, her father through and through. Bluster and pride, anger and noise. The Seven of Wands, jealousy and spite. And finally the Three of Pentacles, alliance and peace, success, stability. She would survive the storm that Tavish sought to raise, and through it, she would grow past him.

Nairna

"I am what they call a mental medium, although I've been known in the past as a physical medium as well." Dorothy Kellings stood by the stone fireplace, a glass of blood red wine in her hand. A gentleman from the SPR had accompanied her and was watching the room nervously from his seat in the wingback chair by the entrance. Nairna had made herself invisible on the far side of the room, listening in fascination to Dorothy's odd American accent, which made everything sound a bit as though all the words were slurred together and slowed down to half-speed.

"I use the mirror to put myself in a trance-like state through which my spirit guides speak." She paused dramatically and looked around the room, locking eyes with the Edinburgh Spiritualists who had been invited to join the dinner and séance. "All mediums have a spirit team of guides who navigate the other side, who connect with the dearly departed."

Nairna was sipping her own glass of wine, which she was acquiring a taste for, and she enjoyed the creeping calm that made her fingertips tingle and her mind quiet.

"I cannot guarantee who will come forward tonight. I can only trust in my guides and allow them to bring the spirits to me." Dorothy sighed dramatically, her flame-colored hair perfectly coifed on top of her head. She stood nearly a foot taller than most of the men in the room, and Nairna could see she wasn't even wearing heeled boots. Suddenly, she felt a hand in hers and her body being pulled forward.

"Come," Rona whispered in her ear. "I want you to meet before dinner. The séance will be immediately after, and I don't want to miss the chance for an introduction." Nairna allowed herself to be pulled along, nerves dancing in her belly.

"Miss Kellings, the Scarlet Sunbird, may I present our ward, Miss Nairna Liath." Rona smiled and nodded at Nairna.

The woman looked down on her with eyes that held a hint of the fire from her hair. She had a faint pattern of freckles across her fair skin, and her neck was impossibly long and thin. Nairna managed a nod and a small, clumsy curtsy. Dorothy Kellings smirked.

"I haven't been known as the Scarlet Sunbird for years. Dorothy will do just fine; you can leave the pageantry." She cast a faint glare at Rona and looked back at Nairna. "This is the child whose talents have been all the talk back in Rochester?" She smirked again. "Hello, Nairna Liath. It is a pleasure to meet you. They say you are a powerful mental medium in your own right."

Nairna stuttered. "I've never thought of it that way, I read the cards mostly, and I'm here to learn."

At that moment a soft and lilting ring filled the air, indicating that dinner was served in the dining room. Dorothy looked to Rona. "I want the girl to sit by me. I have so many questions."

Rona nodded and hurried off to remedy her seating plan before it was too late. Dorothy held out a hand to Nairna, ushering her forward. "Come, dear. Let's talk as much as we can with all these eyes and ears surrounding us. Your talents have caught the attention of the folks at the Society for Psychical Research offices, and stories of your readings have made it all the way to America, so I'd like to know what is going on in this tiny head." She smiled, but the gesture wasn't entirely without malice. Nairna nodded nervously and proceeded to the dining room where she sat next to Dorothy Kellings, and the man who had accompanied her was swapped to a seat next to Rona. He looked none the happier for it.

As bowls of steaming tomato bisque were served, Dorothy stared at Nairna, ignoring the polite questions and attempts at small talk from other parts of the table.

"Who is your spirit team, dear? Who guides you?" Dorothy asked in a voice that brought the chatter of the table to a halt as everyone leaned in to hear Nairna's answer. Nairna suspected they were equal parts interested in anything Dorothy Kellings had to say and secretly entertained by Nairna's obvious awkwardness.

"I . . . don't have guides, not really. I read the cards for the most part. I'm only just now learning about the art of mediumship," Nairna answered, her voice unsteady.

"Nonsense," Dorothy declared as she smiled a viper's grin at the table. "Mediumship is all things. Reading cards, stones, bones, tea leaves—it is all mediumship, and none of it happens without guides from the other side. Perhaps you are a mental medium like I am, and you can use your cards to scry the future, see into a person's heart."

"I can attest to it." Rona spoke from across the table, her expression controlled but firm. "The young lady is exceptional in her ability to see detail, and she's yet to be proven inaccurate."

"Well, quite a vetting, quite a vetting." Dorothy took a sip of the soup, seemingly breaking the spell she had cast on the entire table, as everyone started eating as well, the tension in the air lessening slightly. Nairna's stomach was in knots, but she sipped at the bisque until it was taken away and a plate of roast beef and parsley potatoes was set before her. It was her favorite, but she could scarcely force herself to choke down even the smallest bites as Dorothy turned her attention away from Nairna and chatted with the other guests. She told stories of the Rochester weather and the American Spiritualists. She talked about the streets of New York and the train to the West Coast and Los Angeles. Nairna cast a glance now and then at Rona, who was watching her worriedly from the far side of the table. As the plates were lifted and petite dishes of berries and cream took their place, Dorothy stood and excused herself.

"I must prepare. Please pardon me. I will see you all in a few moments." She gave Nairna a hard stare on her last words as the gentleman from the SPR rose and followed her out to the west sitting room, which was used for séances by the Edinburgh Spiritualists and had been arranged according to Dorothy's specific needs.

"Well, isn't this exciting?" a woman to Nairna's right elbow gushed. The Edinburgh Spiritualists were a small group, and demonstrations from visiting guests were a rare treat. Nairna knew that Rona had been hesitant to invite Dorothy Kellings and hadn't understood why, but she did now. The woman had a current of darkness surrounding her that Nairna couldn't quite place. It was like a faint smell, a perfume of sorts left behind in the air, slightly sour and insidious.

Nairna did not know quite what to expect. She had attended other séances before led by the Edinburgh members. There were none of the tricks and theatrics that she had employed for the sake of earning a pound or two back in her travels with Tavish. These had been quiet affairs that had yielded little fanfare. They had led Nairna to believe that perhaps magic only existed in the cards and rune stones, and the act of calling the dead was best left for the theatre. But Dorothy Kellings was said to be able to channel those who had passed on. Nairna had seen the front pages of the American newspapers with Dorothy's picture and read the interviews she had granted to the Society for Psychical Research.

Nairna knew that Dorothy claimed to have several spirit guides. One was an old woman named Blessed Moons. In the interview, Dorothy had said that once passed, spirits took their soul name, which did not always match their identity when they had been on this earth. In addition to Blessed Moons, there was a little boy named Jimmy, who either had a very pedestrian soul name or had opted to keep his earthly identity. There was also a young woman and the spirit of a slave who had died in bondage during the early days of America. Dorothy said her spirit team came to her as she stared into the reflection of the mirror, and through them she could contact those who came to reach out to their loved ones.

Nairna was fascinated, but she also recognized a show when she saw it. She had once been the principal player in her father's performances, and she wondered how much of what Dorothy Kellings claimed was true. She certainly knew how to command a room, and Nairna still felt shaken from their interaction. She had regarded Nairna so suspiciously: her face a model of politeness, but the undercurrent more akin to malice than curiosity. Nairna's reverie was interrupted as Rona appeared at her side again.

"Come, love." She motioned for Nairna to follow her. "They are ready." As they entered the dimly lit room, Rona leaned in and whispered in her ear, "She has her eyes set on you. She sees in you what I saw, and it scares her, I expect."

Nairna met her eyes and started to ask why. How? She was a seventeen-year-old girl who held no power over anything in this world; she was the least frightening creature in all of creation. But before she could express this thought, Nairna was seated on the north side of the table. The chair at the head was empty, waiting for its medium. Nairna felt a shudder course through her body, and the image of a card flashed across her eyelids. The Queen of Swords, a richly beautiful woman with flowing dark hair holding a sword, a hook-beaked bird of prey leaning over her shoulder. A card of supreme feminine energy, powerful and discerning. But as Nairna watched the vision that floated in her inner sight, the card slowly spun itself upside down. The energy was being twisted, and in its inverse position it had become envious and impatient, cruel.

Nairna opened her eyes to see the figure sitting at the head of the table, her hair fire instead of ink, but the look of a predator was unmistakable.

Nairna

A smallish mirror in an ornate silver mount sat before Dorothy. She looked around the room, lingering on Nairna, who felt the hairs on her arms stand straight despite the warmth of the air.

"In a moment I will ask the lights to be extinguished entirely. I must work in darkness and absolute silence. My guides will speak through me, so I ask you please to address them by the name they give. I do not know who will join us tonight, and I make no guarantees. Do not speak unless my guides ask a question of you."

At that, the gas lanterns were extinguished, and the room sat in perfect blackness. Nairna could hear her own heart beating and the breath of those on either side of her. The image of the Queen of Swords danced before her eyes, followed by the Ace of Swords, also inverse. The card held a fire-framed woman with a single sword on which was speared a skull. It was a card of victory in its upright position, but upside down as it was, it spoke of poor choices, of ambiguity, of disrepair. Nairna felt her body shaking, and she jumped when the scratchy voice rose from the head of the table.

"Hello, my dears . . . hello, my dears . . . I am Blessed Moons. Hello, my dears . . ." There was a low moaning sound and then, "I see a man is here, he is here for his son, a man is sitting to my right, this man is here for you . . . are you there, dear?"

A voice, timid and unsure, rose from one of the Spiritualist members, a man named John. "Yes, I think it could be me. My father passed last spring."

"Yes dear, yes dear, he is showing me a pocket watch, a silver pocket watch, and he says you know what it means, he says you know . . . ," Blessed Moons through Dorothy continued in her scratchy voice.

"I think so. My father's pocket watch, I have it with me now," John said, his voice unsteady.

"He passed suddenly, he passed in his sleep; oh dear, he is showing me that he passed without knowing he had gone." Blessed Moons moaned, the tone exaggerated.

"He did. He died in bed."

"Hello! I'm Jimmy!" A childlike, high-pitched tone interrupted John. It was almost comical in nature, and Nairna suppressed a smile even though no one would have seen it in the pitch-black room.

"Say hello to me!" The voice squeaked again.

Around the table various voices uttered a rather unsure "Hello, Jimmy."

"I have a visitor for a lady who's wearing a red dress; red's my favorite color it is!" Jimmy chirped.

Nairna was confused that Jimmy had a British accent but a rather odd one, the ends of the words dropping into Dorothy's distinct American clip.

"I'm wearing a red dress . . ." A voice rose from the table.

As Jimmy channeled the spirit meant for the lady in the red dress, Nairna found herself feeling altogether strange. Her body began to feel as though it were encased in static, and the voices lost their words and meaning and became nothing but a dull whine. The darkness of the room became an endless pit, and she stared into the blackness watching with fascination as a bright white light came closer and closer. She could not feel the chair below her any longer and wondered if she were earthbound at all anymore. The light came closer still, and the space was filled with a warmth that Nairna had never felt. It seeped into her very bones. Framed by the brilliance, a woman with coal-black eyes and black hair stood with her arms wide. She nodded at Nairna and swept a hand in a circular motion. No sound emitted from her throat, but a single word swirled and danced around Nairna, wrapping her in its soft comfort.

Soon.

Lottie
Aberdare
1866

Children's Rhyme, Author Unknown

The wailing woman walks the grounds
And haunts the mist on Argoll Downs.
If she catches you in sight,
You're not like to live the night.

Lottie

Lottie awoke to her hands and feet numb from cold and her head threatening to split into two. She was on a rough stone floor, and the stale air smelled of urine and unwashed bodies. She tried to turn her head, and the effort caused a wave of nausea to wash over her. She vomited down her chin and, sick with disgust, tried to wipe it away with the hem of her now-filthy dress. Her hands were red and raw, the flesh underneath the nail bed blue. Lottie looked around her, her vision unreliable, foggy at the edges.

She was in what looked to be a jail cell. There was a single barred window high above her. It must be the basement, she realized. There was a single cloth cot and a wooden bucket but no blankets, save for a pile of unclean straw in the corner. Lottie was curled against the stone wall, her legs cramped from the unnatural position. *How long have I been here?* she thought madly. The light overhead was fading; was it the same day? The next? How long had she been gone? What had they given her?

"If yer quiet, the fella who comes on the night shift'll slip you a blanket. If yer quiet." A woman's voice, scratchy and rough, seemed to echo all around the cell. Lottie looked about in confusion, her head swimming and the sick threatening to rise again. She buried her head in her hands to stop the motion.

"Where am I? Who are you?" she muttered, her voice weak, the effort to form the words herculean.

"My name's Georgiana, but you can call me Georgie, they all do, they all do, they all do . . ." The voice ended in a strange little song, a wisp of melody.

"Where am I?" Lottie whispered.

"Where? Why the Aberdare Crown Suites . . . where'd you think?" The voice erupted in cackles, the sound cutting through the space like a knife.

"Is this jail? Is it the workhouse?" Lottie looked up to try to find the owner of the voice. Georgie sat on the other side of the iron bars that divided the room. She was close to Lottie's age, but her skin held signs that her life had been much harder. She was wearing nothing but a thin cotton shift, her skin red and mottled with cold. Lottie started: the woolen shawl she had worn to Aberdare was gone, she only had her winter dress and boots. Her scarf and cloak were gone as well.

"My things . . . where are my things?" Lottie shifted, the nausea swirling again, but less than before.

"Nice things go away here. They fly right through the bars . . . like the spring butterflies, they fly, fly, fly. I blame the concierge. I asked him for a pot of warm mint tea, and he never arrived, never arrived . . . I came here in a fine silk gown I did, finest in all of Wales, made in London it was, blue silk the color of azure, and matching shoes and gloves, oh I looked grand, and look at me now, all alone, all alone, lost my fine things, and the concierge made off with my watch as well. I'm not tipping the house staff. I'm not, I say."

"Georgie, stop yer prattling." A man's voice echoed around the chamber, and Lottie looked up to see an older man with graying hair coming down a stone staircase. He was dressed in the dark uniform and conical helmet that the polis wore.

"I'm in jail," Lottie said in her cracked and frozen voice.

"They said yeh were a smart one. Guess they weren't lyin'." The officer laughed at his own joke and threw a dark wool blanket into Georgie's cell. "Here. If yeh freeze to death on my watch, I have to clean up after yeh. Take a blanket."

"Thank you, kind sir, and now I would like a little brandy, and if you have it, maybe a bit of an aperitif . . ." Georgie grinned at the officer, showing off a mouth full of missing and broken teeth.

"Coming right up, madam." The officer tipped his hat to Georgie and then looked to Lottie. "Here, same deal. If yeh die on my watch, I'm swamped with paperwork. I'd rather yeh not freeze to death quite yet." He pushed a dark wool blanket through the bars. Lottie reached for it and wrapped it around herself. The cold of the outside still hung on the fabric, chilling her even more.

"Why? Why was I brought here?" Lottie said, her voice gaining strength.

"Assaulting Mr. Glasscock. Yeh don't remember? Or is that yer game fer the judge? Watch that one. You'll end up like Georgie here, won't yeh?" He winked at Georgie, who was winding a strand of her filthy hair around her little finger and singing to herself in a barely audible voice.

"Assaulting? I never . . . I didn't lay a hand on him." Lottie paused, the memories of the event foggy. "Not really. Besides, he had it comin' to him." Lottie pulled herself to her feet, her entire body screaming in protest. "I went to talk to him; his men grabbed me and made me drink something . . ."

"Made yeh, huh?" the officer said, eyeing her with a pitying look. "It was my understanding that yeh attacked Mr. Glasscock and his security men, and they had to calm yeh before yeh lost control entire. If yeh just admit to it, the judge will likely fine yeh and send yeh on your way. Mr. Glasscock filed charges, but from what I understand, he asked the judge to be lenient, so if I were yeh, I'd act the mouse and pay the fine. Live to fight another day, as they say."

"He's a liar! Anything I did was well deserved. Yeh don't know what's happened!" Lottie cried, her voice shrill and uncontrolled. "I want to speak with . . ." She ended in a stutter, realizing she had no one to speak to, no one who could help, no one who would even miss her. Even the other women in Cwmaman, they wouldn't miss her for days, and even then, they had no power to help. "There was a woman! In the wool and yarn shop across from the colliery office. I talked to her before he arrived. She can vouch for me, she can tell you, she knew why I was there, she can vouch for me!"

"Do yeh mean Tess Griffiths? Who do you think was the witness to Mr. Glasscock's report? Tess told them everything: how you'd stumbled into her shop, talkin' madness; how she worried fer her own safety is what she said, ran out after Mr. Glasscock. Hell, girl, she saw the whole scrap from her window. She's already signed her papers. She'll not vouch for you; she's already told her truth." The officer paused. Then, glancing at Georgie in the next cell, satisfied she wasn't listening, he leaned in. "Between us, Tess Griffiths'd sign anything that'd help Glasscock not to turn her out on the streets, but what matter does it make? They have their story. You have to wait fer the judge. He'll decide whether to send yeh home, or . . ."

"Or what?" Lottie asked, a fresh fear filling her spine. "Or what? Lock me up here?"

"Or somewhere else," the officer said. "I'd calm myself if I were you. I'll be back with some supper soon. All yeh can do is wait till morning."

Lottie closed her eyes and tried to block out the sound of Georgie's manic humming and the chill of the stone walls. She felt exhaustion take over and curled into a ball on the stiff cot. Strange, fitful dreams filled her head. She saw a girl, a young girl who looked something like herself, but not entirely. Younger than her, smaller. She was standing at the foot of a great, long table. Others sat and watched, their faces shocked and a bit scared. Lottie stood at the opposite end of the table, watching the girl, who writhed and shook as though she were in pain. *Enough! Stop it!* Lottie tried to call to the girl, but her words were lost in the dreamscape. A man stood near her with dark hair and eyes so much like her Elis, his whole countenance so familiar and yet so alien. Lottie felt the whole room spinning away from her, and she opened her eyes to the stone-walled cell and the first streaks of a new day's light.

Lottie

"Step forward, Mrs. Liath." The judge did not even look up from his great wooden pulpit. He sifted through documents and adjusted the glasses on the end of his great, warty nose. There were only three of them in the court that day. Lottie, Georgie, and a man who appeared to still be intoxicated. He could hardly stand on his own, and the officer had to lean him against a wooden pillar to keep him upright.

"Mrs. Liath . . . battery and assault." The judge looked up finally and assessed Lottie. She felt his eyes move over the length of her body, looking at her thin arms and her bloated belly, her pale skin, dirty hair. "It says here you very nearly took out Mr. Glasscock's eye. What do you have to say for yourself . . . and I might add, young lady, it best be an apology so we can send you on your way and get on with it all."

Lottie looked around the room. Officers stood at attention. Georgie swayed back and forth, her lips moving in a silent recitation of whatever was happening in her head. She felt a fire of rage and angst filling her gut. She knew what Elis would tell them, how he'd straighten his spine and tell them all to go to hell, how his voice would fill this chamber. *He was a man*, her mind whispered to her. *Apologize, say you're sorry, go home and figure out what's next.* She opened her mouth, the false apology on her tongue, but then an image flashed before her: the eyes of the woman in the wool shop and the cloaked look in her eyes. Of course, she had lied. Mr. Glasscock had probably threatened her lease, her home. He probably did this every day, the same as he was doing to Lottie and the others from the mine. He would continue to lie and steal and cheat and never care who was hurt in his wake. He would sit in his office and smoke his pipe, and all the while her Elis grew colder in his grave by the day. Elis . . . the grief she had yet to allow herself to feel reared back and crashed like a wave over her. She stumbled in place, struggling to stay upright; in that instant, she could smell him, feel him, the skin of his neck when he held her, the scent of soap and lemon that hung on his skin even when he was thick with coal dust. His hands on her cheeks, the sound of his voice, the shirts that still hung in their closet back in Cwmaman . . . all of it overwhelmed Lottie, and she gasped for air, blind to the courtroom and the judge, the curious eyes of the officers. Even Georgie stopped her strange and silent song and watched, her mouth a bit ajar.

"Mrs. Liath? Are you quite alright? Can I take your silence as an apology and let's be on with it?" The judge's voice was more impatient than concerned. He wanted to get rid of her, to send her back to her cottage that she was surely turned out of now that Mr. Glasscock knew who she was. All their dreams, hers and Elis's, flashed before Lottie's eyes as though she were near death. She saw the trains and carriages, a temple built from solid gold shining in the sun; she saw a manor house in the countryside, far from the coal dust; she heard laughter, a tiny hand in hers; her stomach heaved, the sprite inside fighting to be acknowledged. She opened her mouth, not certain what would come out. In lieu of words, a keening wail filled the room, inhuman and bone-shattering. Lottie felt herself drop to her knees. The sound continued to shriek forth from the depth of her grief and loss, her fear, her anger, her confusion. She saw the girl she'd seen in her dreams dance before her eyes, sleeping beneath a tree; the air was cold, and she was hungry. She reached out to stroke the girl's hair back from her face—so familiar, so new. But nothing. She touched the girl's skin, and it was nothing, no sensation, as though she were a spirit or the girl a vision. The scream that seemed it would never end faded to a quiet sob. Lottie felt her vocal cords shredded by the exertion, the girl in the woods fading fast, the courtroom coming back into focus, and the officer's hands on her arms as she was pulled from the floor.

Lottie

Lottie awoke to motion. She was propped upright, and when she tried to stretch her arms, she found them bound in cloth around her body as though she were hugging herself. Her mouth was covered in some sort of cloth that smelled of strong lye soap. Her eyes were dry and crusted-over; she could barely see straight as she glanced furtively around the space. She was in the back of a carriage, but the sort that the polis drove, with hard sides and wide-opening back doors that locked from the outside. An officer in a dark uniform sat opposite her near the closed doors; he glanced at her as she wiggled in resistance to her bindings.

"Settle yerself, love. Settle yerself. I expect this is all a bit startling." He spoke slowly as though Lottie were either very young or very old. She tried to respond, but the effort made her throat burn with a pain so intense it made tears spring to her eyes.

"Don't try to speak; that's why the mask. Yeh did a nice fine job of shredding yer throat there in the courtroom. I imagine it hurts like the devil. They'll give yeh up when we get to the hospital." He pulled a pocket watch from his vest pocket and scrutinized the time. "Shouldn't be too long now. Yeh've been out like a light fer hours now."

Lottie shook her head and looked pointedly down at the cloth that covered her mouth.

"Yeh need to be careful. They told me to keep yeh from talking," the officer said, his voice concerned. "Can yeh promise me yeh won't speak? Just whisper?"

Lottie nodded vehemently, the motion making her head throb. The officer slid down the long bench and gently pulled the cloth down under Lottie's chin. She felt the sharp pain in her throat again but managed a near-silent whisper. "Where are we going?"

"Argoll Asylum, love. They'll tell yeh more when we arrive. The judge saw what a state yeh were in. Shame about yer husband. Lost my brother to the mines not too far from where they said yeh were from; my mum never quite came back from the loss." The officer gave her a sympathetic nod. Lottie hardly heard his words, her mind was spinning. *Argoll Asylum?*

"Why?" she mouthed. "Why asylum?"

"As I said, love, they'll tell yeh more when we arrive, not too long now." The officer gave her another nod, and Lottie knew it was all she would get from him. There were small windows lining the very top of the carriage, and in the dim light Lottie could see irons around her ankles. She tried to lift her right foot and gasped at the weight of it, the effort sending knives down her throat.

"Just a precaution. They'll take care of all that when we arrive," the officer said. "Yer lucky, yeh know? Could've been thrown in the HMP Swansea; that's a terror, it is. Judge deemed yeh incompetent, sent yeh the other direction. Right good to be glad fer that yeh should be."

"I'm not sick," Lottie whispered.

"Well, yeh're not well either," the officer said as the carriage began to slow. He stood, bending his tall frame to the height of the carriage to look out the small windows. "We're approaching now. Not much longer and they'll get yeh nice and settled."

Lottie felt a jolt of panic rush through her body. It paralyzed her for a moment, and her heart began to beat in a ragged rhythm, her breath short and insubstantial.

"I didn't do anything wrong, not that wrong anyhow," Lottie croaked, her throat burning with the effort.

"Hush, girl. I'm not the judge, and I'm not a doctor." The officer adjusted his uniform as the carriage came to a stop. "Now c'mon, settle yerself."

The carriage doors opened wide, and the dim Welsh sun was enough to blind Lottie entirely. She wondered how long it had been since she was in that jail cell in Aberdare. Days? How long had she been in this carriage? She could smell herself in the confined space, urine and sweat. How the officer had managed it, she couldn't imagine.

A man in an exquisitely tailored tweed suit stood in the doorway to the carriage. He moved back as the officer pulled Lottie down the bench and out into the light. Her legs felt as though they couldn't hold her weight; she fell backward, and the officer's hands caught her before she hit the ground.

"There, there," the man in the tweed suit cooed, his voice a thin tenor. Even these simple words made Lottie's skin crawl. She thrashed in her bindings and fell back against the officer. "There, there," the man repeated. "Sid, can you bring the roller chair here, please?"

Lottie looked desperately from side to side. She was standing on a narrow dirt lane, thick woods on either side. She could smell saltwater in the air, which meant she couldn't be too far from the coast. She wasn't in Aberdare or Cwmaman any longer, and the officer had said she hadn't been sent to Swansea, so where was she? Cardiff? It looked too remote. As she spun away from the officer who was struggling to keep her upright, she was knocked back by the sight of a great stone castle-like manor that rose seemingly straight from the trees themselves. It towered over her, the turrets spiraling into the sky. The arching entryway was heavy gray stone, and the doors dark wood of the sort that looked to defend the inhabitants from an invading army. The woods reached nearly to the stone wall that looked to encircle the place. *How tall?* Lottie thought. *Twenty feet? More? I am going to die here*, she thought clearly and with a certainty that rocked her core. If she was wheeled through those monstrous doors, she would never leave. A thick-necked man wearing crisp, white hospital clothes was wheeling a chair to her, his face impassive, his eyes empty.

"Settle yerself," the officer said firmly as he removed the irons from her ankles.

"Has she been this agitated all the way here?" the man with the insipid voice asked, looking at Lottie as though she were a specimen in a laboratory jar.

"No, sir, calm as a lamb. I expect she'll settle back in soon enough," the officer said, and then, looking back at Lottie, he said a bit quieter, "Won't you, love?" But it was more command than suggestion.

"It's quite an adjustment. We're well accustomed to all manner of reaction when our patients arrive. Mrs. Liath? We will take good care of you here. Won't we, Sid?" the man said. Sid had no reaction other than to move the chair in front of Lottie, where the officer forced her into it, her legs so weak her efforts to resist failed.

"I am Doctor Bothelli. Dr. Theodore Bothelli. It is very nice to meet you, Mrs. Liath." The well-dressed man looked to the officer, who seemed hesitant. "You are free to go, sir. Thank you kindly for your safe delivery of this young woman, and do thank your driver for us. At the guard gate back the way you came, you will find a resting house for the horses."

The officer nodded. "As long as yer settled." He looked to

Lottie and nodded. She thought she could see a hesitancy in his eyes, but he tipped his cap and walked to the front of the carriage to ride with the driver for the trip back.

Lottie thrashed in the rolling chair, her muscles and body so weak it hardly made a difference. "Well, Mrs. Liath," the doctor said, "I understand you have had quite a few days. Let's get you settled into your new home."

"Not my home," Lottie croaked, her throat on fire.

"They warned us about your poor throat. Screamed like a banshee and tore it to shreds, didn't you? Let's give that a rest, and maybe we can find you a nice cup of tea once we are a bit calmer."

His accent wasn't the thick Welsh brogue that Lottie had become accustomed to, and it didn't sound like the Scottish of her home. It was more cultured, crisp, precise. She wondered where Dr. Bothelli was from, and what this castle hidden in the woods held. As though he had heard her thoughts, the doctor nodded to Sid, who began to push Lottie's chair toward the entryway. As they moved, he walked beside her.

"Welcome to Argoll Asylum, Mrs. Liath. We understand you have come to us suffering from melancholia and fits. We can help you here. There are many who share your pain, so many tortured souls." He sighed.

As they approached the stone steps, two more men whose necks were as thick as Sid's opened the doors wide and descended to the chair. They positioned themselves on either side of the rolling chair and lifted it as though it were no heavier than a feather. Lottie felt an ice blade of panic course through her veins. She would never see those woods again, never see anything of the outside world save the tops of the trees on the other side of Argoll Asylum's walls. She would die here, and no one would come to save her.

Nairna
New Town
1901

Excerpt from Byers and Brown's
The Fantastical Life of Nora Grey

To truly understand the significance of the Dorothy Kellings séance in the spring of 1901, one needs to understand exactly what Dorothy Kellings was. Born in 1860 in a small town in Iowa, Ms. Kellings had displayed what had been considered unnatural talents even as a small child. There are even reports of her resurrecting a dead bird. This report led to Kellings's admission to a boarding school of sorts, but as history would tell, it was more prison than education. She left the academy at the age of fifteen and was taken in by her uncle, who worked to attract the attention of the now famous Rochester Spiritualist circle. By the time she had come of age, Dorothy Kellings was a household name in East Coast psychic circles. The Scarlet Sunbird commanded full theaters, and a private reading with her could run as high as $50, or roughly $1,600 in today's terms. For the time, this was considered unheard of. Dorothy Kellings was quickly becoming a legend.

The events as related by the Edinburgh Spiritualist Society and Dr. Edgar Burroughs of London's Society for Psychical Research tell a story of a medium who had lost control of her table, a séance where the display of ability by a mere child so far outshadowed Dorothy Kellings as to cast doubt on Ms. Kellings's veracity entirely.

Upon Dorothy Kellings's return to America and

her circle of followers and fans, her reputation never quite recovered. However, a new story was being told. The story of a young woman, very nearly a child still, who could levitate, move furniture with the power of her mind, and see the future in tarot cards with an accuracy that convinced even the most stalwart skeptics.

Nairna

The world came tearing back into focus with a ferocity of chaos and confusion. Nairna was lying on her back on the floor of the west sitting room, her chair in pieces around her. She could hear Rona, her voice urgent but calm. She could hear Dorothy Kellings yelling obscenities and the gentleman from the SPR, a low male voice interjecting meaningless words here and there. Nairna's head ached. A cool cloth suddenly touched her skin, and she focused her vision to see Marjory, the head cook from the kitchen, hovering over her, wiping her brow. Nairna was suddenly flooded with confusion and fear.

"What happened?" she managed to whisper. The effort it took to speak was herculean.

"Yeh gave them a right fright, you did," Marjory whispered back and gave her a conspiratorial grin. "Let's get you to the other room and let this lot fight it out. I'll get you some tea."

Nairna felt herself being lifted and carried, the angry voices growing softer. She stared in wonder as Marjory carried her along a narrow corridor and down a steep flight of stairs. The tiny door at the bottom opened to the wine cellar that lay below the kitchen.

"Can you walk alright? You hit yer head right well, yeh did," Marjory asked as she elbowed the small door shut. Nairna nodded as Marjory set her on her feet. The world spun for a moment, and she grasped the older woman's arm for balance.

"Easy there," Marjory said quietly. "Let's get you upstairs."

Nairna looked around in amazement. The door they had just come through was nearly invisible, a row of dusty wine bottles in dusty racks blending into the wall and masking the thin seam where the entry existed.

"What . . . ," she stuttered.

"I'll tell yeh all about it," Marjory said as she wrapped her muscled arm around Nairna's shoulder and helped her up the wooden stairs to the kitchen. It wasn't until she helped her onto a worn wooden chair at the kitchen staff's dining table that Marjory paused and took a long look at Nairna.

"Thought it best to get you out of there for a bit. Caused quite a row, you did. We'll just take a minute back here. Kira! Tea!" she shouted over her shoulder to the curious kitchen girl who stood in the doorway of the staff room.

Nairna sat up and realized that there was a growing lump on the back of her head. "What happened?" She repeated the question.

"Here. Drink this," Marjory said in response, handing her a cup of tea. "Wait." She pulled a small flask from her pocket and poured a draught of dark liquor into the cup. "There, you deserve that."

"For what?" Nairna asked. "How did you get to me so fast?"

"The false wall in the bookshelf," Marjory said gleefully, then registered Nairna's confused expression. "Oh, they haven't told you about that yet, have they? Let's just say that the spirits aren't always in the mood to show up on demand, so in the dark, things, people, bells, and the like have been known to mysteriously slip their way onto the table."

Nairna stared at the old woman and then sputtered a disbelieving laugh. Marjory joined in.

"Been known to happen," she said with a wink. "'Course tonight, I was just watching. There's a peep hole right above the *Collected Works of Shakespeare*. Wanted to see what the great Dorothy Kellings was made of, I did."

"What did she make happen? Why was I on the floor?" Nairna took a sip of the tea and cringed at the bite of liquor.

"Miss Kellings? She had nothing to do with you! No, she was just talking in her funny voices, staring in her little mirror. Not sure what to make of that one. What gentleman in Edinburgh doesn't have a silver pocket watch? And it doesn't take a medium to know that John Greenerly's father was Lord Greenerly, whose passing was in the news months ago. No, not sure whether that was communing with the spirits or the *Edinburgh Daily*." Marjory laughed at her own joke. Nairna had always liked the older woman, who'd worked for Rona and Frederick for decades; she'd come with the house, she joked. Her mother had been head cook for the family that owned the property before the Connells. She spent her days bossing about the twin girls who worked as her assistants and making bawdy jokes whenever Nairna ventured into the kitchen.

"What happened? Please tell me," Nairna asked again. She was starting to feel nauseated.

"The table started to rumble, it did. I couldn't see anything, the room so dark as it was, but I could hear it, I could. And then the oddest thing. No one was anywhere near the lamps, and it was still as black as pitch, but there was a light, right there in the middle of the room. Bright like the electric lights, not those old gas lamps in that sitting room. It just hung there like a ball, and that was when I saw you. That was when everyone saw you, I expect." Marjory took a sip from her flask and shook her head, enjoying the telling of the story immensely.

"What was I doing?" Nairna whispered. She feared the answer.

"Floating right out of yer chair, you were! Damndest thing I ever saw, it was, and I've been peeking over top Lord Shakespeare's collection since I was a little girl. And some sort of shadow creature likes of which I've never imagined, thought I was seein' things I did, but there it was, hoverin' like the pair of yeh were sheets on a line. Never saw anything like that!" She slapped her thigh in delight. Nairna felt numb with disbelief. "There you were, floating three, maybe four feet up in the air, big as life it was! And then . . . all of a sudden, Miss Dorothy Kellings stood up and turned up the gas lamp, and down you come! You crashed back down like you were made of lead instead of feathers. The chair you'd been sitting in—well, you saw the condition it was in."

"And then you came in and took me here," Nairna said softly.

"That's the end of the story!" Marjory said. "Thought it best to get you out of the line of fire, so to speak. No one was watching me anyhow, so I whisked you back through the false door. Only one who'll suspect where you are now is Lady Connell. Oh, that Miss Dorothy was angry as a hornet. She was screaming up a storm—still is, I expect."

"She's the Queen of Swords . . . but she's upside down," Nairna said, remembering the vision she had had of the cards.

"That doesn't sound good," Marjory said.

"I'm suddenly very hungry," Nairna said as a paralyzing wave of hunger and weakness overtook her.

"Let's take care of that." Marjory grinned and rose to her feet, calling for the kitchen girls as she left Nairna alone with the image of silky black feathers against a red chest and the woman who wielded its power.

Nairna

Nairna shuffled back and forth in the kitchen, the old stove coughing up its share of smoke. Marjory opened the top half of the Dutch door to let out the stink.

"Keep chopping, girl." She interrupted the nonsensical song she had been singing to herself to glance up at Nairna. "This dinner won't prepare itself."

Nairna continued to split the peeled potatoes in half, chopping them into even squares. It had been a week since the Dorothy Kellings séance and the "incident," as it had come to be called around the town house. Nairna's reputation among the Edinburgh Spiritualists had risen to near-celebrity status. The parlor was full all day and into the evening with the curious and skeptical who wanted to see the girl who had levitated and stolen Dorothy Kellings's thunder. For her part, Dorothy Kellings was busy telling everyone back in Rochester about the obvious fraud that the Edinburgh Spiritualists were perpetrating and how they had set her up for a fool. Whether they believed Dorothy Kellings or the myriad witnesses who had seen Nairna float in the air before crushing a heavy wooden chair with the weight of her body, it wasn't clear. It didn't really seem to matter what the truth was, and Nairna was the worst to ask, as all she had as evidence was a still-sore spot on the back of her head and a memory of the Queen of Swords and her hook-billed familiar.

Today she had feigned a headache and then snuck back to the kitchen, where she knew Rona was unlikely to find her. The women and men in the parlor could exchange their tales of that night all they cared to. Nairna preferred the company of Marjory and the kitchen staff. The mystery of how Nairna had risen from her chair unaided only seemed second to how she disappeared from the sitting room seemingly without a single person witnessing her departure. Rona knew, of course, exactly how Nairna had disappeared and had given Marjory a mouthful about how dangerous it had been to use the hidden door when so many could have seen its existence. But apparently no one had noticed Marjory slip in and carry Nairna out, and no wonder when the great Dorothy Kellings was raising hell on the other side of the sitting room. Nairna knew it came down to a simple truth: people generally didn't see what they weren't looking for, and especially what they cared not to know.

"Nairna? At the rate yer workin', I figure dinner'll be round about next Tuesday," Marjory clucked. Nairna looked up and offered a weak smile. She felt drained, tired to her bones. It had all gone so wrong. Rona had been so busy managing Nairna's newfound infamy that they had hardly spoken about the incident. Nairna had no idea if Rona believed her or not, or if they were soon to be showing her and Tavish the door. The fact that the visitors kept arriving and demanding an audience with Nairna was the only indication Nairna had that perhaps they were on her side in the aftermath of the chaos. For Tavish's part, he was in an agitated state regarding the events of that night. Nairna had endured a frantic lecture as to how her actions were disrespectful to their hosts and they'd find themselves on the street if she kept up with her antics. Nairna had let him rant; Tavish could not understand that the events of that night were beyond her control.

"I'm sorry, I am. A bit distracted. I know they'll figure out where I am soon enough," Nairna said softly. As if on cue, Rona's voice rang out from the hall, calling Nairna's name. Nairna nodded to Marjory, who took the bowl of potatoes from her and nodded to the door.

"You're due on stage, my lady," the cook said with a wink.

Nairna sighed and turned to exit up the pantry stairs to her bedroom. Marjory wasn't wrong; her audience was assembled in the parlor, awaiting her arrival, hoping for wonderment. As Nairna changed into one of the fine silken dresses in her new closet and tidied up her hair in preparation for her appearance, she tried to imagine what it would be to have an ordinary sort of life. Maybe Marjory's niece or daughter, who worked in the kitchen and went home to a flat of her own each night. Invisible, alone, each decision her own. With a deep breath, she started downstairs.

Nairna

"Nairna, I am pleased to introduce you to Dr. Edwin Harrison. He is a guest from London, and he is very interested in speaking with you." Rona nodded gracefully to the gentleman in the crisp woolen suit who rose from his seat by the picture window as she entered the room. He crossed the space effortlessly and instead of shaking her extended hand, he raised it to his lips and kissed her knuckles, a gesture so unexpected and soft that Nairna felt herself blush. The parlour was full of ladies from the Spiritualist Society, including the Fairwright sisters, who looked ready to jump her as soon as the opportunity was offered. Nairna felt the relief of gratitude as she saw Rona head the ladies off to the next room, all three of the sisters objecting loudly and trying to get Nairna's attention.

"You are in high demand. I won't take much of your time, my dear."

Dr. Edwin Harrison had eyes that matched the cornflower blue curtains, and his dark hair served to make his defined features look dignified, striking even. Nairna felt eyes on her as the ladies and men who milled around the room pretended not to be watching and listening to her every word.

"Please sit. May I offer you a brandy?" the doctor asked, and Nairna nodded. He waved at the serving boy who stood near the door, and two crystal glasses of the dark liquor appeared before them as they sat at the table farthest from the other guests. Nairna took a sip and tried not to grimace. Alcohol went straight to her head, and she knew she shouldn't imbibe at all, but the week had been exhausting and another night full of curious eyes and hesitant conversations seemed impossible, even if the doctor did smell of sandalwood and vanilla.

"Dr. Harrison, I don't remember you from the séance last week, so I presume you have heard the stories, which likely means you believe me either a liar or witch, of which I am neither," Nairna said bluntly.

"Please call me Edwin." He smiled, seemingly amused by her brusqueness. "And I don't presume you to be either. However, not many can rattle Dorothy Kellings. I work with the Society for Psychical Research in London. The stories I heard of that night were told to me by my associate who was here assisting Mrs. Kellings. He is not one to be impressed or bewildered, and that night he found himself both."

Nairna remembered the stern-faced little man who had ushered Dorothy Kellings around that night. She nodded. "Can I assume that the psychical research you do is aimed at proving its falsehood as much as its truth?"

Edwin smiled again, and he regarded her curiously, as though he had not expected her to be intelligent.

"Rona speaks so highly of you. I see why now. So many mediums get lost in their own legend. I mean to say, they refuse to acknowledge any possibility that their talents are more a form of empathetic sight reading than a psychic phenomenon." Edwin paused. "Which is why what you did at Dorothy Kellings's séance was so very extraordinary."

"You don't believe Dorothy Kellings is psychic, do you?" Nairna asked, curious.

Edwin looked around the room at the many sets of ears who

were desperately trying not to look as though they were listening. He leaned in until Nairna could feel his breath against her ear, and she felt a rush of blood to her neck.

"Dorothy Kellings is a great showman, and that is what the Spiritualists want, a showman. You are not a showman, but you have perhaps something a bit more important." He sat back.

"And that is?" Nairna said, trying to maintain her composure.

"Talent," Edwin said simply. "You proved yourself to be what we call a physical medium. You manifested an action, and if the accounts of that night are to be believed, you did something that is actually quite impossible. You levitated feet above the ground for several seconds, and you succeeded in smashing an oak chair to bits without harming yourself, as though it wasn't your body that broke the chair at all but your mind. That is quite impossible, and either you are the best showman I have ever encountered, or you have an ability that we have not yet been able to measure."

Nairna took a sip of the brandy. "Perhaps I faked the whole thing. People see what they want to see. Before I came here with Lady Rona, I had quite an act. Ask my father. He's the showman, a natural born circus barker. I made him quite a bit of money all over the countryside, claiming to see the spirits of the dearly departed." She leaned in, feeling the occupants of the room hold their breath. "I never saw a thing."

Edwin locked his eyes on hers for a minute and then smiled. "You do not disappoint, Nairna Laith. You do not disappoint. I know all about your father. I think Rona and Frederick are generous almost to a fault. I would have left him back in . . . Where did they find you? Kirkcaldy?"

Nairna nodded. "I wouldn't have objected," she said, relaxing a bit as the brandy began to soften her edges.

"I believe you," Edwin said, motioning to the serving boy

for another round of brandies. "I think your talents may lie beyond these theatrics, and I would like a chance to see if I am right."

The serving boy exchanged their glasses for full ones, and Nairna regarded the man before her. He was sincere, and he did not want anything from her, as the others did; he did not seek knowledge of a loved one or a secret that was being withheld. He did not look at her like she was a child.

"What do you propose?" Nairna asked.

"Allow me to visit you tomorrow, and if you agree, every day this week while I am here from London. I have some—well, experiments, to put it poorly. Think of them as assessments. I believe that you are capable of so much more than card readings and parlour tricks." He met her eyes, and Nairna felt for the first time since Rona had found her that she had truly been seen.

"I do not know what a physical medium is," she said softly.

"I will show you. Nine o'clock tomorrow? Can I join you for breakfast and then perhaps an interview? A few hours of your time?" Edwin asked.

Nairna nodded. A tone sounded, and everyone began moving toward the dining room.

"Join me?" Edwin said, and Nairna stood to take his arm, feeling for the first time like she was moving forward.

Nairna

"Meet Miss Oleander Hawk Moth," Edwin said as he laid the creature in front of Nairna. She stared at the swirls of leaf green and cream, the ornate pattern that covered the nearly two-inch wings, and the light fuzz that covered the oblong body.

"She's lovely." Nairna had seen the moths before, but not often. The farmers cursed them and all their brethren, as they ate the crops on the vine and could wipe out a field of greens in a single afternoon. Nairna had always rather liked them despite all that. They had no fear of humans; she suspected they had no awareness of much at all.

The moth lay with its wings spread wide on the felt tablet before her as though it were an exhibit in a science display. Edwin sat across from Nairna and watched her as she studied the specimen.

"A physical medium is a rare breed," Edwin began. "While the mental medium claims to read the thoughts, actions, even futures of others, a physical medium can reach into the next world and create. Physical mediums have been recorded as manifesting corporeal forms during séances, manipulating their own bodies so as to levitate, emanating a substance we call ectoplasm, and causing physical effects to inanimate objects, such as breaking chairs." He raised his eyebrows on the last sentence.

"It sounds dreadful, and entirely improbable," Nairna replied.

"Physical mediums have even been known, in extraordinarily rare occasions, to successfully reanimate life forms," Edwin said carefully.

Nairna looked up at him, unsure that she had heard correctly. "Reanimate? Raise the dead?"

"Resurrection, yes," Edwin said.

"And I am supposed to, what? Reanimate this moth for you?" Nairna felt her lips twitching as she suppressed a laugh.

He looked uncomfortable. "Well, that would certainly prove our point. But no. I bring this purely as an example. You see, I represent the interests of people who work far beyond the reaches of psychical research."

"I don't understand," Nairna said.

"Have you ever heard of Countess Carolina Gustav? How is your fifteenth-century Prussian history?" Edwin asked, his voice softening.

"Not good," Nairna responded. "But I have a feeling you are about to fill in the gaps."

"I am." Edwin smiled. "She is the impetus for our research in this area. The countess was, by accounts, an odd child. The official records list her as 'feeble,' but given that she was a rather important asset and highly marriageable, her eccentricities were tolerated and even seen as court entertainment. She evidently had a rather gruesome trick where she would take a dove, twist its neck before a crowd, and then release it into the air where it would fly away unharmed."

"How horrible!" Nairna said, fascinated despite herself.

"Yes, and you'd be tempted to say that she hadn't twisted the poor creature's neck at all, that it was all a trick, and the dove was quite alive the entire time. However, when prompted, she would hand the unfortunate dove to a party guest, have them break its neck, and then proving the bird quite inarguably dead, she would then repeat her trick, and the dove would fly away unharmed."

"And she never had witchery cried against her?" Nairna said in disbelief.

"She was the daughter of a very powerful count, who happened to be at the right hand of the emperor himself, and anyone who cried witchery would have found themselves in a right heap of trouble. Money tainted a great many things then, as it does now," Edwin said. "As I said, she was considered mentally feeble, so no one questioned this behavior. It wasn't until many years later that not even the crown could protect her."

Edwin leaned in, and Nairna ran a finger down the silky back of the Oleander Hawk Moth.

"Countess Carolina married well, as all expected, and had a castle of her own to manage, as was also to be expected. But her son died in infancy, of smallpox or yellow fever. Whatever took him, took him quickly, and the house staff said her cries could be heard all across the grounds. But then the sun rose and the lady's wailing had stopped, and in its place was a baby's cry."

Nairna shook her head. "No. It can't be. She took a servant's baby, surely."

"That is how they explained it in the end. The story goes that the doctor climbed the stairs to the nursery to find the countess holding an infant who looked to be as healthy as a dove released to the sky. Eventually, a serving girl came forward and said the infant was hers and she had relinquished care of the child to the countess as a balm for her grief. But no one in the household could remember the serving girl having a child, and the baby seemed to be a perfect copy of the infant that had perished. All that can be certain was that the serving girl was well paid for her story by the crown, and the countess was moved further into the shadows—no public appearances, no parties, no chance to prove her story true or not."

Nairna stared at Edwin for a long moment. "What utter rot." She laughed. "No one can raise the dead. My Nań used to tell me when I was girl that we look in the shadows for truth that sits on our nose."

Edwin grinned and sat back in his chair. "It is a fantastical story, and your Nań sounds wise. But it's a curiosity nonetheless, and what if it were true? What would that mean for all of the rest of us out here in the world?"

"So you are looking for physical mediums to see what they are capable of?" Nairna asked carefully.

"Exactly. I work with an organization called the Order of St. Cyprian. We are a facet of the psychical research groups here and in London, but we have long arms, so to speak. We aren't looking for the next Countess Carolina, but what you did at Dorothy Kellings's séance was the clearest demonstration of a physical medium's ability that we have on record. So we are curious what else you might be capable of."

"So am I," Nairna replied, her mind lost in the marble leaf pattern of the Oleander Hawk Moth.

Nairna

On the second morning, Edwin brought a curious box full of mirrors and wires. Nairna examined it and looked up at the doctor suspiciously.

"Your Order of St. Cyprian, what is it exactly?" Nairna asked as she poked at the box.

"It is a research society, much like the SPR or the Edinburgh Spiritualists," Edwin replied, his voice neutral and not forthcoming.

"But not exactly, is it?" Nairna looked up, meeting the doctor's eyes. She felt herself flush slightly and looked back to the mysterious contraption on the desk. "Not exactly, are you?"

"No, not exactly, we do much of our work in America, which I think you would rather like. It would suit you."

Nairna caught his gaze again and saw a flicker of a thought appear and disappear behind his irises. She suddenly felt uncomfortable, as though the air had been pulled from the room. She shook the sensation off and again looked at the box on the table.

"What does it do?"

Edwin smiled and, indicating for her to sit, took a glass light-bulb from his case. Fixing the bulb in place, he set to work on the wires until the bulb began to blink, first furiously and then at a slow and steady pace. The mirrors lining the box amplified the light, the effect blinding even in the sun-filled parlor.

"It is a tool, which may or may not work for you, but it is designed to help you to a trancc-like state—a meditative condition, if you will," he said. "Here, try. Let yourself relax and watch the light. It would be better, of course, if the room were dark, but this is just to show you the concept."

Nairna nodded, skeptical. She rolled her shoulders a bit, releasing the tension she felt in her neck and back. With a deep breath, she let her eyes fix on the light emanating from the box. With the rhythm steady and constant, she felt her body begin to feel odd, numb but entirely aware of its senses: the bit of chill air from the doorway, the faint clamor of the pots and pans in the kitchen. She stared at the light and felt her head loll to one side. Quickly she recovered, shaking herself out of the state she had been in.

"Turn it off, please. It is making me feel rather queasy," Nairna said, closing her eyes.

Edwin complied, fidgeting with the wires until the light ceased to flash and went dark.

"What did you feel?" He sat across from her with his notebook, an eager expression on his face.

"Relaxed at first but then like the room was moving, like a ship. What was it supposed to do?" Nairna blinked, tiny specks of bright light apparently burned into her eyelids.

"The light box was developed some years ago for the purpose of mesmerism. For some, it can transport them into a higher state where their abilities are easier to access. Most notably of late it has been used by a man named Dr. Harold Oswent."

"Another history lesson?" Nairna said, taking a sip of her tea.

"A very recent history, if you will," Edwin replied, meeting her eyes. "Dr. Oswent resides in Ottawa, Canada, and has a reputation for surgery without anesthesia, pain-free procedures without morphine or opiates. His secret, he claims, is this box. He lulls his patients into a hypnotic state, and they feel no pain; they recover more quickly and with no side effects."

"Well, you are on the wrong continent," Nairna said. "You should be interviewing Dr. Harold Oswent."

"I already have," Edwin said with a smile. "Dreadful man. His patients consist of young women, and only young women. He claims to be able to cure 'female hysteria' and restore virginity to the impure."

"Oh dear," Nairna said, not able to stop the smirk that escaped her lips. "Yet you are using him as a reliable source."

"In all fairness, I only vouch for his light box. The man himself is a toad," Edwin replied. "The design is quite ingenious, and we have had some luck mesmerizing volunteers during the course of our research in London. But, of course, it is not for everyone. I wonder, though, what would happen if you pushed past the nausea you felt. Do you think you could try?"

Nairna grimaced. "I am willing to try, but if I vomit, you have what's coming to you."

At that point the echo of heavy footsteps filled the room, and Nairna heard Tavish's voice in the hall. He flung open the parlour doors and regarded Edwin as a hawk regards the mouse.

"Well, there she is. My daughter has been keeping to herself lately. And now I see why." Tavish strode to the table, where he extended a hand to Edwin. "You, I presume, are the so-called doctor who is here from London?"

Edwin smiled graciously and rose from the table to shake Tavish's hand. "I am a doctor. I completed my medical training at the Royal College of Surgeons in London. Dr. Edwin Harrison, pleased to make your acquaintance. I am sorry we have not met sooner."

"As am I," Tavish said, his voice dripping with false charm.

"Your presence is not needed here, Da," Nairna said, her temper on its edge. Tavish had been simmering with anger at her for the séance, afraid she'd offended the grand visitors. It made Nairna's blood boil. She didn't care much who she'd offended, and the truth was that he would still be hustling country farmers for their harvest pennies if it weren't for Nairna.

"My girl has a flair for the dramatic." Tavish turned his eyes to Nairna. He looked back at Edwin. "What exactly is it you want with my daughter?"

"To talk to her, learn from her. Your daughter is quite extraordinary, and we believe that she is very talented."

"Because of that show she put on for the American?" Tavish said with a hoarse laugh. "That was clever of her, I will admit, but I handle my daughter's affairs, so perhaps I should be the one you are talking to. What are you proposing for my girl? We're quite comfortable here, as you can see, so whatever you might offer best be appealing."

"You're making an ass of yourself," Nairna said, barely containing her growing anger. "You have nothing to do with this."

"And you think the good doctor here is just interested in your mind, do you?" Tavish's showman charm dropped off abruptly. His eyes turned cold and hard, and he stared down Edwin. Nairna could see the doctor was intimidated and hated her father for it. "Nothing is free, girl. This man wants more from you than he has let be known, and my job is to make sure he pays the proper entrance fee and treats you with the respect you deserve."

Nairna felt a surge of ferocity and rage boil over, her mind going blank. She felt herself rise to her feet, and her voice was guttural when she spoke. "I am done with your entrance fees and your mock concern over my well-being. I am not a puppet whose strings you can pull. I am not your property." She felt years of suffering, hunger, cold, the ache of her knees and toes from her performances all building up in her fingertips. "Leave. Now," she growled.

The next thing Nairna was aware, she was lying on the chaise in the parlor, a cool cloth on her head and Marjory fussing at her ear. Nairna tried to sit up, but Marjory's firm hands propelled her back on the pillow. "Lay back, girl, you gave yerself quite the knock to the head, and there's glass all up yer arm. Give me a chance to pluck it out."

Rona's face appeared over Nairna's eyeline, her expression worried yet filled with wonder. "You don't remember what happened, do you?" she asked.

Nairna shook her head as much as her position allowed, the faint movement sending an ache down her neck through her spine. She winced.

"Let's sit her up," Rona said, and with Marjory's help, they moved her to an upright position where she could survey the damage to the room.

The parlor table where Nairna had been sitting with Edwin was flipped entirely upside down; the chairs lay on their sides. The picture window that overlooked Princes Street had been blown inward and twinkling bits of glass covered the Persian carpet.

"What happened?" Nairna asked, an odd, swirling ache filling her head.

"You got angry," Marjory said simply. "I saw yer father come stormin' in, and I stayed close in case I needed to toss him back out. But turns out yeh did the job yerself."

"I don't understand," Nairna whispered, her thoughts not connecting. Only vague memories of the events leading up to this point remained.

"You did this," Rona said softly, sitting next to Nairna and taking her free hand. Marjory was using a small pair of tweezers to pluck bits of glass from her left arm, tiny beads of bright blood appearing with each successful extraction.

"You did this," Rona repeated. "There was an exchange between your father and Dr. Harrison, and then this. No one saw, but Marjory was close, and grateful we are that she keeps such close track of us all." Rona winked at Marjory, who grinned back.

"If you'd get me that radio I keep askin' fer, I'd have more to entertain me than all yer antics," Marjory said with a gentle humor.

"I couldn't have . . . what are you saying?" Nairna felt tears threatening to well up in her eyes.

"Dr. Harrison is right, my love; you are quite talented and very powerful. You did this. I doubt you even know how you did it. You were angry, and you released all that energy into the room, and well, this happened." Rona stroked her hand as Nairna felt a tear escape down her cheek.

"Edwin, is he hurt? My father?" Nairna asked, her voice shaky.

"They're both fine. Edwin will want to discuss it with you as soon as you are ready, and not before. And your father, well, we think it's best if he keeps his stay outside of the town house," Rona said.

Marjory wiped Nairna's arm with a clean cloth. "There you go, no damage done. For the job you did on the room, ye'd think ye'd be more banged up, but yer fine, yeh are."

"My head . . . ," Nairna said, closing her eyes.

"I imagine this took a great deal out of you. It's natural to feel drained. You should rest," Rona said. "I'll take you to your room."

"I'll bring you up some tea and a bit to eat. Yeh look pallid," Marjory said kindly, giving Rona's shoulder a squeeze as she stood.

As Nairna lay down on her soft bed and as her thoughts began to drift, she felt ice fill her throat. Terror sat like a weight on her chest, forcing her to take soft breaths. What had she done and, more importantly, how? It was overwhelming to think that perhaps it was all in error, a burst of wind or freakish storm that burst through the window and upset the table—not her at all but a force of nature for which she had been given credit. They would see soon enough she was a fraud, a show-man like Dorothy Kellings, and then where would she be? Starving in Kirkcaldy once again? Rolling her eyes into the back of her head for ha'pennies? But she also remembered the feeling of anger and bitterness in her hands, she remembered the pull of the wood and glass, the roar of fear in her father's eyes, and the feeling that she was finally in control of her fate.

Nairna

Edwin approached slowly. Nairna could see a thin scratch on his cheek, the faintest line of red against his pale skin.

"I did that," she said softly.

He raised a finger to his cheek, his eyes thoughtful. "You did. And it was simply magnificent."

Nairna let the silence sit for a moment, watching Edwin as he carefully took the light box out of its case. He was so different from Tavish. Where her father blustered and raged, Edwin was quiet. While Tavish filled a room with his very presence, Edwin was content to observe. He had not reacted to Tavish's attack the day before. Edwin had not risen to Tavish's challenge and anger, but Nairna had. She wondered if she could ever again find the quietude within her that she had once had. The girl who had been content with a bit of bread and goat cheese, a cup of cabbage broth and a warm spot for the night, was gone. Nairna knew she would never again be content with the ordinary life that she'd once known. How could she after her time here in New Town?

"What are you thinking?" Edwin asked quietly, sitting across from her in the soft leather chairs of the study. The glass was yet to be repaired in the parlor, so Frederick had opened this room for their use. It smelled lightly of pipe tobacco and mint, and Nairna felt as though she could live here in this space for a thousand years and never tire of it.

"I'm thinking that I traveled with Tavish for years, following him around like a starving dog. He sold my skills at fairs and carnivals. He told anyone who'd listen that I could talk to the dead, reach the souls of the departed. Remember when we first met, I told you I had an act?"

Edwin nodded, his expression impassive.

"I can pop the joints in my feet and toes—my knees, too. If I concentrate, it can be loud, loud enough to mistake for a knocking on a hard surface. I can roll my eyes back so it looks as though the devil himself has me in his grip. I'm a fraud. I always was. I know the meanings of the cards, but I don't need to see into a person's head to know what they are asking. They wear their wants and desires on their sleeves. All I do is pay attention."

"Could you do it now? Roll your eyes back, pretend to be in a trance?" Edwin asked.

"Yes, I could," Nairna said, looking up at Edwin, daring him to challenge her.

"Why are you telling me all this?" Edwin asked gently. "Are you trying to convince me that you are not who I know you to be?"

"I never even so much as raised my voice to him," Nairna said in a rush, gooseflesh creeping up her arms and down her neck. "Even when I'd watch him drink away the money I'd earned after a fortnight of not eating a thing except the leavings I found behind the shops and farmers' carts. I never challenged him, I never tried to leave. I just followed, thinking he'd change, the world would change, or maybe I'd finally die and that would be that."

"You're not a child anymore, you don't have to bow to Tavish Liath." Edwin reached across the space and took her hand.

"No, I suppose not," Nairna said, staring at her hand in Edwin's, the warmth of his skin, the rough feel of his fingers against her flesh. "What happened yesterday?"

"Didn't Marjory tell you?" Edwin said with a crooked smile. "You got mad."

Despite herself, Nairna smiled back. She felt the tension she was holding in her shoulders and back release, and for a moment she could see herself sitting in the study, holding the hand of a man with cornflower blue eyes. She could be any young woman, and he could be any suitor. She could see herself walking arm in arm with him through the gardens of the portrait gallery; she could almost feel his hand on the small of her back.

"What does your Order of St. Cyprian want with me?" Nairna asked softly, afraid of his answer.

"To see what you are capable of. As for myself, I have far more selfish motives. I want to see you are never beholden to anyone again. To see you never suffer and starve. And to see you leave your tricks behind because you are greater than anyone's imagining."

Nairna felt time stop just for the softest of moments. "Well then," she said and nodded to the light box. "We should start."

Nairna

In the relative dark of the study the effect of the light box was more profound. As the light flashed, Nairna allowed her mind to fall away and her body to relax. She trusted Edwin with her entire self, and she felt the walls she had carefully maintained for so long beginning to fracture.

"Nairna, if you can hear my voice, tap the table with your finger."

Edwin's voice sounded far away, though Nairna knew him to be at her ear. She felt her right index finger lift and fall as though of its own accord.

"Good. Now let yourself give way, in three, two, one." As the voice said one, Nairna found herself in a soft and perfect blackness. Her body felt as though it were floating, her limbs spongy and numb.

"Envision the books on the shelf, Nairna. See them in your mind's eye, see the rows of books, see the colors of their spines, see them lined up row after row," Edwin intoned.

Before her in the silky darkness, Nairna saw the tall rows of books in the study, the image becoming solid before her.

"Choose one, any one you like. Do you see one that you like?"

Nairna watched the wall of books until a forest green spine began to stand out against the others, the title in embossed gold.

"*The Portrait of a Lady*," she whispered.

"Very good." Edwin's voice was lulling, hypnotic. "Now use your mind, pull on the book and see if you can pull it toward you. Can you pull it out just a little, move it just a bit, concentrate on just that book and pull it forward just a bit, just the tiniest inch, just a little?"

Nairna stared at the book in wonder. This place where she found herself was like a dream, but real. She knew her body was sitting in a chair, her eyes staring forward. But her mind was unleashed, she could move, and all the while the books before her were tangible and solid as though they existed in both this world and the next. She reached for the forest green book and felt the texture of the leather beneath her fingertips. With both hands she reached forward and swept across the rows of books, her body hanging in space—not floating, just existing. With the slightest exertion of her arms, she pulled the weight of the shelves toward her, feeling the energy of the books bending to her will.

Suddenly she was snapped back into the waking world by Edwin's shout, his voice pained and even afraid. Nairna opened her eyes. She was still sitting as she had been—firmly in the leather chair, her arms at her side, her feet on the ground, her chin to her chest as though she had fallen asleep. But when she raised her head to see the cause of Edwin's distress, she gasped.

The floor was littered with books. Books that had seemingly hurled themselves from their shelves and now lay scattered in every corner of the study. In Nairna's lap sat the forest green cover, *The Portrait of a Lady*, as though she had placed it there. Edwin stood near the door, rubbing his head, which now had an angry red gash in addition to the scratch on his cheek. Nairna stared at him, words caught in her throat. He locked eyes with her, and his mouth twitched as he spoke in an unsteady voice.

"Well done."

Nairna

"If only we could take her to London or, better yet, Boston . . . we have the most modern means of testing her true ability . . . if it was known what she was capable of . . ." The whispered voices filtered through the door where Nairna was not supposed to be listening. She had not been invited to this conversation, and it angered her. She was seventeen, close enough to adult in any way that mattered except, perhaps, the ability to control her own fate.

"She is a child still, and I'll not have her a rat in your lab, Mr. Harrison." Rona's voice was firm.

"Have you read the papers? Your guest is starting to attract attention," Edwin said flatly, and Nairna heard a rustle of newsprint. "They are calling it the Dorothy Kellings Incident. It started in the oddity column, but now it's right here, on page seven of the daily news."

Nairna heard Rona audibly sigh, her voice resigned. "I saw. And the window, the shattering of the glass and the mess and whatnot, it was all the talk in the square. Our kitchen staff said some of the merchants refused them service at the market. Witchcraft, they said it was."

"Your Edinburgh Spiritualists have always walked a delicate line here, haven't they? What would it take for them to raid this house? Fine you? Charge you with witchery?" Edwin's voice was sharp, almost unrecognizable as coming from the man she knew.

"Please, Dr. Harrison. They haven't enforced that archaic nonsense for a generation." Rona paused. "But you do carry something of a point. She's attracting attention, more every day. The papers from the Americas are telling the story of the Dorothy Kellings Incident, as you put it, every direction to Tuesday. It's a matter of time before it's no longer page seven."

"Can you do the work you do here with the town's eyes on you as they are?" Edwin asked, his voice softer.

"She's a girl, little more than a child. I'll not turn her out because she caused a stir. We can handle page seven, and there are plenty of markets in Edinburgh. My answer stands for now, sir." Rona's voice was firm, and Nairna heard a door click shut as one or both of them left the next room.

Nairna stepped back, frustrated. She stomped down the hall and out the front door to Princes Street, with the carriages passing each other and men and women crowding the sidewalk as they went about their lives. Nairna closed the front door behind her and leaned against the iron banister. It was not even a year ago she had been starving in the cold, yet she couldn't shake the feeling that she had traded that hell for another prison, albeit a far more posh one than she'd ever known. No one asked her what she wanted from her life; no one cared. She was a commodity to this house the same as she'd been to Tavish. Suddenly exhausted, she sank down onto the cold stone step and stared up at the crisp night sky.

"Daughter, what have they done to yeh now?"

Nairna looked up to see Tavish on the bottom step. He wore a new wool suit and matching flat cap. The two might have been incongruous and ridiculous on anyone else, but on Tavish it was cause for a cluster of ladies giggling their way up Princes Street to fall silent as they passed, their eyes lowering flirtatiously in his direction. Tavish was utterly unaware; he was watching Nairna with an odd expression on his face. They'd hardly spoken since the shattered glass and overturned table. Nairna suspected that Rona was keeping him away, but it had pained her that he hadn't checked on her at all. It did not, however, surprise her much. Tavish's paternal inclinations had always been tied to profit, and he was living better than ever thanks to her newfound talents.

"I'm worried for you," Tavish said in a tone that almost sounded caring.

Nairna patted the step beside her. "Join me."

Tavish sat beside her and took her hand in his. Despite everything, Nairna felt herself become a little girl again, in awe of his booming voice and presence.

"Da, when does all this end? I mean, is this my life for all time now? They're inside now, arguing over where I'll go and whatnot," Nairna said softly.

Tavish frowned. "Rona Connell and that doctor have no say over you. I know you hate me at times, but they have to get past me first, and no matter how much glass you try to throw in my eye . . ." He offered her a dark grin. "You are still my daughter, and I will not let a mouse so much as step in yer path were it not in the best fer yeh."

"You can be a bit . . . overwhelming at times, Da," Nairna replied, feeling her mood lift a bit.

"It's the drink. I need to give it up, I do, but haven't and don't really intend to. So occasionally yeh have to know I'll not be as . . . what's the word . . . articulate? Yeh, that's it. Articulate as I could be," Tavish said, standing and pulling her to her feet with him. "Come inside. Not sure how closely the lady of the house follows the news, but this caught my eye."

Nairna frowned as Tavish handed her a cheaply printed periodical. She wasn't familiar with the title: *Clipmalabor Monthly*.

Tavish nodded at her. "Go ahead, read the lead story."

Nairna held the periodical closer and squinted in the dim light. She felt the air leave her lungs as she saw the title.

EDINBURGH WITCHES RULE PRINCES STREET

Nairna looked up at Tavish, her eyes wide. Behind them the door opened, and Rona stood against the light.

"Come in, both of you before you catch yer deaths. Let's take a look at that rag together."

Nairna

Clipmalabor Monthly

EDINBURGH WITCHES RULE PRINCES STREET

From the desk of our esteemed staff writer Miss Clarentine Marchant comes a story of shock and scandal that takes center stage right here in the heart of Edinburgh. Our sources reported the arrival of a mysterious young woman nearly a year ago today to the auspicious town house on Princes Street known to many as a den of witchcraft and debauchery. Our eyes have watched this young creature for months, out of fear for her safety. What use did these so-called Edinburgh Spiritualists have for a young girl, a child? Was she to be a sacrifice to their dark lord? A pawn in their hell games?

"I can't keep reading this," Edwin said flatly, looking at Rona and Frederick on one side of the dining table and then at Nairna and Tavish on the other. "It's utter rot, no one takes this for the truth."

Rona took the periodical from his hands, glaring, and then a sip of her wine. "Yes, it is rot, and they have written rot about us before, but this is, well, it's different. Let me continue."

> We have all heard the rumors of the ill-fated Dorothy Kellings Incident—the stories more fantastic than truth, we are sure. And the mysterious "accidents" that have been occurring at the Princes Street town house as reported by our brave local workmen who were tasked with replacing a floor-to-ceiling window, stained glass that heralded from William Cooper himself.

Rona looked up and glanced at Frederick. "I told you not to hire that man. I had a bad feeling, like he was taking notes the whole time he worked, and look at that!" She jabbed a finger clear through the newsprint. Frederick took the paper from her and grimaced, continuing.

> But never has so strange a tale been told as that of a Cornish tree and what lay buried beneath it. The Venerable Miss Leticia Fairwright tells us she consulted this house of sin and lies out of desperation. The future told to her by the young woman of note in this twisted tale, Miss Nairna Liath, was nonsensical and dismissed as a child's story when it was delivered. But since that fateful day, her story has proven to be far more insidious than previously thought.

"Someone else's turn," Frederick said flatly, handing the paper to Tavish. "I never liked that old bag and her sisters, and this is the final straw." Tavish patted Nairna's leg, his eyes worried. Nairna took a long sip of her wine and nodded to him to keep reading.

> *Told to dig beneath a forked tree for buried treasure and riches unknown, Miss Leticia Fairwright sent her dear nephew to the task. She hoped for the best, her finances drained and her situation desperate. But what the boy found was too horrible to mention. Not treasure, not fortune or gold coins, but rather the decomposed body of a man reported missing from London nearly six months prior.*
>
> *The horror and shock are too much to report for our gentle readers. Suffice it to say that Miss Leticia Fairwright and her sweet sisters are shocked and appalled at the trickery and devil work in this matter. The Cornwall Police are investigating the matter, and the story is sure to break here in Edinburgh within the week, but you heard it here first, dear readers.*

"Heard what exactly?" Tavish interrupted himself, looked around the table, his brow furrowed. "What are they implying exactly? That my girl had something to do with this man's murder?"

"How could she?" Rona sighed, pouring more wine into her glass and across the table for Nairna. "They're implying that we are not a society of Spiritualists but rather a den of witches who can divine for blood. It's nonsense, but the sort of nonsense that the polis find hard to ignore. When did you find this rag, Tavish?"

"They're fixin' to sell it with tomorrow morning's papers. The newsboy gave me one off his cart. Now that I think of it, he smirked when he did it, the little brat," Tavish growled and then looked back to the paper.

What other grisly secrets are hiding on Princes Street? What blood magic is being practiced behind the polished doors? Hidden by austerity and a mask of decency, we know, gentle readers, the comings and goings of the so-called Edinburgh Spiritualists and the newest member of their legion. We watch in the night, so your children stay safe; we listen in the shadows so your loved ones don't find themselves beneath a Cornish tree.

"So-called?" Frederick stood and paced to the window, where he looked out onto the street. "So-called? We *are* the Edinburgh Spiritualists, and we've been around a hell of lot longer than this tabloid."

"Perhaps it will blow over—you are right, after all, it is a tabloid, a gossip rag, mumbles in the wind," Edwin said, offering Nairna a smile. She stared back, expressionless. She felt like her soul was disassociating from her physical body.

"Perhaps," she whispered.

Nairna

Nairna lay in bed, her eyes closed, and wished the day away. She could feel the early morning sun on her face and the winter chill to the air. Normally, these were her favorite moments, the peace before anyone knew she was awake, when her time was hers entire. But today was different. She had a faint headache from last night's wine, and the words from the gossip rag still rang in her ears. Rona had not told her of the building talk about town surrounding her presence at the town house. For the others, this was an inevitability; for Nairna, it felt like a sudden shock. She had walked the streets, come and gone from the town house for a year now, and never known she was being watched, whispered about.

Thinking back, she could pinpoint times when she'd received a strange look or maybe even hesitancy from a stranger, a clerk at the market, or the girl at the tea shop, but she hadn't thought much of it. She was a country girl in a city, that had been it, surely that had been it. Nairna opened her eyes to see the sun steadily rising outside her window. The others had stayed awake long after she had retired to bed, her legs weak and wobbly from the wine that Rona kept pouring. They were afraid of how this would be received, of what it meant for the Edinburgh Spiritualists and their tenuous relationship with the polis. Nairna knew it was her fault they found themselves in this predicament and thought back to what Edwin had said. Boston, America. A fresh start, he'd said, a way to draw the public eye away from the town house.

A sharp rap on the door shook Nairna from her reverie.

"Nairna? Are you awake?" Rona's voice sounded strained.

"Yes, of course, please come in." Nairna called, grabbing her dressing gown from beside the bed.

Rona entered and closed the door behind her. She was dressed for the day, her dark hair neatly coifed, but her eyes were red and her face drawn. "The morning papers are out, and it is as I feared. Come down to breakfast when you're ready but stay away from the windows."

With no further explanation, Rona patted Nairna's hand and left her alone to dress and prepare herself. She knew this was the last time she was to awaken in the town house, last time she would see the sun through her window and Princes Street below. Making sure to keep the curtain obscuring her face, she peeked out the window at the street below. The sight made her gasp. A dozen or more women and men stood on the sidewalk, crowded around the front steps. Some huddled together in the chill morning and pointed at this and that, their mouths moving soundlessly. Others milled about, examining the row of Snow Glories that grew along the walk. Several had cameras around their necks, waiting for a glimpse of what? Nairna could not fathom. A witch? A spirit? *No*, she thought coldly, *me. They are waiting for me to appear.*

She finished dressing and pulled a thick shawl around her shoulders. She cleaned her teeth over the porcelain wash basin on her vanity and tucked her hair into a knot at the base of her neck. She knew this was the last time she would feel this room was her own, the first space that had felt like home since Nań had passed, and it was ending. She could blame Dorothy Kellings, Nairna mused. Except it had little to do with her. The papers hooked into the incident, perhaps, but Dorothy Kellings hadn't caused Nairna to see the strange woman with a face and hair so like her own. And Dorothy Kellings certainly hadn't caused Nairna to levitate. No, whoever's fault this was, it was more Nairna's than anyone else's. Even Tavish was blameless in this matter. A burning nausea at the back of her throat, Nairna made her way to the dining table.

Edwin rose from his seat to greet her, nodding, his forehead creased with concern. Tavish sat slumped in a chair, his eyes closed, and a cup of black coffee before him. Nairna winced at the acrid smell. Rona offered a nervous smile and indicated for Nairna to sit. Edwin poured strong Scottish tea into her cup and sat back, his blue eyes unreadable.

"Dear, we have a proposal for you."

Part III

Lottie
Argoll Asylum
1866

Posting from The Psychiatric Annals of
Harvard University, *circa 1847*

*A glass of congratulations is to be raised to our col-
league, the newly minted Dr. Theodore Bothelli, who
leaves us here in Boston and is headed to study with
the honorable Dr. Soekan of the esteemed Gest School
in Paris and continue his postdoctoral studies abroad.
Further congratulations are due as Dr. Bothelli has
accepted the position of Chief of Psychiatry at the soon-
to-open Argoll Sanitorium and Asylum for the Mentally Distressed, a prestigious appointment and a chance
to bring his worldly education to our friends across the
pond.*

*Argoll Sanitorium and Asylum for the Mentally
Distressed, or Argoll Asylum for short, is being housed
in the newly rebuilt and refurbished Argoll Manor,
located in Wales, outside of the capital city of Cardiff.
A long and illustrious history follows both the manor
and the surrounding area, appropriately known as
Argoll Downs.*

*Congratulations, Dr. Bothelli. A farewell luncheon
will be held at the Cabot Science Library for invited
attendees.*

Lottie

"There you go," Dr. Theodore Bothelli murmured in his unnatural voice.

Lottie rubbed at her numb arms, freshly released from their constraints. Before her a steaming cup of tea in a plain white mug waited. She looked around at her surroundings. Dr. Bothelli's office was lined with heavy, leather-bound books, and a stone fireplace inset into the far wall created a false sense of coziness and safety. There was nothing about this place that was safe, Lottie was sure of it. Still, she reached for the tea as her bones ached, her throat was fire, and her body chilled through. The first sip set her to coughing, and the pain quaked through her, making the hot water splash onto her legs.

"Let us help." Lottie heaved and leaned back as Dr. Bothelli stepped around the side of the desk gracefully and took the mug from her hand, replacing it with a clean handkerchief. "There we are. Now sit quiet; let that cool, perhaps; and I will let you know exactly what is going on. Please don't strain that throat."

Lottie stared at him distrustfully. His face was smooth and unlined, but his dark hair held wisps of gray. He looked like the children's book images of fae who roamed the night woods. She imagined rows of pointed teeth hiding behind his too pink lips, his fingers as long and pointed talons, better suited for ripping apart flesh than pouring tea. But then she blinked, and his talons were just hands once again, and the fangs just bright white teeth, the sort of teeth that spoke of money and plenty to eat all his days.

"May I call you Lottie?" Dr. Bothelli asked as he sat back in his leather chair. Lottie nodded, a slight movement, but his eyes that were more creature than human caught it, nonetheless. "Fine, then. Lottie, we understand that you are expecting? Is that right?"

Lottie nodded again, this time with more strength. A jolt of fear coursed through her as she imagined the sprite inside her having endured all she had seen in the last few days.

"We'll have our doctor examine you and make sure all is well, of course. You've had quite the excitement, and I think once you settle in a bit, you will find that a bit of a rest is just what you need." Dr. Bothelli smiled, those bright white teeth catching the light and once again appearing, for just a flash of a moment, to be more suited to monster than human.

"I want to go home," Lottie whispered, and reached for the tea, the hot liquid quelling the pain caused by the effort.

"Lottie, this may be hard to hear, but you don't have a home any longer. I was told by the courts in Aberdare that your cottage in, where was it?" He shuffled through a file folder of papers, his inhuman eyes skimming the words. "Ah yes, here we are. Cwmaman? Your cottage was in arrears to the colliery, and you were evicted following your incident in Aberdare. Your personal effects will arrive here in the next delivery, as soon as can be done, but I am sorry to tell you that your home is no longer your own." Dr. Bothelli's forehead creased in a mimic of sympathy, and he leaned forward, his tone softening. "Are you alright, Lottie?"

Lottie nodded and sipped the tea. She had figured as much

even back in the jail cell in Aberdare, the first thing that dobber would do was turn her out of the cottage. As far as her things ever arriving in god-knows-where-she-was, she doubted she'd ever see it happen. Not that there was much: a grainy photograph of her mother and Da, a deck of seer cards passed on to her from her mum (and grandmum before that), Elis's work clothes, her leather winter boots—how she wished she'd worn them instead of tryin' to look fancy on her trip to see that *bassa* in the colliery office. The only thing that was worth a pence she'd left with Bryn back in Cwmaman. A copper-plated locket that held no photographs. It had been hers as a girl, and she'd taken it with her when she boarded the train leaving Glasgow what seemed to be a lifetime ago. She'd imagined the images of her and Elis's children inside, p'r'aps a lock of their hair. She'd left it with Bryn, afraid to carry something of even so little value on the road, safer there. She'd never see it again, and p'r'aps it didn't matter.

"Now this is the hard part." Dr. Bothelli paused as though he were looking for the words to fill in the silence he'd created. "The judge in Aberdare sent you to us with what he called melancholia and fits. And as I look at your case file that the officers were so kind to bring, I can see you've had quite a terrible time. You have lost your husband recently?"

Lottie nodded. "Twenty . . . days . . . I don't know how much time has passed . . . twenty-five days?"

Dr. Bothelli nodded. "I see. And you had gone to see the colliery office to inquire about your husband's wages?"

Lottie felt the rage in the core of her being struggling to rise, but her body was too exhausted to react. "He's a crook, a *bassa*. Glasscock denied us all, told me he wouldn't pay," Lottie whispered, her voice rough and broken.

"I understand. The judge chose to send you here instead of the women's prison, and I thank him for it," Dr. Bothelli said with a smile that Lottie guessed was meant to be comforting.

"Prison? I didn't do a thing to deserve it," Lottie mumbled, and took a sip of the tea to calm her throat.

Dr. Bothelli nodded. "I understand you must have been very angry. But you are aware that Mr. Glasscock was sent to hospital because of your anger. And the courts see that as a crime, as it is. But we are here to help you with that anger and help that baby into the world."

"When can I leave?" Lottie growled. She ground her filthy fingernails into the palm of her hand, the pain keeping her from throwing the tea straight at the insipid doctor's face.

"Leave?" Dr. Bothelli said, his voice clinical and detached. "When you are well, you can leave. And not before. We need to evaluate you and get you settled. You will be glad to know that we are practicing the most modern treatments in all of psychiatry here at Argoll. I studied at Oxford, and Harvard in the Americas. I am passionate about the care and cure of psychopathy, and I have the highest hopes for your full recovery. It is my preliminary belief that you are suffering from a sort of nervous exhaustion and pregnancy-induced mood disorder. I think with some rest, and if we can get that anger to release its grip on your mind, we can see real progress here."

"Where is this place?" Lottie whispered. The man's words were daggers drawing pinpricks of blood from her raw flesh.

"Where? Oh my, I do apologize, I thought they had informed you before you left Aberdare. Argoll Asylum and Sanatorium is not too far from Cardiff. We are in what is called Argoll Downs and are quite near the sea, just on the other side of the woods. Argoll Asylum has been in operation for twenty years now. The structure is said to have been built sometime in the thirteenth century as a sort of summer house for Llywelyn ap Gruffydd and has housed royalty for centuries. Turned over to the Church trust, it is now a place of healing and rest. You will see clergy members on our staff, but believe me when I say all are welcome here."

"Fascinating," Lottie muttered, her unease growing with each word he uttered.

"It is rather," Dr. Bothelli said, and he smiled at her as though entirely unaware of her intended tone. "But let's save the history. I am going to have you settled into the infirmary. We will get you cleaned up and tend to your physical self before we address what's going on in that troubled mind."

"My mind is sound," Lottie whispered.

"It will be in time, but let's get you healthy, and then we start our work. Soon you'll be moved to your ward; you will make lucky fifteen on your floor. We have over a hundred in the asylum total, but you won't ever know it, lots of space here, lots of privacy. You are our only expectant guest as of now, but we have had babies born here at Argoll in the past, and our staff is quite skilled." Dr. Bothelli nodded, affirming his own words.

"I'll not have my child in this place." Lottie spat the words at the doctor.

Dr. Bothelli stood and rang a small bell on his desk. The thick-necked guard or one like him appeared in the doorway. "We will discuss the matter once you've settled in a bit." He looked to the orderly. "Please escort Mrs. Liath to the infirmary. Sister Mary knows she is arriving; they are ready for her."

As the orderly wheeled Lottie out the door, she heard a high-pitched scream echoing from somewhere in the stone-walled prison. She jerked her head back and stared up at the emotionless man pushing the chair. Had it been in her head? She placed both hands on her stomach, the sprite within quiet. Perhaps it was dead already, having already found the only escape from Argoll Asylum.

Lottie

The infirmary was a row of bleached cotton cots and bottle-glass windows that allowed the sun to fill the room with a blurry sort of light. The orderly wheeled Lottie to a cot on the end. It was made with clean white sheets, and a dressing gown and stockings sat neatly folded on the end.

"Not till we have a bath." A shrill-toned voice behind Lottie startled her. She turned her head to see a nun in a simple black dress, white coif and head covering. She was younger than Lottie expected her to be, her face still youthful despite that voice that sounded thirty years her senior. "I'm Sister Mary, you can call me Sister Mary, not Mary, or Romanist, or Gibface, or Mutton Shunter. Sister Mary will do nicely. I run the infirmary. You'll meet Sister Therese soon enough; she is in charge of the women's ward."

Lottie found her soiled clothing pulled from her body with inhuman efficiency and speed, her skin scrubbed with stinging lye soap, and herself dressed in a simple white cotton gown and stockings. Sister Mary tucked her into a hospital cot, the sheets clean and crisp. Despite her jumbled thoughts, Lottie felt her body release the tension it had been holding for weeks.

"There. Better," Sister Mary declared.

Lottie could only nod. "I'm not sick."

Sister Mary gave her a long, hard look. "The hell you aren't. I saw you getting out of that paddy wagon. You can't even stand, at least for long. You're in miserable shape. I'd say you haven't eaten a proper meal in maybe weeks, you're underweight for being pregnant as you are, your throat is raw, and I imagine you haven't slept a night's worth of sleep since your husband passed."

Lottie looked up at the nun, stunned. She just nodded. "I can't stay here."

"Sure you can," Sister Mary cried, turning away and walking off down the row of cots. "I'll bring your dinner." She threw the words over her shoulder as she strode out of the room. Lottie was left propped up against the thin pillows, her skin still tender from the harsh soap and hot water. But she felt more herself than she had in a forever's time. The nun was right. She was in miserable shape, but she couldn't let herself get settled here; she had to get out, leave this place. Her child could not be born in this institution. Her thoughts began to run together, and her eyelids drooped. The sun faded to darkness as her eyes closed, and her body sank into the stark comforts which suddenly seemed like the finest lodgings in all of Wales.

Lottie

Lottie felt the sticky blackness of the nightscape all around her. No light penetrated the velvety dreamscape before her. Her limbs felt impossibly heavy. Experimentally, she lifted an arm, then rotated her hand around and around. She was asleep, asleep and her mind was her own. With a tentative delight, afraid that she would awake at any moment, she turned her head from left to right. She was entirely free in this place, weighed down only by the limitations of her own mind. Lottie took one hand and swept it across the darkness; a swath of golden light appeared. She stood and looked through the spot as though it were a window. On the other side, she saw a girl, a girl who looked much like her but also different. She'd seen this girl before, in a dream before, but a dream she'd had while awake. Lottie strained her eyes, but the girl remained blurry, and it was clear she was not aware of Lottie. *This is real*, Lottie thought to herself, the sound of her realization echoing like bells ringing all around her. *This is real, this girl is real.* The absolute knowledge that she was in a dream that had crossed the boundary set by time and the limitations of the waking world was a revelation. Lottie smiled.

The girl was wearing a fine velvet dress, sitting in a parlour surrounded by ladies, older than her but finely turned out; their hair and dress spoke of wealth, of comfort. The girl was looking down at a set of cards, and Lottie was struck with an arrow of knowledge—the cards were hers, the same deck of seer cards that she'd been given by her mother and had belonged to her mother before that. Lottie watched with fascination as the girl drew a card from the pile and laid it in a neat row. Lottie recognized the patterns: gold and pale yellow butterflies, some emerging from moss green cocoons, some with wings spread, six ornate swords intermingled around them, the butterflies reflecting in the silver light of the metal.

Lottie had never used the seer cards; she'd never seen the messages her grandmother claimed were there. Lottie's mother never saw anything in the cards either, and so they had been passed from one to another—an heirloom, a box of pretty pictures with no meaning. But this girl saw. She stared at the cards the same way that Lottie remembered her grandmother had locked her gaze on them. Lottie had been so young when her grandmother passed; the memories were faint but strong, like a stain that never quite leaves the fabric.

The girl looked up, and the women at the table leaned in close, their eyes mystified. Lottie reached out through the smear in the darkness and pressed a hand to the girl's shoulder. The girl automatically froze, and then she felt the tight muscle beneath the velvet dress soften and lean into her touch. The girl couldn't be any older than Lottie herself, but still she felt maternal, protective in a way she had never felt, even toward the sprite growing in her belly. This girl belonged to her; she was her flesh, her blood. She could feel her fear, her pain; she could feel that the velvet dress and posh lodgings were foreign to her, that she was lost inside, afloat in this comfort.

It was as though a cord in her gut was yanked from the depths of the blackness. Lottie was ripped from the parlour and the girl with the black hair so like her own. She was pulled back into the perfect darkness and overtaken with exhaustion. She felt her eyes close, and her whole body drifted, weightless in the space, no thoughts, no pain, no care for what came next.

Lottie

Lottie awoke in the infirmary, her eyes sticky with sleep and her throat dry. She tried to raise her head, but it felt as though a weight was wrapped around her neck. She managed a low sigh.

"Well! Awake, are you?" A voice that Lottie vaguely remembered as belonging to the nun bellowed from across the room. Then Sister Mary's face loomed over her, and Lottie blinked with great effort.

"Where . . . how long?" she whispered.

Sister Mary sat on a metal stool beside the cot, lifting Lottie's head and fluffing the pillows behind her so she could sit upright. Lottie's head throbbed with the movement, and she grimaced.

"Drink this." Lottie felt the edge of cold glass on her lips, and she gratefully accepted water. Her hands shook, but the nun watched approvingly as she drank the whole glass.

"It's odd . . . what . . . ?" Lottie said, trying to identify the spicy, bitter taste to the water.

"Ginger with a bit of willow bark, good for the little one, maybe help you eat something," Sister Mary said curtly, taking the glass and refilling it from a clay pitcher next to the cot. "Here."

Lottie took the glass and sipped this time, looking around the room warily. "How long did I sleep?"

"Seventeen hours all be said," Sister Mary replied. "You haven't moved a muscle in seventeen hours. I imagine you were flat exhausted when you arrived, and now we need to get some food into you."

Lottie shook her head. "I can't stay here."

"You keep saying that. However, you don't have much choice," Sister Mary replied as she stood and looked down at Lottie, her light eyes catching the sun as it came through the infirmary windows. "Once you leave the infirmary, you'll be assigned duties, cleaning and such, so I would milk this as long as you can. The doctor will be in a bit later to check on you; he was the one who said to let you sleep. Now, let's get you to the privy. I don't want to be changing your sheets."

Lottie realized that she had a paralyzing sort of pressure on her bladder, and she grimaced as Sister Mary pulled her to her feet and plopped her back in the wheelchair.

"I can walk," Lottie said, annoyed at the invalid treatment.

"Sure, and I can fly, just not today." Sister Mary whirled her around and set off to a row of chamber pots in small wooden stalls at the far end of the room. She helped Lottie to her feet and stood a respectful distance while Lottie felt a rush of relief greater than anything in recent memory. They made their way back to the bed, and with her brusque efficiency the nun had Lottie back in place before she quite knew what was happening.

"I'm off to get your dinner," Sister Mary announced. "This time, try not to fall asleep before I return."

Lottie lay back on the cot and looked at the ceiling. Seventeen hours. She'd never slept that long in her whole life, not even when she caught the fever back in Glasgow as a girl. She'd had to take care of her Da, who'd been worse off than she'd been, and her mum had relied on her too much to allow any time for the sick. This cot, this prison, felt almost like an indulgence. The dream she'd been pulled from still played behind her eyelids. She saw the girl, not too much younger than she was, who looked so familiar and yet so different. She saw the seer cards and the women sitting around the fancy table. The image had been so clear, as though she'd been there; she had smelled the leather of the fine parlour chairs, felt the velvet of the girl's dress. She'd seen the girl before, in other dreams. What did it mean? Her grandmum in Glasgow had used the seer cards and spoken of dreams. But Lottie had never been one to see anything in the tea leaves other than a mess to be cleaned. Grandmum had talked of the spirits and the fae, but Lottie had never seen anything in the shadows save dust and work. Her mum had been the same; she scoffed at Grandmum's stories, rolled her eyes when she shuffled the seer cards. When Grandmum passed, Lottie had been little, no more than ten. Mum had given her the cards with a wink. "She'd want you to have them. Learn to play a proper game with 'em, yeh hear? The spirits are poor company."

Lottie had brought them with her when she left for Wales with Elis; they had been left behind in the cottage in Cwmaman, and she wondered what had become of them now. Who was this girl in her dreams that had the exact deck of seer cards that Lottie had only seen with her grandmum? She shook her head—silly dream it was, all it was. Her head was a mess, and she needed to get her mind clear, figure a way out of Argoll. To what, though?

As though she had spoken her thoughts aloud, a voice from the other side of the row of cots broke the silence.

"It's not as bad as all that."

Lottie looked up, startled. An elderly woman with a bluish tint to her skin and a mouth empty of teeth grinned at her from a cot across the way.

"Yeh look as though yer lost, but it's not all that bad here. I stay sick, I do. Stay in this bed, the little sister brings me meals, I get a bath ever so often. Better than the workhouse."

The old woman leaned forward, looking back and forth to make sure no one was listening. "Yeh'd do well to stay here. The doctor might want to try his cures on yeh if yeh're too well off, and that's no good for anyone."

"What do you mean?" Lottie asked, feeling a chill on her spine.

"All the newest treatments he told you, I'm sure; all those fancy schools he studied at. He's got lots of ideas, none of them good." The old woman cackled, the sound abrasive and frightening. Lottie startled, and the old woman laughed. "Not so bad here. The little nun is a pill, but she's a sight better than that old witch doctor . . ."

"What're you carrying on about, Lorna?" Sister Mary reentered the infirmary carrying a tray with a clay bowl. "Stop scaring the new girl." With her was another nun in full habit, an older woman with dark eyes and a perpetually concerned look etched on her face.

"Mutton cawl and black bread. I'm afraid this is a regular menu item, so get used to it. The kitchen lacks imagination. This is Sister Therese; she is in charge of the women's ward," Sister Mary said as she set the tray on the small table next to the bed.

"Hello, Lottie," Sister Therese said simply with a gentle smile. Lottie smiled back despite herself.

"Lottie here says she's fine and doesn't need to be here," Sister Mary said curtly as she fashioned a handkerchief into the neck of Lottie's dressing gown.

"Well, just think of yourself as our guest for the time being then," Sister Therese replied softly. "Let us get you well and some color back in those cheeks. Please eat. I'll be back to check on you." The nun nodded to Lottie and turned to exit. "Lorna, you are looking well today."

The old woman grinned and waved at Sister Therese as she exited the infirmary.

Suddenly the smell of the hot food overwhelmed Lottie, and she ate without tasting a thing. The feel of the broth in her throat made her dizzy. She mopped the sides of the empty bowl with the bread and breathed a sigh of relief as she looked at the tray.

"Better?" Sister Mary asked, a sardonic smile on her face.

Lottie nodded. "Hadn't . . . eaten."

"I know. No good for the baby, you know. You need to eat regular meals even if it's a never-ending parade of mutton." Sister Mary took the tray from her lap and started to stand.

"Where are you from?" Lottie asked suddenly. The nun's accent was so strange; it had a London sort of precision, but her words were oddly formed.

"It's been bothering you, has it? My accent, you've been trying to figure it out." The nun stood and looked down at Lottie. "Well, as I told Lorna over there, if you guess it correctly, I will affirm it, but till then, I won't say a word. I like a bit of mystery."

Lottie nodded, still a bit unsure of the young nun. "How long will I be here?"

"In the infirmary? Till we get your strength up. You came in here in low shape. I suspect you're anemic and underweight. I expect that even before all this trouble, you didn't eat half of what you needed. I can see your fingertips and toes have a bit of blue to them; we call it cyanosis. You're not moving oxygen around your system like you should. Likely your body is giving its all to the baby. You need to rest and let us get you back into fighting shape. Was Lorna telling you to stay put? She likes to warn newcomers like she's putting one over on me by staying here as long as she has." Sister Mary looked over her shoulder. "Isn't that right, Lorna?"

The old woman cackled again and flashed her toothless grin.

"Lorna lost her feet in a winter freeze. She can't walk, too weak for the wheelchair, and she's not right in the head on top of it all. She's better off here, but she's not fooling anyone, are you?" Sister Mary asked Lorna pointedly.

"Told her to play possum, I did!" Lorna cried. "Stay away from that slick doctor and his remedies."

Sister Mary rolled her eyes. "If you had kept hold of the sense God gave you, you would be grateful for Dr. Bothelli. He's studied . . ."

"In all the finest places . . . yes, we know, just ask 'im!" Lorna interrupted.

"Well, he has." Sister Mary looked back at Lottie. "He will be in later to see you. Try to stay awake?"

At that, the nun left the room, her efficiency and speed making it look as though she nearly flew over the tiled floor.

"My bet's on America!" Lorna crowed from her cot. "I think she's an American who came here to be all fantsy pantsy and study her medicine. I think she has a lover in one of those London schools for the high and mighty, and she hides out here for the shame of it all."

"You've had a lot of time to think on it, yes?" Lottie said, suppressing a smile.

"Nothing but time, nothing but time." The old woman nodded and then sank into singing a low, soft song to herself.

Lottie closed her eyes. She wouldn't sleep, she told herself, but the old woman's odd little melody danced in her ears, and she felt herself slipping back into the void.

Lottie

The images of the seer cards danced before her eyes, but it wasn't the girl this time; it was her Elis, but not. Lottie floated in a vat of perfect blackness; she was weightless in space, hovering in the nothingness. Images of her grandmum's seer cards swirled around her like a cyclone. She saw a ghostly white swan, three bloody swords ripping apart its wings and neck. She saw four silver moonlight swords surrounding a skull made of pale moonlight-colored leaves. The images danced and spun. Behind them a man—not Elis, she could see that now; a man who had her Elis's eyes but not his spirit—stood behind the cards, outside of the darkness. Lottie looked closer, and the man came into focus. He was tall, his dark hair so like hers. His dark eyes and fair skin were hers as well, but his face could be Elis in the right light, clear as anything. The man was laughing, gesturing wildly, telling a mad story. Behind him sat the girl, and Lottie could see the invisible cord that connected the pair. The girl did not hear the man's stories; she stared off into the distance; she wanted away, far from this place. Lottie saw the upscale parlour she had seen before, but this time it was the man who held audience; he performed and gestured, acting the grand master of ceremonies. Lottie grimaced as she hung weightless in space, watching the image outside of her imagining. She was overwhelmed with a sensation she had never felt before; she could feel the darkness creeping into their waking lives, and she tried to stop it, tried to cry out.

As before, Lottie felt a sharp yank on the invisible cord that held her in this place. She was yanked backward, away from the darkness, away from the figures that felt so oddly familiar, and back into the cold sterility of the infirmary.

Lottie

"Our goal is to try to calm your nerves, which will calm your body, and once settled, your baby will also benefit from your newly found state of health and vigor." Dr. Bothelli spoke with a calculated charm, his hands folded under his chin and his gaze not quite meeting Lottie's eyes but just off to the side. Lottie wondered whether that was on purpose or a sign of his own muddied state of calm.

This was her third session with the doctor. Sid, the orderly, had wheeled her to his office the first two times, but she had walked herself down the hall for this visit. Sid had followed as though she were likely to tip over with every step. Lottie swallowed an urge to swat him away. She felt quite herself now. A week's worth of regular meals, baths, and sleep, and she felt physically better than she had in maybe months. The events that preceded her arrival at Argoll lingered behind a high, thick wall, though—one she built from every last scrap of strength she had. Just as she had in Cwmaman, she did not allow herself to feel the nagging grief. The wave of loss that rose out at sea was forced to crash over and over again against a high rock face of her own creation. She needed to leave this place, but what came next, she had no idea. Her baby could not be born in this place. It would be taken from her, and she would be locked up forever, her child given to the nuns. Sister Mary had simply nodded when Lottie asked if this would happen.

"Nothing to worry yourself about now. You are five, maybe six, months by my calculation, and you have weeks yet to fret about what will become of you," Sister Mary had informed her brusquely, and Lottie had stared in amazement at how such cold words could be spoken without any emotion whatsoever.

She had four months, maybe less, to figure out how to leave this place, how to look calm, settled, stable, and utterly capable of taking care of herself. So she walked to the office herself, at her insistence, thinking the effort might speak to her overall health. But now, as Dr. Bothelli looked at her with his crooked gaze, Lottie wondered if she'd have been better off playing possum, as Lorna kept advising her to.

"Have you ever heard of the Gest School?" Dr. Bothelli paused, searching Lottie's face. She shook her head. "The Gest School operates in France under the tutelage of a man I studied with in Strasbourg some fifteen years or so ago. I had the opportunity to complete my postdoctoral studies with a Dr. Soekan, who was making quite a name for himself in the field of hypnotherapy and his work with the unconscious mind. While this asylum was being built, as a matter of fact, I studied the techniques I would bring to its door. Dr. Soekan is a brilliant physician, and his work with the unconscious mind is groundbreaking." The doctor paused. "Have you heard of hypnosis before?"

Lottie nodded. "I saw it once at a fair in Glasgow when I was a girl. A man swung a polished stone on a chain back and forth, and the girl fell dead asleep." She wrenched her memories for more from that day. She'd been there selling small bottles of her Da's homebrew whiskey, which he made in a tub out back of their flat. It was wretched stuff, and no one who knew better would buy a drop, but plenty of strangers were in town for the fair, so Lottie's pocket had been full of coins. The girl had slumped over and then straightened back up, listening to the man's voice, and then, big as anything, she began to sing, "I Love a Lassie" in a crooked, off-tune voice. The crowd had laughed themselves silly before the man snapped his fingers and the girl stopped her murder of the song and ran off the stage, confusion filling her face.

"I'll not be made a fool of," Lottie snapped, remembering the girl's eyes. She looked as though she'd no memory of what she'd done, and she certainly did not look as though her nerves had been calmed.

Dr. Bothelli laughed, a low chuckle one might have for a child. Lottie felt her anger boiling up, and she stamped it back down. She needed to look as though she were fully recovered. Spitting in the good doctor's eye would not help her case.

"I'll also not be laughed at. I've seen yer hypnosis, and it's a circus side show, it is," Lottie said as steadily as she could manage while swallowing her disdain for the man before her.

"I am sorry, Lottie. I am not laughing at you, truly. And it is true, hypnosis is used by crooks and carnies, though likely the sort you've seen had willing accomplices, part of the act. They behave as though they are bewitched and do silly things—cluck like a chicken, sing a song—and the man looks to be magic. Am I right?" the doctor asked. This time his eyes met hers. He had an excitement in his gaze that made Lottie uneasy, and she remembered Lorna's warning, scattered as it might be, that she should stay far away from his remedies.

"And what is it you want to do?" Lottie asked, suddenly curious. What good would it be to him to make her dance a Snow Mare or sing a silly song?

"Dr. Soekan uses hypnosis as a therapy. He teaches that it is a way to see inside the mind, and if your mind is troubled, it is a way of allowing those troubles to leave your subconscious and bring about relief for the ailing." He leaned forward. "I will use a technique not unlike what you might have seen at your street fair, but once you are relaxed and your mind open to me, I will try to draw your pain to the fore, and we will work on your troubles together, your mentality will improve, and your mind will be clear."

"I see," Lottie said quietly. "And how do I know you'll not have me crowing like a rooster or some other trick to make me look mad?"

Dr. Bothelli looked genuinely surprised at her question. "Why Lottie, what cause would I have to create troubles for you? My research, my studies, my life's work is dedicated to healing troubled minds. Think of it as a purely economic situation, if you like. If my patients all went about singing the *Calon Lân* at the top of their voice or dancing a jig, do you think I'd still have a job? They want doctors who can heal, not a sideshow barker." He smiled.

Despite herself, Lottie smiled back. What was the harm, after all? If she did sing or dance and act the fool, there was no one around to lock her up any further than she was already, and it couldn't be any worse than her display at the courts in Aberdare.

Lottie found herself lying back on the narrow sofa that sat adjacent to Dr. Bothelli's desk. He sat over her in a still-backed chair, his face engaged and alive with purpose. She had a brush of sympathy that bordered on affection for the man; he was young for a doctor, at least the ones she'd known, who had all been gray and bearded old men. He was like a child with a new trick he couldn't wait to play with. The fact that Lottie was the plaything was unsettling, but she swallowed her discomfort and looked up at the small silver ball hanging from a chain that he held before her eyes.

"We are going to concentrate on the orb, and you will listen to my voice. Trust me, Lottie, and listen to my voice."

Lottie watched the silver orb swirl in slow circles. She heard Dr. Bothelli's voice, soft and steady; she heard him counting, slowly and then quickly, slowly and then quickly. She tried to focus past the orb, but the light from the oil lamp on his desk began to fade, his voice began to change—it was deep and far away, the numbers were out of order, and the room grew increasingly dark. She felt the tug of sleep, but different, intentional, and stronger, it dragged her into a darkness that was highlighted only by the flash of the silver orb, the light appearing in the periphery of her vision, here and there, gone and back. She felt the last bit of resistance fall away as she fell entirely into the darkness, her world a void, only the low drone of the doctor's voice interrupting.

Lottie

The flash of the silver orb moved through the blackness, cutting the perfect darkness. Lottie was weightless, hanging more than floating, as though gravity itself had ceased to exist. She heard the low drone of the doctor's voice from a great distance, the low pulse of words. She turned in the black, away from the words, and stared into the void. It was as though her eyes were closed, the absence of light was so perfect in the moments between the flashes of the silver orb. Lottie felt her hands and fingers move. This wasn't a dream, not like before; she was in control entirely of her mind and body. Experimentally, she propelled herself upward and away entirely from the low hum of the doctor's voice. She felt her body move through the air, thick and warm; it held her suspended in space. Lottie pushed herself upward still, as though she were at the bottom of a lake and swimming through a mire. She began to see a light at the surface, faces, shapes. She swam further up, trying to break the skin of the vision. The flash of the orb was gone entirely now; only the dim light from what lay beyond illuminated the space. So close, so close. Lottie reached upward, stretching her fingers to the surface. The faces blurred. She could see lips moving but heard no sound. She had to push herself upward still.

She burst through the caul, the thick blackness clinging to her skin like a membrane. The faces flashed into focus. The girl with the black hair and eyes so like her own sat before her, her eyes wide; a woman with hair the color of lamb's blood sat at the front of a long table, her lips moving soundlessly. Lottie looked around at the others sitting around the long table, their faces rapt and enchanted. Only the girl with the black hair and eyes looked directly at her, transfixed. Lottie looked to the blood-haired woman at the head of the table. A small boy wearing a newsboy's cap was whispering in her ear. Instinctually, Lottie knew that only she could see him, and he could see her. With a jolt, she realized that even the girl with the black hair and eyes did not see her as a form—maybe a sense of her presence, but not as she was. The little boy finished his message and then looked up at Lottie; he grinned, his mouth gap-toothed, and the stench of rot rising up from his gut. He nodded at Lottie and then at the blood-haired woman, and Lottie knew what he was trying to say. She could talk to the woman, and she would hear. She could whisper in her ear the same as the boy did, and she could say the words to the women and men who sat around the table. A chance to speak to the black-haired girl, a chance to ask her for a name, a reason she kept appearing.

Lottie moved closer, her feet not quite using the ground as a surface; she moved much as she had in the void from which she had come. Closer to the blood-haired woman, closer still. The boy opened his mouth, and darkness poured out; he was laughing, a wicked sound that chilled Lottie's soul. They were not the same; he was not of this earth, not anymore; he was spirit, and Lottie was something that she had yet to define. He had no earthly form to return to, and Lottie's lay somewhere on the stiff-backed sofa, lost to a silver orb and the low hum of a doctor's intent.

What is this place? She tried to speak to the boy, but the words clung to the back of her throat. The boy nodded just the same as though she had made sound.

In-between.

His response was not voice or sound but a throb that began in the back of her neck, a certainty of words that she had never felt before. Lottie looked to the blood-haired woman and then realized what it was she needed to do. She did not wish to send a message to the black-haired girl; she wished to speak to her, directly to her. Lottie turned and faced the girl, who rose from her seat, staring blankly.

See me.

Lottie projected the words to the girl, who registered a look of shock and fear in her bottomless eyes. Lottie knew then that the girl could see her form, and it looked to be spirit and mist, not flesh. She was not as the boy was; she was real. She was here by a trick of the devil or the angels, didn't matter which. She looked into the girl's eyes and saw herself and her mum and her grandmum before that. She saw her Da and all that had come before her. This girl was her blood, and she would meet her soon. She lifted her hand, moving it round and round, stirring the energy in the room. She could feel the veil between the worlds thick between her fingers. The girl rose from the floor, her feet suspended in air. Lottie stared deep into her eyes, willing her to come to her, to feel the touch of her hand.

Soon.

Lottie sent the word across the space to the girl just as she felt the invisible thread that bound her to her mortal frame recoil and pull her backward. Lottie felt herself sucked back into the silky blackness, back down into the abyss, back into the pitch darkness that surrounded her entirely, but now the silence was broken by a voice—a voice full of fear, full of things that had gone wrong in her absence. Lottie opened her eyes, jolted by her abrupt return to the waking world, and saw Dr. Bothelli's wide eyes staring down at her.

"Lottie? Lottie, can you hear me?" he repeated.

"I bloody well can. I expect it worked, then?" she snapped, her head swimmy and starting to pulse with a pinpoint of pain in each temple.

"Thank god." The doctor sat back. "Lie still. You gave me quite a scare. I've never had a subject fall into such a deep state. I couldn't reach you at all. You didn't respond to any prompting or touch."

"I didn't cluck like a chicken for you, then?" Lottie asked, knowing full well the doctor was genuinely frightened but not caring to make him feel better.

"Lottie, I have to know. Did you see or hear anything while you were in the hypnotic state?" Dr. Bothelli asked, clutching a small notebook, ready to record her answer.

Lottie paused. She had traveled through a window into another world, another time, where a child who carried her and Elis's blood lived. Lottie knew now the dreams she had were far more than exhaustion, more than night terrors; they were windows as well but not as clear as this, never like this. She could be free from this place in a way she had never imagined— if not her body, her mind could sail away from Argoll and into what lay beyond.

"Nothing," Lottie said. It was her secret, nothing to do with the doctor. She would keep her hidden world to herself, and soon she would find a way to leave this place. Soon.

Nora (*née* Nairna)
Boston and Thereabouts
1901

From The Bell Island Historical Register

Bell Island has retained a rather enigmatic reputation since its official completion in 1685. Commissioned by the Duke of Kinross, who was sent to the new world by William III, its roots were already auspicious. If the stories surrounding their departure are to be believed, the duke and duchess were sent to Boston at just the right time, and not a minute too late to avoid the rumors that continued to surround them. Duchess Loreana Dewit née Bell had a penchant, it seemed, for the occult. Duke Dewit's close friendship with the king had helped them avoid scrutiny, but nonetheless, the pair were sent as ambassadors to the new world, their official mission to start a colony in New England that represented the good word of the king and crown. Hence, immediately upon their arrival, the scarcely inhabitable land nearly twenty miles off the coast of Boston, now known as Bell Island, was procured, and construction on what was the most extravagant house of its time began. The colony would take shape over time. However, the duke and duchess never built the "New Kinross" that had been intended and always had their sights on a life well away from others.

Bell Manor enjoyed a relatively quiet few years until the hysterics of the 1692 incidents in Salem and all of Essex County. Lady Loreana Bell, who had inscrutably and not without scandal reverted to her maiden name during her time in the new world, of-

*fered a vocal defense of the accused girls, as is re-
corded in the official Essex County court record. When
the first accused girl, a young house servant charged
with bewitching her employer in Ipswich, went missing, no one suspected Lady Bell. When subsequent
girls disappeared from the Andover jail, everyone
suspected the girls had simply bribed the guards. It
wasn't until several years after the trials that a sailor
on a merchant ship bringing supplies to Bell Island
claimed he had seen the missing young woman from
Ipswich, who went by the name of Rose McNarny.
The claim was summarily dismissed, however, seeing
that Bell Island lay past Outer Brewster and The
Graves and was notoriously difficult to navigate. The
merchant supply ships only ventured there every two
months and not at all during the storm season.*

*The sailor's story was largely panned, but still the
rumors of an island full of lost girls grew. The mystery surrounding the grand manor only grew as stories from contractors and construction crews spread
about passages that led nowhere, staircases that
ended in midair. Duke Dewit died in 1701. Bell
Manor became the full property of his widow, Lady
Loreana Bell, and slowly it slipped into obscurity.
Occasionally a story would arise that defied explanation. But the island was largely forgotten, and being
as inaccessible as it is, it escaped many of the horrors
wrought upon the Americas by its history. Lady Bell
died at the impressive age of one hundred. Her daughter, also named Loreana Bell, took control of the
mansion, and her daughter after that.*

*There were no employment records for the staff of
Bell Manor, yet the merchant ships and the occasional
contractor sent to the island for repairs reported a full*

and lively household and a growing village in the valley near the manor. All the residents were notoriously closemouthed, and one would have no option but to believe they had sprung from the rocky soil itself if it weren't for the ghost stories told by The Graves lighthouse keepers about the midnight passages of tiny vessels done in secret, with no record of their voyage or their passengers. It was said the island was inhabited by those who had been spirited away from a dark fate. Much like the girls back in 1692 who had seemingly vanished without a trace from their Andover jail cells, the residents of Bell Island had all left their former lives at just the right time, much like the original Lady Loreana Bell.

The arrival of Nora Grey on Bell Island in 1901 was never recorded in official immigration documents. Much like those who had arrived at Bell Manor before her, Nora Grey's time on Bell Island is clouded in mystery. All that can be said with any assurance is that whatever danger drove Nora Grey to America, her presence was well hidden by the crags and rocky coast as had been done for hundreds of years.

Nora

Bell Manor was a maze. Nairna, now Nora although it still felt awkward on her tongue, was lost again on the third floor where she had been tasked with collecting the tea dishes from the West Guard Observatory. Instead of ascending the winding stone staircase that led to the circular watchtower where a pair of gentlemen with convoluted New York accents sat and watched the horizon, Nora had found herself in a seemingly endless hallway of staff quarters. Now only a quarter of the rooms were occupied; Bell Manor employed far fewer house servants than it had in its inception back in 1685. Anyone who could have pointed her in the right direction was downstairs at work.

Nora stamped her foot in impatience and frustration. They had been at Bell Manor for months, and she was still as lost as the day she arrived. Lady Bell had stopped reprimanding her—in truth, Lady Bell was unlikely to reprimand anyone—but she wore her emotions on her face, with none of the cool charm that Rona Connell had carried. Nora was assigned to the house staff, and if she did not make an appearance soon, she would earn the ire of the head housemistress, and the glares of the other girls who would have been doing Nora's work all this time.

Nora gritted her teeth and tried another doorknob. It was locked, but none of this looked right anyhow. The entry to the West Guard Observatory had been at the end of the hall in Nora's memory. She remembered a plain wooden door, on the other side of which was a narrow staircase that led to another wooden door, which opened to the tower. Trying to contain her frustration, Nora walked to the end of the hallway and stood for a long minute. This house confounded her. She and Tavish had been given a thorough tour all those months ago, and where Tavish had committed the entire floor plan to memory at first glance, Nora was constantly wandering the halls and running into locked doors.

"Lost us again, huh?"

Nora whipped around to see the younger of the two watchmen grinning at her from out the door across from her.

"We rang the kitchen a bit ago, and when no one showed, Gus said he betted it was the new girl, and I said likely it was, as you're the one who spends her afternoons wandering the halls in this place." He grinned again, and Nora couldn't help but smile back. He held the door for her as she walked past and up the stairs.

"There ya are!" Gus nodded as she entered and crossed to the tea tray. "Thought you might've gotten lost. We've been watching your father hard at work." The man chuckled as Nora collected the dishes and teacups.

Nora paused and looked out the window where the watchman was pointing. There Tavish was. He wore the dark dungarees and buttoned work shirt that designated him as part of the grounds crew, but instead of doing anything useful, he was leaning against the stone garden wall, smoking a cigarette.

"There he is," Nora said, stepping back. "Between his ways

and my lack of direction, we'll be out on the street before long," she muttered.

"I wouldn't worry none," the watchman said, glancing over his shoulder. "Lady Bell's put up with a lot worse than the pair of you. The things we've seen up here—am I right, Gus? Nah, you're doing okay. Besides, Lady Bell doesn't hire so much as she adopts, so you're here for a reason, am I right?"

"I suppose that's true," Nora said softly. The watchmen grinned, and Gus offered friendly nods as she took the dirty dishes and descended the stairs, hoping she could find her way back to the kitchen.

She was here for a reason; the two watchmen were not wrong. And she was Nora, not Nairna, and Tavish was still Tavish. His paperwork might say different, but he refused to use the new name, and Nora relented. He wasn't the reason they'd had to leave Scotland, after all. As far as the watchmen or the head housemistress or any of the others save Lady Bell knew, she and Tavish had immigrated to Boston through Ellis Island in New York. They came from Glasgow looking for a better life and were lucky enough to be second cousins to the head gardener, hence their employment at Bell Manor. No one came to Bell Manor by accident; the entire staff and the village itself all carried their own story, and in that their own secrets. It went without saying that Nora and Tavish had never met the head gardener before and were no more related to him than Robert the Bruce. But it was what everyone had been told, and on Bell Island no one asked questions. Nora had learned that on day one of their new life in America all those months ago when she'd stepped on board the small ferry to Bell Island.

Nora wound her way back to the kitchen, stepping over one of the many overgrown, long-furred cats who wandered the manor with an air of entitlement and eternity. She dropped the tea tray next to the sink where one of the kitchen girls grunted acknowledgement. Nora then took her cleaning pail and set off to the library. It was her favorite task on the long list of things she was to accomplish in a day's time here at Bell Manor. Every day, after luncheon and before the late afternoon hour, Nora was to sweep the wooden floors, dust the surfaces, and replace the vases of roses and daisies that were dotted throughout. The library was a grand room; it reminded Nora of the sort of place a duke or earl would have sat with a glass of brandy had it been back in Edinburgh. Books lined every available surface, and winding metal staircases led to upper levels on which you could walk along a narrow balcony for even more books.

It was a notorious task, and Nora knew it was hers because there were a thousand cracks and crevices, busts and figurines that needed dusting, and the books themselves seemed to grow particles to spit into the air as fast as she swept. But all that aside, it was her favorite place to be; it was quiet, and she never felt eyes on her, never felt the cracks of fear at the base of her neck that she could never quite shake since she and Tavish had left Edinburgh.

Tavish told her she was foolish—that her nightmares, her nerves, were wasted energy. He had told her that as they stood in the line for the customs agent at Ellis Island, their paperwork courtesy of Dr. Edwin Harrison and the Order of St. Cyprian in his pocket.

"No one's so good as to figure where we're at," he'd whispered in her ear as she stood in the line, visibly shaking despite the ferocious and stifling heat that filled the cramped immigration center. The air had smelled like a thousand things, none of them pleasant; around them a thousand languages bounced off the walls; strangers looked at them and looked away, everyone caught in a thousand problems they had left behind.

The ship had been miserable, but Nora had known it would be. Rona had managed to get them a room together, but it was in steerage just the same and scarcely had room for the two bunks it held. Nora had spent the weeks at sea vomiting into a bucket and ignoring Tavish's admonishments. It had been Nora's doing that had led to their hasty and unplanned departure from Scotland, and although Tavish made no mistake he was delighted to be receiving a free trip complete with room and board at the other end, he made a grand show of proving to Nora that she was a creature in need of protecting. It was as though she were a child again, but as Tavish had never been around much during her actual childhood, he'd failed to see that not all children are helpless, and even fewer are docile.

Despite Tavish's claims that no one was so savvy as to ever figure out where they might be, Nora still felt a newly familiar fear every time she turned a corner or heard her new name spoken aloud. As she carefully polished a row of ceramic doves, she felt as though she were back in the chaos of Ellis Island as the customs agent had examined the paperwork while looking up occasionally and then back down where he would turn a page and then look back up again, to scrutinize the papers as though the letters themselves were foreign and not the Queen's English.

"All in line?" Tavish had asked nervously.

The man in the dark uniform had looked up at him and then at Nora.

"One moment. You have an appointment, so it seems." His face was utterly impassive, but Nora had felt a wave of barely contained panic nonetheless as he stepped from behind his counter and disappeared into a tiny office.

"Settle yerself, girl," Tavish growled in her ear. "They said it was all arranged; just trust it. Yer gentleman friend is the one behind all this. I hope yeh trust him."

Nora's fear was replaced with anger at Tavish for mentioning Edwin. Before she could respond, the uniformed man reappeared.

"This way, both of you," he said in a weary and disinterested voice, indicating the office.

"Told you it was all arranged," Tavish whispered. "Settle yerself. We'll both look mad otherwise."

In the office was a bald-headed man whose stacks of documents were threatening to bury him alive. He looked up at the pair of them and then back at their documents before him. "Not often we get a genuine VIP through this trough," he muttered.

"What do you . . . ," Nora had started to ask, but Tavish elbowed her sharply, silencing her query.

"Someone has spared no expense is all I'm saying," the man said as he stamped two forms, the impact shaking the table and threatening to upset the delicate stacks of paper. "Welcome to America, Miss Nora Grey. I believe a ferry has been arranged for you both. I'm sure you'll enjoy your time in Boston and thereabouts."

The papers had, for all intents and purposes, given them not only new identities but an entirely new life. As they boarded the ferry that would take them to Boston and another even farther to Bell Island, Nora felt her old life fall away. She was not the girl who had left Glasgow port with a hood over her head and her face hidden. Her life was entirely new now, none of the old ugliness left behind, even if Tavish seemed determined to treat her as though she were still in a nursery.

Nora finished the library and was exiting out the side door to the back hallway just as Lady Bell was entering for her afternoon reverie, a black-and-white spotted cat at her heels. It wasn't a bad life overall, Nora thought as she wound her way back to the house staff's supply room. Her talents grew every day; there were days when she could feel the very thoughts of others buzzing on the surface of their skin. There were whispers in the corners of every room at Bell Manor, and Nora wondered what she would see if Edwin were to place the flashing light before her now. Before she stepped onto the train bound to Glasgow where she would catch the passenger ship, he had assured her that Bell Manor was a fresh start, a place where she could grow her talents in peace. The gossip that followed Nairna Liath had nothing to do with Nora Grey, after all.

So she worked without question and found a deep peace in the monotony of the routine. No one expected her to perform, no one looked at her with wonder or fear; in fact, no one noticed her much at all. And the best part of it all was that every week, three dollars were deposited in her very own house account, which—it had been explained to her upon their arrival at Bell Manor—her father could never access. The money that Nora earned was all hers, and if ever she wanted to cash out her account, no one could stop her. From their cottage among the staff quarters in the back of the manor house, Nora could see the ocean and the sea birds that swooped and rioted at the shore. Sometimes, especially when Tavish was absent, she pretended the cabin was all her own, and this was life—a small life, to be sure, but a quiet one. In another universe she could see herself growing old here, lines and crevices deepening on her hands and face as she polished the floor of the grand library and expertly wound around the crooks and corners of the manor.

She found the memory of Edwin Harrison and his cornflower blue eyes grew more distant every day. In those early miserable days on the ship, and even here on Bell Island, Nora had found herself lost in thoughts of when he would arrive and join her, what life they might have together. Now, with even the scant bit of time between them, she found herself caring less and less. Perhaps she didn't need another man to take care of her. Another man with his plans and ideas, even kindhearted ones as Edwin's might be. It wasn't so very different from Tavish, not really. It had been Nairna Liath who had harbored a girlish crush on Edwin. Nora Grey was a different woman entirely. Nairna Liath allowed her life to be dictated by others. Nora Grey could, perhaps, carve out a life for herself.

Nora

Lady Loreana Bell was an imposing figure. She stood nearly six feet tall, and her dark hair, streaked with gray, was swept back from her face, giving her features a stern appearance. Her skin was the lightest shade of cocoa, which made her golden hazel eyes appear almost ethereal. She was not beautiful in a traditional sort of way—she was far too frightening to be such—but she was a woman that Nora knew she would never forget no matter how many years she lived.

Nora had met her before this night when she and Tavish had been mysteriously summoned for dinner at the main house. Lady Bell remained a somewhat elusive figure in the manor. On the night Nora and Tavish had arrived at Bell Island, Lady Bell had been at the dock, wrapped in a woolen cloak that was scant protection against the pelting rain and wind. She had hustled them into a carriage led by a single Clydesdale horse; in the rain, it had been a terrifying sight. Nora had felt herself frozen in place as stories of Nan's *puca*, the shapeshifter said to roam the lowlands, filled her head. But she had climbed into the carriage with Tavish and ridden silently to the manor, Lady Bell coldly regarding them the entire trip. Even Tavish had had enough sense not to try to speak. They both knew they were not only guests but in great debt to Lady Bell.

Once they had arrived at the manor, Lady Bell had whispered something to the doorman, who whisked Nora and Tavish into the butler's pantry, which set off the main kitchen. It was a casual sort of sitting room designed for the days when the butler and head housemistress would conduct business and meet with staff to manage the running of the house. By 1901, however, the butler was also the doorman, the footman, and the handyman. The head housemistress served to manage the cooks, the cleaning staff, and do the work of all the lady's maids in one. The house had pared down its once extravagant staff, and it ran despite the skeleton thin crew that supported the work.

The butler/doorman/handyman, who Nora would soon learn was named Clarence, led them to the pantry where they sat on soft chairs and wrapped themselves in the blankets that Clarence provided with a warm smile. Lady Bell joined them after a few minutes, carrying the tea tray herself. She set it down, poured three cups, added lemon to each without consulting anyone, and nodded at Nora and Tavish before she ever spoke a word.

"It's late. I like not to bother the staff unless necessary." Her voice was deep. If one had not seen the speaker, they might have thought her a man.

"Of course . . . we are very grateful, " Tavish began. Lady Bell waved him silent.

"It is my duty, as it was my mother's before me, and hers before that. You are both safe here, but I do expect you to help with the care of the manor. I trust that will not be a problem," she said without asking.

Nora nodded. "Of course, we are happy to do whatev—"

Lady Bell waved her silent as she had done Tavish. "You will be paid. I abhor free labor, and I do not wish you to feel beholden to me, or anyone for that matter." She regarded Nora for a long minute. "You made some very powerful friends in Edinburgh. Do you even know how powerful they really are, I wonder?"

Nora shook her head. "Edwin . . . Dr. Harrison is from the Society for Psychical Research in London, he arranged for ou—"

Again Nora was interrupted by Lady Bell's spider-like hand. "Dr. Harrison is the mere tip of the iceberg. Have you heard of the Order of St. Cyprian?"

Nora nodded, sipping her tea. Her bones were chilled to their core, and she was trying not to rattle the fine china. "Dr. Harrison did not tell me much about them, only that he was a member."

"You will learn all you wish to know soon enough. I understand you were causing quite a stir in Edinburgh, enough to become an issue to the local Spiritualists. I've always found the Scots to be an especially superstitious bunch. Your fresh American names, your passage across the Atlantic, your time here at Bell Manor is all a gift from the monastic heads of the Order. Your Dr. Harrison must be quite taken with you . . ." Nora felt herself blushing, and Tavish shifted uncomfortably in his chair, but Lady Bell's eyes narrowed slightly. "Or you must have something that he wants very badly. I would practice caution, child. The Order of St. Cyprian is rarely so magnanimous."

"Magnanimous?" Nora searched her mind for the word. "But I'm certainly not anyone's rival. I am hardly even a medium. I read the cards, that's all . . ."

"Hardly all you can do. And when you are capable of as much as I have been told you are capable of, you are always someone's rival." She paused. "You are well read. That's good. I hope you will feel free to read whatever you like from my library. A sharp mind is your best weapon."

"I don't understand . . . ," Nora said, feeling the chill in her bones move up and down her spine.

"You will. But for now, Clarence will show you to your cottage, where I had them bring you some proper clothes for the work you will do here. There is a bit of dinner waiting for you as well. Pay no mind to the cats you will see in the manor and the grounds; they have been here for far longer than I can account for and will remain after we are gone. I will take good care of you for as long as you wish to remain here. Some of my guests stay for years, some for generations, and some pass through back to the mainland before the season has ended. Bell Island is a bit like Avalon; it exists just beyond the mist and out of mind."

Since that odd night, Nora had not spoken with Lady Bell and had hardly seen her except as her grand shadow passed to and from the library. But her presence was everywhere in the manor house. The staff spoke of her only when necessary and always with reverence. Lady Bell demanded a spotless house but did so with grace and loyalty, not fear of retribution.

This invitation to dinner with a mysterious guest was the first communication Nora had had from Lady Bell in all the months she had been on the island. Her fingertips were shaking with anticipation as they entered the kitchen to find Clarence sitting on a tall stool in the kitchen while the cook and the kitchen girls hustled about.

"Good evening," he said with a friendly nod. Clarence's skin was shades darker than Lady Bell's, and his rough black hair was peppered with streaks of gray. Nora nodded back, and Tavish took off his felt bowler hat as he entered.

"Looks like you two have a visitor," Clarence said as he rose to his feet and motioned for them to follow.

"Clarence, do you have any idea who it is?" Tavish asked.

The old man shook his head. "Lady Bell will introduce you, I'm sure. Don't worry." He turned to give them both a look that was both curious and guarded. "No harm will come to you here. Lady Bell wouldn't stand for it."

"That's a comfort," Tavish muttered. Nora shot him a look as they entered the drawing room adjacent to the dining room.

Lady Bell was dressed in a simple dress of green silk, and Nora was glad to see she was not inappropriately casual. A man rose from a high-backed chair and stepped forward as Nora approached.

"You must be Nora Grey," he said with a tight smile. Nora shook his extended hand and looked to Lady Bell.

"Thank you both for joining us. Nora, this is Karl Mendis. He is an associate of your friend Dr. Harrison in London and was part of the team responsible for bringing you to my island. Karl, may I present Nora Grey and her father . . ."

"Tavish Grey." Tavish stepped between Nora and the man.

"It is a pleasure to meet you both. I have much to tell you. Shall we?"

Nora watched Karl Mendis closely as they took their seats in the drawing room and Clarence offered small glasses of brandy from a silver tray. The man who had come all this way to meet with her was a vapid, squat little fellow. He was likely no more than thirty, but he had skin so pale it seemed nearly translucent. His hair was an absence of color and eyes nearly perfect voids. The overall effect was the appearance of a much older man. His pale skin was pockmarked and pitted, the uneven terrain highlighting every wrinkle and crevice. A strange energy rolled off the man; it set her on edge. She regarded him curiously. When he caught her staring, instead of looking away, Nora found herself asking, "Your accent, you're not from Edinburgh. London, then?"

"Yes, I am from London," Karl said with a nod. "I was sent on business from our mutual friend Dr. Harrison."

"Of course," Nora responded.

A soft bell rang, indicating that dinner was served. Nora rose and found herself sitting in a fine oak chair at a dining table that she was more accustomed to polishing than eating at. A bowl of blood red soup sat before her. Karl took a spoonful and sat back with a satisfied expression on his face.

"Just marvelous," he said warmly. Lady Bell continued to eat, her face expressionless.

"Nora." He turned his attention from the soup. "Do you know who St. Cyprian was?"

Nora shook her head, the food before her swiftly cooling, her stomach in knots.

"He's a myth, according to the Catholic Church," Karl said, raising his spoon again. Nora watched as soup dripped from the spoon and splashed back into the bowl.

"There was never a bishop of Antioch named Cyprian according to the official records, and how could there be? After what he did." Karl smiled, baiting the question.

"And what did he do?" Tavish asked impatiently.

Karl cast Tavish a look that made Nora realize that Karl would have far rather met with Nora alone. She was suddenly grateful for Tavish's bullish presence and Lady Bell's silent command of the room. As she watched Karl Mendis slurp the thick soup, she saw a flash of the intent and thoughts that filled his head and knew that his ill-kept presence was but a front; the man was a viper and would strike anything that impeded his path.

"The official story is that before Cyprian was the bishop of Antioch, he was a magician who conjured a devil at the behest of a young man who was desperately in love with a young woman named Justina. The story also goes that Justina recognized the devil for what it was, and the plan was thwarted, her maidenhead saved." Karl smiled, his lips stained blood red.

A serving girl appeared and began to clear dishes in preparation for the main course. Nora hadn't touched a bite. Her skin was cold, and she looked to Lady Bell for a sign that she shouldn't follow her instinct to run straight out the heavy wooden front entrance and into the night. Lady Bell's eyes bored into her, and in her right ear Nora heard a whisper of a voice.

Even snakes are rendered impotent in my garden.

Lady Bell twitched her lips in the smallest of smiles, and Nora felt the ice in her spine turn to steel. She shifted slightly as a plate of steaming greens from the manor garden and poached fish was set before her.

"What an inspiring story," Nora said, as she met Karl's stare.

"Oh, that's just the beginning. The bad part if you will. Cyprian was angered by this girl's . . . oh what is the word? Tenacity? And so he summoned the devil himself to prove that he, a great magician, was stronger than a mere maiden." Karl took a big bite of the fish, bits of flesh falling back to his plate.

"And was he?" Nora asked.

"A maiden is never just a maiden in such stories. What would be the point of telling them if she were?" Karl laughed at his own joke, but his voice grew stern as he scraped his fork along the china plate, making gooseflesh rise on Nora's arms. "Justina defeated the devil himself by making the sign of the cross. Cyprian was so awed by the power of Christ that he gave up his dark ways, converted to Christianity, and eventually became the bishop of Antioch. The Feast of Cyprian and Justina is a holy day to many, myth though it may be."

"Fascinating story," Nora said evenly.

"Yeh, fascinating. What exactly is the purpose of it all?" Tavish interrupted, his expression one of a wolf ready to defend its den.

"I am sorry, my good man." Karl nodded to Tavish. "I do not mean to leave you out of the conversation in the slightest. It is just that it is such a unique pleasure to meet our Nora Grey. You have been much talked about in London, young lady."

"What exactly do you talk about?" Nora asked.

"The thing about Cyprian—his pre-bishop days, of course,

before he denounced magic—is that it is impossible to summon a demon, and even more impossible to call the Devil himself, especially for such a petty cause as love, or lust as it might be better termed," Karl said, his gaze never leaving Nora's.

"You'd do well to watch your tongue around my daughter," Tavish said impatiently, his temper rising quickly.

Lady Bell stood abruptly. "We'll take our coffee in the drawing room. Though I'd prefer wine, as I suspect you would as well." She looked to Nora, who felt the air she had trapped in her lungs release.

Karl rose, his lips disappearing in his smile. "Wonderful. And dinner? Simply grand. Wine and coffee sound lovely. I can finish my story."

"I trust your story has a purpose," Lady Bell said. Her voice was ice.

"Everything has a purpose," Karl said as they moved back to the silken wing chairs of the drawing room.

Nora wrapped her hand around the wine goblet that Clarence offered her. She would be hungry later, but now her body felt like a bow, tensed and ready to snap.

"My story has a distinct purpose. I represent the Order of St. Cyprian, based on the exploration of Cyprian's true magic and separating truth from fiction." Karl leaned forward, his face intent. "You see, Cyprian did not raise a demon; this is a thing that cannot be done. A demon is a creature of mythology, as is the devil. These are fairy stories for religious zealots and children. No, his magic was real, not the stuff that feeds the Catholic masses. What Cyprian did was something that I believe our Dr. Harrison spoke to you about, Nora, once upon a time."

Nora shook her head. "I don't understand."

"Think," Karl said. "Remember when Dr. Harrison showed you a beautiful butterfly?"

Nora closed her eyes slightly and saw the swirls of green and cream. "It was a hawk moth, an Oleander Hawk Moth."

"Yes, that was it," Karl said. "Do you remember why he showed you the moth, what special talent he was fishing for in you?"

"Regeneration," Nora said, her eyes snapping wide open. "Is that what Cyprian did? He brought someone back from the dead?"

"If the stories are to be believed, yes. He did," Karl said, sitting back with a satisfied smile.

"And that is what you want from me?" Nora said, her voice sounded tinny and hollow in her ears.

"Yes, yes, it is."

Nora

"I can't imagine what would lead any of you to believe I am capable of such a thing," Nora said bluntly. Her entire body felt as though it were vibrating.

Karl regarded her for a long moment. "I was not present, but if the accounts of your experience with Miss Dorothy Kellings are to be believed, you summoned an entity. An entity that was seen by multiple people in the room. An entity that had a full body, a face, and even a voice. You controlled or perhaps were controlled by this entity for the expanse of more than three full minutes." Karl leaned forward, intently staring at Nora. "Do you have any understanding of how rare this accomplishment is?"

Nora shook her head slightly. She could feel Tavish's discomfort. He was shifting in his seat, obviously uncomfortable with the tone of this meeting.

"And furthermore," Karl continued. "Furthermore, Dr. Harrison has reported even more fantastical abilities. You tore apart the library in Edinburgh, didn't you, young lady?"

"What is this?" Tavish said in confusion. Nora cast him a look that silenced his questions.

"It wasn't like that . . . I . . . ," Nora stuttered.

"And you shattered a window without ever laying a hand on the glass." Karl sat back and took a long sip of his wine. "Regeneration is a big word. There are so many aspects to what you do that align with the studies that we at the Order have conducted for hundreds of years. However, in recent history, we have not had the pleasure of so talented a medium. We have a vested interest in procuring your time."

"Do I have a choice?" Nora asked, glancing at Tavish, who sat oddly silent.

"My dear." Karl chuckled. "You always have a choice. You and your father are not prisoners here. You are free to catch the next ferry back to Boston; you can sail back to Scotland if you like. You can return to reading tarot cards at county fairs and begging for scraps. It would be a deep shame, but it is your choice. You would be an independent agent, so to speak, if you returned home; you were bringing a bit too much attention to the Edinburgh Spiritualists. You could always join us in London—we'd be happy to host you—but the new world brings with it new opportunities, and I think you will find that once you step foot off this island, the world is your oyster. And we at the Order of St. Cyprian are beyond excited to represent your interests."

Nora's body felt as though it were made of ice. "And what do you mean by that?"

"Helping you to live up to your potential. That is all, my dear; your interests are our interests." Karl regarded her with his snake-like eyes, waiting for her response.

"Cartin' me 'round like a show pony? Throwing me on stage like Dorothy Kellings and the like?" Nora felt her temper rise and with it the brogue that she tried to keep carefully tapped down.

"A show pony? Never, my dear," Karl replied with calculated concern. "We would like to arrange a certain number of public appearances—tastefully orchestrated, of course, nothing so brash as Miss Kellings's performances. Your abilities appeal to our passion for research, and research needs funding, which comes largely from our loyal patrons, who we would very much like you to meet, and perhaps if you could see it in your heart to give them a little preview of what they might be funding, well, all involved would be on a winning team."

"Miss Grey's presence here at Bell Manor is a matter of confidentiality." Lady Bell spoke, her voice cutting the air and silencing Karl Mendis instantly. "If the girl wishes to stay here and leave the public circus behind, she is welcome, as is her father. Bell Island is open to all who wish a life away from the public eye."

Karl Mendis nodded and looked to Lady Bell and back to Nora. "Of course. It is your choice, and please do not misunderstand, we would never do anything to compromise your presence here. What was considered a scandal in Edinburgh is simply seen as stardom here in the West. Would you believe, Miss Grey, that there are those who move to America just to seek the sort of attention that you are hiding from here on this island? But to each his own. I hope you will agree to work with us, hone your talents, build a new life here in this new world. You have a new name, and with our help, you can reenter the world as a new person. Tell me, Miss Grey, you have read about the American Spiritualists? The Fox Sisters? The teachings of Franz Mesmer? The lovely Miss Cora Scott? You could be a part of this world, Miss Grey. You could be its leader. You have a natural, albeit untrained, talent that exceeds anything that spins in their circles."

Nora put her lips to her wineglass and let the liquid scorch her throat and warm her chest. The quietude of Bell Island called to her. She could see a path that led to her own little cottage on the manor grounds, her hair graying and joints stiffening with time and honest work. She would never be hungry or cold or want for a sense of belonging. It was safe. At the same time, Nora felt a shudder of not-unwelcome excitement as she pictured another path. The rush of energy as the books flew from the library shelves, the limitless chasm she had glimpsed as the woman with eyes so like her own stared at her from across the void at the séance. What was she capable of? What existed in that perfect blackness? She contained multitudes the likes of which she had only started to imagine. Nora closed her eyes, and in the darkness the image of the hawk moth took shape, its green- and cream-swirled wings beginning to slowly move, the dust of disuse and death staining the perfect darkness. The creature moved in uneven strokes through the blackness of her mind, a dead thing reborn.

Nora opened her eyes. "What do I need to do?"

Nora

"Dorothy Kellings showed early promise," Karl said as he shuffled a deck of playing cards. The light was fading outside, and soon the night chill would overwhelm the island. It had been three days since their dinner, and Nora had insisted on keeping up with her house duties in service to Lady Bell. That left the late afternoon hours to sit with Karl Mendis, the same as she had done with Edwin in what seemed like another lifetime back in Edinburgh. Unlike with Edwin, however, Nora took no joy from these sessions. Karl proved himself to be humorless, and Nora knew she would never entirely trust the rotund little creature. He possessed none of Edwin's charm, and even as she questioned what connection she might have had with Edwin, she missed everything about those afternoons in Rona's parlour.

"She showed potential as a young woman, just about your age," Karl continued, breaking Nora's reverie. She looked up at him resentfully.

"She brought a bird back to life," Nora said. "That was what Edwin told me, like the Prussian countess?"

"A bit. But unlike Carolina Gustav, Dorothy Kellings only performed her miracle once, and her bird wasn't entirely dead," Karl said as he set the deck of cards before Nora.

"Not entirely dead? So alive then? So she didn't resurrect anything?" Nora replied, remembering Dorothy Kellings's mocking tone and cold eyes.

"Well, not entirely alive either, so somewhere in-between perhaps?" Karl said, cutting the deck and lining the two halves side by side. "Allow me to explain. I was not present; it was one of our American sisters who reported the incident. A blackbird had flown straight into a glass pane; it lay on the steps motionless, stunned, its heart beating out of its tiny chest. As it was reported, Dorothy Kellings was just a girl then, younger than you are now. She picked the creature up in her hands and whispered something to it that our colleague could not hear, and the blackbird immediately sat up, regarded Miss Kellings as though it were replying, and then flew away."

"It's not a very fantastic story," Nora said with a frown. "That is what sparked such interest in her?"

"No, not that alone. Dorothy Kellings was touted as 'The Scarlet Sunbird' by her uncle—who, I might add, reminds me a bit of your father. In the retelling, a common and stunned blackbird became a rare Scarlet Sunbird that dropped out of thin air, conjured by Dorothy Kellings. She brought the creature back to life, and it appeared as her familiar in those early years. At least until it actually died and obtaining another became problematic. The uncle hauled her around the Rochester Spiritualist scene, where the girl was performing séances and summoning the dead. She was advertised as a natural physical medium." Karl pointed to the cards. "Choose one from each pile."

Nora flipped two cards over. A nine of hearts and the two of spades. She didn't know where Karl was going with this exercise and was far more interested in what he was saying than whatever he was attempting to show her.

"What did she do in her séances?" Nora asked.

"First, tell me what you feel from those cards. What are your impressions?" Karl asked.

"Tell me a story first, then I'll let you know," Nora said, and Karl suppressed a small smile. He didn't seem to mind that she was outstandingly rude to him, and it only encouraged Nora to keep pushing her limits with the little man.

"Fine. You can look this up on your own. There's an entire volume on Dorothy Kellings in Lady Bell's library, but I will share one story. She must have been near to twenty years old when this happened. A public séance at the Albany Opera House, every seat full. Dorothy sat on stage bound to a chair with rope, so no one could claim trickery. The newspapers reported that a substance began to emit from the very walls of the theatre. It had a foul smell and burned the skin of those that touched it. It was as though Dorothy Kellings was willing it into being."

"Ectoplasm," Nora said quietly. "I've read a bit about this."

"Well, that was just the start. The gas lights flickered, and the theatre was dark. Then a moment later they were again at full light, and a woman in the front of the audience pointed to the opera boxes and screamed." Karl paused, obviously enjoying the dramatics of the story. "In the first box, closest to the stage, sat one Mr. Roland Washington."

"And who was that, and why did he make the woman scream?" Nora asked, imagining the hysterics of the crowd.

"Well, in life one can hardly say. But given as though Mr. Roland Washington was six years in the grave, he was very scream-inducing."

Nora shook her head, laughing softly. "It's ridiculous. I saw her at work; she's an actress. Roland Washington was likely an actor, and the ectoplasm a trick of the theatre. People believe what they are told to believe. They were told she would raise the dead, and so they saw the dead risen."

"Like I said, early promise. By the time she was selling out opera houses, the execution of her craft was becoming . . . questionable for our purposes. But here's a story you won't find in Lady Bell's library, and then you really must cooperate. I am trying to prove a point with these cards, truly I am," Karl said, and Nora nodded.

"When the Order first met Miss Scarlet Sunbird, she was sixteen years old. Her uncle had brought her to London and to the Society for Psychical Research—hoping she could earn him a fine penny, I'm sure. Young Dorothy's first test was to guess images on cards that were obscured from her view. It was more a test of what lengths her caretaker would go to cheat, truth be known. But Dorothy, according to those that were there, ignored the cards entirely. Instead, she took the hand of the man who held them and in a voice not her own spoke to him about his childhood, how she was sorry to have had to leave him, sorry for the illness in her lungs, the childhood spent in the orphanages. You could say it was a parlour trick, easy enough to look up the history of a man and know his mother had died of the consumption when he was five and he'd spent his childhood in the church dormitories. But it was her voice that caught our attention. It wasn't anything that could come from a child. It was a woman's tone, a woman who was dying, a woman whose lungs were already dissolved by the illness that would kill her. It was . . . not of this earth. So actress she may be, but there is a core of her that can cross the veil and back again." Karl paused, looked down at the cards and back up at Nora. "Enough stories. What do you see?"

Nora looked down at the nine of hearts and the two of spades. "I see a terrible poker hand."

"No. What do you see?" Karl pressed. "You cannot be beholden to your cards. You need to be able to read any cards that are presented to you, and you need to see the deeper meaning in simple symbols."

Nora looked again, the simple pattern staring back at her.

She closed her eyes, and in the blackness she saw the image of a tall and thin tower, the sky a burnt apocalypse behind it. No life stirred behind the darkened windows; any secrets it held were part of the very fiber of the stone.

"I see playing cards," she replied, the image of the black tower pulsing in her mind. She did not trust this man; the tower was a dangerous place, full of distrust and betrayal. The secrets this man and his Order hoped to uncover were hidden within its walls along with everything that was lost to mankind, all the wars and senseless death, suffering, loss—all this resided within the walls of the tower. The power to pull a life back from the veil was an unnatural act, a defiance of the order of the world. Still, despite all this, she felt the fluttering of the moth's wings behind her eyelids.

Later, as she lay in her bed in the cottage, Nora reached for the extinguished candle at her bedside. She had pinched it dark over an hour ago and had lain still, staring at the blackened wick, since then. Feeling a tingling in her fingertips that extended up her forearm, she reached out, brushing her skin against the wax. The flame sputtered and then rose high into the air as though it were shocked at its own existence. Nora smiled to herself. A thing reborn, what was once dark was now light.

Lottie
Argoll Asylum
1866

Notes on the International Psychical Society of Oxford's Official Examination of Spirit Sighting #A827 — Also Known as the Wailing Woman of the Argoll Downs

Presiding Investigator: Dr. Rodney Naandaro, chief of presiding investigations
Incident Date: November 11, 1911
(from the field journal of Dr. Naandaro)

The incident was reported by a Mr. Walker and his wife (see file notes), who reside on the land known as Argoll Downs and have for generations, wherein they operate a small farm. The farmhouse is a simple structure, the likes of which one would expect. No obvious reason for the disturbances can be easily determined. No electricity or running water on the property that could be responsible for disruptions, and while there are farm animals present, none of the sort that would be likely to cause disruption.

The letter sent to the IPSO stated that the incident was a regular occurrence, and it tended to coincide with the moon waxing full. The report stated that a woman wearing a white or otherwise pale gown walks the downs, a wailing cry emitting from her, though no facial features are visible. The vision is described as a mist-like substance. When questioned as to how many months this sighting had been noted, Mrs. Walker scoffed and said the "wailing woman," as she called her, had always been there. The letter to the IPSO was prompted not by the sighting of the "wail-

ing woman" but rather a new disturbance that had recently threatened the safety of the farmer and his wife's infant son.

I will stay the night in the child's nursery, where it was reported by the couple that the mist-like image of the "wailing woman" has been appearing over the baby's cradle at night during the time of the waxing full moon. The vision, as reported, does not make her customary "wail" but rather stands silent, reaching for the child. When questioned as to whether this vision had appeared in the presence of other children in the house, Mrs. Walker replied that their son was the first child in the house in generations. Family lore spun stories of changelings and ghostly goings on, and as a result children had traditionally been kept from the premises until they were of a toddling age. Mr. and Mrs. Walker, who are not of a superstitious mind (see file note for official statement), scoffed at what they termed "fairy stories" and have kept their infant son at home.

In line with the procedures of the IPSO, I will stay the night to observe the happenings and, in doing so, determine whether further investigation in this matter is warranted.

Lottie

"Lottie, we're going to try again, but with a few safety precautions. Can you hear this bell?"

Dr. Bothelli held up a brass handbell and shook it back and forth vigorously. The racket it clanged out made Lottie jump back.

"Yes! Yes! I'd have to be deaf to not hear that," Lottie grumbled. Sid had collected her after her breakfast of plain porridge and unimpressive tea. She had been moved from the infirmary to a small room in the women's ward. It was utilitarian and clean. The residents kept to themselves, and Lottie had been surprised to find a small package on her bed. Items from home, a wooden box containing her grandmum's spirit cards, and three handkerchiefs that miraculously still smelled of Elis. Lottie had nearly broken down when she'd clutched them to her chest.

"Just had to make sure. In our last session I found it very difficult to pull you out with simple verbal commands, so I need to make sure we have a noise you will hear even when you are deep in your own subconscious." Dr. Bothelli placed the brass bell carefully on the desk and looked at Lottie with a pleased expression on his face. "I have to say, you demonstrated one of the most malleable minds for mesmerism I have ever encountered. I was very excited to work with you again, and given your condition, I believe our work together will be of better use than chores."

"I've been warned that I'd do well to play sick rather than be the subject of your therapies," Lottie said pointedly. "Why would people warn me about that?"

A look of momentary annoyance or even anger flashed across the doctor's face and was almost instantly gone. He smiled, revealing his too-perfect teeth. "No one likes to take their medicine. That's a truth that remains whether you're a child or grown. My therapies force my patients to confront their demons, and it's not always pleasant. But I have such great hopes for you, Lottie. Your mind is so open. I feel you can experience true healing once we really face your troubles."

"Perhaps," Lottie said uneasily. Dr. Bothelli ushered her to the stiff-backed sofa, where she lay back with her head on a velvet throw pillow. He sat in a chair next to her just like the last session. The brass bell was on the side table. He held the silver orb on its chain in front of her.

"Are we ready? Before we start, Lottie, I want you to trust me completely. The unconscious mind is malleable, but it is still your mind. I cannot force you to do anything. I cannot plant thoughts or actions in your mind. It doesn't work like that. I am just a guide, walking you through the museum that is your subconscious. You are in control of your actions, and I will not see anything without your permission. Mesmerism is a greatly misunderstood art. I want you to think of it as a sort of balm, a meditation, prayer. You are setting aside all the troubles of your waking life and allowing your mind to be clear from confusion. Together we will help you face what is causing your malady." The doctor's voice was soft and soothing. Lottie nodded, already feeling the tips of her fingers and toes fading gently into static.

"Now watch the orb, and when I snap my fingers, you will close your eyes and let yourself fall back, back, back. Only the sound of the bell can awaken you. All other sounds are background. Let them fade, watch the orb, and now, close."

Lottie's eyes fell closed of their own volition. She heard the doctor's voice, but the words blended into a soundless murmur. She was back in the inky blackness, floating weightless in a liquid darkness. She saw the face of the black-haired girl before her and swam toward it—this other version of herself, this other dimension where she was free from these troubles. She propelled herself through the darkness until she felt the skin of the next world against her flesh. The faint flash of the silver orb sailed through the darkness, and the doctor's low hum vibrated behind her. Ignoring it all, Lottie tore at the skin, and it gave way. She found herself in a room where the black-haired girl was reading cards in the same grand parlour she had seen before. Three older ladies in fine dresses sat before her. Lottie could not hear their words, but their mouths moved back and forth, question after question.

Lottie hovered in the room, aware that no one could see her, not like the last time when the girl had stared right at her. She was a spy in this vision, although she saw gooseflesh on the back of the girl's neck as she drew closer and knew the girl sensed her presence. The cards on the table made Lottie's skin crawl. Her seer cards, the same cards that sat in her dormitory cell on the ward floor. The same cards she'd never learned to read, but now they were clear as words on a page. The Ace of Swords, inversed, glared back at her, and Lottie was pulled from the grand parlour and out, out, out. The thread that connected her to the earthly place was pulling her furiously, and for a moment she thought it must be the doctor calling her back. But no, it wasn't the stiff-backed sofa and the doctor's sparsely decorated office where she landed but in a cold and bitter field. Night was swiftly approaching, and gnarled, dead trees surrounded her. The ground was frozen and dead, devoid of seed or life. A crumbling cottage sat in the distance, cold and unused. Lottie stared around the plane and found herself transfixed by a gnarled and forked tree. Its blackened and dead trunk stretched upward and then split into two long fingers that wrapped their way into the mist. Beneath the tree, beneath the frozen and ruined soil that held its dead roots, Lottie saw blood and flesh. She felt the tear of a knife in her neck, felt the sticky warmth of her own blood dripping down her arms and chest. Whatever lay beneath that tree was not to be disturbed; this was cursed ground, and its discovery would bring only misery. Yet it cried out to her; it wanted to be free from this place; it wanted to be found.

The cord snapped back, across the rigid and freezing landscape, back into the grand parlour where Lottie saw the three women standing to leave, their faces relieved. Whatever the black-haired girl had told them had soothed their souls. Lottie grasped her way through the space to the girl's ear.

"The forked tree is death. It's trapped here; it wants to be released."

The girl brushed her pleas away, as though a mosquito or maybug had been at her neck. Lottie tried again. "It wants release!" She was screaming the words, but the sound that she emitted was little more than a breath. In desperation, Lottie pulled at the girl, who scratched at the spot on her skin, momentarily distracted. As she opened her mouth to again roar her warning, the deafening clang of the brass bell echoed through the parlour. Lottie was hurtled back into the perfect darkness;

the reflection of the silver orb like a twisted moon sailed back and forth in the space. The clang of the bell again, and Lottie felt her spirit slam back into her physical body. She gasped and felt herself falling. This time the scream found its full voice as it left her lips.

Lottie

"Can you describe the room?" Dr. Bothelli was scribbling furiously in his journal. Lottie sighed and sipped at her tea.

"It was posh, the likes of which I've never set foot in—velvet, fine wood. It was a wealthy house, not ostentatious but wealthy." Lottie rubbed her temple with her free hand. She still felt the urgency of the message she needed to tell the black-haired girl as though her very life depended on it. She'd begged the doctor to put her back under the mesmerism spell with the silver orb, but he had said no, too much too soon. He wanted instead to talk endlessly through all she'd seen and heard.

"Lottie, this is important. You say you saw what you believe to be a version of yourself? Can you tell me any physical differences? Were her mannerisms different in any way?" The doctor leaned forward intently.

Lottie sipped the tea, annoyed with the flushed focus of his questions. She could not determine if he believed her or if this was all part of some grand psychological profile he was building. She was sharing far more with the doctor than she was comfortable with, but it seemed that the price of admission to the world of these visions was to let the good doctor in, to share what she saw and felt. Perhaps the only way out was through; perhaps at the end of his notes and files there was freedom. There was also a part of her that hoped that maybe, he might have some insight into what she was experiencing—the sense of urgency, the lucidity, the sense that this alter-realm was more real than her current reality.

"She seems younger by a bit, not much. And she's not exactly my face but so similar, as though she were my kin, a sister perhaps, or a daughter . . ." She trailed off, looking down at her swollen belly, where the child lay quiet for the moment.

"Is there any indication of anything that would not fit in a parlour room of today? Anything that perhaps seems to be out of place?" the doctor asked.

Lottie thought on it. The room was, as she had told Bothelli, formal and of a wealth she had never been privy to. Everything seemed out of place for her life, any way she looked at it. "How do you mean?" Lottie asked, confused.

"There's a theory not just about mesmerism but about mental unrest in a broader sense that I learned from my mentor, Dr. Soekan, during my time in Paris. He was a brilliant man and a revolutionary mind in the field of psychiatry and the disturbances of the senses. He believed that mesmerism was a tool with which we could unlock not only our subconscious but also our other selves, a way to travel past the earthly plane, if you will." Dr. Bothelli's brow was knitted in concentration as he explained.

Lottie shook her head. "Other planes? My physical self stayed right in this room, did it not?"

"Of course," Dr. Bothelli answered, looking down at his journal. "The visions you are seeing in our sessions and the depth of your immersion into your own mind is unlike anything I have ever encountered. Dr. Soekan was working on a theory in his studies that was considered too controversial for most, and I do so wish he could examine you. Have you heard the word *reincarnation*?"

Lottie shook her head. "I haven't."

"Some believe that when you die, your soul is reborn into another mortal body. It differs from the prevalent view of heaven and hell and the lot. Are you a religious woman, Lottie?"

Lottie shook her head again. "My mum and da were Catholics once upon a time, but by the time I was of an age to know anything, they'd fallen away from the church. They had a chapel in Cwmaman, for the miners and their families. Elis was a Christian, but he never attended the services, and I never had an interest either. I suppose we would have baptized the baby had things been different, seems only right." She moved her hand over her belly, and the baby kicked back in response.

"Reincarnation goes the other way from most Christian teachings of where our souls go after we die, and it is not my intent to offend." Dr. Bothelli paused, hesitant.

"Dr. Bothelli, I am entirely unsure of what may become of us after we die. I want to believe my husband is here with me now, but I haven't a shred of evidence for it. I've never felt so alone in my whole life as I have since he passed. I know what the Catholics believe, and I know the Anglican take on it, too. If there's a heaven or a hell, then be on with it. You'll not offend me with another option." Lottie set the teacup on the side table and shifted uncomfortably, her back aching.

"Dr. Soekan studied in Strasbourg with some of the finest minds from the East, and the concept of reincarnation became central to what he hoped one might attain from mesmerism. The idea is that when we die, our spirits go on to inhabit another body; we are reborn into the world as a newborn babe, entirely ignorant of the life we led before. But on some level, it's as though that person you used to be stays with you, gnawing at your subconscious, and the struggle between what you were and what you are now can lead to various mental disruptions." Dr. Bothelli paused. "Do you follow?"

"I believe so," Lottie said. "Like the soot from a fire that stains the walls, it's always there, whether we see it or not."

"Yes, in a way." The doctor nodded emphatically. "I believe that when you descend into the mesmerized state, you might be seeing a former life, a past life."

Lottie let the words sink in, the face of the black-haired girl so vivid in her mind's eye it was as though she were in the room. Could that girl be her in a time gone past? What did the warnings mean? The urgency?

"Doctor, as I told you, I believe the girl saw me, the others in the room as well. If I was just reliving a memory, how did they . . . ?" Lottie said softly, her mind spinning.

"It may have seemed that way, but if I am right, it was your own mind recognizing itself. This is most exciting. I am going to send a communication to Dr. Soekan and try to convince him to come and meet you. You could be the key to unlocking the unconscious mind, Lottie."

Later, as Sid led Lottie back to the ward, she played the events of the mesmerism session over and over in her mind. It was too present, too urgent. The doctor's claim that it was already passed, or perhaps nothing more than a construct of her disturbance, felt hollow. The girl felt far too real, as did the black-haired man who Lottie felt she had known her whole life. But if the belief of it all led to more sessions and the chance to escape the reality where she was imprisoned, Lottie would pretend to believe in anything.

Nora
Boston and
Thereabouts
1901

Internal Memo: International Psychical Society
RE: Dorothy Kellings and Nora Grey

The Old South Meeting House will host a spectacle on the evening of Sunday, October 13, 1901. Invited guests only as this is a subject of investigation, not public entertainment. Dorothy Kellings will be traveling to Boston from her home in Rochester, New York. Nora Grey is unknown to many of our American members but has an impressive file on happenings in regard to recorded incidents occurring in Edinburgh, Scotland, under the tutelage of Dr. Edwin Harrison and the Society for Psychical Research, based out of London.

It is not known how long Miss Grey has been in the United States, only that she is to be accompanied by a mentor from the SPR by the name of Karl Mendis.

Invited guests must show proof of invitation and allow their personal items to be searched. This is a research event, and lights, or other devices can tamper with the results.

The International Psychical Society looks forward to this partnership with London's Society for Psychical Research. Please contact the head office (see file notes) for questions and concerns. Only select members of the press have been invited, and guests are asked to honor the nature of the event as we benefit from the experience of our honored guests.

Nora

Nora shifted uneasily, trying to alleviate the stabbing pain in her back. The elaborately carved wooden chair in which she sat was made for form, not function. The card table in general was made for show—beautiful, handcrafted show, but nonetheless. It was dreadfully uncomfortable, but it did set an appropriate atmosphere. The oil lamps reflected off the walls of the library, and the moon shone through the tall windows, creating shadows and shapes on the walls. She sat with Karl, Lady Bell, and Mr. Stanley Corder, the gentleman from Boston who had just arrived that morning. Mr. Corder had been introduced to Nora as a liaison to the International Psychical Society and had teased that he carried news. However, he had kept that news silent all through dinner and now as they sat around the card table waiting for Nora to demonstrate her abilities.

Nora straightened her back and watched the candle flame before her. Mr. Corder had a series of "challenges," as he called them—basically skills other physical mediums had successfully demonstrated that he wanted to see if Nora possessed. She knew she would disappoint. Apart from the incidents in Edinburgh, Nora had done little more than read the seer cards since her arrival. Even Karl Mendis with all his cultish talk seemed a bit bored.

"Nora, I would like Mr. Mendis here to talk you through a light relaxation, and then we will direct your attention to the teacup at your right elbow," Mr. Corder said in a maddeningly slow pace, as though Nora were a child.

"What is it I'm expected to do with the teacup?" Nora asked, trying to keep the edge off her voice. She knew Lady Bell had a vested interest in her abilities, and for her sake if no one else's, she wanted to do what was being asked of her.

"We'd like you to tip it over. But any movement you can do at all—without physically touching it, mind you—is outstanding. Just concentrate on the teacup, and try to focus your mind. This skill is known as psychokinesis, and according to Dr. Harrison's reports, you are quite skilled at it. You shattered a window, threw books from the shelves to the floor."

Nora nodded, uncertain. "I suppose that's true, but I was . . . it was different. I was, well, angry."

Lady Bell suppressed a laugh, and Karl shifted in his seat. "We'd like to teach you to harness that skill without anger. Much of our research is focused on the hypothesis that our mental states, our psychosis, our disturbances can manifest in a physical form. Have you heard the term *poltergeist* before, Nora?" Karl asked, leaning forward.

Nora shook her head.

"They're a sort of specter, or ghost if you will, but a spirit that is more of a trickster. The poltergeist is a spirit that breaks things, throws books off shelves, that sort of thing to get attention, much like a child might. We are researching the concept that poltergeists—or these trickster hauntings, which are reported quite often—are actually the manifestation of one's mind, and not a spirit at all. If we can teach you to harness this anger that brought about the other incidents, it would go very far in proving that other cases such as this were the product of the mind, not the supernatural." Karl paused. "Do you understand?"

"Yes, I think so," Nora said. "But it still might help if you did something to set me off. Is my father about? He has a knack for infuriating me."

Lady Bell's guffaw escaped her lips this time, and she nodded approvingly at Nora, then took a sip of the gin she had in her own teacup. Mr. Corder shook his head and offered Nora a conciliatory smile.

"Let's try this first, Nora, and then we can resort to, well, other measures."

Nora nodded and watched as Karl readied himself to mesmerize her. Tavish was around, though; Nora could feel his presence lurking outside the library doors. He'd been allowed at dinner but not asked to this session, and he was quite put out about it. Karl had told him he was a distracting presence, and he'd wanted to curl his fingers into a fist. In fact, Nora had seen his hand twitching with the urge and had been flooded with his angry thoughts. But Tavish had stood down and politely agreed to join Clarence for a game of cards in the butler's pantry. But he hadn't stayed put; he was listening at the doors, waiting for a chance to interject himself.

Karl pulled a multifaceted crystal on a silver chain from his pocket. He held it high over the candle in the center of the table so the angles caught the light and cast rainbow shards around the room. He began to swing the crystal in a circular motion, slowly and methodically.

"Nora, watch the light. Let your mind empty of the day's thoughts, and just watch the light. Focus only on the light. Let the world fade away and watch the way the light reflects. Watch the light, let your thoughts fly away, empty your mind completely."

Nora watched the crystal and felt her arms and legs becoming not numb but rather like they were floating. Her head, too, felt as though it were weightless, her body insubstantial. She ceased to feel the chair below her; she was suspended in space, comfortable, stable.

"Nora, I am going to count down from ten. When I ring this bell, you will not move a muscle, but you will focus on the teacup to your right. Ten, nine, eight, seven . . ."

Nora felt herself spinning and her eyes closing. In her mind's eye, she could see the others at the table; she could see the teacup, the spinning crystal, the candle. Their thoughts were like string candy, winding out their heads like the spools of woven sugar at a carnival. They were all looking at her. Some thoughts were dark. Karl thought her dreadfully plain, that she resembled a boy more than a woman; she could see the thoughts spin out of his head. Lady Bell was thinking of her grand house and the island; looking to Nora, she felt what one must feel from a mother for the briefest flash of a moment, and it made her want to reach out to the woman, take her hands. Stanley Corder had a knot of flesh in his chest, right near his heart, that pained him when he stood or moved too quickly. She could feel it, growing, poisoning his blood. He would die, and soon, and never have any idea of the cause. She saw his face ashen and gray, surprised at his own demise.

"Six, five, four . . ."

Nora could hear Tavish pacing the hall outside the library as though he were walking circles around the card table. His thoughts were of despair; he was useless, lost; he'd be sent away, back to Edinburgh. Nora saw he was afraid that he'd be back on the streets, wandering the countryside and working for ha'pennies at the country fairs again. She felt the memory of hunger pains and the sharp Scottish wind.

"Three, two, one . . . alright, Nora, concentrate on the teacup. Can you see the teacup?"

Karl's thoughts spun around and around his head. Nora could

see them in the dark, bright red and gold threads. He thought her a waste of his time; he didn't believe what they had said happened in Edinburgh. And deeper still, she saw a swirling storm of demons behind him—St. Cyprian's demons dancing in a mad, crazed circle. He believed that until he called the demons the way his false saint had, he would be forgotten, lost.

"Nora, can you move the teacup? Even a little?"

Nora opened her eyes and stared at the teacup next to her right hand. The cyclone of thoughts melded together and took voice, overlapping fears and pains, criticisms. The voices became louder and louder, deafening. Nora felt her breath caught in her throat; she gasped and felt the very air suffocating her. A hand pressed against the back of her neck, and Nora exhaled all the anger and resentment that she had swallowed. The woman was here, in her strange dress and with eyes so like her own; she was standing behind her, and her hand was on Nora's neck. Nora felt a calm wash through her body. They wanted a show; they wanted her to move a teacup.

With the steady comfort of the woman's hand on her skin, Nora shifted her gaze from the teacup and closed her eyes in concentration. She heard astonished gasps from the others at the table, but she did not dare look. She pushed harder, feeling pinpricks of pain in her temples; she raised her hands, directing the energy, and held it balanced in her palms. When she opened her eyes, the card table was hovering a good six feet above the ground, the teacups were all steady on the surface, even though the table wobbled back and forth in the air. Karl Mendis was out of his chair and running in circles around the table, trying to find where it was being lifted. Mr. Corder was rubbing the space near his heart where the lump grew. Lady Bell stared straight at Nora, a smile on her face. She gave her a simple nod of permission or approval, Nora could not tell which, but she felt the hand at the back of her neck gently stroke her hair.

With a flick of her hands, Nora sent the card table flying

across the room, the teacups and candlesticks falling to the ground as it traveled. It smashed against the library doors where Tavish had his ear pressed. She heard a surprised yowl from the other side of the wood as he was pushed backward by the force. The card table was as sturdy as it was elaborate, it lay largely unharmed on its side, tottering back and forth slightly from its flight. The dark wood floor was littered with broken china and candle wax.

"Will that do?" Nora said simply, folding her hands in her lap.

Nora

Nora sat in the kitchen with Clarence and Lena, the kitchen girl. A manor cat with mottled ginger fur lay curled in front of the stove. They each had mugs of rich red wine from the oak barrel in the back pantry. After the library incident, Mr. Corder and Karl Mendis had excused themselves and excitedly scuttled off with their notes. Lady Bell had offered Nora a simple nod and whispered good work before she'd gone up to bed. Tavish had stayed with Nora and the others in the kitchen for a bit but was far too agitated to sit still. It was the first time that Nora had seen him genuinely flustered. She couldn't tell if it was because she had glimpsed inside his head or if the evening had actually rattled him. The man who had spent his adult life pretending to be a water diviner or selling his daughter's seer card readings to strangers was shaken to pieces by what had happened in the library.

"Why do you figure he's so bothered now?" Lena asked. "Pardon me for sayin', but I thought that was what you all did back in Scotland? You know, séances and the like?"

"I can't say, not for sure," Nora said. "I think perhaps he

didn't really believe me until tonight. The things we did back in Scotland, the séances, they were . . . I'm ashamed to say, but they were false. We were grand pretenders. I could spin my eyes clear back in my head, say the spirits did it. And even the other things that happened in Edinburgh, I think part of him thought them to be tricks, but tonight it became a bit more real."

"Do you want it to be real?" Clarence asked. "You struck me as awfully happy to settle into being a house girl when you arrived—not that there's any wrong in that; this is a good place to settle into. But you won't stay at dusting the library and fetching tea for the watchmen at this rate."

Nora paused. Clarence was right. Tonight she could have done nothing, and eventually the International Psychical Society and all the others would have perhaps lost interest, but now . . . she had made an ordinary life impossible.

"I thought when we were taken in in Edinburgh that it was the nicest house I had ever seen, but here, here it's different. I am quite happy fetching tea and dusting. I think mostly I'm happy not to be under anyone's thumb, to have a say in what I want, what I do." Nora looked at Clarence, crow's feet lining his eyes, streaks of silver in his rough hair. "You've spent your life here?"

"All of it that mattered. I was a young man when I smuggled my way into the bottommost hell of a shipping freight out of Georgia and found my way to Bell Island. I woke up in a bed with clean sheets and a warm meal and the assurance that the slave catchers would never find me. I started my life that day. Everything before that? It was what my mother called the *nusu uhai*, or a ghost life. When I saw this house, this island, I woke up for the first time. I saw that same sort of relief in your eyes when you first arrived here to Bell Island. Are you sure you want to leave?" Clarence topped off Nora's mug with more wine.

"In a way I do," Nora said. "I don't understand this place, not entirely, but I feel safe here, and I've never felt safe."

"They say the island's haunted," Lena said in a low tone. "The sailors who bring the supplies say it's haunted and they don't dare step foot on shore for fear the wandering spirits will drag them to their grave." She giggled and sipped her wine.

"Enough of that wine for you, young lady." Clarence looked at Lena in mock admonishment and winked at Nora. "Ghost stories are part of what's kept this island safe. I am grateful for them."

"Clarence, you said Lady Bell welcomed you to the island? That was a lot of years ago. Lady Bell is not so old, so how?" Nora's voice trailed off.

"The previous Lady Bell, our current Lady Bell's mother, welcomed me to the island. A Lady Bell has always managed the island and always will as long as the ghost stories hold up. Lena here was born on Bell Island, so she doesn't even exist as far as the rest of the world is concerned." Clarence patted the girl's hand, and she grinned at him.

"My parents were born here, too," Lena said proudly. "None of us exist, not really, do we?"

"It is safer that way," Nora said quietly, sipping the wine. The idea of being born in a hidden place where no one knew you existed sounded like a perfect sort of life. As the night hours ticked closer to dawn, Nora knew she had ruined her chances at anonymity when she threw the card table against the wall. But for now, she let the warmth of the wine wrap itself around her as she allowed herself to feel safe and loved, if even for a short time.

Nora

"We've been sent an offer," Karl said from across the dining table, where Nora and Tavish had joined him for breakfast. Nora's head ached from the wine, and she was nibbling on a piece of toast and trying to ignore the smell of the rich food spread out before her.

"What sort of offer?" Tavish asked, his voice guarded.

"The sort we oughtn't turn down." Karl cleared his voice and took a sip of his coffee. "Dorothy Kellings has been stewing about Miss Grey since the séance in Edinburgh, and she's convinced the Rochester Spiritualists to fund a séance in Boston for the two of them. Closed to the public, invited guests only. The International Psychical Society is hosting, so it will be limited to their researchers, some academic types from Harvard, and a few very select members of the press. This is a great opportunity for our organization. A demonstration of psychic talents, with some of the best minds in the world as witness. And a chance to bridge the rift with Miss Kellings."

"And why do we want to do that?" Tavish asked, looking to Nora questioningly.

"I was not present for the Edinburgh séance, but I do understand that Dorothy Kellings is a bit, well, abrupt. She is also the connection to the Rochester Spiritualists and their wealth of knowledge and research. This is a wonderful opportunity for all of us, " Karl replied.

"Aren't I supposed to be a brand-new person?" Nora asked. "New name and hidden off on this island and all? Weren't you planning on some grand reintroduction or some such?"

Karl smiled, but it didn't extend to his eyes. "Well, your reputation seems to have preceded you. There is no harm to our friends in Edinburgh, and a reintroduction by the still-great Dorothy Kellings is more than we could have hoped for."

Nora closed her eyes and sipped her tea. Her head was pounding. She had stayed up till far too late with Clarence; even after Lena said her goodnights, the two of them had sat silently, grateful for the company.

"How does this benefit me?" Nora asked. Glancing at Tavish, she could see that his gruff exterior was close to breaking.

Karl paused, then carefully spoke. "Nora, you were brought here at the expense of the Order of St. Cyprian, the Psychical Research Society, and the Edinburgh Spiritualists. A great many people have invested their time and money into making sure you are meeting your potential. Did you think you would be left here to play the housemaid for the rest of your life? You have more untapped potential than I have ever experienced. I will admit, I was skeptical. The incident in Edinburgh sounded too fantastical to be true. I thought you to be a fraud—a clever one perhaps, but a fraud. Dr. Harrison's judgement is clouded when it comes to you; he's quite fond of you; I think you know that. His account of books falling off shelves and broken windows read to me as a bit exaggerated, wishful thinking." Karl sipped his coffee, his face thoughtful. "But last night was extraordinary. We were seeking only the most basic demonstration, and you manifested psychokinesis in a way that I have never even read about. I know that the stories from Edinburgh were not fanciful. In fact, now I wonder if they downplayed the details."

Nora cleared her throat. "Lady Bell has made it quite clear I'm welcome to stay on at Bell Manor."

"And spend your days as a maid to the lady of the manor? That's a fine slap in the face to all those that have worked to get you here," Karl said bluntly.

"Wait just a minute here," Tavish interrupted, his voice simmering with hostility. "You sat across from us that first night and said we were free to catch the next ship back to Scotland. You didn't give a fig what happened to my girl when you thought it was all bullshite, did you? We don't owe you a lick. Nora didn't ask for any of this. She was asked to join that circus in Edinburgh. We were happy enough in Kirkcaldy; we had a life of our own."

"A life on the road, in the cold, going from place to place. The reports I read state that your daughter was half-starved when the Edinburgh group found her. That was the result of your loving care, Mr. Grey, so you might watch what you say about how happy you were before you both were pulled from the gutter." Karl's voice held an edge.

Tavish started to rise, his face growing flush with anger. Nora cast a glare at Tavish, and as their eyes met, she saw all the frustration and pain in his night-black eyes. She felt a flush of anger at both of the men.

"I'll do it. But only because I would like to talk with Dorothy Kellings again; she has made a life out of this strange talent. But Karl, your group of demon hunters and resurrectionists? What are they hoping comes from this event?" Nora shifted her gaze to stare directly at Karl, whose face was a mask of professionalism.

"The Order of St. Cyprian welcomes the opportunity to continue our research into the potential of psychical abilities and the application of those talents. We continue to be your devoted servants and will work tirelessly to ensure your safety. We carry no expectations for this event or any other appearances that may occur." He nodded, and Nora knew him to be sincere.

"Then arrange it. My father will come to Boston with me, but I want separate accommodations. I am not a child who needs a nanny. I want someone to stand as security wherever we are to be housed and at the location of the séance," Nora said with authority, leaving Karl and Tavish to simply nod. "But for now, I'm going back to bed and would appreciate not being disturbed unless absolutely necessary."

Nora did not wait for permission. She stood and left the table, crossing back through the kitchen, where she gave Clarence's hand a squeeze as she passed through. He smiled warmly and went back to his work. In the cottage Nora lay down with a cool cloth on her head and closed her eyes. A chance to meet Dorothy Kellings, the Scarlet Sunbird, again, but this time as an equal, not a little girl to be talked down and condescended to. She would find out what it took to harness this talent and turn it into a life, free herself from the men who sought to twist and manipulate her talent for their own.

Lottie
Argoll Asylum
1866

New Brunswick Journal of Healing and Medical Arts,
June 1887

New discoveries regarding famed researcher Franz Soekan have come to light and are of great interest to this journal and the study of mesmerism in a medical capacity overall. By way of background, Dr. Soekan was the founder of the Gest School in Paris, France, and head researcher until his untimely death in the spring of 1867.

New documents and recordings of Dr. Soekan's mesmerism therapy sessions and his work with the unconscious mind are available at the Cornwall Medical College Library and will be on public display through Thursday. The records are of particular interest to the field of study of psychokinetic and psychic manifestation reports and their connection to the subconscious mind. Dr. Soekan, in his lifetime, worked tirelessly to prove the connection between a heightened state of agitation, or mania, and what had previously been labeled as psychic phenomena.

Dr. Soekan's work was left unfinished and thought unpublishable due to the macabre circumstances of his passing, which occurred in Wales during his tenure at the Argoll Sanitorium and Asylum. Much news was made at the time of his passing, as it occurred following intensive research sessions with the former director of Argoll Asylum, Dr. Theodore Bothelli.

Reservations to view Dr. Soekan's research and writings can be arranged through the Cornwall Medical College information office.

Lottie

Dr. Soekan was a rotund little man with a round face and bushy sideburns that stretched into his neck. Lottie couldn't help but think of the children's stories of Toad and Hog that her grandmum used to tell. Whether Dr. Soekan was the toad or the hog, Lottie withheld judgement.

"Lottie, my dear, I am told that you are of particular interest to Dr. Bothelli and particularly suggestible. Are you familiar with my work?" The man spoke in an odd rhythm, and his eyes seemed engorged by the tiny spectacles that balanced on the end of his bulbous nose.

Lottie shook her head. She was annoyed; she'd been annoyed since she'd been brought here this morning by Sid and made to sit in Dr. Bothelli's office for a good hour before anyone had arrived. The baby kept kicking her bladder with a ferocity that made her wince, and if she did not see the inside of a lavatory soon, there would be an entirely different sort of result to whatever experiment the doctors had planned for her.

"You have been here nearly a month. Is that correct, Mrs. Liath?" Dr. Soekan said slowly, looking at papers in a file.

"And it is estimated that you are six months along in your condition?" A brief flash of disgust passed across his face. Lottie wanted to slap him, but she held her hands in her lap. Her child was not a bastard; she had been married, and proper. Her child was due its respect, not the judgement of Dr. Toad and Hog.

"I am," she said simply. It was best to get through this and get on with whatever they had planned for her. The sooner Dr. Toad and Hog left, the better. Lottie could not look at the man without her skin crawling.

"Alright, Lottie, we are going to test today to see how your emotional state is connected to your unconscious mind. It is a simple mesmerism. All you need to do is follow our directions. Are you ready?" Dr. Bothelli asked, his eyes holding an unspoken question. Lottie regarded him curiously. "Lottie." He started as though he could not find the words. *A rare occurrence for one who loved the sound of his own voice*, Lottie thought darkly. "Lottie, you may feel a bit of pressure. The idea is whether the physical affects your mental clarity. But I assure you, this is all for the goal of helping you, and helping us understand your unique talents. We have your best interests at heart . . ."

"Goodness!" Dr. Toad and Hog interrupted. "What are you going on about?"

"Yes, what do you mean?" Lottie asked anxiously, watching Dr. Bothelli's eyes. He was bothered by this. Lottie felt a chill in her fingertips. The baby kicked again. "Could I possibly take a moment before we start . . . I have to . . ."

"No time." Dr. Toad and Hog shook his head; he was getting increasingly frustrated. "We're behind schedule already. You'll have to wait."

"Surely we can allow Mrs. Liath a moment to . . ." Dr. Bothelli interjected.

"Dr. Bothelli, are you aware of how valuable my time is?

Are you willing to calculate that and add it to my consultation fee?" Dr. Toad and Hog's voice was ice. "I expect you would like to proceed. The sooner we start, the sooner we are done." The doctor fixed his bug-like eyes on her, devoid of empathy.

Lottie nodded. Whatever she needed to do to make this end she would do. The pressure in her bladder suddenly subsided as the imp in her belly shifted position in agreement. She sighed with relief. As before, Lottie lay back on the stiff-backed sofa, and Dr. Bothelli held the silver orb before her. She could see Dr. Toad and Hog sitting behind him, but she tried to block out the idea that the man was watching.

"You know how this works, Lottie. Watch the orb, back and forth. I am going to count back from ten, nine, eight . . ."

The orb swung back and forth as Lottie felt her eyes close. The flash of silver continued behind her eyelids, and she was weightless. She felt a jolt of excitement as the pull of the invisible cord began to drag her toward the alternate world she had been longing for—another version of herself perhaps, another planet far away from here.

"Seven, six, five . . ." The doctor's voice was a low hum in the distance. Lottie didn't need his countdown. She ruled this world; he was only the key to enter. Once here, the doctor and all men were rendered useless.

"Four, three, two, one . . ." More words followed, but Lottie was flying through the blackness, the doctor's voice a meaningless hum. Lottie felt the tug of the skin that separated this world from the next and looked around to see herself in a darkly polished leather and wood library. The scent of tobacco filled her nose, and she spun in circles to see the walls lined with leather-bound texts. In the center of the room the black-eyed girl sat, a man before her. This was the same man from the dream where the glass had shattered and filled the room. Now the man was calm and there was no sign of the other, the black-haired man who also held such familiarity. It was just these two, and Lottie felt a danger for the girl she had not yet felt. This man saw her as a commodity, a product. She could see it in his face; he was weighing her benefits and deficits with every action and response. The girl sat, a glowing sort of box before her. Lottie stared in amazement at the box, it flashed and blinded her. It occurred to her that the girl was also being mesmerized, and this was her version of the orb. Fascinated, Lottie drew closer, staring at the box and feeling its pull.

The black-eyed girl's face went slack as she entered what Lottie imagined was her own weightless blackness. *How utterly fascinating*, Lottie thought as she placed a protective hand on the girl's shoulder. They were both in another realm, both in the in-between. How many worlds existed between here and there? Was there another where Lottie and the baby lived in a cottage near a creek? A quiet and perfect life? Could she pull her way to that reality if she only imagined it into being?

A sudden shock of pain rocked Lottie's body, and she looked down to the hand that was resting on the girl's shoulder. A mark on her hand was growing increasingly red and harassed. The pain was one of twisting flesh, and Lottie saw the skin rise and circle angrily, the blood beneath pooling. Lottie cried out, and the girl shook. *She can hear me!* Lottie thought as the pain repeated. She tried to pull her hand from the girl, but it was heavy, weighted, as though it were tied in place. Lottie jolted again in pain, the skin rising and twisting, leaving a blood red mark underneath her pale skin. Again and again, Lottie cried in confusion and fear, ripping her hand off the girl's shoulder. She held the injured hand before her and with the full force of her body willed the phantom attack to stop.

She saw the twitch of the books on the shelf before her scarcely a moment before they took flight. Lottie stared in astonishment as the books sailed through the air as though a thousand arms were throwing them. Desperately, Lottie waved her arms, and the books veered away from the black-eyed girl, falling at her feet but not hitting her. The man ducked and cowered and recovered to sitting as the girl opened her eyes. Lottie felt the wrenching pain in her hand again and then was dragged back, back, back. The faint ringing of a bell in the background, and the flash of the silver orb in her sight. Back, back, back until she was slammed into her waking self. The pain in her hand returned, this time as a recovering pain, the pain of an injury already inflicted. Lottie opened her eyes and stared up at the two men looking down at her.

Lottie

"Oh dear, my word." Dr. Toad and Hog's face was a mask of disgust. Lottie looked down at her hand and saw an angry red welt where she had felt the pain.

"Wha—?" she murmured, but was cut off by Dr. Bothelli rushing to the door and summoning Sid.

"She's wet herself. We will need housekeeping. Please take her back to the ward." Dr. Bothelli's voice was flustered and brisk. Dr. Toad and Hog was scribbling notes in a journal and looking at a broken hurricane lamp that lay on the floor.

"Doctor?" Lottie started to sit up, but her head swam, and she paused. Sid appeared in the doorway and nodded to the doctor. Lottie felt the warm wetness on her shift and realized that her full bladder had, indeed, been a problem. Despite the reaction of the two doctors, Lottie couldn't help but suppress a smirk. Disgusted so easily, the both of them—how had they done any medical training? Wasn't the human body a mess of urine and blood? She held her hand before her face. The mark was starting to fade a bit, but how had it happened? What had attacked her, and was it in the vision or here in this office? Had the books really flown off the shelves in the other world where the black-eyed girl lived, and what had become of the hurricane lamp that lay in pieces on the floor? Lottie's mind was spinning, and as Sid lumbered across the room and silently helped her to her feet, she stared at the two doctors, whose reaction to her wetting herself seemed a bit overdone. Surely in a mental asylum this wasn't the worst thing that Dr. Bothelli had witnessed?

Sid took her arm and helped her across the room. As the door closed behind her and Lottie was left in the hall, she looked at her hand again. The mark was still agitated, and she could see the darkening parts where a bruise would surely form. What had happened while she was unconscious? Sid escorted her back to the ward, unlocked the door to the hall, and then locked it behind her. Lottie made her way to her room and pulled her soiled shift and undergarments off. Once changed, she made her way to the laundry where whoever was on laundry duty would be made to deal with the doctors' mess. Lottie did think of it as the doctors' mess; whatever had transpired in that room went far and above her bladder.

Sister Therese appeared in the doorway of her room as Lottie returned.

"Heard there was a bit of excitement," she said simply.

"I wet myself, but you'd think the doctors had been raised in a different world entire. The way they reacted . . . ," Lottie said softly.

Sister Therese cast her a curious look. "It's not an uncommon sight; we are a hospital, after all. We had a girl one year who used to smear her own feces on the walls. Dr. Bothelli didn't seem flustered by that one much. What else happened in your therapy?" she asked, her voice neutral.

"I have no idea. My hand is hurt, but I don't know how, and there was a broken lamp, but I don't think I moved about. I can't really sit up too quickly now; if I'd thrashed about, I think I'd know." Lottie looked to the nun, who had concern in her eyes.

"I don't like that the doctor from Paris is visiting, not at all.

I've heard stories of that one. He works with the Spiritualists, I heard tell—devil's work if anything at all," the nun said and then turned to leave. "Remember, you tell me if you feel these treatments cross a line. Before Argoll, I worked at Haydock. The things they did in the name of science. I've seen things done to patients that I'll never be redeemed for not stopping. I'll not have that again."

Lottie nodded, and as the nun left, she curled up on her bed. The Welsh sun filtered through the glass of her windows, and Lottie pulled Elis's handkerchief from under her pillow. Holding it to her nose and smelling the faint scent of her love, she closed off this place, these walls, and imagined a life in that cottage by the creek, her Elis holding their child, all three of them far from this place.

Lottie

"And you trust her?" Dr. Soekan asked without looking up, his brow wrinkled and his eyes expressionless.

"Yes, I do," Dr. Bothelli said, glancing at Lottie and Sister Therese. "I trust the sisters with all the care of our wards."

Dr. Toad and Hog looked up and examined Sister Therese as though she were an insect to be mounted with a pin on a board. "It's not the care of the girl I am concerned with. I need to know that the examination will not be biased; that if there is trickery at play, it will not be ignored or perhaps encouraged." He looked down at his copious notes again. "I would feel best if one of my men did the inspection. The sister can witness it to make sure no improprieties abound."

"Absolutely not." Sister Therese stepped forward, and Lottie could see her hands shaking with anger. "This inspection, as you are calling it, is the very definition of impropriety. This is a hospital, and while this girl is here to account for her actions, she is a patient receiving care, and I will not allow it." The sister turned to Dr. Bothelli. "Doctor, you might well remember that the funding for this asylum, including your salary, comes from the diocese, and they will not take well to this report, not at all."

Dr. Bothelli's face was torn; he looked to his mentor, then back to the nun. "Dr. Soekan, I am afraid I have to defer to the good sister; she is right. The church is our patron here at Argoll, and they would not approve of this inspection at all, especially if it were done by a man. I will allow the inspection, within reason, and insist it be performed by Sister Therese and Sister Mary from our infirmary. And Lottie, if at any time you feel overburdened by this process, you only need tell the sisters." He nodded, solidifying his point.

"Very well." Dr. Soekan sighed. "Let's just get on with it."

Lottie followed Sister Therese out of the office and down the long hall to the infirmary. She went here weekly to see Sister Mary about the baby. The sister measured Lottie's stomach, felt her pulse, asked about aches and pains. But the nun wasn't really a doctor or even a nurse, so Lottie still worried that the nymph, which was coming up on its sixth month now, would be born with any number of maladies. Still, she reminded herself that she wouldn't even be getting this care if she were back in Cwmaman. She'd be lucky to see a midwife; doctors were scarce in the colliery.

However, this was not a visit to talk about the baby. Dr. Soekan wanted a mesmerism session, and prior to the session, he wanted an inspection to determine if Lottie had wires or strings or some other magical contraption hidden under her dress or god knows where. To Lottie's horror, he wanted to search her naked body for evidence of trickery. Lottie had stayed silent and kept her horror to herself, but the idea of Dr. Toad and Hog or his men, who had arrived with him from Paris, so much as touching her made her skin crawl. A week had passed since the last mesmerism session. Lottie had been told that a lamp had inexplicably moved along the surface of the desk and fallen to the ground while she had been displaying agitation in her mesmerized state. The implication, of course, was that Lottie had somehow moved it.

Lottie didn't know whether to laugh in their faces or cry. It was witchery what they were accusing her of, and back in Glasgow, especially in the outlying countryside, she'd known of women who'd been jailed for less, even killed. The very idea that she broke their damnable lamp was ridiculous. It was the doctor's idea to put her in the mesmerized state, and the things she saw there were not a reality. As much as she wished the black-eyed girl was flesh and blood, Lottie knew it to be a vision. As real as this other realm seemed, she knew it to be a place apart from her waking world. She was no conjurer, the thing they attributed to her was impossible, and impossible feats were dangerous for a girl like her. She had no intention of telling Dr. Toad and Hog any of what she had confessed to Dr. Bothelli about her visions, though she was sure he knew from the reports of the prior sessions. She would not add to his file; she would not damn herself.

Sister Therese opened the door to the infirmary and allowed Lottie to pass through first. The only patient in the ward was Lorna.

"Back again! Back again! Told you! Play possum! In for it now!!!" Lorna screeched. Sister Mary cast her a look that silenced the old woman and ushered Lottie and the older nun to the back.

"Let's get this done then," she said with her usual briskness. "Looking for what exactly? Wires and tricks?"

"They provided a list," Sister Therese said with a resigned tone, pulling a cream-colored piece of paper from her pocket. "Wires, strings, any metal attachments to the skin . . . this is ridiculous. They want us to inspect her in her most private areas to see if she's hiding guide wires." With great frustration, the nun refolded the list and put it back in her pocket.

"What is it they think I've done?" Lottie said softly, looking at the floor. The idea of even the sisters looking all over her body was making her grow chill with dread.

"Sit," Sister Mary said. "Here, take some cider." She poured apple cider into a glass and handed it to Lottie. "I propose we take no part in this preposterous action. We sit here quietly for a bit, you'll drink your cider, and then we'll go back and assure them you haven't hidden an ironmonger's shop in your belly button."

Sister Therese nodded and sat next to Lottie. "Yes, I think that will do fine." She turned to Lottie. "You didn't do a thing. A lamp fell and broke. They likely left it near the edge of the desk. I told you before I hate that this Paris doctor is here. I've read about him, I have. He's obsessed with the idea that in a mesmerized state one can manifest things, move objects and the like."

"Dr. Bothelli called it a poltergeist," Lottie said, sipping the cider and feeling relieved at the nuns' defiance.

"The devil has many names, and you're not to blame for their lamp. Bad enough they hurt you, even if it wasn't too terribly bad. I'll not be sad when that one boards a train back home," Sister Therese said, her voice tense.

Lottie looked down at her hand. The mark had faded, but there was a faint yellowing bruise still remaining. Lottie had discovered that Dr. Toad and Hog had taken a clamp and twisted the skin on her hand while she was mesmerized, the purpose of it being to spark strong emotion and drive her to psychical action. Lottie had stared at Dr. Bothelli when he had disclosed this to her finally. She now understood why he stuttered and stumbled before the session, full of half-apologies, trying to justify what he was about to partake in. She had no reasonable understanding of what he meant by psychical, and his explanations of ghosts and poltergeists made her think of her grandmum and all the superstition and foolery that she believed in. But the broken lamp had only encouraged the doctors, as though Lottie had had anything at all to do with that.

As she followed Sister Therese out of the infirmary and back to the office, Lottie tried to silence the doubts that refused to lie silent. The images, the girl, that house, and all the things she'd seen, it was real either in this world or the next. And the doctor's therapies were her only key to get there.

Lottie

"All is in order?" Dr. Soekan asked brusquely as Lottie and Sister Therese reentered the office.

"Yes," Sister Therese said, calmly handing the doctor his list. "None of the items listed were present."

"We should begin," Dr. Toad and Hog said, looking at Lottie with a mixture of curiosity and disdain. She cringed.

"I'll not have her injured again. Her hand is still bruised; it's barbaric." Sister Therese straightened her back and spoke in a way that made Lottie glad she was in her good wishes.

Dr. Bothelli silenced his colleague who had opened his mouth in response to the nun. "Sister Therese, our therapies are for the benefit of the patient, and it is never our goal to cause harm. Dr. Soekan's therapies are new and quite innovative, and I assure you no harm will come to Mrs. Liath." With that, he shuffled the nun out the door and shut it behind her, leaving Lottie standing uncomfortably in the space, her heart beating rapidly.

"I'd like to sit," she said quietly, feeling her knees getting weak.

"Of course, in fact, lie down here on the sofa," Dr. Bothelli said, taking her arm and helping her across the room.

"Mrs. Liath, we are going to try a different approach this session. I believe Dr. Bothelli has talked to you regarding our goal with your therapies?" Dr. Toad and Hog sat next to Lottie, and she could smell cigar smoke on his vest. It turned her stomach, and she swallowed her nausea.

"He's spoken of poltergeists, ghosts, and the like. I know you think I broke your lamp. I didn't, sir. I swear to it." Lottie spoke quickly, the words spilling out.

The doctor held up a hand to silence her. "My student, Dr. Bothelli, got a bit ahead of himself in talking to you of such things. It is my belief that your grief, the melancholia that brought you to this place, is affecting your conscious mind, and by accessing your unconscious and teaching it to take command of your rampant emotions, you will find your way back into the world. Now wouldn't that be nice? A letter to the courts saying your mania and madness is cured, that you are no threat to anyone? You and your child could go anywhere you like, back to your family, in—where are you from, dear?—Scotland?"

Lottie nodded suspiciously. "My family wants nothing to do with me, but I want my freedom from this place."

"Of course you do, dear." Dr. Toad and Hog spoke slowly, as though Lottie were a child. "There are opportunities in the world for a girl such as you. You might even remarry. Who is to say? But without that letter of health, without our therapies, you'll live out your days in an institution, perhaps here, perhaps somewhere else. But you'll never be allowed to keep a child in this sort of place. Now I know you don't want that, do you, Lottie?" The doctor's voice held an edge, and Lottie stared at him in horror.

"So I submit to your therapies or there's no hope of me ever leaving this place with my child?" Lottie whispered.

"Lottie, you knew this from the start." Dr. Bothelli sat next to Dr. Toad and Hog. "It is my duty to treat you and make sure you are fit to reenter the world, and because of your circumstances, I have to convince the courts of that, too. So yes, you do have to submit to therapies to cure your melancholia, your violent outbursts, and I believe you are in the best possible hands."

Lottie nodded, her skin cold. Sister Therese could do nothing to protect her from this, whatever it was they had planned for her. If she denied them, she would never leave Argoll. Her child would be farmed out to the orphanages. If she allowed them to do their work and experiment with her mind, she might lose her soul to whatever force led their studies. Lottie closed her eyes and felt her fear as a thick pit in her throat.

"Then let's get started," she said quietly.

Part IV

Nora
Boston and Thereabouts
1901

From the Boston Ledger—*Letter to the Editor,*
circa November 1901

Dear Sirs and Madams,

It is with the greatest alarm that I write in response to the recently published coverage of the so-called mesmerist Nora Grey and her exploits in Boston in October of this year. As a Christian woman, I object to the affirmation of such carrying on and speak for a great many of your readers when I express my fear that the Boston Ledger *is in danger of turning to what is commonly held as tabloid journalism, common gossip and fanciful stories told more for shock value than for the intent of informing the reading public.*

There is no doubt that Miss Nora Grey and her fellow charlatans have quite a future in sideshows and carnivals, where godless audiences will no doubt find delight in her tricks and exploits. But there is no room in professional journalism and a Christian public for such nonsense.

The very idea that these articles appeared in the Boston Ledger *is not only appalling but an affront to the very idea of integrous journalism. Not one but a series of articles about a girl, little more than a child, and a circus act wherein she managed to fool a room full of men and women twice her age—it is an outrage. Perhaps Miss Grey's adventures would be better suited to the fiction pages of a* Pluck and Luck *or* Galaxy Science Fiction. *But I expect a news organization such as the* Boston Ledger *to operate with more veracity.*

Sincerely,
Mrs. Winston Carmichael

Nora

The ship from Bell Island to Boston Harbor made Nora vomit three times. Each time, Tavish grimaced with disgust and fetched her the means to clean herself up. Nora took to sitting on the deck, even though the winds were fierce and drowned out all sound. Going below deck for even a minute turned her stomach, so she sat in an alcove off the captain's watch, wrapped in a blanket and hoping to spot land soon. She could see clearly why Bell Island had maintained its secrecy. Too harsh a journey for the ferries that ran clear out to The Graves, Bell Island seemed to have a bit of Avalon in it, except instead of peaceful and mysterious mist hiding its existence, there were choppy waters and waves that threatened to sink the shipping freight that was taking them to the mainland.

Karl Mendis was equally unhappy with his sea legs and periodically joined her in the alcove that barely blocked the wind. Only Tavish seemed unaffected. No one else had accompanied them, but more from the Order of St. Cyprian as well as the Psychical Research Society would be on shore. Nora still did not have a solid understanding of why this was so important or what was expected of her. Karl had explained that as both she and Dorothy Kellings were known to be physical mediums, the attention would be on manifesting objects, perhaps even living creatures. Nora had scoffed at the notion and then had been made to read of the physical medium Isaiah Tobedy, who had, according to witnesses, manifested a violet-backed starling during a session in Rochester five years ago. It was even more spectacular and harder to prove fraud as the violet-backed starling was native to the African continent. It reeked of Dorothy Kellings's blackbird turned Scarlet Sunbird, and Nora found herself wondering how many innocent birds had been made to play along with the game of Spiritualism.

Nora had wanted to ask if they had bothered to check if any pet stores in the Rochester area had been selling violet-backed starlings and whether anyone named Isaiah Tobedy had purchased one. But Karl Mendis had been adamant that the incident as recorded by the Rochester Spiritualists had been concrete. Manifestation of a living creature was possible, and the subtext was such that it was expected in the Old South Meeting House in two days' time. Nora had also read more stories of the great Dorothy Kellings and how she had made her first demonstration of automatic writing during a séance in Philadelphia at a supposedly haunted town house. She had been the same age as Nora was now, and the incident had only added fuel to her fame. Nora was fascinated by the idea that the dead would speak to you through writing, or that one could channel the thoughts of spirits.

She thought of the black-haired woman who had appeared to her so often in her trances, whose hand she often felt on her shoulders. Was she a spirit? Was she a manifestation of Nora herself? Her soul? Dorothy Kellings was very vocal about her spirit guides, and as much as she questioned her motivations for instigating this séance, Nora was looking forward to speaking with her. Karl had no natural talents of his own besides being unpleasant, which he was very good at. Dorothy Kellings might be a fraud, but so was Nora, or she had been. She could still roll her eyes to the back of her skull and stand on her toes if needs be, but for over a year now, those talents had been allowed to go dormant. She thought of the night she spent sitting quietly with Clarence in the kitchen of Bell Manor, how nice it would be to disappear in a place hidden by the waves and wind. More than anything, Nora wanted a life where she answered to no man, a life that was entirely her own. One where Tavish and all the Karl Mendises of the world held no sway over her. She knew without being told that the only way to that end was to prove herself more powerful, more terrifyingly capable than the men who sought to profit from her. She needed to inhabit the same sort of space that Dorothy Kellings had carved out for herself. Fraud as she might well be, she needed the Scarlet Sunbird if she was ever to free herself. Once that happened, she could decide what came next.

In the distance Nora could see the shore, and a loud horn sounded, making her jump. It wouldn't be long now before they entered the harbor. Nora could already see the shapes of other ships on the waterline. She had a dinner planned with Karl Mendis and his associates tonight, and tomorrow she was to meet with Dorothy Kellings. There were to be chaperones to the meetings, so that no one could claim any corroboration or theatrics had been designed. Nora wondered if the fire-haired lady would really consent to that; she hadn't struck Nora as one who was known for her cooperation with the rules men made.

The séance was to be held at the Old South Meeting Hall, which Karl had been delighted to tell her had been a meeting place of the American revolutionaries and, even before that, a hall where witch trials had occurred. It was said to be haunted by the spirits of those who had been sentenced to death within its walls. Nora doubted that the spirits, if they existed in that place, cared much to haunt the scene of their trial. If she were a spirit, Nora thought absently as she watched the shoreline approach, she'd haunt the source, go right for the bastards who had hung the noose.

"Miss Grey? We're approaching, best if you come inside the cabin." A crew member leaned out the door and nodded at her politely. Nora pulled herself to her feet. Karl had been here a moment ago—she must have been so lost in her thoughts, she hadn't seen him go back to the cabin. It was hard to keep her mind on one thought; it wandered from place to place, perhaps a bad sign considering what was expected of her in two days' time. She took a deep breath of the salt air and hoped it would be enough to keep her gorge down until they docked.

Nora

The men at the dock were as dull and dry-looking as Karl Mendis. Nora had little wonder that the whole of the Order of St. Cyprian was entirely composed of wretched little men whose grasp was exceeded by their greed. Nora nodded greetings and allowed her bag to be taken by a man in a black uniform. A carriage pulled by a single Clydesdale horse was waiting for them.

"They couldn't have sent a motorcar?" Karl growled at his associates. A tense conversation continued among them as Nora climbed into the carriage with Tavish behind her.

"If I had to place a bet, he was looking to impress you with all the modernities of the big city," Tavish said quietly. "You feeling a bit better? You were as low as I've ever seen you out there. Worse even than the trip across the Atlantic."

Nora gave him a faint smile. "I think the trip from Bell Island is rougher than the entire Atlantic. No wonder it stays hidden."

Tavish tapped her knee with two fingers, a gesture he used to make when they were traveling across the lowlands back home in the back of some cart or a farmer's wagon. Nora felt the familiarity of the touch flood her body with a feeling she hadn't had for so many months. The feeling that they were a team, partners, friends even. Tavish had been a thorn in her side for so long it was easy to forget he was also a father and lost himself most of the time. Nora leaned into his shoulder, and she felt his body relax. They were a team here, the only remnants of home, of where she had come from, perhaps where she belonged. These men who were arguing about motorcars and profiting off her, they weren't family and never would be. Tavish, for all his warts, knew her, had nursed her through flu and hunger. He'd caused a great deal of her pain, but he had also been there to hold her hand, and he tried to keep them afloat.

"I promise you that more suitable accommodations will be made for the rest of our trip," Karl grumbled as he climbed into the carriage. "We're headed to Young's Hotel, which is a fine establishment. I expected more for your arrival."

"Mr. Mendis, my daughter and I are hardly impressed with motorcars and linen sheets. I am here to assure you treat both of us, but especially her, with the care and respect that is due," Tavish said steadily, and Nora found herself silently applauding him.

"Of course," Karl muttered. "The dinner tonight will give you an opportunity to meet my associates from London, as well as acquaint yourself with our American branch. The Rochester group will be arriving later tonight, and you will have the opportunity to meet with Miss Kellings at that time."

Nora barely heard him. Out the window, she was watching the city go by. Edinburgh had been grand, but Boston was twice what she had seen in her time there. So many people walked the street, and motorcars bobbled their way around the horse-drawn carriages. Karl was going on about the history of the city, the American Revolution, and such. Nora was ignoring him entirely, fascinated, as she watched women walk down the street in fashions that Nora had only seen on Lady Bell. Not even the fine ladies back in Edinburgh had carried themselves with such confidence. As they pulled up to Young's Hotel, Nora felt entirely overwhelmed. The noise of the street, the voices, the rumble of the motorcars, all of it surrounded and distracted her. She felt Tavish take her by the hand and pull her to the hotel entrance, and she allowed herself to be led. Nora felt as though if she were left to her own devices, she would just stand in one place forever, absorbing the life of the city.

More hands to shake as they entered, more men from this society or that, all well-dressed, all staring at her as though she were a fish caught in a net. Nora turned to Tavish and was about to ask him to arrange for their rooms when a voice cut across the lobby and silenced everything in its path.

"Miss Grey, I'll meet you in the lounge. I imagine you could use a drink. I know I could."

Dorothy Kellings stood in the lobby, her eyes catching the light from the grand chandelier and her hair piled on top of her head in an impossible configuration.

"Go and clean yourself up, and meet me in the lounge. Leave your nannies."

With that, Dorothy Kellings turned and strode through an entry into the lounge. Nora smiled and looked to Karl. "I'll take my key now."

Nora

Dorothy Kellings sat at a corner table, staring out the window at the street traffic. A martini glass sat next to her hand, and she was tapping her finger rhythmically.

"Hello," Nora said simply as she approached.

"Hello to you," Dorothy replied without shifting her gaze from the street. She turned her head to appraise Nora and then glanced at the door. "Your handlers let you go?"

"I didn't give them a choice," Nora said, taking the seat opposite Dorothy.

"Good girl. The child I met back in Edinburgh would have never stood up for herself. I'm glad to see you're growing up." Dorothy motioned to a waiter and pointed to her drink and then to Nora. He nodded and scuttled off.

"They said you weren't arriving until tomorrow," Nora said.

"I came a day early. We need to have a talk," Dorothy said, glancing up as the waiter delivered martinis to her and Nora. Nora eyed it suspiciously; she couldn't afford to have her mind clouded. Dorothy watched her and then laughed.

"You need to lighten up, have a drink, relax a little. I won't bite, not this time." She sipped the martini and then regarded Nora with a critical gaze. "You're such an insubstantial little thing. You've never met the Fox Sisters—oh they're older now, but in their day? They silenced a room just by entering it. You do not. You are more shadow than light, but that might be in your favor."

Nora took a sip and grimaced. The clear liquor tasted like cleaning fluid. "You said you weren't going to bite."

"Oh my dear, I'm not biting, just observing. You have an advantage being plain: no one will see you coming," Dorothy said, still staring at Nora, her gaze softer but still with an edge.

"And they see you coming?" Nora asked sardonically, enjoying the back and forth.

"Yes, they do." Dorothy's lips twitched in a hint of a smile. "But I had a chance to play it your way. None of this is real." She gestured to her hair and face. "I am lucky that ambrotypes and the like were outside our budget when I was young, or you'd see a plain, little brown-haired girl that lived in the shadows, much like you. This, the hair, all this, this was a product of success. I had a reputation to uphold, after all."

"The Scarlet Sunbird?" Nora asked, taking another sip, the bite of the liquor stinging her tongue in a pleasant way.

"The one and only. It was a dreadful creature, truth be told, nearly bit my ear clean off." Dorothy pulled her crimson hair back a bit to show a line of scars on her right ear, thin lines that crossed the smooth flesh. "I knew you when we first met because I was you. A girl with a bit of talent and a lot of men who wanted to own it. So I pretended and allowed their lies to become my story. It made me very wealthy, very famous, and very unhappy." She regarded Nora for a long moment. "I expect we are more alike than we are different. Except you have a chance to own your life here and now, and I have a chance to take mine back entirely." Dorothy gestured to the waiter for another round of drinks. "I have heard such stories about you.

Even before I met you in Edinburgh, the Spiritualists were going on and on about this girl, this child they'd found in the wilds of Scotland. And now? They're over the moon. They tell me you not just flipped a table but threw one. True?"

"I suppose so," Nora said.

"And I heard that back in Edinburgh you broke a window, sent glass flying. They say you sent a library sailing across the room." She paused, her brow furrowed slightly. "How did you do it?"

"Truthfully, I have no idea," Nora said. "I was angry each time, and . . . there's a woman . . ."

Dorothy leaned forward, her face intent. "Yes? Your spirit guide?"

"I don't know who she is," Nora said. "She looks just like me."

"I believe we all saw her that night in Edinburgh. And yes, she does look like you. You've never talked to your guide?" Dorothy said, draining her second martini and waving at the bar for a third.

"I don't know how," Nora said quietly.

"All mediums have guides. We are sensitive to the other side, sensitive where others are deadened. Our contact to the next world is only possible through guides, spirits who have crossed over or perhaps spirits who have only ever lived in the next world. Most mediums have many guides; they serve different purposes, they show you different things. You are operating on rage now, anger at the men who are controlling you, anger at your little world. I don't know, but I can say with authority that until you allow your spirit guide in, until you meet her and know her name, until you trust each other, you will not progress. You will throw books and break windows and fade back into the shadows." Dorothy looked up and nodded at the waiter, who left behind a fresh drink. "I want to help."

"Help?" Nora asked, hesitant.

"This séance has been planned by so many groups and so

many men, and they think they can control what comes out of it. They have representatives from the International Psychical Society, the Society for Psychological Research, the Rochester Spiritualists, and god knows who else. The local press is coming, and a few rich voyeurs. They expect us to call the spirits, make a bird or two appear, and tell the fancy old ladies in the audience hello from their departed husbands. I have a better idea." Dorothy smiled; it was full of mischief.

"What do you have in mind?" Nora asked. As the liquor warmed her throat, she felt more free than she'd ever been.

"How would you like to meet your spirit guide?"

Nora took a moment to ponder the question.

"Yes, I think that would be fine," she said, and returned the smile.

Lottie
Argoll Asylum
1866

Internal Records: Argoll Sanitarium and Asylum

Presiding Doctor(s): Dr. Franz Soekan and Dr. Theodore Bothelli
Patient: #189LLF
Diagnosis: Melancholia and fits of rage—danger to self and others
Patient Overview
Mrs. Liath was admitted to Argoll under judge's orders suffering from melancholia and rage-induced fits. She was deemed by the judge to be a danger to herself and others and unfit for either release or Swansea Women's Prison as she is expecting and the health of the unborn child is a considerable factor.

Previous sessions have proven that Mrs. Liath is particularly susceptible to mesmerism and has a highly suggestible mind. This may be the result of a simple intellect or perhaps pregnancy-induced hysteria. Under Dr. Soekan's supervision, experimentation is to be done to see the extent that Mrs. Liath's heightened emotional state plays a part in her ability to accept mesmerism. By doing so, it is hoped that her melancholia and mania will subside and the patient will be deemed healthy mentally and physically.

It has been determined by the presiding doctors that it is in Mrs. Liath's best interest to receive extra therapy sessions and be allowed to forgo the customary work detail normally assigned to patients. For the foreseeable future, Mrs. Liath will be the focus of intense study for the purposes of unlocking the connection between hysteria and her mental prowess.

Noted by Dr. Theodore Bothelli

Lottie

"Mrs. Liath. Good morning to you. I trust you are well?" Dr. Soekan spoke briskly. Bothelli followed him into the office, a pensive look on his face. It was funny, Lottie thought distractedly, he seemed to have lost years since Dr. Toad and Hog arrived. The ever so official man she'd met on that first day at Argoll now had the air of a student trying to impress the headmaster.

"We're a bit short on time. I'd like to get started. Today we would like to try something a bit different." Dr. Soekan sat opposite Lottie. A red vein had broken on his cheek, making him look as though a tiny lightning storm had wrought its damage on his skin. Lottie stared at the mark, feeling as though she were already half-mesmerized.

"Dr. Soekan has brought with him a device that is the very height of scientific advancement, and you are lucky to be able to benefit from it today." Dr. Bothelli offered a stiff smile that didn't extend past the borders of his mouth.

Lottie looked at her arms and then at the doctors. "You don't plan on bruising me?"

"Lottie, you make it sound like we enjoy hurting you, but this is important research and we are making such progress. Just yesterday, you moved a teacup three inches during a session while mesmerized. Dr. Soekan recorded the phenomenon. It's nothing we've ever seen before." Dr. Bothelli's voice was low and soft, as though he were comforting a petulant child.

Lottie took a deep breath. A clean bill of health, a chance to leave this place with her child.

Dr. Soekan nodded to a simple-looking wooden box on the desk. One side had a hand crank, and there were wires running from either end, leading to small metal disks. She looked at the doctors suspiciously as Soekan lifted the lid to reveal copper-colored gears and more wires.

"The Davis and Kidder's Magneto-Electro Machine for Nervous Diseases," Dr. Soekan announced proudly. "This is the very peak of scientific achievement in the treatment of nervous disorders, female hysteria, and melancholia."

Lottie shook her head, beginning to understand what they had planned. "You mean to electrocute me."

"Nothing of the sort!" Dr. Soekan looked to Dr. Bothelli. "This has been widely used at Yale Medical College as well as Columbia University and vetted by the very finest minds in psychiatry. It simply stimulates your nervous system and, in doing so, helps you to heal those psychical wounds. In our case, we are hoping it will also stimulate your natural talents. If you can move a teacup with the mild stimulation we have been giving already, imagine what you could accomplish!" He smiled broadly, already imagining his published study in the *New England Journal of Medicine*, Lottie thought darkly.

"So you mean to electrocute me?" Lottie repeated her question, her voice ice.

"My dear, this machine does not electrocute anyone." Dr. Bothelli took a step forward and sat next to her, keeping his eyes level with hers. "It delivers mild electric sensations, nothing more than what happens when you touch a doorknob after you've built up a static charge on your finger. You are perfectly safe."

Dr. Soekan cut him off. "Let's get started."

"Wait." Lottie turned her head to the impatient Soekan, whose face had morphed from excitement over his machine to annoyance at her hesitancy. "Wait, that hurts. It hurts when you touch a doorknob and you get a shock. You mean to hurt me with no regard to my baby."

"Lottie, your child is perfectly safe, and the stimulation given by the machine is mild. It simply excites your nervous system so that you can reach a higher state of consciousness, and thus healing." Dr. Bothelli spoke slowly, as though he were trying to convince himself as well as her.

"But you aren't so concerned with healing, are you?" Lottie asked stiffly. "You are interested in your research, how many teacups I can move while you mesmerize me and twist my skin into a knot. You are more interested in me being cooperative and maybe, if I am a very good girl, you will let me leave this place, not because I'm well but because you've used me till you had no more need. Isn't that more the truth?" Lottie spat the words at the two men.

Dr. Soekan's toad face grew red with anger, but he contained it. They needed her to cooperate, at least a bit, for their experiments to work. "Young lady, you need us if you are ever to leave this place. So it seems that we both have something the other needs. We need your cooperation, and you need to trust us. Trust that we are your best chance at living a life outside of this place with your child. Without that trust, and without your cooperation, you will spend your days here in this asylum, and your child will leave with the good sisters for the local orphanage. Or maybe it won't make it even that far."

Lottie felt her spine stiffen. The baby kicked as though it

heard the doctor's words as well. "What do you mean by that?" she whispered.

"The incinerator on the back border of the asylum has been used to burn more than just rubbish. That is all I am saying, Mrs. Liath." Dr. Soekan tipped his head, as though thinking.

Dr. Bothelli looked like a man caught in the middle of a storm. He turned to Soekan and sputtered. "Doctor, I do not see the point in this conversation. There is no need to scare the girl, and you are spreading falsehoods about the workings of this institution."

"Falsehoods? Am I?" Dr. Soekan asked brusquely. "Mrs. Liath's child is not the first born in this hospital, not the first to suffer the maladies of birth, and not the first to be disposed of. I am not, in any way, threatening the girl. I am, however, telling her some truths about what will come to pass if she does indeed live out her life here in Argoll, and what will happen to a child born in this institution who is not perceived as viable."

Lottie felt her whole body shaking. Either she went along with the doctor's plan or what he said was true. She would give birth here, with only Dr. Bothelli and the nuns to help. If her baby lived, she would never see him or her again. If it was sickly or carried any number of maladies too great for healing, it would be burned. She knew the doctor's words to be true. Of course, that might happen no matter what she consented to, but she had a feeling that the choice that was laid before her was less a choice and more a consideration of how forceful the two doctors needed to be in their "treatment."

"I understand your point," Lottie said softly, nausea creeping into her gut. "What is it you want from me?"

Lottie felt Dr. Bothelli's hands guiding her to lie back on the stiff sofa. She was racked with exhaustion and anger. Dr. Soekan's vile face appeared over hers.

"I want you to concentrate on the orb and let yourself be mesmerized, nothing that we have not practiced before. When you are deep in your hypnotic state, I will send the magnetic-electro stimulations through these two electrodes, which you will hold in either hand. You will not feel a thing, your child will be perfectly safe, and we will see how the stimulation of your nervous system affects your psychical talents. Simple really. I want you to concentrate on this pot of flowers, right here next to you on Dr. Bothelli's desk. As we guide you through the mesmerism, concentrate on those flowers, and let's see what you can do. Yes, alright, yes. Let us begin."

Lottie felt paralyzed by her emotions, a nagging voice in the back of her head told her that no amount of cooperation would ever mean that she left here with her child. What if that promise had always been empty? What was stopping her from clawing Dr. Toad and Hog's eyes clean out of his skull? She stared at the pot of flowers, feeling as helpless as she had ever been. She felt two cold metallic disks being placed on the palms of either hand.

The silver orb dropped down before her eyes, and Lottie tried to breathe. The shape swung back and forth, back and forth.

"Lottie, I want you to concentrate on the orb, watch it move, and I want you to fall back into it as though you were swimming in a lake, just fall back into it, and follow the sound of my voice." Dr. Soekan spoke softly as Lottie felt the silky blackness surround her.

Lottie

The blackness encircled her, pulling Lottie back, back, back into a feeling of weightlessness. She felt the presence of the black-eyed girl, and she pushed herself toward it as though she were swimming for shore. Only in this world did the despair ebb, did the immediacy of her situation not overwhelm her. In the far distance, she could hear Dr. Soekan's voice speaking in a rhythmic tone. She ignored it entirely. It became a ripple in the darkness, the words indistinguishable, texture to the background of wherever it was she found herself.

Lottie found herself in a room that was filled with shadows. It was as though there were bits and pieces of different rooms all thrown together. She could see a grand library, impossibly high walls filled with leather-backed books. She could also see what looked to be a church, perhaps, a tall pulpit of dark wood and bright, white paint. None of it fit together, and Lottie looked down to see where her feet landed. They were nowhere, a solid plank of sheer night. She was in neither place, not really, yet she was in both.

A woman walked toward her from the blackness. It was not

the girl or the man that Lottie had felt drawn to before. This was an older woman, her hair matted and gray. The figure grinned, and Lottie could see gaps where missing teeth were. The eyes were voids, unseeing pits, yet they focused entirely on Lottie, and the woman kept inching closer and closer, holding out a hand. The flesh was gray, dead, stiff already. Lottie recoiled in disgust, but the woman just offered a toothless grin.

They're asking for you.

The woman's lips never moved, yet Lottie heard the words all around her, the voice broken and cracked.

Who?

She responded without words; the thought sailed from her mind into the void. In response, the old woman reached out and took Lottie's hand, the dead flesh touching hers. To Lottie's surprise the touch was not cold, not stiff, but warm and alive. The old woman pulled Lottie along, closer and closer to what looked to be a church: the other scene, the library, was still behind her. Lottie wanted to ask what this was, where she was, what she was being taken to. In the very far distance the doctor's voice faintly continued on. Lottie hoped he would prattle on for a bit longer so she could see what she was being called to.

The black-eyed girl sat at a table. Across from her was the fire-haired woman who had been present in a vision some time before, how long Lottie did not know. Time ran differently here, she could feel it; maybe it was months, perhaps it was years or minutes. The fire-haired woman sat with a straight back, her gaze fixed. The old woman pulled Lottie forward and then leaned down to whisper in the fire-haired woman's ear; she looked up and grinned at Lottie.

Go ahead. You have permission.

Lottie started to object. Permission to do what? But then it washed over her—this woman was offering herself as a means to speak, a body for her floating spirit. Lottie felt a twist of fear, and the old woman smirked at her as she pulled her forward, thrusting her into the fire-haired lady's flesh. Lottie tried to scream, to run, to move, but she was frozen. She opened her eyes and could see she was looking through the space as another saw it. The black-eyed girl stared back at her, and Lottie could feel her heart beating; she, too, was afraid.

In the girl's eyes she could see everything. She saw a library, two men and a different woman sitting round a table. She felt the girl's rage, she felt herself standing behind her, her hand on the girl's neck. She saw the table rise in the air and fly through the air, she felt the satisfied triumph of the girl, and Lottie almost laughed aloud for it. The girl was speaking to her, and Lottie understood what she was saying, but it was as though she were a thousand miles away, the words garbled as though they were coming from deep underwater.

I am no spirit. I live, I am no spirit.

Lottie tried to shout, to scream the words as she realized who the black-eyed girl was, who the man with the matching hair and eyes was, how they saw her.

I live, I live, they've locked me in this place.

Lottie struggled and felt herself becoming more and more enmeshed in the body she had inhabited. She had control over her hands, her neck, she could turn her head and look at the astonished faces of the onlookers. What was this place? What had become of this girl?

Nora. The girl's name was Nora Grey. It hadn't always been; it was what the girl called herself now, in this place. Nora. Tavish. That was the man's name. Tavish. She felt her baby twist and kick in her belly, a spirit child in a spirit body. He was sitting in the front row, his face pale with shock.

I live, I live, I live.

Lottie screamed the words as loud as she could, knowing

they were little more than a whisper for all the effort. Suddenly, a sharp jolt of pain racked her body. It emanated from the palms of both hands, and Lottie knew exactly what was happening to her corporeal form back in the doctor's office. All so she could move a pot of flowers? The doctors had no idea what she was capable of, no comprehension of the places she traveled under their mesmerism. Lottie steeled herself. If they wanted a show, she would give them a show. She felt an army of voices behind her; she was not a spirit, but perhaps she commanded them just the same. With the last burst of her energy, she commanded them to destroy the flowers, the doctors, to tear, rip, claw everything in their path. She allowed her anger to overwhelm her.

The last words she heard from the girl Nora's mouth were "You're Lottie Liath." Lottie then knew that this girl and herself were blood. She was no spirit, but this girl was her kin, her granddaughter, her blood. How this had come to pass, how she had traveled across years and the impossibility of time to be here, Lottie did not know; she only understood her anger. She heard the sound of claws ripping wood, then behind her, the table flew across the space in the dark library. In another reality, a pot of daisies exploded on a desk, a lamp fell to the floor, a teacup inched across a table. Lottie raised her voice to scream, but the sound was aborted as the tug of her reality, her time, her present tore her backward. The church-like room, the library, Nora, Tavish, her son, her child grown—all the faces disappeared. She felt herself leaving the fire-haired lady's body, bits of the woman's flesh psychically intertwined with hers.

"Lottie? You will awaken now. You will open your eyes and awaken."

Lottie found the act painful and exhausting. The room was a sight. Broken glass and flower petals covered the floor. Dr. Bothelli's desk lay on its side, all the contents in a pile. The electrocution box was a sad pile of gears and wires in the corner. The chair that one of the doctors had been sitting in was in pieces, jagged bits of wood littering the floor.

"What? What?" Lottie stuttered. She felt a bone-deep weariness that she had not experienced since she was brought here. The baby kicked and flipped in her stomach, agitated and angry.

"You moved the daisies," Dr. Bothelli said simply.

Nora
Boston
1901

Internal Work Order Originating from the Boston Carpentry and Construction Union—Author Unknown

> Date: October 14, 1901
> RE: Repairs to the Old South Meeting Hall
> Dear Sirs,
> This letter is to confirm the work order submitted for various repairs to the Old South Meeting Hall. We were informed of the need for urgent attention to this matter at a quite early hour, and our men investigated the site before 8 a.m. We have a list of what we believe are necessary repairs (see attached itinerate list). We were also informed of the need for secrecy, particularly regarding the media or any other curiosity seekers.
>
> It is not our typical custom to discuss repairs and carpentry jobs with the media, and I do not see how this job will be any different. We are, however, concerned with the extent of the damage done, in particular to the walls of the Old South Meeting Hall, and are submitting a special work order for a deep cleaning of the surfaces. The walls appear to be coated in a sort of substance the likes of which our men could not determine. They will need to be scraped and repainted, and as we do not know the origin of the damage to the walls, we are asking for increased hourly rates to atone for the potential danger to the health of our workers.
>
> We expect the order to be complete by week's end, and as per our agreement, the extent of the job as well as the details will remain a subject discussed between our two offices.
> Thank you.

Nora

The Old South Meeting Hall was a beauty of dark wood and crisp, white walls. A towering pulpit reigned over a maze of pews. An oblong table had been set in the small space that surrounded the pulpit, a chair at each end—one for her and one for Dorothy, so they could face each other. Three candles burned, equally spaced from each other on the table's surface. Oil lamps were dimmed but not dark, casting shadows around the room. The invited guests and researchers sat in the front pews, filling the first five rows on either side. Nora was led by Karl down the aisle in a bizarre mockery of a macabre wedding service and seated in one of the chairs. A moment later, Dorothy Kellings walked in, accompanied by a lady from her Rochester group. She, too, was seated.

All these details were at Dorothy Kellings's request. She had insisted on the low light, the long table, the two chairs, and the entry ritual. They had no magical meaning, she had told Nora—it was theatrics and setting a mood. Dorothy had been right. Nora could feel the tension in the air as the audience sat attentive, barely containing their fear and excitement. Dorothy had also insisted that once they were seated, no one interfere unless instructed by her to perform a particular task. Once complete, no one was to speak or move unless one or both of their lives were in danger. She had not stipulated how one might know their lives would be endangered, but Nora hoped the edict was more theatrics and not premonition.

Dorothy looked up at Nora, and the two women stared into each other's eyes while minutes passed. Nora could feel the tension building.

"I am here to channel the spirit guide of Nora Grey," Dorothy announced, her voice strong and full of authority. She kept her eyes locked on Nora. "Cecil, please, the light box."

A man who Nora knew to be part of Dorothy's entourage from Rochester set a light box similar to the one that Dr. Harrison had back in Edinburgh on the table. It was shielded so the flashes of light would only be visible on either side, for Dorothy and Nora. This, too, had been rehearsed the day before, and Nora settled in for what was to come next. Cecil stood behind the table and nodded to Dorothy.

"I will darken the light box as both Miss Kellings and Miss Grey's chins drop to their chests. I will then call to Miss Grey's spirit guide, who will manifest here for us tonight. We must all stay silent and not interrupt this window to the spirit realm." Cecil spoke to the room, then nodded to both Dorothy and Nora.

The light began to flash slowly and rhythmically. Nora watched as the bright descended into darkness and then again, and again. She felt her fingertips growing numb, and her body began to feel as though it were attached by a string and floating above, slightly outside of her corporeal self. In the distance, she heard the low hum of Cecil's voice, and the flashing light darkened, leaving only the candles.

"Welcome, spirits, welcome to our house. Welcome, spirits, welcome to our house."

Nora lifted her chin and looked up at Dorothy, whose eyes caught the light of the fire. She had a golden sort of glow that surrounded her skin, and behind her Nora saw a shape, a figure who tottered forward in the darkness. It was an old woman with long, gray hair, her face aged and lined. Nora felt as though her body were floating above her chair. Everything but the light from the candles, Dorothy, and the figure behind her disappeared, lost in utter blackness.

The old woman locked her eyes on Nora, dark and blank. They were dead eyes, eyes that saw nothing of this world but existed only in the next. She leaned forward until her cracked and dry lips were inches from Dorothy's ear, and she whispered silently, keeping her gaze locked on Nora the entire time.

Dorothy's body shuddered, and her eyes closed.

"Greetings, all. Greetings, all. I am Blessed Moons. I summon the spirit that surrounds Nora Grey. Come, spirit. Come to our space. Talk to us, spirit; let yourself be known. None will harm you, none will harm. Come, spirit. Come to Blessed Moons. Come, spirit." The voice was ancient and rusty.

Dorothy shuddered again, her entire body convulsing. Nora could see Blessed Moons reaching behind her, extending a hand to the darkness. Nora felt her arms leave her side and float to shoulder level. She watched Blessed Moons pull an invisible force forward and then whisper again in Dorothy's ear. A shadow—no, not a shadow, more of a disruption in the black, a shimmer, a break in the continuity of the fabric of the room — moved next to Blessed Moons and settled itself over Dorothy's body, sitting down in the chair as though Dorothy's physical form were not there. Suddenly Dorothy's eyes flew open, and her face was panicked. She looked from side to side, trying to move Dorothy's arms and legs, but Nora could see the resistance, the struggle in Dorothy's body that prevented the force from taking her over entirely.

"Where am I? What is this place?" Dorothy spoke, her voice

entirely different from Blessed Moons's. It was higher, younger, and scared.

"Who are you?" Nora asked. The sound of her own voice felt as though it were coming from a far distance.

"You. It's you. Who? How am I here?" Dorothy's mouth moved with the strange voice.

"I am Nora Grey. You are my spirit guide. What are you called?" Nora asked.

"I'm no spirit. I'm trapped here in this place; they've locked me in this place." The voice was angry beneath the fear, and indignant.

"But you are a spirit. You have crossed to the next realm. Who are you? What are you called?" Nora asked again. Dorothy had told her that spirit guides often do not want to be named and to insist until her guide relented.

"You are the spirit. You are! You are the spirit. I live, I live," the voice insisted.

Nora felt her shadow self growing larger, expanding. Her physical body was a sliver of flesh in the center of her expanding mind. She stared at Dorothy Kellings's face, so full of wonder, so full of fear.

"Speak your name, spirit," Nora said again.

"My name is Lottie, and I'm no spirit. I live, I live, I live." The voice spoke again, desperate this time. Nora opened her mouth but was silenced as Dorothy Kellings's fire hair began to grow black; the careful coif on top of her head turned black as Nora's and fell past her shoulders in lank, unwashed strands. Her face, too, changed. It became thinner, her skin pale, her light eyes darkened to night black, and Nora found herself staring at a version of herself, the version that she'd seen since she was a girl, in her dreams and in visions. She saw the face she had always thought to be her imagination.

"Lottie," Nora repeated. "You are Lottie Liath."

"I live. I live. I live," Lottie said insistently.

"You do not. You are spirit. You died, you are spirit, you walk with me now. Let me give you a voice," Nora said, watching the girl's face twitch with confusion and near hysteria.

"You haunt me. I am not spirit. You are a devil or a ghost. I am not dead." Lottie's voice cracked and broke. "I live, I live, I live, I live."

The black hair and eyes melted off Dorothy's face as though held there by candle wax. Dorothy appeared again, her hair fallen around her shoulders and her face contorted in pain.

"Lottie!" Nora cried, trying to draw the spirit back, but Lottie Liath was gone. As Cecil set the light box out, and Nora felt her mind and body once again become one, she felt the spirit ripped from the room, sent back to her darkness.

Nora

The Old South Meeting Hall had erupted into chaos. Nora woke on the floor next to her chair. She could see the shape of the table that was on its side, and the candlesticks were rolling back and forth on the floor. All around her, she heard voices, some frightened, some pitched with excitement. She could make out Karl's above the din.

"Let's leave now, everyone. Please make your way to the doors; we need to take care of our mediums. This session is now over; please make your way to the door."

Nora sat up, her head throbbing. She could see Dorothy slumped in her chair, her eyes closed, her body slack. Nora looked around at the room, and her head spun. The walls were coated in a sort of gel; it gave off a faint glow, and the smell was ghastly. This was the same substance Rona Connell had talked about, the ectoplasm that Nora had dismissed as a parlor trick. There were deep scratches in the wood floor beneath her, as though a tiger had taken its great claws and raked them across the wood. Overhead the chandelier still swung wildly, and Nora could see paint and plaster chipping away and falling to the ground. The oil lamps still burned, but they had been brightened somewhat, showing another claw mark across the front of the pulpit. The white paint was scraped away, and the bare wood showed beneath, five perfect claw marks, a phantom paw that had reached into this world and tried to destroy it. Nora pulled herself to her feet, surveying the scene. The floor was scratched with the phantom claws in other places, too, and chunks of wood were chipped away from the columns that supported the balcony seating. Nora steadied herself and sat on the edge of her chair.

Cecil was tending to Dorothy, wiping her face with a cloth. Her eyes fluttered, and she straightened up and looked straight at Nora. Her face was confused, and Nora wondered if her head was pounding the same as Nora's was. Nora heard Tavish's voice in the distance—angry, incoherent words—and she felt suddenly better for it. His heavy footsteps made their way to her chair, and suddenly his eyes met hers.

"Nairna, my girl, my girl, are you alright? I've never seen such a thing. Can you answer me?" His voice was a model of barely contained panic.

"Da, I'm fine. I think, anyhow . . . what happened here? I saw Lottie . . . Lottie Liath," Nora whispered, her strength gone.

"We all saw her. Damndest thing I've ever witnessed. Damndest thing anyone's ever witnessed, I'd wager." Tavish cupped her face in his hands. "Can you stand? I want to get you out of here."

Nora nodded and looked to Dorothy, whose cheeks had a bit more color now, and who was sitting a bit straighter.

"Well done. I understand your guide made a smashing entrance," Dorothy said, her voice betraying her weariness.

Nora nodded. "What happened here?"

"I have no idea, but I am sure there will be no shortage of men who want to tell us about it." Dorothy rolled her head from side to side, stretching, and then looked up at Cecil. "Take me back to the hotel. I need to rest." She looked to Nora. "You should rest as well. You're famous now."

With that, Dorothy made her way out the doors and disappeared. Tavish helped Nora to her feet, and she walked on legs that felt like rubber to the exit. Karl reentered the building as they approached. He looked at her, a flash of concern in his eyes. "You're alright, then?"

Nora nodded. "I suppose so. The audience was pleased?"

Karl grinned. The expression looked alien on his sour face. "You could say that. This is the last time you get to be a no one."

Nora looked to Tavish, who grimaced at Karl. "Let's get her back. She's just a girl, for god's sake. I have no idea what happened back there. I need a drink."

On the ride back to Young's Hotel, Nora leaned against Tavish's shoulder, and he held her hand in his, stroking her fingers gently.

"My girl, it's not the right time to ask, but you said the name Lottie Liath . . . it can't be. It can't be," Tavish said in a gruff whisper. "My whole life, the thing I wanted most was my family. I asked god until I stopped believin' in the bastard. I asked anyone who might know what became of my mother. And now, what is it that happened tonight?"

"I don't know, Da. She's been with me for a time now. I didn't know who she was. She's guarded me, she's a part of me," Nora said softly, her head spinning.

"All this time, I've not had a whisper of knowing she was there. Not a dream, not a hint. I . . . I . . ." Tavish's voice broke with emotion.

"I know, Da. I know. I don't understand any of this," Nora replied, squeezing his hand.

As she lay in a hot bath, Nora tried to remember what had happened in the room. She'd seen the black-haired woman, Lottie Liath. The only stories she'd ever heard of her grandmother had come from her Nań, whose whispered stories were spun from gossip. She told of how Tavish's mother had given birth in a Welsh asylum somewhere on Argoll Downs, which Nań said was a dreary and dreadful place, and infant Tavish had been shipped to Glasgow in hopes that he'd be taken in by family. But as it had turned out, Tavish had spent his youth in orphanages and workhouses. Lottie was never heard from again. Had she lived out her years in the asylum? Or died in childbirth? Perhaps she had been set free from Argoll Downs entirely and had a history no one could even guess at. Nora wanted it to be true but knew it was more likely that Lottie Liath was buried in a potter's field somewhere on the Downs.

I live, I live. Nora closed her eyes and plunged her head under the water. What had Lottie Liath meant? If she had not died in Wales as Nań had always said, where was she? Was she still locked away in Argoll Asylum? An old woman lost in her mind? If she was dead, what had happened to her that she did not know she'd passed? What story had died with her?

Later, as Nora lay in bed, the oil lamps extinguished and the night quiet, she allowed herself to fall into a deep and dreamless sleep. She saw the silky blackness in the back of her mind's eye and fell entirely and wholly into its depths. No memories, no dreams, no visions permeated her rest. She slept as though it were the last night of her life as she knew it.

Lottie
Argoll Asylum
1866

Excerpt from Ghostly Tales and Spirited Fright,
Volume 10 (Spring)

The tale comes to us from Argoll Downs, and it's one that's been passed back and forth at plenty a campfire: the Wailing Woman. You're likely to have heard the basics. Woman wearing a long white nightdress wandering the downs; she's been seen walking the downs as well as in the surrounding manors. She seems to be drawn to children and is the root of the superstition regarding babies and the curse of Argoll Downs. The curse states that infants are in dire danger on Argoll Downs, as the Wailing Woman will appear by their bedside screaming her senseless anger and scare the soul right out of them. It bears noting that despite the locals' defense of said curse, there is no evidence that children of any age are in any particular danger in Argoll Downs.

Other tales contradict this telling. They tell of the same lost woman in the same ghostly white nightdress; however, in this version the screaming and the anger are absent. Instead, the figure is calm, sad even. The woman appears at the bedsides of children seemingly just to watch them sleep, the way a mother might do.

Whatever the intent, the Wailing Woman is a fixture of Argoll Downs the same as a daffodil or a red kite, a symbol of Wales itself. A legend that lives in the Welsh sun and soil and grows with each passing year.

*Tonight we join the legions who have tried to un-
ravel the history behind the Wailing Woman: who
she was, how she died, why she remained. Tonight's
addition is part history lesson, part folklore, and it
tells the story of an asylum, a lost woman, and a mysterious death in the winter of 1867.*

Lottie

Lottie limped back to her room, her energy entirely gone. She collapsed on her cot, too tired even to follow the sound of the voices in the corridor to the dining hall. The good doctors had been simultaneously horrified and ecstatic at her performance. Lottie couldn't make heads or tails of it. Her hands and arms ached from the shock of the electric currents.

She'd left the vision with the idea that she'd spoken more than had actually left her mouth, and that the way she appeared to Nora Grey and the others in her reality was such that they thought her a spirit. Lottie pulled the blanket over herself, shivering in the icy room. Maybe she was spirit; perhaps she was dead, and this was her version of hell. She didn't understand the passage of time. She'd been in the vision for what felt like minutes, but near the whole day had passed; hours were gone, and she'd never felt it. The doctors said she was in an unconscious state and hadn't moved at all until the end when the room was destroyed. Even then, Dr. Bothelli told her with wide eyes, she hadn't moved a muscle, not even an eyelid.

The events in the vision also were out of order—different

rooms, different places, but she was there simultaneously. Nora Grey was there, too, and unless she, too, were caught in some sort of hellscape, she also could not be in two places at once. The entire thought made Lottie's head spin. She knew she ought to eat, but the idea of standing and walking, then listening to the other women from the ward chatter on, was more than she could bear. A knock at her door made her jump, but her body was so tired it barely registered the surprise.

Sister Therese stood there with a tray. A bowl of soup, bread, and a hot liquid, so hot Lottie could see the steam rising from the mug. Lottie pulled herself to a sitting position, every muscle in her body screaming in protest.

"Didn't see you with the rest; thought you might be feeling a bit peaked." Sister Therese set the tray on the small table and helped Lottie up and to the chair.

"Now eat. You can't go missing meals, not now. That little one will be taking everything you have." The nun put a spoon in Lottie's hand and then sat on the edge of her bed, watching her eat the thin vegetable soup. It tasted more of water and salt than anything, but Lottie hadn't realized how hungry she'd been.

"I'm concerned," Sister Therese said after a time, as Lottie was swallowing the last of the bread and sipping the tea.

"As am I," Lottie said softly, turning the chair to meet the sister's eyes.

"I want you to know I spoke to the Mother Superior. I told her I disagree with the treatments they are putting you through, the bruising on your arms, the hours they keep you in that room. It's indecent." Worry lines framed Sister Therese's face.

"Sister, can I ask you something? Something unsavory?" Lottie said hesitantly, Dr. Soekan's words still rolling around her mind.

"I suppose," the nun said, her expression confused.

"I heard from . . . well . . . I'd like not to say who, but they said that there's an incinerator out back of the asylum, and, and . . ." Lottie choked on the words.

"There is an incinerator—it's for trash, as we don't have another way being this far out in the downs. What is the rest of your question? What else did this person tell you?" Sister Therese sat up a bit straighter, leaning in.

"They said, they said that if my baby were sick, or abnormal in any way, that it would be likelier to be burned alive than placed in an orphanage when it's born, and I'm like to die or be locked away till I do." Lottie spat the words out in a rush.

Sister Therese stared at her for a long moment, her eyes unreadable. "It's a horror what they told you." She patted the bed next to her. Lottie made her way to the nun's side, still holding the cooling mug of tea.

"Lottie, I will do everything I can to keep you safe here. I believe with every fiber of my heart that I was placed by God above to protect the souls and bodies of the women who pass through the doors. You are cooperating with your treatments; you are dealing with your grief and your loss. You are clearly calm and wanting to get better. I do not see why you would not be released with your child when the time comes." The nun took Lottie's hand and squeezed it. Lottie winced from the ache left by the electrodes.

"They had a box. It was meant to send electrical shocks. They said it wouldn't hurt none, but it did. They lied." Lottie lowered her eyes, frightened to utter the words, of what would happen to her if the doctors were angered. She drank the last of the tea, the warm liquid filling her chest.

"That man cannot leave soon enough. It's barbaric. I will speak to the Mother Superior," Sister Therese said, and she stood. She took the empty mug from Lottie's hand and placed it on the tray. As she exited the room, she turned to Lottie. "Get some rest. I'll see what I can do about getting you to see Sister Mary tomorrow in lieu of more 'treatments.' It's time to see how you're doing anyhow."

Lottie nodded appreciatively. She slipped into a dressing gown and extinguished the oil lamp. In the darkness, some of the pains of her body quelled, and she played back Sister Therese's answer to what Dr. Soekan had told her about the incinerator. The sister hadn't said it wouldn't happen. She had just said she was here to protect her. What did that mean? And why would the doctors ever let her leave? No one was likely to miss her if she lived and died here in Argoll. And if Dr. Toad and Hog wanted a bigger response, what if he wanted the sort of thing that she saw in her visions, tables throwing themselves across rooms? What would he do then?

Lottie

Sister Mary regarded her suspiciously.

"You've lost weight since you were last here," she said with a hint of accusation. "You've been skipping your dinner."

Lottie shook her head. She had measured as nearing her eighth month, but the nun wasn't exactly sure, said Lottie might be farther along than she was measuring, that the baby was small.

"Not on purpose. I've been so tired," Lottie said by way of excuse.

"You can't be so tired so as not to eat," Sister Mary said, "or I'll park you next to Lorna there and let her chew your ear off. She's on a new theory, says she thinks the doctors are really lizard people and not humans at all. Isn't that true, Lorna?" Sister Mary turned her head to where Lorna was rocking back and forth in her bed slightly, a grin plastered on her face.

"True! It's true! You can tell by their scales. Lizard people through and through." Lorna howled.

"That should be incentive enough to take better care of yourself." Sister Mary winked at Lottie and handed her a thick, woolen sweater.

"Thank you," Lottie said, surprised.

"No need. You need to keep yourself warm—no colds, no fevers now. And I had this old thing lying around with no one to wear it. So here you are. Besides, I'm a nun. I'm supposed to give all my worldly goods to the poor." Sister Mary offered a hand to Lottie to help her stand.

"Well, in that case, you should thank me for being poor and helping you fulfill your duties," Lottie said with a smile.

"I'll not go that far," the nun said, her tone light. "Come back anytime. I'd say based on where you thought you were when you arrived that you were in your seventh month, and the baby's small, but something about the position of the little imp makes me think he or she might be a bit farther along. Just a feeling. If you continue to lose weight, I'll have to call in a midwife from Cardiff to talk some sense to you."

"Cardiff is that close?" Lottie asked, surprised.

"You can get there and back in a day if needs be. But I'd rather not have to call for reinforcements, so it would be nice if you'd start eating proper," the nun said with a frown.

"Understood. If I want to know about the lizard people, I'll be back," Lottie said, and Lorna laughed as though she would burst.

Sid stood in the door. "Time for treatments," he said dully.

Lottie followed, the seed of a plan beginning to form in her mind.

Lottie

Lottie worked quickly and quietly, the breakfast bell already sounding. If she didn't make an appearance in the hall soon, Sister Therese would look for her, which is exactly what Lottie was hoping for, but to ensure she was taken to the infirmary and not the dining hall, Lottie needed to work fast. She pulled the edge of the metal piping that lined her bed cot and managed to clear a sharp, clean edge. Lottie took a deep breath and sliced her finger down its side. The blood welled to the surface immediately, and Lottie felt her vision swim momentarily. She shook her head, willing her mind to cooperate and be stronger than her ragged body. Careful not to drip, she moved her hand right below the swell of her belly. She grimaced with disgust and the sheer perversion of it all as she wiped the thick blood from her throbbing finger on her gown. Hopefully it would create the illusion she was hoping for. Sister Therese would take her immediately to the infirmary, where even if they found nothing to be amiss, she would likely spend the day in a bed next to crazy Lorna, just to make sure.

Her arm ached from the previous day's treatments, wherein

Dr. Toad and Hog had held a lit candle to her arm until the flesh blistered. He had been delighted when an end table had flipped on its side while Lottie screamed in pain. Lottie couldn't take any more treatments; she had to get out. This plan, however ill-thought, had to work; it had to be just right. Sister Therese, true to her word, had tried to get her pulled from treatments altogether and admitted to the infirmary. The doctors had disallowed it, and while Sister Therese swore to take the matter to the diocese, Lottie feared what the two doctors could do in the meantime. It had to stop now. She needed an incontrovertible reason to be admitted to the infirmary. This had to work.

Lottie heard the other women in the hall, shuffling their way to the dining hall. It would be just moments before she was missed. As neatly as she could, Lottie wrapped her finger in a strip of cloth she had ripped from her bedsheet. The bleeding was already slowing, and she hoped it would stop entirely before it gave her away. The baby kicked and squirmed in her belly, Lottie rubbed the swell with her uninjured hand. *Trust me*, she murmured soundlessly to the imp. *It just might work.*

Sure enough, she heard a knock on her door, and Sister Therese appeared, blocking the light from the hall.

"It's time to rise, the others are already on their ..." She stopped as she saw the stain on Lottie's nightgown. "Oh dear. Sit tight, love. I'll get Sid."

An hour later, Lottie was settled into a bed next to a sleeping Lorna. Sister Mary had examined her and, though confused, had simply declared it to be routine spotting and assigned her bed rest. She had not discovered Lottie's cut finger, although Lottie suspected that the sister knew something was amiss. Something in the way she had regarded Lottie made her think that she had not been quite as clever as she had wanted to be. No matter, she had found herself exactly where she wanted.

No one would be interfering with her for the rest of the day—no treatments, no doctors, and no one watching to see if she was in the dining hall at suppertime. She wondered why she had not thought of this before, although it would have been a temporary kind of solution. A reprieve for the night, and not a means to get her child to safety.

The day passed quickly. Lottie allowed herself to doze, half-dreams of the flat where she'd grown up in Glasgow creeping into her thoughts. She woke and ate the lunch of stewed cabbage that Sister Mary served her and Lorna. Lorna was unnaturally quiet, staring straight ahead. No raucous laughter, no talk of lizard folk. Lorna stared and muttered wordlessly to herself, and Lottie gave her peace. In truth, it was for the best. If Lorna raised a fuss later in the night when Lottie needed her to be quiet, it would all fall apart.

After the sun had set, Sister Mary returned to collect dinner trays and make a final check of the infirmary. She slept in an adjoining room, and Lottie knew she would have to wait until Sister Mary was satisfied her charges were well asleep before Lottie did anything. The sister paused as she cleared Lottie's stew bowl and mug from her side table.

"Lottie, I'm happy to officially report that you should be on bed rest. You could stay here till the baby arrives," the nun said with concern. "It wouldn't even be a lie, not really. You are obviously worn, and I can't have you slicing yourself up every time you need a rest." She cocked her head and raised her eyebrows.

Lottie felt her stomach sink. "You won't be calling in a midwife," she whispered.

"Gah, girl, I'm not stupid. I'm not sure what your game here is, but you're welcome to stay in this ward till the baby's born. I can see to it." Sister Mary shook her head. "I'll put a bandage on that finger."

"What after that? Where does my baby go? What happens to

me?" Lottie felt tears in the corners of her eyes, and her throat was welling shut, cutting off her words. "What happens to us?"

Sister Mary sat on the edge of the bed and took a small kit from the pocket of her apron. She reached for Lottie's hand, gently unbinding the rough bandage. "It's a clean cut—a scratch, really. A miracle you got as much blood out of it as you did." She cut a short length of cloth wrap from her kit and methodically wrapped the finger. "I'm not in the habit of locking the infirmary door at night. No need, really. If anyone were to give me trouble, the guards need to be able to get in without a fuss, and no one much expects the patients to be up and about in this part of the hospital." She clasped Lottie's hands in her own. "I'm a deep sleeper. Or can be under the right circumstances." She leaned into Lottie's ear. "The guard at the gate is named Willem; he's a good man, has children of his own. He has a carriage and horses. I don't know what he's willing to do to help you, but I know he's sympathetic to what a mother is willing to do to protect her child. I delivered his youngest. I've never seen a man who loved his family more." Sister Mary looked around. Satisfied that Lorna was in her own world, she lowered her voice. "The kitchen storeroom is on the first floor. Follow the back hallway. There's a door for deliveries that leads out back. The cook sleeps across the hall."

She stood, taking the dishes, then turned and left the room without another word. Lottie lay in bed, afraid to breathe. *It could work. It might just work.* The guard gate was an eternity away, and Lottie wondered if she'd even be able to make it out the front door, much less the rough road she only half-remembered from her trip here. She'd been in the back of the paddy wagon, hadn't even seen the route, she'd like to end up frozen in a ditch rather than on a horse headed to Cardiff. The voice in the back of her head was relentless. *You have to try*, it whispered soundlessly, echoing in her head. If she didn't, if she allowed her child to be born in this place, they were both dead already.

Lottie

Lottie discovered that her clothes had been neatly folded and placed next to her bed. Included was a thick pair of woolen socks to line the insides of her boots, a warm sweater, and a matching scarf. Lottie knew the nun had left them and would have left more if she'd had the means. She dressed quickly and slipped out the unlocked door, wrapping her head in the scarf. The baby kicked in her belly, as though anticipating the flight to come.

The imposing dark wood door loomed in front of her as she hurried down the corridor from the infirmary. The back hallways led away from the front door. Intended for servants in the days when this was a grand manor house, they were designed to be invisible. Lottie had little trouble finding the storeroom, the cook's snores echoing into the hall. Lottie quickly and quietly slipped inside and surveyed the space, shelves full of sacks of flour and beans, dried fruit and crates of potatoes. A rat scurried across the floor, as surprised as Lottie at the interruption. Lottie cringed and silently shuddered. Any sound could wake the cook and ruin her chance.

The back door squealed in protest, and Lottie cringed at the sound, but still the cook's snores echoed in the hall. As she peeked out into the frozen night, Lottie had a sudden rush of paralyzing fear. What if there were guards posted at the door? She would have to circle around the manor house to get to the road; they'd surely see her no matter how dark the night was. *No one is standing guard outside on a night like this.* Lottie heard the familiar voice whispering in the back of her head. She hoped she was right. The door screamed on its hinges as she closed it and stared into the darkness. She'd been at Argoll long enough for the winter to give way to the early spring rains, though the night air carried the same chill. Freezing rain poured from the night sky, and the mucus in her nose immediately froze, forming what felt like ice crystals on her face. The wind whipped past, so cold Lottie was nearly paralyzed by it. Still she pushed herself onward, grateful for the thick socks Sister Mary had left. She had no time to worry if someone had heard the door or seen her in the hall. Lottie forced her feet to move, and she managed a sort of loping run, the best her swollen belly would allow her. She circled around the manor house, the dark stone melding into the darkness, giving the impression that the night and the house were one. She was relieved to see that the voice in her head had been right—there were no guards standing at the front doors. She knew they were likely just on the other side, though, ready to move if there was the least bit disturbance outside. She forced herself to keep moving, a sharp pain streaking through her belly, the skin growing taut like a drum. The sensation stole her breath, and Lottie stopped at the entrance to the road, trying to catch some air in her lungs, her stomach pulsating and the baby kicking its tiny feet directly into her rib cage. She swallowed a scream and kept moving forward.

She limped down the road for an eternity, the damp creeping past her boots and the thick socks, winding its way past the woven strands of her sweater, her belly pulsating, the pains moving in rhythm with the tightness that wrapped itself around the swell. Lottie knew it was too early. She knew that if she went into labor out here on the winter road at night, they were both as good as dead. She'd never even make it back to the asylum; she'd be lucky to haul herself off the road and die under one of the grand oak trees that lined the dirt road. She had to keep moving toward the faint golden light she could just make out in the distance. The guard gate, it had to be the guard-house where a man named Willem lived with his wife and children. Where a man named Willem might take mercy on her when he saw her pregnant belly and knew what was like to happen to the child. A man she'd never met with a wife and children that she never knew existed held the key to her escape; they were the only means she had of fleeing this place, of trying to save her baby, of ensuring that she would never again be hooked to the electric shocks or have her skin twisted with the metal tools in the doctor's bag.

Lottie put one foot before the other and kept moving toward the glow of the guardhouse. Her fingers had lost feeling some time ago; they felt as though they could snap off like twigs any moment, as though they were no longer a part of her body but a separate entity, an attachment that could easily be removed and replaced. She inched her way toward the gate, which was in view now. She saw the cottage to the side and the lantern glow from the oil lamp hanging over the doorway. The guard shack where Willem spent his days was empty; he was in for the night now. Lottie could veer to the right where she saw the stable that held the sleeping horses. She could leave now and never be seen, but she knew she would not be able to so much as throw a blanket over the horse's back, much less climb atop. Her blood was barely moving as she reached up with an immobile hand and rapped on the wooden door of the cottage. She didn't feel her skin tear from the effort; the cold congealed the blood from the scrape immediately. Her belly seized in pain and protest, and she felt herself falling forward as the door opened and a woman wrapped in a blanket over her nightdress screamed in surprise.

Lottie's last sight was the woman's shocked face and a man looming over her shoulder. *Willem*, Lottie whispered, *you have to help me, you're the only one who can help me.* Unsure of whether the words were in her head or if she spoke them aloud, Lottie closed her eyes and allowed the darkness to overtake her.

Lottie

Lottie awoke in grainy blackness. Only a faint glow of day-light entered from a dirty window high above her. She felt around in the dim light and discovered she was on a thin cot on a stone floor. There was a sheet and a blanket. She was wearing the same sort of shift as she'd left in, but this was ill-fitting, and she assumed she'd been changed by the nuns. But why was she here? How had she been caught? Maybe the guard had found her and taken her to Cardiff and this was a hospital room—although a poor one it was, she observed. Her head pounded, and her mouth was dry. Lottie looked around the room wildly. There was an oil lamp in the corner. She fumbled her way to it, and the room was illuminated with light. A simple metal bucket in one corner that she cringed at, knowing its purpose. The cot, the sheet, a blanket, and that was it. What had become of her? Who had found her passed out from cold and pain outside the guardhouse?

She didn't have to wait long for an answer. The wooden door rattled from the outside, and Dr. Soekan appeared in its frame. Lottie's heart sank, and she felt the baby kick in frustration or anger in her belly.

"Thank goodness you're awake. You gave us a good worry, young lady," the doctor said, his voice an imitation of sincerity.

"Where am I?" Lottie whispered.

"Why safe at Argoll, of course," Dr Soekan said, and smiled, enjoying the position she was in. "I trust you are ready to resume your therapies, now that you are clear from distraction."

"I . . . I . . ." Lottie stuttered the words. She had no response for his directive.

"You are out of options, my dear. The gate guard was surprised as anything when you showed up at his door. He sent for us straight away—afraid for your health, he was. Sister Mary swears the infirmary was locked tight, so we know you must have picked the lock—carryover from your previous life, I suspect." The doctor paused, and Lottie felt a streak of ice shoot down her spine. No one knew she was here, she realized with utter terror.

"I'm not in the infirmary," she whispered more to herself than the doctor.

"No, you are not," the doctor replied simply.

"What of Sister Therese?" Lottie whispered, realizing that wherever she was, no one but the doctors knew she was here.

"Sister Therese is an untrusting soul and would get in the way of our progress. She was already stirring up trouble with the diocese, claiming we were abusing you. Can you imagine? So while we work, it's best not to have her involved. She thinks you ran clean to Cardiff. That was your plan, wasn't it? Imagine you, in your state, stealing a horse, climbing on a horse! Oh Lord." The doctor chuckled, and Lottie cemented any doubt that she truly and utterly hated the man.

"Sister Therese is praying for you, and you are so close, I'm sure it will work wonders. Right now, my dear, you, me, and Dr. Bothelli have a very special secret. And until we have finished our therapies, and I have documented all our progress, it's us three that will keep it. Now, my dear, I have some medicine to help you sleep." The doctor stepped forward and Lottie slammed herself against the wall.

"No, no, no, no, no!" she screamed.

"Worried about the baby? I wouldn't. The baby is like to be stillborn, happens so often when the mother is under such stress." The doctor pulled a needle-pointed syringe from his pocket, and Lottie wrapped her hands around her belly. The last thing she remembered was the pain in her thigh from the needle and the growing darkness of her cage.

Nora
Boston and
Thereabouts
1901

New England Courier, *October 14, 1901*

And now the matter of the Spiritualist session with mediums Dorothy Kellings and Nora Grey. The event was held at the Old South Meeting Hall just last night, and this reporter was most honored to have been asked to attend. The evening began with the use of a tool deemed a "light box," a sort of contraption that has a flashing light at either end, used to plunge the mediums into a mesmerized state. The conversation that took place following mesmerism could have been called pedestrian and even a disappointment for an audience if it had not been for the extraordinary transformation of medium Dorothy Kellings. She appeared as a dark-haired girl similar in appearance to Miss Nora Grey.

What occurred next is beyond any reasoning: it was as though an invisible beast were tearing the room apart. This reporter witnessed firsthand deep scratches appear in the wood floor and walls, seemingly without cause. Miss Dorothy Kellings, seemingly under the control of a spirit, insisted she lived and was no specter. As the session progressed, a table was overturned and Miss Nora Grey thrown to the ground. It was as though the events of the night were centered around Miss Grey, as the moment she became unconscious, the phantom events ceased, and the energetic malignancy disappeared.

No word has been given as to future session dates

with Miss Nora Grey or Miss Dorothy Kellings, but this performance is sure to make an impact on the Spiritualist scene. Not since the Fox Sisters have we been so delighted and amazed by the psychical showings.

Nora

Nora sat in a stiff, wooden chair in the sitting room of the Shen Mansion, built in Providence's historical district back in 1790. It was technically a town house, but one that took up an entire city block and included jutting towers, a hand-laid stone façade, and an interior courtyard that had been named the "gem of New England." Days had passed since the Old South Meeting Hall event, and Dorothy had already booked Nora for twelve dates, each of which paid between $20 and $50 a session—Dorothy taking a manager's cut, of course. Karl hadn't objected; he realized he was far out of his element in these dealings. Since the séance at the Old South Meeting Hall, Nora was receiving more newspaper and radio attention than any Broadway play.

Nora sat in the North Wing of the Shen Mansion, surrounded by ladies in fine lace embroidered dresses and men in neatly tailored suits. Some were the bourgeoisie of Providence society; two were from the *Providence Tattler* and *New England Courier*, respectively. The reporter from the *Courier* was the same young, overly ambitious woman who had covered the Old South Meeting Hall event and had sealed a deal with her paper to follow Nora Grey on her first tour down the East Coast. She was positively buzzing with excitement.

Nora's job was to channel the spirits of the unfortunates who had met their end, their necks broken in different ways, in different eras throughout the Shen Mansion's history. Of course, there were others who had died on the premises, pedestrian matters such as heart attacks and choking on unchewed bits of dinner, but the focus would be on the four dead girls, all under the age of eighteen, who were said to wander the halls and scream obscenities from the North Tower.

Nora hadn't wanted this job. Her guide was unreliable. She didn't show Nora spirits or insight into the next world—in fact, Lottie Liath didn't even profess to be dead. Dorothy said it was a matter of persuasion; when she appeared, demand she do her job as a spirit guide, be firm, teach her to meet her purpose. *What if nothing happens?* Nora had asked. *It didn't matter a bit*, Dorothy said. *All they want is a show.* Then she reminded Nora that if all else failed, Nora still had a bag of tricks to fall back on: roll her eyes back in her head, rise on her toes, and appear to levitate. Everyone at the table wanted to believe, and so they would. Besides, they could always claim the elements weren't right, it was too damp or too chill, and the proprietors of the mansion would pay to have her back when the clouds had cleared or the humidity dropped. It was all bank to them, too; the grisly business of death tourism would keep lookie-looks coming back on promise alone.

Tavish had stayed quiet and said he'd wait for them at the hotel. Once he'd arranged for his daughter to give the gullible a show, and now she'd moved past him. There was something else, too—a brokenness that weighed on him. He'd grown up an orphan with nothing but the ugliest rumors of his mother, and now she was present in a way. He hadn't asked Nora anything about Lottie Liath since that night, but Nora could see the questions in his eyes. For the first time in their lives together, Nora thought he looked tired and old. There were lines around his eyes that had never appeared before. He carried himself with a resignation that made him unrecognizable as the man who left Glasgow to cross the Atlantic.

Dorothy cleared her throat, signaling that the séance would begin. The ladies and men all stirred in quiet excitement. The young journalist from the *Courier* looked as though she would launch clear off her chair in anticipation.

"We will use a light box, a modern contraption created to lull the medium into a mesmerized state. You will see a flashing light, which will be directed at Miss Grey's face. It is imperative that no one interrupt the process in any way. If you need to leave, please do so now." Dorothy paused dramatically and nodded to her assistant, Cecil, who appeared from the shadows and placed the light box before Nora.

"As Miss Grey is lowered deeper and deeper into the mesmerized state, I will guide her in an attempt to contact the spirits of the girls who died in this house. Do not interrupt or interject. Speak only if spoken to by myself or Miss Grey. Are we all understood?" She cast her gaze around the room, her practiced ferocity silencing anyone who might have even thought of speaking.

The box began to flash, slowly, rhythmically. Nora felt herself being surrounded by darkness. The oil lamps disappeared from view, and she felt as though her limbs had gone numb and her spirit grew outside her skin. She took a deep breath as the last connection to her flesh fell away and she felt as though she were floating inches above her seat. The flashing stopped, and the room became entirely black. Nora stared into the void, willing Lottie Liath to come to her. In the very far distance, she could hear Dorothy's voice, slow and steady.

"Spirits, join us, talk to us, show yourselves. Spirits, all are welcome in this space, all will be heard."

Nora felt a familiar tug and then a hand on her shoulder. She breathed out in relief. Her guide had appeared.

"Lottie, Lottie, are you here?" she asked quietly.

"I see what you see. But I am no spirit," Lottie answered, whispering in her ear. "I have passed through time and space, past pain, past all the pain, to be here. I see what you see."

Nora reached up with considerable effort and placed a hand on Lottie's phantom grip. The skin was ice cold, dead flesh, already stiff. She paused, then asked, "We have assembled to call the spirits of those who have died in this place. Can you call the spirits of the girls who died in this house?"

"I have no skill to call the dead. I'm trapped here. They locked me in this place," Lottie answered. "But I see four girls, sitting at this table. They are lost; they cannot speak."

"There is a woman in an umber dress to my right. Please raise your right hand to be level with your eyes." Nora spoke loudly, not sure how far away the figure she saw really was. Space and time were different in the realm she was in.

"The littlest of them all sits in her lap. This woman looks like her mother did in life; she wants her mother," Lottie whispered. "Such a dear little thing. She was tricked. She was told she could fly. A malignant creature, fae or goblin, lives in this house; even now it lives in the attic, waiting for those that it can whisper lies to."

"Does she tell you this? How do you know?" Nora asked as everyone sitting around the table trembled with nerves.

"What does she tell you?!" a woman burst out, her excitement barely contained.

"Quiet!" Dorothy Kellings boomed. "Do not interrupt the process." The woman shrank back, but her face was still animated.

"Lottie, who tells you these things?" Nora repeated as Lottie's image faded in and out.

"I just, I just know. No one tells me. It's just truth, it just is . . ." Lottie's voice was insubstantial and small, fading back into the shadows.

Nora spoke loudly again, addressing the woman in umber, aware that her voice was almost a shout. "The girl who sits with you wants comfort. Do you feel a weight on your lap? Wrap your arms around the girl; she wants the touch of her mother."

A loud gasp filled the space, followed by, "I feel her, I feel something, oh she smells of soap. My girl, my baby girl is back." A low sob and a rustling at the table. Nora could feel Dorothy settling down the guests.

"Spirits, give us a sign, show us you are here," Dorothy cried. Behind Nora, Lottie shuddered. Her hand tightened on Nora's shoulder, pinching her skin. A loud *clang* filled the space, and Nora felt Lottie's grip release, her own body shrinking back down to fit her flesh, the hard wood of the chair beneath her, and then the flashing of the light box again, until she opened her eyes. Cecil quietly removed the box and disappeared back to the edges of the room.

"My god! My god!" The woman in the umber dress was on her feet, pointing at the center of the room. "My child! My girl!"

The others were staring in delighted horror at a tiny object in the center of the table. The young journalist was madly scribbling in a notebook, her face awash with excitement.

"STOP!" Dorothy commanded, and the room fell quiet. She stood and reached to the center of the room, grimacing a bit as she picked up what appeared to be a gold tooth, a molar that would have been in the back of someone's mouth. "A tooth," she said simply.

"My Cara! My Cara!" the woman in the umber dress cried. "It's her tooth! Dropped by the spirits! I felt her in my arms. I held her, smelled her hair!"

A finely dressed gentleman next to the woman also stood to examine the gold tooth. "Our daughter Cara passed to the next world last spring. She was fifteen; she had a gold tooth. It was buried with her when she passed. But that . . . it looks . . ."

"A gift from the spirits," Dorothy said with authority.

Later, Karl helped the women and men file out of the room. The journalist recording the answers to her many questions was the last to leave. Nora looked to Dorothy, who sat next to her at the now empty table.

"Whose tooth is that?" Nora asked.

"Cecil's," Dorothy said. "Don't worry, he won't miss it. I'll buy him another after our next session in Charleston."

"I'll not have it. I won't be a fraud anymore. The girl was here. Lottie told me she sat in the woman's lap. It wasn't a fifteen-year-old, though. It was a child, the child who died in the tower." Nora rubbed her temples.

"That's fantastic. And I know it's just who you were supposed to contact, but that woman? Her husband is a surgeon, a well-known one at that. They've spent more money trying to contact their deceased daughter than we'll ever earn in a lifetime. We were able to give them something they will never forget. You know they paid an extra $10 before they left? Not to mention the word of mouth. I expect we will book five more sessions just off tonight's performance."

Nora locked eyes with Dorothy. What once intimidated her now just infuriated her. "I said I won't have it. I'll not play the fraud. It happens again and I'm out."

"The world itself is a fraud. We are ghosts moving through a landscape that is more nightmare than heaven. None of what we see every day is real, none of what we suffer is real. It's a construct. Everything we love is already lost to us. The sooner you realize that truth, the happier you will be and the sooner you'll let go of this noble idea of honesty. Everyone lies. Do you know that woman, the one with the lost daughter, all the grief, all those tears? That fine woman was in the papers two years before her daughter passed because their housekeeper had gone missing. She said the woman had run off with a man, and no one thought twice about it until a neighbor's dog dug up a body in the backyard. Turns out the housekeeper had been performing some, well, additional duties, and the lady of the house grew tired of it. No one was ever charged, no one cared about another immigrant dying. So before you feel too terribly guilty about that woman and the notion of truth, just remember that the housekeeper was someone's daughter, too."

"It's not my place to pass judgement, and I'll not justify it by saying she had it coming. I'm done pandering in gossip and stories." Nora looked at Dorothy in shock.

"Gossip? Stories? It's the truth. Cecil does research on all the guests of all the sessions well in advance. I do not like to be surprised." She paused and looked at Nora for a long moment. "You are going to be so successful, and in turn, you will give me a new life."

"Always what I can do for you, isn't it? I'm surprised you and my father don't get on better than you do," Nora said, an edge to her voice.

"Sometimes I forget you have only recently joined the civilized world. Calm yourself. We're done here. Let's have a drink." Dorothy stalked out of the room, leaving Nora fuming.

The guests gone, Nora walked to the carriage with Karl.

"Just a moment please," Nora said quietly and walked past the carriage to the entrance to the grand garden that surrounded the mansion. She stared out at the darkness, spiny outlines of the roses stark against the moonlight. *Everyone we love is already lost to us.* Dorothy's words rang in her ears. Perhaps the Sunbird was right, and there was no point in anything beyond the most basic and immediate happiness. But perhaps there was a place beyond all this, a world where her life was hers entire. She could walk away from Dorothy Kellings. There would be uproar and angry men, but Nora hardly cared about that. Yet she knew there was something she needed to accomplish before she did. She had no idea where she would go if she walked now: her path was still clouded, and Lottie Liath had more to say. Somewhere out there was the answer that Nora wanted; until she was sure of it, she would stay, just a little longer.

She turned and walked back to the carriage where Karl waited. He regarded her quietly. "There's a mention of you in the *New York Times*," he said as he helped her into the carriage. "It seems Miss Kellings has finally found her true talent."

Nora

Charleston blurred with Jersey City, and then Norfolk and Baltimore and New Hope. They would take a train to the station, where they were met by carriage or the occasional motorcar. The hotels became increasingly nicer, until Nora stopped catching her breath at the ornate chandeliers and hotel lounges. The sessions were held in old churches, country houses, a funeral parlor in Brunswick, and an old orphanage in Middlebury. It wasn't until the days had turned into weeks, and then half a year had disappeared entirely, that Nora found herself at the House of the Seven Gables in Salem. They'd taken a water ferry from Boston Harbor, and Nora had found herself wishing the boat were back out to sea, heading to Bell Island and away from the chaos her life had become.

Their hosts were the Salem Historical Society, who could scarcely afford the fee that Dorothy was negotiating for Nora's appearances. Karl now had an entourage of researchers from the International Psychical Society accompanying him, and a couple of gentlemen who hailed from the Order of St. Cyprian. They had hoped Nora would finally accomplish what other mediums had not; they had hoped to see regeneration, manifestation of the dead to the living. They had been disappointed in their pursuits but fascinated by Nora's communication with Lottie. The scrutiny of the sessions on the part of the Order members had become so intense that Dorothy had been forced to abandon her cheap parlour tricks. She still passed on Cecil's briefings about who Nora's guests were and what grief, hopes, prayers they carried with them. Nora tolerated it only because she knew how unnecessary it was.

Lottie was with Nora nearly every minute of every day now. All the months before, she had to be called, and even then there was not always an appearance. Now Nora felt Lottie's presence constantly. Her breath had become ragged, her spirit appearance faint, but her presence was strong. She no longer insisted she wasn't a spirit but begged Nora to allow her to die. Nora did not tell Dorothy of these visits. Dorothy would have found a way to monetize it, and Nora couldn't bring herself to sell the spirit's pain for profit. Instead she tried to comfort Lottie. *You are already dead*, she said, *you can move past this*, secretly hoping she might. Without a spirit guide, Nora was just another girl with a talent for the seer cards. But still the spirit remained, and the answer that Nora sought was still just out of her grasp. Every appearance, every night spent before the light box and the fascinated masses, Nora could feel it just beyond her fingertips. There was an end to this, just a breath away, and she had to keep going until she knew what all this meant, what torment kept Lottie from passing through to whatever came next. There was another part of her that she could not deny, perhaps shameful—a part that loved the wonder in the faces of the dazed onlookers. She had spent her entire life invisible, and she would be happy to do so again soon enough. But for now, it was a relief to be seen. The girl who had spent her first seventeen years in a sort of half-life, as a spirit of her own making, was now a phenom in her own right—not a Sunbird, something far grander. It was a bit like the waves on the Atlantic, crashing toward shore and then collapsing into foam. She wanted to see what came of it all, and then she could walk away. That girl could return to the quiet life she'd found for a short time far out in the sea, away from the noise of the city. She could go back to being invisible and never doubt what she was capable of ever again.

Tavish helped her off the ferry. He looked ragged as well. He'd taken to drinking far too much, but unlike the old days when the drink turned to either rage or celebration, he would just grow quiet. Ever since the appearance of Lottie, he had curled inward.

"I never had a dream of my mother, not a one. I never felt her spirit, nothing. I was alone my whole life until I met your mother," he told Nora. He didn't outright say it, but Nora knew he felt cheated; it was his mother who guided Nora's visions, and never once had she reached out to him. He passed it off by playing the skeptic; he scoffed at Dorothy's theatrics and pretended not to see Cecil and his deception. They were other versions of himself, after all. The game they played in America was one he had mastered in Scotland, only they were able to keep Nora in fine clothes and fancy hotels.

"Miss Grey! A delight, just a delight!" A slender woman in a practical dress met them at the dock. "We have a carriage for you. You will be my honored guests at the Nurse House, very close to the sight of the séance."

Nora nodded and shook the woman's hand. At her shoulder, Lottie's breath was labored and had a sour smell to it. "Thank you. You've met my father, Tavish Grey?" The woman extended her hand and exchanged niceties as Nora watched Dorothy fuss at the porters over the bags. Dorothy was reveling in this new life. She took a healthy cut of every session, and Nora knew she would not live on the road for much longer. She would soon have enough money to buy a house in New York

City, and her reputation as the elite manager of the Fantastical Medium Nora Grey would carry her for years. Nora found herself looking forward to that day. Dorothy was a creature of opportunity, and while Nora could see through the crusted exterior now, she knew that Dorothy held no loyalties to anyone but herself. She had seen Nora as a means to an end. Her career had been waning, and now it was solely hers—she owed no one.

"We have a dinner prepared for you at Nurse House. Come right this way to the carriage." The woman, who introduced herself as Mattie Wardwell, hustled them along and out of the chill wind. Once everyone was seated and the carriage in motion, she smiled, which made her face only look thinner and more sticklike. "The Nurse House once belonged to the daughter of the accused witch Rebecca Nurse. Mary Elizabeth Nurse lived there with her husband and children, and the house stayed in the Nurse family clear to the present day, where it is overseen by the Historical Society," Mattie said proudly.

"Fascinating," Dorothy said. "We will have privacy once we arrive?" It was less question and more demand.

Mattie looked taken aback but recovered quickly. "Of course. The second floor is entirely yours. Dinner is ready and waiting. We will leave you to prepare and fetch you for tomorrow night's session. I know the Historical Society would love to host you for breakfast or perhaps a tour of . . ."

"Miss Grey needs to rest and prepare." Dorothy cut her off, and Nora felt a stab of anger about the crestfallen look she saw on Mattie Wardwell's face. In her ear, Lottie grumbled and muttered, her voice faint. *Almost time, almost time, almost time*, she repeated. Nora tried to ignore the sound. Lottie didn't make any sense when she was like this. When a session started, and Cecil turned the light box on, Lottie became more coherent, focused, her presence stronger. In the times between sessions, she cried quietly, asked for it to end, talked of the cold, of a doctor, of pain and blood. Nora was exhausted from the telling of it all. It was pain on an endless loop, and she was power-less to help her grandmother avoid whatever fate she had already met, powerless to help Lottie accept the bizarre present in which they both found themselves. Nora could feel the wave reaching the shore; it could not hold for much longer. Lottie could not bear much more, and Nora could not carry the burden of know-ing much longer. Even in the moments when Lottie's voice qui-eted, Nora still heard her whimpers of misery and pain echoing in her ears.

Nurse House was a simple and solid farmhouse on the edge of the old town area. The House of the Seven Gables was within walking distance, but Nora knew Dorothy would insist on a carriage and fuss over every detail as though she were in New York City and not a hamlet outside of Boston. Nora picked at her dinner and tried to ignore Dorothy's chatter as she went over the details of the session with Karl. They became so engrossed in their discussion and the arrangement of the room and lighting that they didn't even notice Nora slip away from the table. Tavish looked up, though, and she lifted a finger to her lips, nodding to him as she quietly exited the dining room.

Outside, the night was chill. It would be the new year soon, and the wind was as cold as it would ever be, whipping around the edges of the farmhouse. Nora had grabbed a thick wool cloak as she went out, and now she wrapped it around herself, aware she looked the part of a Salem witch even as she prepared to perform as one. Lottie hung at her shoulder, making a wheezing sort of breath. She hadn't spoken since the dock, but her breath had been labored, and Nora could feel misery rolling off her in waves. Nora came to a bench under a low branched tree, and she sat, enjoying her anonymity, the knowledge that no one knew where she was and no one could interrupt.

"Lottie?" Nora spoke quietly even though the walking path and the streets were empty. "Lottie?" she repeated.

The wheezing sound turned to a rasp in response.

"Lottie? Can you speak? Can you show yourself?" Nora asked. The wind picked up a pile of fallen leaves and blew them into a cyclone. The air felt positively frozen, and Nora could smell the snow hiding in the clouds. "Lottie, I need to see you, to speak to you." In response, there was a low moan in her ear and a faint pressure of fingertips on her arm. "Can you show yourself?" Nora pleaded.

Next to her, a filmy figure began to materialize, Nora could see matted and filthy black hair, a torn and dirty white shift, a belly bulging huge and swollen. Lottie's face was gaunt, her cheekbones poking through her skin. When she'd appeared before, Nora had not seen this version of her, a phantom pregnancy, suffering even as she dwelt in a place that should have been immune to pain.

"What's happened to you?" Nora whispered, a lump forming in her throat at the wretched state of her grandmother.

"Any day now, that's what Dr. Toad and Hog says, any day now." Her voice was so faint, it was scarcely more than a current of air that whistled past Nora's ears.

"Who is Dr. Toad and Hog?" Nora asked, struggling to keep her voice steady, grief forming a fissure in her throat as she spoke. Even in this state, Lottie had a biting sort of wit.

"Soekan. Dr. Soekan, he keeps me here, all locked away. The sisters think I ran, they think I'm gone, but I'm here, here, here, hidden away by Toad and Hog. The sisters were so good to me. They protected me as long as they could. Sister Therese was going to help me to keep the baby, at least for a time, until I could be freed, she is so kind . . ." Lottie's spirit form leaned against Nora's shoulder.

"Lottie? I don't want to do this anymore," Nora whispered. "I want to go home."

The spirit looked up at her, the eyes vacant spaces, as substantial as mist. "Glasgow. Not Wales. Wales is not home. I fear

I will be trapped in Argoll Downs for all eternity. Are you afraid of dying?" Her voice danced around Nora, ebbing and dipping like a fall leaf.

"Yes. Lottie, you do not have to stay in Argoll Downs. You can go home to Glasgow or anywhere you like. You are not bound to this world any longer." Nora spoke carefully, aware that she was giving her guide permission to leave, to render her utterly ordinary.

"You say such things as though I can master concrete and steel. I am trapped here, you are a dream in a dream, and I spend so much of my time trying to sleep away this life. They wake me and run their experiments, and then I sleep. I would welcome death if it took me now, but the baby . . . the baby needs to go home to Glasgow, maybe my Da is still alive, maybe it would be different for the baby there. I think it's a boy, I think I saw him grown . . ."

Nora watched as the figure disappeared completely and then, like a light catches the dust, reappear in a barely visible shadow. "It is a boy. You named him Tavish. He grows up in Glasgow. He goes home."

"He's all I have." The words hung in Nora's ears and then sailed away on the wind. The figure dissipated, and Nora was left alone. She knew Lottie would return; the near-constant presence of her guide had just gone dormant for a few hours; it happened every day, almost as though the spirit slept. Nora shivered and pulled her cloak around her, the winter wind whipping through the lane. She stood, stepped out into the walking path, and headed back to Nurse House.

Tavish was standing on the steps, bracing himself against the cold. As Nora approached, he shifted his gaze from the night sky to look at her. His eyes conveyed a weariness that Nora had never seen in him before.

"By the time those two had noticed yeh'd snuck off, they'd planned the next six months of yer life, I swear. I always knew

I wasn't treatin' yeh right, back home. I knew it. I thought at the time, yeh were young, yeh'd be fine, it was all we had to keep ourselves out the streets." He paused and looked down at Nora, deep rivets around his eyes. "If I was ever close to the likes of them, I need to say I'm sorry. I didn't realize."

Nora pulled the cloak around herself, let his words sit in the silent, frigid air that lay between them.

"Da, we're better fed than we've ever been. I'm wearing the finest dresses. The places we sleep, oh lord, I would never have imagined such a place in all my life back in Scotland, even with the Connells. It's not so bad, and it's not your fault. I don't have to do this any longer than I want, and I think it might come to an end sometime soon . . ." Nora trailed off, the image of the pregnant and suffering Lottie haunting her.

"Before it ends." Tavish's voice was low and uncertain. "Before that, I've been too afraid to ask. My mother, all I knew was the ugliness whispered by the monsters at the children's home. I . . . I don't know exactly what I'm asking . . ."

"She can't see much of anything when she comes through. It's like looking through a tunnel. But she's seen you. She knows who you are. She's confused, though; she thinks she's alive still, and I'm the ghost." Nora spoke cautiously, choosing her words one at a time. "The baby is all she cares about. She wants the baby to go to Glasgow, and she hates Wales with a passion." Nora looked into Tavish's dark eyes, which held tears in the corners. "She sees you, but for her, you're not born yet; she spends all her days worrying."

Tavish swallowed hard, tears escaping down his rough cheek. "The stories they told me, you wouldn't believe the stories. She was a night girl, they told me. I was a bastard, she was insane and tried to drink a gallon of lye to abort me; she had a dozen more like me, bastards strewn all over the moors."

Nora shook her head and clasped Tavish's frozen hands. "No, no, no. All that is rubbish. She loved you; she wanted a life with you more than the stars themselves. She's lost now, trapped by men I can't see, can't hear. All she speaks of is you. She wants you in Glasgow; she mentioned family, her father and mother. She didn't want you to go to the orphanage. You're no bastard; you were loved, are loved. She says you're all she has."

Tavish looked up, his face twisted in grief. "I used to pretend she was a great lady in Wales, maybe the daughter of a lord who'd had to give her baby away against her will. Someday, a fine lady and gentleman would ride up to the gates and demand that I be returned to them, and all the monsters who lived behind those walls would have to watch me walk away; they'd see I had a real family. I knew it was rubbish even when I was young, but it kept me going."

"She was no daughter of a lord, but Lottie Liath was a lady. She fought for her friends, she fought to keep you safe. She was fearless and better than those who are keeping her wherever she is. Your blood is strong." Nora allowed herself to sink into Tavish's arm that wrapped around her shoulder, and for a minute it was easy to forget all the minutiae that had led them both to this place.

"Let's go in. No use in catching the grippe out here in the cold." Tavish turned and opened the door, and Nora followed, steadying herself against whatever might come.

Lottie
Argoll Asylum
1866

*(Note: Shot on location on Argoll Downs; base
camp was the ruin of what used to be Argoll Sanitorium and Asylum, in operation from 1841 to 1899.
Licensing and filming permissions available upon request.)*

*Trevor Makalmany: Do we have a show for you
tonight! We are here, on location in Wales, just a few
hours outside of Cardiff in a bit of wilderness that
makes you feel as though you are a million miles from
everywhere.*

*I am standing on what used to be Argoll Asylum.
Opened with the support of the Catholic Church in
1841, it served as a sort of nineteenth-century psych
ward for the court system as it existed in the day. Patients were assigned to Argoll Asylum if the presiding
judge deemed them mentally feeble, unstable, or not
fit for the regular prison climate. This was, as you can
imagine, a somewhat subjective sort of test.*

*While there are reports of male prisoners—or pa-
tients, if you prefer—residing at Argoll Asylum, by the
winter of 1866 the population was entirely women.
The scandal that occurred in early 1867 sealed Argoll's
fate, and while it remained in operation for another
thirty-two years, it was converted to a women's refuge and served as a sort of early rehabilitation center
under the direction of a group of nuns from the Order*

of the Blessed Rose. The head of the reinvented Argoll Asylum was a nun by the name of Sister Therese Magdalene Alfonsius, a hero figure for early suffragettes, as well as a champion of the poor and impoverished.

Lottie

Lottie drifted in and out of consciousness. In her dreams she was living in Glasgow, and her grandmum was still alive, but she wasn't a child; she was as she was today, baby and all. Grandmum made her bone broth and sat her in the good rocker by the fireplace. They talked for hours, although to Lottie's frustration, she could never remember the words when she awoke. Elis was at work, somewhere in Glasgow, a nameless and faceless job where he was safe and alive. Lottie clung to sleep when she felt herself drifting up toward the surface. But always she was pulled back into the stark day, the cold of the basement cell, the cot, the sheet, the blanket, the bucket. Lottie counted the items over and over, and then she'd count the number of stones on the floor and in each row on the wall. She counted and counted until she could sleep again. Dr. Bothelli brought trays of food that Lottie ignored until hunger or thirst overcame her. Sometimes he brought fresh linen. He lingered in the doorway, unspoken words on his lips. Lottie hated him only a pence less than Toad and Hog. There was something that bound him to that devil, and she could not figure the sort of cowardice that ruled him. Before Soekan had arrived, Bothelli had been a different man, and now he was no more than a lackey. She wondered with grim humor how the grand fellows at his fancy universities would regard him now. She knew what Sister Mary would say. She could feel her skin retreating back, growing tighter, a frame for her bones that stuck out at peculiar angles. Only her belly grew, and the baby, despite Dr. Soekan's repeated assurance that it would be stillborn, kicked and fought, as though it knew it were entering hell on earth.

Lottie was trying to claw her way back to sleep when Dr. Soekan entered the cell. The doctor was carrying a small pail and a rag, which he set at Lottie's feet.

"There you go. Wash up. Time for your therapies."

At least once a day, the doctor interrupted her malaise for therapies—the silver orb, the box that ran electricity through her fingertips and shot pain through her veins. A command to move a cup or a flower. Lottie had learned early on that it was the only time she was like to have anything pleasant—a mug of tea, a blanket—so she would refuse until they offered a bribe. This time, though, Lottie reached for the rag and pail and wiped the grime from her face and arms. She could smell herself and longed for the too-hot baths that Sister Mary was fond of. The idea of the dirt and stench rinsing from her hair, her skin clean and soft again. Lottie sighed. No bath, just a pail of freezing water and Dr. Soekan staring at her impatiently.

"I'd do better with a cup of tea," Lottie said, as she wiped the exposed skin on her calves. "And a clean dress and another blanket."

"Let's just see how you do today, Lottie," Dr. Soekan said in a paternal voice that made Lottie's skin crawl. He took the pail and rag and set them outside the door. "Come with us."

The doctor pulled Lottie to her feet and down the basement hall to the next room, where there were three chairs and a small table set up. The first time they had transported her here, Lottie had screamed her throat raw, but she'd soon learned they were deep enough under the asylum that no one would ever hear her, and the screaming was all for her own benefit. Still she screamed sometimes, on the off chance Sister Therese was near or maybe the cook had been made to go to the root cellar. She screamed sometimes just to hear her own voice, because it was something the doctors hated, and something she could still do even if her throat ached after.

This time, though, she did not scream. She just limped along beside the doctor and allowed him to sit her at a chair opposite them. A hot mug of tea was set before her, and Lottie saw there was a teapot and a plate of lemon cookies behind the doctor. She gasped with surprise.

"Treats to those who cooperate. It's all we want from you, my dear," Dr. Soekan said in a slow, careful voice as though Lottie were a petulant child. "Today, I'd like you to tell me what you see when you are in the mesmerized state. I will be asking you questions, and I want you to try to answer: what you see, maybe smell, touch, if there is anyone with you. No detail is too small."

"How long have I been here?" Lottie asked.

"How long since you tried to kill yourself by running into a storm without a coat or proper shoes or any way of seeking relief?" Dr. Soekan said steadily, never breaking his gaze at Lottie. "Is that what you mean?"

Lottie swallowed the answer she wanted to give. "Yes," she muttered.

"It's been three weeks, give or take. You have been to this room many times, and we have seen such marvelous sights. You are advancing the science of mesmerism more than you will ever appreciate. And now that you are safe, and we are un-interrupted, we can truly do the work that will change the way we see the mind." Dr. Soekan cocked his head, regarding Lottie. "Go ahead, have some tea." She reached with shaking hands and sipped, the warmth flooding her throat and straight to her stomach. The baby kicked and twirled in response.

"Where is Dr. Bothelli? Don't you need your *giolla* for your 'studies'? Or is he starting to see what a monster you actually are?" Lottie kept her voice steady, her words venom.

"My *giolla*? I'm afraid I'm not familiar with your quaint Scottishisms, my dear. Dr. Bothelli will join us shortly. He was needed upstairs for a bit; after all, he has an asylum to run. Do not worry, my dear." Dr. Soekan's eyes belied his simple response. Lottie suspected that Dr. Bothelli had more objections than his mentor would like. He had lingered the last few nights he had brought her meals, and she could see the distress in his eyes mixed with fear, but of what? Surely Dr. Toad and Hog was not so powerful that he could undermine Dr. Bothelli's life the way he had hers. But maybe he was; perhaps that was what kept Bothelli from acting on the hesitation that emanated from his fingertips as he slipped her an extra blanket or the mug of cider he'd delivered with last night's meager supper.

"*Giolla* means lackey, servant, serving boy. He's not entirely sold on your experiments, is he? In fact, I haven't seen him en-tirely comfortable since you started bruising and burning me in the name of science, and now . . . he might turn on you entirely, might he? What would the sisters say to that?" Lottie sipped her tea, her hands shaking with a combination of fear and anger.

"Lottie, we wish you no harm, but the opportunity to study one under duress and truly measure how stress, strain, mental despair can create a sort of physical presence is groundbreak-ing. You have demonstrated an incredible psychical gift which I doubt you ever knew you had. We are helping you to awaken. You will help so many. If we can only understand the root of pain and suffering, we can learn how to manipulate the mind, how to use mesmerism to heal any condition under the sun. Dr. Bothelli will be known far and wide once we've published in America. Once our study appears in the *New England Journal of Medicine*, Dr. Bothelli can write his own future. He is far from a serving boy. I am going to make him a household name, and you will be the reason. Do you have any concept of how important this work is, Lottie? You are changing the very fabric of the medical world." He sat back and looked proud of himself.

"And when you're done with your experiments? When you've discovered all you wanted to know?" Lottie whispered, clutching the mug.

"Do you know who Dr. William Morton is, my dear? Of course, you do not." Dr. Soekan's voice was that of a father reading a bedtime story to a toddler. "Not that long ago—1846, in fact—Dr. Morton made history by using ether to anesthetize a surgical patient. Can you imagine the horror of surgery before Dr. Morton's advances? The pain? The idea that you could feel the blade cutting your skin, the agony of every stitch, every nerve on high alert to what was coming next?" Dr. Soekan's face was animated, and he stared at a point far beyond Lottie's head as he spoke, lost in his own thoughts. Lottie set the mug down, her hands shaking too much to hold it steady. Dr. Soekan continued. "Do you know what he had to do to get to that miracle? Every medical advance comes at a price. In you we will learn how to manipulate pain, suffering, disease with the power of our minds. You will make Dr. Morton's advances look like a child's toy. Do you realize how important this work is? I assure you that Dr. Bothelli does, no matter how soft-hearted he may be. He is young, and he does not always understand that great work such as ours is never without sacrifice." Dr. Soekan leaned forward, his eyes imploring.

"What happens to me? To my child?" Lottie whispered. "Are we to be the sacrifice?"

Dr. Soekan pursed his lips and gave Lottie a small, sad shake of the head. "Always jumping to the worst conclusion, even when there are so many good things to be had right here. Now Lottie, we should begin, and there might be a treat at the end."

Lottie swallowed the chill in her throat and did as she was told.

Lottie

"Alright, Lottie, watch the orb, and let's count backward. I want you to remember that you need to listen to my voice, you need to hear me and respond. I want to know what you see, what you feel, I want to know where you go. Ten, nine, eight . . ."

Lottie felt the tug into the blackness. She was accustomed to ignoring Dr. Toad and Hog entirely, but this time she tried to keep him more present even as she felt herself pulled into another parlor, candlelight and dark wood as they always were, but this was a room Lottie had never been in. It had a claustrophobic feel, and she hated it immediately.

"What do you see, Lottie, what do you see?" The man's voice echoed around the chamber, and Lottie wished she could tune him out, ignore him entirely, but she needed to survive a bit longer. She needed time, so she would try.

"I see, I see . . . ," she murmured, and as she hovered in the room, figures appeared as though they'd always been there—Nora Grey and others, the fire-haired woman and a man with skin so pale he looked more ghost than man. She'd seen all of them in dreams, in and out of consciousness over the last weeks, new rooms and new crowds each time. Sometimes Lottie could only whisper in Nora's ear; sometimes she saw others the way she'd seen Blessed Moons; sometimes it was nothing at all, and all she could do was hover in the space, watching Nora and praying against all that was probable for relief. But this time, this time, she saw four little girls all crowded around a woman in an umber-colored dress. Their skin had a grayish tint, their eyes were voids. Lottie knew they were spirits, and had been for so very long.

"What do you see, Lottie?" The doctor's voice echoed. She realized with a jolt that Nora asked her the same thing; her voice was tinny, distant, the result of Lottie staying on the edge of the vision. How she longed to immerse herself, to feel as though she were in this time, this place.

"They've trapped me here. I'm lost, lost, lost." Lottie reached for Nora, whose face twitched, and she knew that the girl had heard her. Maybe the doctors had, too. "I have no skill to call the dead. I'm trapped here. They locked me in this place. But I see four girls, sitting at this table. They are lost; they cannot speak." Lottie watched the children and saw their lives play out before her. Two had died as children; the others were older when they passed but stayed as little girls in this realm. They were angry and lost. One little girl thought the woman in the umber dress was her mother; her mannerisms, maybe her hair or her eyes or anything at all, had sparked something in the spirit. Lottie smiled despite herself.

"Such a dear little thing. She was tricked, she was told she could fly, a malignant creature, fae or goblin, lives in this house; even now it lives in the attic, waiting for those that it can whisper lies to." Lottie watched as the little girl climbed into the woman in the umber dress's lap. The woman remained quite unaware, sitting riveted as Nora looked to Lottie.

"Lottie, what do you see? Describe where you are." The doctor's voice distracted Lottie, and she felt she was drifting in two halves, one in the parlor with the little dead girls, another in the cell-like basement of Argoll Asylum. She disassociated, each half answering the questions asked of it. Put together whole, she'd never remember entirely.

"She wants her mother to hold her," Lottie whispered furtively in Nora's ear before she felt the tug and was thrust backward, flying through the darkness, all the way back to the horrible room and her captors. Lottie opened her eyes and released a long-held breath. She felt weary, her arms heavy, her head pounded.

"Excellent work, my dear." Dr. Soekan had a grin on his face. It made him look more devil than man, and Lottie wished for the strength to lift the mug of now-cool tea and throw it.

Dr. Bothelli now sat across from her next to his mentor. Lottie was confused. When had he entered the room? How long had she been in a mesmerized state? "You said you were in a parlor. Do you know where?" Dr. Bothelli interjected, writing in his notebook.

Lottie looked at him imploringly, begging him to see past Dr. Toad and Hog and become the man she had first met at Argoll—imperfect, pompous yes, but also good intentioned, kind-hearted. He met her gaze and looked back to Dr. Toad and Hog, conflicted, but not nearly so much as to override his loyalty to his mentor. "I have no idea." Lottie sighed. "I never know where I am when I see the things I see. I told you already, I see a girl. Her name is Nora. I don't know where, when, how she is. She might be a figment of my imagination. I think she is my blood, my kin, but I do not know how that is possible. Sometimes I can see my child, grown into a man. I think I see him. I think these things, and I think I may be going mad." She started shaking, tears rolling down her cheeks. Dr. Soekan reached across the table and patted her hand. Lottie pulled it back, revolted at his touch.

"My dear, time is bendable, it is breakable, it is a thing much like this scarf." He pulled the wool scarf from his neck, and

Lottie had a flash of how the strong and healthy version of herself would have strangled him to death with it. Dr. Soekan, unaware of this urge, continued. "We are here." He held the scarf out straight and indicated a bit of the checkered pattern. "And we are here." He nodded to another spot a ways away. "We are in all places at all times. The beauty of this science and why you are so important is that you can help us navigate the mind, and in learning to understand our minds, we can travel within time. You already do it. It's a miracle by any definition, and we are working to make your miracle a reality for all. Don't you see how important you are, Lottie?" Dr. Toad and Hog's face was alight with excitement.

Lottie fought back the words she wanted to say and pointed at the cookies behind the doctors. "Can I have those now?"

Later, as Lottie lay on her cot staring at the crack of moonlight that filtered through the slit of a window, she allowed herself to fall back into the darkness, to feel herself descending through time, through worlds. She suspected that all the things she saw in her mesmerized states were out of order, dots jumbled in a cup, poured out like a child's jacks. She had seen Nora Grey look so adult-like, so coifed and mature. She had seen her as a child, thin and suffering. Why she saw her out of order, or at all, was a mystery, but she knew the young woman who carried her blood was like to be her child's only hope.

As she fell into sleep, she found herself in a dream. She sat with Nora Grey on a park bench. It was night, and the snow fell around them, catching the moonlight. She was cold, but the warmth of Nora's shoulder and arm wrapped around her warmed her through and through. Nora's sweet voice echoed through her, soothing her. Lottie could feel her strength draining from her body. She didn't have the time she needed to make things right; if only she could stay in a dream all her days, if only.

Nora
Boston and
Thereabouts
1901

Salem Tattler, *December 1901: Excerpt from the Local Dear Agatha Advice Column for Ladies*

Dear Agatha,
I am writing to raise a call for action in our community. Recent events have proven that there are forces afoot who seek to undermine the Christian community we have all struggled to build here on auspicious ground. Our forefathers claimed this land as a refuge for Christian souls, and it seems that there are outsiders hellbent on turning Salem into another Rochester, or perhaps New York City.

The recent events at the House of Seven Gables have been splashed around in newspapers and journals spreading as far as Los Angeles, California. I ask you, what can be done to protect our community from this sort of unwanted scrutiny? We already struggle under the yoke of our past, and much discussion in Christian meeting groups has occurred over what good would be done for our children and young families if we were to stop glorifying our bloody past and close the museums and stop catering to the grisly tourist trade that our town attracts.

Recent events at the House of Seven Gables have already been responsible for an uptick in visitors hoping to get a glimpse at the scene of the crime, hoping just to stand in the room where such atrocities were said to occur. Every penny we ac-

cept from these ghouls is support for charlatans and fraud doers and will encourage more of the type to enter our doors. I say we close our docks and refuse to serve anyone who is here on the ghastly business of worshipping Nora Grey or any of her kind.

Perhaps we can work together to pass a measure and save our town and, along with it, our souls.

Sincerely,
Aghast in Andover

Nora

The House of Seven Gables was humming with energy by the time Nora and her entourage arrived for the session. The local Salem residents had braved the cold and were crowded outside for a glimpse of Nora as she exited the carriage and entered the house. Karl had, of course, made sure there was press invited, and they waited in the doorway, respectful and wary. The young woman from the *New England Courier* had been with Nora through the entire tour, and she felt like she should know more about the young woman than she did. But the journalist kept to herself for the most part, stayed a respectful distance from Nora, and wrote absolutely glowing reports of the séances and sessions. Karl considered her a model member of the press. In addition to the *New England Courier*, the *Salem Tattler*, *Boston Globe*, and *New York Post* were present. Guests had paid five dollars a head for the privilege of attending the session and were inside being briefed by Cecil, who Nora had grown to tolerate if not particularly warm up to.

The house had an old-world sort of charm that was born in simplicity. Nora could tell that Dorothy hated it immediately.

It was not ostentatious, and its history was not particularly macabre. Dorothy favored locations like the Shen Mansion, where the history spoke for itself and, no matter what occurred, the guests were like to see shadows jumping at them from the corners on their own, no help from Nora required. But the House of Seven Gables? Apart from what Dorothy considered an inordinate sort of pride that Nathaniel Hawthorne had visited the premises often, the house was rather benign as far as old spaces went. Nothing particularly dramatic had happened in its walls, and despite the grisly history of the town, the house stood near the town center, an unimposing presence, quiet even.

Nora liked it immediately. The loud, active spaces like the Shen Mansion were deafening when she was in a trance state. The more she became accustomed to the light box and the weight of the hypnotism, the more spirits had begun to surround her when she was in a trance. The last session before Salem had been at what used to be a flu ward in a closed sanitarium in Ithaca. Nora had been left with a headache that lasted three days after the session, the echoes of the lost and dying screaming in her ears. Lottie had sat across from her in her spirit form, her eyes sad and full of knowledge. Not much had occurred at the session, in truth. Candlesticks had moved across the table, a chair overturned, but still it was hailed a triumph by the *New England Courier*, Nora's biggest fan.

Nora knew Dorothy was banking on a bigger showing tonight and suspected Cecil had planted some of his nefarious tricks in the room. Nora hated the trickery and was always relieved when Cecil's talents were not needed, but she also understood that this was a business, a performance, and tickets wouldn't sell for long if all the audience saw was an overturned chair. She had an odd feeling about tonight, though. As suspected, Lottie's dragging and anguished presence had returned hours after she had disappeared in the snow on their first night in Salem. But she hadn't spoken, and her breath was uneven. Nora couldn't see her physically, but her mind's eye had a clear vision of her wan face, her swollen belly; she felt the pain of the occasional but not regular contractions that racked Lottie's spirit form, the nausea, the fear. Nora wondered how much her guide had left in her. Dorothy was unconcerned. When she had been the medium of the night, she had operated with several spirit guides and felt that another would appear in time if Lottie disappeared. Nora wasn't as positive; her talents were less skill and more a connection. Once that connection was broken, perhaps Nora would go back to simply being a girl with a set of seer cards. Nora wondered if she would miss this life she had cobbled together with the Scarlet Sunbird or be glad for the quiet.

"Miss Grey!" Mattie Wardwell met them as they exited the carriage and ushered them past the crowd, who reached out to Nora as she passed. She took the hand of a little girl who was so wrapped up in woolen cloaks she was more bear than child. The girl looked up, two large and astonished eyes beneath the layers of cloth. Mattie Wardwell patted the girl's shoulder. "Come, Ellie, let the good lady pass. She's quite busy tonight." The child smiled and ducked back into the crowd. Nora looked up and suddenly felt a rush of air around her. Lottie's breath was at her neck, and the world was spinning. She stumbled backward and was caught by Tavish, who steadied her and kept his hands firmly on her shoulders.

"Let's get her inside. This chill will do us all in," he grumbled to Mattie Wardwell, who hurried the group past the crowd and into the house. Nora felt as though her knees had turned to jelly. She sat on a hard wooden bench that lined the entryway as soon as the door shut. A pain shot through her stomach, and she doubled over.

"Nora? What's wrong?" Tavish knelt down as Dorothy hurried the guests and members of the press into the next room.

Karl's face appeared next to Tavish, his pale skin mottled with the cold.

"I don't know, I just feel out of sorts," Nora said quietly as the pain subsided and the nausea passed.

"We need to call this off; she's not well." Tavish stood and indicated to Dorothy, who had just reentered the room.

"Out of the question. A reporter from the *Washington Post* is here. He's a skeptic who worked with Houdini, and if we impress him, none of us will ever need to muscle through anything again, but tonight? There will be a showing." Dorothy's tone was inarguable. She sat next to Nora. "Is your guide present?" Nora nodded. "Then use it," Dorothy said with authority, taking Nora's hand. "Use whatever you're feeling. Tell a story with it."

Nora nodded. "I'm fine. Let's get started. Sooner we start, the sooner we'll be done."

With Tavish at her elbow, Nora stood. She was filled with a sort of grim inevitability, as though a cycle were coming to a close.

Nora

The séance was to be held in what had once been the formal dining room. Dark wood floors with an elaborate throw rug accented the meticulously restored molding and carefully chosen drapes. A large oblong table fit easily into the space, even leaving room for a comfortable chair and ottoman by a fireplace, which was lit at Dorothy's request. The room was warm, and Nora felt the ice thawing from the tips of her fingers and ears as she entered the space. The guests were already seated and watched her expectantly. Early on, Nora had eschewed the idea that she needed to be the first one into the room, with time to meditate or prepare. That had been a trick of her old life back in Scotland—setting the mood, making the mark feel like there was a process so complicated they couldn't possibly understand.

The fireplace provided a warm glow to the room, and three lit candles on the table cast shadows across the walls. Lottie's fingers dug into her shoulder, and Nora could smell unwashed flesh, rotted teeth, and sour breath. Another pain coursed through her body, and Nora doubled over, clutching her stomach. The guests at the table all gasped while Nora tried to catch her breath. It was a pain she had never experienced, sharp like a knife but radiating down her stomach and across her back, up her spine. She was paralyzed, the skin of her stomach taut like a drum, an immense pressure that welled up from inside, making Nora feel as though she was going to rip in half. And then, as suddenly as it appeared, it was gone, and Nora was left gasping for breath.

"Miss Grey's spirit guide is particularly active tonight, ladies and gentlemen," Dorothy said from her position at Nora's right hand. "It is imperative that we all stay silent and still while Miss Grey enters a trance state. Only then will we learn what this restless spirit desires. Do not speak unless Miss Grey addresses you, and keep your hearts and minds open to whatever may come." Dorothy's voice was rhythmic and lulling, pulling the audience into their own form of a trance. All Nora could see were eyes in the darkness, eyes staring at her, eyes expecting so much from her, eyes doubting her. She was suddenly overwhelmed with an urge to run out the door and into the swirling December snow, but her feet stayed planted on the ground as Cecil placed the light box before her and it began to flash. Nora heard Dorothy's voice as she spoke the words that were more for the audience than Nora at this point. Nora's head became heavy, and Lottie's form appeared at her side, her belly swollen, her eyes empty and dead. Nora reached up to Lottie and took her hand, which had a slight corporeal presence to it that normally did not exist. This figure was not just air and mist but tonight had taken on bone and skin. Lottie looked down at Nora and shook her head.

"I'll not survive the night," she whispered.

Nora

"Please stay silent, please keep your seats, our medium is under the influence of her spirit guide, please stay seated."

Dorothy's voice seemed a million miles away, a faint hub in the space. Nora looked around. She was no longer in the warmly lit room at the House of Seven Gables but in a cold metal and concrete box. There was a slit of a window high up on a wall, the floor was stone, and the air was so cold Nora could see her breath. Lottie was leaning against the wall, both hands pressing onto the cold surface, and she was suppressing a scream from deep in her throat.

Nora walked to her, feeling that her arms and legs were not entirely her own. On the periphery of her vision, she could still see the dining room of the Salem house, the dark wood, the astonished faces of the women and men who sat at the table, but it was only on the edge. In her immediate sight were Lottie and this cage of a room where she was imprisoned.

"Lottie?" Nora said softly, and the girl turned her head to look.

"How are you here? How are you real?" Lottie gasped, her face full of fear.

"I don't know where I am," Nora replied, looking around her. "What is this place?"

"Argoll . . . the sisters think I ran away, but the doctors . . . they locked me down here for weeks. They run their experiments, do their work; they know I'll die, they know it." Lottie moaned as a contraction from her extended stomach racked her body and Nora knew what she had felt earlier—she had been channeling Lottie's pain, her anguish.

"Lottie, what happened here?" Nora asked.

"Happened? It's happening right now." Lottie groaned and slid to the floor where there was a thin and filthy cot mattress and blanket. "I've been here for weeks. The sisters think I'm dead or I ran, but I'm here, here."

"Oh Lord," Nora whispered and sank to her knees. On the periphery of her vision, she could see she had risen from her seat at the table and was now kneeling before the fireplace. All the eyes from the table followed her every move, wide and frightened. Nora shook off the awareness and focused on what was immediately before her: Lottie and the stone floor of her prison cell.

"Save me," Lottie wailed, and a flood of blood-tinted liquid gushed from under her thin shift, soaking the mattress and winding its way through the cracks on the stone floor.

Nora was frozen with indecision. She had no idea what to do. She'd never helped a woman through childbirth, never even seen it done. She knew the midwives back in Inverness had wanted buckets of boiled water and clean cloths, none of which were present here. She placed both hands on Lottie's knees. This was a vision of an event, she reminded herself, this already happened; she couldn't make it better or worse, but even so, it felt immediate, real, present.

"Jesus!" Lottie screamed, and another rush of fluid, this one bright with blood, poured out onto the floor. "It's time, I can feel it, I'm dying, the baby . . ."

"Will be fine," Nora said in a voice more certain than she felt. "The baby is fine because I am here with you now, and without this baby being just fine, I wouldn't exist. So stop yer worryin'. I'm here to make sure this baby is fine." Nora took both of Lottie's hands and squeezed.

"Yer an angel," Lottie whispered.

"I'm not, and I've no idea where I am or what to do, so yer not allowed to be thankin' me either," Nora said.

Another contraction shook Lottie's body, and she convulsed on the floor, inhuman screams coming from her lips. Blood, thick and black, pulsed from between her thighs, and Nora could feel Lottie's skin becoming colder and colder.

"Stay awake, Lottie, stay awake, it's so close, so so close," Nora shouted, adrenaline in her veins. She was only vaguely aware of the activity on the edge of her vision, in a warm room many years in the future where women and men were watching her every move in fear and horror.

Nora let go of Lottie's hands and lifted back her shift, trying to see if the baby was emerging. The area was a mess of blood and fluid, but Nora could just make out the top of a head, appearing and then disappearing back up into Lottie's flesh.

"I can see the head!" Nora cried, her excitement fierce. Lottie gasped and grasped at the edges of Nora's skirts. "You need to push. It's time to push! Your baby is going to be fine; he has to be."

A contraction shot through Lottie like lightning, and her screams drowned out the sound of the key in the door and the rattle of the latch. Nora did not hear the two men enter the space until one of them gasped. She turned her head to see utter terror on their faces. One was a squat, red-faced man; the other younger, townie-looking. She couldn't take too much mind of them, though, as the baby's head was suddenly thrust into her waiting hands, and then a tiny shoulder.

"Lottie! He's coming, you have to push, he's almost here!"

Nora was entirely in this moment. The awareness of her reality on the periphery of her vision was entirely obscured, the improbability of what this was entirely washed away in the excitement of the moment.

"Lottie! Again! He's almost here!" Nora repeated as Lottie shook with another contraction, her screams filling the room and making the two men wince. Nora felt the warm, solid weight of the baby slide into her hands, its tiny foot emerging last. His eyes were closed, and under the blood and gore of birth, his skin was gray.

"Lottie! It's a boy, like I told you it would be. A boy, he's here. Oh Jesus, he's here." Nora pulled at her petticoat, using the fabric to wipe the baby's face and mouth. A moment that lasted mere seconds but felt an eternity passed as Nora realized the baby was not breathing; he was tiny, so small he could have fit in just one of her hands, and his chest was still, his eyes closed. But that wasn't possible. This was Tavish, and he lived. He lived and went on to be her father. He lived.

"Nora? Nora?" Lottie lay on the cot with heaving, exhausted breaths. "I don't hear him. Nora, why isn't he crying?"

Nora felt her heart racing, and her hands shaking. The still form before her had no breath, no life, no heartbeat. "I–I . . . don't know. I don't know what's wrong." Nora looked up at the two men pleadingly. They looked at her as though she were a demon, and Nora realized for a moment that the way Lottie appeared in her world was how they viewed her. A vision, a ghost, a monster.

But Tavish had to live, he had to survive, because without his breath, nothing else existed. Nora frantically wiped the baby clean of the blood, his skin smeared with the violence of birth. He had a topknot of night-black hair, and Nora knew that under those still lids were eyes that matched, eyes that could charm or convince, eyes that could hold enough love to make up for the horrors of the world. But he had to live, he had to breathe.

Nora steeled herself with determination and looked Lottie in the eyes. "Don't you worry. This baby lives, this baby survives, he has to." With one hand Nora began to massage his tiny chest, not pressing too hard for the fear that she'd crush the feather-weight bones beneath the skin. She curled herself around the infant, surrounding him with her warmth until her lips rested next to his tiny, perfect ear. "You live, you hear me, you live and you go on to do such things as I could never repeat. You live and you leave this place, you disrupt and interfere, everyone who meets you loves you immediately, you can convince anyone of anything with your smile, you get all in the way of my plans, but you live. I need you, so you have to live."

With a gasping sigh, the baby sprang to life and with a sputtering cry spat out a milky goop that landed all over Nora's cheek. She felt tears streaming down her cheeks as the tiny creature flailed his arms and legs, his lungs loud and angry. His eyes opened, great, dark pits that focused on her and screamed the louder for it. Nora reached for the blanket and wrapped the baby tight, navigating the cord that still connected mother and child, handing him to Lottie who pushed herself up against the wall. Her face was damp with tears, and her skin so pale Nora could see blue veins pulsing in her cheeks. Nora ignored the muttering of the two strange men and set about fixing Lottie's shift and looking for another blanket to wrap Lottie in.

"Get me more blankets. Now," Nora commanded, throwing a glance to the men who pressed themselves against the wall and pointed at her as though she were a demon.

Just as she looked back, a flood of thick, pulsing blood coursed from Lottie's thighs, pouring out onto the stone floor. Lottie's face went slack, and her eyes fluttered. Nora could see she was trying to stay conscious.

"His name is Tavish." Lottie looked at the two men. "He is to be sent to Glasgow to live with my family. Send my belongings with him; it's all he'll have to remember me." Lottie looked at Nora. "I know not what this is, except that it's impossible."

"Perhaps," Nora said softly. "Perhaps it is." She reached out and stroked Tavish's tiny head as another wave of blood gushed from Lottie's body, and Nora saw the cold stone cell, the dying woman and her baby, the two doctors who suddenly rushed into action all fade, turn to mist where a moment ago they had been brick and stone. Nora felt herself fall back, and her head hit the dark wood floor of the formal dining room of the House of Seven Gables.

Before she lost consciousness, she heard the chaos of the guests and journalists being hustled from the space. A hand took hers and held it gently. Tavish's face appeared over hers, his night-black hair and matching eyes scared but very much alive.

Lottie
Argoll Asylum
1866

The wailing woman walks Argoll Downs dressed in a white gown. Her hair is long and black as the night. Her eyes are the voids of the dead, and it is said by the locals that if you look into them, you'll be struck dead in an instant. It was thought that the Wailing Woman was a remnant of my ancestor's time, a twelfth-century machination; perhaps she'd been a serving girl or mistress to the great Iorwerth ab Owain himself. Perhaps she'd lost a child, perhaps it had run darker than that. Was she a murderess? Guilty of infanticide? And now damned to wander the downs in search of her own cursed soul?

It seems not. The story as rigorously researched by the Pemberley Research Society seems to date to the nineteenth century, allowing old Iorwerth a reprieve for any misdeeds, this time anyhow.

The first sighting of the Wailing Woman originates at a farmhouse on Argoll Downs, not far from the original Llewellyn manor, where many years later a sort of underground catacomb would be discovered, thought to have been part of the Argoll Asylum, later known as the Argoll Refuge Manor.

The family in question had an infant child whose nursery was one door over from his parents' bedchamber. On the night of this recorded tale, Miss Hel-

edd Evans heard a cry from her infant son that set her nerves to edge. She rose from bed, and upon looking in on the nursery, she observed a woman standing over the child's cradle. Thinking at first the figure was an aunt of Mr. Evans who was visiting the farm-house, she approached the form, only to see it was translucent in places, and the air surrounding it was ice cold.

As the figure spun to regard Miss Evans, it opened what Miss Evans could not describe entirely as a mouth, as it had no form or shape, but no matter, the cry or wail that filled the room caused a water glass on a shelf to shatter, and Miss Evans blamed it all her remaining days for damage to her ears.

The figure disappeared, and Miss Evans did not re-port the matter until a short time later, when the child was stricken with influenza. Even though the infant survived the illness, Miss Evans remained stead-fast that the "wailing woman" had set the sickness upon him.

This concludes the first recorded story of this mys-terious specter. Other sightings over the years seem to be centered around children, and a popular super-stition is to keep infants from the downs until a cer-tain age.

It is interesting to note, however, that while the Wailing Woman has been spotted at the bedside of children who later became ill, it seems only fair to point out that the families affected by this experience sought preemptive medical attention based on their fears. It has been noted, and will be noted again, that none of the children the Wailing Woman has haunted have died; in fact, they were at a great advantage *when they did become ill, as their parents had already sought treatment.*

Believe what you will, readers, but it is the assertion of this ghostly scholar that the families of the Argoll Downs perhaps owe the Wailing Woman a debt of gratitude. Perhaps she was warning them of sickness to come, sickness that lay in the infant's lungs, dormant and waiting to strike. Perhaps this is a healing spirit, an angel rather than a demon.

Or you can believe the more popular and perhaps more entertaining tales of the Wailing Woman, a bloodthirsty child killer who eats the souls of infants and drags them to hell.

Your choice, gentle readers.

Lottie

"His name is Tavish." Lottie looked at the two men. "He is to be sent to Glasgow to live with my family. Send my belongings with him; it's all he'll have to remember me." Lottie looked at Nora. "I know not what this is, except that it's impossible." Lottie felt the warmth of her son at her chest, and her words found a strength she was rapidly losing.

Nora hovered, not quite specter, not quite present. Her touch was ice, the feel of her skin as though she were made of finely stretched fabric, dry and stiff. But she was here, she had breathed life into the infant, she'd cleaned the gore of birth from his tiny face with her own skirts, she was straddling this world and her own, she was as much spirit as Lottie had been in her visions. She spoke, but a wave of pain, a stabbing cramp from her gut, overwhelmed Lottie, and when she opened her eyes, Nora was gone, and Lottie knew that she would never see Nora Grey again.

Dr. Soekan ran from the room. He'd been frozen in terror throughout, so much so that Lottie smiled faintly thinking of it. Dr. Bothelli knelt by her side, his eyes once again those of the man who had shown her a modicum of kindness. Lottie saw the cord that had bound him to Dr. Soekan had been severed, the doubt that had plagued him overriding the spell of obedience he had been under. Perhaps they both were free now, Lottie thought deliriously.

"Doctor, you have to get my boy to Glasgow," Lottie whispered, her eyes fixed on her child. She could feel the sickly warm rush of blood between her legs, and she knew she would be gone soon. She'd close her eyes and never see this child again, not in this life.

"Lottie, I . . . we'll get you to hospital, we'll get you better." Dr. Bothelli reached a tentative hand out and gently stroked Tavish's tiny cheek. "Dear god, what have we done?"

"I'll be gone in minutes," Lottie whispered. Feeling her strength draining rapidly, she leaned forward and kissed her child. She could see Elis's chin, her eyes and hair, Elis's nose. She knew what he would grow up to be; she'd seen him, handsome and striking, and his daughter would be the famous Nora Grey, beautiful and kind, and she would live a long life free from the suffering that Lottie had known.

"You have to promise me. You'll get my child to Glasgow." Lottie looked up, breaking her gaze with her child for a moment to meet Dr. Bothelli's eyes. His face was streaked with tears.

"But Lottie, you said your family wanted nothing to do with you. Will they raise the child?" the doctor asked, his voice cracking.

"I don't know. I don't even know if they are still living, but if he is to be put in an orphanage, I want him to be home, in Glasgow—not here, not Wales," Lottie said with as much strength as she had left. "Don't let Soekan burn him. Don't let that man touch him."

Dr. Bothelli covered her hand in his. "I promise. I'll take him to Glasgow myself. I'll make sure he is safe."

Lottie pulled the infant to her. With her last bit of strength, she kissed his tiny forehead, then looked the child directly in his great, dark eyes. "You'll have to find the life for yourself that I wanted to give you. I'm with you always, I love you always."

With that, Lottie felt herself falling backward into the silky blackness of the mesmerism sessions, but this was different, there was no end to the fall, no invisible cord connecting her to the earth. She felt herself fractured into pieces, bits of her consciousness scattered to the wind. She walked the downs, looking for lost babies, babies who would surely die if she did not save them. In another self she sat by the fire with her grandmum, watching as the old woman read the seer cards and murmured their truths. She lost part and particle of time; she was connected to nothing and everything. In yet another self she felt a hand in hers and looked to see Elis beside her. They stood on that lane in Glasgow where they'd first touched, so many years ago now. He pulled her toward him and whispered a word in her ear.

"Exquisite."

Part V

Nora
Boston and
Thereabouts
1901

Internal Memo: Order of St. Cyprian Working in Cooperation with the International Psychical Society

Date: December 31, 1901
RE: Nora Grey and complications
Dear Sirs,
   Since the outstanding events demonstrated earlier this week, we have remained in Salem, Massachusetts, hosted by one Madeline Wardwell of the Salem Historical Society. Miss Grey has not felt well enough to travel, but despite her ailments, which we believe to be psychic in nature, she has demanded a session be held tonight, before the turn of the new year. The session, at Miss Grey's insistence, is to be frustratingly private. Only myself, Miss Kellings, Tavish Grey, and inexplicably, a journalist from the New England Courier *are to be in attendance. What Miss Grey hopes to fulfill at this session is a mystery; she has said only that she feels her spirit guide is now gone. It is this researcher's opinion that her physical ailments brought on by the very dramatic events on the night of December 27 are clouding her judgement on the matter.*
   The significance of the events on the night of December 27 cannot be overstated. You will, of course, have seen the news coverage, particularly that of the New York Times *and its far-reaching syndicates. A girl who was gaining prestige slowly was catapulted to infamy in the course of an hour.*

The manifestation of not only a full body apparition but also what appeared to be a psychic window to another dimension or perhaps another time is unheard of. Miss Grey became a part of the scene before us, effectively transporting herself to this other dimension. The spectators and press watched as Miss Grey delivered an infant in what looked to be a prison or asylum of sorts. While the vision presented itself as grainy, unfocused, perhaps dream-like, the physical qualities of the dining room in which the séance was being held were quite real.

The temperature—which had been quite comfortable, overly warm even—dropped suddenly and without explanation, the warmth returning only after the vision disappeared and Miss Grey collapsed. An ectoplasm-like substance, very similar to what stained the walls at our first successful session at the Old South Meeting Hall, was found on the walls of the dining room. It emitted a foul smell, much like a birthing room or hospital surgery ward. There was no doubt as to whether Miss Grey was immersed in the vision or that the specters witnessed in the vision were aware of Miss Grey. Two male figures expressed a deep and sincere fear of Miss Grey. The young woman figure, who has been noted as Miss Grey's spirit guide "Lottie," was also aware of Miss Grey's presence. An infant boy was born, seemingly stillborn, and in what was the most extraordinary act witnessed in my entire career, Miss Grey seemingly breathed life into his lungs.

This incident has already reached a peak of public interest that I have never witnessed, and

*subsequent investigation will be made to
eliminate all possibility of fraud or trickery.
Tonight's session is at Miss Grey's demand, and
another report will be filed as soon as is possible.*

    Thank you,
    Karl Mendis

Nora

"And what after?" Dorothy asked the question with an air of resignation.

"I'm done. Nora Grey is done," Nora answered simply. "I have earned you enough money to buy that house in Manhattan I know you had your eye on and to make sure you will be quite in demand from here on out. But I'm done. After tonight, it's over."

"Queens, actually. It's a town house in Queens, and it's magnificent. You're welcome to stay whenever you like." Dorothy gave Nora a wry smile. "I suppose this worked out rather well for both of us. I already have a meeting with a girl in Cleveland who claims she can bend spoons and talk to the dead via automatic writing. I have a feeling she'll be remarkably dull, and Cecil will have to work overtime to make her sessions anything more than terrible, but it's work." Dorothy paused and then, choosing her words carefully, continued. "You don't have to quit, you know. I know you think your spirit guide is gone, and she may very well be. But you may find another, and you can always fake it until that happens. No one would question you, not now."

Nora shook her head. "No tricks. This last session is something I need to do, and I'm not even sure it will work. Just the girl from the *Courier*; that's all the press. She's earned it, and whatever she writes as my eulogy will be enough to carry you through to whatever comes next."

Dorothy shrugged and sat back, sipping at the martini she'd ordered from Mattie and grimacing. "Remind me never to come back to this hole in the woods. Terrible drinks. And what of Karl? And the psychical groups?"

"I have an offer for them, too. I haven't forgotten my debt," Nora responded, staring out the window at the falling snow. Despite Dorothy's opinion of Salem, she found it incredibly beautiful and far enough away from the city that she could almost see herself staying, almost. Nora, however, had other plans.

"I heard your handsome doctor from Edinburgh wanted to come out and visit. Dr. Harrison, was it?" Dorothy flashed her a conspiratorial grin, and Nora swallowed a laugh.

"It's funny how uninterested I am in anything to do with men now. Remarkable, really. Edwin was the first man to really show me any attention, and even then, I rather doubted his sincerity, but now? I truly couldn't care less. I have other plans for myself. Plans I think Lottie would approve of."

"Can I assume it has something to do with the letter from Madame Bell?" Dorothy asked, sipping her gin.

Nora nodded. "You can assume that. All you need know is that I plan on closing this chapter and disappearing."

Dorothy nodded thoughtfully. "Well, I suppose we should prepare."

Nora

The journalist from the *New England Courier* was named Edith Parks. Nora felt like an ass having not known that until this very last session. She'd never read the coverage written about her, especially now that her name was blowing up headlines and selling through newsstands. Edith was positively glowing with excitement as they settled into the parlor at the Nurse House. Mattie Wardwell had made sure the room was arranged just the way Nora requested. A small round table, a single candle, and seats for herself, Dorothy, Karl, Tavish, and Edith Parks. This was the last session she would do for the press, and its secrecy would sell even more newspapers than the last grand show.

Nora entered the room after the others had been seated. Her mind felt calm, determined. She had one last task, one last thing she could do for Lottie, a last way to make everything right. As she sat, she nodded to the others at the table.

Dorothy spoke in her rhythmic and calming voice. "We are here to channel the spirits; we are here to contact the dead. Please do not speak to Miss Grey unless she addresses you, please do not interrupt in any way, please do not interfere with the trance state which Miss Grey will enter. We are witnesses to the beyond, nothing more."

With that, the light box began its rhythmic and hypnotic flashing. Dorothy controlled it this time, no Cecil. Nora felt her chin becoming heavier, her mind fading to the warm blackness where normally Lottie would meet her. Not this time, though; this time she was on her own, and she would have to guide herself through the darkness to where she needed to go. As the world became entirely black, the flashing stopped, and Nora heard Dorothy's voice in the distance.

"Greet us, spirits; greet us here. Grant us audience, greet us here."

Nora felt a tug in her chest and followed the sensation. She had a very particular person she needed to find in the mist, one who had crossed over long before in Nora's timeline but in her own lived still. Nora pulled herself through the blackness until the cold and chill of the dank stone walls and stone floors began to permeate her body. She was in the cellar room where Lottie had given birth and died. But this was not where she needed to be. Nora turned to the door, which now stood open with no occupant to jail any longer. Nora walked tentatively, aware that her feet were only barely touching the ground. Up a steep flight of stairs, through a thick wooden door, and down a long hallway to a main room. No one knew Lottie was hidden away for all those months; no one could have heard her through all that wood and stone. It was what the sadists posing as doctors had counted on, but their secret was no longer protected by this place. Lottie had proven herself to be a force to be reckoned with.

Nora looked around her: dark wood floors, institutional décor, an office that must belong to the younger of the two doctors Nora had seen before. But it wasn't these men that Nora needed to reach. No, she needed to find another that Lottie had whispered about in her ear as she lay suffering in her cell. Another that would make sure justice was done. Up the stairs, up and up. Nora trusted the tug in the chest as she put one foot in front of another. She could feel the quiet presence of the one she sought, somewhere behind one of these closed doors, somewhere in this maze of a manor house turned hellscape.

Sister Therese was just as Lottie had described, her face lined with age, her eyes kind and concerned. She wore a nun's simple habit, a rosary at her waist. Nora watched her as she sat at a wooden desk in a dormitory room; she was writing, her hand moving gracefully across the page.

"Sister," Nora spoke as loud as she could, knowing the sound would be as soft as whispers in this realm. The nun looked up and then dismissed the faintness of the call, going back to her writing.

"See me," Nora said, pulling all the energy she could muster into her corporeal form. She was faintly aware of Dorothy's voice in the next world, of the figures surrounding the table, but they were worlds away. What they saw of this vision, Nora had no idea.

"See. Me," Nora repeated, and the nun spun in her chair, staring at Nora with a look of sheer terror.

"Lottie? Oh dear Lord, Lottie?" the nun said softly, crossing herself.

Nora shook her head. She was not Lottie, but she was here to help the sister discover what had become of her. She was here to ensure that Lottie Liath would not be forgotten, that perhaps a bit of justice could be found. Nora stepped closer to the nun and leaned in, her lips inches from the sister's ear, and then she told her story.

Nora

It was a week later that Nora found herself standing with Tavish on the dock in Boston Harbor. It was newly 1902, and Nora swore she could feel a new life hiding behind the frozen Boston sky. The Bell Island ferry would depart any moment. It was rare for it to make a winter supply run but not unheard of, and this time it had a particular reason for braving the winter sea. The sailors wouldn't speak of it to anyone; they had been properly bribed and their silence bought by the current Lady Loreana Bell, who knew the importance of keeping a secret.

The official reason for Nora's departure according to the International Psychical Society was for her health. Given the extensive and explosive nature of her newly found fame, she was overcome with exhaustion and in need of a doctor's ordered rest. It had been decided by Nora, Tavish, and the Psychical Society that it was best if Nora were to take her repose in the quiet of Bell Island, far from the talk of her groundbreaking and utterly fantastical séances that were selling through the newsstands and clinical journals.

The unofficial reason was known only to Nora and Tavish. It had arrived in a letter that Nora had burned after it was read and would never be spoken about to anyone other than her father. Tavish, for his part, was planning to stay in Boston; he had secured work in a tavern in Old Town and had allowed Nora to buy him a small town house on Copp's Hill. He was welcome to visit Bell Island with the summer ferry. But now he stood in the freezing cold, waiting to say goodbye to his daughter.

"I still can't believe that all those psychical types are actually going to leave you be," he muttered.

Nora smiled. "They're not entirely. The Order of St. Cyprian has long been friends with Lady Loreana Bell, and I don't see why that will change. They will be welcomed on Bell Island. I've agreed to hold private sessions for the purpose of their research. But no more shows; it's on my terms now."

"I suppose so." Tavish took Nora by the shoulders and looked down at her. "I don't know what it was I saw on that night. I only know it was a miracle and there is a shortage of those in the world, so I'll have you know I won't easily forget."

"I'd hope not," Nora said softly, reaching up and taking his hand. "And you're welcome if you ever want to give up this city life. You can even stay in the big house."

Tavish chuckled.

Nora smiled and kissed him on the cheek before she boarded the ferry. Tavish waved from the dock and stayed in the freezing cold wind until Nora could no longer see him in the distance. It was only then that she went below deck to the relative warmth of the dry storage room and curled up on a cot with a thick blanket around her shoulders. Lady Loreana Bell's letter had arrived before the séance at the House of Seven Gables, and Nora had burned it hours before the session began. Perhaps it had given her the strength to let Lottie go, to see what lay beyond the life she'd been living then. Following instructions, she had burned the contents, but the words stayed fresh in her mind. A chance at a new life, a chance for everything she had thought impossible.

Sister Therese
Magdalene Alfonsius
of the Order of the
Blessed Rose
Argoll Asylum
1867

The Cardiff Sun Times, *Week of January 1, 1867*

It is with sadness and shock that we report the untimely passing of Dr. Franz Soekan here in the first week of our new year. Dr. Soekan was the founder of the prestigious Gest School in Paris, France, and specialized in mesmerism and the treatment of mental afflictions and maladies. He had been working at the Argoll Sanitorium and Asylum for the last few months.

The circumstances surrounding Dr. Soekan's untimely passing are a matter of mystery. His body was found in the cellar of Argoll Asylum. Officials are currently attributing his death to a snake bite.

Dr. Soekan studied in Strasbourg, France, and served as a faculty instructor in the medical college of Strasbourg University. He left to start the Gest School in Paris, which is heralded as a place of innovation and psychiatric research. He is survived by a brother and will be remembered by his many students and colleagues.

Services are to be held near Paris, France, at Chartres Cathedral on January 7, 1 p.m. Flowers and gifts of memorial can be sent care of the Gest School.

Sister Therese

The figure appeared dressed in a fine gown, the style something Therese had never seen. The colors were muted, the lace skirt. The color of the figure's skin was muted as well, pale but as though it were just slightly out of focus. Black hair swept up in a stylish coif, black eyes and a strong face.

"Lottie? Oh dear lord, Lottie?" Therese crossed herself and prayed that the vision was flesh and blood, that the girl was alive, well, thriving. But even as she spoke the words, she knew it was not Lottie. This figure was slim, no expectant belly; this figure was healthy, safe, strong, where Lottie had been broken and scared. The figure shook her head and approached.

The spirit's voice was soft as a breeze, the words danced in and out of the space, filling Therese's mind. She listened as the woman in the fine dress who looked so much like Lottie told her a story of a pregnant woman locked in the cellar of the asylum. A woman who had died in childbirth and whose infant was in danger. The figure talked of where the woman's remains had been hastily thrown in the hope they'd get eaten by the creatures of the Downs and forgotten. Therese listened with horror and disgust as the figure told her why the men had locked Lottie away, how they hoped to use her talents, her ability to contact the next world, to move objects with her mind. How they hoped to exploit and research her as though she were a specimen in a lab and not a woman who suffered and died at their hands.

"Do your worst," the figure whispered before it faded back into mist. Therese shook herself and steadied her hands. *Lottie, dear sweet Lottie.* She'd disappeared so many weeks ago; the doctor had said she'd escaped all the way to Cardiff, been caught, and sent to a hospital to see her through the end of her pregnancy. Had the girl been locked in the asylum all this time? Could that be true, and Therese had never found her, never even looked? Why had she so willingly believed Dr. Bothelli even when he looked pale and drained? *Guilty.* Therese realized what his wan appearance had been all these weeks—it had been guilt, and now Lottie was dead, and her baby was god knows where. Dr. Bothelli hadn't been seen by any of the staff for several days, so where had they taken the child?

Therese marched out of her room and up to the infirmary.

"Where is he?" she demanded of Sister Mary, who sat at her desk, going over papers.

"Who?" She looked up, startled.

"The doctor. Dr. Bothelli. He's been gone for days now. Where'd he go?" the nun asked, pacing back and forth.

"He left two nights ago. Carriage house said he was bound for Glasgow, left in the early hours, still dark out. I only found out when I needed his signature for the pharmacy in Cardiff. Can't say he'll be back anytime soon. Why do you need him? I had to get his colleague, that Dr. Soekan fellow, to sign my orders. He's a gruff sort, even more so than when he arrived," the nun said, her face surprised at Therese's forcefulness.

"I . . . do you know if he had a parcel with him? A bundle, a . . . ," Therese stuttered.

"A what? I haven't the faintest. As I said, I only heard of it after he'd already gone. What's gone mad in you?" Sister Mary asked, putting her pencil down.

"I . . . think something terrible's happened. And Soekan is to blame. Dr. Bothelli isn't innocent, but I think he might be trying to right things, as much as he can. But Soekan, we need to do something, something for Lottie."

Sister Mary regarded Therese for a moment. "He'll continue his 'experiments,' his 'science,' won't he? Here or in Paris, he'll continue till another girl runs away in the night. Won't he?" she said softly.

Therese nodded. "'These have chosen their own ways, and their soul delights in their abominations.'"

"Isaiah 66:3," Sister Mary replied. "What do you have in mind?"

Sister Therese

Sister Therese stood before the tiny stone cell, still stained in Lottie's blood, the twisted blanket cast to the side. They'd taken her body out a hidden door that led to the Downs and dumped it just inside the woods. Therese and Mary had found her easily enough. The cold had preserved her; she looked as though she'd been living moments before, her skin intact, no sign of rot. The animals hadn't found her yet; she was unscathed. The gravedigger had gladly taken an extra pence for the unsavory task of digging a grave in the still frozen ground in the asylum yard. No potter's field for Lottie. With only Sister Therese and Sister Mary to preside over the burial, Lottie would be buried in the yard proper, next to the resting places of the Llewelyn family and those who had lived on this land after them. Therese paid another pence of Dr. Bothelli's money to have a small plaque carved:

A WOMAN OF GOD AND A WONDER TO ALL

No name, nothing to object to should anyone want to object. She didn't know if it was a sin or if the diocese would send her away for the act—if they ever learned of it at all, that is. There was no one to tell except Sister Mary, and she was as distraught as Therese. The plaque was small, embedded in the earth; flowers and polly vines would grow over it come summer. Lottie's resting place would likely be hidden forever, and perhaps that would be fine; she could rest quietly with the royalty of Argoll Downs for eternity. *Lottie would rather like the mystery of it*, Therese had thought with a smile as she said her goodbyes and swore she would do what the spirit who'd looked so like Lottie had commanded her to do.

Now, as she stood in the cell where Lottie had died, where she'd said goodbye to her child, Therese knew she had to steel herself. It was a sin, perhaps—she had no right to say who died and who lived—but she had a responsibility to protect the most vulnerable, and that meant that Dr. Soekan, Dr. Toad and Hog as Lottie called him, needed to be stopped.

The adder snakes were still in hibernation from the winter; it had taken a bit of persuasion, but eventually Sid had been willing to help Sister Therese and Sister Mary in their task. The big man dug into a burrow at the base of a rotten tree stump and quite successfully found three adders wrapped around each other, fast asleep and quite cooperative. Luring Dr. Soekan into the cellar where the adders awaited had been surprisingly simple. Therese had simply left the cellar door open, and the good doctor had entered as he finished up his business for the night. She and Mary had formulated countless ways to get him back to the prison-like room where Lottie had perished, but after all their scheming, all it took was an open door.

Dr. Soekan likely never knew what hit him when the first snake bit. The three adders had awoken confused and angry in the cellar room. Soekan might not have been the cause of their ire, but he became the target. They left the doctor's body where it lay; when the polis arrived, they disposed of the snakes; and Therese felt pity for the poor creatures who had become pawns in their plot. But in the hierarchy of guilt she carried, they ranked relatively low.

Multiple bites from three snakes had assured the poison worked its way through Soekan's blood, killing him swiftly. He had been rendered unconscious after the first few strikes, and even if Therese hadn't waited until dawn to contact the polis, he would never have woken up, stuck in a permanent dream, which was more mercy than he showed to Lottie. At least that was what Therese told herself. She wasn't sure if there was enough penance in the world entire to make up for what she'd participated in. Whatever the consequences might be for her soul, Therese knew no one would ask too many questions. What cause would two nuns and an orderly with a simple mind have to harm a grand doctor like Franz Soekan?

Therese sent for the polis in the morning, claiming worry over the doctor missing breakfast. Sid said he'd seen the doctor enter the cellar the night before, and in minutes the doctor's body had been found. *A terrible accident is what it was*, that was what the officer said with a sad shake of his head. *City folk don't realize how dangerous the countryside can be. He must have stumbled upon a snake burrow*, Therese had agreed, and the polis had nodded in agreement. *A real shame.*

"I'll make it better, Lottie," Therese whispered as she stood in the cell, surrounded by the evidence of horror. Dr. Bothelli was on his way back from Glasgow, where he'd delivered a very special package to the Smyllum Park Orphanage. Lottie's parents had been deceased, but the baby was back in Scotland where Lottie wanted him. When the doctor returned, there would be changes. Therese could feel it. Never again would the walls that surrounded the asylum be a prison; in their place it would be a refuge meant to keep the evils of the world out, not locked inside.

Lady Loreana Bell
Bell Island
1902

Excerpt from The Bostonian Historical Register:
Chronicles of Bell Island, *circa 1902*

Lady Loreana Bell transferred the ownership of Bell Manor, the surrounding properties, and subsequent assets and holdings of the estate to her daughter, also named Loreana Bell, in January 1902. The island remains in the Massachusetts statehood, but all property on the island—including structures, businesses, farms, and livestock—were listed as under the sole proprietorship of the new Lady Loreana Bell. It had not been known that Lady Loreana Bell (Sr) had a daughter prior to the court filing, but as of January 1902 all holdings will be the sole responsibility of Lady Loreana Bell (Jr).

Not much is written about the residents of Bell Island, except that it was recorded by a sailor who manned the January ferry that transported Lady Loreana Bell (Jr) to the island that she was met with great enthusiasm by what looked to be members of Bell Manor and Bell Village alike. Where the good lady had been or what life she had been living prior to her return to the island is all unknown.

Lady Loreana Bell
1902

Lady Bell was enjoying a brandy in the dark wood library. Her mother sat in the chair opposite her, a matching drink in her hand. It was starting to thaw outside, and green was starting to appear on the edges of the trees and ground. Lady Bell loved this time of year the most, the time when new things began. Her mother was playing cards, and the quiet slap of the solitaire hand caught Lady Bell's attention. Her mother looked up and smiled. She had run this house for two decades before this last winter, when she'd handed the reins of the island over to her daughter. And the older woman was enjoying her retirement. She spent her days playing cards, and when the warm weather arrived, she'd walk the grounds trailed by island cats.

Lady Bell and her mother did not look alike, but none of the residents of the manor or village seemed to notice. Lady Bell was fair-skinned where her mother was dark, but the same intensity, intelligence, and passion lived in their eyes. It was clear they were cut from the same cloth even if not related by blood. Lady Bell, for her part, was finding her feet in the running of such a grand estate. There was an immense amount of business to be done, and people to take care of, but she relished the work. It was a quiet life, an important one. She kept people safe, protected, unseen. She made sure that Bell Island continued to exist just beyond the mist, an Avalon for those in need.

Author's Note

A few years back I became curator to my very Scottish family's historical records, which include a thousand handwritten letters, albums of aging photographs, and a few handwritten attempts at family trees. It was a puzzle made only more complex by the myriad and varying stories that had been passed around the dinner table since I was a child. They contradicted each other, were often full of impossible events, and nearly always ended with a claim to royalty.

My favorite was that of J.H. Atkinson, my great-grandfather and the reason I grew up in the Colorado mountains and not the Scottish lowlands. His stories were a stark contrast to the brave and daring deeds that were often regaled, the royals we were related to, the microscopic parcel of land we were deeded as a many-greats heir to Lady Jane Grey.

No, J.H. Atkinson was a different sort of famous, more like infamous. According to the recorded history, he made his way across the Scottish lowlands claiming to be a water dowser and spiritual medium. As he was neither, his efforts were not appreciated, and there exist verifiable records of his legal woes. He was made to repay farmers and even saw the inside of many a jail cell.

Now this is the recorded history, but the stories told around the dinner table paint a different man, one so charming and witty that he could talk a beggar out of his coppers, one that could make the dearly departed appear just to have had the honor of seeing his face. But his charms were not without danger, and there came a time when it was very inconvenient for J.H. to remain in Scotland. My personal favorite tale is that of J.H.'s abrupt departure.

It so goes that Great-Grandpa J.H. was riding his Clydesdale (did I forget to mention that he was also the best horse breeder in the land?) through a storm the likes of which had ne'er been seen. The horse was a beast, a regular Kelpie, twenty hands high if the stories are to be believed (and they are best not . . .). The lightning lit up the sky, the thunder crashed with the fury of the heavens (and maybe a few farmers . . .), and it struck J.H. down as he rode across the moorland. The man was taken entire in a flash of light and fire, and all that was left was his sapphire pinky ring, which is all that was found atop the Clydesdale as it charged, rider-less, back to town.

There are a few holes, the most obvious being that his corporeal form would soon after appear aboard a ship headed to America with my great-grandmother at his side. Lesson not learned, upon J.H. and his bride's arrival in the United States, he immediately started up his old tricks. This time, he claimed to be a spiritual healer and mesmerist with a vintage business card, to boot. As he was, again, neither, he again found himself on the wrong side of the law and pulled yet another great escape. This time he perished in a West Virginia coal mine, no body found, like the Clydesdale and the lightning, gone in a flash of light and fire. His grieving bride, my great-grandmother, was expecting and made her way to Lyons, Colorado.

This is not quite the end of the story, however. Just like after that storm on the moorlands, Great-Grandpa J.H. is rumored to have made a miraculous recovery, as some years later there are still more stories of a man matching his talents, touting his skills as a spiritual medium and clairvoyant.

The evidence to prove these comings and goings varies; most lies in stories told around the table and in front of a warm fire. This is the best sort of history, one that has one foot in reality and one in the ether. For those of you invested in hard facts, take heart that there is very little evidence to say these things did not happen either. *The Entirely True Story of the Fantastical Mesmerist Nora Grey* is a celebration of the possible and the impossible, a what-if exploration of a world where his talents were real, and they brought him fame and fortune instead of a life on the run. Much of the Spiritualism Movement lives in this realm somewhere between the extraordinary and the imagined. Nora Grey is the real deal. J.H. might not have been, but his spirit lives on in her story.

Acknowledgments

Writing this story was a bit like stepping off a cliff and hoping I would learn to fly on the way down. It was a huge leap of faith, and the fact that it exists here in book form with this amazing team of people behind it is pretty extraordinary. Writing and publishing is an industry that forces you to believe in magic—you have this little seed, along come your fairy godmothers and wizards, and sorcerers, and all of a sudden . . . you have a story. Then that story is twisted and changed and edited and revised, and it's made into a book. A whole universe exists where there once was a void, and that's pretty magical.

I will be forever grateful for everyone who believed in this story and worked to make it what it is today. Thank you to Kensington Publishing, especially Elizabeth Trout, for taking a chance on *The Entirely True Story of the Fantastical Mesmerist Nora Grey*. My team at Paradigm Talent, my literary agent Katelyn Dougherty, Caja Leshinger, Matt Snow—thank you for believing in this work and pushing it even when I felt like I was plunging headfirst into the chasm. Thank you to Carolyn Pouncy, and all the editors, artists, and eyes at Kensington and Paradigm who have given your energy, your talent, and your time to *Nora Grey*.

A lot of research went into this work, much of it from the annals of family history that I am now the curator of. Thank you to my mother for this honor and forgive me for the creative license, but I really do think the ancestors would enjoy their fictionalized narratives. If I get haunted later, I'll eat those words. Thank you to Lisa Morton for her fantastic nonfiction book *Calling the Spirits: A History of Seances*, which served as my guide through this fascinating world. Thank you to all my friends in the Horror Writers Association: your hearts, your passion, and your talents are also pretty magical.

Last but not least, my husband and my son are with me in the seedling stage of book ideas. They listen to me muse about it for an interminable amount of time, they lose me to the writing of it for months on end, and then they get to talk me out of my tree when we get to the stage where someone is going to actually read it. I love you, I see you, I appreciate every itty bitty thing you do. Thank you.

THE ENTIRELY TRUE STORY OF THE FANTASTICAL MESMERIST NORA GREY

Kathleen Kaufman

ABOUT THIS GUIDE

The suggested questions are included to enhance your group's reading of Kathleen Kaufman's *The Entirely True Story of the Fantastical Mesmerist Nora Grey*

Discussion Questions

1. This novel is both historical fiction and magical realism. How does Kathleen Kaufman achieve her unique writing style? What details does she use from each genre? What do each add to the emotional quality of the story?

2. Both Nora and Lottie are othered by society because of circumstances and abilities. What parallels do you see between the two women, and how does each handle her obstacles?

3. The book ends with Nora choosing a life of obscurity and eschewing the fame and fortune that her abilities have brought her. What drives her to that decision, and why does she choose this path?

4. Dorothy Kellings plays many different roles with Nora: she is a nurturer, a partner, and a business manager. Discuss the complicated relationship between these two women. Where does the power dynamic lie?

5. Lottie's story of institutionalization was all too common for its day. What leads to her commitment to Argoll Asylum? Consider the sequence of events that led to her courtroom appearance. Discuss what other options might have been open to Lottie.

6. Discuss the father-daughter relationship between Tavish and Nora. In what capacity is Tavish a protector? In what ways does he exploit her talents? What drives the loyalty and familial bond that lie between the two?

7. If you could ask Nora, Lottie, Dorothy, and/or Tavish any question, what would it be, and how do you think they would respond?

8. Nora Grey has to deal with the advantages and trappings of fame at a young age. How does this change her perspective on what she wants from life? Is this comparable to young celebrities in today's world?

9. What do you think happens to Nora, Dorothy, and Tavish after the book concludes?

10. If you could travel back to the historical setting of either Nora's or Lottie's story, where/when would you go, and what would you do or see?

Also by Sara Cate

SALACIOUS PLAYERS' CLUB
Praise
Eyes on Me
Give Me More
Mercy
Highest Bidder
Madame

SINFUL MANOR
Keep Me

THE GOODE BROTHERS
The Anti-hero
The Home-wrecker
The Heartbreaker
The Prodigal Son

BEAUTIFUL SERIES
Beautiful Monster
Beautiful Sinner

WILDE BOYS DUET
Gravity
Free Fall

BLACK HEART DUET
Four
Five

COCKY HERO CLUB
Handsome Devil

SPITFIRE
Burn for Me
Fire and Ash

WICKED HEARTS SERIES
Delicate
Dangerous
Defiant

the
Good
Girl
Effect

the
Good
Girl
Effect

SARA CATE

sourcebooks
casablanca

Published by Sourcebooks Casablanca, an imprint of Sourcebooks
1935 Brookdale RD, Naperville, IL 60563-2773
(630) 961-3900
sourcebooks.com

Cataloging-in-Publication data is on file with the Library of Congress.

Printed and bound in Canada.
FR 10 9 8 7 6 5 4 3 2 1

This book is dedicated to your praise kink.

Author's Note

Salacious Legacy is a second-generation series that takes place twenty-five years after the events of Salacious Players' Club. This series will feature some familiar faces and will reference events in the original series, but this is an entirely new series and can be read on its own.

For those who would like to make connections between this series and the original, a family tree has been provided.

Welcome to Legacy.

Salacious Family Tree

Eden · Jade · Clay

Jack St. Claire · Elizabeth Bradley · Scarlett Bradley

Ronan · Daisy

Julian Kade · Amelia Kade

Hunter Drake Isabel

Phoenix Scott   Austin Scott   Weston Scott

Garrett Mia

Liam Porter

Emerson | Charlotte

Maggie | Beau

Prologue

Jack

"Everyone's here," I say as I find a seat in the back of the
dimly lit bar. "Did you all get the email too?"

"Yep," my best friend Phoenix replies next to me.

"Sure did," Weston adds while scrolling on his phone.

At the corner of the booth, Julian and his sister, Amelia, sit in
silence. Julian is doing so as a form of defiance, while Amelia is
silent most of the time anyway. She's chewing on her lip, looking
more uneasy by the second.

Neither of them wants to say anything about this mysterious
email their father sent everyone yesterday asking us to meet at
Geo's bar promptly at eight. Ronan Kade co-owns the sex club
where I've been working for the past seven years. He's also my
godfather, and his son, Julian, has never been my biggest fan.

The feeling is mutual.

It grates on my nerves to see the pretentious, haughty expression on his face. Julian and I might have grown up together, but it
doesn't change the fact that I find him to be infuriatingly snobbish
and full of himself.

"So do you think he's coming?" I ask, scanning the group around me.

"Yeah, right," Julian snaps. "He's not coming. He's probably on a yacht halfway across the world right now. He sent this email to trick us all into meeting here."

To trick us all into talking to each other, I think without saying it out loud.

"And what about your sister? She's on the email too," Julian says as if it's a weapon to use against me. He's cruelly pointing out that my own sister isn't speaking to me. She won't return my calls, let alone step foot in the same room I'm in.

My younger sister, Elizabeth, took my wife's death last year as hard as I did. She looked up to Em like a true sister and even lived with us during Em's brutal passing. But when she needed me the most, I went to a dark place for a long time. I should have been there for my sister and my daughter, but I just couldn't. I could hardly be there for myself.

And now, my only goal is to get my four-year-old daughter out of Paris and go back home where we belong. If this email from Ronan means what I think it means, I might have my opportunity.

"We don't need to wait for Elizabeth," I mutter under my breath, assuming she won't show.

"We should wait for everyone," Phoenix says, softly placing a hand on my arm. I can't make eye contact with her because I know she's right.

Just then, the heavy door swings open, and I turn to find my sister slipping into the room. She doesn't make eye contact with anyone as she approaches our table, sliding into the empty seat silently. Her black hair is pulled tight into a bun at the back of her head, and her expression is harsh like it's filled with pain. The sight guts me.

No one speaks—the six of us stationed around the table in the back of a dark speakeasy as if we're awaiting our grim fate.

"Now what?" Phoenix asks first. I look at her, our expressions mirrored. She's been my best friend for years. She followed me to Paris after college and is currently the only person at this table who I think actually likes me.

As for the others, Julian and Amelia were raised here, although their parents are American. My sister came for a ballet program. And Phoenix and Weston came out here to work for the club a few years ago.

I'm starting to feel restless as the awkward silence engulfs the table. My hope is that Ronan is about to announce his official retirement, naming his son his successor, which would mean I'll be free to leave. There's not a chance in hell I'll work for Julian Kade.

Just when I'm about to suggest we call Ronan, my phone buzzes.

As does everyone else's.

We all look down in unison.

"It's an email from Dad," Amelia says softly with a smile.

Julian rolls his eyes without picking up his phone.

"I'll read it," I say, clicking the notification.

"*Dear Kids*," it starts, as if we're a bunch of teenagers and not a group of fully grown adults in our twenties and thirties.

> *This message is for all six of you: Julian, Amelia, Jack, Phoenix, Elizabeth, and Weston—*
> *This letter is a long time coming, and I'm sure you've guessed by now what it's about. With the help of my business partner, Matis Moreau, I've managed L'Amour for the past two and a half decades. It is time for me to officially retire.*
> *I've spoken to Matis about this, and we both agree that you should make the club yours now.*

"Wait," Julian interjects with a scowl. "Who? Who the fuck is going to own the club?"

I scan the beginning of the email again, searching for the answer.

"I think he means...all of us," Phoenix replies.

"All of us?" Amelia asks. "Own the club together?"

"Fuck this," Julian mutters, tossing his phone back on the table and picking up his drink.

With a disgruntled sigh, I continue reading.

I've known you all since you were born. Your parents created a legacy, and you were raised together like a family. You came to Paris with a dream, and you've all worked so hard at L'Amour. But what I see now are six adults who have lost their way. You've grown apart, and each of you has lost something you can never replace. I know how that feels.

I see your potential. Each of you brings something special to the table. If you really worked together, you could make a club even better than what your parents created.

There is nothing more powerful than family. The six of you are a family, whether you see it or not. There are three of you missing from this letter—Liam, Austin, and Scarlett. They are choosing another path for their lives, but this offer extends to them, should they choose it. And I hope they do.

Across the table, my sister huffs, and I look up to find her clenching her teeth angrily. Trying not to let it affect me, I continue reading.

That is why I am passing the club down to all six of you. You can do what you want with it. Change the name. Make it yours. The only catch is that you have to run it together for at least a year. If one of you pulls out, the ownership reverts to Matis, and he'll sell the property.

This isn't a punishment. It's an experiment. I watched your parents' club save lives, and I'm hoping this one will save yours.

One year. That's all I ask. After the year is up, you can do what you want.

I'm begging you to give it a shot.

Find your family, and make this your home.

Sincerely,
Ronan Kade

My jaw hangs open as I stare at the email. The rest of the table is silent as we let this news settle in.

Suddenly, I see my plans of leaving Paris slipping through my fingers. If I leave, the rest of them lose out on this opportunity. Do I really want that on my head?

I scroll through the message again. "There has to be some catch."

"Well, that settles it." Elizabeth stands angrily from the table. "Looks like none of us are getting the club after all."

"Now, wait a minute," Amelia pleads with a hand toward Elizabeth. "Are we not going to consider it at least?"

"Consider what?" Julian barks. "The six of us are more likely to sprout wings and fly to Neverland than work together and create something that could actually succeed."

"Not with that attitude," Weston replies sarcastically. He's hardly looked up from his phone this entire time, and I doubt he's even interested in what has been presented to us. Everything is a joke to Weston. He's here to party, and everyone knows it. If he doesn't get a crack at owning the club, he'll just tend bar here at Geo's or at one of many other bars in Paris. He doesn't have nearly as much riding on this as the rest of us do, and his cutting tone grates on my nerves.

"Maybe Dad is right," Amelia says sweetly as she wrings her hands and glances around the table. "Maybe we could own it together. It could work."

She barely gets through the sentence before her brother rises from the table. Weston is right behind him.

"What a waste of time," Julian complains.

There is disappointment on Amelia's face, but all I see is my sister sitting next to her. My sister, who I haven't even been in the same room with for over a year. Who knows if I'll get this chance again? If I want to repair my relationship with Elizabeth, working side by side with her on this club might be the only way to do it. This could be different than just seeing each other in passing like we do now. We'd be in meetings together. She'd have no choice but to speak to me.

But how the hell am I going to rally the rest of this group to join me? If I let them leave and Ronan's offer goes up in smoke, then Elizabeth will go back to ignoring me, and it could be another year before I get her in the same room as me again. I can't let that happen.

"One year," I say, and everyone freezes with their eyes on me. "One year," I repeat, standing from my seat. "I mean…what do we have to lose, right?"

"What's the point?" Phoenix asks with a tilt of her head.

"The point is…Ronan is right. We could make something great. We all bring something different to the table. Amelia has the design and marketing skills, and West can run the bar. Nix has the business brains. Elizabeth…"

My sister doesn't turn my way, even after I utter her name. Swallowing my grief, I continue.

"Elizabeth has danced in shows all over Paris. She can head the entertainment."

"And what about me?" Julian asks from behind me.

Turning away from the table, I stare at him. Standing at my height, I am toe-to-toe with the one guy I can't stand. The idea of working with him repulses me, but this isn't about me. It's about making this harebrained scheme work in hopes of getting my sister back.

For her, I can endure a year with the most pretentious, arrogant, self-absorbed asshole in Paris.

"You, Julian," I say, clapping a hand on his shoulder. "You'll be my partner."

"Your partner?" he asks with a scoff.

"Yeah. You and I will manage it together. And after the year's up, those of us who want to leave can leave. Then you'll have it to yourself."

He scrutinizes me. The room is bathed in awkward tension as we wait for his response. It's all up to Julian now. The one person who needs this the least. He lives a comfortable existence thanks to his rich inheritance.

We're at Julian's mercy now.

His brow furrows as he considers it with a scheming expression.

"Fine," he says eventually. "I'll do it." Quickly, he averts his attention from my face, and I know I should react, but I'm too confounded. I never expected him to actually agree to this.

"Wait, so we're really doing this?" Phoenix asks.

"I guess we're really doing this," I respond.

I look over to my sister, who still won't look at me. Instead, she smiles softly at Amelia, who is trying to stifle her excitement.

"I'll get us a round of shots," Weston announces as he goes to the bar, slipping behind it like he owns the place. And considering most of us grew up here and have known the owner since we were kids, he sort of does.

Meanwhile, the rest of us are still standing around the table. Low chatter and nervous mumbles fill the space while I let this all sink in. There's a twinge of guilt in my gut because I didn't do this for the club or the others. I don't care whether the club thrives or fails, and I don't genuinely believe Ronan's message about finding some deeply hidden worth in working together. These people aren't my family. My family fell apart the day my wife died.

Now, there's only one family member I'm concerned about in this room, and I'm doing it for her. Running this club with

Elizabeth means getting to see her and talk to her and hopefully repairing our broken relationship. Once I do that, I'm taking my daughter back home to California where we belong. The rest of them can do what they want with the place.

One year. I can get through one year.

Weston returns a moment later with a tray full of shots. Knowing Weston, they're cheap crowd-pleasers, as if we're a gang of kids fresh out of college and not a meeting of mature business owners. Judging by the white appearance and sugar-coated rims, I assume they're Lemon Drops, and I was right.

"To the new club," Phoenix cheers as she holds one up.

"Wait," Amelia cries, and we all lower our shot glasses. "Dad said we could rename it. So what should it be?"

The answer comes to me immediately.

"Well, he said our parents created a legacy. So I say we do the same."

"Legacy," Phoenix replies with a proud smirk.

"I like it," Amelia chirps.

"To Legacy," Weston cheers.

"To Legacy," the rest of us echo. Then we all throw the shots back, even my sister, who has replaced her angry scowl with an expression that looks vaguely like warmth and hope.

This whole venture will surely be a disaster. We've worked under Ronan and Matis for years, but have we really learned enough to do it on our own? We don't have what it takes to recreate what Emerson Grant did nearly thirty years ago. Maybe if our hearts were in it, we could. But like Ronan said, we've lost our way. We're all fighting for something other than this club. Our motivations go far beyond this business venture. But with any luck, my plan might work.

And just like that, the Legacy is born.

Rule #1: You'll almost always find something exciting inside a book.

Camille
Ten months later

"Bonjour, Marguerite," I call, pressing open the door of the bookstore. After dropping my bag under the counter, I stretch my arms over my head and move toward the aisles.

The early autumn temperatures have dropped, so the room is still cool with the shutters closed. Pulling them open, I let the heat of the morning sun shine through the dusty windows. Popping my earphones in, I flip through the music app on my phone, landing on an '80s pop playlist and hitting Play. Pat Benatar guitar chords blast into my ears as I grab the cart full of books and push it toward the Littérature section.

Working at the used bookstore doesn't pay much, but it's enough to cover my half of the rent at the flat that I split with an obnoxious and annoying woman who works at the boulangerie. And I like working with books. At least with them, I can escape this mundane life for a moment. The measly pay is enough to get me by until I can get out of this village for real and go somewhere better. Maybe London. Maybe Paris. Maybe Rome. But it's not like a lonely girl with no parents, no money, no education, and no skill can just pick up and leave the village where she grew up. My stubborn curiosity and poor drawing skills wouldn't get me far.

So until then, I'm stuck at this boring job in this boring village, living this boring life.

It takes me a few hours to get the cart full of new donations put away, but to be honest, I'm going slow on purpose. If I hurry, then I won't have anything to do, and hardly anyone comes in now that summer is over, so if I finish too quickly, then I'll *really* be bored.

Marguerite is at the checkout desk now, handling customers, while I peruse the books in the romance section because they have the best covers and titles. After peeking around to make sure no one is watching, I slide a book from the shelf. The spine is pink, and the text is bubbly, and on the cover are a pair of lips blowing bubble gum.

Blondie shouts "Call Me" in my ear as I pull a pen out of my back pocket. After another quick glance around, I flick open the front cover of the book and draw a tiny black cat with a spiky mullet blowing a bubble on the inside. It makes me chuckle as I finish the doodle before closing the book and sliding it back into place.

The drawings are just something I've always done. My father used to call them my little signature. He'd find them all over the house when I was young, shouting at me from the kitchen when I'd forget the rules: no furniture, no walls, no floor.

"Tu as encore fait des bêtises, Camille," he used to shout. *You've been causing trouble again, Camille.*

But he'd still find tiny black cats or snakes or turtles popping up on a dinner plate or the leaves of a plant. He wasn't *really* mad. He was never really mad.

I smile at the memory as I walk down the aisle.

My pen goes back into my pocket as I run my fingers along the shelf. I don't know what it is about the next book that catches my eye. It's an old one that hasn't been picked up in years; I know every untouched book on these shelves by heart now. But something about it grabs my attention today.

It has a dark blue leatherette spine with the title *Le Passeport*, which is a boring and strange title for a romance novel. But then I get the idea to draw a gorilla with a suitcase and bucket hat on the inside, so I slip the book from the top shelf.

As I thumb open the front cover to find the title page, something falls from between the pages and lands on the floor. I put the pen back in my pocket as I lean down to retrieve the beige envelope. I stare at it curiously, turning it over to see the messy, scrawled handwriting on the front.

It's addressed to a woman—Emmaline Rochefort.

The top of the envelope is ripped open, so as the song in my ears changes to something slower and more romantic, I put the book back on a random shelf and peer into the envelope. Inside, there is a folded piece of paper and a small square photo.

It feels like an invasion of privacy, but I can't help myself as I pull them both out. Flipping the photo over, I stare down at the couple smiling back at me. It's a young, handsome man with his arm around the shoulder of a beautiful brunette woman. They're both grinning, cheeks pulled tight from ear to ear and bright, pearly white teeth showing.

They appear so happy it's almost hard to look at them. Two very real people in what looks like the throes of a blissful moment together. One small photograph has captured that, so now it's like they're inviting me to be a part of the moment too.

Tearing my eyes from the photo, I look at the letter next. It's folded beige paper with scribblings all over it, from the front to the back.

At the very top, it says, *Dear Emmaline*.

The letter is scrawled in messy English.

I can't stop thinking about you, it starts. But I stop reading there. It would be an invasion to keep reading.

Turning it over, I find the closing sentence sweetly signed:
Love, Jack.

"Camille," Marguerite calls from the front of the store.

I quickly shove the letter, envelope, and photo into the pocket of my jacket before I answer, "J'arrive!" Then I dash up to the front of the store and Marguerite hands me a list of tedious tasks.

For the rest of my shift, I think about the letter and the couple. How did the envelope end up in a book in our small used bookstore? Who still writes love letters anyway?

The temptation to read it is almost too much to resist. And every free moment I have, I pull it from my pocket and glimpse another line.

I miss you so much.
I never expected to fall in love with you.
Please come back.

On my lunch break, I walk down to the bakery to buy a quiche. My rude roommate, Ingrid, is working, and she barely acknowledges me as she tosses me my lunch.

I don't reply as I take it and walk out the door. On the table outside, I pull out the letter. Instead of inspecting the message, I look at the address listed on the envelope.

The woman, Emmaline Rochefort, must have lived here in Giverny.

The man, Jack St. Claire, has an address in Paris.

How did an English-speaking man in Paris end up writing a love letter to a French woman in a small village? The answers might be in the letter itself, but for some reason, it feels forbidden to read it. It's so personal. So intimate. Whatever he wrote on that paper is meant for her eyes only, even if it did somehow end up in the bookstore where I work.

Maybe it never made it to Emmaline. Maybe someone else found it and opened it, using it as a bookmark and discarding it between the pages when they lost interest in reading it.

Maybe Emmaline did read it and has been looking for it all

this time. If that book has been on our shelf for years, then what became of the couple in the photo?

Since I can't bring myself to read the letter in its entirety, I decide to pull out my phone and look up their names instead.

David Bowie croons "Starman" into my ears as I type *Emmaline Rochefort* into the Google search bar first.

Of course, she's not the only Emmaline Rochefort. So I scroll through the results page, finding old women and teenage girls in various locations around the globe. But eventually, a social media page pops up, so I click on it.

The image at the top of her page is of her and a little girl. Immediately, I can tell the woman on the screen—with the pearly white teeth and warm, congenial smile—is the same woman in the photo. It's eerie, really. Finding some stranger online from one small photo and a name.

From there, I scroll, and my heart sinks.

I miss you, Emma.

You're in our thoughts forever.

Gone too soon. Prayers for your family.

Comment after comment after comment of some random person online sending messages to an account as if they can speak to this person beyond the grave. I'm hit by a twinge of grief.

Not for this woman I don't even know, of course. But seeing this immediately brings back memories of my father's restaurant's social media page. One day, it was filled with photos of his famous pan-seared fish, and the next, it was flooded with messages like these.

Gone too soon.

Prayers for your family.

We'll miss you, Laurent.

Messages he'll never read but words of sorrow that just needed to be expressed.

I glance down at the photo on the table. The happy couple stares back up at me.

The woman in my photo is dead.

Judging by the comments on her page, it happened only two years ago.

For the rest of my lunch break—and then some—I delve into this woman's life. I manage to scroll far enough to see past the in memoriam comments and see tidbits of her real life. Pictures of her with her daughter, an adorable toddler with bright blue eyes and brown hair set in bows on either side of her head.

And then I find what I'm really looking for. It's a photo of the beautiful woman, adorable little girl, and a dashing man standing together on the steps of the Sacré-Cœur. They are bundled in wool jackets and hats, and like the small photo on the table in front of me, they look happy. They look like they're in love.

Even without reading the letter, I feel some sense of comfort in knowing this happy couple stayed together. Even if she passed away. Even if the ending wasn't exactly happy. Even if I still have no idea what that entire letter says, I'm glad to know they got married and had a child.

After my lunch, I try to put my little obsession away, but I still carry it with me for the rest of the day. When my shift ends at four, I leave work and stop by the market to pick up some food and a bottle of wine. My roommate doesn't cook or bother me much when I'm in the kitchen or dining room. She does, however, hog the TV in the living room and plays her nauseating reality TV shows far too loud.

So I pick another playlist and keep my earphones in as I cook, this time listening to '90s grunge. Nirvana shouts through "Heart-Shaped Box" as I doodle on the wine label and wait for my pasta to cook.

All the while, I think about the couple. How do people find love like that? What did that woman have to do to get a handsome, seemingly successful, and, from what I can tell, normal man to give her so much attention? The only men I can get to look my way are creepy old men or chauvinistic young guys who only see tits and ass and fail to notice I have a face and a personality.

My dating life has been abysmal, to the point now where I turn down every single advance, even if the other person seems halfway decent. Every date I go on lacks connection. I won't settle for a life of contentment with someone else just to have a partner. I want fireworks and magic. I want to stare into someone's eyes and feel seen. I want to find a soul that matches mine.

I'm glad my pretty woman in the photo found love. Good for her.

After my dinner is done, I take it to the dining room table and browse more photos of the woman's social media. It's out of boredom and curiosity. This isn't an obsessive stalker thing. I'm not a creep. I'm so entranced, though, that I don't even hear Ingrid come in from the living room.

"What is that?" she asks, nodding toward the letter under my phone.

"Nothing," I reply, tugging it closer.

She takes a step closer and tries to reach for it. In a panic, I abandon my phone and fork to rescue the letter and photograph, spilling my wine in the process.

Ingrid rolls her eyes and chuckles to herself as I check to make sure the letter is intact. It's at that moment that I realize I might be a little too obsessed with this random piece of mail I found in a book today.

But I feel like I know Emmaline and Jack.

Not to mention I am in possession of something that once belonged to her. Something special. What if he's been looking for this letter? It's silly of me to think this way, to think that some strangers in a photograph mean anything to me.

What if I could return this letter to him? It may seem insignificant to most, but he clearly loved her enough to write it. He must be sick with grief, and this letter could be one small token of remembrance.

It's a wild idea, but my life is so boring and mundane that wild ideas feel like a lifeline. Wild ideas feel like hope. Because why not? Why can't I take the train to Paris and give this man a letter I found?

Why wouldn't I?

If he were mine, I'd want someone to do the same for me.

Rule #2: Get out of town once in a while.

Camille

"THE TRAIN TO PARIS DEPARTS IN FIFTEEN MINUTES."

I'm buzzing with excitement, standing on the train station platform. I've latched on to this wild idea as if it's a hot air balloon taking flight. If I let it go, I'll drift off into space. Instead, I hold tight and try not to look down.

The letter is tucked safely away in my pocket. Every few moments, I shove my hand in to make sure it's still there, sometimes rubbing it softly with my thumb or picking at a corner as if it's a safety blanket.

When the train doors open, I climb aboard and find a quiet seat in the back. I called into work this morning at the bookstore, telling Marguerite I had a bad case of food poisoning. It's a one-hour train ride to Paris, and my plan is to arrive in the city, go straight to the apartment listed on the envelope, and return the letter. Perhaps I could spend a couple of hours around the city before boarding the train tonight and coming home.

Still, after much deliberation, something about this plan feels off. It's as if I can't fully commit to it because part of me doesn't want to come home at all. This is the first time I've properly left home in years. It feels like a taste of adventure when what I really want is a lifetime of it.

Papa used to say I was like a little hummingbird, constantly flitting from one place to another, and that someday I would fly too far if someone didn't hold me down. I was always running off, sneaking out, staying out too late, and ditching school. I certainly didn't make it easy on him. But he was never too angry. He'd shake his head with a tsk, but he was never one for punishment.

The memory stings my eyes. I don't feel much like a bird anymore. Ever since he died, it's like my feet have been glued to the village. That part of me died with him. The Camille he once knew, who had enthusiasm for life, perished the moment he did. Would he be disappointed in me if he knew how much I've changed? That I lost my luster. That the responsibilities and weight of adulthood without him tied my feet to the floor. Would he be let down by the woman I've become?

During the train ride, I pull out my phone and browse some more about my mystery couple. I've done so much research on the woman, Emmaline, that I've barely done any research on the man. Suddenly realizing that I might see him today, I decide to try to find something about him.

In the photos with her, he's not tagged.

In her friends list, he's not listed.

Even when I search his name, results pop up, but none of them are the man in the photo.

It's like he's a ghost.

For the rest of the journey, I busy myself with checking my appearance in the selfie camera of my phone, taming my stray curls and wiping the ink smudge from my cheek. Digging into the bottom of my purse, I find an old lipstick and swipe it across my lips. I'm not usually one for makeup, but I want to look nice today. One should always look beautiful in Paris.

By the time the train arrives, I'm feeling far too flustered and tightly wound. From the train, I have to take the Métro to the 18th arrondissement, where the address listed is located.

As I climb up the stairs from the underground, it suddenly hits me that I'm really here. I'm really doing this.

It's a short walk to the apartment building, and as I walk, I enjoy the stroll through one of my favorite areas of the city. The art and culture come alive here. Walking alongside tourists and locals on a narrow sidewalk, I pass by a market bustling with energy and a small children's park where the kids laugh and play while their parents watch from the sides. The hills in Montmartre make for a beautiful view of Paris.

Then, before I know it, I'm standing in front of his building. The leaves of a large cherry tree fall around me as I stare up at the apartment building. Emmaline's letter is still safely stowed away in my pocket. Nervously, I climb the stairs and find the main door unlocked. I realize at this moment that it's possible he doesn't even live here anymore. He could have moved, especially if this letter is from before they were married and had their child.

And even though I came all this way to give him this letter, there's a subtle sense of relief at the idea that he might not be on the other side of that door. Then at least I could keep the letter guilt-free. I'd have a funny story and a day in Paris to look back on.

Still, I climb the stairs to the second floor and gently rap my knuckles against the surface. My limbs are shaking, and it's as if I forgot how to breathe entirely. Behind the door, I hear a little girl shouting something I can't make out, and a woman replies in an assertive tone.

The door flies open, and to my surprise, a beautiful woman with long red hair stands before me. She has a businesslike appearance to her with black trousers, black flats, and a thin white blouse tucked into her pants.

"Bonjour," she says in a polite greeting.

Struck by the sight of her, I hesitate before reaching my hand in my pocket. "Uh...I—"

"You must be here for the nanny position," the woman says in hurried English, cutting me off. "Please, come in."

The hand in my pocket freezes. *Nanny position?*

Just then, a small child pops up to the right of the redheaded woman. She has piercing blue eyes and perfectly combed brown hair that reaches her shoulders.

"Bonjour," she greets me sweetly.

I return the sentiment softly. Then the woman steps backward, allowing me space to walk into the house. Still frozen with uncertainty, I stammer some more. "I, uh..."

"Please, come in," she urges.

It's her authoritative tone that shakes me from my stupor. I don't understand why, but I take the steps forward into the stranger's apartment.

Think, Camille. What are you doing? Why are you here?

"My name is Phoenix Scott," the woman says with an American accent. "I'm Mr. St. Claire's business partner. I'll be conducting the interviews for the position. What is your name?"

I blink rapidly as if I've forgotten my own name.

Interviews.

Positions.

"Parlez-vous Anglais?" she asks as I stand here like a fish with my mouth hanging open. I've never been more confused in my life.

"Oui," I stammer. "I mean...yes."

"Good." She gives me an uncomfortable smile and a nod. "And your name?"

This isn't what I'm here for at all. I'm here to return a letter. I'm here to meet the mystery man in the photograph and return something from his late wife. I'm not here to apply for any job.

But for some reason, I find myself holding out a hand toward the woman. "Camille Aubert," I reply.

"Enchantée, Camille." She seems pleased that I managed to finally remember my name, gesturing for me to follow her into the apartment.

My jaw drops even more as I take a look around and notice just how stunning it is. The ceilings soar with ornate crown molding, and large windows bathe the space in warm, natural light. Looking down, I stare in awe at the herringbone wood floors and expensive-looking rugs. My fingers drift along the back of a plush velvet upholstered sofa.

It's a big difference from the small, boxy two-bedroom I live in.

Just then, I hear heavy footsteps from above, and I glance up toward the staircase to see someone walking by. It's clearly a man in a dark blue suit, but at this angle, that's all I can make out. In a flash, he's gone.

"Was that...Monsieur St. Claire?" I mumble awkwardly.

The woman glances up toward the stairs. "Yes, but he won't be coming down," she answers in a rush.

"Oh."

"Please have a seat," she says, guiding me toward the sitting room with two oversized armchairs near a marble fireplace. I sit down in one of them, and warning sirens continue to go off in my mind.

They say that I'm going to be in trouble for even sitting down. I'm a trespasser. An interloper. I'm not supposed to be here. I only came to return a letter. And now I'm sitting in their home under false pretenses.

The last twenty-four hours of my life, I've been obsessing over this family. I know far more about them than they know about me, and something about that feels very wrong.

I should go, but as I sit in this beautiful room in this luxurious apartment, I can't bring myself to leave. I'm not harming anyone. I can apply for the job. It doesn't mean I have to take it.

The woman with the interesting name returns and hands me

a clipboard with a stack of papers on it. "Fill these out, please. And then we'll get started with the interview."

Biting my lip, I take it from her. "Yes, ma'am."

As I'm filling out the papers on the clipboard, I keep glancing up at the stairs, wondering if I'll get a glimpse of the man again. Every few moments, I hear his voice, deep and muffled. It makes me wonder what he does for work. Why isn't he the one conducting this interview?

It takes me nearly thirty minutes to complete the paperwork, which is a considerably long time to spend on something I shouldn't even be doing. The woman and the little girl seem to have escaped into another room of the home, leaving me alone. Every time I contemplate giving a fake name or wrong answers, I choose not to. Instead, I scribble every single answer with conviction as if this is a job I actually want.

There are more footsteps upstairs, and the curiosity becomes too much to bear. Setting the clipboard on my seat, I stand up and glance around cautiously to be sure I'm alone. Then I quietly tiptoe toward the stairs.

I just want a small glimpse. I'd only like to lay my eyes on him—for reasons even I don't understand.

If I'm caught, then I can simply claim confusion or say I got lost. Climbing up the stairs one by one, I get about halfway, and it's high enough to just peek into the office on the left.

And there he is. He's pacing the room and speaking, sounding frustrated and controlling. I assume he's on the phone, but I'm not focused on his words. Instead, I'm staring at the broad expanse of his shoulders and the sharp line of his cheekbones.

He's even more handsome in person than in the photo. But there's a darkness in his eyes, heavy circles underneath, and new wrinkles at the corners. He's aged, and not just by time. The effects of grief are apparent in his weathered features. His posture is rigid and straight, and I watch the way his right hand balls into a fist before releasing, over and over again.

"I'm Beatrice," a small voice says from behind me, and I let out a startled yelp.

Spinning around, I stare at the little girl at the bottom of the stairs.

She's standing politely with her small hands clasped in front of her. "But everyone calls me Bea."

I open my mouth to reply, but first, I glance back up toward the second floor in time to see Jack St. Claire glaring down at me. Heat and embarrassment pulse through my veins. A moment later, he slams his office door, and I am riddled with shame for spying on him.

Taking a deep breath, I turn back to the little girl and descend the stairs toward her.

"Enchantée, Bea," I reply with a half-smile.. "How old are you?"

"I'm five. Are you going to be my new nanny?" she asks. She has on a lavender chiffon dress with pristine white tights and shiny black Mary Jane shoes. Her hair is meticulously combed with a part on the side and a matching purple bow pinned just above her ear.

"I don't know," I reply as I kneel down in front of her. "Can I tell you a secret?"

She nods emphatically.

"I've never been a nanny before," I whisper. "I didn't even know I was going to be applying for this job today."

I'm not sure why I come clean to a child, but Bea smiles widely at me when she hears my confession.

"That's okay," she chirps with a grin. "Do you like unicorns?"

This makes me chuckle. "I love unicorns."

"And fairies?"

"Of course."

"Want to see my room? It's painted with fairies and unicorns."

"I should probably wait here," I start, but the girl takes my hand and tugs me along with her. Her shoes clap loudly against the floor as she pulls me deeper into the apartment, down a hallway, and into one of the bedrooms.

The room is, in fact, painted with fairies and unicorns. The entire back wall looks like a scene out of a fairy tale, with lush green trees, toadstools, and a castle in the background.

"This is amazing," I whisper as she hops up onto her bed, kicking her feet beneath her.

"My papa works a lot," she says. "Phoenix says I need someone to play with when I'm not in school because Papa is too busy to play with me."

There's sadness in her voice when she says this that tugs on my heart. I suddenly remember that this poor child lost her mother at only three years old. She probably doesn't even remember her.

Something I can relate to. My mother didn't die. She just decided she wasn't fit for motherhood and rarely came around as I was growing up. But at least I had my father, who was always present, always enthusiastic about raising me, and always there to be the parent I needed.

But poor Bea has a father who is too busy to spend time with her, so they have to hire someone to come into their home and give her the attention she deserves.

And she's so desperate for that attention that she's latching on to a random stranger. I remember doing the same.

I stand in the doorway of her room, not comfortable with going inside. "I'm not going to be your nanny," I say softly as I cross my arms over my chest.

"Why not?" she asks. "Why don't you want to be my nanny?"

"Well, it's not that I don't want to. It's that…" My voice trails, unable to find a good enough reason for her. "Your papa is going to find you a very good nanny. I'm sure a lot of people have applied."

"He'll pay you a lot of money," she says, and it makes me chuckle. "And you can stay in our extra bedroom. And we can bake cookies and have sleepovers and play games."

"That sounds very fun," I reply softly, which isn't a lie.

Just then, I hear footsteps behind me, and I turn to find the redheaded woman coming toward us.

"I'm sorry," she says. "I was on a phone call. We can do your interview now."

Giving Bea a small wave, I leave her and follow the woman back out to the sitting room. Phoenix takes the opposite seat from me as she glances down at the packet I just filled out, assessing my answers with a strict, tight-lipped expression.

"Do you have experience with children?" she asks.

"I curate the children's department at our bookstore, but other than that…no."

She glances up at me skeptically. "Any certifications…or training?"

I shake my head. "No."

"What makes you qualified for this job?" she asks plainly.

Somewhere in the midst of this whole mix-up, I found myself actually wanting this. And why shouldn't I? I want to work in this home and live in this city. I want to pull my feet from the cement they've been stuck in since my father died and actually live my life. This could all be a mix-up, or it could be fate.

My hands are clutched in my lap as I glance back up toward the stairs again. Then my eyes dance over to where Bea is peeking out from the hallway. And the answer comes straight from my heart.

"I didn't have a mother growing up," I say. "So I can under-stand what life is like for Beatrice. I know what it's like to feel like a part of you is missing, but I was lucky enough to have a father who instilled confidence in me. I may not be…certified or trained, but I'm trustworthy and curious and fun. And I'd love her like my own."

Bea grins at me from the hallway.

Just then, something draws my attention to the stairway again, and I glance up to find a man standing there, watching me from the second-floor landing. He has intense dark eyes and a wide, stoic stance. The way he's staring at me sends chills down my spine.

Without saying a word, he walks away again as if he was just caught spying. He leaves me feeling cold and strange after gazing at me so intensely.

Phoenix doesn't even notice his presence. She just notes something on the paper before smiling back up at me. "That was lovely. Thank you." After a minute, she adds, "You should know the position is live-in. Beatrice would require around-the-clock attention with breaks, of course, in the evenings and on Sundays. I think that's all for now. Do you have any questions?"

Questions? No. I'm still reeling from this entire encounter. My only question is how on earth did I end up in this job interview? Instead of asking that, I shake my head.

"Great," she says as she stands. "We will be in touch."

I stand from the chair and wave goodbye to Bea, glancing up at the stairs one more time, but he's not there.

Then I shake the woman's hand and walk out the front door. On my walk back to the Métro line, I can't stop thinking about the man's eyes as he stared at me. And about the sad way Bea spoke about him in her room. And about how strange it is that I just applied for a job I didn't even come here for.

The letter is still hiding in my pocket.

I no longer feel bad for not giving it to him. I don't feel bad for actually wanting this job now. And it's not because I want the money or the life in Paris. It's because something about this home and this family feels right.

It feels familiar.

It feels, in some small way, as if they need me.

Rule #3: Don't look back.

Camille

WHAT JUST HAPPENED? I'M IN A DAZE ON THE WALK FROM JACK'S apartment to the Métro station as if I've just woken up from a dream. Pressing my hand over my lips, I stifle a giggle as I relive the entire thing.

Was it wrong of me to apply for that job? If it was, I don't care. When was the last time I did something so bold? It might have just been a job interview, but it felt like breaking the rules. And I nearly forgot how fun breaking the rules could be. It's not like I'll get it or ever see them again.

Or will I? What if I really do get the job? What if I really do move to Paris and work in that luxury apartment? I might not have gone there intending to apply for a job, but I still want it—I want it *bad*. Working in that home, spending my days with the cutest little girl I've ever seen, living in Paris, and making better money—it's not wrong of me to want this.

Not to mention I am perfectly qualified. Okay, so I've never been a nanny before, but how hard could it be? I can cook and clean. I can make sure that she stays safe and entertained. Honestly, what else do I need to know from there?

With a renewed sense of invigoration in my bones, I walk. Although I was headed toward the Métro station to take me back home, I don't continue there, not right away. Instead, I walk to the center of Paris, taking my time to breathe in the city. Strolling along the Seine, I buy a dusty old book from one of the stands, and I think for a while that my dad would be proud of me.

For one entire day, I'm not stuck in the same old boring routine.

Sitting on the edge of the river, my feet dangling over the wall, I pull the letter out again. I still don't read it, but I stare at the picture. On the other side of the river, there's a couple cuddled together, giggling so loudly they distract me from my thoughts.

Loneliness settles in like mud seeping into my pores, caking every part of me with this solitude. It's not just that I've been stuck in my village for the past two years—it's that I've been utterly alone throughout it all. The friends I did have I pushed away. When relatives call, I don't answer. I've isolated myself, and it took me this long to realize it.

As the sun starts to set over the city, I make a promise to myself. Even if I don't get this job, I need a change. I need to get out of Giverny. I need to meet someone. I can't keep living my life like this, hidden in the shadows while the world passes me by through dirty bookstore windows.

With a renewed sense of purpose, I board the train for home. With my head pressed against the glass, I watch Paris disappear into the distance. "I'm coming back," I whisper quietly to the city as if it can hear me. As if it will miss me.

Then I close my eyes as I relive every moment in that home. The adorable way Bea pulled me into her room, the smile on her face when I answered the interview questions.

The heavy gaze from the man on the stairs.

I only saw his face in passing, but the man I saw did not

match the one in the photo. The man in the picture is young and exuberant. The one who glared at me, making me shrink in my seat, is a hardened, reclusive shell of a man.

Even still, he was handsome.

Not that it matters. I doubt I'll ever see him again.

———————

The next few days pass in a sullen, boring haze. When it sinks in by the end of the week that I truly am *not* getting that job, it hits me harder than I expected it to. I'm not sure what hope I was clinging to, but part of me genuinely thought he was going to hire an unqualified, inexperienced woman to care for his precious five-year-old daughter.

I'm sitting at a table in the back of the store, doodling a lizard climbing the side of the Eiffel Tower on the inside of a pamphlet, when I glance up and see a familiar face passing through the front door.

Jack St. Claire strides into the small, musty shop as if he owns the place. He doesn't see me at first as he marches straight to the front desk.

My jaw drops, and heat floods my cheeks as I tear my feet down from the table and nearly tumble over in my chair, knocking a stack of books to the floor in my clumsy attempt to be discreet.

Ducking down to pick up the books, I watch him through the aisles of the store as he speaks to Marguerite. It's the most I've been able to look at his face since that moment in his house.

He has a soft five-o'clock shadow, a dimple in his chin, a heavy brow line, strong cheekbones, and a flat, emotionless expression on his face.

My eyes drift downward and latch on to the gold band gleaming around the ring finger on his left hand. *His wedding band.* My heart stutters at the sight of it, and a strange feeling courses through me. Is it jealousy or pity? Hard to tell.

Suddenly, I start to panic, thinking I've somehow been caught. He knows I took the letter from the book. He knows I manipulated my way into his home. He knows I lied about everything.

Except…I didn't lie about anything.

I am wholly innocent, but just seeing his demeanor and hearing his voice make me feel as if I've done something wrong. Chills break out over the exposed flesh of my arms and neck.

He speaks loudly in English to Marguerite, and she stumbles her way through a response. I can't make out what they're saying, but I hear my name. My fingers grip the desk tighter as I spy from beneath the table.

What is he doing here? Did he really come all this way to check up on me?

Marguerite makes a confused face as she glances around the store. When her eyes find me in my hiding spot under the table, she points, and my cheeks burn even hotter. I let out a stifled groan as Jack's fervent gaze locks with mine.

Thanks, Marguerite.

Swallowing my pride, I stand from the floor, quickly stacking the books I knocked over to busy my shaking hands. He's still speaking to my boss at the front. She answers in quick, pleasant responses, nodding her head with a smile.

Then he's making his way toward me, his footsteps heavy and pronounced. As he reaches the table where I stand awkwardly, he glances down at the pamphlet I was doodling on. I snatch it up and shove it into my pocket to hide my childish sketch.

He lets out a disgruntled sigh, and I nearly choke on this sense of inadequacy. It dawns on me how odd it is that he came all this way. Back to an old used bookstore in his late wife's hometown. To the very bookstore where his letter ended up.

"I'm Jack St. Claire," he states, and I bite my lip at the sound of his voice, deep and husky. I am practically shrinking in his presence, so I press my shoulders back and lengthen my spine to make up for the commanding loftiness of his stature.

"I know who you are," I reply quietly.

For a while, he seems ready to say something but doesn't. I can't help but wonder why this man is standing in my place of employment. He looks so out of place here. After a moment of staring at me without an expression on his face, he states plainly, "My daughter likes you."

"Me?" I murmur, touching my chest.

He nods. I'm filled with warmth at the thought. Picturing her in her pristine purple dress and shiny black shoes makes me smile.

"I like her too," I reply before pinching my bottom lip between my fingers to hide my grin.

"She must speak only English in our home. Will that be a problem?"

My brows furrow, confusion piercing my ability to think clearly. Disoriented, I shake my head.

His next words don't do much to clear up my confusion. "I did a thorough background check on you."

Funny. I did one of my own on you too, I think but definitely don't utter that out loud.

Sternly, he continues. "You never went to university. Never left this town." At this, he glances around the small, cramped bookstore, and I stiffen with a hint of defensiveness. Is he judging me? My spine straightens a little more.

"I stayed to help my father with his restaurant," I reply, although I'm not sure why. I don't owe this man an explanation of my life choices.

At the mention of my father, he glances back into my eyes as if he knows. Was that part of his *thorough* background check? Again, he looks like he wants to say something but stays quiet.

There is something so intriguing about him, and I don't buy for a second that he's as cold and emotionless as he lets on. Behind those dark eyes is the smiling man in the photo. He's in there somewhere. There are layers hidden beneath Jack's facade, and I have the photo in my pocket to prove it.

Finally, he bluntly states, "You start on Monday. Phoenix will call you with more information."

Time stops as I blink at him numbly. I start on Monday. Start what? Did he just tell me he's hiring me as a nanny?

"Wait, what?"

The broody veil lifts momentarily as he clarifies, "You got the job, Miss Aubert." But then it's quickly replaced as he settles his brows together. "Don't let me down."

Just when I expect him to say more, he lets out another growly sigh and turns on his heels before marching out of the bookstore without a goodbye. He says something in a kind tone to Marguerite before disappearing through the doors.

I'm standing in shock at the entire encounter, and she seems frozen in the same manner. It's like he put us both in a daze, and we can't seem to snap out of it.

Marguerite finally makes her way over to me before placing her hand on her hip, saying, "When were you going to tell me you were applying for other jobs?"

Blinking, I shake myself out of it. "Um…I didn't mean to. It accidentally happened."

"Well, you accidentally got the job. Congratulations."

"Marguerite, I'm sorry," I say, letting my shoulders melt away from my ears. "I can turn it down."

"Psh," she says, waving a hand at me. "Look at this place. Does it look like I need you? You're taking a job in Paris with *that* man. If you turn it down, *I'll* take it."

Suddenly, it's like everything hits me at once. Placing my hands on my cheeks, I stare at the old woman with eyes shot wide.

I got the job.

I'm moving to Paris.

I'm living with Jack St. Claire and his daughter.

All because I found a picture in a book.

"Don't panic," she says with a shake of her head. "You're

young. Your father wouldn't want you wasting away here in this old town. Go. Have an adventure."

The mention of my father has my head snapping up. Thick emotion builds behind my eyes because I know she's right. My father would definitely not want me to stay here when I have the opportunity to go somewhere new.

I clear my throat before responding. "I can...finish the week."

"Finish the week?" she asks incredulously. "I don't want you finishing out the *day*. You need to get home and pack. You're moving to Paris. Go draw all your little animals there. Leave one on the Eiffel Tower for me."

I let out a giggle before leaping around the table and wrapping my arms around the woman. She pats my back sweetly before shooing me away.

"Merci, Marguerite," I say with excitement. Then I grab my purse from under the central desk and dash out the front door.

Rule #4: Don't get carried away.

Camille

On my next trip to Paris, I have a lot more with me than just one handbag. Okay, it's not much more, only a rolling valise filled with clothes and a backpack with my electronics. It's a little depressing to see everything I own fits into one small suitcase, but I'm on a mission to change that. I'm moving to Paris to build a life, a real one.

Once I save up some money working for the St. Claire family, I'll have the means to get my own place in Paris. Eventually, I could find another job here. Maybe I'll meet someone, and we could travel the world together. Who knows what my new future holds? The possibilities alone are more exciting than anything I've done in the past two years.

My feet are leaving the floor, Papa. And there's no one to hold me down.

I've been in contact with Phoenix since Jack showed up in my bookstore out of the blue last week. She's helped to set everything up so that when I get off the train at Gare Saint-Lazare, there is a driver outside waiting for me. I have never in my life seen a man in a black suit waiting for me with my last name printed on a white card, but there he is. I stifle a grin as I wave at him awkwardly. He helps me load my things into the trunk of the car and ushers me into the back seat before we take off toward the apartment in Montmartre.

It still feels like a dream.

Phoenix is standing out front with Bea when we pull up to the building. The little girl, clothed in a slightly more casual blue dress today, hops up and down excitedly as the driver opens my door. As soon as my feet hit the cobblestone street, Bea comes running toward me as if we're old friends reunited. It tugs at my heart to see how quickly she's latched on to me.

"Camille!" she squeals as she throws her arms around my legs.

"Bonjour, Bea," I say as I lean down and give her a proper hug. Her hair is still as immaculate as it was last time, and it makes me wonder if she ever lets it get messy. Is this little girl always so prim and proper? Does she ever get the chance to be a kid?

"I told Papa to hire you," she says with a giggle.

"I'm glad you did," I reply.

After greeting Bea, I stand and shake Phoenix's hand again. She seems so serious with strict posture and very practical clothing.

"How was your trip?" she asks.

"Très bien, merci," I reply, wincing at the reminder that Jack said strictly no French in the house. Technically, we're still outside, so hopefully she'll let that slide on a technicality.

Phoenix doesn't react. "The driver can bring your bags inside, and I can give you a tour."

Bea links her little hand in mine as we follow Phoenix into the building and up the stairs toward the apartment. Once we enter, I find myself immediately looking toward the stairs for a sign of Jack. The apartment is quiet, so I assume he's not here.

"This will be your room back here," Phoenix says, and I follow her through the apartment. It takes me by surprise again, just how large the home is with two levels, two sitting areas, two dining rooms, one grand kitchen, and a hallway full of doors.

As she presses open one of the doors, I peer inside to find a pristine and practical bedroom. One bed, one dresser, one nightstand, and an en suite bathroom.

"This is lovely," I say as I take a look around. I imagine myself living here. It's not much, but it's a start.

"I've printed out everything we agreed upon already here," she says as she hands me a packet. "Including your hours, house rules, payment, and numbers in case of emergency."

As I take the packet, I quickly scan through it, but none of it is new. We've already discussed all this.

"Beatrice attends primary school from eight thirty until four. You will need to drop her off and pick her up. Monsieur St. Claire works mostly in his office upstairs during the day. The apartment must stay relatively quiet while he's working. There's a children's park down the street."

Bea hops excitedly at the sound of that. Surely, she has some play clothes, because I can't imagine her at the park in these pretty dresses.

Phoenix continues to elaborate on all the rules and expectations, and I want to stop her and assure her that I have everything under control. But she seems so determined, I let her finish.

"Do you have any questions?" she asks.

"No," I reply with my hands gripped together behind my back.

She hesitates briefly while staring into my eyes, and I can tell she wants to say something. "Bea, go play in your room," she says to the little girl.

Reluctantly, Bea listens, sprinting down the hall to her own room, leaving Phoenix and me alone.

After breathing a pensive sigh, she says, "Monsieur St. Claire is a private man. It's best you don't go upstairs or bother him unless it's important. Don't ask about his work or where he goes at night."

Well, that sounds very ominous and not at all comforting. My brows furrow as my heart suddenly starts hammering in my chest. "Okay…" I should probably pry for information, but what if I do and she decides I'm too nosy and Jack changes his mind about hiring me? It was my stubborn curiosity that got me this job—I'm not about to let it ruin it at the same time.

"He hasn't dealt with the death of his wife well, so he might come across as a little cold and mean. It would be wise of you to give him his space."

Consider my curiosity piqued. *Leave it be, Camille.*

"I understand," I murmur.

"You have my number. If you need anything, call me. I live just two blocks down."

"Everything is under control," I say with a nod.

When she lets out another sigh, her shoulders relax.

Before she walks away, I ask, "Has Bea ever had a nanny before?"

She shakes her head. "No. Jack never wanted another woman in the house."

"So who normally watches her?"

Her mouth sets in a thin line. "Me. Other friends. Her aunt."

"What about her father?" I ask, sensing that she's hiding something.

After a contemplative look, she replies, "Like I said, he didn't handle Em's death well."

Before I can ask her to elaborate, Phoenix walks out of the room and down the hall toward the front door. I'm left to wonder what exactly that means.

⁕────◦◦◦◦◦────⁕

Once Phoenix is gone, I find Bea sitting on the floor of her room. There is still no sign of her father. I'm not sure if that means he's asleep or at work…wherever that is.

Suddenly, it hits me that it's just me and her. I'm really doing this. I'm really her nanny. Until this evening, I am responsible for this little girl that I don't even know. For now, I can put my curiosity about Jack St. Claire aside and focus on her.

Bea's room is tidy and simple. Other than the fairy mural painted on the wall, it's a very traditional girl's room. There's a large dollhouse against the wall with a small bucket of toys next to it. Bea is lying on the floor with two of her dolls, playing quietly.

"What are you playing?" I ask, leaning against the doorframe with my arms crossed. The urge to use French is strong, but I refrain. Although I know English, French is what I'm accustomed to using at home. This might be difficult to get used to.

"With my dolls," Bea replies playfully.

My stomach growls as if on cue. I read somewhere in my very lazy research on taking care of children that they thrive on structure. And while Bea's home seems to be very strict and controlled, I have a feeling her life is anything but structured. If what Phoenix said was true, then Bea has been cared for by family and friends sporadically to cover the gaps that her mother's death left behind.

Step one—create a routine.

Glancing down at my watch, I see it's just past noon. "Are you hungry?"

She glances up from the floor. With a cute little smirk on her face, she nods.

I hold out my hand for her, and she jumps up from the floor and takes it. We walk together into the kitchen, and I find an apron hanging on a hook behind the door. After slipping it over my head, I open the fridge and scavenge for something to prepare for lunch.

The kitchen is poorly stocked, which is something I assume will be my responsibility starting today. Step two—make a grocery list tonight and go shopping tomorrow.

"There isn't very much in here," I say with a wrinkle between my brows.

"Papa normally orders in."

"Orders in?" I reply with a gasp. Slamming the fridge shut, I turn toward Bea. "Well, lucky for you, my father owned a restaurant, so I know how to cook."

It takes me a while to scour the kitchen, but eventually, I find enough to prepare a simple stir-fry lunch with eggs and vegetables. As I'm working, Bea watches from the stool.

Everything just feels right. I have a new job in Paris. An adorable little girl to look after. Excellent pay.

"Are you a…" She stumbles over her words. "What's the person called who cooks for other people?"

I turn to find her mouth twisted up in a quizzical expression. With a smile, I reply, "A chef?"

"A chef," she repeats. "Are you a chef?"

"No," I say, shaking my head. "I was a waiter sometimes, but not a chef."

"You don't want to work there anymore?" she asks innocently.

A pang of regret stings as I turn my attention back to the stove. "After my father died, the restaurant closed."

"Oh," she mumbles sadly. "Did he go to sleep like my maman?"

Shit. The kitchen falls into a heavy silence, and the change in mood is my fault. I didn't really want to cover death on day one of my new job. It's slightly concerning that she thinks her mother went to sleep, but maybe that's how they explained it to her innocent mind. Who am I to complicate that?

"Um…yes. I think we need some music," I say to change the subject. Going into my backpack, I pull out my portable speaker and place it on the counter. After connecting it to my phone, I pick an upbeat playlist, and "Girls Just Wanna Have Fun" blasts through the kitchen.

Bea begins smiling and dancing in her seat as I continue cooking. *Crisis averted.*

"So what do you like to do?" I ask, turning toward her.

She shrugs.

"You like arts?"

"Sometimes we do art at school," she replies.

"What about sports? Or music?"

"At school," she repeats.

"Hm," I mumble to myself.

"Tante Elizabeth is a ballerina," she says, and I turn to her with interest.

"That's nice," I reply. "Does your papa ever take you to her shows?"

Bea slumps in her seat. "No. Papa doesn't take me anywhere."

"Nowhere?" I ask.

She shakes her head. I can see sadness creeping in on her face, so I decide to change the subject—again.

"Well, I love arts and crafts and sports and music. So we'll have lots of fun."

This makes her grin excitedly. The song changes, and the next one is an upbeat pop song that suddenly has us both dancing and singing along.

The next thing I know, Bea is hopping around on the floor, shaking her hips, and trying to sing along with the words. She twirls so fast in her pretty blue dress that her hair bow flies across the room. It makes me laugh, so I crank up the volume and take her hands, spinning her around the kitchen as we giggle with excitement.

I lose track of time as we dance. I lose track of *everything*. Warmth blossoms in my chest at the sight of her grinning from ear to ear. When was the last time she smiled like this? Hell, when was the last time *I* smiled like this? If this is what being a nanny is like, then I am certain I will love every second of it. All I must do is create a routine and keep her happy. That's it. How hard could it be?

Lost in the moment, I'm singing along to the lyrics, incredibly off-key, when I spin around and let out a scream.

Slamming my hand over my mouth, I stare at Jack in the doorway, watching us both with a displeased grimace on his face.

"Turn it down," he barks angrily.

But then, out of the corner of my eye, I catch sight of smoke billowing from the pan on the stove.

"Le riz!" I shriek as I run over and turn off the flame. I try to stir the contents, but it's futile. They're charred and stuck in a smelly black mass at the bottom of the pan.

"Papa said to turn it down!" Bea shouts at me.

Clapping a hand on my forehead, I dash over to the speaker, but Jack marches over and beats me to it. We reach for the device at the same time, our hands colliding as his clicks the button first.

Then the room is bathed in tense silence with the stench of burnt rice in the air.

Jack is wearing a tense scowl, the cleft in his chin more prominent as he frowns at me. This job is about to be over before it even started. Frazzled and caught off guard, I start rambling apologies in French.

"Je suis désolée. J'ai commencé à faire à manger, nous nous amusions beaucoup, et je n'ai pas fait attention. Je suis une très bonne cuisinière en principe, et…"

"English," he bellows in frustration. "Miss Aubert, I thought I made it clear that we only speak English at home."

My mouth hangs open as I stare at him in surprise. Does he not speak French?

"I'm sorry," I stammer in English.

He settles his enraged eyes on me. "It's only your first day, and you're trying to burn our apartment down. I'm starting to worry that you can't be trusted."

I square my shoulders, my brows knitting together. "We were dancing, and I got distracted."

I stare defiantly up at Jack. He's tall, but he doesn't intimidate me. I tip my chin up to try and make myself taller, but it's no use. For what feels like an eternity, we do nothing but glare at each other.

"This isn't a game, Miss Aubert."

I catch a hint of grief in his dour expression, and I realize as I stare at him that he's not just a cruel, angry man. There is pain there. I want to dislike him for the frigid, bleak exterior he presents to the world, but I'm too intrigued.

This is not the man in the photo. This is not Emmaline's husband.

"I know it's not a game," I say, challenging him.

I'm being obstinate. I know that, but I can't stand the thought of yielding to his irrational mood. It's bad enough that he won't even let Bea speak her mother's language in their home.

"Please don't make me regret hiring you," he commands softly.

As his gaze moves away from my face, it travels down to his daughter as she stands hesitantly near the counter. I watch the way he regards her, remorse etched into his features.

With a sigh, he turns his back on us and leaves the kitchen. His footsteps echo through the apartment as he climbs the stairs to the second floor.

After a moment, I reach for the speaker and turn it back on, clicking the volume button until it's low. The music begins to play again, and I turn toward Bea with a forced smile plastered on my face.

"Still hungry?"

She nods.

"You like burnt rice?"

She giggles.

Smiling down at her, I walk over to the sink, scrub out the blackened saucepan, and prepare it for another batch. The entire time I work, I can't stop thinking about Jack and the way he stared at me. Like we could speak a language with our eyes alone.

I wish I could tell him what an ill-tempered, miserable grump he is. He'd probably tell me what a foolish, immature brat I am.

So I guess in that case, we really shouldn't talk to each other at all.

Rule #5: Don't go poking around where you're not supposed to.

Camille

THE NEXT DAY, I DON'T SEE JACK AT ALL. HE'S RECLUSIVE IN HIS own house, but with that sour attitude of his, that's just fine with me. I don't need his broody, menacing eyes watching everything I do, barking orders in that cruel tone of his. I can do my job just fine without him around.

I take Bea to school in the morning and then take my grocery list to the store to restock the pantry with the money Phoenix left me for food and supplies. After putting Bea to bed last night, I spent hours meticulously making a routine, planning meals, and making lists.

Getting back to the house with heavy paper bags under each arm, I hoist them onto the counter and glance toward the stairs for signs of Jack. I hear nothing, so I assume he's gone. Being alone in the house has me on edge. Not knowing if he's really up there or not. Not knowing if he'll just come down and berate me for something else I've done wrong.

After picking up Bea from school in the afternoon, I hear him up there, secluded to one floor of his own home. And as curious as I am, I follow Phoenix's strict orders never to pry or go poking where I don't belong.

Then another day goes by without seeing him.

And another.

And another.

His relationship with his daughter is nonexistent. That's the most bizarre part. If they pass each other in the house, he'll greet her coldly, but there is no affection. No tenderness. No relationship between them at all.

He's a ghost, and she's come to accept it.

As for me, I've settled into a comfortable routine. Every morning, I take Bea to school, and every night, I tuck her into bed before preparing for the next day. And for the most part, I'm really happy here. Bea reminds me so much of myself when I was younger, except for the fancy dresses and perfect hair. She's curious and playful. She loves to laugh and use her imagination. With every day, she comes out of her shell more and more.

Our favorite activity together is, by far, drawing. I'm teaching her how to do little doodles like I do. She leaves them for me, so when I go to bed every night, I find folded pieces of paper on my nightstand—one a beret-wearing whale and the next day a panda sitting on a bed of flowers.

On my fifth day in Paris, I finally have my first night off. Phoenix comes over around 6 p.m., relieving me of my duties for the night.

As much as I love this job, I've been looking forward to this all week.

"Go have fun," she says, practically ushering me out the door.

I've been to Paris before. I spent the weekends here with friends when I was a teenager. But this will be my first time here alone as an adult with money. And I am taking myself out on a date.

I've always sort of prided myself on being somebody who is comfortable spending time alone. I could go to movies and shows alone. I could travel alone. And I could live alone if only I could afford it.

I have a reservation at one of the more sought-after restaurants in Montmartre. So I put on my best dress—a modest black knee-length A-line—with comfortable ankle boots good for walking, and I head out by myself. The restaurant is only a ten-minute walk from the apartment, but I take my time, savoring the taste of freedom on my tongue.

Passing by the Sacré-Cœur, I sit on a nearby bench at the bottom of the steps as the sun sets, and I watch the tourists as they pass. Families. Couples. Friends.

I like being alone, I do, but sometimes I wish there was someone next to me whose shoulder I could rest my head on. Someone who would let me hold their hand as we watch the sun set over Paris. Someone who would listen to me tell stories about the trips I took to the basilica as a kid with my father. Someone who would pull me away from the crowds to kiss me under the shade of the tree growing up the side of the hill.

As I stand up to head toward the restaurant, a nice couple asks me to take their picture, and I do. It makes me think of Emmaline and Jack, and I have to brush off the sadness that begins to creep in.

My reservation is at a small restaurant off the beaten path. It's family-owned and quaint, but it has the best foie gras I've ever tasted. And as I sit at the small table, drawing a mermaid on a napkin, I think about Jack.

There's something so sad about how deeply this man grieves. I still have the picture of him and his late wife in my purse. I tell myself that I carry it around with me to prevent someone at the house finding it, but I think the real reason is that it's become sacred to me.

I never knew Emmaline, but I somehow feel as if I did. I could tell by the photo that they loved each other. But I see it even more in the way he's withdrawn himself from his own life. I'm confident this is not how she would have wanted him to go on.

Especially since they have a little girl to look after. How long can he really keep this up? How long can *I* look after this child with no interaction with her father?

My meal is delicious, but I'm a little bitter that my obsession with Jack St. Claire has clouded my mind and my entire night. I was supposed to be spending tonight relaxing, not thinking about him and how to drag him out of this cage of solitude he's locked himself in. Of course, it's not *his* fault I can't stop thinking about him, but I'll blame him anyway.

After my dinner, I take a stroll through the city, and I consider slipping into one of the bustling bars for a pint. It's a lively night with people milling about on the streets, and I'm not ready to let this evening go. Who knows? Maybe someone will buy me a drink. Maybe I'll actually get to talk to someone other than a five-year-old this week.

But just as I'm about to enter a pub that looks promising, I spot the familiar gait and stature of the very man I can't stop thinking about.

Jack St. Claire is walking briskly down the road in front of me, taking a turn onto a quiet side street. Driven by curiosity, I abandon the bar I was about to enter and follow him. I'm far enough behind that he can't hear me, and there are people on the street who seem to be heading in the same direction as we are.

I'm dying to know…what does Jack get up to in his free time? Where on earth does he go? Phoenix said not to pry, but I'm not prying. It's not my fault if I just happen to see Jack walk into a building late at night.

At the end of the small street just off the main square is what appears to be a bustling nightclub, and I pause in astonishment as I watch Jack march confidently inside. The club is nestled at the bottom of the building, the lower-level facade painted in discreet matte black with an awning and people milling around on the street outside. Voices and the bass of music echo through the narrow city street as I slowly approach.

He's going to a nightclub?

I know nearly nothing about this man, but from what I do know, I find this slightly odd. No matter how hard I try to conjure up an image of him dancing, I can't seem to do it. It just doesn't fit.

After continuing my way down the street, I stand in front of the building and try to make sense of it. There's no name on the door. No other bars or businesses nearby. When I catch the eye of a group of men lingering near the door, I turn my back and cautiously walk up the street. I could go back to the apartment. I could spend the rest of my evening at a different club or bar. I could do literally anything else, but for some reason, I'm moving toward the door of the club.

There's a bouncer at the door who takes a long look at me before stepping aside to let me pass. I nearly turn away, intimidated by the deafening sound of music and people inside. I don't belong here. This is not my scene at all.

The main floor of the club is incredibly loud and a little dark. There are crowds of people everywhere, and I have to squeeze my way through to find an open area where the bar stands off to the left with a dance floor to the right. It appears like any normal club, and as I make my way to the bar, I glance around, searching for my mysterious employer.

I'm not sure what I would even do if I saw him. What if he sees me? I could play it off as coincidence. Or he could accuse me of stalking him and fire me on the spot. Either way, I'm still looking for him.

"What are you having?" someone asks to my left. Turning, I find a woman behind the bar. She's beautiful with spiral brown curls and big, dark eyes.

"Just water for now, please."

"You got it," she replies, turning away to fill a glass.

I continue scanning the room for Jack, but it's so crowded, and I just can't imagine that he's standing amid the horde of people here.

When the bartender returns with my glass, I decide to be a little nosy. Resting my arms on the bar, I lean toward her. "This is a long shot, but does anyone named Jack happen to work here?"

"Jack St. Claire?"

My heart hammers in my chest. "Yes."

"Well, he owns the place," she replies, and my eyebrows shoot upward.

He owns this club? It's certainly not what I expected for his job, but it all makes sense. His strange work hours, his constantly being gone at night.

"Do you have a meeting with him?" she asks.

I clear my throat, feeling uncomfortable. "I actually sort of work for him."

"Oh," she says with a wide-eyed, knowing expression on her face. "Well, he's probably downstairs."

"What's downstairs?" I ask.

"The club," she replies with a chuckle.

I glance around me. "Isn't this the club?"

She laughs again. "You must be new here."

Isn't it obvious?

She points across the club, and I follow her finger to see an elevator guarded by another man in a black suit. "Tell him you need to meet Jack. He'll let you down, and you should probably be able to find him in the back somewhere."

"Thanks," I stammer awkwardly. After drinking the water, I follow the bartender's instructions.

What on earth is down this elevator that needs a security guard, and why is Jack down there? Why is that considered the club and not this?

I've never been more confused in my life. Warning bells are going off in my mind, and I suddenly remember Phoenix giving me stringent instructions not to ask about his job or go poking around where I'm not supposed to. And yet here I am, standing in a club, or above a club, that Jack apparently owns.

You're causing trouble again, Camille.

Perhaps if I were better at following instructions or listening to warnings when I'm given them, I would turn away now and go home. I would put all this to rest and let my curiosity subside.

But I am none of those things.

Instead, I'm reckless and nosy, and I wouldn't recognize a boundary if it slapped me in the face. If this is how I lose my job, then this is how I lose my job, but I can't turn away now.

"I'm here for Jack St. Claire," I say to the man by the elevator. Then I point back at the bartender. "She told me to tell you that."

He lets out a grunt as he nods at the bartender. Then he jabs his finger against the button, and the doors slide open, allowing me into the elevator. I'm practically shaking as it takes me down alone. Once it opens, it takes everything in me to step out.

It's immediately a little quieter and even darker as I exit the elevator and walk down a narrow black hallway. A red neon sign above the inky black curtain ahead simply says *Legacy.*

Something about this has my insides screaming, *I don't belong here.*

What if Jack is in the Mafia, and I'm about to walk into some secret meeting where everybody in the room will turn to me with guns drawn? What if it's some seedy underground dealing of drugs or other black-market goods? What if it's a kinky sex dungeon and I walk in on something I really shouldn't see?

As all these thoughts swirl anxiously around in my mind, it is a sudden reminder that I don't know who I'm working for. I could be employed by a very dangerous man, and I would have no idea.

Not that it matters. I love Bea already, and I would take care of her even if her father were some drug-dealing Mafia killer.

As I slip through the dark curtain at the end of the hall beneath the sign, what I find is nothing like I expected. It's not nearly as crowded as it is upstairs. There's still music playing, but it's slower, more sultry, and not as loud. The lights are dim, but they're also a pinkish shade of red, and the entire room has a sense of sexy energy about it.

There is distorted glass and ornate fixtures on a half wall around what looks to be a dance floor. I follow it around, watching the strange movement of the people, unable to make out what kind of dance this is.

As I reach the other side, I stop and gawk in surprise. I can't believe what my eyes are seeing. There are people on the dance floor, but not many, maybe twelve or fifteen. They're moving to the music in a way that is both natural and unnatural.

It takes my eyes a moment to realize that most of them are completely nude. And the rest are hardly wearing anything at all.

The small mass of bodies grind and rub against each other to the beat of the bass. Their hands roam over each other's bodies. One of the naked women has her legs wrapped around a man, her arms hanging around the shoulders of another, and it's definitely not a *dance* they're doing. The man's thrusts match the sultry beat of the music, and I can just make out their moans from here.

It's salacious without being grotesque or vulgar. In fact, it's almost beautiful.

"So it *is* a kinky sex dungeon," I whisper to no one.

"You keep staring like that, you're gonna get yourself kicked out," a voice says from behind me.

My body feels flushed, tight, and hot as I spin around to find another small bar, much like the one upstairs. The man talking to me is a very handsome young bartender with nearly pitch-black hair. He appears to be my age with dimples and a coy smirk as he leans against the bar.

I quickly scan my periphery to be sure I haven't just been caught staring at the dance floor...or sex floor, I guess. "I'm sorry," I stammer as I rush toward the bartender. My cheeks are on fire, as are other parts of my body I don't want to acknowledge at the moment.

He chuckles. "First time?"

Silently, I nod.

First time what? I don't know. First time in a kinky sex dungeon, yes. First time my curiosity has gotten me in trouble, not even close.

"Need a drink?" he asks.

"Desperately," I whisper as I rest my arms on the bar, not daring to turn back toward the erotic display in the middle of the room.

"Want me to fix you up something? I could surprise you." Judging by his accent, he is also from America, like Phoenix and Jack.

"Yes, please," I reply as I toy with my hair to busy my hands.

"Did you come alone?" he asks.

"Yes," I whisper.

"Normally, new members get a tour and a guide. Did you not get a tour?"

I clear my throat, uncomfortable again. New members? Am I supposed to be a member? *Good God, Camille. What have you gotten yourself into now?*

"Um, no," I reply, stammering.

"All right, well, this isn't much of a tour, but that's the dance floor. Those are VIP booths, and there's a BDSM room in the back, but if you wanted to rent a private room, you'd have to talk to the host."

As he slides my drink across the bar, I try to absorb what he just said, but none of it is really sticking.

A private room? BDSM?

Trying to keep my cool as I let all this register, I take a sip of the purple drink and realize that Jack St. Claire owns a sex club. That's what all this is about. Now it makes sense why Phoenix didn't want me asking any questions.

"Feel free to go take a look around," he says, "but don't be doing any of that gawking stuff you were a moment ago. Just play it cool. A pretty thing like you, I'm sure you won't be alone for long, but if someone gives you any trouble, just signal to any one of the security guards, and they'll help you out. Got it?"

"Got it," I reply, feeling embarrassed and more nervous than I've ever been. I nearly chug down the rest of my drink, convincing myself that I'm going to leave as soon as I'm done. After slipping a note over to pay for my drink, I stand from the stool, clutching my purse to my chest as I slowly make my way around the club. I'm expecting that at any moment, someone is going to realize that I'm trespassing and kick me out.

As the bartender said, there are large circular booths off to the right with high backs and low tables so that people inside are hidden from view. Passing them, I see a doorway leading deeper into the club.

The noises from within stop me in my tracks. It's not music I hear anymore but the unmistakable sound of something smacking flesh. The bartender told me not to gawk, and I am doing my best, but I am definitely out of my element here.

The room is sectioned off with high walls and space for people to walk around them. Other guests like me are meandering around them, watching. I pass by each one, not fully absorbing what I see. It reminds me of a museum, people perusing the art, but instead of paintings and sculptures, it's whips and bondage.

There's a man paddling the ass of a woman bound to a bed. Judging by the sound of her voice, she both loves it and hates it.

There's another woman suspended from the rafters wrapped in rope with her hair tethered to her ankles. I can't quite make sense of that one, so I pass it by for the next.

What I find in the last booth stops me in my tracks.

Jack St. Claire is standing near a wall covered in paddles and other tools I don't recognize. He's shirtless with his back to us and a pair of dark jeans hanging on his hips. I can't take my eyes off the cords of muscle cascading from shoulder to shoulder and down his spine. There's a glisten of sweat on his skin, and I'm too struck by the sight to move when I know I should.

A woman kneels on the floor at his side, but I don't even look at her. Jack reaches for something along the wall, a bundle of black corded rope, and I spot the gold wedding band on his left hand.

As he picks up the rope and slaps it against the other palm, I flinch. The girl on the floor looks acquiescent. Then Jack turns around to regard her, and I watch as he softly pets the top of her head and the line of her jaw with adoration. She practically melts under his touch.

Hiding myself behind a couple, I watch them with fiery interest. The woman leans into Jack as he begins to unravel the rope in his hand. She lifts her wrists on his command, and he softly whispers two words that course straight down my spine.

"Good girl."

Lips parted, I find myself wondering what it must feel like to be in her position, to be so adored and treated so gently by him. To feel his touch, his attention, his gentle praise.

He mumbles something else to her I can't understand, and I wish that I could.

And then his eyes lift, making their way out to the crowd where a small group of people is standing, myself included. I do my best to hide, ducking behind the couple in the darkness, but it's too late.

His eyes meet mine. It feels like being struck by lightning. Dread floods through me as his eyes widen in shock. His nostrils flare and his chest expands as he takes a deep breath, and I ready myself for his wrath. He mumbles something to the girl before slamming the rope in his hand to the floor.

Shit.

He stomps angrily toward me, and I find myself backing up as if I could escape him. One of his hands latches around my upper arm, and I shriek, "Let go of me!"

"What are you doing here?" he says, his eyes searching my face.

"I… I…" No words come out. There's not a single excuse I could come up with, so I give up on the futile attempt to talk my way out of this one.

"You don't belong here," he says in a growly reply. Silently brooding, he drags me deeper into the room instead of the way we came, and I find myself digging my heels in as if I could stop him.

"Why not? I can go where I want!" I shout.

"Not here you can't," he argues as he continues dragging me through the deep recesses of the club until he finds a door. Grabbing hold of the knob, he tears it open and shoves me through.

"Stop it!" I'm engulfed in fear as he drags me up a set of stairs in the back of the club. It all happens so fast. He slams open an exterior door, and suddenly, we're outside.

"What are you doing?" I scream.

He lets go of my arm and blocks the door we just escaped through. His eyes bore into mine with intensity, rage pulsating through his features. "Why can't you just listen?" he grits with exasperation.

Huffing, I stare back at him, lifting my chin with all the defiance I can muster. "Why would I listen to *you*?" I snap. "You're not my, my…"

"Your boss?" he growls, leaning closer.

The chemistry between us is electric, his chest heaving as he glares at me. I forget how to speak, no response on my lips. I don't know what I was about to say to Jack, but I'm disarmed when he calls himself my boss. All this time, I've fabricated this connection between us, all because of some photograph. That's what drew me into this club. What had me following him, desperate to know as much as I can about him. And I discovered *far* more than I ever imagined.

But he is just my boss. Nothing more. Nothing less.

And if I don't listen, I risk losing the best job I've ever had.

"Go home." He points toward the street, away from the club, like I'm a dog that must listen to his commands.

"What is wrong with you?" I ask, my voice shaking with emotion. He doesn't react or answer. When it's clear that he won't move until I leave, I sigh as I take a step away.

Tears moistening my eyes, I turn my back on him and walk away from the club toward the road that will lead back to home.

Rule #6: Beware of those who lurk in hallways in the middle of the night.

Camille

After the incident in the club, Jack continues ghosting us. No surprise.

He continues to haunt the house. His existence consists of nothing but noisy footsteps upstairs and occasional appearances as he passes us for the door.

I'm just glad I still have my job. The morning after the club, I woke up humiliated. What was I thinking, following him into that place? Why on earth did I stay after I realized what it was? Maybe I was digging deeper into Jack's life for more than just curiosity. Maybe I was trying to find pieces of Emmaline there. Or maybe…a place for myself.

This new piece of information about Jack, that he owns a sex club, settled in with shocking ease. Why did I never see it before? Seeing him standing over that girl, shirt off and control etched into his features, suited Jack so well I can't get the image out of my mind.

Part of me wonders if he's embarrassed for being caught at the club, but I think it's more than that. I can't stop replaying the moments when he dragged me from that basement out the door. There was so much anger in his eyes.

He clearly did not want me to be there. And I can't stop wondering why.

Was it about keeping his work life private?

Or was he trying to protect me from something?

I hold no judgment against Jack or anyone else for the life he leads in his personal time. His kinky business is his kinky business, and I would probably be mortified to find him watching me in that sort of situation.

Granted, I'm not exactly doing those things in public, but still. This is one time where I need to keep my fervent curiosity in check.

On the following sunny Saturday, I decide to take Bea to the small craft fair in town not far from the apartment. She's wearing a green-and-white-plaid dress with a white buttoned cardigan and her usual shiny black Mary Janes. I tried to talk her into a more practical outfit for a day in the city, but she was adamant about her choice. At only five years old, she has better style than me, and she's quite passionate about it.

As we walk through the crowds, Bea's hand is clutched tightly in mine. There are artists with easels set up, painting as they sell, and some even do commissioned portraits right there in the plaza.

"I'd like to hang a painting in my room. Will you help me pick one?" I ask, browsing the selections.

"Oui," Bea replies excitedly. She wastes no time pointing to a small watercolor painting of the Moulin Rouge in a red matte frame. "I like this one," she says.

"I like that one too," I reply.

The artist steps out from behind his easel and greets us with a smile. "Two for fifty," he says, and Bea beams up at me.

"Does that mean I can get one too?"

"Go ahead. Pick one out for your room," I say.

She steps into the artist's stall and starts browsing his selection of paintings.

"These are really lovely," I say to him.

"Merci," he replies. "Are you an artist?" he asks.

"Me? No," I say. "But I love art."

Which is true. I've never really wanted to be an artist. As much as I like doodling and sketching, I've always had an appreciation for art but never really wanted to make it something I do professionally.

I don't think everything needs to be perfected as a skill. There's nothing wrong with just enjoying something for the sake of enjoying it. We don't need to become better at it, and certainly not perfect.

That was a lesson my father ingrained in me.

As I watch the old man paint another beautiful landscape of Paris, I remember my father. He used to say that he wasn't a perfect cook and his restaurant wasn't a perfect place to eat, but he fed people, and he made them happy, and that was enough.

And yet there is always a voice inside me that strives for perfection. It's as if he was trying to convince me to embrace my flaws, but I couldn't. When I look in the mirror, all I see is a girl who is too messy, too loud, too wild, too silly, or too ignorant.

And deep, deep down, I know my mind is trying to say that if I were better, then my mother wouldn't have left.

With a hint of sadness, I hand the man a fifty-euro note and turn to see if Bea has picked out her artwork yet. But when I glance down at the area where she should be and find it empty, panic explodes inside me like a bomb going off.

My head snaps in every direction. "Beatrice," I call. "Beatrice!"

Dashing out of the stall, I glance back and forth down the marketplace in desperate search of her. How could I have let her out of my sight? What have I done? I've only been on the job two weeks, and I've already lost her. She was right here.

"Camille!" her tiny voice shouts for me.

Spinning around, I find her standing with her arms latched around a beautiful woman's neck in a loving embrace. Heaving a deep sigh, it feels like all the blood in my veins begins to slow, as if losing her for just a second has completely rewired my entire nervous system.

"You scared me to death," I say as I rush over toward her, grabbing her hand and pulling her away from the woman. "Where did you go?"

"I'm sorry." She pouts. "But I saw my tante Elizabeth." She looks up at the woman, who gives me a stern expression.

"Your aunt?" I ask.

The woman puts a hand out toward me. "Je m'appelle Elizabeth. Je suis la sœur de Jack."

My eyes widen as I take in the woman before me. This is Jack's sister?

And not only that…but she speaks perfect French.

I don't see a resemblance, but she is as stunning as he is handsome. She's slender but short with dark brown, nearly black hair pulled up into a tight bun at the back of her head. She's wearing a loose crop top that hangs off her shoulder, exposing what looks like a sports bra underneath. She has a Louis Vuitton handbag slung over her right shoulder. She is exquisitely beautiful.

Bea did tell me she had an aunt who was a ballerina. I put out my hand to shake hers.

"Je m'appelle Camille," I say, introducing myself.

"You're her new nanny?" she asks.

Her French is so flawless that it sounds native, which I find slightly odd, considering Jack doesn't speak it at all.

There's skepticism in her expression as she regards me.

"Yes, I'm her new nanny. I just started two weeks ago."

"And losing her already," she says in a snappy remark.

"She ran off," I reply defensively.

"Well, it's about time my brother finally hired someone," she says.

Your brother, I think. I'd love to pick her brain to understand that man. I wonder if he is as much an enigma to her as he is to me. Is he cold and impassive to her too?

"Is Jack here?" she asks, glancing around.

I let out a huff of a laugh. "No." The idea that Jack would venture out with me and Bea is downright comical. Her brow shoots upward at my outburst. I don't want to talk badly about Jack in front of Bea, so I casually reply, "He's very busy at work."

She slowly nods as if she understands. "Yes, he is."

"Tante Elizabeth works with Papa," Bea says with adorable innocence.

My eyes flash over to Elizabeth as they widen. "I thought you were a dancer," I say.

"Part-time," she replies. "Jack and I do work together as well."

All I can think about is that club, wondering where precisely this woman, his sister, works while he's in the basement petting women on their knees and doing God knows what else.

"But we don't need to talk about work anymore," she says, looking down at Bea with a wink.

"You speak French so well," I say. "Have you lived here your whole life?"

"No," she replies. "I moved here when I was eighteen. It was actually Bea's maman who taught me French. She was a good teacher."

There is a spark of despair in my chest, seeing the way she looks at the little girl. Even if Elizabeth moved here when she was eighteen, she can't be any more than twenty-three now. So it's still quite impressive how fluent she is. Bea's mom must have been a very good teacher.

The woman leans down to Bea and mumbles something softly to her in English. I give them their moment, stepping back before Elizabeth stands up again to say, "I think I'll take Bea tomorrow if that's all right. She's been wanting to come up to the dance studio for a while, and I figure you'll probably be off on Sundays."

"I am," I say. "Phoenix was going to come over for the day, but—"

"I'll tell her," Elizabeth says. "I'll see her today."

"Okay," I reply. "It was nice meeting you."

"It was nice meeting you too," she says. A hint of a smile crosses her face before she turns and leaves Bea and I standing in the market.

———◦◦◦———

Later that evening, as Bea and I are doing a puzzle at the table in the living room, the front door opens, and Jack walks in.

"Bonsoir, Papa," Bea calls to him.

I pause, watching for his reaction. He stands at the door in the foyer of the apartment, his eyes on his daughter at the table next to me. My attention is glued to him, waiting for him to give her something. This poor child just needs a parent. A touch of affection. Attention. *Anything.*

But he's staring at the two of us sitting here as if this is somehow offensive to him. As if us just existing is hurting his feelings in some way.

"Hello, Bea," he says, replying to her in English in a raspy, grief-stricken voice.

Normally, when Jack comes and goes from the apartment, it's a beeline straight from the front door to the stairs. I've never known him to go to the kitchen or her room or anywhere else in the downstairs portion of the home.

But this time, I notice him hesitating. He stands statue-still and regards us as if he's mentally considering doing something other than fleeing the room. In my mind, I'm begging him to walk over to her. Touch her hair, kiss her head, smile at her.

"How..." He clears his throat. "How was your day?"

Bea and I both freeze, taken aback by the sudden conversation from him when he's stayed so quiet before.

"Super," Bea replies enthusiastically. Then she rattles off more in French, and I notice him wincing before holding up a hand.

"English, Beatrice."

She halts her story as she stares up at him apologetically. "I'm sorry, Papa."

The room is thick with tension as he rubs his forehead before opening his eyes and glancing at me. I feel as if I've done something wrong. Just by being here or just by being…French?

Then his expression morphs into remorse. He looks lost. The hard shell dissipates long enough for me to get a glimpse of the broken, aching man underneath.

"It's okay," he says to the little girl. He hesitates before nodding stoically and marching toward the stairs, climbing them quickly as if to escape us.

My eyes dash over to Bea, watching her reaction. She is only five, still so little. She's just a baby, really. It's so unfair that she's already been dealt such a hard hand. Losing her mother and now essentially her father. Although he lives here, he's not here. He's not present. He's not raising her.

I glance down at my watch to see that it's already 7:30.

"It's bedtime, little Bea," I say.

"Aw," she whines. "Five more minutes?"

"No, I'm sorry. We're actually a little late as it is. I should have had you in bed fifteen minutes ago. Come on. Let's go get pajamas on."

It didn't take long, but Bea is getting comfortable with me now, which means she likes to push back against my authority. It makes everything more difficult. Bedtime, dinnertime, and getting ready for school in the morning. I think I underestimated how difficult caring for a five-year-old could be.

After a lengthy and tiring negotiation period and a tiny tantrum, I finally have Bea settled in her bed, her book read, and her teeth brushed. I brush her hair from her forehead and *boop* her softly on the nose before leaving the room and shutting off the light.

"Camille," she whispers.

"Yes?"

"Can I have a hug?" she asks, and my heart splinters at her words.

"Of course," I reply without hesitation. Rushing over to her bed, I sit on the side and gather her up in my arms. She hugs me tightly, her tiny arms gripping my sides as she burrows her head against my chest.

It suddenly dawns on me just how broken this poor family is. It's daunting to think I'm here to help take care of her when what they truly need is so much more, far beyond my abilities. They need each other.

She releases the hug first. Then she lies back down and nestles herself under the blankets. Clearing the emotion in my throat, I stand from the bed again and head to the door.

"Good night, Bea," I say before leaving.

"Good night, Camille," she replies.

As I wait for her to fall asleep, I busy myself cleaning the kitchen, preparing my meal list for tomorrow, and doing some light doodling on my notepad in the kitchen.

Hearing Jack's footsteps upstairs, I fight the urge to march up there and give him a piece of my mind. I want to yell at him to snap out of it. Stop being such a ghost. Be a father. But then again, who am I to judge? I fell apart and stopped living the day my dad died too. Processing grief is hard enough, but being a parent at the same time is unimaginable.

As I turn away from the counter, I nearly scream at the sight of Jack walking into the kitchen. I freeze in place, expecting him to say something to me. Instead, he does just the opposite. He walks right past me as if I don't exist.

My mouth opens, silently watching him as he opens the fridge to retrieve something to eat. I'm dying to speak to him, and I have so many questions, but this is truly the first time he and I have been alone together since the night at the club.

I need to say something. It would be irresponsible to let this opportunity to speak to him pass me by. But what do I say? I can't actually tell him to snap out of it. But maybe if I could cultivate some relationship with him…

Wringing a dish towel between my fingers, I quietly mumble, "So…that's where you work?"

He doesn't respond as he continues to rifle through the fridge.

"At the club, I mean. Is that what it is? A club?" I continue awkwardly. "I wouldn't know. I've never been anywhere like that before. It's not really my…thing, but it's fine if that's your thing. I'm not judging."

I'm rambling, and it's humiliating, but I can't stop now. Still, he ignores me as if I'm not even in the room, and my molars grind at the sheer boldness.

"I didn't mean to follow you," I say, which is a lie. "I was just…curious. I had no idea it would make you so angry. I didn't mean to trespass. My father used to say—"

"Please, for the love of God, stop," he snaps loudly as he stands up straight.

My words are clipped, my voice stopping abruptly as I stand frozen, shame and embarrassment washing over me.

I fight off tears as he finally turns toward me. When he sees the wounded expression on my face, his features soften. He almost looks remorseful, as he should. I've never met someone so cruel before.

"I'm sorry," he grumbles to himself, letting his head hang and rubbing fiercely at his brow. "Just please…stop talking."

Obeying his command, I close my mouth tightly as I try to swallow my pride, but it's futile. I won't bend to Jack's will—not like this. The persistent thoughts bubble up anyway.

"What is wrong with you?" I plead. "Why are you so cruel?"

He glances up at me with surprise, but I can't bear to look at him for another moment, so I storm out of the kitchen, rage and anguish coursing through me. Slamming the door, I hide away in my bedroom, hoping he doesn't follow me.

I don't understand why I care. So Jack St. Claire is a jerk. So what? He's just my boss, and he pays me well to do my job. So why can't I let it go? Why do I feel this persistent need to understand him?

It's because of that *stupid* photo. In my passion, I rip it from my purse. Clutched between my two hands, I grit my teeth as I start to tear it in two. But I stop myself before I can do any real damage. The smiling couple stares back at me, and for the first time, I hate them both.

Why am I so obsessed with this man? This family. Why have I conjured up this image of Jack St. Claire in my mind to be someone who is actually lovable instead of the emotionless, cruel monster of a man he is? How on earth did Emmaline love him so much? The disappointment of his character is the most frustrating thing I have ever felt.

I manage to stave off the tears as I get ready for bed, fuming all the same. Jack's footsteps echo through the apartment as he climbs up to his second floor again, and I curse his name with each one.

When I finally get into bed, I am unbearably restless. The creaking of the floorboards upstairs keeps me up. That and the memory of Jack's hurtful words. I realize now how much he dislikes me, and it stings. I know it shouldn't, but I can't seem to avoid feeling his scorn whenever I'm around him. Eventually, I fall into a light, dreamless sleep.

Sometime in the middle of the night, I'm awoken by the sound of a floorboard creaking. By the sound of it, someone is walking just outside my bedroom.

I stiffen as I wait for another creak.

My bedroom door is open, just a crack, so I can hear Bea if she wakes up. And maybe that's who's in the hallway now.

The room is dark, moonlight shining through the window as I stare at the opening, trying to make out if anyone is standing there watching me.

When another floorboard creaks, I sit up. My heartbeat is

thrumming quickly in my veins. I have a feeling I know exactly who is standing on the other side of my door.

The only thing I don't understand is *why*.

Sure, there is something ominous and mysterious about Jack St. Claire, but nothing dangerous. I don't get the feeling that he would hurt me. I'm not scared of him.

When I stand up from the bed and place my feet on the floor, I do so with the intention of proving myself wrong. I want to quiet the doubts in my head. There's nobody standing in my hallway. He's not waiting for me on the other side of that door. It's all just the creaks of an old apartment.

I tiptoe slowly across my dark room. Pulling the door open, I let out a quiet gasp as I make out the tall, dark figure hovering in the middle of the hallway. My breathing quickens, and I search his face for a sign. When our eyes meet, it's like an electric current.

"What is it?" I whisper, but he doesn't respond.

In what appears to be today's clothes—a tight black T-shirt and a pair of dark slacks—he looks so sad, so lost. There are heavy circles under his eyes and a sheen of moisture on his cheeks.

The only sound between us is our breathing, and the only scent is his delicate cologne. I fight the urge to pull him into my arms like I held Bea earlier. His pain radiates off him like a blazing fire, and I wish I could make it go away.

As I wait for him to make a move, it's as if I'm standing at the edge of a cliff. One small quake or gust of air would be enough to push me over the edge. All the anger I felt toward him earlier has dissolved and morphed into pity.

When Jack takes a step toward me, I suck in a gasp, and when he crowds me against the doorframe, I let him.

His eyes have not released their hold on me since the moment I walked out of my room. It's almost impossible to stare at someone so intensely, but Jack's gaze has a strange sort of comfort to it. It's odd, the way we can stare at each other as if we're staring into each other's souls. I could never do this with anyone else. It would grow too uncomfortable, too awkward, but with him, it makes me feel at ease, seen, like I'm not so alone.

His hand lifts, and I hold my breath as he strokes his thumb softly over the side of my face. The touch alone is enough to send sparks down my spine. A heat burns in my belly, arousal blooming between my legs.

His eyes, his touch, his presence speak a language I don't comprehend. What is he trying to say? Is he sorry for the way he yelled? Does he want me in some forbidden way?

I have no idea what's going on or why I'm reacting this way. It's his nearness, the intimacy of being able to look into his eyes for so long. The gentle silence between us when nothing needs to be said but everything needs to be felt.

He touches my cheek delicately as if unsure what to do. It gives me the courage to lift my own hands, resting them softly on his chest. His heart beats steadily against my fingers.

And I keep waiting to see if he'll kiss me or if he'll touch me more.

Or if he'll drag me into my bedroom and let his lips say what his mouth can't.

Would I even want that? It's like he's suddenly making me forget that he's rude, grumpy, and miserable.

Because right now, what I see standing before me is just a man—a man in pain.

"I never should have hired you," he whispers, jolting me from my fixation.

His words are stabbing and painful. My brows furrow, and my hands fist his shirt in anger. "What did I do?" I reply, but he moves his hand over my mouth to keep me from speaking.

Eventually, he releases his fingers from my face and turns his gaze away from mine. It feels like being doused in ice-cold water. He steps away, and I find myself reaching for him.

"Wait," I whisper. "Don't go."

I have no good reason for wanting Jack to stay. With the way he's treated me, it's the last thing I should want, but I can't bear the thought of him going back to the torment of his loneliness.

Ignoring my request, he walks quietly down the hallway back to the stairs.

Just like that, he's gone, and I'm left reeling from the most bizarre yet intense sensual encounter of my life. As I slip back into bed, pulling my covers tightly over my body, I'm left wondering if maybe my obsession with Jack St. Claire isn't so one-sided after all.

Rule #7: Rules were made to be broken.

Camille

As Bea eats her breakfast the next morning, I lean my elbows on the kitchen counter and draw a ghost in a suit with a top hat on the front of my grocery list. I hear Jack's footsteps upstairs, but he hasn't come down. If I were to guess, I would say that he's going to be a phantom again, quietly haunting the house as he comes and goes without a word.

I didn't sleep well last night, and it shows. Mid yawn, I hear a door slam upstairs. Bea and I glance at each other as we wait for his footsteps that never come. I wish I could say I'm dreading the moment I'm face-to-face with him again. But I can't.

In fact, I'm dying for it.

As I walk Bea to school, she holds my hand in hers, squeezing my fingers as she hops clumsily around the cracks in the cement.

"Tu crois aux fantômes?" she asks innocently. *Do you believe in ghosts?*

"Ghosts?" I reply.

"Like the one you drew this morning," she says with her tiny mouth screwed up with curiosity.

"Oh." I laugh. "Yeah, I guess I do."

"Do you think my maman is a ghost?" Bea gazes up at me with those big, innocent blue eyes, and I have to swallow down the tension in my throat. How on earth should I answer this question? Perhaps these are the sorts of things *real* nannies are trained for.

"Um… I don't know. Do *you* think she's a ghost?"

"Oui," she replies plainly. "I can hear her walking around sometimes. She comes into my room when I'm sleeping."

Comes into her room? Could this have been a dream? I'm struck with confusion, wondering why the hell this little girl would think her mother is traipsing around their home, but then the memory of last night comes back, and it all makes sense.

Jack.

Even his five-year-old daughter thinks he's a ghost. He must slip into her room after she's asleep to check on her. Perhaps that's why he was downstairs last night, lurking in the hallway with tears soaking his face.

I wouldn't tell Bea that, even if I knew for certain the only haunting spirit in her house is her father. If she wants to believe it's her maman, then who am I to correct her?

"That's lovely," I say as I kneel in front of the girl. "I'm sure that if your maman were a ghost, she would watch over you so you're never alone."

Bea shrugs. "I hope she takes care of Papa now."

"Why is that?"

"Because I have you," she chirps happily before wrapping her arms around my neck.

I hug her back, trying to hold back the tears that are threatening to spring free.

Without another word, Bea releases my neck and bounds away, running toward her teacher by the front door of her school. I'm left reeling as I kneel on the sidewalk outside.

Feeling a little lifeless myself, I stand and walk mindlessly back to the house. This is normally when I'd do the shopping and the errands, but I can't seem to focus on work today. There is an electric buzz under my skin. I'm not sure I want it to go away.

When I get back to the house, I listen for movement upstairs, but it's quiet. He could be sleeping. Or he could be gone.

Going up to his room is forbidden. I've been told this more than once. But after last night, I feel at liberty to investigate. If he's going to prowl outside my room while I sleep, I can snoop a bit in his while he's gone.

Besides, rules were made to be broken, right?

The house is silent as I climb quietly up the stairs toward the second level. The floor of the landing at the top creaks as I reach it, and I pause, waiting to hear his scolding voice. When nothing comes, I assume it means he really is gone.

Frozen in place, I peer around. The second floor has an open sitting room to the left with a leather sofa, ottoman, and rug. There is a beautiful painting on the wall and a fresh bouquet of flowers on the table near the window.

Facing a long hallway in front of me, I see one door ajar and what looks like an office on the other side. There is a desk and an empty chair.

I take a quiet step toward the room, carefully pressing the door open to find my suspicions correct. It's his office. The desk is immaculate and tidy. The computer on the desk has a large screen that is currently black and a notepad on the surface near the keyboard.

Tiptoeing into the room, I sneak a peek at the notepad.

Talk to Logan about security.

Scanning the rest of the desk, I notice a framed photo by the monitor. I pick it up and stare down at the woman in the picture. She's the same woman in the photo I own.

She's beautiful with dark brown hair braided loosely over one shoulder. She's sitting in a chair near a window, and unlike my photo, in this one, she's not smiling. And yet she looks so peaceful. Her hands are resting on her full, round belly, and I try to imagine the moment the picture was taken.

In my mind, I picture him standing in the middle of the room, telling her how gorgeous she is. In my mind, Jack is kind and loving. He speaks to her with compassion and warmth. In my mind, Jack is a real person and not a cruel, soulless apparition of a man like he is now.

Then I imagine it's me standing by the window, hugging my perfect round belly, feeling his loving gaze on my face as he snaps a photo of me. It's a cruel trick my mind plays on me, and the moment the tormenting idea settles in, I shove it away. That's not real.

Quickly, I put the frame down, snapping myself out of such a dangerous fantasy.

Turning away from the desk, I walk out of the office, peering down the hallway and waiting for any signs of life. When it proves safe, I ease back out of the room, leaving the door the way I found it.

Across from the office is another door. With my hand on the handle, I slowly ease it open and peek inside to find a bathroom. It looks untouched, so I quietly edge back out and close it without a sound.

Moving down to the next door, I pause and question my own sanity. What if he's in here? What if he's sleeping? What on earth am I going to do if he catches me and fires me for breaking the rules and trespassing into his private space—again?

That would tear Bea up.

I should turn away now. A wise woman certainly would.

And yet I'm resting my hand on the next door, the last on the left. I'm a fool for this, but I can't help myself. Moving at a speed that could only be categorized as agonizingly slow, I turn the handle and press open the door.

What I expect is a bedroom. I expect a bed, a dresser, maybe a pile of laundry on the floor.

What I don't expect is an empty room with dark gray walls and ornate crown molding. There are deep purple velvet drapes hanging over the windows. Aside from an upholstered chair and a velvet bench, the only piece of furniture in the room is a large wood antique wardrobe.

I glance behind me at the closed door I haven't opened yet, which I assume now must be his bedroom.

So what is this?

I step into the empty room with piqued interest. There's a round, plush rug in the center of the room and strange gold hooks in various positions along the ceiling.

There is something so odd and yet comforting about the room. But what on earth is the purpose of it? Some sort of meditation room perhaps? Then I'm instantly reminded of the small station in the dark sex club where I found Jack. My memory conjures up images of paddles, ropes, and other tools I don't yet know the names of.

Crossing the space toward the window, I pull back the thick curtains to let in some light. There's a beautiful view of the city from this spot, and I take a moment to stare at it.

Was this the window she stood in front of for that photo? I picture her standing in this spot as he snapped the image.

I've never met someone as mysterious and strange as Jack St. Claire. I know I should let it go and just do my job, but I am enamored by him at every turn. I can almost see the man beneath the monster. But with every discovery only comes more questions.

Like what is this room used for? What is he hiding up here?

And what is inside this wardrobe?

I know I shouldn't open it. And maybe in some way, I already know what's in there.

It was curiosity that led me to open that letter. Curiosity that led me to Paris in the first place. Curiosity that led me to the club the other night and curiosity that brought me into this room.

But is it possible all these things are really just breadcrumbs?

Is it possible Jack is inviting me down this path, tempting me to take a closer look every chance I get?

He could have locked this door. He could have shut me out entirely. But he hasn't.

With that, I cross over the thick rug and stand before the large armoire. I rest my fingers on the metal handle before giving it a gentle tug. It pops open, and I hold my breath as the light shines into the small space.

But before I can get a glimpse of what is waiting inside, a large hand with a familiar gold band around the ring finger presses against the wood, slamming it closed. I let out a yelp in fear, but when I try to back away from the furniture, I hit a giant wall of muscle and anger.

Freezing, I shrink into myself as I wait for his reprimand.

Speak to me, I think. *Yell at me. Punish me. Give me something.*

His breath is warm against my head and his chest solid against my back.

"I'm sorry," I stammer.

"You don't belong in here," he whispers with his mouth near my ear, and my heart rate picks up in a panic. For some very odd reason, I'm not afraid of Jack. I probably should be, but in my heart, I know he won't hurt me. "Why are you always breaking my rules?" he demands.

I can't respond, so I don't. But I want to argue. I *do* belong here. I found my way here by some invisible force. Here in Paris, here in this house, here in this room.

Then, to my surprise, he asks, "You want to see what is in there, don't you?"

Staring at the ornate wood of the armoire, I nod.

With a hand around my waist, he tugs me gently backward so I'm flush against his body as he grips the handle of the wardrobe and pulls it open. My breath is shaky as I stare into the dark void behind the door.

But it's not quite what I had anticipated. There are gold hooks along the backside with various ropes and ribbons draped over each one. My brows furrow as I try to make sense of what I'm looking at.

Admittedly, I sort of expected things like paddles, whips, gags. Things like I saw the other night at the club. But these are different. Far less intimidating, if I'm honest.

Perhaps I should be afraid of what I'm seeing, but I'm not.

"Is this what you were expecting?" he whispers in my ear.

I shake my head.

"Are you still curious?"

I nod.

"Go ahead."

It takes me a moment to realize he's telling me to touch them. With a tremble in my hand, I reach out and run one of the black ropes through my fingers. It's coarser than I expected it to be.

Immediately, I remember the woman I witnessed at the club being bound so tightly she couldn't move a single muscle. These ropes surely would have itched and burned.

Even that thought doesn't dissuade my curiosity.

I want to ask what he does with these. Is this a sport to him? Or is it all about sex? Hundreds of questions swirl around in my mind, but if I learned anything from Jack's behavior, it's that he doesn't like it when I speak. Something about my voice triggers him in a way I don't understand, so I stay quiet.

Boldly, I pull the rope from the hook and let it drape over my fingers. When I think about it wrapped around my wrists, warmth sparks between my legs. As if he can read my mind, he lets out a low, rumbling growl, and my knees grow weak.

The warmth in my core blossoms into a burning heat, pulsing between my legs. It's like a spark of life in parts of my body I didn't know existed until now.

What is happening?

Jack leans into me, and it's much like the moment in the hallway last night. Slow, blazing tension engulfs us as if the world has completely stopped turning and some feverous tidal wave is sweeping us away.

Show me, I chant in my mind. *Please show me.*

His nose is pressed against the side of my head, and he takes a deep inhale as if he's trying to pick up my scent. My eyes drift closed as the heat deep within my body continues to pulse, pulse, pulse.

Then, without warning, he stiffens, pulling himself away and snatching the rope from my hands. He hangs it on the hook with a huff and slams the door loudly, making me flinch.

"You're not going to show me?" I ask in astonishment.

"No."

"Wait!" Reaching out, I grab his arm and try to turn him toward me. He glares down at my hand on his skin as if I'm a leech. "Why not?"

"Not me. Find someone else."

"I don't want to find someone else."

Immediately, he winces as if the sound of my voice pains him. It only enrages me more.

"What is it you're hiding?" I shout. "What is this room? Why did you leave it unlocked if you didn't want me to—"

The words are stolen from my lips as he turns toward me and thrusts a hand against my mouth. Holding me by the back of the head, he crowds me as he silences my words without reason.

Staring into my eyes with fire, he leans in as he growls, "Please stop talking."

My brows lift as I stare up at him. Instead of arguing or fighting more, I nod against his fingers.

Time passes slowly as he just holds me, one hand pressed over my mouth, the other at the back of my neck. I am entirely at his mercy.

He holds me close, his mouth just inches from mine. Again, we share eye contact in a way that I couldn't possibly with anyone else.

I keep waiting for him to relent and give me what I want, which, to be fair, even I don't understand. I want Jack to *show me* things I don't know how to vocalize. I want him to let me into his world. I want to be the one at the center of his attention like that woman was for a brief moment at the club.

But at the same time, I wish he'd hold me in his arms with affection. I wish he'd share the heavy weight of his grief with me.

There's familiarity in his eyes like he can feel the same thing I do. I just wish he'd let it all go. Instead, his expression hardens again.

"If I find you in this room again, you're fired," he mutters angrily near my face.

Then, without warning, he releases me, and I try to reach for him again, but he's already stomping out of the room and into the one on the opposite side of the hall. The door slams shut, and once again, I'm left standing alone, reeling from another bizarre and intoxicating moment with Jack St. Claire.

Rule #8: Always do your research.

Camille

JACK DOESN'T COME OUT OF HIS ROOM FOR MOST OF THE DAY, which is really no surprise and nothing out of the ordinary.

Around dinnertime, as Bea and I are sitting down to eat, he finally descends the stairs. Like always, his little girl greets him.

"Bonjour, papa!"

"Hello, Bea," he murmurs in English.

This is what he does every night, except tonight, he falters on his way out the door.

Then, for the first time since I've worked here, he smiles at his daughter. It's a soft, affectionate smile, but it's enough to set my heart on fire with hope.

His eyes find mine. Neither of us says a word to each other, but we share a small, silent connection before he eventually turns away and marches out the door.

Like every night, I resume my duties taking care of Bea, giving her extra attention and affection to make up for what she should receive from her father. But throughout the entire evening, as I give her a bath, put on her pajamas, and tuck her into bed, I can't stop thinking about what happened today in the room upstairs.

After Bea has gone to sleep and the house is quiet, I brew a cup of tea and cuddle up on the couch in the living room downstairs. Rain pours down outside, tapping against the window as I pull a blanket over my legs and set my laptop on it. Music plays softly on the speakers as I open it and stare at the blank search engine screen. There's so much I want to know and yet so much I'm afraid to know.

Not afraid in the sense that it could hurt me but afraid in the sense that once I go down this path, there's no turning back. As if whatever I learn here might change me forever or, at the very least, change my perception of Jack. Not that my perception of him is all that good to begin with.

Heaving a sigh, I type two words into the search bar: *rope bondage*. With a wince, I hit the Enter button. Immediately results in the form of photos, videos, and websites pop up on the page.

I expect the results to be explicit and pornographic. And while some of them are, the majority of the results are more aesthetically stunning than I thought they'd be. I scroll through site after site after site, proclaiming *beginner's guides* and *what you should know about rope bondage*.

Some of it is mainly about sex, being tied up during sex, and being restrained to things like beds, bars, walls, and chairs. But that doesn't feel like it applies to what Jack had upstairs.

I click on a site that looks promising. *The Art of Shibari,* it says. And the images that greet me the moment I click the button are beautiful. The first is of a woman with her hands fastened near her shoulders in an intricate web of knots and ropes.

For something that looks like it should be excruciating, her face shows a solemn expression of peace. For what feels like hours, I read and scroll and read and scroll some more, absorbing every ounce of information I can on this unique practice.

But even after all my research, I struggle to find the purpose.

What is the point? Why do people do this? Is it all about the intricate knots and ties? Is it in some way meant to turn the participants on? Is it for sex? Is it for show? The websites all claim that being tied or being *a rope bunny* is a form of submission meant to put the person being tied into something called a *subspace*, which I still struggle to understand.

Does Jack really have an entire room upstairs devoted to this? Who is he tying up and why? Was this something he and Emmaline once did together?

Then I remember holding the ropes in my fingers as Jack stood behind me. There was a moment in which I could almost feel them tied around my arms. And that image alone sparked such arousal inside me. And not just an arousal for sex but an arousal for something so much more potent. Something that aroused more than just my body but my mind too.

The clock in the top corner of my laptop says that it's already past midnight. I've completely lost track of time and spent far too long doing this research. I close my browser, shut my laptop, and try to stow away this curiosity.

Even as I climb into bed, I know that I won't be able to put this new information away so easily. I can't stop thinking about what it would be like. And how I swear there was a moment today, particularly the growling noise Jack made, that made me believe he might want this too.

Like me, he was imagining me bound and tied for him. And he liked it. Hell, *I* liked it. It's not like I want him to hurt me or degrade me. And so what if I did? What's wrong with that? At least it's what *I* want.

Is that what I want?

I can't help that I'm so curious by nature. For all I know, after five minutes of trying something like this, I'd realize that I hate it, and I'd never want to do it again. But how will I ever know if I don't try?

And who on earth would I ever try it with if not him? I picture myself going back to that club to find another partner, perhaps the cute bartender, to introduce me to something like this.

I'm sure it could be exciting. But then what?

Sleep evades me as I toss and turn in my bed. Deep down, I know that the reason I can't fall asleep is because I'm still listening for the door, wondering if Jack will find his way to my hallway again. Maybe he'll go a bit further this time.

How has Jack St. Claire infiltrated my psyche so much in such a short time? Why can't I stop thinking about him? I'd like to believe that I'd find peace if I could just let him go and focus on my job, on Bea, the house, and my new life in Paris. But all that only feels like one half of my life now, as if he's somehow taken up so much space in my mind that I'll never be able to truly move on until I've unwrapped the mystery around the man.

But how can I when he won't even let me speak? The moment I open my mouth around him, he silences me.

I wish I understood why. Why does he shut me out? Why won't he give me a chance? And why on earth do I care?

I don't know what time it is when I finally decide to throw back the covers and climb out of my bed. It's mostly stubborn tenacity, or maybe it's a need to feel closer to him, that has me pulling the letter out of the desk drawer.

Even after all this time, I've never fully read it. Only skimmed a few lines. But there's a burning interest inside me that won't let me let it go. It's not about knowing their relationship anymore. It's about understanding *him*.

Sitting at the desk with my legs folded in front of me, I read his letter to his late wife.

Dear Emmaline,

I know what you're going to say. No one writes letters anymore. You'll call me cheesy or an old romantic, but I don't care. You deserve so much more than a text message or an email. You should know that a man who adores you sat down at his desk and wrote you a letter by hand to tell you just how much he loves you.

And you know that I do. I love you.

I never meant for this to happen. In only one year, I fell head over heels for you. Did you think I really went to all those ballet performances because I suddenly loved ballet? I was there for you. Every time.

You brought so much joy to my life, Em. I was a miserable, boring man before you came along. My heart is telling me that you feel the same. And I know if we really gave this a shot, we'd be happy together.

I miss you so much, and you've only been gone two weeks.

Paris doesn't shine the same without you.

Please come back.

Yours,
Jack

PS: I'll even learn French for you.

I read the letter three times, trying to imagine that cold, hardened man upstairs writing it. It just doesn't match the version of Jack that I know. Did her death really take such a toll on him that it changed him from a romantic, loving person to…this?

Setting the letter down on the desk, I can't stop thinking about everything I know about him now. It's like he thinks that he died along with her, but he didn't. He's still here, and he still has a life to live. A daughter to raise. And I can't help but think that shutting me out is just another way of hiding.

My mind is reeling, and there is too much I need to say to him. Opening the drawer, I pull out a piece of blank paper and a pen. If he likes to handwrite letters, fine. I can write one too.

My hand flies as I scribble out everything I want to say to Jack. It's a messy string of conscious thoughts, and I don't care that it's not eloquent or well-spoken. He needs to hear what is on my mind.

When it's all out and it's taken up two pages, I read back through the letter. I don't change a word. I don't know if he'll even read it, and at this point, I don't care. But I hope he does. I hope he listens, and I hope he considers what I'm asking of him.

It's nearly two o'clock in the morning when I fold the letter and walk it quietly up the stairs. He must still be at the club, because every room is empty. It takes me a moment to decide where to leave the letter. It needs to be somewhere he will find it immediately.

I step quietly into his bedroom. The room smells like him, immediately bringing back memories of last night in the hallway or earlier today in the room across the hall. I take a deep breath, breathing him in because I can. *Expensive cologne. Leather. Soap and musk.*

What I'm doing now could be a huge mistake, and it could cost me my job. But after the last few days with Jack, I have a feeling it won't come to that. He may act like he wants me out of his life, but the way he held me today said differently. He wanted to show me. He just needs a little nudge.

Standing next to his bed, I stare down at the nightstand where a single photo of him and Emmaline and baby Bea rests in a frame. I'm stabbed with a twinge of guilt in my gut, realizing that she's not here. That although she is gone, he is still another woman's husband. Is this wrong of me? To ask what I'm asking?

Ignoring the photo and swallowing down my guilt, I rest the folded letter on the nightstand with his name scrawled across the front in my messy handwriting. It looks so out of place. I have no doubt he'll notice it immediately when he comes home.

With that, I'm overcome with a sense of relief. Absolutely nothing could come from this, and at least I would have expressed myself. At least I said what was on my mind. Whether or not he reads it or cares, I did what I could. Leaving his room, I close the door behind me and quietly tiptoe down the stairs to my own. Crawling into bed, I tell myself that whatever happens now, I need to let him go. And even as I drift off to sleep, I know in my mind that there is no way that is happening.

Rule #9: Never say what's on your mind, and for God's sake, never put it in a letter.

Jack

"WHAT ABOUT THIS ONE?" I ASKED, HOLDING A BLUE LEATHER-BOUND *book in my hands.*

Em turned around and glanced at it. With a shrug, she shook her head.

"No, I couldn't get into it."

"To the donation bin it goes," I replied, tossing it in the box full of other books, old sweaters, and a pair of barely worn ballet slippers.

We were standing in Emmaline's apartment in Giverny, packing her belongings on a warm Sunday spring morning. There was some generic classic rock song playing on the radio. The smell of coffee, fresh flowers, and her perfume wafted through the air. It was only my second time being in her home. The first was the trip I took three months prior, delivering her home after her yearlong teaching internship in Paris.

The second time was this particular memory. Packing her things to move in with me.

A two-carat diamond on a gold band sat on her left ring finger. Seeing it shimmer in the light had my heart beating faster in my chest. I moved closer to her, wrapping my arms around her waist and kissing the side of her neck. She giggled like she always did, a sound like a warm breeze or a sip of champagne.

"Are you happy?" I asked.

Turning toward me, she kissed my lips and softly mumbled, "Very happy."

As I pulled away, I tried to find the truth in her eyes more than just in her words. She looked back at me for a second before her attention flitted down to my lips and then to the ring on her finger.

"Very happy," she softly whispered again.

It sounded true enough.

I scroll through another photo on my phone, scrutinizing all Em's smiles and the memories captured in the pictures. On my desk, my computer displays another month of dismal stats and numbers. Ever since we took ownership of L'Amour, recently renamed Legacy, it's been slowly sinking into an unprofitable mess. As someone who worked for L'Amour under the direction of Ronan and Matis for seven years, I should know how to fix it.

I should be focusing on that now instead of romanticizing the past, but this is what I always do.

I search for a distraction. Work is my distraction from my grief, and my grief is a distraction from my work—a vicious cycle.

Neither is what I should really be focusing on.

"Knock, knock," a soft, familiar voice calls from the doorway. I peer up from my phone to see Phoenix leaning against the frame with her arms crossed and that familiar, concerned look etched into her features.

"Hey." I set my phone down and wait for her to continue, although I'm pretty sure I know what she wants to ask.

"How are things?"

I knew it.

"Fine," I murmur without meeting her eyes.

Phoenix is the type of friend who can see that I'm drowning but doesn't know how to pull me out of the water. Instead, she dives in and swims next to me. She's been by my side, shoveling work and distraction my way since Em got sick because she knows it's the only way to get me through.

Right or wrong, I love her for it.

"How's the new nanny working out?" She steps into the office and sits in one of the chairs facing my desk.

My molars clench at the mention of the nanny. "Bea loves her," I say, sounding more displeased about that than I should.

"That's good," she replies before clearing her throat. Out of the corner of my eye, I can see Phoenix chewing on the inside of her lip, and it's blatantly obvious just how worried she is.

After Em died, I begged Phoenix to take my daughter. And for a short time, she did. For me.

It was a cruel request, and I'm not proud of it. To ask my best friend to help me and hurt me at the same time. To take the person I love most in this world because I couldn't be the father Bea needs.

I nearly died right along with Em when my daughter wasn't in my house for six whole months.

But I didn't die. Instead, I buried myself in something new. Something to distract me. Something that gives me control and forces me to focus.

I found a love for bondage that made everything hurt just a little less.

I thought I was better. That is until Bea returned home, and I realized that I still didn't have what it takes to be a father to her.

"I'm glad it's working out," she says softly. "But you know if it doesn't…she can always come back and stay with me."

I hear my daughter's voice in my head, and sorrow builds painfully in my throat. The adorable way she greeted me as I left the apartment. The hope and love in her eyes.

She just wants her father.

I won't give her up again.

"Thanks, Nix," I say, my voice thick and raspy with emotion. "But it's getting better."

She forces a smile. "Good. You know I'm always here for you."

"Thank you," I say on an exhale.

"Now, go home. There's nothing you can do to fix this mess tonight," she adds, gesturing to the financial reports on my desk.

"I will," I mutter lowly.

With that, she leaves my office, and I'm left with nothing but shame and regret.

I usually take a car back from the club, especially at nearly four in the morning.

But I need a moment to think, and the quiet, early mornings in the hilly district of Montmartre are the perfect place to do it.

Throughout my entire walk, I think about this new nanny.

She was hardly qualified in the first place, but now she's proved herself disobedient, insubordinate, and nosy.

Not to mention there is something that borders on inappropriate between us that is both of our faults.

I should fire her. But I won't.

What I said to Phoenix was true. My daughter likes her new nanny. There is laughter in our home again. She smiles more now. What kind of asshole would I be if I took that away from her?

Besides, it's only six more weeks until the yearlong contract with the club is up and we are free to leave. It might have been heartless of me to hire a new nanny with plans to leave the city before the year is up, but I'm a desperate man in a desperate situation.

The city streets are still wet from the late evening rain, and I find something so relaxing about that. The way the cobblestones glisten under the streetlights and the cars on the road sound against the wet concrete.

I will miss this city when we go. I'll miss the way Paris feels, embracing me with memories. But I won't miss it at the same time. Because even the rain on the city streets taunts me with moments from our past, like the night Em and I were caught in the rain, coming home from dinner. How she asked me to kiss her under the downpour because it was *romantic*, although I still don't understand why.

But I did it anyway.

I used to hear her laughter in my mind so much more, echoing through our house and down the halls. Now I hear Camille's instead, and it grates on my nerves. Her presence alone seems to be erasing the memory of my wife. And she has no idea.

Even the feel of her body against mine today. The soft curls of her hair against my cheek. The sound of her footsteps against the floorboards. The pinkish-red hue of her lipstick.

Fuck, I hate the way she tempts me. I'm a monster for what I want, not only because the poor woman is so naive, so innocent, and so new. But also because I want to reach for her in memory of reaching for Em.

I have to brush these thoughts aside. No more lurking in the hallway outside her door at night. No more pushing boundaries with her. No more lingering eye contact.

Put all these feelings away for good.

When I reach the house, I creep down the hall before disappearing upstairs. I briefly hover in Bea's doorway before approaching her bed. My daughter sleeps peacefully, clutching a stuffed unicorn in her arms.

There's an ache in my chest as I stare at her, the same way I do every night. I wish more than anything it had been me to go instead of Em. If she were here, she'd smother our daughter in comfort and affection so she'd never feel my absence. I wish I could do the same, but I don't know how. I don't know how to reach through my own pain to ease my child's, and I feel like a failure for it.

My mother raised me alone until I was seven. She made it seem so easy, but I don't know how to do this without Em. I'm terrified of saying the wrong thing or messing Bea up somehow. This grief feels like a disease I don't want her to catch.

She's better off without me.

After gently kissing my daughter's head, I tiptoe out of the room. Pausing in the hallway, I glance down at the closed door where Camille sleeps. Part of me wants to linger there again for reasons I don't understand.

It's the strangest thing. It's like there is a line of invisible rope from her to me, and it tugs me relentlessly closer to her.

God, I need to get out of this city.

Turning my back on her room and ignoring the bond between us, I creep up the stairs to the second floor. I loosen my tie from around my neck as I walk into my bedroom, closing the door behind me.

I notice the piece of paper on the nightstand right away. Pausing in the middle of my room, I stare at it.

At first, I consider that it's a note from my daughter. Or perhaps a drawing she made in school today.

Upon closer inspection, I see my name scribbled in black ink with messy yet feminine handwriting. Tearing off my tie, I toss it on the dresser before picking up the letter and staring at my name, written by her.

Jack

Slowly running my thumb over her handwriting, I imagine her scribbling my name on this paper. I hear her voice in my head as I read it over and over again.

What is this hold she has on me?

I unfold the two pages and find a letter written inside. A panic takes over as I consider that this is her resignation letter, not that I would blame her. I've been terrible to her. Sitting on the bed, I read the words in a rush.

Dear Jack,

You say I don't belong here, but you are wrong. I do belong here. I don't know why I came up to your room today, and I don't know why I opened that armoire, but something was calling me to.

What I found today in that room has made me very curious, and I know you are the best person to teach me. Whatever it is, I just want to feel what it's like.

I've done my research. I know what it is you enjoy, and I'm not some naive virgin who is afraid of being hurt. I know it doesn't have to be about sex, so I'm not asking for anything inappropriate. We can keep things innocent.

I think you want to teach me. I felt the way you touched me today. I heard the way you reacted. You can deny it all you want, but we both know that this could be good.

One thing you should know about me is that I'm stubborn. I don't give up easily, and I always put up a fight. So the more you push me, the more I push back. The more you try to silence me, the louder I will be.

And since you won't let me speak, this is the only way to reach you.

I'm trying to be patient with you. I will give you grace and patience while you work through whatever it is you need to work through, but you and I have more in common than you think. Because I think you're as stubborn and curious as I am.

If you don't want me to talk to you, that's fine. I won't. But I still want to know what those ropes feel like. I want to know what it's like to let you tie me up in them. I want to know what it feels like to submit.

Please.

Show me.

Camille

A rumbling groan climbs its way out of my body as I run my hand over my five-o'clock shadow. I read the letter nearly ten times before deciding how the fuck to feel about this.

Those last two words make my cock twitch in my pants: *Show me.*

Does she even know what she's asking of me? She thinks this doesn't have to be about sex, so she clearly doesn't understand what it would feel like to be bound and submissive for another person. Because it might not *be* about sex, but it's definitely going to blur some very serious lines.

"No," I say to myself as I set the letter on the table. "Absolutely not."

I sound out of my mind, speaking to no one in the room as I stand from the bed and pace the empty space. Part of me wants to march right back downstairs and tell her emphatically that this is out of the question.

She's my employee. I'm her boss.

My daughter is our only priority, so abusing this working relationship would only put Bea in harm's way. The right thing to do would be to keep things professional and tell Camille that we cannot do anything that would be considered inappropriate.

But as I unbutton my shirt and tear it from my shoulders, I imagine her long blond curls braided down her naked back. I picture her small wrists bound behind her. I picture a blindfold over her eyes and her empty mouth at the right height to take my cock.

"Fuck!" I bark as I bury my fingers in my hair. *What am I doing?* I can't think things like that. That is exactly what I should *not* be doing.

Trying to distract myself, I go to the bathroom down the hall and close myself in. I don't have to remove my pants to know my cock is stiff and pulsing with need.

"Stop it," I berate myself, trying to carry on with my normal night routine before going to sleep. By the time I've finished brushing my teeth, my cock has managed to soften to a manageable state.

I'm a monster for even having to think that.

Dammit, Camille. How could she ask me that? She really has no idea the effect she has on me, and clearly, neither did I until this moment.

Returning to my room, I know there won't be an ounce of rest for me until I respond to her in some way. So I go down the hall to my office and sit in the dim room with only a small lamp on the desk to illuminate the blank white page.

With a pen in my hand, I quickly scrawl my reply. But every few lines, I decide I hate my response, and I tear the page from the pad and ball it up before throwing it in the trash. Every excuse feels wrong.

It would be inappropriate.

I am your employer.

Contrary to what you assume, I do not share these feelings with you.

Wrong, wrong, wrong.

Just once, I decide to write something without letting my mind stop me. I write her a response that *feels* right. The words fly across the page, and by the time I finish, I know that I should not, under any circumstance, give her this letter.

For nearly an hour, I contemplate what I've just written. The sun starts to crest the city through the windows when I mumble, "Fuck it."

Folding up the pages the same way she did, I scribble her name on the front. In a pair of dark joggers, I quietly tiptoe down the stairs, rushing to deliver the letter before she wakes.

With one last moment of hesitation, I slide the letter under her door.

There is no turning back now. My regret and I make our way back upstairs and into my bed.

I am not a man of impulse. I don't make decisions lightly.

But this woman seems to have scrambled the wires in my brain. I find myself almost obsessed with her in a way that can't be healthy.

And when she reads that letter today, she will know.

Rule #10: Be a man of your word.

Camille

I don't sleep well all night. The image of that letter on his nightstand haunts my dreams. Even my subconscious imagines him opening it, fuming with anger that I had the audacity to speak my mind to him.

When my alarm goes off at half past six, I climb reluctantly from under the covers to face the day. Ambling tiredly to the door, something crinkles under my feet as I reach for the door handle.

I glance down and stare at a folded piece of paper on the floor.

Realizing that it's a letter is like a shot of espresso to my heart. My name is written on the front in his handwriting. In a rush, I pick it up and stare at it.

Oh my God, he wrote me back.

He wrote me back.

I have to take a moment before reading his response. Bracing myself for disappointment, I consider that what is inside is probably his very formal request to never speak of this again.

Biting my lip, I cautiously peel it open. Then my eyes ravenously read his response.

Camille

When I said you don't belong here, I meant that you are far too sweet and innocent to know what you are asking me to do.

And I stand by this assumption.

If you think any of this could be accomplished without sex, then you have no idea what it is I would do in these demonstrations. You have no idea who I am or what I like.

If you are so certain that I am the man to teach you, then I think you should know what you're asking. So if you are so curious, then I will tell you now.

First of all, you would be naked for me, stripped of every ounce of clothes on your body. Your hair would be braided down your back so it does not get in the way. You would start on your knees for me, blindfolded, and you will not speak unless I tell you to.

I would bind your arms and legs in a harness so that you could not move them.

You would be completely and utterly bound for me. Every one of your senses would be heightened.

Do you understand? You would be at my mercy, Ms. Aubert. I would own you.

If you think that would not involve sex, then you don't know what you are getting yourself into.

I'll be clear so that you understand.

When I have you tied up, I will want to fuck you.

And when you are tied up for me, you will want me to. In fact, you'll beg for it.

You'll beg for my cock in your sweet, dripping little cunt.

If this letter scares you—good. It's meant to.

I am not a kind or gentle man, Camille. And I'm no fucking teacher.

I want you to fully understand what you ask of me because there is no chance of us going down this road with any part of it remaining innocent or appropriate.

So tell me. Are you still curious?

My hands are trembling as I hold the paper. Blood heats my body like lava as I read the filthy words again and again and again, gasping each time I imagine exactly what he would do to me.

Out of everything I expected him to reply, this was definitely not it.

Gauging my reactions, I try to determine exactly how I feel about it.

I know how I *should* feel. Alarmed. Disgusted. Terrified.

But in truth, I'm none of those things. In fact, I've never felt more excited.

He said he wanted his letter to scare me, but it doesn't. He thinks I'll be turned off by his perverted words, but I'm not.

Tiny footsteps steal my attention, so I shove the letter into the drawer of the desk and quickly compose myself, ready to face the little girl who needs my attention.

Coming out of the bedroom, I find Bea standing in the hallway, still in her pink satin pajamas and her hair a mess.

"J'ai faim," she mumbles sleepily as she rubs her eyes.

"What would you like for breakfast?" I reply, forcing a smile.

She shrugs as she shuffles into the kitchen. Quickly donning my apron and cleaning up, I begin to make breakfast for Bea and myself. She colors quietly in her sketchbook while I work, and I worry that she can sense my discomfort.

I don't feel as calm and comfortable as I normally do. In fact, I dread this entire day. It's Saturday, which means I have to entertain her all day while her father sleeps upstairs. We won't have a single moment to discuss whatever this is.

And we won't have a single moment to do any of those provocative things he spelled out in his letter.

Get it together, Camille.

I'm not here to screw Jack St. Claire in my free time. I'm here to take care of this precious little girl without a mother. I'm here to help this family.

After serving Bea her breakfast, I sit down across from her and pick at mine. My stomach is too knotted to eat.

My gaze flicks to the stairwell every few minutes, wondering if he is going to come down at any point today. What on earth would I do if he did? Just act normal? Act like he didn't explicitly spell out how he would do deplorable and enticing things to me?

I don't know if I can do that.

After breakfast, Bea goes to her room to play. I set out her dress and tights for the day and help her to get cleaned up. Everything feels like going through the motions. I'm just passing the time.

Once she's settled, I pat her on the head delicately. "I just need to get dressed. Then we can go to the park."

"Okay," she chirps excitedly. She's quietly playing with her dolls as I slip out of her room and down to my own.

Once I'm hidden behind the door, I rush to the desk to read the letter again. My fingers graze my lips as I devour every word once more. I can't help but imagine him doing all these things to me in elaborate detail. I've never felt more turned on in my life.

Finally, I sit in the seat and pull out a new, blank notepad. Just like last night, I tell him everything straight from the heart.

Dear Jack,

I am still curious, and I don't scare easy.

I am not an innocent or naive woman.

If you think I don't want the things you've described in your letter, you're wrong. I want all those things, and I'm not afraid.

I want to know what it feels like to be bound the way you promise. And everything that comes with it.

So tell me. Are you a man of your word?
Or was this all talk?

Camille

When I'm done with my response, I quickly get dressed. After twisting my messy curls into a clip at the back of my head, I emerge from my room and tell Bea to get ready to leave.

While she's busy getting her shoes on, I scurry up the stairs with my letter. My fingers are shaking as I tiptoe down the hall toward his room. Then, just as he did sometime last night or early this morning, I slide my letter under the door for him to read when he wakes.

There's no taking it back now.

———◦❧◦———

Bea and I come home from the park in time for lunch. I take a peek up the stairs and see no sign of Jack at all. I assume if he works all night, then he would probably sleep all day.

I can't help but imagine my letter still lying on the floor, waiting to be read.

"What's wrong?" Bea asks when she finds me sitting on the sofa with my face in my hands, distressed about what I've written in that letter.

I plaster a fake smile on my face as I shake my head. "Tout va bien," I reply, trying to assure her that everything is fine.

There is an expression of concern on her face, and I'm plagued with guilt. It dawns on me then that all the adults in Bea's life have either left or retreated in their grief. She needs me to hold it together for her.

So I quickly shove away all thoughts of Jack and the letters, and I give her my full attention. After making lunch together, we spend the rest of the afternoon working on a puzzle, then reading a book, and finally, she settles down in her room for quiet time.

When I check on her after fifteen minutes and find her asleep, I breathe a sigh of relief. As much as I love spending my days with Bea, I am more exhausted than not.

I'm wiping down the counters in the kitchen when I hear movement upstairs. He's awake—reading my letter at this moment. I freeze, waiting in anticipation. I can practically hear my heart thumping in my chest.

With a humiliated squeak, I cover my face with my hands and wait for his response. A long time goes by in silence. I continue to clean the kitchen, then prep for dinner. My eyes flash to the stairwell again and again.

I'm leaning against the counter when I hear his steps coming down. That invisible string between us pulls him nearer and nearer. The house is so quiet that I can barely breathe. I fully expect him to pass by the same way he does every day, but I hope he doesn't.

When he appears in the doorway to the kitchen, all the air is sucked from the room. I see him so rarely that every time he stands before me, I am reminded of just how handsome he is. Dark hair, a chiseled jaw, piercing eyes, and a little dimple in the center of his chin.

He stands in silence, staring at me. The words in our letters hover around us like promising threats. Then I glance down and see my last letter held tightly in his hand. My breath hitches in my chest.

As he takes one menacing step after another toward me, I lean into the counter pressed against my lower back. He doesn't stop his advances until his body is flush against mine, and I have to practically bend backward to hold his stare.

He lifts a finger and presses it to my mouth to keep me quiet.

As if I could speak. I can hardly breathe.

His eyes bore into mine as he brings his mouth closer. I'm thrown off by his proximity when he whispers, "You are a stubborn little thing, aren't you?"

Silently, I nod, making him crack a smile. It's the most warmth he's ever given me, and I'm hungry for more.

"You're playing with fire, you know that? I can't seem to say no to you, although I should."

His fingers drift away from my lips, but I don't open my mouth or utter a word.

"I am a man of my word, so I will show you. But that's all. A simple lesson. Anything more would be inappropriate. So we'll see just how curious you are."

I suck in a breath, forcing myself to remain calm.

"Midnight. Upstairs. Understand?"

Again, I nod.

"Good girl," he replies, and it has me melting against the cabinets.

The effect of those words alters my brain chemistry. They have me wanting to pull him closer, bury myself in his arms, and do whatever he wants as long as he praises me like that again.

I never want his body to move away from mine. I'd like to spend the rest of the day pressed against him, feeling his gaze bore into me like basking in the warmth of the sun.

Regardless of what I want, he pulls away anyway. I watch as he walks out of the room, a disgruntled wrinkle between his brows. My eyes catch on the gold ring on his finger, and I'm reminded of how *wrong* this is. I'm panting in the kitchen, waiting for my body to recover from what just happened.

Moments later, the front door opens and closes, and I know he's gone. And I'm left knowing that the next time I see him, it will be under very different circumstances.

Rule #11: Always trust your gut.

Camille

THE CLOCK MOVES AGONIZINGLY SLOWLY. IT FEELS LIKE DAYS between when I put Bea to bed at 7:30 and midnight. I try to busy myself by doing my normal nightly routine around the house, but my actions are clumsy, and my body is unbearably tense. I break a dinner plate in the kitchen when drying the dishes because I can't seem to suppress the tremble in my bones.

I don't want to back out. I want to do this.

But I lied when I told Jack I wasn't scared. I'm *terrified*.

I'm reminded of the time when I was only twelve, and some of the cruel boys in my year called me a baby because I was too scared to jump over the shallow channel behind our school. I was scared out of my mind, but I refused to back down.

And when I landed in the hospital with a broken ankle, my father scolded me for always acting without thinking. I am too reckless. Too careless. Too foolish to know when I'm getting myself in over my head.

I always was, and I guess I still am.

That's what got me this job in the first place.

And now I'm about to embark on something I don't even understand with a man who is way out of my league and far more experienced than me. Jack scares me in a way that I like.

I waste the last hour before midnight leaning over the kitchen counter, doodling a swan hanging by its feet in knotted rope.

Jack has been gone since he left this afternoon. So when the door opens at half past eleven, I watch nervously. I can hear my pulse in my ears as he walks into the apartment, glancing toward the kitchen briefly before climbing the stairs to his room.

Should I follow him?

I decide to wait it out, wringing my fingers in anticipation.

At precisely 12:00 a.m., I climb the stairs without looking back. The doors at the end of the hall are open, and I pause when Jack passes from one to the other.

Forging ahead, I continue down the hall until I reach the room on the left, the one with the dark walls and plush carpet. Bracing myself one last time, I make eye contact with him as I enter.

Jack is rolling up the sleeves of his shirt. "Close the door," he says, so I press it shut behind me. Then I'm standing just a few feet away from him, waiting for what comes next. "Come here," he says in a clipped command.

Licking my lips and keeping my gaze on his face, I close the distance, meeting him at the center of the rug. Gazing up at him, I roam the features of his face—his handsome green eyes, his full pink lips, his gentle, patient expression. There is something soft about him tonight, and it no longer feels as if I'm trespassing into his space. He's inviting me in.

He's not glowering at me like I'm a nuisance or petulant brat. He's giving me a calm warmth.

This is the Jack I've been dying to see.

"You're here because you wanted to see what it's like to be bound, so that's what I'm going to do. You are new to this, so I'm going to use restraint, but at any time, if you don't like what

I'm doing or anything hurts or feels numb, I want you to tell me. Understood?"

Knowing that Jack prefers silence, I nod instead of speaking.

Touching my shoulder, he slowly turns me around so my back is to him. I take a slow, shuddering breath as he gathers my hair at the nape of my neck.

With deft fingers, he begins to section my hair into parts as if he's done this a thousand times. While he works to braid it, he speaks. Meanwhile, I just have to remind myself to breathe.

"I've been thinking about what I put in that letter today, and I want you to know that I do not plan on fucking you, Ms. Aubert. It was wrong of me to write that. I am fully capable of showing you what you want to experience while keeping things professional. Understand?"

I'm flooded with disappointment, which is a little surprising. Reluctantly, I nod.

He works to braid my hair down my back, his fingers moving quickly. There's something so calming about it that it seems to settle the nervousness inside me. He ties a small black ribbon around the end of my braid before resting his hands on my shoulders. Then he leans in until his mouth is near my ear as he adds, "But it doesn't mean I won't want to."

Tendrils of hope cascade down to the base of my spine.

He leaves my back and walks over to the wardrobe, pulling it open. I don't move from my spot as I watch him.

"When I thought about it more, I realized this might be a perfect solution for both of us. You want to know what it feels like to be tied up, and I need a willing person to let me. This does not make me your Dom, understand?"

I nod, although he never turns around to see me.

"This is an intricate and elaborate practice with many different layers and variations. I don't want to be your teacher, Miss Aubert. I'm not interested in showing you how to tie these things yourself. If you choose to learn more, you'll have to find someone else."

I want to tell him that I have no intention of learning with anyone else. Instead, I whisper, "Why do you do it then? If not for...sex."

He turns toward me with his expression pinched together in concentration. "It...settles my mind. Gives me some sense of control." His voice is low and steady, and I have to swallow down my nerves and a hint of arousal at hearing him speak so intimately.

Why is he so desperate for control? What is on his mind that he needs to quiet?

I want more. This obsession only grows stronger with the breadcrumbs he leaves me. This man, with so many shades and so much complexity, draws my interest like no one ever has. *Who are you, Jack St. Claire? Show me.*

"Why are you so interested in trying it?" he replies keenly.

"I'm curious, maybe to a fault."

His mouth twitches with the hint of a smile. "You've mentioned that."

He pulls a black silk ribbon from the cabinet. As he brings it over to me, he pauses, his eyes cascading down my body. He seems to realize that I'm still fully clothed.

"You'll need to take these off. Leave on your bra and underwear." He clears his throat as I quickly tug my shirt over my head and shed my pants, throwing both in a pile in the corner. I watch his molars grind as he stares at the messy pile of clothes.

Suddenly, I'm standing half-naked in front of him while he's fully clothed, and it's incredibly vulnerable and uncomfortable. I can practically feel my nipples tighten under my thin bra. He must notice too, because his attention lingers there as if briefly hypnotized. I grow warmer with every passing second that his eyes are on me.

Shaking himself out of it, his gaze finds mine. "Before we start, I need to know you understand that this requires a great deal of trust between both of us. You trust me to keep you safe, and I trust you to communicate with me if anything feels wrong. Nod if you understand."

So I do.

I know I have no good reason to trust Jack. I hardly know him. He's only proven himself to be self-centered, rude, and detached. But he's slowly opening up to me. As vulnerable as I feel giving my trust to him, I know he feels twice as vulnerable by letting me in. My instincts are telling me that he won't hurt me. And I always trust my gut.

"Normally, I'd want you blindfolded. It will heighten your senses and build trust, but I don't think the first session is the right time to do it."

My brows soften as I stare at the black ribbon. "I can handle it."

Reaching out, he touches my chin. "Not yet."

With that, he drapes the black ribbon over the handle of the door, and I fixate on it longingly. Why am I so intrigued by the idea of being robbed of my sight? Why on earth am I so eager to hand over all my trust to this man?

"We're going to start with a basic tie, just so you can feel what it's like. Hold out your wrists," he says. His voice is soothing yet rough, and I find something like peace in his commands. He's not bossing me around or barking orders at me. He's giving me guidance, making his instructions easy to follow.

Suddenly, I am eager to please.

So I hold out my wrists.

He steps away to pull a bundle of black rope from the wardrobe. My heart picks up speed at the sight of it. A second later, two strands of the rope are draped over my arms. He winds them around again and again, moving at a pace that is not rushed but not slow either.

I find myself watching his face instead of his fingers, thinking about how he said it quiets his mind, and I can see that already. He's obviously very experienced in this, and I find comfort in that.

As he works, my curiosity gets the better of me, and I close my eyes, eager to feel what it would be like. The moment my vision is gone, the rest of my senses heighten. The scent of his cologne becomes more potent, and the feel of his fingers on my skin grows warmer.

It's the same feeling I would get as a child when I'd fall asleep in the car, and my father would bring me into the house, barely waking me as he set me into my bed. It's a feeling of safety. It's complete confidence in knowing the person with the most power over me is the one person who would never hurt me.

"Open your eyes, Camille," he says, and I do, taking a deep, slow breath, realizing that I have been holding it. Why? I don't know. Our gazes meet, and I worry that he's about to scold me. Instead, that hint of a smile reappears on his lips, and he shakes his head. "You never listen."

"Yes, I do," I argue.

"Fine," he says, tugging gently on the binds around my wrists. "Prove it. Keep your eyes open and your mouth shut."

My brows furrow with offense at his rude demands. But I intend to prove to him that I can obey simple orders, so I keep my lips pressed together and my eyes on the ropes.

He continues to loop and knot and loop and knot, and it's far more complex than just a simple tie. It winds halfway up my forearm. The binds are not tight, but as he knots them together, I try to move them and find that I can't. There's a part of me that wonders if I should be panicking. Anyone in their right mind would probably hate this, but I don't.

In fact…I like it.

"Nod your head if you're feeling comfortable."

Quickly, I nod.

"Do you want me to release them?"

I shake my head.

"No numbness or tingling?"

Shake again.

"How do you feel?"

Lifting my attention to his face, the connection between us is strong, maybe stronger than ever as I open my mouth to reply, "I want more."

His jaw clicks as he clenches his molars and exhales through his nose. I see his pupils dilate, the restraint apparent in his expression. "I'll give you more, but we'll start slow. Now, close your eyes."

On a trembling exhale, I do as he says, reminding myself to breathe. He steps closer, the heat of his body radiating against my bare skin.

"I'm going to touch you now," he whispers.

I tense in anticipation. *Touch me? How?*

Then the backs of his fingers cascade down my arm, leaving goose bumps in their wake.

"Notice how everything feels so much more intense when you can't move. Can't see. Can't pull away."

My stomach tightens. *What is he doing to me?* Slowly, I nod.

His touch moves back up my arm, cresting my shoulder and traveling across my collarbone. I let out a gentle gasp, and he growls lowly in return.

"Imagine being pleasured like this. Imagine pleasuring *someone else*. Being used. Being fucked."

I start to feel dizzy as his touch dances down the center of my breasts, over the thin bralette, and then to my navel. I'm practically shivering and finding it surprising how gentle he's being. It's not what I expected. If it's not about sex to him, then why is he torturing me like this? Is it because he enjoys my torment or because he wants me to know what we're missing out on? There is a pulse between my legs as I soak my panties, desperately wishing he would stop talking about pleasuring me and just do it.

Then he grips the knot around my wrists and jerks me roughly toward him. I let out a yelp as my body slams against his. My eyes fly open and connect with his. The rough domination sends heat coursing through my body, culminating between my clenched thighs.

"See how much control I have over you?" he mutters. His mouth is so close to mine that his lips move against my skin. "Imagine your entire body covered in these knots. Imagine not being able to move an inch as I use you. Do you like the sound of that, Ms. Aubert?"

Shuddering, I nod. My lips part when I feel his breath on my mouth. In my mind, I'm pleading, begging him for more.

Kiss me, please. Take back everything you said earlier about showing restraint, cover me in those knots, and use me like you want to.

Of course, I don't utter a word. The moment is too delicate to disrupt. I know that's foolish of me, to want to be thrown in the deep end when I don't even know how to swim, but I can't help this desire. I can't help the way Jack makes me feel.

Watching him come to life from just a man in a photo to a closed-off ghost to *this*. Someone who looks at me with so much potent attention, I want to drown in it.

It's as if he can read my mind. Or maybe he's just thinking the same things I am.

With his hand still on the ropes, he moves his body closer to mine, his rock-hard bulge pinned against my leg. I let out a gasp. But as soon as he's touching me, he's gone. With distance between us, I want the hard surface of his body against mine again. I want to feel the proof of his arousal, but he won't let me. That would be crossing a line, one he promised he wouldn't cross, and that was something I wasn't supposed to feel.

To distract me from what I just felt, he tugs the bind on my wrists downward as he says in a tight, raspy tone, "On your knees."

I quickly obey, moving to the floor. I've never felt my heart beat so fast in my life.

"Good girl," he says with a low growl. His free hand pets my hair, and I start to sway.

How can he have me so compliant with just a few commands and words of praise? It's like being hypnotized. I'd do anything just to please him.

For the first time since I walked in that door, I'm filled with a sense of danger. Not at risk of being hurt but at risk of loving this too much. In danger of never wanting this to end. And winding up very brokenhearted.

Rule #12: Show restraint.

Jack

THIS WAS A MISTAKE. I NEVER SHOULD HAVE BROUGHT HER UP here.

I'm corrupting this sweet, innocent woman, and for what? My own sick, twisted pleasure? Because I've been dying to see her in knots since she showed up at my house a few weeks ago? Because everything she does drives me out of my mind? Because everything about her reminds me of Em.

But Em wouldn't have done this. Em was never as curious or interested in this lifestyle, regardless of my job. All this—the room, the wardrobe, the obsession with bondage—was just part of my ever-growing and unhealthy coping mechanism since her death.

So maybe if I tarnish and corrupt and defile Camille, she'll no longer appear to me like a ghost of the woman I married.

Fuck, what is wrong with me?

Just another dark path this grief wants to lead me down. But I meant what I said. If I could just keep my restraint, then she would be the perfect person for me to practice on. She is curious for more as much as I crave this outlet. What I should have seen coming is just how much *more* I want with her.

Now, she's on her knees, bound and beautiful, and I said I would hold back, but *God*, I don't want to. I'd like to show her exactly what it's like to submit. I'd like to make her body mine.

But as tantalizing as it sounds, I also know how incredibly unfulfilling it is. It's like chasing a high I'll never find.

"Nod if you're still comfortable," I say as I release her hand and take a step back.

She nods, but I notice the way she reaches for me, wanting me back within her grasp.

For some reason, I give her what she wants, stepping back toward her so she can feel my presence.

I never let the sub have control. What is wrong with me?

Reaching down, I softly pet her hair. She leans into the touch, soaking up my attention.

I can't help it, but I find myself saying the things I absolutely should *not* say. "Do you know all the filthy things I could do to you at this angle?"

She lets out a breath as she nods.

"Stand up," I command, swallowing the temptation to *do* all those things. Taking her by the wrists, I help her to her feet. With the extra rope from her binds in my hands, I hook them over the suspension loop hanging from the ceiling.

Then I tug on the rope, and she lets out a squeaking sound as her body extends, leaving her on her tiptoes. I quickly tie the rope with a quick-release knot so she's locked in place, barely able to stand. Immediately, she starts to sway, her head hanging back. From this angle, I can see the pulse in her neck, rapidly beating under her tender flesh.

Her breasts look exquisite in this position—petite, tan circles peeking through the sheer fabric of her bra. I can't help myself as I reach out and draw my fingers along the ridges of her rib cage and up to the small mounds of her breasts.

She lets out another sound like a whimper. So I pinch the small bud between my fingers. What the fuck am I doing?

"Would you like me to stop?" I ask.

She shakes her head.

Good girl, I think. I won't say it out loud. I don't want her to think she's being praised for enduring something. It would only encourage her to lie for my benefit.

Bringing my body flush with hers, I continue to play with her small tits just to see the way her breathing changes as I do. God, what a weak man I am. It's only the first session, and already I'm losing my control. I was so full of shit when I told her it wouldn't be about sex. That's *all* I can think about.

She's trying to keep her pleasure sounds in. Maybe she thinks I don't want to hear those the same way I don't want to hear her voice. I like the idea of her obeying me so intently.

"Do you like it so far?" I ask with my face near hers. "Being tied up and teased?"

She nods only a little, unable to move her head and neck as much with her arms pressed up around her ears. She does, however, let out a small sound again as I pinch the sensitive bud.

I can't get over how beautiful she looks like this. Most people are uncomfortable their first time. They fight against the ropes or struggle to find a comfortable position, but Camille seems to melt into this bondage like she was made for it. Like she was just waiting for me to show her.

"Is this what you wanted me to show you?" I ask, trailing my fingers down from her chest and around to her back.

She nods.

"There are so many more things to try. More positions, more knots, more…opportunities. Would you like that?"

"Yes," she cries out on a whimper. "Please."

With that, I spin her around so that her back is pressed to my chest. The chains above her rattle as she struggles to regain her balance.

My cock aches as I press it against her ass. I'm going to hell for this.

Her head falls backward so she's resting it on my shoulder. She's struggling to keep the sounds in now. Little whimpers and whines of desire escape her lips. And they only get worse when my greedy hands take their fill, roaming her body.

What I wouldn't give to slide down these panties and fill her up. I'd like to see her try to stay quiet then.

No matter how hard I try to restrain myself from rubbing my stiff length against her, I can't seem to stop. It feels too good. She is too perfect.

She cries out with need, and it only urges me on. So much for restraint. That's long gone now. We have slipped past the edge of control, and we're both giving in to base needs here. I'm grinding against her as she writhes against me, hungry for more.

Then she mumbles something incoherent to herself in French, and it's like having someone snap me out of a daze.

What the fuck am I doing? This is my daughter's nanny.

I'm a fucking monster.

My hands release her body, and I take a step back, forcing deep breaths into my lungs.

I'm supposed to be the one in control here, and she has me falling to pieces.

"That's enough," I snap.

She lets out a gasp, turning her head to find me, although she can hardly move with her arms still stretched toward the ceiling.

"What? No. Don't stop," she pleads.

"We're getting carried away," I say as I pull the rope loose from the ceiling, and Camille nearly tumbles to the floor.

"Wait," she whispers, quickly catching herself and closing her lips.

"You wanted to know what it feels like, so I've shown you."

I work to undo the bind on her wrists, but she's shaking her head emphatically. "Show me more, Jack. Please. You know you want to."

My head snaps up, and I stare at her. "That's exactly the problem. I never should have touched you like that. I was supposed to show restraint. You are my employee, my daughter's caretaker. I have to think about her, and I lost control, but I have it back now."

Once her wrists are free, she immediately reaches for me. But I grab them before she can put her hands on me. It's taking everything in me to hold back when all I want to do is let go.

I inspect her hands and wrists for any swelling or bruising, but other than some basic rope marks, she appears fine.

When I look into her eyes again, I remember why I wanted the blindfold on her in the first place. There is an intensity in Camille's gaze that always stops me in my tracks.

It's like she can see into my soul. It makes it so much harder to hide from her. She looks at me like she knows me.

I've never found that with anyone.

Quickly, I look away.

"There are plenty of people at the club who could show you more, but it won't be—"

To my utter shock, Camille lunges forward and places her hand over my mouth like I have done to her so many times before. My eyes widen as I stare down at her in surprise. Even she looks surprised by her own audacity.

"Please stop saying that," she mumbles. "I don't want anyone else to show me, and I don't think you do either."

After a moment, she eases her hand away from my mouth and steps back. Looking down at the floor, she presses her lips together, and I can't even find it in me to argue with her because she's right. I hate the idea of someone else touching her.

At this point, I should lead her through some aftercare, but we didn't go very deep into the scene, so I think it's safe to assume she's okay. With nothing left to say or do, we stand in awkward silence, not looking at each other or speaking.

I decide to be the one to leave first.

"That's enough for tonight," I mumble. Turning my back on her, I walk to the door before adding, "Good night, Camille."

Just as I disappear into my room on the other side of the hallway, I hear her softly reply, "Good night, Jack."

The moment I'm alone, I run my hands through my hair and question where the hell my sanity has gone. I hear Camille's footsteps down the hall and then the stairs. Once I know she's gone, I collapse onto my bed and put my face in my hands.

There's a photo of my wife watching from the nightstand, and her stare feels like daggers of grief and regret. I don't know how others are able to move on after the loss of their spouse, but I never will. I can't let Em go. I will *never* let her go.

Tonight was just a game. Another meaningless moment with a stranger that scratches an itch and fills some superficial hole inside me. From the moment Em died, I've buried myself in the bodies of others like some sort of sick penance because I'd rather feel this than soul-crushing grief.

But tonight didn't feel like the others. Something about Camille was different.

Maybe it's because she's my employee, and I wouldn't let myself fuck her.

Maybe it's because she's the first French woman I've been with since Em.

But either way, it doesn't matter because it's never happening again. There is only one objective on my mind. Finish the year at the club, hand it over to Julian, and leave this country forever.

Only then will Bea and I be truly free.

I can't let myself get sidetracked and distracted by a beautiful, curious woman who seems to set my soul on fire without even meaning to.

Rule #13: Be careful what you ask for.

Camille

I HAVE NEVER FELT MORE TIGHTLY WOUND IN MY LIFE. I SCURRY down the stairs from Jack's room and bolt into my own, shutting the door behind me as I force myself to take long, deep breaths.

There is a warm, resounding pulse throbbing between my legs, begging me to relieve this ache. With my back against the door and a feverish need thrumming in my veins, I slip my fingers down the front of my panties.

The rest of my clothes are balled up in my arm, and I drop them to the floor as I stare up at the ceiling. I should feel ashamed for this, but I can't help myself. With my toes curling against the hardwood floor, I rub fiercely on my aching clit.

It's not enough. It dulls the pain of arousal, but it doesn't give me what I want.

Imagining it's still his body against my back instead of this door, I turn my head, trying to find the scent of his cologne in my braided hair. Then I curl two fingers deep inside me.

It's still not what I want, but it's enough to feed my imagination, to imagine that it's him thrusting himself inside me. It's him touching me while I'm bound and strung from the ceiling. It's him finding pleasure in my body.

I know he wanted it. I could feel the evidence of his desire. So I search my memory for the sensation of his hard cock pressed up against me, seeking friction in my body.

Biting my lower lip, I penetrate myself in rapid thrusts, chasing this trail of pleasure. My free hand pinches my nipple through my bra, remembering the way he did, imagining it's his hand there now. With a muffled moan, my body begins to spasm, seizing in this tight, almost torturous sensation. I have never come so fast in my life. I can hardly breathe as the waves crash over me again and again.

The shame settles in after the orgasm crests and fades. What on earth is wrong with me? Was it just because what we did upstairs was so erotic and sensual? Or is it because something about Jack St. Claire ignites a fire inside me?

I have always found him attractive, but now it's clear the chemistry between us is so much more than that.

When my body feels somewhat normal again, I peel myself away from the door and sneak into the bathroom. I can't even look at myself in the mirror as I wash up and get ready for bed.

The entire time, I'm writing a letter to him in my mind, voicing everything I want to say about tonight and what I want after tonight.

Jack was spooked by his own desire, afraid he was losing control, and I intend to convince him that there's nothing to be afraid of.

When I go back into my room, I sit down at the desk, and I write the letter.

Dear Jack,

What are you so afraid of?
    If you think because I am your employee and your daughter's

caretaker that I am not also just a woman who feels and desires and craves the same things that any other woman does, then you're wrong.

I know you think it's inappropriate for us to continue with what we did tonight, but I disagree.

If you let me show you, I will prove to you just how good I can be. I can follow orders. I can be submissive. I can draw a line between what we do during the day and what we do at night.

As one of your employees, I can keep things professional. I will do my job, and I will do it well.

But after dark, I don't want to be your employee. I want to be the one who submits to you, who kneels, who obeys. If you don't want sex to be involved, then I can show restraint too—the same way you did tonight.

Because I know you have so much more to show me, and I am eager to experience it all. There is no one else I'd be more comfortable with.

So I am begging you, please show me more.

Staring down at my letter, I bite my lip as I consider how to sign it. Just signing my name doesn't feel right anymore. After tonight…after feeling what it's like to be praised by him, I realize that I want to sign it a different way.

Taking a deep breath, I hold my pen as I scribble out the last line.

Your good girl.

With that, I fold up the letter and take it back up the stairs. No longer afraid of telling Jack what is on my mind, I slide the letter under the door.

I'm playing with fire. I know it, but for the first time in my life, I want to feel what it's like to get burned.

I flip an omelet onto Bea's plate, sprinkling it with salt and cheese before delivering it to where she sits at the table in her school uniform. Her tiny legs swing under her seat, and I find it so adorable. I pat her head affectionately as I set the plate down.

"Bon appétit."

"Merci, Camille," she replies.

Bea is obviously fluent in French, and I notice the way she's eager to use it with me when we're at home. In public and at school, she speaks it without restraint. For some reason, Jack says it's off-limits at home, and I wish I understood why.

She has school today, and since I stayed up far too late with Jack in the *bondage room*—as I'm calling it now—I am feeling a little sleep-deprived this morning. It didn't help that I could hardly sleep after our session ended, too strung out and excited about this new dynamic between us. Sitting down next to Bea with my espresso, I try to wake up.

While she eats, I hear footsteps on the stairs, and I freeze. Bea does too.

Then we both turn at the same time to find Jack standing in the doorway to the kitchen in a nice dark blue suit, freshly showered with wet hair and the scent of aftershave wafting into the room.

He never comes down to the kitchen in the morning.

"Morning, Papa," Bea says with a guarded expression.

"Morning, Bea," he replies. Then his eyes find mine.

After last night, seeing him in the daylight feels like staring into the sun. It burns with intensity and a hint of awkwardness, and I know I should look away.

Regardless, I promised him that I could keep things professional. I swore to him in that letter that I could put up a boundary between day and night activities. And I need to prove that to him.

So I quickly stand from the table.

"Sit down. I can make you breakfast."

"I have a meeting to get to," he replies.

"Coffee then?"

Staring at him intently, I let my eyes dance over to Bea, hoping it conveys to him that he needs to do this for his daughter.

I think he gets the message because he takes a deep breath and walks over to the table. Sitting down in the seat next to her, he glances at me expectantly.

"How do you want me—I mean it. How do you want it? Your coffee I mean," I stammer, rubbing a hand over my tired eyes.

Bea giggles at me as I stumble over my words, and when I glance over at the both of them, I see Jack's mouth twitch with a threatening smirk.

"An Americano, please," he replies with a grumble.

Just hearing him ask for something fills me with purpose and excitement. I rush over to the machine, quickly preparing his coffee while he and Bea sit in awkward silence behind me. When I glance back, I notice him staring at her with adoration as she eats her breakfast.

He loves his daughter. I believe that. He just struggles to show it.

A moment later, I'm passing the Americano to him. Our fingers brush and his eyes meet mine as he mumbles, "Thank you."

Bea smiles up at him, her legs still kicking back and forth under her chair. Jack's movements are stiff and uncomfortable, his shoulders tense as he takes a sip from the cup.

It's not perfect. It's not even great. But it's progress. And that's something.

As I clean the dishes in the sink, I realize for the first time I might actually be able to help this family. Maybe I'm here for more than just watching Bea and learning something kinky and new from Jack. I might actually make a difference in their lives.

At this moment, I think about the woman in the photo. And call it fate or divine intervention, but it's almost like she left that letter for me on purpose. I can repair her family in her absence.

Rule #14: Don't be afraid to prove how good you are.

Camille

On my way back from taking Bea to school, I get lost in a daydream, thinking about last night. This discovery has filled me with new life. Especially when I still have so much I've yet to experience.

Jack St. Claire is gorgeous, rich, and older—and the one person I can't get involved with.

For one, he's far out of my league. Two, he's still grieving his late wife.

And three, I'm his daughter's nanny.

I meant what I said in that letter. I can separate work from pleasure. But pleasure from love? That sounds harder.

If anything romantic were to grow between us and it didn't work out, I would be forced to leave, and it would crush that little girl. And after everything she's been through, that would haunt me forever. Not to mention it would ruin my grand plans of getting out of Giverny and starting a new life.

So I can keep my heart guarded. It shouldn't be hard with

such an emotionally unavailable man. He would never let me in anyway.

In just a few short weeks, I've seen a new side of Jack. He was so elusive and grumpy to start, and now I'm seeing this softness in him. I see the desire and humility that he thinks he's hiding so well.

Jack is just a man. And I may never know the pain he's endured, but I can still see who he is underneath it all.

I imagine what it must be like to see all of him. To have Jack St. Claire without restraint. Even if he shuts out the world, I love the idea of him letting me in. And for someone who is not supposed to be getting romantically attached, it does sound awfully nice in my head.

When I get back to the apartment, it's quiet and empty. Jack had meetings today, as he said during breakfast. So I have the house to myself.

And while I do need to do some shopping for supper, I also desperately need a nap to recoup the sleep I lost last night.

I quickly clean up the kitchen and set my list on the counter where I can find it later. Then I go to my room.

Distracted by the promise of a nap, I nearly forget about the letter I left Jack last night. So when I walk into the room and find a folded piece of paper on my pillow, I let out a gasp.

Of course he's responded. These letters appear to be the only way we can truly communicate.

I open it quickly and start reading.

Camille,

I am not afraid of anything. It's become clear to me that neither are you.

But since you are so intent on proving your ability to separate your role as my employee from your role as my submissive, then I will give you the opportunity.

There will be rules.

Rule #1: You cannot tell anyone about our sessions.

Rule #2: We will meet for one hour each night at midnight upstairs.

Rule #3: No sex.

I can prove my restraint if you can prove yours. I lost control last night, and I will not do it again.

If any of these rules are broken, the deal is off. No punishment. No second chances.

Let's see if you can prove just how good you are.

Jack

Biting my lip, I smile down at the letter. The promise of more sessions fills me with excitement. Now I don't know if I'll be able to sleep at all.

Dropping onto the mattress, I hold the handwritten note against my chest as I close my eyes. With thoughts of ropes and blindfolds and the scent of his spicy cologne, I drift off to sleep.

"What do you want to be when you grow up?" Bea asks with her hand in mine as we walk home from school. She prances along the sidewalk, trying to jump over cracks in the pavement.

I laugh as I smile down at her. "I am already grown up."

She sneers up at me in confusion. "No, you're not."

"How old do you think I am?"

"I don't know," she replies with a shrug. "This many?" She holds up both of her hands, showing ten fingers, and it makes me giggle.

"Not quite, little Bea. I'm twenty-four."

She appears momentarily shocked before bouncing along beside me. "But you can still grow up more."

"I guess so," I say.

"So what do you want to be when you grow up?" she asks, repeating the question.

"Hmm…" I screw up my mouth. "I don't know. I used to work in a bookstore. Before that, I worked at my father's restaurant. Now, I'm a nanny for a curious little girl. I don't know what I'll do next."

"I want to be a ballerina like my tante Elizabeth," she says, pointing her arms over her head in a messy little ballet move.

"Why don't you take lessons?" I ask.

"Because Papa doesn't like it."

My brows pinch inward. "Why not?"

She shrugs. "I took lessons when Maman was sick, but when she went to sleep, I stopped."

Everything in me tenses. Why does it seem like every innocent conversation makes its way back to her mother? I'm terrible at this.

And why on earth does she think her mother went to sleep? Is that what Jack told her? Maybe she's too young to understand death? What the hell do I know?

I wish I could take away all Bea's pain and give her the normal, happy childhood she deserves. I can't imagine what it must have been like to lose her mother at only three years old.

"If you want dance lessons, I can take you."

"You can?" she asks excitedly.

With a sigh, I realize it might not have been wise of me to make such promises. What if Jack doesn't change his mind? She's not my daughter. But then again…it's not like he would notice anyway. He barely knows his own child.

I can't help that I have this overwhelming need to make Bea's life as good as it can be. And if ballet lessons are what she wants, then somehow, I can make that happen for her.

When we get back to the apartment, I write *ballet lessons* on the to-do list I keep in my bedroom. I plan to look into it later when I have some free time. I'm sure I have Jack's sister's contact information somewhere. I'll call her later and ask if she can recommend something for Bea.

I should ask Jack first. But what if he says no? I'm not sure if that's something I want to risk.

While Bea plays with her dolls in her room, I stare down at the to-do list, mindlessly sketching a polar bear ballerina on the bottom. For some reason, I get the urge to look at the photo of Jack and his wife again, so I check to be sure I'm alone before opening the drawer and fishing the original letter and photo out.

It's the first time I've looked at it in a while. And it feels strange to see Jack with her now. Now that it feels like some small piece of him belongs to me. Even if he and I will never be romantic the way they were, Jack is opening up to me. He's giving me a piece of himself, no matter how big or small that is.

But as I stare at the woman in the photo, Emmaline, I realize that I feel a closeness to her too. It's strange, really. I never knew her, and I never will. But I care about her in a way that I can't describe. I love her daughter with a sense of protectiveness already.

I'm living in her house and building a relationship with her family. Would she like me? Or hate me? I know I'll never fill the hole she left or live up to her, but in some strange way, I want to make her proud.

I want to prove that I'm good enough.

Rule #15: Legacies are not about turning a profit.

Jack

JULIAN IS SITTING SMUGLY ACROSS FROM ME AT THE TABLE, AND I glare at him as Phoenix stands at the front of the room, going over the dismal numbers from last quarter.

Everything with the club is going to shit. It's his fault, and he knows it.

"We need to cap attendance lower and increase security," I say when Phoenix is finished.

"How is capping attendance going to improve these numbers?" Julian asks.

"We were overcrowded last weekend, and it created security issues," Phoenix adds, taking my side.

"So we increase security," Julian argues.

"Increasing security doesn't change the fact that the building can only hold so many," I reply with a tense, angry tone.

"Nobody wants to go to an overcrowded sex club," Elizabeth says flatly while staring at her phone.

"Exactly," I say, glancing over at her and hoping she'll look at me for even one second. She doesn't. "It should be more exclusive,"

I say, straightening my spine and loosening my tie. "We're not even vetting membership anymore. We can't have a sex club that's full of unchecked, drunk partiers. That's not how Ronan and Matis ran L'Amour, and that's not how we should run Legacy."

Julian shakes his head without looking at me. I see the way his jaw clenches as he heaves a sigh.

He hates me, and that's fine. I'm not doing this to get in his good graces. I'm doing this to prolong my godfather's legacy and set my sister up for success after I leave. I can't walk away knowing she'll have Julian's mess to clean up later.

"So what are you suggesting?" he asks. "We close down the club and only open to a select few?"

"Yes," I reply confidently.

He finally turns my way. "It's easy for you to say, Jack," he bites back. "You're not here half the time, and if you are, you're fucking around in the BDSM room. And we all know you've got one foot out the door already, don't you?"

It grates on my nerves to hear him talking about my plans and my life like he knows a damn thing about me. "And what about you, Julian?" I fight back. "You're not here out of the goodness of your heart either. We all know you're just here to have a place to party and get laid."

"Enough, both of you," Phoenix snaps from the front of the room.

Elizabeth lets out a huff.

As of now, it's only the four of us. Amelia and Weston don't bother to even show up to most meetings.

Everything we started nearly one year ago is falling apart. It's embarrassing. Our parents left us the keys to success, and we're throwing them away.

I just keep telling myself it doesn't matter. I'll be gone, back home in California soon. At least I tried to work with the team to make it better. At least I stuck around for this long. But no one can expect me to endure this any longer.

"Why don't we all just accept defeat?" Julian says dramatically.

"Do you even care about this club?" Phoenix asks with a shake of her head.

"No, obviously not," he replies sarcastically. "I don't care about anything, right?"

"Let's just finish this meeting," I say, rubbing my forehead with a sigh.

"I think this meeting is over," he mutters, standing from the table and marching out the door.

What a prick.

Elizabeth doesn't say anything to either of us before she leaves too. Phoenix and I are left alone in the conference room above the club.

She stares at me with exhaustion in her eyes. "What a mess."

"Why is he such a self-indulgent asshole?" I say with annoyance.

"The two of you can't hold a civil conversation to save your lives," she replies with a tilt of her head.

"Me?" I say in disbelief. "You think I'm part of the problem?"

"It doesn't matter what I think," she replies. "But we can't run this club when you two do nothing but fight at all our meetings."

Maybe she's right. But he's the one who wants to run this place into the ground. He makes all the wrong choices, doing what *he* wants instead of what is right. He doesn't care about anyone but himself.

As for me, I've been under a lot of pressure lately. I'm failing as a father and now as a business owner. Nothing I do seems to go right. Maybe that's why I'm actually considering taking on my daughter's nanny as my submissive. Because at least that I know I can't fuck up. That is something I excel at.

I let out a sigh. "We only have six more weeks left of this," I reply.

"Then what, Jack?" she asks as she drops into a chair. "I can't run this place by myself. Julian isn't going to change his ways.

None of the others even care anymore. What if…" Her voice trails as she stares down at the table, quietly tapping her finger against the wood. Chewing on the inside of her cheek, she lets the sentence die.

"What if…what?" I ask.

"What if Ronan was wrong about us?" she says, finally looking up at me.

"What do you mean?"

"Our parents created something great, but they were best friends before they started Salacious. Half of us can't even get along, let alone run a business together. He wants us to find our family, but let's face it. Your sister won't talk to you. Mine is with Liam, and God only knows where they are. My brother is a mess. Your godbrother hates you. We are *no* family. And maybe we never will be."

Leaning my elbows on the table, I stare at my best friend as I let those words sink in. She's right. We are no family.

"Nix…" I say carefully. "Was that…why you agreed to this? For family?"

She has always been the smart one—the only true business owner here besides myself. I had always assumed her motives were economically driven. So this…is news to me.

She slumps back in her seat. "I don't know," she confesses. "Maybe. That letter he sent us was inspiring."

I scrutinize her. This isn't what I expected to hear, and knowing this changes things for me. This whole time, I assumed my best friend would be fine on her own once I left, but now…I'm a little worried.

"Listen," she says, sitting up. "I can find another job. I can make a business work just about anywhere. But this, the idea that we could bring together our oldest friends and somehow outdo what our parents created, was the first time a business venture sounded like more to me. And I was excited about that."

I let out a huff. "Outdo Salacious? Nix, we can barely turn a profit."

In the nearly thirty years since Emerson Grant and the rest of his team opened the doors of the club in Briar Point, California, they have turned the sex club industry on its head. Phoenix's parents alone helped branch out the brand into six more clubs across America and set a precedent that was revered for its integrity and inclusivity. They created far more than a legacy, and the mere idea that we thought we could follow that is embarrassing.

"But maybe it's not about profit, Jack," she argues. "Maybe it's about creating something special."

For some reason, my mind instantly goes to Camille when she says that. I would love to bring her here. It's a thought that's crossed my mind more than once. If she genuinely wants to learn more about this lifestyle, then she deserves a safe and inspiring place to do that.

But she deserves better. Everyone does.

"What are you thinking?" Phoenix asks, noticing me deep in thought.

"I'm thinking you're right. But we only have six weeks left. What do we do?"

"We shut down and start over. And we do it right this time," she replies.

"Julian will never go for that."

"Fuck Julian," she argues.

My brows jump upward at that. I'm normally the one cursing his name.

Before I can respond, Phoenix continues. "We can have vetted membership this time, exclusivity, and standards. Drink minimums and *real* workshops for those who want to learn."

I know she's right. Hell, Phoenix always is. But I still feel as if I'm lacking the motivation it takes to pull this off.

"You want me to call them all back in?" I ask.

She scoffs. "They won't listen. Let's give it the rest of the weekend, and then we convince them."

"If we leave Julian to his own devices, he'll get the club shut down on his own. What if we get out of the way and just let it happen?"

"That's maniacal, Jack," she replies with a nervous laugh.

"I don't care. He wants to pull in a crowd, then let him. He'll overcrowd this place, make a mess of the whole club, and Matis will have no choice but to step in and shut it down."

Phoenix is chewing her lip again. She doesn't like this idea, I can tell. But I love it. I think I've been wanting this for a long time, to let Julian truly crash and burn. And once he does, Phoenix and I will have free rein to make the choices that need to be made. Let that spoiled brat see what it's like when he finally does get his way.

Rule #16: Sometimes, being good is hard.

Camille

WHEN I FIND JACK UPSTAIRS TONIGHT, I'M ONLY SLIGHTLY LESS nervous than last night. I've worn a robe over my undergarments to make getting undressed easier. I've also braided my hair already to save time. Although if I'm honest, there was something inexplicably hot about having him do it.

He's pulling ropes out of the wardrobe when I enter. Again, he's in a button-down shirt with the sleeves rolled up and a pair of dark slacks. Without a word between us, I close the door, locking it before pulling off my robe and hanging it on a chair in the corner.

"Start on your knees," he says with his back to me. "That is your default position, understand?"

He seems tense tonight, although I guess he's always tense. Nodding, I find my place at the center of the rug. Lowering to the floor, I take a deep breath and mentally prepare myself.

If you had told me a year ago that I'd enjoy being silent and submissive for a man, I would have told you you'd lost your mind. But I find solace in knowing that this isn't about what *he* wants. It's about what *I* want. It's about connection. Safety. Comfort.

I like the way it feels to give up control, and I won't apologize for that.

When he turns around with a black ribbon, there's hesitation on his face, and I silently pray that he's deemed tonight a good time to start using it. I even shut my eyes and wait for him to blindfold me. Instead, I hear him pulling out ropes, and I open them to find the blindfold hanging on the doorknob again. Disappointment washes over me.

I want to ask him why he normally uses a blindfold. I've done my research, and I know it's not common practice. It's just something Jack likes, and I wish I understood why. Is this another form of control? When it feels like most of my connection with Jack shines through our eye contact, I'm dying to know what it would be like to be with him without that. Would I feel as close to him?

"Same as last time," he says, turning toward me with ropes in hand. "Nod for yes. Shake for no. Speak up if anything hurts, burns, or starts to feel numb. Understand?"

I nod.

There is stress written on his face. He carries it in the tight furrow of his brows and the tense movement of his shoulders. Pride swells inside me that I get to be a part of the thing that calms him.

And to be honest, it calms me too. As I wait silently on the floor, he moves around me, gathering things, and that overwhelming loneliness I felt when I first moved here is gone. There is silent comfort between us, and in a way, that's better than sex. This is more intimate.

When Jack kneels on the floor in front of me, it takes me by surprise.

"I want you to feel a leg tie tonight. Sit down with your legs extended in front of you."

I do as he says with my bare legs on the rug pointed toward him. When his fingers touch my right leg, I flinch slightly, and he glances up at me cautiously. I don't know why I did that, but the sensation of his fingers on my thigh was electric.

"Are you ready?" he asks, and I nod with confidence.

This time, when he grips my leg under my knee, he moves slower. I savor the feel of his fingers against my skin as he lifts my right leg until it's bent with my foot on the floor. Then he winds the rope around my ankle, moving much like he did last night, deft and assured. I watch his face as he loses himself in the practice.

Ever so slowly, his tight muscles relax, and the stress melts away.

As much as I love the silence between us, I wish he'd talk as he works, but Jack St. Claire is a closed book. I'm dying to know things like where he learned this and what makes him love it. Has he ever been tied up? Does he normally have sex with the women he binds?

Was this something he did with his wife? Did she enjoy it as much as I do? Something about that sparks a sense of jealousy in my gut. I desperately want this to be something only he and I share, but those are dangerous, reckless thoughts to be having.

All the while, he winds the rope around my ankle, looping and tying it with skillful fingers. The room is quiet. Instead of waiting for his voice, I just let myself drown in his scent and presence.

Once he has a secure tie around my ankle, he touches my upper thigh, and I let out a squeak as he presses my ankle backward, bending my knee until my thigh is flush with my calf.

"Does that hurt your knee at all?" he asks.

I shake my head.

Leaning back, I put my hands on the floor behind me as he works to wrap the rope around my thigh and leg, binding them together. Every time his fingers brush the upper part of my leg near my panties, there's a lightning strike of arousal through my veins and goose bumps erupting across my skin.

The longer he works, the more I relax into his ministrations. I can't move my right leg at all, and it's such a new sensation.

And no matter what we both say about boundaries and lines separating work from pleasure, being this close and giving over this much control creates a sensual energy between us that he can't deny.

He seems to read my mind, leaning closer to knot the rope at my upper thigh. "I want you to feel what it's like to give up control. There is something about the leg binding that is more intense than the arms. Perhaps because you can't get away. Or because it makes you truly rely on me. Do you sense how different this feels?" he asks as he continues wrapping rope in circles up to my bent knee.

As I nod my head, I wish he'd look at me. Being tied in this position makes me even more vulnerable. I wish I could express to him just how much I love this, like slipping on a perfectly fitting dress.

I have a feeling my next letter to him is going to be more detailed than the last two.

He doesn't speak anymore as he begins looping the rope in the strands already wrapped around my legs. It's clearly a move to secure the binds. Testing the knots, I try to extend my leg, and it won't budge.

Chills cascade down my spine at that sensation.

He works in silence, and it's obvious by the slow, steady way he moves that he enjoys this. I have my silly doodles, and he has this. The signs of his tension from work are all gone.

When he tucks what is left of the rope into the crease between my thigh and calf, I wait for his next move.

His hands drifts softly over my leg as if he's admiring his own handiwork. The words that leave his mouth next have my heart practically jumping into my throat.

"You look beautiful like this," he whispers.

There's a pulse between my legs as I let his compliment sink in. Unable to stay quiet for another second, I whisper, "Thank you."

"I wish I could show you off," he adds.

"Show me off? Where? How?"

Sitting back on his knees, he lets out a sigh. His lips quirk with a crooked smile. "Curious as always. You'd like that, wouldn't you?"

I nod energetically. "Yes."

The thought of being shown off by him sends a thrill down to my core. Not only the idea of being so admired and treasured but also for people to know that I belong to him…it sounds incredible.

His fingers find my face, dancing gently down my jaw. "I'd cover you in rope and put you on display like my own little masterpiece."

I nod again, although he didn't ask a question.

"If we could have a session at the club, would you come?" he asks.

Yes, yes, yes, I think, conveying it with yet another head nod.

He chuckles. "You're not afraid of anything, are you? I've never met anyone like you."

Warmth floods my body all the way from the top of my head to my core. When he looks at me like that, like he truly sees me, it's exhilarating. Every moment with Jack is like cracking open another thin layer. I'm still miles away from the real person hiding under there, but every day, I get a little closer.

But I wish I could tell him that I am afraid. I'm afraid of ending up alone. Of feeling stuck again. Of falling head over heels for him and having my heart broken. I'm always afraid—I'm just too reckless to show it.

"I'd like to bind your other leg too," he says, stroking the back of his hand along the left thigh.

I nod my head, assuming he's looking for consent.

As he works on the other leg, I know that we have definitely gone over an hour, but he doesn't seem rushed or annoyed to be here. He's settled in close to me as he works, wrapping, looping, and tying until both of my legs are immobilized.

I'm well aware that the more tied up I am, the more aroused I am. I know he won't, but God, I wish he'd take advantage of me in this position. Force me to my back and use my body for his own pleasure while I can't move.

I start fidgeting on the floor, just thinking about it, and I don't even notice until he says, "Hold still."

He steadies my leg by holding my knee. There's more to bondage than sex, I know that from my research, but my experience so far is that they go hand in hand. Or perhaps that's just Jack's effect on me.

A man who craves control has full control over me. And yet the more control he has, the more I see him losing it. It's evident in everything he does, even when he doesn't realize it—his lust-filled gaze on my chest and between my legs. The evidence of his arousal last night as he pressed his hard length against me.

My excitement isn't because of the ropes alone—it's because of *him*.

He stands from the floor, letting his eyes rake over me. Leaning back on my hands, my knees are parted just enough that he has a filthy view of me bound like this. When he reaches into his pocket, I know exactly what he's reaching for.

Pulling out the sleek black phone, he holds it up. "Can I take a picture? Just for myself. I mean…of the knots, of course."

I bite my bottom lip tightly to keep from smiling. Staring up through my lashes, I nod. And as he holds it up, the camera pointed at me, my nipples pebble tighter and my panties grow wetter. The thought of him enjoying these photos later or wanting to capture this moment forever ignites a fire inside me.

With that, I stick my chest out and let my head hang. If he wants a sexy picture, I'll give him a sexy picture.

He lets out a low growl as I let my knees fall away from each other.

"Stop it," he barks, and I grin wickedly. "You know exactly what you're doing." As he leans over until his mouth is near my ear, he adds, "You promised, remember?"

Suddenly, I'm flooded with disappointment. I did promise. With a pout, I close my legs.

Of course, he's referring to the promise I made in that letter to keep things strictly professional and show restraint. Tempting him with sexy, spread-leg photos is not showing restraint.

"You don't play fair," he says as he starts to untie my right leg.

There's a part of me that loves the idea of being such a temptation to him, but there's another part of me that hates disappointing him. I want to be his good girl, like I said I was.

But if being good means not getting what I want, is it even worth it?

Rule #17: Aftercare is essential.

Jack

"FEELING OKAY?" I ASK.

Camille is sitting on the counter downstairs in the kitchen, wrapped in her short white robe and guzzling a glass of water like it's medicine. Her feet glide slowly back and forth, her single braid resting over her shoulder.

She nods, watching me over the glass.

"Aftercare is important. Don't let anyone try to skip it, understand?"

I'm an asshole for skipping it before, and if I'm going to be introducing her to the basics, then aftercare must be involved. I hate to think of Camille finding another partner at the club or somewhere else who doesn't take the time to ensure she's okay after a rope or submissive session. Although if I'm honest with myself, any vision of her at the club with someone else irritates me.

I cross my arms over my chest as I stare at her. I've come to love this silence between us. It's as natural as speaking with anyone else, this intense eye contact without any of the awkwardness.

But at the same time, I'm dying to know what is going on inside Camille's head. I want to hear her thoughts and opinions on everything we're doing. Even more...I want to hear her thoughts and opinions about *me*. Does she find me as intriguing as I find her? Does she think about me at night while lying in bed? Does she want *me*, or is this all about the bondage to her?

This is dangerous. As fascinated as I am by Camille, I can't let anything romantic happen between us. For my daughter's sake, I need to keep it together.

"Before you go to sleep, I want you to write me a letter telling me how tonight felt. If you didn't like anything, put it in the letter. Is that clear?"

I keep my tone flat and commanding, but it's a cover. What I really want to do is settle between her legs, stroke her cheek softly, and ask her to spill every thought in her head.

Nodding, she takes another sip of the water. Then my eyes cascade down her body, landing on the rope marks written across her legs. They are fucking beautiful. It's a shame they'll fade away by morning.

My hands twitch, wanting to trace the lines on her skin.

Quickly, I snap out of it, focusing on her face instead of her bare legs.

After her glass is finished, I take it, setting it in the sink before returning to her. Stepping close, I lift one of her legs by the ankle and inspect her foot for any damage from the knots. It's definitely *not* an excuse just to get to touch her again.

She bites her bottom lip as she often does—driving me absolutely mad—while I gently run my fingers over her ankle. It's more intimate than it should be, and I sense the tension filling the space between us.

In just a few short weeks, this woman has somehow found her way under my skin and into my brain. I'm supposed to be keeping things professional, but I can't stop thinking about her nearly every moment of my day. I think about keeping her safe, keeping her here, keeping her content.

I think about her adorable button nose and the light freckles cluttered down the slope. I think about her beautiful, big blue eyes and the way she tends to tip her chin down so she's often staring through her thick lashes. I think about her full pouty lips, often covered in pink or red lipstick, and the way she pinches the bottom one between her teeth while she concentrates.

It feels so wrong. Em has only been gone two years. What is wrong with me?

I've lusted after plenty of women since my wife passed. In fact, that was my coping mechanism of choice for a long time, but this is different. I never cared about them.

Any other woman would have obeyed the basic rules I set—stay out of rooms, don't pry about my job, don't ask any questions. Camille broke every damn one, but I'm not nearly as angry as I should be. Instead, I'm fascinated by her. If she wasn't so fucking cute, maybe I'd have less patience.

When I look at Camille and see the kindness in her eyes, especially her kindness toward *me*, which I don't fucking deserve, I feel myself slipping. I should be ashamed of how I've behaved. Those damn rules were meant to keep people like her out of my life, and now I find myself actually enjoying our time together. I'm glad she broke them.

She is infuriatingly curious and stubborn. I've never met someone so strong-willed in my life. My daughter adores her, and it's obvious the feeling is mutual. I can't find a single fault with this girl, and even when she pisses me off, it's so goddamn endearing I can't be mad.

The way I'm starting to feel about Camille frightens me. I have to keep her at a distance, or someone is going to get hurt.

Quickly, I clear my throat and drop her foot.

"Looks good. Now go to bed and get some sleep. But not before you write me that letter, understood?"

She nods as she jumps off the counter, coming toe-to-toe with me. "Yes, sir," she says, and my resolve crumbles.

As she stands so close, I worry that she can see everything I'm hiding. No matter how cold and closed off I am with her, I fear she can see past all that and will know my secret—that I adore her. Even when I know I shouldn't.

"Good night," she whispers before moving around me and going to her room. The sound of her voice drags me from the reverie.

I go into my room, closing the door. Trying to busy myself, I check emails and clean myself up in my bathroom. Every few minutes, my eyes drift to the door, waiting for the appearance of the folded-up white piece of paper, but it never comes.

Minutes drag into hours, and I start to grow irritated.

Where is she?

I know I should go to bed and forget it. Get her out of my head. Go back to living my own life.

But I can't. I've grown addicted to her handwritten scribbles on lined paper. I want her thoughts and feelings.

I gave her an order, and she didn't obey.

After trying to sleep and forget it, I give up after another hour when it's clear there is no sign of peace until I face her.

It's sometime around three in the morning when I march out of my bedroom and down the stairs. I creep slowly down the hall, careful not to wake my daughter. When I reach Camille's door, I find it open just a crack.

What has gotten into me? This is the second time I've lurked outside her door in the middle of the night like some kind of creep. Granted, last time I was drunk, but still. This isn't right.

And I blame her for getting into my head. For being too beautiful. Too captivating. Too perfect.

I press open the door of her room to find it dark and quiet. By the light coming in through the window, I see Camille's blond curls strewn over the pillow. Tiptoeing closer, I hover over her and watch her as she sleeps, hugging one of the pillows to her body.

Still mostly naked, her bare leg is draped over the pillow. The way it's nestled against her body makes my dick twitch in my pants.

Part of me wonders if I could just fuck Camille and get it out of my system. I could lose interest in her the same way I do every other woman I take to bed. But what if I don't? What if one of us gets attached?

It takes everything in me not to crawl into her bed right now. She'd welcome it, I know it. Although if she didn't want me, that would make all this so much easier. But I can tell by the way she moves around me, the way she submits so beautifully, the way she spread her legs for me for that photo—she wants this as much as I do.

Walk away, Jack.

Finally listening to the voice of reason in my head, I turn my back on the beautiful woman sleeping in her bed and walk toward the door. On my way out, I notice the piece of paper and pen on her desk.

She did write the letter, or at least she started it.

It's too dark to read in here, so I snatch it off the desk and carry it with me as I slip out of her room, closing the door to the same place it was when I found it.

Then I walk down to my daughter's room.

Standing in the doorway, I watch her sleep. It's like my heart is no longer in my body but now across the room in that bed. As I watch her sleep, I just keep reminding myself—she's safe, she's alive, she's happy. That's all that matters. She doesn't need me. I can't watch her for long before the shame and regret start to creep in.

Swallowing my pride, I close her door and head back up to my room. When I get there, I crawl into my own bed alone and read what she wrote.

Dear Jack,

It feels wrong to call you Jack now. Should I call you sir? I liked calling you that downstairs.

Sir,

I smile to myself at that. I've been called sir before, but hearing it from her is different, and I like it.

You told me to write down everything I was feeling tonight, so here you go.

For reasons I don't fully understand, I love what we do upstairs in that room. It doesn't make any sense. Being tied up should be terrible. It should make me feel afraid and panicked, but it's the opposite. I'm relaxed and at ease, and for that short time, my mind is just quiet.

If I were with anyone else, I think I would be afraid. They could hurt me or take advantage of me, and I would feel like a fool for putting myself in that situation. But I know you won't hurt me. How do I know that? I'm not sure. But I do.

I guess what I'm saying is...I trust you.

And the only other man I trusted was my father. All little girls should be able to trust their fathers.

But then mine died. Which was the most deceitful thing he's ever done. He left me alone in this world, and now I have no one.

So now I'm letting a grumpy American man tie me up in his secret room.

This letter has gotten off topic. So I'm definitely going to throw this away and rewrite it in the morning.

And since you'll never read this, I'll just say... I desperately want to know what it feels like to be fucked while tied up, and I'm sad that you won't ever let that person be you.

God, I hope you never read this.

———◦◦◦◦◦———

I read that last part over and over, unable to keep the grin off my face. Even though this just makes me want what I can't have even more.

There is so much in this letter to love. For one, the fact that Camille loves being bound. Everything she describes here is exactly what she should be feeling when in bondage.

Second, getting a glimpse into her life and the death of her father feels like getting a gift I'm not worthy of. Camille is not just some mechanical figure to fulfill a role. She's a living, breathing, real person with a real history. She knows grief.

And like she's already told me in her letters, she has desires and dreams like every other woman.

We are tiptoeing too close to this line we're not supposed to cross, but I can't help it. Something about her draws me closer. She makes me want to throw out all my rules, boundaries, and goals just to have a moment to feel her, touch her, taste her.

With that, I lean back on my bed and close my eyes, holding her letter to my chest as I slide my hand into my briefs and take hold of my cock. It's already thick and pulsing with desire.

I reread the last line of her letter as I stroke myself. I hear her voice in my head, saying how much she wants to be *fucked*—that word exactly. And not just fucked by anyone but fucked by me.

I hold the letter to my nose, searching for her scent like a dog as I stroke myself faster.

In my head, I have her hog-tied and bound in that room across the hall. I picture her body laid out before me, and I can touch her all I want. I imagine myself playing with her cunt, slipping inside her just to hear the noises she'd make. I picture myself licking and nibbling every inch of her body.

My cock tightens, but I hold back, wanting to let this fantasy play out a little longer.

Then I remember the picture on my phone. Quickly, I drop the letter on the bed and grab my phone from the nightstand. It takes me a moment to open the app and find the photo I snapped, and it's enough to have my cock leaking at the tip.

Her bent legs are parted, and I can just barely make out the shape of her pussy through the thin fabric of her white panties. I can see the tuft of hair above her clit and the lines of her folds, a hint of moisture darkening the fabric.

I let out a groan as I stare at this image, feeling like a deviant for all the depraved things I'd like to do to her.

When I imagine it's her lovely cunt and not my fist that I'm fucking, my body starts to strain and seize with my climax. My head is thrown back, and my breathing shallows as I spray my chest with the sticky white jets of my own cum.

This is what she does to me. This is the mess I've become because of that one woman.

But even if I know that firing her and cleaning my life of her would solve all my problems, I'd never do it. I'm only a man after all.

Rule #18: Never turn down a day in Paris with the handsome man you work for.

Camille

THE VERY LAST THING I WANTED TO FIND THIS MORNING WAS A written response from Jack slid under my door. But the moment I woke up and noticed the humiliating rough draft of my own letter gone and saw his, I was filled with mortification.

He must have snuck into my room in the middle of the night to take it. The thought of him sneaking into my room should probably bother me a lot more than it does, but I'm too distracted by the memory of what I wrote in that letter.

Now, as I stand in the kitchen, watching Bea color at the table, I'm remembering everything I said and wanting the earth to swallow me whole.

It's bad enough that I shared something so personal with him, like my father's death, but then I had to make it worse by telling him how much I want to be—

"Can we do something fun today?" Bea asks, interrupting my thoughts.

"Of course," I reply. "What would you like to do?"

She shrugs. "I don't know."

It's Saturday, and since I've been here, Bea's routine has been nearly the same every day. We haven't done a single thing out of the ordinary.

"What if we take the Métro into the city?" I ask. "We can go to lunch and see the big park."

"With the boats in the fountain?" she replies excitedly.

"Yeah. We can see the boats."

Paris is beautiful in the fall, especially now that the leaves have started to change. And since we have a respite from the rain on this late September day, it feels wise to take advantage of it before it grows too cold outside to enjoy a sunny day in the park.

Bea wiggles excitedly in her seat. Instantly, my thoughts go back to Jack. He should really be the one to spend time with her today. I wish he'd come with us. I know how much she'd love that.

I pull the letter from my back pocket and read it again.

My good girl,

I think this was my favorite letter from you. You seemed to have forgotten to deliver it to me, so it's a good thing I found it on your desk.

I'm sorry to hear about your father. That must have been difficult. And I understand the resentment you feel toward the one who left you. Being the survivor is incredibly unfair.

I've read this letter nearly a hundred times since I found it only an hour ago. And that line strikes a nerve every time. Here's a man so torn up by his grief that he can hardly look at his own daughter, and yet he's suddenly baring his soul in a letter to me.

How did this happen? And how do I protect it so that I might be able to hear more from him?

Your reactions to and reasoning about the bondage are perfect. I'm glad you like it.

And I'm glad you trust me. That is the most important part.

Don't give that to just anyone. Make them earn it.

As for that last part of your letter...

I wince, biting my lip and remembering what I wrote. The filthy, dirty words that *no one* was supposed to read.

I wish that person could be me, but we have to show our restraint. There are rules to follow and lines we cannot cross.

My daughter seems to really like you, and that's more important to me than my selfish desires.

Also, you should talk like that more often. Tell me what you want.

You should always be honest about that.

I want to write my response before we leave, but Bea is already bouncing excitedly and clearly restless to get out of the house for the day. So my letter will have to wait.

We're by the front door, tying the laces on her shoes, when we hear footsteps coming down the stairs. Bea and I look up at the same time to see Jack walking down. He's casual today in a pair of dark jeans and a Henley-style shirt that fits snugly over his shoulders and pecs.

I force myself to look away.

"Hi, Papa!" Bea says with a smile. "We're going on the Métro!"

Jack halts with skepticism on his face. I hesitate to explain more before I remember this isn't a bondage scenario where I answer in silent nods and shakes of my head. I have to actually explain to him where I'm taking his daughter.

After clearing my throat, I mumble, "Bea wants to go into the city. I'm taking her to the Jardin du Luxembourg. If that's all right."

"Of course," he replies quietly.

"Come with us, Papa!" Bea chimes in before rushing over to his side and taking his hand in hers.

He stares down at her as if he's just now meeting her, a glimmer of warmth in his eyes.

I can see him deliberating, and I wish I knew what was going on in his head. The reason—or is it fear?—that keeps him from wanting to be around her. Is he afraid that being around Bea will hurt, like losing his wife all over again? Is he filled with so much grief that he doesn't even know how to love his own child anymore?

Either way, I just know the answer isn't to avoid her and push her away.

"If it's all right with your nanny," he says before glancing up at me.

I'm struck as I open my mouth, unable to reply right away. "Uh…of course," I say finally. "Do *you* want to take her? Just you two?"

"No," he blurts out. "You should come."

"Yes, you have to come, Camille," Bea says sweetly.

"D'accord," I reply under my breath.

Bea cheers, jumping in place as her father and I put on our shoes, getting ready to leave. I do everything in my power to avoid his eye contact. Normally, I can stare into his eyes and feel so comfortable, but right now…in this setting, I can't possibly look at him.

We walk in silence down the street. Bea carries on with her usual chatter, holding my hand as Jack walks behind us. And when we board the Métro, he sits on the opposite side as she cuddles close to me.

Seeing him in this environment makes me laugh a little. I don't suspect that Jack is the type to ride the Métro very often. He probably has personal drivers or takes taxis if he needs to get around, but I've always loved the city's transit. This is what it was made for, so it feels like a privilege to use it.

His eyes find mine for a brief moment on the journey, and I quickly look away. My cheeks heat when his attention doesn't shift, and I'm reminded of the things I said in that letter. Not that he hasn't also said dirty, sexy things to me in his letters too. His first letter to me was the filthiest thing I've ever read. But that was a different time. That was before we found this new dynamic together. Before I became his bunny, and he became my rigger.

I feast on the sight of his ravishing smile, his gaze averted.

These past few weeks have been like watching Jack come into the light. Slowly, he's emerging from the depths of wherever he's been hiding. My overwhelming interest in him started as curiosity and has blossomed into something more. He's not at all who I expected, and even now, the ice is slowly chipping away from that cold, brutal man I encountered when I started.

When we reach the park, Bea runs ahead of us in her sandy tweed coat and pink tights, eager to eat up the free space and sprawling pathways through the large garden. Geese scamper by as she chases them around an island of green grass and a stone statue.

This garden has always been my favorite. My father brought me here as a child, and I distinctly remember gasping in awe as we came upon the massive palm trees, uncharacteristically planted right in front of the old palace. Colors burst along the walkways in pink and purple flowers blooming in perfectly landscaped artistry.

Bea seems to be equally as enamored as she dashes ahead.

"Beatrice!" Jack calls in a panic when she slips around a hedge and out of sight. The moment she hears him call, she turns back and returns to where we can see her. I jog ahead to be closer to her, but the sound of his voice in such a fatherly, protective tone stays with me.

With Bea's hand in mine, we meander our way through the park until we reach the large fountain where white sailboats are drifting across the water. Jack steps away and returns a moment later with one of the boats for Bea to sail. She sets it on the water with an enthusiastic giggle and a beaming smile.

Then he leans over and demonstrates how to use the large stick to push the boat onto the water. I stand back and watch them, savoring the way he speaks to her, explaining how the wind pushes the sails. She touches his hand, and I wonder if it's the first moment they've really spent together since his wife died.

As she plays, he and I find a bench to sit on together and watch her. He seems at ease, and when I glance his way, I see the love in his eyes as he watches his daughter play. I'd like to ask him so many questions—like why has he been so distant with her? Why won't he be the father I know he wants to be?

Instead, I keep my lips pressed together tightly, and I let him have this moment. Whatever I have to say, I will put it in my next letter.

After the park, we get lunch at a nearby café. The three of us share a Margherita pizza and three bottles of Coca-Cola. Jack is sitting across from me, and I can't stop marveling at how sexy he looks as he leans back in the small café chair, his wool coat draped open to reveal the tight shirt over his muscled pecs. With a pair of pitch-black sunglasses on, he stares out at the people passing by, and I can tell that he loves Paris. He fits in well, as if he was made for this city.

"L'addition, s'il vous plaît," he mumbles to the server as he walks by, and it catches me by surprise. Staring at Jack with wide eyes, I watch as he pulls out his wallet and hands the man his credit card.

Does Jack know French? It's a simple phrase that I'm sure most tourists learn to ask for the bill, but hearing him speak my native language has an effect on me. Is he doing this on purpose? Making me fall for him when he's very explicitly said we shouldn't.

After collecting our things and standing from the table, Jack drapes his jacket over his forearm as the day has grown warmer with the clear skies. We continue to stroll around the city, stopping in the shops Bea wants to see. It all feels so comfortable and intimate. To anyone walking by, we look like a regular family. A man and his wife and their young daughter.

Shamelessly, I love that idea.

If only they knew I'm just the nanny to a grief-stricken man and the daughter he barely knows.

Everything always looks better on the outside.

When we finally board the Métro for the ride home, it's far more crowded than when we rode it earlier. There are no places to sit, and Jack and I have to stand with Bea pressed between us to keep her safe.

She holds my hand as we squeeze in closer at one of the stops to let even more people on. When a rowdy group of young men board, I feel a hand on my lower back, and I look up at Jack to realize it's him. He's holding me close to his body while glaring protectively at the men, and it sends a thrill through my bloodstream.

As the train starts to move again, I stumble a little toward him, and his grip tightens. My gaze lifts slowly to his face and his to mine. It feels like I'm being granted access to this connection between us.

Just like the night in the hallway and the moment in the kitchen when he gave me his letter, it's as if Jack and I exist alone, separate from the rest of the world, when we allow ourselves to feast on the sight of each other. It's a feeling so palpable I never want it to end.

I smell his cologne and see the flecks of green and brown in his eyes. His fingers are still on my back, and for the first time since he placed them there, he moves them slightly back and forth. It's not much, but to me, it feels monumental. Just a subtle reminder of his touch. A hint of affection.

What is he doing? Doesn't he realize what moments like this do to me? They obliterate boundaries and lines and rules. This longing is so much louder than all those reasons why we shouldn't get involved with each other.

Unable to bear it anymore, I turn my head away from him, glancing down at Bea, who is nestled by my side.

Then Jack's nose brushes against my head, and I hear him breathe in the scent of my hair. Suddenly, I wish I could tie *him* up, because then I could force him to stay away from me so I never have to know what it's like to feel his affection.

Rule #19: The only person you have to prove your loyalty to is yourself.

Camille

Sir,

I don't want to cross that line either. Being Bea's nanny is the best job I've ever had. In fact, it feels like more than a job. I care for her very much, and I agree. If things became complicated between us, it could end badly, and Bea would be the one to pay the price.

I can show restraint.

Thank you for the condolences regarding my father. He died three years ago. He was opening the restaurant one day and had an aneurysm. The doctors said it was instant. I'm glad there was no pain, but I can't explain how strange it was to speak to him one second, and then he was gone the next.

You would have liked him. He was grumpy too but always nice to me.

He used to call me his little hummingbird because I was always moving from one place to another. I guess you've found a way to make me sit still, and I like it.

I'm glad you came to the park today. Bea loved having you there.

So did I.

Your good girl

I CURL MY TOES AGAINST THE PLUSH RED CARPET AS JACK WORKS. He's doing a chest harness tonight, something he explained when I first walked in. This one isn't as restraining—yet.

He's winding two threads of rope around my body, knotting them at my back and my stomach in various places. It brings him so close, and I get to breathe in his scent and feel his touch without it being like it was on the Métro today.

That moment frightened me. The last thing I want to feel is how heavenly it is to briefly experience something I can't have.

When we're up here, the lines are drawn and we are stepping into roles with defined parameters. It's easy.

Today was different.

He refrained from using the blindfold again, touching it briefly when he was pulling out the ropes, and I held on to hope that he would finally deem the trust between us worthy. Instead, I close my eyes, letting the darkness engulf me as he works. His nimble touch sends me into a state of relaxation. I can tell by the way Jack is working that he's getting just as much enjoyment out of this as I am.

I feel like his doll, something he can play with. He's winding rope around my body like it's his favorite hobby.

My arms are above my head, giving him access to my torso when my fingers brush the brass loop hanging from the ceiling. Without uttering a word, I turn my head up toward them.

"Those are suspension hooks," he says, noticing my curiosity. "We won't use those for a while. You're not quite ready for that."

I press my shoulders back and stand up straighter at that,

which makes him chuckle as he works to loop the rope into a small knot around my rib cage.

"You don't like being told you can't do something, do you?"

I shake my head.

"Well, I didn't say you *couldn't* do it. I said you can't do it *yet*."

I let out a huff and press my lips together.

"We'll work our way there. Someday, you can."

I nod softly, pleased with that answer.

"Sometimes, obeying me means being patient. It means doing what I say but also not doing what I forbid. Understand?"

I hesitate. This is the one thing I don't want to hear. Not because I want to disobey him but because listening when I'm being told what I can't do isn't something that comes as naturally to me. Call it stubborn pride or fierce independence, but following orders is far easier than following restrictions.

Isn't it enough that I keep quiet for him? That I nod and shake my head quietly and do what I'm told, standing still as a statue for him as he ties me up?

Suddenly, Jack jerks hard on the harness wrapped around my torso. I fly toward him with a gasp. His face is close to mine, much like that first night in this room before we found our restraint with each other.

"I said understand?" he repeats with his mouth near mine.

My jaw clenches, and my nostrils flare, and as much as I wish I could argue and rebel, I'd much rather hear his praise than his discipline. So with reluctance, I nod.

"Good girl," he rasps with a wicked smile against my cheek. That phrase works to thaw some of the ice inside. "I think we should do some exercises to practice restrictions," he says, and my interest piques at that. "Tell me, do you ever touch yourself after these sessions?" he asks.

My cheeks grow hot, and I swallow nervously.

"Answer the question. Yes or no?"

Dragging in a shaky breath through my parted lips, I nod.

"Don't be embarrassed," he says before leaning in from behind me. His lips are next to my ear as he adds, "So do I."

Arousal floods the space between my thighs, so I clench them together tightly. The thought of Jack getting so turned on by this time with me that he has to pleasure himself afterward is enough to make me want to climax right here. Sparks of excitement dance down to my belly.

Why is he telling me this? How is this showing restraint?

"From now on, I don't want you touching yourself. Understand?"

My brows furrow. I even turn my head toward him, although I can't see him. But this rule doesn't make any sense. How would he even know if I did? Is he going to come check my panties for signs of pleasure? Is he going to install cameras in my room to watch me?

"I'm trusting you to follow these rules, Camille. Do you think you can do that?"

Slowly, I nod.

"Do you understand why I'm telling you this?" he asks, tucking the loose end of the rope against my back.

I shake my head.

"Because I want you to be devoted to this. I want your full trust, and if you break that trust, I may never know, but you will. You'll know that you can't be trusted. That you can't follow the rules. That you aren't really a good girl."

My jaw drops with a gasp as I turn toward him, showing the offense of him even saying that. That sentence alone strikes a chord in my chest. He's right. I would know. So this isn't really a rule for him—it's a rule for me.

He chuckles again. "I trust you'll follow the rules then."

After he's unwound the ropes from my chest and our session is over, his new rule sits heavily on my shoulders. While I am determined to follow it, there's also a sense of dread there too because it means no relief for me.

Wrapping my robe around my body and tying it at the waist, I pull the letter out of my pocket. He's wrapping the ropes in a figure-eight pattern to store them, so his back is to me. I consider handing him the letter, but that feels odd.

Instead, I walk out of the room and slip it under his door like I always do. Then I make my way down the stairs.

My body feels tight and ravenous for something it can't have. The few moments of pleasure I get after our lessons is the one thing I look forward to most, and now that's been taken away.

I'm lying in bed, restlessly kicking the covers off every few minutes, only to pull them back up the next.

Following restrictions is terrible.

Maybe I'm not a good girl. Maybe I *thought* I was when the instructions were simple, and he whispered the phrase in my ear seductively. That would trick anyone into thinking they were submissive and obedient.

But I'm not. I'm defiant and stubborn and rebellious.

And I am certainly *not* the type of woman who lets men dictate what she can and cannot do when she's alone.

The creak in the floorboard outside my door catches my attention, so I freeze in my bed and listen. There's another.

I slowly throw back the covers and slip out of bed. Tiptoeing, I make my way to the door and peek through the narrow opening. I can barely make out his form in the hallway through the darkness, but it's enough to have my heart hammering in my chest.

Pulling the door open, I stare at him through the darkness. He freezes with a folded piece of paper in his hand. But my eyes don't go to the letter; they stay glued to his eyes instead.

He takes a step forward, but he doesn't breach the opening to my room. I take a step toward him until our bodies are nearly flush with each other.

Just like the last time I caught him in my hallway, we stare at each other for no other reason than just to savor this quiet, peaceful silence together.

His hand lifts, and instead of touching my face again, he drifts his fingers down the side of my arm. When he reaches my wrist, I flex my hand, hoping to feel his touch against mine.

"Are you being a good girl?" he whispers, leaning forward. His eyes dance over to my bed and back to my face.

With my chin held high, I reply, "Of course."

"Good," he whispers, his lips twitching as he fights a smile.

Then, because he's cruel, he backs me up until my spine hits the doorframe. His body presses against me, and a jolt of realization washes over me—he's about to break the rules and cross the line. He drifts his fingers over my stomach and down. I stop breathing entirely as his featherlight touch breezes over the core of my panties. He doesn't touch my clit, but I swear I can feel him hovering over it.

"Does that feel good?" he whispers.

With an ache in my core, I nod. "Yes."

"I'm sorry," he says, and I glance at him with confusion. "I shouldn't torture you like this, but I want to see how strong you are."

"You don't play fair," I mumble indignantly. He's just turning me on more to make my challenge even harder. It's cruel and heartless and *so* fucking sexy.

When did I give this man so much power over me? And why do I love it so much?

His wicked lips touch the side of my neck, sucking delicately and sending chills down my spine.

"Jack, please," I beg.

I hear the crinkle of paper, and I look down to see him dragging the letter softly over my skin and then across the pebbled center of each breast. It's excruciating.

When he tears his hand and his body away from me, I let out a pained whimper from the ache of his absence.

Then he hands me the letter. And I snatch it from him reluctantly.

I scowl when I hear him laughing to himself.

"Like I said," he mumbles. "I'm sorry."

I mumble curses in French as he retreats into the darkness. I slam his letter on the nightstand, too angry to read it right now. I don't care what he has to say.

"Espèce d'enfoiré cruel," I grumble to myself, punching my pillow. "Salopard malfaisant!"

Sleep doesn't come easily. My body is wound tight with need, and I'm far too angry to allow myself to drift off.

I never touch myself to relieve the ache before sleep finds me, though. So I guess I really am a good girl after all.

Rule #20: You deserve to be shown off.

Camille

My good girl,

I'm sure I would have liked him. He raised a headstrong woman, and I can't imagine that was easy.

Especially not with you.

I can tell by the way you reacted to my restrictions tonight that you didn't like it. But rules are easy to follow when it's something you want to do. The harder the restriction, the stronger you are for sticking to it.

The more of a good girl you are.

Here is the good news. If you do obey, then you will be rewarded.

And it will be more than just some light praise. I'm not sure yet what your reward will be, but I'll be sure it's something you want. I'll make sure you enjoy it.

Thank you for letting me tag along today. I've been so busy with work lately.

Bea's mother was usually the one to organize outings like that.

I'm glad you're here.

How do you feel about going to the club tomorrow night? It's your night off, isn't it? I can arrange for Phoenix to stay with Bea. You deserve to be shown off a little.

Let me know what you think.

Your Sir

LAST NIGHT WAS GRUELING. I WOKE UP IN THE MIDDLE OF A SEXY dream covered in sweat and practically crawling out of my skin, but I made it.

And this letter from Jack is reward enough. The idea of going with him to the club has me practically jumping out of bed.

Not only is today my day off, but his sister Elizabeth has agreed to watch Bea during the day. Which means I'll have a chance to talk to her about ballet lessons.

I get Bea ready in the morning and prepare her a bag with everything she might need for the day. Jack is still upstairs, probably sleeping, when the door buzzes.

"Let's go, Bea," I say, ushering her out the front door. When she and I appear on the front steps of the building, Elizabeth looks surprised.

"I was hoping we could talk out here. Can I walk with you?" I ask.

Elizabeth looks confused before hesitantly nodding. "Sure."

Bea walks in front of us as I talk to Elizabeth. Unlike the last time I saw her, her long black hair is down, and she's wearing a red wool coat and high black boots. She really is stunning, and it makes me feel immediately inadequate in my joggers and T-shirt.

"So," I say as we walk. "Beatrice has mentioned wanting to take ballet lessons."

Elizabeth turns toward me in surprise. "And Jack said she could?"

I wince. "I haven't spoken to him about it."

She lets out a sigh. "He won't change his mind."

"But what about what Bea wants?" I argue, trying to keep my voice low.

"It's not up to us," Elizabeth replies.

"I just don't understand why," I say.

When we come upon a small market, Elizabeth stops. She fishes in her pocket for some coins and hands a few of them to her niece. "Bea, will you go inside and pick yourself out a treat? I don't have any good snacks at my house."

"Can I get candy?" she asks excitedly.

"No," I say, but Elizabeth answers at the same time.

"Yes."

When I glance at her, she shrugs. "Auntie privileges."

"Fine," I say, and Bea cheers before rushing into the store.

Once we're alone, Elizabeth turns toward me and says, "When I was sixteen, I came to Paris for a ballet program, and I lived with my brother. Emmaline was one of the teachers in that program."

"That's how they met," I say with a subtle gasp.

"Yes. After a year, she had to move home to Giverny, but Jack was already in love with her. He begged her to come back to Paris. So she did. Within a year, they were married, and Bea was born. That's when she found out she was sick. I stayed with them through it all. She fought for three years, but the cancer wouldn't go away."

Tears prick my eyes as I turn to see Bea still perusing the candy section in the shop. Poor Emmaline. Poor Jack. Poor Bea. Poor Elizabeth. One cruel disease left so much despair in its wake.

"Em never danced after she came back to Paris, and my brother blames himself for that."

"So he won't even let Bea take lessons?" I ask.

"Jack won't do anything that reminds him of Emmaline. I'm still in shock that he hired you."

"Why?" I whisper.

"Because you're French."

My lips part, and I stare at Elizabeth as everything suddenly makes sense. That's why he won't let me speak. He can't bear to hear my accent.

It feels like something in my heart both shatters and expands at the thought of my presence bringing Jack any pain. When did I start to care for him so much that the idea of hurting him hurts *me*?

Bea comes bounding out of the shop a moment later, and I'm still reeling from this revelation.

"Listen," Elizabeth says with a sigh. "I can take Bea to the studio with me on my days with her. I'll give her lessons. But you can't tell Jack."

"Okay," I say excitedly. "Thank you so much."

She looks down at her niece with love in her eyes. "I just want her to be happy."

"So do I," I reply.

With that, Bea waves goodbye as she and Elizabeth walk away together. On my stroll back to the apartment, I can't stop thinking about Jack.

This whole time, I've watched the real Jack come out of his shell, and my suspicions were correct. He was never truly as cruel and cold as he let me believe. He was just protecting himself. Closing off the rest of the world so he never had to feel that pain again. And the distance he puts between himself and his daughter isn't neglect. He's protecting her.

When I walk in the door of the apartment, I expect it to be empty. But when I turn a corner and see Jack standing in the kitchen, I freeze.

Neither of us say a word as we just stare at each other. For the first time, we are alone—truly alone. And it feels like a test.

I promised I could keep things professional. Those were the rules.

Suddenly, the thought that Jack and I could do whatever we

want, and I know how much we both want to, seems so tempting it hurts. But I intend to prove to Jack that I have a strong will.

So head held high, I walk into the kitchen without a word. His eyes are on me as I pass by him and go to the fridge, pulling out a carafe of juice and placing it on the counter. When I open the cabinet and reach up to retrieve a glass, I feel him step up close behind me.

His body brushes against mine, and for a moment, I think he's trying to taunt me or even may be about to break the rules. Instead, he pulls down one of the glasses I can't reach and sets it on the counter.

"Merci," I whisper quietly before wincing at the reminder of what I learned today.

"You're welcome," he replies before pulling away.

I pour myself a glass of juice and lean against the counter as I drink it. He sips his coffee while we both stand in comfortable silence. Finally, he's the first one to break it.

"Phoenix will be here at nine. I don't want to be seen leaving together, so I'll be at the club already, waiting for you. Understand?"

I nod, holding my glass to my chest. My teeth pinch my bottom lip as I think about it, being back there and with him this time.

He used the phrase *showing me off*, and something about that feels both exhilarating and terrifying. I'm not sure if it's about how good I look in the ropes or if it's about how well I behave for him, but thinking about either one makes me feel the same way I do when he calls me his good girl. Like for the first time in my life, I know exactly what I have to do. I have someone who appreciates me and values me. I'm not alone.

It's foolish, but I can't help it. I love the idea of belonging to Jack in some way.

I wonder if he feels the same. Does he like the idea of belonging to me? Maybe we don't express it in the same way, but this is a two-way street. If I am his, then he is mine. And not romantically or with any sort of commitment, but we share something that binds us. It's in the way we can stare into each other's eyes. The way he knows what I'm thinking without me having to speak a word. The way we trust each other.

He seems to notice my contemplation because he sets his mug down and approaches me. Staring down into my eyes, he tugs my lip from between my teeth softly with his thumb.

"Don't be nervous," he murmurs quietly. "You are perfect."

All the air in the room is suddenly gone, and it feels like I forgot how to breathe. He reaches up and tucks a stray curl behind my ear.

"Do you trust me?" he asks.

It takes everything in me not to crawl into his arms and hold him tight. I'd like to bury my face against his chest or in the crook of his neck and just squeeze away all his pain after learning what I did today.

I nod, but it makes his eyes narrow, and I worry that I did something wrong.

Then he utters the two words that strike me.

"Say it," he whispers.

He wants me to speak? Why now?

Now that I know my voice and my accent bring back harmful memories for him, I can't find it in me to hurt him. And yet he's asking me to.

Gazing into his warm green eyes, I gently reply, "I trust you."

The muscles of his face relax as he nods. "Good. Then I'd like to blindfold you tonight. If that's okay with you."

How can something so simple and so innocuous feel so monumental? The idea of putting one more ounce of control in his hands excites me more than I would have expected it to.

"Yes," I answer without hesitation. "I want you to."

"I hope you know that I do want more," he adds with a wince of pain in his expression. "You have no idea how much I want. But I don't trust myself. Because once I go further, it will be a slippery slope. First, I'll touch you. Then I'll taste you. Then I'll fuck you. And all the rules we set out will be for nothing. We just have too much at stake. I'm sorry."

"We can have both, Jack," I plead. "If we make it just physical, I know we can keep things just like this. In the daytime, I'm your daughter's nanny. At night, I can be more. I can be *so much* more, Jack."

Eyes narrowing, he clearly considers this. Touching my cheek, he gently strokes it with the pad of his thumb. Then without responding to my idea, he adds, "I would never hurt you. I hope you know that."

"I know that."

When he stares at me like this, like I mean so much to him, it makes me wonder if he still sees her. Do I just remind him of his late wife, or has Jack started to see me for me?

"I meant what I said in that letter," he says. "I'm glad you're here."

The moment is delicate and breakable. One small gust of wind could shatter it into a million pieces. So neither of us moves.

"I'm glad I'm here too," I reply softly.

I watch his face for a reaction, a sign of pain or grief, but there is none—only intimacy and warmth.

I have no experience with being a nanny, but I'm pretty sure it's not supposed to be like this. This is more than crossing the lines with what we do upstairs. This is different. I meant what I said—I am glad that I'm here. This home feels like my own now, and it probably shouldn't, but I can't help it.

"Perfect," he whispers again.

My eyes watch him intently as he pulls away, leaving me feeling breathless and hot. And a little confused.

"Nine o'clock," he says as he moves toward the front door. Before disappearing through it, he turns back to me and adds, "Don't be late."

And then, just like that, he's gone.

Rule #21: The wanting is the best part.

Camille

THE CLUB IS DARKER AND LOUDER THAN I REMEMBER. THERE IS A line of people outside along the street, and I find it strange how rowdy it feels once I get inside.

This doesn't seem like the kind of place Jack would own.

Once the bouncer by the door lets me in, I move immediately through the thick horde of people toward the elevator that leads to the basement. I give my name to the security guard by the doors, and he lets me in immediately.

When I reach the basement of the club, I have to squeeze past more people to get to the back, where I found him last time. The large room where the various exhibition booths are is just like it was last time, only a bit more crowded.

When I spot Jack near the last stall, he smiles at me before catching himself and pasting that stoic expression back on his face.

I cross the room toward him. When he lifts a hand toward the space where he'll be performing the bondage on me, my skin erupts in nervous goose bumps. There is a large, padded bench in the center as well as ropes situated on hooks along the back wall.

Just like the room in Jack's apartment, there are suspension beams and hooks. I can't wait until we can start using them.

I stand toe-to-toe with him as he stares down at me. "Take a deep breath," he says. Then he starts unbuttoning his shirt.

I can feel people watching us from around the room, and it's unsettling to have half of their attention.

"Don't worry about them," he says. "They'll be looking at you soon enough."

I bite back my smile as I bask in his attention.

"Take off your clothes," he murmurs. "Just like normal."

Just like normal, I think as I peel off my dress in a crowded room. There is nothing normal about this. While I'm feeling anxious, Jack seems to be cool and calm. He is my anchor in this sea of uncertainty.

When he turns me around to braid my hair, I close my eyes and try to siphon some of his serenity in this situation. But when I open my eyes, I notice a woman watching me with interest. She's holding a drink and talking to a man while her eyes stay fixed on me. She smiles as if she finds all of this very amusing, and I don't like the way it makes me feel, so I close them again.

He wants to show me off.

I keep reminding myself of this, hoping it will settle my nerves.

Once my hair is braided, he reaches for the black ribbon hanging nearby. Our eyes meet in a quick glance as he strings it through his fingers.

"Ready?"

Letting out a long sigh, I nod.

When Jack drapes the blindfold over my eyes, his presence burns more potently. His breath, his touch, his warmth. I focus only on him, putting all my trust in him like I said I would. But having one sense taken away only heightens the others, which means the room becomes louder and hotter, and it's nothing like the room we do this in at home.

As I kneel on the padded bench, I wait for Jack to place the ropes around my arms or torso. Instead, he wraps his arms around me, firm, warm muscles engulfing me tightly.

"You're shaking," he whispers. "We don't have to do this."

I shake my head. "I want to do this."

He tears the blindfold off and forces my chin upward. "Open your eyes, little bird."

At that name, a gasp slips through my lips, and I pop my eyes open, staring up at him in surprise. Little bird, like what my father used to call me. Like I told Jack in my letter.

"I've got you," he whispers.

My brows pinch inward, because none of this makes sense. Jack brought me here to show me off. To tie me up. Not to make me feel so seen it brings tears to my eyes.

"We can stop," he says, his arms still wrapped fiercely around me.

"I don't want to stop," I whisper in return.

"Are you sure?"

I nod.

"I want you to tell me if you start to feel uncomfortable," he says, softly running his knuckle across my cheek.

"I will," I say under my breath.

This time, when he puts the blindfold over my eyes again, I am much more at ease. My shoulders melt away from my ears, and the tremble in my bones fades.

Then he starts wrapping the doubled cords over my body, starting with my torso and moving up to create an X shape between my breasts. This rope is a bit coarser than normal, creating a slight itch against my skin, but I focus on the burn of it instead of letting it bother me. The friction creates tighter knots, feeling more secure against me.

As he finishes up the chest harness, I hear the crowd around us quiet. Without seeing them, I can tell they are watching us.

He's showing me off.

I lose track of time as he binds my wrists behind my back, attaching them both to the harness. I lose myself to the nimble expertise of his fingers, touching me everywhere. There's an ache in my shoulder, but the longer I sit like this, the more my body melts into the position, and the discomfort dissipates.

When he ties something at the end of my braid, I know what's coming next.

"Hold very still," he says. Then my head is forced back as my hair is bound to my wrists, leaving my neck exposed. "How do you feel?" he asks, running a hand softly over my shoulders.

"Good," I reply.

Then he leans in until his mouth is near my ear. "You should see the way they're staring at you," he mumbles softly. His hand closes around the front of my throat, and I let out a gentle whimper. He's leaning over me from behind, touching me because he can. Because I let him tie me up and surrendered my body to him.

I wish he'd do more.

Even if sex is off the table, I want to savor every single touch. Every single moment that Jack is in my presence feels as good as sex to me.

With one hand at my throat, the other trails down my body, lightly drifting over my breast and belly. When he reaches my panties, my body tenses, and my breathing accelerates.

"I have you all to myself now, don't I?" he whispers in my ear. "I could do whatever I want."

I fight a smile as I lean back into him. What used to feel like torture feels like heaven now.

Touch me, tease me, make me want it. The wanting is the good part.

A moan escapes my lips as he slides his hand into my panties, and I nearly forget there is an audience watching.

"Is this breaking the rules?" he asks as his finger barely kisses the sensitive bud between my legs. "I can't tell."

My skin breaks out in a light sweat as he continues to tease me with his touch. Then his fingers dive deeper into my panties, and I jolt with anticipation, but my body is stuck in this position with nowhere to move.

And when he drags his finger through my folds, finding them soaked, he growls loudly in my ear. "God, you're so wet, little bird."

I don't know if the room has grown quiet watching us or if the blood pounding in my ears is just so deafening I can't hear them anymore, but it's like Jack and I are the only two people who exist right now. With his hand between my legs, touching the most intimate part of me, nothing else matters but this moment.

He continues to tease me, running his finger through the moisture, sliding between the lips of my core without penetrating me, and it's driving me mad with need. What I wouldn't give to have him inside me.

The wanting has turned into needing, and needing hurts.

"You have been a very good girl for me, haven't you?" he asks as his finger slides a little deeper.

I whimper against him as my neck starts to ache from stretching backward. The pain and the burn and arousal all blend into one until it's everywhere and I can't tell one from the other.

"Is it time for your reward, little bird?" he asks, sinking his middle finger to the first knuckle.

I fidget as a throaty, guttural sound escapes my lips. "Yes, please," I beg.

"Shall we show them what good girls get?" he growls in my ear as his finger sinks deep inside me.

I groan loudly, trying to move although I'm completely bound. He holds me upright, and all I hear is his breathing in my ear as he slides his digit in and out, picking up speed and using his palm to rub against my clit.

"You are soaking my hand," he says, only turning me on more.

The muscles in my thighs grow hot as I clench them, struggling to keep them apart when all I want to do is squeeze them together and ride out a much-deserved climax. Instead, my body surrenders to him, letting him wring out my pleasure like I'm a doll for him to play with.

"I'm almost there," I squeak as I fidget some more.

"Oh, I can tell," he whispers, kissing my neck.

His hand picks up speed, holding a steady tempo that draws all my attention and every ounce of blood in my body to that one sensitive spot. Pressing the heel of his palm against my clit, he draws quick, tight circles until the sensation explodes behind my eyes and my muscles seize with white-hot pleasure.

"That's it, little bird. Let it go. Come for me."

I let out a screaming gasp as my body answers to him, coming hard against his hand. My hips are thrusting and writhing as he continues the movement, letting me float through the climax for what feels like forever. My head is stuck in the clouds, focused only on the sensation and the need. But as I come down, I'm flushed with humiliation.

I just had a full-blown orgasm in *public*. People are watching. I'm mostly naked, blindfolded and tied up, and I just let Jack St. Claire get me off like some horny cat in heat.

"Oh my God," I mumble as I try to turn my head toward him. The tight rope at the end of my braid keeps me from moving much at all.

"That was beautiful. Don't be embarrassed."

"I've never…" I stammer.

I didn't even feel him pull his hand out of my panties, but the absence of his touch is cold and aching.

I can't drag air into my lungs fast enough. Everything hits me so hard, and I start to tremble again.

Once the thrumming in my ears subsides, I hear people speaking, but my mind doesn't comprehend their words, just their presence.

"Focus on me, Camille," Jack says, his fingers deftly working to release my knots. "You're doing so good."

Somehow, Jack feels closer to me now, like what we have is more significant than lust. Maintaining these boundaries between physical and emotional has made us stronger somehow. That's when it hits me—he touched me. He walked right over that line and listened to what I said today. We can be sexual and intimate with each other and still stick to our rules of never letting it affect my position or his daughter.

"How are you feeling?" he asks, pulling the blindfold from my face.

To my surprise, my eyelashes are wet when I blink them. I give him a solemn nod.

He leans in, nearly touching his forehead to mine as he says, "Use your words, little bird. Let me hear you."

I have to swallow down the rising emotion in my throat. My chest is still heaving, and goose bumps cascade across my entire body. "Good," I say, although it doesn't feel like enough. Gazing up into his eyes, my mouth cracks into a smile as I add, "I feel great."

Then Jack aims that brilliant, beaming crooked grin of his on me, and I begin to melt. "Good," he replies. "Now sit down. I want to massage your shoulders because I know they're sore."

I can't help but bite my bottom lip as I sit down on the bench with my back to him. He covers his hands in warm oil and slips my bra straps to the side before kneading his fingers gently into my shoulders. I let my head hang forward and savor his touch and how good it feels as his fingers loosen the tight muscles.

"The club isn't normally like this," he says as he works. "We're going to be making some changes around here, and I wanted to bring you in before we shut down."

My eyes pop open. "Shut down?"

"Temporarily," he adds gruffly.

Jack continues massaging my shoulders and down my back, and the temptation to push the boundaries of our relationship is prominent. Surely, if he can get me off in front of a crowd, I can ask more about his work now.

"How did you end up owning a sex club in the first place?" I ask.

He doesn't show any hesitation as he lets out a huff. "It belonged to my godfather, who passed it down to me. In fact... my mother runs one back home."

I giggle to myself. "The family business?"

"I guess so," he replies with a chuckle. "I know it sounds strange to others, but it's not strange to us."

"I don't think it's strange," I reply. "I assume you've been learning this stuff for a long time then."

"Bondage? Yes, but it wasn't until a few years ago that I started practicing it. It was...a coping mechanism." He adds that last part, and I know that it's a struggle for him to be so vulnerable and speak about his wife's death. Not wanting him to close me out again, I change the subject.

"So why are you shutting the club down?"

"Well, my godfather didn't just pass it down to me. He passed it down to six of us to see if we could run it together, the six children of the original owners of another club back in California. A club that did superbly better than this one is."

"It's not going so well?" I ask.

"Not at all. Everyone has different ideas about what this place should be. And the worst of all is my godfather's self-indulgent son. So I'm going to let him run this place into the ground so we can start fresh."

My brows furrow.

When I don't respond, he pauses, his hands on my back. "You think I'm wrong for doing that, don't you?"

"I don't know anything about running a business, but to me, that decision sounds like it's coming from a place of spite. If your godfather gave you this club to run it together, I don't think he'd want to hear that you let it fail just to prove a point."

I bite my lip, hoping my first time truly speaking to Jack about his work didn't just end in failure from my outspoken, arrogant mouth.

He doesn't speak, letting his fingers trail softly over my skin. My shoulders don't ache anymore, but my heart does.

"You're right," he mumbles quietly.

"I'm sorry," I say, spinning toward him. "I shouldn't have said anything. I'll go back to being quiet."

The corner of his mouth lifts. "No, I like to hear your voice."

"You do?"

We're lost in each other's eyes when someone starts shouting across the room, and a fight breaks out. The room instantly erupts into chaos, and Jack quickly pulls me into his arms.

Rule #22: Even Doms have to learn to take orders.

Jack

"Stay here," I order Camille as I shove her behind me.

A fight has broken out somewhere in the club, creating pure chaos on the floor. If people aren't running *from* the fight, they're running *to* it, phones drawn and ready to record.

What a fucking mess.

I push through the crowd to eventually find two men brawling on the floor. Everyone around them is cheering or recording as if this is some sort of sick sport.

Glancing up over the two men, I make eye contact with Julian. My teeth are clenched and my nostrils flared as I glare at him, his expression mimicking mine.

"Break it up!" I shout, reaching down to drag the man on top off the other.

"Everyone back up!" Julian bellows. He starts pushing people away from the circle as I hold the men apart.

Finally, security shows up to handle the crowd. Once the two men are detained, I march over to the bar and slam my fist against it. "Shut it down."

Weston puts up his hands in surrender. "I wasn't planning on serving anymore."

"What are you doing?" Julian argues. "We can't shut it down. It's only eleven!"

Spinning on him, I jab a finger against his chest. "I told you we were over capacity. I told you we had to limit alcohol and prohibit phones, but you wouldn't fucking listen."

"You know everything, Jack. Sorry, I forgot!" He replies in a huff.

Ignoring Julian's immature argument, I turn back toward Weston and reiterate, "Shut it down."

"Yes, boss," he replies, which irks me, but I don't have time to deal with that. I need to get this place cleared out before something really bad happens.

"Help me get everyone out of here," I say to Julian. "We have a liability on our hands."

"I'm not shutting it down just because one little fight broke out," he replies with his arms over his chest.

"One little fight?" I can't believe what I'm hearing. "Julian, we almost had a riot."

"You're being overdramatic."

"And you're being a child," I snap, regretting it as soon as it leaves my mouth.

I just wish I understood why Julian is the way he is. Arrogant, inconsiderate, selfish.

I don't fault his father for this. I think it's just the world in which he was raised. His parents are good people. His mother is a fucking saint. But without meaning to, they raised one hell of a spoiled brat.

Turning away from the bar, I work to usher the guests out of the club. After making my way over to the DJ booth, I motion with my hand across my throat, telling him to cut the music. A moment later, the room is bathed in silence, the only sound the collective *boos* from the crowd.

When I turn back, I find Julian helping with a disgruntled expression on his face.

I work my way to the edge of the crowd along the wall and through the door to the backstage area. My sister is stomping angrily with a look of rage on her face.

I'm quite certain there is nobody meaner on this planet than Elizabeth, and I'm not just saying that as her big brother. Judging by the look on her face, whoever is on security tonight has just been subjected to a massive serving of her fiery rage.

She stops in front of me with her hands on her hips. "You need to get this place under control," she barks. "I can't subject dancers to this, Jack."

"I'm handling it," I argue.

"Are you?" she replies with a tilt of her head. "Or are you just fighting with Julian?"

Speak of the devil, he suddenly appears behind me, staring at Elizabeth with a flat expression.

She points a stern finger at both of us as if I'm not nearly ten years older than her. "You two need to get over your bullshit and learn how to work together before someone gets hurt!"

With that, she shoves past both of us, stomping away on a mission.

The entire reason I took on this club last year was to work alongside my sister and hopefully repair the broken relationship between us. And nearly that entire year has gone by with very few words and absolutely no progress. But it's not something I can focus on right now.

She's right.

I turn toward the man at my side and let out a sigh. "Help me empty this place out."

"I don't take orders from you," he replies coldly.

Tired of his shit, I grab him by the collar and shove him hard against the wall. He doesn't seem the least bit surprised. Glaring through half-closed eyes, he glowers at me as I get in his face.

"I don't know what the fuck your problem is," I bellow. "But I have people here who I actually fucking care about, and I will not rest until this shithole is empty and they are safe, understand?"

He pushes me away, straightening his tie. "It's always about you, Jack. *Everything* is about you."

"Fuck you, Julian."

"No, fuck you, Jack."

With that, he turns on his heels and marches away. I'm left huffing in anger.

When I leave the backstage hallway, I find Camille standing where I left her. Her brows are lifted, and her arms are wrapped around herself, and it kills me to see her looking scared. Rushing over to her, I place my hands on her arms.

"Go home. I have to clean this up."

"I can help," she mumbles softly.

At the sound of her voice, I wince. Just a few minutes ago, I wanted to hear her speak. But right now, with everything falling apart, I bristle at the sound.

"No," I say sternly. "You need to get home. It's late."

I watch as she chews on her bottom lip, and I can tell she doesn't want to leave me. Truth be told, I don't want her to leave me either. In only the past few weeks, I've become accustomed to her nearness in a way that surprises me. I don't want distance between us. The way it feels to be in her presence is like a drug to me, and I can't get enough.

But right now, I have work to do.

"Go," I say again, and finally, she nods and obeys.

It takes Julian and I nearly three and a half hours to clear the club. By the end of the long and grueling night, I can't bear to look into his eyes, or anyone else's for that matter.

I feel like a failure. Everything Camille and Elizabeth said stings with truth. I was supposed to instill faith and guidance in everyone but most of all my sister. She can still hardly stand me.

THE GOOD GIRL EFFECT   183

As Julian and I reach the top floor of the now-empty club, we freeze as we come face-to-face with Matis.

Matis was the original owner of L'Amour, which he opened nearly thirty years ago in his early twenties. And although he gifted the club to us just one year ago, he's stuck around as a bit of a mentor for the rest of us.

And judging by the very disappointed look on his face, he's not happy. I don't blame him.

"What happened?" he asks in his thick French accent. "Capacity should only be three fifty, and I hear you were over five hundred."

From the corner of my eye, I can see Julian's jaw clench. He won't admit it was his fault, and at this point, there's no reason to throw blame.

"You know better," Matis says, pointing his glare at me.

"It was a long night, Matis. Let's talk about it tomorrow." I try to walk past him, and he places a hand on my chest, shoving me back.

"No, we talk about it now."

Exhausted, Julian and I collapse into the chairs of a nearby table. Matis pours himself a drink and comes over at a leisurely pace. When he sits across from us, it's as if I'm about to be scolded like a child, and I hate it.

"Shouldn't we call in the others?" Julian asks.

Matis takes a sip of his drink and shakes his head. "You two are the problem," he says flatly.

"Us?" Julian asks.

I don't bother responding because I know he's right.

"You two were supposed to be the leaders. Partners, remember? But you make terrible partners."

"We don't get along," I reply coolly.

"You don't have to get along. You don't have to even like each other. Because it's not about *you*, it's about the club. But you've both sabotaged that to get back at each other. And that's not fair to anyone."

With my elbows on the table, I rub my brow. "I have been trying to tell him we need stricter enforcements and more control over capacity, but he won't—"

"Enough," Matis barks, so I stop speaking. He looks exhausted too as he leans back in his chair. All of this is such a mess, and I hate the disappointment on his face. Suddenly, I'm very glad Ronan isn't here to see this. Matis's disappointment, I can handle. But my godfather's…

Suddenly, I remember Phoenix's words in the office that day. *What if Ronan was wrong about us?*

It pains me that she somehow thinks any of this was *her* fault. Or Weston's or Amelia's or Elizabeth's. Because it was never any of their fault. It was mine.

"If I didn't know any better," Matis adds, looking at Julian this time, who is sulking silently in the seat next to me, "I'd say you're purposefully trying to sabotage this club."

"Why would I do that?" he replies.

"I don't know," Matis says in a calm tone. "To ruin something your father loved. To make Jack look bad."

Julian scoffs but doesn't reply. I stare at him with my brows pinched, suddenly wondering if either of those could be true. I've never known Julian to have a strained relationship with his father, so the first one seems strange, but to make me look bad…

That does make sense.

But who am I to judge? Haven't I done the same?

Rule #23: It's okay to let go sometimes.

Jack

I DON'T CALL THE CAR BACK FOR A RIDE HOME AFTER WE'VE LOCKED up. I'm the last one to leave, and I decide to walk home instead. It's only a few hours until sunrise, and the streets are quiet.

When I arrive back at my apartment, I walk in to find it dark and quiet. My kitchen smells like cleaning chemicals, and my sink shines with the absence of the dirty dishes I left in it this afternoon.

Instead of going directly up to my bedroom, I stare at the living room, remembering a time when I once lived here too. But now I've turned into a ghost in my own home.

Tearing the top few buttons of my shirt open, I walk to the kitchen and pour myself a glass of red wine. I can't stop staring at how clean the sink and countertops are. And although I know it's something I pay Camille for, I can't help but feel like shit for it. I can't take care of my own house. I can't take care of my own child.

And for what? My job? The one I'm failing at?

I'm failing at everything.

There's a drawing stuck to the fridge, and I pull it down,

smiling at the black cat wearing a red beret like some Le Chat Noir recreation. It's obvious this is my daughter's artwork, but it reminds me of the small drawings that have been appearing around the house on notepads and takeout menus and even at the bottom of a few of the letters Camille has written.

I'm growing too fond of this woman in my home. I'm aware of it. She is both adorable and sexy all at once, and I haven't been this attracted to a woman since Em. Taking her on as a bondage sub was a mistake. Thinking I could keep it professional was a joke.

I'd give her everything, throw caution to the wind if I didn't worry that my attachment to her wasn't just some side effect of this grief. What if I'm reaching for her because I miss reaching for my wife? How cruel of me. How careless.

What I did tonight, making her moan and whine with pleasure under my touch, was reckless. But I can't stop thinking about what she said—we could draw the line. We could still have everything we want and stop it there. Can't we?

I want to believe I can touch her and bury myself in her body while maintaining a professional boundary. This desire has become so much more. It's become a *need*.

And the more I deny myself, the more tense and miserable I become. For her sake, I'll endure it. For both of their sakes—hers and Bea's. What kind of man would I be to ruin what they have?

After my first glass is empty, I consider going to bed, but I reach for the bottle to pour another one instead. Then I carry it to the living room, where a basket of my daughter's toys sits in the corner. Dropping onto the sofa, I let the silence envelop me. The only light is the moon's glow shining through the large windows. And in this dark, quiet, midnight space, I haunt my own home.

The long year weighs on my body, and I know something has to change. I can't keep going on like this. The only question now is: do I leave the club, call it a loss, and move back home?

That is the smart choice. It would put much-needed distance between me and Camille.

My eagerness to leave Paris has dissipated recently. After Em died, I couldn't wait to get out of here. I couldn't stand to be in this house, let alone this city.

But I think it was the trip to the park the other day that changed things for me. Seeing Bea happy. Hearing her speak her mother's language again, living so happily in the city Em loved, made me realize that getting away from our pain here means leaving the good too.

I can't just tear my daughter away from the only home she's ever known and expect it to fix everything. She is too young to feel the painful memories here the same way I do.

A door opens down the hallway, and I wait with bated breath to see who will appear. When Camille steps quietly into the living room, I release a sigh of relief. Just the sight of her, arms wrapped tightly around herself, brings me a sense of peace I didn't expect.

She doesn't say a word as she comes closer. She's dressed in nothing but a long T-shirt and underwear, and I try to swallow down the arousal brewing in my blood, seeing her like this. Her long, wavy blond hair is draped over one shoulder, and she looks so fucking beautiful in this moonlight it should be criminal.

I'm only human. How on earth am I supposed to resist her when she looks at me like that?

I'm in shambles on the couch, and she can see it as she approaches. Leaning over, she places a hand on my knee and reaches out to brush my stray hair off my forehead. Then she cups my cheek and stays silent as she stares into my eyes.

I've never in my life met someone who seems to be and do everything I need. There's no way I do the same for her, but she offers so much of herself to me, and I just don't deserve it.

"What am I doing?" I mutter in the darkness. I don't know

why, but I have this need to express everything to her. "My job is a mess. I'm a terrible father. My life is falling apart."

She presses her fingers to my mouth to silence me. "Shhh…"

Then she slowly lowers herself to her knees between my legs, softly resting her cheek against my thigh.

I don't breathe as I stare down at her, struck by the sight of her kneeling for me. I didn't even have to tell her to do this, but she just knew. Somehow, she knew exactly what I needed.

"How are you so perfect?" I whisper.

A tender smile plays on her lips as I pet her hair.

"Say something, little bird."

"I don't want to talk," she replies. "I just want to be what you need."

"You are," I say without hesitation. "You are exactly what I need."

Her hands drift up my thighs, and my cock twitches. "Then let me be what you *want*."

"Camille," I say in a warning. This is dangerous. We're about to cross another line; I can feel it. It's all moving too fast, and I don't care anymore.

I want to believe that in this quiet space, in the middle of the night, between just us, rules and boundaries don't matter.

"Let me make you feel good," she whispers as she rises up. Her hands move to the button of my pants, and when I hear the zipper go down, there's not a reason in the world I could think of that would be good enough to stop her.

My head falls backward on the couch as all the blood in my body courses straight into my cock. Filled with heat and arousal, I shut out the world as Camille reaches into my pants and wraps her hand around me.

I let out a groan as she softly strokes my cock to life. "That feels good," I mumble under my breath.

Within a second, it's rock hard and throbbing. Panicking, I grab her hand to stop her.

"We shouldn't be doing this," I say in a raspy whisper. "What I did to you today was under very different circumstances. When we're in a scene, it's one thing, but this—"

"Hey, it's okay," she replies as she pulls my hand away. I look down, feeling the tension and pain etched into my features. She rubs a hand down my thigh as if she can see into my mind. "It's just us."

Those three words feel like water being doused on the fire of anxiety inside me.

It is just us.

We are the only two people in this room. We might as well be the only two people in the world.

With her hand wrapped around my cock, she gazes up at me as she leans down and runs her tongue around the head. I let out a low growling sound as I watch her slather my length in saliva.

"Oh God, Camille," I groan.

Burying my hand in her hair, I keep my eyes on her as she takes me into her mouth. I almost can't believe what is happening. And it's not just the sensation of warm, wet heaven that drives me wild but the look of eager desire on her face as she does it.

Camille yearns for me the same way I yearn for her. She wants this, not as a duty or gift but because it brings her pleasure too.

"You like that, little bird?" I manage to utter as I watch her bob her head up and down on my shaft.

She hums around my cock as she nods her head.

"You love my fat cock stuffed in that little mouth of yours?"

My filthy words seem to excite her, and she rises up, moving faster and tightening her lips around me. Her tongue swirls around the head, hitting the most sensitive spot that makes my hips jerk and my heart hammer harder in my chest.

"Fuck," I groan, throwing my head back and surrendering myself to the sensation. "Don't stop, little bird."

I'm lost in the euphoria. She is so perfect, so beautiful, so *mine*.

With her small hand wrapped around the base, she keeps up her motion, drawing my body tighter and tighter. Any moment, I'll explode.

But I don't want this moment to end. Because I know once it's over, she'll return to her role as the person off-limits to me. And we will step back over to the safe side of this line we were never supposed to cross.

She pulls her mouth from my cock, kissing the shaft as she mumbles softly, "Don't hold back. Give it all to me."

I squeeze her hair in my hand, fighting the urge to come.

"Where are you going to take it? On your face or in your mouth?" I ask.

She grins up at me wickedly. "Wherever you want it."

"Don't," I say, moving my hand from her hair to her jaw. "Don't be so perfect. I can't fucking take it."

My praise practically makes her glow. Then she returns her sinful mouth to my cock, sucking and stroking, and all I have to do is imagine my cum dirtying her perfect face, and it sends me reeling into my orgasm.

"I'm coming, little bird," I say in a strained tone. With my hand on her jaw, I pull her mouth from my dick and stroke myself quickly. I'm washed away by pleasure as my cock shoots white spurts of my seed all over her face. The first drop lands across her cheek and then the next on her lips.

I should be disgusted for the way I'm treating her. Using her and staining her and treating her like nothing more than a toy for my pleasure, but when she darts her tongue out to taste the mess I've left on her lip, I know I'm fucked.

She hums with my taste in her mouth just as my climax fades. Overcome with desire, I drag her onto my lap. I want to kiss her and fuck her and make her mine forever. I want reckless, foolish things with this woman.

It was never like this with Em. I never felt so depraved and overcome with lust the way I am with Camille. I never felt so *close* to Em. Camille doesn't deserve this version of me. She is too pure and beautiful.

Tearing my shirt off, I use it to wipe her face clean. "I'm sorry."

"Sorry?" she murmurs. "For what?"

How can I explain? I couldn't possibly.

So I keep my mouth shut as I pull her into my arms, stroking her back and telling myself it's not too late to step back over that line and go back to the way things were. I can still make things right.

"Nothing," I whisper. "You are such a good girl, you know that, little bird?"

She rests her cheek on my chest as she hums pleasantly.

I wish I could tell her she's so much more than that. Not just good.

She's perfect. She's wonderful. She's everything.

Rule #24: The truth will always come out.

Camille

A week slips by since the night at the club. A week since the night Jack and I crossed that line—twice.

I can tell Jack is putting a wall between us again. Although we still do our bondage sessions every night upstairs, there is no more touching, no more indulging, and no more breaking rules. I think he's proving to himself that he can behave, even when he doesn't want to.

That night in the living room still crosses my mind nearly every hour of every day. I have always been the one to make the first move with men, but never men like Jack St. Claire. Touching him outside the sessions was a risk. But I wanted to show him how good it could be. Which I did.

Now he wants to show me that we can still maintain our working relationship. Which we are.

But I'm growing restless again. It wasn't just about the lust that night. It was about the connection. About giving him exactly what he needed. It was about *us*.

This morning, I dropped Bea off with Elizabeth again. She's taking her to the studio for her second week of lessons. Bea hasn't been able to stop talking about it since she started last week. Luckily, Jack is never around to hear it.

I'm racked with guilt for lying to him about Bea's lessons. Maybe if I knew his concerns were justified, I'd feel more. But Bea has found a way to connect to her aunt and her mother, and I will defend her right to do that. Even if it gets me fired.

Now that I'm alone for the day, I'm feeling even more on edge than before. I've had all week to think about that sexy, forbidden night and no way to relieve my aching need. How much longer can Jack really expect me to endure this? I'm dying.

Maybe he's forgotten. And in that case, it would be justifiable to break the rules. I mean…this is unreasonable.

Walking through the silent house, I go to my room and stand in front of my nightstand as if it's a bad omen I'm forced to face.

I could just reach in and pull out a toy. It probably wouldn't even take me more than a second.

I'd still be a good girl. I went this long, and that is very impressive.

Biting my bottom lip, I reach down and pull the drawer open.

"What are you doing?"

I let out a scream as I turn around and find Jack standing in my doorway. My heart is beating so fast, I can feel it in my ears. Heat flushes my cheeks as I grab my chest and stare at him. "You scared the hell out of me!"

He chuckles. "Sorry." Then he nods toward the nightstand again. "What are you reaching for in there?"

"Nothing," I say with a quick shake of my head.

He smirks as he crosses his arms and leans against the doorframe. He really can't look that good and still expect me to deprive myself. It's not fair at all.

"Really? Nothing?" He steps into the room looking haughty, and I have to bite down harder on my lip to keep from grinning.

"Because it looked like you were about to get something out of your drawer there."

I take a step back, guarding my nightstand. "No, I wasn't," I argue.

"You wouldn't," he says as he steps up to me, running his fingers down my arms. "Because you're a good girl, and you don't break the rules."

I have to clench my teeth together. "I *am* a good girl. How dare you imply otherwise?"

As he leans in with a devilish smirk, I get a whiff of his cologne, and it makes my knees start to weaken. "I suppose you want your reward soon."

"I thought..."

"You thought what, little bird? That the night at the club was your reward?" Then with his lips against my ear, he adds, "You'll find there are *many* rewards when you behave."

"I do behave," I reply, tilting my chin as he brings his lips closer to my neck. I don't know if he intends to actually reward me or if he's just playing with me, but when it's just me and him alone, those boundaries and rules don't apply. And I am just fine with that.

"Actually, I think I have an idea," he says as he pulls away and stares down at me. My jaw is clenched as I meet his stare, hoping his idea isn't another form of torture for me. But judging by the look in his eye, he's not in the mood to torment me.

No, I can tell by the lightness in his demeanor that Jack is here not out of duty or purpose but because he wants to be. He's in my room for *me*.

"Maybe I'll just watch you reward yourself," he whispers playfully. "That's not breaking the rules."

I let out a whimper at the idea of Jack watching me. And as embarrassing as that sounds, I would do it. Mostly to just get off but also to do it knowing he likes watching.

"You're not serious," I reply, searching his face.

"Why not?" he asks. "Unless you really don't want to."

My lips purse and my eyes narrow. "Really?"

Instead of answering me, he leans past me and opens my bedside drawer. I squeeze my eyes shut in horrified shame as he rifles through the random items before finding what he was looking for.

"Here we go," he says with amusement.

As he lifts up the sleek black vibrator, I peek through my clenched eyes to see the smug look on his face.

"Go ahead," he says, his breath soft against my neck as he presses the toy into my hand. "If you really want to, I won't stop you."

With shaking hands, I wrap my fist around the vibrator. Then I drop onto the bed behind me. Sitting up, I stare at him with my bottom lip pinched between my teeth.

I do really want to, and there is a sense of comfort with Jack now that I'm not entirely opposed to the idea of masturbating while he watches. If anything, I think the real reason I'm holding back is because he's not telling me to do this as my Dom or my boss. He's here with those gentle eyes, more alive than I've ever seen them, because he wants to be. And the problem with that is…it blurs lines. It's not so easy to separate work from pleasure when work becomes pleasure.

But I am nothing if not reckless and stubborn. So I lean back on one hand and click the button of the toy so that it comes to life in my hand. His face lights up with excitement as he watches me slip it down the waistband of my loose pants. My eyes close the moment it touches my clit.

This won't take long at all.

The buzzing is too intense at first, so I squirm on the bed. When I open my eyes again, I find that Jack is no long standing near my legs but hovering over me, staring at my face as I bring myself to the brink of ecstasy.

He doesn't say a word as he watches me, more enthralled with the expression on my face than what's happening between my legs. And I was right. It doesn't take long at all. Within minutes, I'm pulsing and shaking, feeling the sensation take over as my climax slams into me.

His lips hover just a breath from mine as I come, moaning as I reach for his mouth, but he won't kiss me. Instead, he pulls just out of reach.

His mouth curls into a smirk as my orgasm starts to fade and my muscles relax. When I'm done, I click the vibrator off and collapse onto my back.

Still lingering over me, he looks at me as if I'm the most intriguing thing he's ever seen.

"I've never met anyone like you."

"You told me to!" I bark at him as I sit up and get in his face.

He only laughs at my outburst. "I know I did, but most girls would be too embarrassed, but you...you're exceptional."

"Great, you think I'm weird now," I reply with a huff.

"I think you're amazing."

I roll my eyes at him, but it's impossible to keep the smile from my face. He drives me wild. But the more I sense the real Jack coming through, the more I like him. He is at times coarse and rude, but only when he needs to be—like that night in the club when a fight broke out. But he's also playful and kind, and I get the feeling he was far more the latter before his wife died.

As sad as that is, I take a sense of pride in knowing that I helped to bring that part back out.

"Any chance you've got another one in you?" he teases as he climbs over me, and I'm starting to get the feeling that my day off will be spent with my boss when my phone buzzes in my pocket. I wince. Nothing could be more important than this right now.

Jack stands as I pull my phone out of my pocket and see Elizabeth's name on the screen. She's never called me before. I'm sure it's nothing.

But what if it's not?

"Something wrong?" he asks.

I don't want to worry him, not when I'm so close to getting what I want. So I silence the call and toss it aside. He's giving me an expectant look, and I hope he's ready to pick up where we left off.

Only a few seconds go by before she calls again.

Filled with concern, I swipe the call to answer it. "Allô?"

"What on earth took you so long to answer?" Elizabeth snaps at me over the phone line.

"I'm sorry. What's wrong?" I ask.

"Bea fell in ballet class and busted her lip."

"What?" I reply in shock as I sit up. "Is she okay?"

"She's fine. She's just crying for you," Elizabeth replies, sounding annoyed.

"For me?" I ask.

"What's going on?" Jack asks in a panic.

I glance up at him, suddenly realizing that I'd have to lie to him if I didn't want him to find out how Bea hurt herself. I can't do that. I can't lie to him anymore, especially about his own daughter.

"Bea fell. She's fine, but she wants..." I let the words trail off as he stares at me. None of this feels right. I don't finish my sentence as I turn my attention back to the call with Elizabeth. "I'll come get her right now."

"Okay. We're at the studio. I'll send you the location."

Shit.

"I'm on my way." When Elizabeth hangs up, I feel sick. Standing from the bed, I shove the vibrator in the drawer. "I have to go get her," I say to him, moving toward the door.

"No, I should go," he replies as he follows me. "She's my daughter."

"We'll both go," I say, not looking him in the eye as I throw on my coat and slip on my boots.

"How did she hurt herself?" he asks as we walk through the

front door. There's something different about his voice, a subtle worry in the tone.

"Umm…" My voice fades as I look down at the directions on my phone. "They're at the dance studio," I say, walking down the street.

"I know where that is. I'll call us a car."

He pulls out his phone and steps away to make a phone call, and I'm pacing in place, nervous and dreading what he'll do when he finds out the truth.

It's nothing, I tell myself. She was just dancing. Why would he be mad about that?

I don't know, maybe because I signed her up for lessons against his wishes.

"He'll be here in five minutes," he says. When he notices me gnawing at my bottom lip, he comes up to me and places his hands on my arms. "Relax."

Just when I finally have Jack opening up to me and showing me kindness, I lie to him and get his daughter hurt. At the very least, I owe him the truth.

"I have to tell you something," I say, looking up at him.

His brows furrow, pinching together in concern. "What? That Bea asked for you, not me?" he asks with a shrug. "I'm not worried about that. I figured that—"

"Not that," I reply.

He tilts his head in question.

Swallowing my guilt, I just come out with it. "I asked Elizabeth to give Bea ballet lessons at her studio."

"You did?" he asks, looking confused. "But why wouldn't you ask me?"

"Bea said you already said no," I reply nervously. "So we went behind your back. I'm so sorry."

At first, he doesn't look angry. He just appears confused. As he releases my arms and backs away, I see the anger start to form on his face like a slowly evolving expression. His jaw clicks as he grinds his molars. His eyes focus on nothing at all. And he never looks my way.

When the car arrives, he ushers me inside. On the entire ride over to the studio, he's quiet, and it's honestly worse than if he just yelled or argued with me. I hate that he's just stewing painfully in the seat next to me.

By the time we arrive at the dance studio, I'm so anxious I could jump out of the moving vehicle just to escape the tension. We rush inside and find Bea sitting on a bench outside the dance room with a bag full of ice pressed against her lip. She's in a pink leotard, tights, and soft ballet slippers.

"Camille!" she squeals when she sees me coming.

Internally, I wince, but I don't let it show. I open my arms with a grateful smile as she sprints down the hall and runs into my tight embrace.

"Are you all right?" I ask.

She whimpers against my side. "My lip was bleeding!" she wails. Her cheeks are splotchy, a sign that she's been crying. It breaks my heart.

"Let me see," I reply, pulling away to look at the damage. She sticks out her bottom lip in a pout, and there is a definite split, blue and swollen. "Does it hurt?"

She nods with tears in her eyes.

Jack is standing a couple of feet away, and I can practically feel how stressed and uncomfortable he is. I wish he'd come closer to her, show her some attention.

Just then, Elizabeth walks out of the dance room. I notice immediately the way she won't look at her brother. "Feeling better, little Bea?" she asks.

Bea nods before leaning her head on my arm.

"Ready to go home?" I say.

She nods again.

"Get your things then."

She runs down the hallway toward a room where her bag must

be stored. I'm left alone with Elizabeth and Jack, and the air is so thick I'm choking on it. I could tell that the relationship between the siblings was strained, but I had no idea it was this bad.

A moment later, Bea comes sprinting down the hall toward us. She practically leaps into my arms, and although she's five years old, I find myself holding her so she can rest her head on my shoulder.

At the moment, I don't care that she seems to seek comfort in me instead of her own family. I don't care that I'm not her mother or aunt. I'm her caretaker, and I'm going to do just that. I'm going to show her comfort and love her and do everything she needs, regardless of whatever these adults have going on.

When we get back to the car outside, I put Bea between me and Jack. He continues to stew on the way home, and I know he's angry with me. I only hope he tells me because the last thing I want is for things to go back to the way they were before.

Rule #25: Bring out the fight in him.

Camille

JACK GOES STRAIGHT UPSTAIRS WHEN WE GET HOME. IT BOTHERS me so much, but I can't say anything. Not around Bea.

Although it's technically my day off, I spend it with her. We play in her room and cook dinner together, and the whole time, I just keep thinking about the brooding man upstairs.

When I lay Bea down in bed at the end of the day, she asks me to stay with her. So I do. Sitting on the chair next to her bed, I softly brush her hair until she closes her eyes.

After a yawn, she whispers, "I wish you were my maman."

She clutches my hand in hers, and emotion stings in my throat. Leaning toward her, I softly whisper, "No one could ever replace your maman."

"But you can," she says, and I quickly shake my head.

I wish I knew the right thing to say, and it's very likely that I'll mess this up somehow. No one trains you for moments like this. And maybe there is no right thing to say.

Moving toward her side, I sit on the edge of her bed as I stare down at her, fighting back tears. "I'm sorry that your maman got sick. I know she would want to be here with you more than anything. And no one else could possibly replace her, but you have so many people who love you just as much as she did. You have your tante Elizabeth. And your papa. And me."

"And my grand-mère," she says sweetly before continuing to rattle off grandparents and aunts and uncles, making me smile.

"Exactly." Leaning down, I press my lips to her forehead. "Bonne nuit. Fais de beaux rêves."

"Bonne nuit," she mumbles sleepily.

Leaving the room, I turn off the light and shut her door. Once I'm alone in the downstairs level of the apartment, his presence upstairs calls to me. I already know Jack is the type to bottle up his emotions and hide. He doesn't want confrontation or to actually face those feelings.

But that's not me. I can't just bury this guilt and pretend it doesn't exist.

I try to busy myself for a while, cleaning the kitchen, doing dishes, prepping meals for the week. But none of it is a true distraction because he's still there at the forefront of my mind. It's like I'm waiting for him to come down and give me a piece of his mind, but it's futile. He's not coming.

Nearly two hours after I put Bea to bed, I decide I can't take another second, and I march right up those stairs. I refuse to let him crawl back into the shadows and be a moody phantom like he was when I first arrived.

He's not in his office or in his bedroom, so I barge right into the bondage room and find him winding ropes and putting them away in the wardrobe. My eyes catch on the gold band on his finger, lancing me with a yearning I can't stand.

"No session tonight, Camille," he says with his back to me.

"I'm not here for a session," I argue.

He glances over his shoulder at me. "Then you should get to bed."

Stomping over to him, I grab his arm and force him to face

me. There's grief and pain in his eyes, and it both kills me and angers me. Why is this man so intent on enduring this agony alone? Why does he punish himself like this?

"You're mad at me," I say through clenched teeth. "So tell me. Yell at me. Scold me or punish me or something."

"Go to bed."

"No," I argue. "How can you live like this? This anger and pain eats at you like a cancer."

The moment the word leaves my mouth, I wince. It was a slip of the tongue.

Squeezing my eyes shut, I stammer, "I'm sorry. That was a stupid thing to say."

"Good night, Camille."

My eyes pop open to find him walking away, and I quickly grab his arm to haul him back. "What? Stop!"

As he turns on me, I see the struggle in his expression. The excruciating conflict. "You think I want to be angry at you?" he snaps. "You are the last person I want to be angry with."

"It doesn't matter if you want to. You *are*. So tell me."

"Fine," he growls painfully as his expression morphs into contempt. "You want to hear how mad I am?" He corners me into a wall with a sneer. "You didn't just disobey me. You betrayed me. And not with just anyone but with my *daughter*. You knew I didn't want her taking those classes, but you did it anyway."

Even though it hurts to feel his wrath, I love it. I want more. Seeing the anger on his face only fuels mine more.

"Well, then maybe *you* should come down from this room once in a while and actually *talk* to us. Then I could have spoken with you about it. Show you care!" I argue, moving to my tiptoes to get into his face.

"You think I don't care? You have *no idea* how much I care about her," he bellows with a pained expression.

"Then let her take ballet lessons!"

He growls angrily as he paces away. "You're overstepping. You are *not* her mother."

"You don't think I know that?" I fight back.

"So you have no say in what she does or doesn't do," he barks.

It's strange, but hearing him fight for Bea feels oddly satisfying, even if I'm the one he's fighting with. And even if I know I'm right.

"I don't care if I'm not her mother," I say, standing tall. "I'm going to do what's best for her no matter what."

When he turns back toward me, glaring through rage-filled eyes, I keep my chin held high. He huffs, exhaling hard through his nostrils and pressing his lips together. "You are too stubborn," he grumbles. "Too strong-willed. And you don't know your place."

"I don't care," I declare.

"I should fire you for this."

I have to remind myself to breathe and not to cry as I stare back at him. I don't want him to see me react to that.

"Are you?" I reply, feeling the threat of tears. I don't know what I'll do if he does.

With an exhale, he turns away, keeping his back to me. "No."

After a long, tense moment, I ask, "Why not?"

Maybe it's foolish of me, but I want to know why he would keep me after I distinctly disobeyed his orders. I don't deserve this job anymore, but in my heart, I hope he's keeping me around for more *personal* reasons.

It's a foolish thing to wish, especially when all our boundaries are getting blurred. If I can't do my job well, then what am I here for? What am I to this family?

"Because she wanted *you* today," he mumbles under his breath.

The tears I've been trying not to cry suddenly brim in my eyes, and it only takes one blink to make them spill down my cheeks.

"Is that all?" I ask, my voice just above a whisper.

He doesn't respond. Instead, he turns toward me and sees the moisture on my face, reacting with a pained flinch.

"I don't think we should do the bondage anymore," he says with a heavy sigh.

I have to bite my teeth together tightly to keep from hiccupping with a sob. Even though I know he's right. We can't cross these lines. There *are no* lines anymore. We've obliterated them. It all just hurts too much.

No matter how much I try to hold back my emotions, they still keep spilling over. I'm not strong enough to keep them in.

"Fine, Jack," I reply with a shaky voice. "Let's just go back to the way things were before when you hated the sound of my voice, and you never came out of your room, and you lived like a shadow in your own house. Back when you hated me. It was much easier that way."

With nothing left to say, I turn on my heels and rush out of the room. I don't even make it to my room before I lose it. Sobbing in my hands, I close the door behind me and throw myself into my own bed, crying against the pillow.

Today was a testament to the truth. Jack and I can't have a physical relationship and keep things professional. We can't separate our work from our feelings. We can't have both.

Because at the end of the day, I know that if I had to choose between having him or having her, I have to choose her. Every time. And I know he feels the same.

Rule #26: Open the door.

Camille

I MUST CRY MYSELF TO SLEEP BECAUSE I WAKE IN THE MIDDLE OF the night feeling drained, physically and emotionally. Lying in the silent, pitch-black room, it dawns on me that I am falling for Jack St. Claire. I don't know when it happened or what I'm supposed to do with this information now, but all I know is that I am on my way to loving him.

And I had no idea love was supposed to hurt so much.

Sitting up, I look at the clock and see it's nearly three in the morning. I climb from my bed, intending to go to the desk to find a piece of paper and a pen, when I hear a creak in the hallway.

I freeze, my hand halfway to the desktop.

Everything inside me feels too raw to know how to handle this. If he is out there, then what? Is he just creeping into my hallway to see me? To talk to me?

If we can't keep doing our sessions, then surely we can't keep doing *this* either, right? Whatever *this* is.

I take a step toward the door. It's closed, so I press my hand to the surface, knowing he's on the other side. Can he feel me standing here? Does he know how much I want to reach for him?

We didn't ask for this. I only took a job, not intending for the chemistry between us to be so visceral. Who are we to fight against it?

I hear another creak, this one even closer. Then something soft scratching against the door, and I know he's there, likely suffering the same agony I am.

For a while, we both wait. And in each passing second, I realize that I have a decision to make. Open this door or keep it closed. If I open it, I welcome in more confusion but also indulgence and maybe...love. If I keep it closed, then it could—and probably should—stay closed forever.

When my hand lands on the doorknob, I know there is no choice. Not really. Not where he is involved.

Twisting it, I pull the door open and stare into the dark hallway at the man lurking outside. He looks into my eyes with intensity, and somehow, I know he feels the same way I do.

"I never hated you," he says, and it's almost silent. Then he takes a step toward me so I can feel the warmth of his body.

"I want to believe that." We are standing at the precipice of something grand, ready to jump.

His hand lifts to touch my face the same way it did that first night I found him here.

"We really shouldn't do this," he whispers so quietly the words drift off into the darkness.

"I don't care," I reply.

"Neither do I."

With that, he wraps a hand around the back of my neck and drags me forcefully into his arms. We don't utter a word before our lips crash together.

His kiss tastes familiar, although it's the first one. Our tongues collide in harmony like we've been doing this for a hundred years.

I squeeze my arms around him tighter as I kiss him deeper, trying to get every single morsel of him, his nearness, his touch.

As he lifts me from the floor, I wrap my legs around his waist, and he devours me with both his lips and his hands.

Stumbling into my room, he closes the door behind him until we're alone.

When he groans against my mouth, I tighten my legs around his waist, and heat blossoms in my core for him.

He has one hand on my ass, squeezing it hungrily as the other slides up my spine to hold the back of my head as leverage to kiss me even deeper.

We are a storm, a violent force of nature that can't be stopped.

It's only seconds after he drops me onto the bed, draping his body over mine, that we start tearing each other's clothes off. He only breaks the kiss long enough to pull my shirt over my head. I do the same with his, letting my hands skate their way down his chest, over his pecs and abs and then back to his face to bring his mouth back to mine.

As he works to unclasp my bra behind my back, he grinds his hips against me, and I let out a purring sound. He's already hard for me—*for me.*

My bra unclasps with a pop, and he quickly swipes it from my body before moving his ravenous lips to my breasts. They are small, barely a handful, but I don't bother feeling self-conscious because he moans and growls with his teeth around my nipple as if he loves it.

The cool metal of his ring slides along the sensitive skin of my breast, and I'm ashamed of the way it causes the warmth in my belly to grow into a blazing fire. Moisture pools in my panties, and I find myself moving against him, needy for more. But he's intent on teasing me, drawing out my arousal to torture me with it.

He moves his mouth to the opposite breast, humming as he sucks and nibbles on the sensitive bud. His hips keep up their grinding so that we're both writhing in need.

When his lips move downward over my belly, he kisses me tenderly until he reaches the waistband of my pants. I feel breathless as goose bumps cover my flesh.

This can't be happening. But it is. And it's happening so fast.

He hooks his fingers in the waistband and tears my pants off with passion, taking my underwear with them. I am exposed and naked, something that feels so right and so wrong at the same time.

I barely get my pants kicked off before he's growling hungrily against my core. There's not a moment to breathe or think as his warm, wet mouth brings me to the brink of pleasure.

"God, you have no idea how long I've wanted to do this," he mumbles against my sensitive flesh. Then he sucks eagerly on my clit, and I start to lose my mind.

Slamming my hand over my mouth, I hold it in when all I want to do is scream. He's rubbing his coarse jaw against my sex, and it burns. But it's such a *good* burn. It's like he's trying to cover his face in the moisture between my thighs. The sensation has me so vulnerable and self-conscious while he's delighting himself in my arousal.

Holding my legs open, he licks and sucks the most intimate part of me as if it belongs to him. And at this moment, it does. All of me belongs to him. My body, my heart, everything.

And he proves it as he forces me into a fast and violent climax, no matter how much I fight against it. My legs start to tremble as I'm assaulted by the intensity. I've never felt my heart pound so fast.

The moment my climax recedes, I reach for him. He retraces his steps with his mouth until he reaches my lips.

I'm eagerly fumbling with the zipper of his pants, and he's helping to undo them. When we finally have them loosened, he wrestles them off and then lies back down on top of me, one naked body against another.

His lips taste like me, and it only heightens my arousal.

"I'm on birth control," I whisper against his lips.

"I'll pull out just in case," he replies. "I just need to fuck you now."

Hearing those words from his mouth causes goose bumps to break out over my skin. He *needs* to fuck me, as if he couldn't stand to live another moment without it. I want to believe it's more than physical. I want to believe he needs me in more ways.

Boxing me in with his arms resting on either side of my ears, he kisses me as his cock finds my core. I'm already so wet for him, mostly thanks to his mouth, that he slips in an inch without trouble. Then he moves slower, letting my body stretch and accommodate him.

We are breathing the same air as he thrusts himself in, one slow inch after another. I wrap my legs around his hips, my heels digging into his backside as I try to force him deeper. I need more.

As he reaches the hilt, pressed in as far as he can go in this position, he freezes. Lifting his head up a few inches, he stares into my eyes.

"We've done it," he whispers. "We crossed the line."

I know we should feel bad about that, but at this point, it feels like a relief. The damage is done.

"There's no going back now," I reply with a smile.

Pulling back, he grinds his hips forward, pressing slowly inside me as he says, "I like breaking the rules."

A moan is pulled from my lips as he does that again, slowly thrusting his hips fluidly, and I savor every second of having him inside me. "Me too," I whisper on a gasp.

Finding my hand with his, he intertwines our fingers and presses them into the mattress above my head. Then he starts to pick up speed with his hips, finding a rhythm as he moves. My body seems to know this rhythm well, following him down a trail of pleasure.

We keep our voices low, but I find it more and more difficult the faster and harder he moves. When the bed starts to squeak from the motion, he stops.

The next thing I know, he's pulling out and rising from the bed. He reaches for me one second, and then I'm being hauled back into his arms. He hoists me against him like I weigh nothing. My legs wrap around him again as he carries me to the wall, pressing my back to the cool, hard surface. Then his cock finds its home again, and he impales me on his length, fucking me hard into the solid wall.

I cling to his neck as he thrusts, finding places inside me I never knew existed before. I've had sex with men, but never anything like this. Never with such passion and lust. Never with such a connection and chemistry. Never with such need and love.

I don't want this to end. I want Jack St. Claire to lay claim to my body, bury himself inside me, and never leave. I want my body to be his home.

My back is pressed flat against the wall as his eyes find mine. Even in the nearly silent room, I hear his heavy breathing and quiet grunts, and I kiss them right off his lips. Our mouths are entangled as he continues to pound into me, the friction from his body sending me into another spell of heat and desire.

"N'arrête pas," I murmur against his mouth. "N'arrête jamais."

I don't even realize I'm mumbling in French, begging him not to stop in a language he doesn't even speak.

"I won't," he whispers in return, and my eyes pop open, staring at him in disbelief. Now is obviously not the time to ask him if he really does speak French, but I'm so struck by this revelation that I almost miss the goose bumps erupting on my skin and the torrent of sensation coursing through my body.

My back arches, and I cling to him tightly as it all becomes almost too much to handle.

He lets out a growl as he pulls out, staring down and panting. I'm still gasping for air as he sets my feet on the floor, kissing me hard on the mouth. My limbs are weak, and my body feels like ice melting into water.

But he's not done with me yet. Spinning me around, he tugs my hips back and enters me again. I have to press my hands to the wall to keep myself upright as he thrusts fast, hitting new spots and making my body sing an entirely new tune. I can only hold on as Jack makes me feel things I've never felt before.

My free hand covers my mouth again because it's all too intense. When I sense his body begin to tense and tighten, he quickly pulls out. A moment later, the warm jets of his cum land on my back.

When he's done, he wraps a hand around my throat and pulls me upright, pressing my back to his chest and kissing me on the side of the neck.

"You are so perfect," he whispers, moving his mouth to my ear and then my lips. "So perfect."

Turning my head, I lean into him as I stare into his eyes. Our bodies are warm with a sheen of sweat, pressed up against each other as we gasp for air together.

I have never known sex to be so consuming. And I don't want to think about anything but this moment. Not tomorrow or the next day. I don't care about the consequences. I just want to savor this feeling of being so close to him that it feels like we are one.

Jack disappears from behind me and goes into the bathroom. When he reappears a moment later, he has a warm, wet washcloth that he uses to clean my back.

After he's done, he pulls me toward the bed. We both know we can't sleep together here, but we can just lie together for a little while.

So as he drapes me over his chest, holding me close without saying a word, I know that's all we're doing, savoring a good moment for what it is—a moment.

Rule #27: Moms have all the answers.

Jack

CAMILLE BREATHES QUIETLY AGAINST MY CHEST AS I BRUSH THE soft curls from her face. For a while, I lose myself in gently stroking her back, feeling each vertebra of her spine under my fingers.

She's fast asleep in my arms, and I am trying not to feel the creeping guilt and regret. Every moment with her is like a dream, and sex was no different.

After my wife died, I coped with bondage. It was a form of control—a way to busy my mind so I never had to feel pain. A distraction. I was convinced that if my body could still feel something good, then I wasn't completely broken and lost to the world. And while there was always sex too, it was never about that. It was always about trying to manipulate and control what I could while my life felt so out of control.

But with Camille, it's different. She gives me the control and the emotional connection. She lets me dominate her, but I swear she lets me feel so safe with her at the same time.

It wasn't just physical pleasure tonight. It was a connection I haven't felt since Em.

Stronger even.

And that only makes me feel worse. It's only been two years since Em died. Isn't it too soon to feel this way about someone else?

Would it be better if I fucked Camille and felt nothing at all? Like all the other women.

Either way, I'm an asshole.

Kissing her softly on the forehead, I roll her away and tuck her comfortably under the blankets. Then I climb out of her bed and dress quickly.

As I stand over her, watching her sleep, I get an idea. Turning to the desk, I pull a piece of paper from the stack and pick up the pen she has lying beside it. Quickly, I write out a message.

Little bird,

Last night, I told you you were too strong-willed, and I was wrong. I like your strong will. I like how stubborn you are. I like that you fight with me when I'm wrong.

It makes your submission that much sweeter.

I hope you still want to continue with our lessons upstairs. I know we crossed a line last night, but I don't care. The view from this side of that line is exquisite, and I'm not ready to go back.

I know we've said it before, but I mean it this time. We can maintain our professional relationship. And have our fun off the clock.

I'll be good if you can be good.

What do you think?

If you're in, then I'll see you at midnight.

Your Sir

PS: You're cute when you come.

With a smirk, I fold up the letter and set it on her nightstand with her name written across the front.

On my way back to my room, I stop at Bea's door again, peeking in on her. I'm instantly assaulted by guilt as I watch her sleep.

When I look at Bea, I see Em. I see the way she held her after we brought her home from the hospital. I see the way she sang songs with her at bedtime. I see all the beautiful dresses Em would put her in and obsess over, a trait even Bea has held on to. And all it makes me feel is sad that she's not here with her daughter anymore.

I'm selfish to be moving on so quickly. All I have to do is keep my word to Camille—no relationship. Just sex and work, and that's all.

I can't give her my heart, not yet. No matter how much I want to.

It still belongs to my wife.

When I wake up, my phone screen is riddled with messages. The fiasco in the club has caused a rift in the team, and I've been putting it off for too long.

I know it's up to me to bring the team together for one last attempt to make this work. But I'm stuck, lacking the drive to swallow my pride and work with the one person I do not want to work with.

I climb out of bed, ignoring the messages as I shower and get ready for a busy day. The entire time, I'm not thinking about work, though—I'm thinking about last night.

How good it felt when she leapt into my arms.

How delicious her cunt tasted.

How she had to cover her mouth to keep from screaming.

I wish I could relive last night over and over instead of going into work today, but life is unfair, and I can't.

After I'm dressed, I move toward the door, ready to leave, when I notice the letter lying on the floor, waiting for me. With a grin and far too much foolish hope, I pick it up and read it.

Sir,

You already know how good I can be.
   See you tonight.

                              Your good girl

I bite my bottom lip, my cheeks straining with a smile as I let out a groan. Can I really make it to midnight? I'm counting down the seconds already.

Placing the folded letter on the dresser, I wish I had time to write her back, but I don't. I'm already late as it is. Besides, there's not much to say, and if someone gave me a pen and paper right now, all I would do with it is lay out in explicit detail exactly what I'd like to do with her.

I'd rather just show her tonight.

Bea and Camille are out of the apartment when I pass through the lower level toward the front door. When I reach the street, starting on my short walk to the club, I pull out my phone and check my notifications. There are things from Phoenix and Matis and Julian, but more importantly, there's a text from my mother.

It says nothing more than *Call me*.

With a tense sigh, I hit the Call button and wait as it rings.

"Hello, my love," she says as she picks up the call.

"I was wondering when you were going to catch wind of everything," I say without greeting.

"Catch wind of what?" she replies.

"What happened last week at the club."

She lets out a sigh, and I wait for her response. She might try to deny she knows anything. My mother likes to pretend I can do no wrong, so I wouldn't be surprised if she avoids the conversation altogether.

"Technically..." she says. "Ronan told me last week."

"I knew it."

"What kind of mother would I be if I called my son, who lives on another continent, to lecture him about his job?"

"So you do want to lecture me?" I reply with a chuckle.

"No, I do not. I want to make sure you're okay."

My mother is one of the strongest, wisest, most fiercely independent people I know, but she never fails to handle conflict with such grace, and to be honest, it irks me to no end. Especially when I feel like I'm losing my fucking mind all the time.

When Em died, I just wanted to lash out at the world. I was so wild with grief that I could hardly hold myself together, and I envied my mother to the point of bitterness because of it. Why couldn't I be more like her? I'm her son. I should have been stronger, like her.

"I'm okay," I say flatly, hoping it convinces her.

"Can I tell you something?" she asks.

"Of course," I say as I reach an intersection, waiting to cross.

"Emerson and I did not always see eye to eye. I had a certain way I thought things should be done, and he fought with me a lot on those things. We were two very stubborn business partners, and sometimes we butted heads so much, I thought the club would have been better if I just ran it alone."

"Is this the part where you impart some great wisdom about how I get over this feud with Julian?" I ask as I cross the street toward the club.

"Nope," she replies. "Because I don't have the answers, and some days, running that club was just hard. Emerson and I were good friends, and still we struggled to work together. But the club always came first. At least we had that in common," she says. I can hear the sound of dishes in the background, and I wonder if it's either of my other parents in the kitchen beside her.

"Well, that's the difference," I say with a sigh. Reaching the club, I stand out front to finish my conversation with my mother before going in. "Julian doesn't give a shit about the club. He never did. You know what Matis said the other day? That Julian is purposely sabotaging it to make me look bad to Ronan. Can you believe that?" I ask.

"Is that what you think he's doing?"

"I wouldn't be surprised," I reply.

"Why would he do that, though?" she asks. "Julian has a good relationship with his dad. Ronan gave that boy the world growing up. Why would he need to sabotage you?"

"Hell if I know. He just hates me."

"Julian has never hated you," she says, and I freeze, furrowing my brows.

"What are you talking about? Yes, he did. Ever since we were kids."

"He adored you, Jack. You were much older than him, and he looked up to you. But for some reason, when you two grew up, you had this contempt for him. Maybe it's because Ronan adored him so much, and until Julian came along, you had Ronan to yourself. In fact…it would almost make more sense for *you* to want to sabotage *him*."

I'm standing on the sidewalk outside the club, staring at the trees blowing in the breeze as I let my mother's words filter through my mind, hunting for truth in them.

"I wouldn't do that," I say, not entirely sure it's true.

"I know you wouldn't," she replies sweetly. "I'm sure you and Julian will work this out. I know how much you want to move back here, but I also know you don't want to leave it like this. So you'll figure it out. You always do."

"Thanks," I mumble, scratching my brow. This conversation has left me even more unsettled than I already was.

In the background, I hear a gentle voice asking something.

"Jade wants to know if you got the dresses for Bea," she says, changing the subject.

"Uh...yes," I reply, although to be honest, I'm not entirely sure. I haven't been present enough in my own home to know whether or not the gifts from my family have arrived. "Tell her thank you," I add.

"I will," my mother replies.

Another round of guilt assaults me as I think about how distant I've been from them all—my parents and my littlest sister, Scarlett. I didn't just turn into a ghost at my own home. I stopped existing everywhere.

I grew up in such a happy, lively home, and I'm an asshole for depriving Bea of that. Up until I was seven, it was just me and my mom. She worked full-time, and still, she was so present. Those years were happy.

Then she got married to Jade and Clay, giving me not just another mom but a dad too. I had three parents, and I can't even give my daughter one.

Camille is trying to coax me back into Bea's life, and I just have to stop fighting it. Then maybe Bea can call for me when she's hurt. I'll be the one tucking her in at night. I'll be there in the morning when she wakes up.

Even I know I don't need to move back home to have that. I don't even need to stop grieving my wife.

"You still there, baby?" my mother asks on the other end of the line.

"Yeah, but I'm about to go into work. I need to have a meeting with Julian."

"Good," she replies, sounding pleased. "I love you very much."

"I love you too," I say.

After I hang up the phone, I don't move. Maybe it was this new revelation about Julian, or maybe it was the way it felt last night with Camille, but a new sense of energy flows through me.

I've been drowning for years, sinking too deep to try and swim out of it all. For the first time in my life, I realize I can turn it all around. I don't have to drown anymore.

With that, I take a very long, deep breath, and I walk inside.

Rule #28: It's okay to smile again.

Jack

THE CLUB IS EMPTY AND QUIET DURING THE DAY. AS I PASS through toward the second-level stairs, I hear Weston doing inventory behind the bar. Amelia is shuffling around with some sort of bright pink fabric draped over her arms. Somewhere in the building, I know my sister and Phoenix are hard at work too. I pause, admiring how dedicated they all are to this place.

They took Ronan's message to heart. They're not just trying to survive the year; they're working to make Legacy even better than Salacious.

It's time I did the same.

The club has three levels. The street level, which Matis and Ronan purchased about ten years ago, used to be a restaurant. They've since transformed it into a nightclub that hides the one below.

The basement level of the club is where the old club, L'Amour, got its start. It has surprisingly tall ceilings and an open, airy vibe for a place hidden underground.

One floor above the street level club is where we have our

meeting spaces and offices. There are also rooms up there that are good for private events and parties.

Reaching the second level, I walk down the hall, passing the offices until I reach Julian's. He's sitting behind the desk, his feet propped up on the surface. His attention is on the computer until he notices me standing in his space. Then he freezes and glares at me expectantly.

"Can we talk?" I ask.

I watch the light leave his eyes and his shoulders tense. "Sure."

Closing his door behind me, I walk into his office and have a seat in the chair across from him. Suddenly, I can't stop thinking about what my mother said, about how I was the one with more motive to sabotage Julian and not the other way around. Have I been doing this unknowingly? Have I ever given a proper moment of actual dedication to this club?

Or did I curse it to fail immediately?

Julian and I are locked in a stare-down as he waits for me to speak. I'm not ready to have a heart-to-heart with him yet, and I still can't stand the insolent brat, but it's time we start defining what our priorities are.

I let out a deep sigh.

"You and I and every single person on this team want the club to do well. The problem is us," I say.

He doesn't move. Still as a statue, he glares at me. So I continue.

"We can dislike each other all we want, but we can't keep letting them pay for it."

"So the minute something goes wrong again, you can just throw me under the bus?" he replies flatly.

I have to clench my fists under the table to settle myself.

"We both failed this club, and we take the fall together."

"Fine," he admits, putting his feet on the floor. "What do you suggest?"

"We don't open tonight," I say, watching his brows lift in reaction. "In fact, we don't open for the next four weeks."

"Four weeks?" he shrieks. "You're out of your mind."

"We need to start fresh. Reinvest what little profits we have and give it one last shot."

"After a whole year, you want to start fresh *now*?" he asks.

"It's our last chance, isn't it?"

"Do you even care?" he replies. "You're leaving as soon as the year is up."

"I do care," I snap in return. "That's why I'm here, sitting in your office, trying to come up with a plan to save this place before it's too late. So are you in or not?"

My tone is impatient and annoyed. But I can tell by the look on his face that he's at least listening to me.

"Okay, so we close down for four weeks. Then what?" he asks.

"We redesign everything. We'll bring the team in and do it right. We have to stop treating this like a place to party and turn it into something we can be proud of. A club with class and integrity."

He rolls his eyes. "You just want to recreate Salacious. Then let them buy it and do it themselves."

I shake my head. "No, I want something better."

He shoots me an unimpressed look. "How on earth will you do that?"

"We're in Paris, Julian. The fucking City of Love. The most goddamn romantic city on the planet. Our club should reflect that. We can bring in people from all over the world and stop treating our club like a place where local people come to get drunk and laid. But we have to do it together."

He stares at me, and although there's no real expression on his face, I can see him mulling over the idea. The fact that he's not shutting it down or replying with some quippy, cutting remark means that he's excited about it.

Without responding, he reaches into his drawer. I wait as he pulls out a pad of paper, a couple pens, and then a bottle of whiskey.

"It's a little early to start drinking," I say, peering down at the two glasses he placed on the desk.

He pours a significant amount into each. "We're going to need something to take the edge off. Otherwise, I'm afraid we might kill each other before this meeting is over."

With a shake of my head, I reach for the glass and take a sip. I mean, he's not wrong.

For the next four or five hours, Julian and I map out an entirely new plan for the club. We don't leave the room once, and we finish the bottle of whiskey.

To my surprise, we don't fight as much as I expected. We still disagree and call each other names, but we get the job done. In fact, it's a relief to be able to speak my mind with him and understand him better.

By the time we come out, it's early afternoon, and we break the news to the rest of the team. We're not opening tonight. We offer severance to the staff, send them home, and then bring the rest of the owners in to hash out the plan.

It takes hours, day creeping into night. And as I watch the clock march steadily toward midnight, I know it's time to cut it off.

By the time everyone leaves, there is a new energy in the group. Even Elizabeth looks happy, smiling at me for the first time in what seems like years. It feels amazing, but I can't enjoy it without the harsh, stinging guilt that it should have happened sooner. It's my fault that I couldn't do this for them months ago.

I apprenticed under Matis and Ronan for years. I knew better. I had the keys to making this place succeed all along, but I was too stubborn to make it happen.

But for now, I do my best to shove those feelings aside. We close up the club, turning away the angry partygoers who usually come in around this time.

I stroll alone up the street toward my apartment with my jacket hanging over my arm. I hear the click of heels on the pavement as Phoenix rushes to catch up to me.

"Should I even ask?" she says as she strides up beside me.

"Ask what?" I reply.

"What changed your mind."

"Can't I just be in a good mood?" I say, glancing sideways at her with a smirk.

"You?" she asks, aghast. "No."

"Well, I am," I reply casually as I walk.

"West said he saw you with a new girl in the club last week. Does that have anything to do with your good mood?" she asks, bumping my side.

"Maybe," I reply without looking her in the eye. Phoenix wasn't there that night because she was with Bea, and Phoenix is the only person, aside from my sister, who would recognize Camille as my nanny. And my sister doesn't walk around the club, thankfully. It's not the kind of place you want to run into your sister. If she is there during opening hours, she stays backstage with the performers.

When Phoenix doesn't respond, I glance her way to find her smiling softly next to me. Out of the blue, she wraps her arm around mine and rests her head on my shoulder.

"What's up with you?" I ask.

"It's good to see you smiling again, that's all."

My chest warms, hearing her say that. I haven't always been a broody asshole. Before Em got sick, I didn't haunt every room I stepped in with gloom and melancholy. I was livelier and happier.

"It's good to be smiling again," I mumble as I squeeze her closer.

Rule #29: Sex makes everything more fun.

Camille

I DON'T KNOW IF I SHOULD BE ON MY KNEES OR NOT. PART OF ME wants to, knowing that that's how he might want me. But then another part wants to watch him walk through that door. I want to be standing, watching his expression as we face each other for the first time since last night.

Pacing the room in my robe, I wait for the sound of the door, reliving every moment of last night in my head for the thousandth time today. I've read his letter enough to have it memorized.

It feels daunting—to have my heart growing so attached to him but knowing that it can never be anything more than physical. It's still so early. Too early to make commitments and change the dynamic of our relationship.

If I tell Jack how I feel and he feels the same, what happens to poor little Bea if things don't work out?

If I tell Jack how I feel and he *doesn't* feel the same, could I still work for him?

We are already pushing the boundaries and playing with fire.

But if we can promise to keep things like this and have fun in our free time, then we might actually be able to make this work.

Suddenly, the door opens downstairs, and I freeze. Standing in the middle of the room, I watch the door, listening as he crosses the living room and climbs the stairs.

When he appears a moment later, we both stare at each other. I'm dying to know if he still wants me here. Has he changed his mind? Maybe work was too stressful, and he doesn't want me tonight.

In a rush, he marches into the room and pulls me into his arms. Kissing me fiercely, he moans into my mouth, and I melt into his embrace.

My arms wind around his neck as I let him practically lift me from the floor. His kiss is ravenous, sucking and nibbling on my lips. He buries one hand in my hair and wraps the other around my waist.

I am flooded with heat and desire, and when his right hand sinks lower, gathering up the bottom of my robe and running his hand over my bare ass, I whimper into his mouth.

I can tell his fingers are searching for the fabric of my panties, and when he finds none, he groans again. Pulling away, he tugs off the belt, and the robe drifts open, revealing my naked body.

With a pained expression, he dives back in for another kiss.

"Why are you so perfect?" he mumbles against my lips.

I want to tell him I'm not perfect. Far from it. But I love that he sees me that way. I just dread the day when he realizes that I come with flaws like everyone else.

His hard length grinds against me, and just the reminder of what he's hiding behind those slacks has me growing wet between my thighs.

"I don't know if I have the strength to be patient with you tonight," he says as he backs me up to the upholstered bench.

"You can have me however you want," I reply.

Just when I think he's going to give in and skip the bondage in favor of just having sex instead, he holds me by the hips and pushes me gently away. My lips miss his immediately.

"No, I need to do this right. You came up here for a session, and I'm going to give you a session."

With a tilt of my head, I smirk at him as I clarify, "I didn't come up here *just* for a session."

He laughs a little, and it makes me realize how much I love his smile. I don't get to see it often enough.

"Little bird, we have opened things up to a whole new world of possibilities now, and I intend to have some fun with you."

Biting my lip, I grin at him. "I like the sound of that." Then I drop my robe so I'm standing naked in front of him.

He takes a deep breath, obviously struggling to restrain himself. "Come here." Grabbing me by the hand, he tugs me toward him, but before I can kiss him, he spins me around and gathers my hair into his hands.

As he braids it down my back, I close my eyes in anticipation of how it will feel to have him bind me tonight. Once he's done, he ties the end with a black ribbon from the wardrobe. But before moving away, he brushes my braid over my shoulder and leans in to press his lips gently against the back of my neck. It sends shivers down my spine.

Everything with Jack feels brand new.

After my hair is braided, he starts to pull out the ropes and blindfold from the wardrobe. I'm surprisingly excited to see the blindfold again. I miss how much it heightened my senses and made everything feel so much more intense.

"Have a seat on the bench," he says, and I do.

Sitting on the center, I wait for him. I'm more excited to be in this room than I've ever been—more, even, than the first time.

First, he drapes the blindfold over my eyes, and I love the way it feels as the anticipation and relaxation wash over me. Before moving away, he whispers, "You know the rules. Tell me if anything hurts, and just say stop if you need a break."

I nod without responding, just like I used to.

A moment later, his lips press against mine.

Then he turns me lengthwise over the bench, guides me to my back, and lifts my feet onto the surface. I hear him kneeling in front of me, and I savor the silence between us. It's comfortable like it always is. As he starts to bind my ankles together, I try to discern which technique he's using. A basic double column, I assume. I try to guess where he's going with each tie he finishes, deciding if it will be a frog tie or a futomomo—all things I've learned in my spare time research on top of what we do in here. I'm not interested in doing any of the bondage myself. I am a rope bunny, through and through. But I do love knowing more about it—my new obsession.

Jack isn't binding my ankle to my thigh tonight. Instead, he starts on my wrists next, doing another simple double column.

The feeling of familiar peace settles in, and I honestly wonder if he knows how much I love this. Trusting him so much. Wanting him to have complete control over me. Knowing that I'm always safe with him.

After my wrists are bound, Jack brings my knees to my chest. With the sensation of vulnerability and exposure, there's a pulse in my core, knowing exactly what awaits me once he has me fully bound.

He wraps my bound arms around my legs so I'm tied into a ball. "How do you feel?" he asks.

"Good," I reply, although my voice is a bit shaky.

He continues tying, doing what I assume is a quick-release knot around my legs and arms, restricting my movement even more.

"Deep breath," he says, and I pull air in slowly to my lungs. He does this to check that it's not too tight and that I can still breathe freely.

Once he's done, he steps away, and I lie frozen on the bench. The room feels cool on my skin, especially the exposed parts between my legs.

"Look at you," he mutters darkly. "Completely at my mercy now, aren't you?"

Arousal blooms in my belly when I hear the sound of him removing his clothes.

"Do you like it, little bird? Being bound like this for me?"

I nod.

The sound of his pants hitting the floor across the room echoes against the walls, and I let out a small gasp. When he touches me, I try to lean into it, but I can't move. He starts at my shoulder, running his fingers softly over my arm and then down my folded legs.

I feel his eyes on me, like warm rays of sunlight. Then his fingers slide through my folds, finding the pooling moisture there, and I mewl with need.

"So wet for me already," he breathes, and I fidget against the ropes. I *need* him—his touch, his body, his cock.

"Please," I whine.

Of course, he doesn't give me what I want. Instead, he slides a finger inside me, and I have to muffle my own cries by biting my lip.

"Is this what you want?" he asks.

I shake my head.

"What do you want, little bird?"

He's teasing me, and I'm afraid that if I tell him what I want, he won't give it to me. It has to be what *he* wants.

"Go ahead," he says, thrusting harder. It feels so good and so dirty, but I need more.

"Please fuck me," I mumble quietly.

"You think you've earned that?" he replies.

I nod eagerly.

When he pulls his finger out, I hear him spit. The warm saliva drips through my folds and down to my ass. I have never felt so depraved and sexy at the same time. I try squirming again, but I can barely budge in these restraints.

It's a feeling of surrender, and I know that if I didn't trust Jack so much, it would be harrowing and frightening. Instead, I am so aroused because I *want* him to use my body without my control. I get as much pleasure out of his pleasure as he does.

With the feel of his cock against my core, I hold my breath. He enters me slowly, and I let out a long, needy moan.

"Is that what you wanted, little bird?" His voice is strained, as if he's so overcome with the sensation that he can hardly speak.

"Yes," I cry out.

"God, I wanted it too," he says as he pulls out to the tip and thrusts back in. "I thought about being inside you all day. I couldn't wait to get home and fuck you again."

He starts to pick up his speed, but the position is awkward, and I can tell he's not getting in as deep as he wants. He pulls a few ropes, and they start to slacken so I can straighten my legs. With my ankles still bound together, he lifts my legs and puts them over one shoulder.

Jerking me to the edge of the bench, he pounds into me so hard that I nearly scream. My back arches, and my head grinds into the upholstery as I struggle to move. It's so intense and so exquisite, and the restraints just make everything better.

Even though I'm no longer tied up in the fetal position, my wrists and ankles are still cinched together, restricting my movement, so I couldn't get away if I tried.

Not that I want to.

But him taking that away only heightens my arousal in ways I can't believe.

"You better be quiet, or I'll gag you," he says as he pistons his hips. His cock hits a spot inside me that creates a wild ache of pleasure, driving me wild.

I hold my tied wrists over my face as he fucks me, moving faster and harder until I can barely breathe. He's using my body like it's a toy, and I can't believe how much I love it.

"Look what you do to me," he growls. "This is what you've turned me into."

He pulls his cock out and takes a few long, heavy breaths as if to keep from coming. Then he turns me onto my side and enters me again.

The new position feels less intense but just as good. I swear I could let him fuck me forever, in every position, at every angle. I could never tire of this. Being with him is more natural than being without him.

But he's only here for a moment before I'm being flipped again, this time onto my knees. With my face pressed into the upholstery and my hands below me, he enters me again.

This position gives him more leverage to pound harder and faster into me. I've never loved rough sex before, but it was never like this. The cushion muffles my cries as he brings me to the brink of ecstasy, and before I know it, I'm shuddering and moaning through an intense and unfamiliar orgasm.

I've never come like this before without even touching my clit. But it's the angle of his cock and the restraints and the sounds he's making that seem to make a perfect combination to turn my body inside out.

My spine arches as my muscles seize. As the pleasure assaults me, I shut my eyes and see stars swimming in my vision. And I'm so overcome by my own orgasm that I don't even feel Jack pull out and release onto my back again.

When I come to, he's slumped over me, trying to catch his breath too.

"Fuck," he groans.

Turning my head to suck in a lungful of air, I wait for the tingling sensation all over my body to subside. Before I know it, he's cleaning my back, then lifting me into his arms. Cradling me in his arms, he pulls the blindfold from my face, and I blink up at him in a pleasure-filled daze. The dim room blurs as I nuzzle into his side, his warm lips against my temple. After setting me on the bench sitting upright, he gets to work on my ropes.

Sweat-soaked and wrung-out, my hair is a disaster as I stare down at him on his knees, untying my ankles. When he's done, he kisses the marks the ropes left, and my heart lurches with love.

This is going to be impossible, because if he doesn't want me to fall in love with him, then he should try not to be so perfect all the time.

Rule #30: Don't try to do everything alone.

Camille

JACK TURNS ON THE SHOWER AND TESTS THE WATER, WAITING FOR it to get warm enough. We're both standing quietly in his bathroom. I'm leaning against the counter with my robe wrapped around me. My wrists and ankles still wear the marks from the ropes, and they're a little sore but nothing terrible. Definitely worth the ache.

"It's ready," he says, reaching for me. I step up to him and let him pull the robe from around my shoulders and lead me into the stall.

After he removes his own robe, he follows me in. As we both stand close together under the stream, he stares down at me with a soft smile before leaning down and pressing his lips to mine. For a few moments, we just kiss and let the water soak us.

Before things can get too heated, he pulls away and reaches for the soap. I watch as he lathers up a washcloth and uses it to clean my back, then my shoulders and arms, working his way down to my legs. His touch is gentle and attentive, and I love being taken care of by him like this.

After he rinses me off, I take the washcloth and try to do the same to him.

"I can do it," he says, pulling away.

"Let me," I reply.

He hesitates before finally nodding and turning his back to let me lather soap across the broad expanse of his shoulders. When I apply a little pressure to the crevice of his neck and shoulders, I'm appalled to find the muscles nearly rock hard.

"My God, Jack," I whisper.

Using the soap as a lubricant, I massage his shoulders, pressing my fingers into the knotted muscles. He winces but doesn't pull away.

"I'm under a lot of stress at work," he says.

"This is more than just stress," I reply. "How do you live like this?"

He hangs his head as I continue to massage, running my fingers along his spine and up to his neck. Slowly, he starts to relax. I see his shoulders melt downward, and his body begins to sag.

"It's my fault," he mumbles sadly.

"What is your fault?" I ask.

"I let the club go to shit. I should have known better. I didn't work hard enough because I think, deep down, I wanted it to fail. Not to mention I work so hard I can't even be a father to Bea—"

"Stop," I plead with him. Releasing his shoulders, I move to his front to face him. Taking his sad face in my hands, I force him to look at me. "This is too much pressure for one person. So your first year of running a club didn't go perfectly. It was your *first* year, Jack. And to be thrust into all this alone after losing your wife…"

I realize it's the first time Jack and I have ever truly spoken about his wife. Hell, it's the first time we've truly spoken about anything at all. And when he doesn't stop me, I continue.

"Don't try to do everything alone," I say. "And Bea is doing fine, but she does miss you."

His brows sink when he hears this. "I shouldn't have been so harsh about the ballet lessons."

"She's your daughter, Jack," I say, tilting my head and staring into his eyes. "You don't have to justify anything to me."

Gathering me up in his arms, he kisses my forehead. As he holds me against his chest, I wrap my arms around his waist. For something that's supposed to be just sex, this feels so right.

"You know…her birthday is next week."

Immediately, I pull away. "Whose?"

"Beatrice's."

My jaw drops. "We should do something for her."

"I was thinking the same thing. But I don't know what…"

"Has she ever been to the Disneyland in Paris?" I ask excitedly.

He responds with pinched brows and the broody expression I know so well. "No. You think she'd want to?"

I stare up at him. "What little girl wouldn't want to go to Disneyland?"

I can see him trying to formulate an argument, but the words never come out. Instead, he sighs. "Fine. I think…she would love that. But you have to come too," he adds.

Biting my bottom lip, I try not to feel too enamored. He's only asking me to come because I can help take care of Bea. It's not at all because he wants me there for more personal reasons. Or at least that's what I tell myself.

"Okay, Monsieur St. Claire. I'll come too."

Using my thumb, I drag the pad across his wrinkled brows until he eventually relaxes them. Relenting with a smile, he leans down and kisses me again.

⸺◦◦⸺

While Bea plays with her dolls in the living room and I wait for the chicken dish to bake in the oven, I draw mindlessly on a letter I'm working on for Jack. It's a frog with mouse ears in the bottom corner of the paper.

The front door opens, and I look up as Jack enters the apartment. We haven't seen each other since last night. He spent some time at work today while Bea was at school.

Our eyes meet immediately.

"Bonsoir, Papa!" Bea calls from the floor.

He pauses as he looks down at her, and I watch him intently, remembering our conversation in the shower late last night. Goose bumps cover my skin as he walks toward her and leans down to place a kiss on her head.

"Bonsoir, Bea," he whispers softly.

Emotion stings my throat as I force myself to look away. It might not seem like much to anyone else, but that small gesture was monumental for both of them. I busy myself with checking on dinner when I hear him walk into the kitchen.

"Smells good," he says.

"Thanks," I reply, glancing up at him briefly. "It's just a roast chicken with potatoes and carrots."

When I finally turn around and truly meet his gaze, it feels loaded and strange. After last night, when we were both so comfortable touching and kissing each other, refraining from doing that now is difficult. And it wasn't just the sex. It was the intimate conversation after. If anything, that was far more significant. Those are the moments that make it hard to maintain this working relationship.

"Will you be joining us for dinner?" I ask hesitantly. I don't want him to feel pressured to, but also…I'd love it more than anything.

"I left work early for a reason," he says, loosening his tie. "I told them I want to be home for dinner every night."

This takes me by surprise. I turn my head toward him and meet his eyes again. A small smile grows on my face, but I try not to overdo it. "I think that's wonderful."

Captured in a fragile moment, the two of us stand here, delicately dancing around the awkwardness of our now confusing relationship. Then he backs out of the kitchen and walks to the stairs. "I'm going to go get cleaned up."

"It'll be ready in fifteen minutes," I reply.

When the timer goes off, I pull the dish out of the oven and finish preparing the sides. I call for Bea to set the table, and as I so often do when it's just her and me, I do it in French.

"D'accord," she replies, getting up from the floor and rushing into the kitchen.

"Lave-toi les mains," I add, peeking at her from over my shoulder as I carve the chicken.

Out of the corner of my eye, I see Jack standing near the dining room table, and I pause, waiting for him to tell us to speak in English around him—as he so often does.

But this time, he stays quiet, only watching Bea as she stretches onto her tiptoes to reach the sink and cover her tiny fingers in soapy bubbles.

My eyes cast over to him again, and this time, he glances up at me. I wonder if he notices how much he's changing. I should be so happy about it, but for some reason, it gnaws at me. He's not the broody, miserable man I knew, and I should be excited about that. So why am I so nervous at the idea that everything is changing?

The next thing I know, something sharp slices across the edge of my palm, and I wince in pain, dropping the knife on the counter as I grab my hand.

"What happened?" Bea shrieks.

I squeeze the side of my hand as I rush toward the sink to run it under the cold water. As the pain starts to throb and pulse, I keep my eyes squeezed closed so Bea can't see my reaction and panic.

"Let me see."

I open my eyes and find Jack standing next to me. He pulls my hands from under the faucet and pries my grip off the cut area. Afraid to look at it, I keep my gaze trained on the ceiling as he inspects the wound.

"It doesn't look too deep. I don't think you need stitches. Bea, go into the closet and get the first aid kit."

"Okay, Papa," she replies, dashing off down the hallway.

"Does it hurt?" he whispers with his lips close to my ear. Now that we're alone, I look up at him and nod.

Then he leans down and presses his lips to my hand, apparently not afraid of my blood. My chest warms with longing moments before Bea dashes back into the room with the red plastic kit.

"Dinner is going to get cold," I complain as he works to meticulously dry and bandage my hand.

"It will still be delicious," he replies placidly.

"Are you okay, Camille?" Bea asks as she huddles in close to my side, watching her father work.

"I'm fine," I reply, smiling down at her. "I should be more careful."

"There," Jack says, sealing the bandage around my hand. "Now you go sit down at the table and let me and Bea bring you dinner."

I give him a defeated sigh. "I can do it."

"Sit," he commands, giving me that dominant tone that causes my thighs to clench and my toes to curl.

Pressing my lips together, I quietly abide, walking over to my chair as Bea and Jack work to set the table and serve the meal. It's cute, watching them work together. He instructs her which cutlery to use as she asks him to pull down the plates for her. It's the most I've seen them interact in a while.

Again, I think that I should be happy about this. This is how they *should* be. How they probably would be if Emmaline had never died.

Of course, this makes me think of the picture again. The smiling woman who thought she had her whole life in front of her. She should be the one sitting here now, watching her husband and daughter in the kitchen.

But if she was still here…I wouldn't be.

What a terrible thing to think.

But I can't help it because this moment is so beautiful. And that's a dangerous idea to let in. If this is how it's going to be now that Jack's home for dinner every night, I fear it will be far harder to maintain our boundaries than I expected. Because right now, this doesn't feel like a nanny, her boss, and his little girl. It feels like a family.

As they both come parading into the dining room, Bea carrying three plates and Jack holding the casserole dish with a pair of pot holders, I shove the sad thoughts aside and smile at them for a job well done.

"Papa made sure you didn't get blood on the chicken," Bea blurts out as she sets out the three plates on the table.

I laugh out loud. "Bonne idée."

"Papa, sit next to me," she says as she crawls onto one of the chairs, sitting on her knees so she's taller.

I can tell that Jack is trying not to grin too much as he takes the seat next to her. Then he looks up at me as he picks up his fork. "Bon appétit."

For a moment, everything feels right.

And there's something about that that feels so wrong.

Rule #31: You can't be in a bad mood in the happiest place on earth.

Jack

"How many membership applications are we currently at?" I ask, glancing across the table at Phoenix.

She scans her computer before looking back up at me. "Just over two hundred," she replies.

"It's too low," I grumble.

"I agree," she says.

"We have to make it clear to them that we've changed. The clientele we need doesn't want to be associated with some trashy nightclub."

"I'll get Amelia on it," she says, standing up and walking away.

I'm sitting at the conference table alone when I notice my sister walk past the open doorway. After briefly drumming my fingers on the table, I stand up and follow her down the hall.

"Elizabeth," I call. She pauses before realizing it's me and continuing on.

"What, Jack?" she replies coldly.

When she slips into her office, I follow her. She won't look up at me as she stands behind her desk, sifting through papers in her hand.

"The new stage design looks great," I say, starting with a compliment.

"Thanks," she snaps, "but it was mostly Amelia's work."

"I know," I reply, "but I also know you had a hand in it as well, and it looks great."

She lets out a sigh before looking up at me. "Anything else?"

God, she hates me. My sister has grit. She gets it from our mother. Her ability to hold a grudge is astounding. Of course, I'm glad she's like that. She doesn't take shit. She doesn't give second chances when they're not deserved, and she has no problem walking away when someone does her wrong. All qualities, I think, that are paramount for a woman in her position, but as her brother, someone who *has* done her wrong, I wouldn't mind a little grace.

"Actually, yes," I say with a sense of unease. "Camille and I are taking Bea to Disneyland next week for her birthday. I thought you might like to come."

All the contempt in Elizabeth's features melts into compassion. "Really?" she asks. "And *you're* going?"

I nod with a sigh. It stings to hear her ask that, rightfully so. "Yes, I'm going."

She watches me, studying me as if I'm a new foreign creature. "Has this new nanny put a spell on you or something?" she asks.

Shuffling my feet and clearing my throat, I put my hands in my pockets as I lift my chin. "Maybe. Is it that bad?"

"No," she replies. "I quite like it. Let me check my schedule," she adds, "but I would like to go."

Inside, I'm practically screaming. An entire day spent in close company with my sister after two years of the silent treatment. This feels like a miracle. I ran a club with her in hopes that I could get this much, and all I had to do was offer to take her to Disneyland.

"Excellent. Beatrice will be thrilled," I say, trying to keep my cool. "I will, uh, I'll get you a ticket then."

"Okay," she replies.

With that, I walk out of her office, feeling a bit more hopeful than when I walked in.

—◦◦◦◦◦—

Bea is wearing a long-sleeved auburn corduroy dress with a tweed coat and a black bow in her hair—and the biggest smile I've ever seen on her face. Pinned to her dress is a massive round button proclaiming that it's her birthday. Emmaline was always so meticulous about Bea's style, even as a baby. She must have had hundreds of dresses for her before she even turned one, far more than she could wear.

Somehow, that affinity for fashion stuck with our daughter, even after Em passed. At only five, Bea picks out her own clothes and dresses herself every day. I'm not sure she even knows this is something she inherited from her mother. Regardless, it warms the hell out of my heart.

As we walk through the park, she swings between me and Camille, gripping our hands like a small monkey. Elizabeth is staring, and I know how it looks. I glance down at my daughter, and she beams back up at me. Who am I to push her away? Especially after two years of doing it every day.

Admittedly, theme parks and Disney attractions are not quite my style. This is definitely something Em would have pushed us to do, though. I probably would have agreed to it begrudgingly.

But I have to say, something about it reminds me of my childhood. Time spent with family, even when it was just me and my mom. A time when things were simpler and gray clouds didn't hover over even the happiest of days.

Bea seems so happy, and I'm envious of her ability to put the sadness aside to make room for the joy. For me, it feels like every ounce of my joy tastes bitter and undeserved. Why do I get these moments while Em does not? How can I smile if she's still gone?

"Can we go on the merry-go-round?" Bea pleads while simultaneously tugging us toward the ride.

"Of course," Camille replies, smiling down at Bea.

"Will you ride it with me?" Bea asks.

"Yes," Camille says as she glances up at me.

I release Bea's hand, and the two of them walk briskly over to the line, leaving Elizabeth and me alone. We hover near the outside of the ride, standing in tense silence as we watch them.

When Camille helps Bea climb onto one of the horses, they both wave to us, and I wave back with a grin. Suddenly, Elizabeth glances my way. I catch myself smiling too brightly, so I clear my throat and press my lips together.

"I like her," Elizabeth says flatly as she glances back at them and the carousel slowly starts to spin.

"She's good for Bea," I reply without emotion.

Elizabeth nods. "I think she's good for everyone."

Should I feel bad for hiding the fact that Camille and I are also fucking like animals every night after she puts my daughter to bed? It's just sex. It doesn't get in the way of her job at all.

So it's no one's business.

Of course, I'm also harboring the fact that I do really like this woman. I love the way she challenges me and isn't afraid to stand up to me when I need someone to argue with. I like that she puts my daughter first in every scenario. I even love those little fucking drawings I find all over my house.

I like the way it feels to stare into her deep blue eyes and know that I can be at ease with her. And the way I can speak to her without the weight of judgment or condemnation.

Sex doesn't complicate things. These feelings are what complicate things.

"What is that supposed to mean?" I ask.

"I think you know what it means," she replies. "I mean...sure, you hired a nanny for Bea, but I think you both need her around."

"It's not like that, Elizabeth," I reply, clenching my jaw. "And it isn't easy, watching someone else take care of my daughter."

"No reason to get defensive," she argues. "I'm not saying it's easy. I'm saying it was a good move."

Though I don't reply, my expression begins to grow tighter and tighter.

Suddenly, a soft hand lands on my arm. "Hey," she mumbles softly. "It's okay. I didn't mean anything, Jack."

"I know," I reply raspingly as I run a hand over my face, trying to relax the grimace.

She's still watching me, but I keep my eyes trained on the spinning ride, forcing myself not to grow too agitated. I don't want to ruin Bea's day with my mood.

"And for the record," Elizabeth adds quietly. "If there was anything more between you two—"

My head snaps in her direction. "Drop it."

"I'm just saying..."

"I said drop it," I grit through my teeth. I just want her to stop talking. Stop saying what I know she's trying to say. It's all too much, too hard, too painful.

"That would be okay too," she whispers, finishing her sentence.

I open my mouth to argue when I hear my daughter giggling. "Papa!" she calls.

Quickly, I turn my attention back to the carousel in time to see Bea and Camille go around again. Forcing a big fake smile on my face, I wave to them.

Elizabeth doesn't say anything else as we watch the ride come to a stop and the girls climb off and run over to us.

"I want to ride another ride, Papa!" she squeals.

"Okay," I reply with a lopsided grin. "Whatever you want. It is your birthday after all."

The four of us take off toward another ride, and it's hard not to feel a sense of peace. For now, I can shove aside everything Elizabeth was saying. I know what she was implying is true, but it doesn't make it any easier to accept. I know I can move on after Em's death. I know I can find love again, but at what cost?

Especially when all I've really wanted is to leave Paris and take Bea back home, where we belong. That is what I still want, isn't it? Everything feels so convoluted now—with the club and with Camille. It's not as black-and-white as it once was. Maybe once we're in California and the memory of what we lost isn't hanging over us like a dark cloud, things will feel clear again.

As we walk, I glance over at Camille and realize just how attached to her I've gotten already.

Which means…that if I do go back home and try to move on, it won't just be Em that I'd be trying to move on from.

Rule #32: It's okay to pretend.

Camille

JACK IS SMILING, LIKE *REALLY* SMILING. HE'S HOLDING BEA UNDER one arm, helping her reach a large balloon from one of the vendors standing in the crowd. She giggles loudly, and Jack presses a kiss to her cheek with more love in his eyes than I've ever seen. This is not the same man I first met. It's far more than just him coming out of his shell. Jack is healing.

Did I have a part in this? Did my presence at the house somehow convince his heart to repair itself? I guess it really doesn't matter. He's getting better for *her*, which I think Emmaline would appreciate.

"Oh, the teacups!" Bea shouts excitedly as she pulls us through the park. I take one look at the dizzying ride, and my stomach turns just watching it.

"I couldn't possibly," I stutter as my feet stop so she can't tug me toward it.

"Me neither," Jack replies as he stares at the ride with a grimace. Then he glances at Elizabeth. "You can take her. Don't you spin for a living?"

She rolls her eyes as she takes Bea's hand. "It's a little more sophisticated, but sure. Come on, Bea. They can't handle it, but we can. Let's show them how it's done."

The little girl giggles as she takes her aunt's hand. Elizabeth glances toward the line and then back at us. This one is a bit longer. A sign above the queue displays that it could take up to forty-five minutes.

"Why don't you two take a walk or something? I'll text you when we're done," Elizabeth suggests.

I glance up at Jack and shrug. "I would like to do some shopping."

"Okay," he relents before looking his sister in the eye. "Don't take your eyes off her for a second."

She rolls them again, an expression she uses often. "We'll be fine. Go," she says as she shoves Jack away.

"Wait, Papa," Bea calls, running back toward him. "Hold my balloon, please."

He stiffens, looking at the large mouse-shaped pink balloon.

"I'll hold it," I say, saving him.

As I reach for it, Bea adds, "Tie it around her wrist, Papa. So she doesn't lose it."

I scoff with offense as Jack chokes out a laugh. "Yes, sweetie," he replies, taking the ribbon from her tiny clenched fist. She dashes off to join Elizabeth, and Jack takes my hand while stifling a grin. "I have experience," he adds so quietly only I can hear it. Slowly, he wraps the ribbon around my wrist in a double loop before glancing up at me with a handsome, devilish look in his eye.

"Very funny," I say, pressing my lips together. Why must he make it so hard to keep myself from falling for him?

I keep close to his side as we make our way through the park. His hand rests protectively at the small of my back. We mostly stay silent, and it's clear neither of us know how to navigate our relationship in broad daylight. It's different when we have Bea as the center of our attention. But when we're alone, we can't be the same *us* we are at night.

I glance awkwardly up at him, and he briefly meets my gaze. More than anything, I'd like to link my hand with his and walk like we're a real couple. Like I truly mean something to him.

When we come across a large gift store, I slip inside and start browsing. He stays close behind me when a small pink box catches my eye. It's a jewelry box with a red rose on the top, and when I open it, the music starts playing, and a small ballerina twirls slowly.

I let out a small gasp as I stare at it. "I had one of these when I was a little girl," I say with tears in my eyes. "My papa gave it to me for my birthday, and every year after that, he would put a gift in it for me."

Jack steps up so close behind me that his chest is pressed against my back. With a soft exhale, I close my eyes and lean into him.

"That's beautiful," he whispers. "We should get it for her."

Blinking the moisture away, I turn my head to stare up at him. "We?"

"I mean…you," he says, correcting himself. "You should get that for her." But even as he says it, his hand slides over mine so we're holding the jewelry box together.

As I stare into his eyes, I fight the urge to kiss him here. It would only take one small movement. I could lift onto my tiptoes and press my lips to his. It would mean nothing, just like all our kisses.

At least to him, it would mean nothing.

To me, it would mean everything. It would mean that I've found someone who doesn't think I'm too much or too stubborn or too nosy. Someone who chooses me. Someone who thinks I'm *perfect* just the way I am.

Instead, I turn away and take the box to the checkout counter. After paying, I walk with Jack out of the store. Without a destination in mind, we just meander through the park in silence.

"I can't believe she's six," he says suddenly, and I glance up to gauge his expression. He seems contemplative, watching a family walk past us. "It goes by so fast."

"She's amazing, Jack. You should be proud," I say.

"I am." His response is immediate, and I can hear the pride in his tone. There is no doubt in my mind that he loves Bea more than anything. It was questionable when I first arrived and he would barely even look at her, but as time has gone by and I see that he shows as much love as he can, I realize just how much pain he was in. But there is no question of his adoration for his daughter.

He laughs. "I was nothing like her when I was a kid. I gave my mom hell, but Bea is so smart and resilient."

"And funny," I reply with a smile.

"She gets that from her mother," he replies, and I don't let the mention of Emmaline sour the mood. Instead, we hold our smiles, even through the sadness.

"And her tantrums from you?" I ask, turning to make eye contact with him. There's no doubt that as adorable as Bea is, when she doesn't want something, she makes sure everyone knows it. It's incredibly frustrating as the person trying to discipline and nurture her. But as someone who loves her, I hope she stays strong-willed forever.

"Yes, I'm afraid so," he says with a nod.

The air between us is light, no longer pinning us to the ground. And when I let out a sigh, I softly add, "I do love her."

His affectionate eyes are on me as he quietly replies, "I can tell you do."

Then, to my surprise, his hand brushes my wrist. And just when I think it was a mistake, he slides his palm against mine and intertwines our fingers. I nearly stop.

We can't do this. What if we're seen? What if people get the wrong idea?

But I don't argue. I just let him hold my hand, savoring the feel of it. As people pass us by, I know we look like a real couple, and I wonder if he's as proud as I am.

It's only fifteen minutes, but for the entire walk, we just stroll hand in hand like it's normal and we can. But before we reach the area where we parted from Elizabeth and Bea, Jack stops and tugs me under the shade of a tree.

"Wait," he whispers as he stares down at me. I look ridiculous with this large balloon tied around my wrist, but those beautiful green eyes of his make me forget everything.

"What?" I reply softly.

"I just want to kiss you once, out here in the open, in broad daylight." His fingers stroke my jaw, and I try to keep myself from collapsing into his arms.

"Why?" I ask, wanting to understand what is going through his mind.

"Because..." His words trail off, and I'm hanging on each one, dying to hear him tell me that I mean something to him, more than just a woman to tie up and have sex with. More than just a nanny or an employee. More than whatever we've been up until this point. "I want to pretend for one moment that we can."

His head dips down, and our lips meet softly. At the delicate touch, my heart surges. My hands wrap around his waist as I lean into him. I don't care about the consequences or the reasons why we shouldn't do this.

His tongue slips out, tasting my lips. I part them and let him in. It's innocent and sweet, neither of us letting it grow too heated. But this kiss isn't about sex or desire. It's about so much more.

Around us, there are people laughing and whimsical music playing. It's not a kinky bedroom or a sex club, and we are not the same people we are when we slip into those roles.

This kiss is not between a Dom and his sub. A rigger and his bunny. Or a boss and his employee.

It's between us—Jack and Camille. And as his tongue rubs

softly against mine, I realize that's what he meant about wanting to pretend we can.

Jack and Camille cannot kiss—not in broad daylight. Not anywhere.

He has a little girl to protect, and I have a job to do. But just for one moment, we can pretend.

The vibration of his phone buzzes loudly in his pocket, so we break the kiss and pull apart slowly. My eyes stay closed as Jack fishes the phone out and answers it.

"Hey. Where are you guys?" he asks.

I hear Elizabeth's voice on the other end, telling Jack where to meet them. Just like that, our moment of pretending is over. He hangs up and stares down at me with a sigh.

"They're by the castle," he says.

"We should go meet them," I reply.

He glances down to my lips briefly before moving back up to my eyes. I briefly wonder if all this is in my head. Does Jack truly care about me as a person? Does he want this for more than just a moment? Even if we could take a risk and try to make it work, would he want that?

I know I do.

Hesitantly, he nods.

"Yeah, let's go."

Rule #33: Everyone has fantasies they haven't discovered yet.

Camille

BEA'S BIRTHDAY WAS ON TUESDAY, AND IT HAS THROWN OFF OUR entire week. It's been three days since the theme park, and it feels like I can't seem to catch up. The housework has fallen behind. Dinner every night has been a disaster. And Bea has been extra moody, making the rest of the house extra moody.

It was worth it, though. Getting to walk through the park with them and feel like a part of their family was a dream. Watching Bea open my gift to her later that day and feeling her arms wrap around me tightly was the best feeling in the world.

I don't know a thing about being a nanny, or at least I didn't when I got this job. But I can't imagine anything more to it than this. I love her like she's my own, and I dread the day she and I ever have to say goodbye. I don't know if I'll be around until she finishes school and goes off to university. But I can't help think about the future.

How long can I really do this? Won't I want to eventually get married and have children of my own? And what if Jack wants to start dating again? What will become of me?

The thought of living the next ten years in that spare bedroom while loving Jack St. Claire in secret with these faintly drawn boundaries sounds torturous. But not as much as falling out with him and losing Bea forever.

Both scenarios terrify me; suddenly, the future feels like a disease we can't outrun. It will either be a long, agonizing death or a quick, painful one. Either way, it's going to hurt.

Eventually, I'm going to have to make a choice. Stay here and devote my life to this family as a nanny, or save my own heart and say goodbye before it grows too attached.

Who am I kidding? It's already too late for that.

Every night, Jack and I have the same routine. I put Bea to bed and wait for him to come home. When he does, I slip upstairs, where we lose ourselves in ropes and sex. We know each other's bodies now like devoted lovers. We have seen each other at our most vulnerable.

I have become Jack's hobby.

We usually talk after sex, but it's always about work or my life before I came here. It's never about the future or *us*—although I'm not sure there is an *us*.

These are the thoughts that plague my mind as I walk back from dropping Bea off at school. The weather is starting to grow bitter as winter approaches. The leaves of Paris have turned gold and copper, and with every gust of wind that blows, the trees drop even more. They skitter noisily along the ground. It's a cruel reminder that everything changes, and time stands still for no one.

When I get back to the house, I hold on to a small hope that Jack will still be there. I want to kiss him in the daylight again, even if we're not in public. I can't stop thinking about the gravity of that kiss and everything it represented.

But when the door of the apartment closes behind me and his jacket is not hanging on the hook, I know he's already gone. The house is empty and quiet, and all the chores I need to do are waiting for me.

With a sigh, I go to the kitchen to get started on the meal prep for dinner tonight when I see the lunch container Jack normally takes to work still sitting on the counter. *Maybe he is still here.*

"Jack?" I call, but I'm met with silence.

I stare at his lunch, contemplating it. I could take it to him. I know where he works; I've been there twice before.

Surely, that wouldn't raise suspicions. I'm just doing my job.

Plus, I'd get to see him again.

It really doesn't take much more convincing than that. I slip my shoes and jacket back on and take his lunch out the door with me. The club is only a twenty-minute walk from the apartment. I think he walks most of the time too.

When I get to the club, the first thing I notice is that they've changed the sign above the door. Now it's sleek pink over black, displayed above the grand-looking double doors. There are construction workers going in and out when I slip through the door unnoticed. Standing in the main room of the club, I marvel at the changes.

Before, it just looked like any nightclub—harsh strobe lights, silver fixtures, black furniture. But now, it looks like something out of a movie. It screams dynamic luxury and energetic opulence. Lush magenta fabric and ornate onyx fixtures fill the space. There is an intricate black crystal chandelier hanging in the middle of the room. This is no longer their parents' club.

I'm staring with my mouth open when a handsome, slender man with chin-length blond hair and dashing almond-shaped eyes passes by me. He stops when he sees me.

"Hello there," he says slyly. When he grins, his face practically glows with mischief.

"Bonjour," I say out of habit. "Is Jack here?" I hold up the lunch case, and the blond man eyes it skeptically.

"He is," he says carefully before taking the lunchbox from my hand. "Jack didn't tell me he was dating anyone."

My eyes bug out wide. "Oh, I'm not his—I mean, I'm just the nanny."

The man takes a keen interest, stepping toward me. "Just the nanny?" When he smiles, he's disarmingly handsome in a way that I fear could be weaponized and used against unsuspecting victims who suddenly find themselves falling in love and handing over their hearts.

Shuffling my feet, I glance around the empty club to see if I can spot Jack instead of looking into this man's villainous eyes.

"I'm Julian," he says. He has an interesting accent. Clearly American but with a hint of French.

"I'm Camille." I put my hand out to shake, but with a coy smile, he lifts it to his mouth and kisses the back as he winks.

"Enchantée, Camille."

"Are you French?" I ask, too curious to resist.

"Afraid not," he replies. "J'ai grandi à Paris."

He grew up in Paris. I wonder briefly if he is the man Jack has mentioned during our late-night talks when he complains about the son of his godfather, who often gives him trouble. This man looks like he gives a lot of people trouble.

"So," he says as he extends his arm. "Would you like a tour?"

"A tour?" I ask.

"Yeah. We can give Jack his lunch, and you can have lunch with me." When he smiles, it creates sharp dimples in his cheeks, so charming it's like I'm getting sucked in by the spell he's putting me under.

I mean…why can't I let this handsome man give me a tour? Things with Jack are not real. He's made that very clear. We have sex without commitment, but that doesn't mean I can't even speak to other men.

"A tour would be nice, but I'm afraid I have to get back to work before lunch."

His smile grows wider. Then I notice his gaze dance upward to the second floor, where there's a line of covered windows. It makes me wonder if Jack is up there.

But before I can ask, Julian puts out his arm, and I loop mine through. He smells divine, like rich cologne. Suddenly, I imagine myself marrying a wealthy man—never having to worry about anything again. No more work. A luxe apartment in the city. People to serve me instead of the other way around.

Is that what I want more than working for Jack and Bea? My head says yes, but my heart says no.

Julian gives me a comprehensive tour of the upstairs, showing me the new dance floor, bar, and VIP section. Then he shows me the speakeasy-style door that leads exclusive members downstairs to the adult club by way of elevator. As we both step inside, he presses the button and leans against the back wall.

"I'm sure you know by now that our parents had a club themselves, but ours will be better," he says with a smug tone.

"How so?" I ask with a flirtatious smirk. Jack's already told me everything, but I want to humor Julian. I want to get to know the man who has driven Jack so out of his mind.

"Well, first of all, we won't only let in the wealthy." He brushes a strand of blond hair from his forehead. "We plan to have a sliding scale fee system and vetted membership in order to be more inclusive and accessible. That was *my* idea."

"Oh really?" I reply, pressing my lips into a grin.

That was totally Jack's idea.

"And heightened security, of course. We want the club to be safe and welcoming to *all*."

"That's good," I reply. I don't tell him how I've already found my way inside without even trying.

The elevator doors open, and Julian leads me down the dark hall toward the club I've been in before. But this time, when I step through the curtain, a gasp slips through my lips.

"This…" he says as he waves a hand over the newly refurbished club, "is my pride and joy."

My jaw drops as I glance around the room. It looks stunning down here. With the same classy, timeless ambience as upstairs, this section of the club screams youth and style. It's not just luxurious in a way that's intimidating. The walls are painted black with bright pink graffiti logos. The decor is all in jewel tones and minimalist. The dance floor is mirrored, and the booths around it are soft-looking and comfortable. Definitely room for…all sort of activities. If I were to come to a sex club, this is the kind of place I'd want to visit. Like some multisensory playground of pleasure.

Julian leans back against a low wall, crossing his arms over his chest as his eyes rake over me.

"You'll have to come see it when it's open," he says in a flirtatious tone.

"I don't think my boss would allow that," I reply with a smirk.

"Then you'll come as my date. He can't say no to that. He doesn't own you."

My expression falters as I bite my lip and look down. *He doesn't own me.*

"You don't even know me," I reply with a tilt of my head. "You just want to bring me to hold something over Jack's head."

He laughs in response but doesn't bother to argue.

"Come on. I want to show you something," he says.

I'd be more alarmed if we were alone down here, but there are so many people coming and going, workers and people dressed like Julian. I briefly worry that Elizabeth will find me here like this.

As Julian takes my hand in his, he guides me toward the back of the club, but when his eyes catch on the lingering rope marks on my wrists, I snatch my hand away and quickly cover them with my sleeve. Even though I know he saw them, he pretends he didn't.

I don't normally wear my scars for so long, but some of the ropes from last night burned into my skin while Jack and I were going at it a little too roughly. He scolded me afterward for not telling him they were so tight, but I couldn't make him understand that I loved the burn. Still, he was upset with me.

"This is my favorite part," Julian murmurs quietly.

I hold my breath in anticipation. He doesn't lead me to the bar or the dance floor or any of the closed rooms. Instead, he takes me toward a blank wall at the back of the club. I'm confused as I stare at it. It's covered in a grid of thin black floor-to-ceiling bars fastened to the plaster. There are what look like cuffs hanging from various spots of the structure.

When he notices my confusion, he picks up something from a bowl nearby and places it in my hand. And it only puzzles me more. It's a large red silk handkerchief.

"What is this?" I ask, to which Julian smiles.

With his lips near my ear and his hand around mine, chills run down my spine. "You hold this in your hand, and then you walk toward the wall."

He guides my movements, and I force myself to swallow as he corners me toward the metal grid. I stop breathing altogether as he lifts my right hand and fastens it in one of the black leather cuffs.

"The rules are that as long you are holding that red silk," he says seductively, "then whoever comes along can do whatever they'd like to you." Then he fastens my left hand in another black cuff. Suddenly, I'm bound to the wall, and I can feel my pulse thrumming loudly in my ear.

His hand slides up my leg, and I let out a yelp. I should feel terrible for the arousal building inside me, but I can't help it. It's not really him that I'm drawn to but the idea of what he's proposing.

"You mean…" I squeak, looking over my shoulder at him. He's so close our mouths nearly touch.

His hands are on my hips now, and he gives them one quick jerk, slamming his body against my ass and making me moan. I am absolutely shameless for how turned on I am right now. I should not be here with him. I should be with *Jack*.

"Imagine being fucked by complete strangers," he mumbles near my ear. "Used freely for anyone's pleasure. Is that…a fantasy of yours?"

Is it? I've certainly never thought of that before, but this feeling right now has me thinking that I have fantasies even I haven't discovered yet.

I seem to be so captivated by it that I find myself whimpering. "Yes."

Suddenly, the next voice I hear isn't Julian's, and it isn't nearly as pleasant or quiet.

"What the fuck?" Jack bellows angrily. His voice has a growly sound to it.

I gasp loudly as I struggle to spin around to find him.

"Oh, hello, Jack," Julian says, and judging by the way he said that, he's not at all surprised or horrified by my boss's sudden presence in finding us like this.

In fact, I'm starting to think I've been set up.

Rule #34: The more stubborn the will, the sweeter the submission.

Jack

I've known anger before. I'm familiar with outrage and impatience and possessiveness.

But I have *never* felt this. Seeing Camille, *my Camille*, strapped to that wall with Julian's selfish, indignant, smug hands all over her created an explosion of passion inside me.

My brain doesn't compute reason or rationale. It doesn't ask questions or work to formulate excuses. It just sees her, and something primal takes over.

Julian stands off to the side, his arms crossed as he laughs to himself. My fingers fumble to remove the straps around her wrists, but my hands are shaking too much.

I hear her stammering something anxiously, but I'm not listening. They're apologies and excuses, I know that much, but I'm not interested in those.

Once her arms are free, I snatch the red silk from her fist, waving it in her face with flared nostrils and furrowed brows.

When she sees the anger in my eyes, her chest expands, and she grows a few inches taller.

That's it, baby. Fight with me.

"Don't you wave that in my face!" she shouts, snatching the fabric from me. "I can do whatever I please."

"Think again, little bird," I argue, getting even closer to her.

"I do *not* belong to you."

My hand snatches her arm, and I toss her over my shoulder while she screams in displeasure.

"Jack St. Claire, put me down!" she hollers as I drag her away from the wall and away from Julian, who is still watching us with enthusiasm. I bet he's proud of himself for this, but I'm not concerned with him right now.

I intend to carry Camille from the club like I did the first time I found her here unexpectedly. That's what I *should* do, but we pass down the long hallway of rooms, and I know I'll never make it to the exit. What did I really expect? That I could just deposit her on the street and somehow return to my work upstairs as if nothing happened?

No. We are either going to fight this out or fuck this out. Or both.

The rooms are all still unlocked, so I throw open the door of the first one and hoist her inside while she bangs her fists against my back. As I set her down on her feet, she doesn't rest for even a second, flying straight toward me in anger.

"What is wrong with you?" she shrieks.

"Me?" I argue. "What is wrong with *you?* What are you doing here? And with *him?*"

"I was bringing *you* your lunch," she says, punching her finger against my chest. "But it doesn't matter what I was doing because I don't belong to you!"

My hand flies to her mouth, covering it in a rush as I back her against the wall. Her eyes are wide, and I can feel her panting breath against my palm. Getting close to her face so our bodies are flush, I mutter angrily, "We both know that's not true, little bird."

Her hands claw at my chest as she tries to push me away

while also scratching through the fabric as if she wants to hurt me. Behind my hand, she's trying to argue, but her words are muffled and incoherent.

I press my body to hers as her eyes meet mine. There is a fire in them, torrid passion blazing behind the irises. Neither of us can grasp where the fury ends and the arousal begins.

"No one else can touch you," I say as I swipe open the top button of her blouse. "No one else can even fucking look at you." My fingers continue, slipping open one button at a time until she's no longer clawing at my chest but mimicking my ministrations.

Suddenly, we are furiously undressing each other, but my hand is still pressed over her lips to keep her from speaking.

"Do you understand me?" I ask as I slide my hand around her waist under her shirt, my cool palm against her hot skin. "You are mine, little bird. No one else's."

She doesn't respond as she slips my shirt from my shoulders, obviously eager to touch me but not eager to answer my question.

Somewhere in the recesses of my mind, there are warning signs trying to remind me that we're not supposed to say things like this to each other. I can't make commitments and promises to this woman. But they are too distant and faint to acknowledge, drowned out by this need to have her.

I replace the hand over her mouth with my lips. She kisses me back, mercilessly biting my bottom lip between her teeth. Her obstinance radiates through the kiss, and it makes me want to dominate her even more, but I know I need to earn her submission to get that. I can't force it.

As we kiss, trading bites and moans, we work off each other's pants. She still won't answer my question, refusing to adhere to my unfair requests.

Before we go any further, I stop her with a grip around her throat. Pressing her to the wall, I force her to look up at me. She's still tenaciously angry, and I want that.

"Tell me what I want to hear," I growl.

"No," she argues with her chin raised.

I pepper it with kisses before pulling away and trying to force her again.

"Say it, little bird."

When she tries pushing me away, I notice tears springing to her eyes. She's upset, and I understand why. I'm being unreasonable. Asking for more than I've offered to give. Demanding something from her without earning it first.

And while I watch her struggle, both with me and against me, I realize that I have to do something I never thought I'd be able to do again. Because if I don't, I'll lose her for good.

Covering her body, I bring my face so close to hers that she can't look away. Her fiery gaze bores into me as I whisper the words—it's like I'm trying to hide from them.

"You want me to tell you I belong to you too, right?"

With her chest heaving, she nods.

I press my forehead to hers, breathing her air and feeling her heart pound. "You don't want me, little bird. Don't you see what a mess I am? You deserve so much better."

Her lip trembles as she stares at me. "Don't say that," she whispers, holding her head up higher and waiting for me to say what she wants to hear. "I do want you, Jack."

The tired beating organ in my chest stutters at the sound of her saying that to me. I had to know it was true before, but hearing those words from her lips hurts as much as it heals.

"You want me to say that I am yours as much as you are mine, but you must know it's true. Don't you see what you've done to me?"

Her expression softens as she looks up at me. The fire is still there as she whispers, "Then say it."

I don't hesitate. "I am yours."

There is disbelief in her expression as she winds her arms around my neck and practically leaps into my arms, kissing me with as much fervor as before.

Mumbling against my mouth, she pleads, "Then take me, Jack. Make me yours, and I'll never touch another man again."

A low growling sound escapes my lips at that response. Picking her up off the floor, I carry her over to the dresser against the wall and set her on the surface. Her legs wrap around me as I kiss my way down her neck, nibbling and licking as if I'm trying to devour her. I want to mark her and leave her covered in bites and bruises to prove to anyone who dares to look at her that she is taken.

I'm rough with her body as I move my lips to her breasts, squeezing her flesh tight enough to make her feel how much she means to me. And when I bite the tight bud of her nipple, she throws her head back and whimpers. "Harder."

I'm coming undone, being torn into a million pieces until all that remains is a base, carnal version of myself with only one motivation—*her*.

My fingers tear at her panties, ripping them off or maybe in half. I can't tell, and I don't care. I just need to get to her cunt and taste her. Dropping to my knees, I throw her legs over my shoulders as I jerk her body to the edge of the dresser and loudly devour the divine paradise between her legs.

Every inch of her body belongs to me. My woman. My delicious pussy. Even the cries of pleasure that pass through her lips are mine.

Her screams are loud, and her body thrashes as I suck fiercely on her clit. I realize it's the first time I've had the pleasure of hearing her sounds during sex. We usually have to stay so quiet, but now, she's giving me everything. And I fucking love it.

Her fingers grip tightly to my hair at the scalp and pull until it makes my eyes water. I welcome the pain. I *need* it. I moan loudly against her.

While my mouth is busy between her legs, licking up her scent and covering my face with it, my fingers work to undo my pants. A tight, overwhelming arousal crawls down my spine as I wrap my hand around my cock, pumping as I feast on her cunt.

"Please," she cries in a needy whine. "I need to come." Her voice is strained, her head hung back as the word draws out like she's been possessed.

"Come on my tongue, little bird. Let me taste it."

I slide my two middle fingers into her tight heat, curling them as I thrust hard. She practically levitates off the dresser with her legs wrapped tightly around my head.

As she screams, her pussy pulses and tightens with her orgasm, and it's the most delicious thing I've ever tasted.

"Good girl," I praise her, letting her ride out the entire wave of pleasure on my mouth and hand, but as soon as the climax has crested, I stand and kiss her fiercely on the mouth. She's unafraid to taste herself, kissing me back as I settle myself between her thighs.

When the warmth of her cunt welcomes the head of my cock, I hold her by the back of the neck so she is forced to stare into my eyes. Then I thrust inside, pressing myself as deep as I can go.

This is proof that I'm hers. The way she takes every inch is all the proof I need that her body is my home.

Staring down, I watch my cock slide back inside her. It's a feeling I've never had with any of the women I've been with before, and I know that Camille will always be the exception. If, God forbid, I lose her, no one will ever come close to her perfection.

I understand the weight of that realization. But it's too heavy to carry at the moment, so I shove the thought aside.

Instead, I focus on the pure bliss of being inside her, finding the rhythm in her body, tasting her lips as I move.

"Fuck me harder, Jack. You won't break me."

With a punishing grip on her hips, I pick up my speed and intensity. She takes me in her arms, and I bury my face in her neck, getting off on the scent of her skin and the reminder that she's mine.

"Look what you do to me," I mumble against her skin. "You are mine, little bird. No one else can have you. No one else can touch you."

"Yes," she cries out, her legs wrapping around me tighter.

Usually, I'm eager to make it last, but not today. Today, I need to fill her up. This isn't sex for pleasure. It's sex for control. I'm marking my territory and staking my claim.

"I need to come inside you," I mumble with a whimper, feeling the pulse in her neck against my cheek.

As she holds me closer, my hips still pounding relentlessly against her, she moans with each violent thrust. "I'll take all of it. Give it to me."

I growl louder as my climax approaches. The dresser creaks and trembles under our weight, but all I can think about right now is filling her up. Images of her swollen belly, my child growing inside, another seed planted to prove that she belongs to me, fill my mind. Within seconds, I'm coming hard, and instead of pulling out like I always do, I use her tight cunt to squeeze every last drop of my cum out of my body.

Her legs tighten around my waist to hold me there. My lips move up to her mouth, kissing her again, this time more breathlessly.

"Jack," she whispers, so I pull my face away and stare into her eyes.

As she strokes my cheek, I know she wants to utter words she can't. And I know what those words are because I want to proclaim them too. But even after acknowledging our feelings today, we can't speak those words to each other. Not without the inevitable heartbreak that would follow.

It doesn't matter that I love her or that she loves me. It doesn't change anything—not really.

It just makes the stakes so much higher.

Rule #35: Someone will think you're perfect—flaws and all.

Camille

JACK IS LYING ON HIS BACK WITH MY BODY DRAPED ACROSS HIS chest like a blanket. We never do this, cuddle in bed together after sex. But words like *never* and *always* don't last long with us. As it turns out, we're very bad at following rules.

I wanted to tell Jack that I love him. The words were on the tip of my tongue, but I held back. Why? I almost forget now why we can't be together. If we love each other like I think we do, then what could possibly stand between us? We might be worried for Bea's safety, but can we truly expect to keep her safe from all heartache forever? Isn't that unreasonable?

And even if things don't work out with Jack, it doesn't mean I can't be a part of her life in some way.

Jack is worried for her because she's already lost so much. That I understand, but protection from loss is not what she needs. Knowing that the adults in her life love her and will be there for her without fail is what she truly needs.

But if that's the only reason we can't be together, then why is there a nagging sense of guilt gnawing at my insides? Is the letter I found from him to Emmaline really a secret so dark that it would tear us apart?

No. But the fact that I've kept something from him this long might be.

We're lying in silence, both of us clearly deep in thought, when he finally speaks.

"We're having a grand reopening in two weeks. I'd like you to come with me."

I lift my head. "Really?"

He nods, those dark green eyes holding me and keeping me safe and warm.

"People will see us together. Elizabeth and Julian and Phoenix…"

"I don't care," he mumbles as he lifts a hand and brushes a curl behind my ear.

"But…" I start, but then his fingers press softly to my lips to quiet me.

"Let me worry about them."

This idea that he wants to bring me as his date is both terrifying and exhilarating. It's everything I want and everything I'm scared of at the same time. Am I ready to be Jack's girl for real? Because if we show up together, then I will be. No one brings their child's nanny to a sex club *professionally*.

Without responding, I crawl up closer to him and press my lips to his. Somehow, we went from casual sex and kinky sessions to being a somewhat real couple. But for how long? And what about Bea? These are all questions that won't leave me alone, but do they all need to be answered now?

Pulling my lips from his, I rest my head on his pillow and stare into his eyes. When we're like this, it's as if I exist in his mind as much as I exist in my own. But for so long, we could never truly speak to each other. So much of our relationship until now has been in letters and in sex. There are so many things I want to express and understand about him. Layers of Jack St. Claire I'd like to peel back to get to the real man underneath.

I know his heart already, but I want to know his mind too.

He strokes my cheek as I work up the nerve to speak. If I ask too much, will he push me away? He's done it before. When we first met, he was a frozen block of ice, but now that he's thawing, will he let me truly see him?

"Can I ask you something?" I whisper.

His brow furrows. "Of course."

"Why did you hire me?"

He turns to face me, sliding an arm under my head. We're so close, we're breathing the same air. Our naked bodies are entangled, and there's not an inch of me not touching him.

"It was what you said about loving her like your own," he mumbles. "I don't ever want to replace Beatrice's mother, but I wanted my daughter to be loved like she still had one. After Em died, I couldn't take care of Beatrice. She stayed with Phoenix for six whole months, and it was the worst six months of my life. I want my daughter, but I couldn't be the parent she needed. I was failing as a father, so it was like Bea had no parent at all. I didn't want her to just have a nanny paid to take care of her. I wanted to find someone to truly love her."

"You're not failing as a father," I say, mostly because I hate to see him hurting.

"I was," he replies without hesitation. "I still am, it seems."

I press my hand to his cheek. It's incredible how falling in love with someone means feeling their pain as if it's your own heart breaking.

"You are allowed to fall apart, Jack. You lost the love of your life. It's okay to fall down sometimes."

He winces as he touches my hand. "I know, but I never wanted to get back up."

"Even now?" I ask.

Staring into my eyes, he pulls me closer and grazes his lips against my forehead. "No. Not anymore."

I squeeze my arms around his waist. In a couple of hours, I

will have to leave and pick up Bea from school, but until then, I'm going to savor this moment. It's daylight, and he's holding me. He's admitting things to me that make this relationship between us feel real.

And what could be better than this? Being in love. Feeling so close to someone and almost forgetting what lonely feels like.

Feeling bold and comfortable with Jack now, I whisper, "Will you tell me about her?"

He noticeably tenses. Maybe he finds it strange that I want to hear about his wife, someone he loved probably more than he'll ever love me. But I do want to hear about her. It might seem bleak, but knowing someone he loved means knowing *him* a little more too.

"She was…the softest, kindest person I had ever met," he says. "When I moved to Paris, I wanted a life like my parents had—love, kids, my own happily ever after. And when I met Em, I fell in love with her immediately. She was my sister's dance instructor and the most beautiful woman I had ever met."

Resting my cheek on his shoulder, I smile. Strangely, it warms my heart to hear him say that. To know that Jack has a warm, loving side. I've seen it briefly, but Em had it all the time.

"She made me learn French before we got married," he says with a chuckle.

I sit up and gawk at him. "So you do know it."

When he smiles, there are soft wrinkles around his mouth, and it's so stunning my heart practically stops in my chest. "Yes, I do know it, but I'm very bad at it."

"So why did you never let me speak?" I ask. "Even when I spoke English, you silenced me."

His smile fades and is replaced with an expression of shame. Stroking my jaw, he says, "Because that accent of yours reminded me of her. Hearing your voice in my house brought back too many painful memories. It was like she was still here…but she wasn't."

My brows pinch inward. "Do you still feel like that?"

"No," he replies, shaking his head softly. "You do not remind me of her, Camille. If that's what you're afraid of."

Is it? I don't want to be a replacement, but was I truly afraid that's what I am to Jack?

"Well," I say, resting my chin on his chest. "If you say she was soft and sweet, then I'm quite sure I don't remind you of her. It sounds like we are very different."

He smirks down at me, running his fingers through my hair. "You are soft and sweet too, but yes, you are very different as well."

For what feels like forever, we stare at each other. My heart is so incredibly full and so terrified at the same time. Am I jumping into this too soon? Giving my entire heart to someone is terrifying. What if he breaks it or I'm reading the situation wrong? Or we get into a fight so big we can't recover from it? Life felt so much safer before I knew what it was like to love Jack St. Claire.

Out of nowhere, he softly murmurs, "You are perfect."

It's a compliment meant to make me feel better, but it only makes me feel worse. I can't be perfect, and I certainly can't be held to that standard. Soon, he'll learn all the things I do and say are not perfect, and he'll fall out of love with me.

"I'm not, though," I argue. "I'm not perfect at all. When my father died, my whole world fell apart too. I had plans to leave the town I grew up in. I was supposed to see the world and live a full life, but I shut down the same exact way you did.

"Growing up, most people would say I was too loud or I asked too many questions or I was just…too much. And I *am* too loud. I *do* ask too many questions. Sometimes, I just don't know when to stop, and every person who came into my life left because they couldn't handle me. Even my own mother." My voice quivers with emotion.

"My father was the only person who stuck around. The only

one who loved me for me. And then he died, and I had no one. So I'm not perfect. I don't want you to think I'm someone I'm not, Jack. I have so many flaws."

Tilting his head, his features grow serious. "My God, Camille, is that what you think? You are not too much, not at all. Not for me. I know you have flaws, but you misunderstand me. I adore your imperfections. I love that you are impulsive and headstrong and you speak without thinking first. And I love that you are so curious that sometimes it gets you into trouble. I knew it the minute I walked into the kitchen and found you burning the rice to dance with my daughter. Those flaws are what I adore. When I say you're perfect, I don't mean that perfection defines you. I mean you define perfection."

I can't speak. I can hardly move. In one moment, he silenced all my fears. There's not a coherent thought in my head as I capture his mouth in a kiss and feel his arms wrap around me tightly, like a bird that might fly away if he doesn't hold me down.

"Fuck me again, Jack," I whisper needily against his lips. Pulling back, I stare into his eyes, mine brimming with tears. "Let's pretend that we never lost them and there is no pain or grief. For just a few minutes, let's pretend we can be together."

Without a response, he simply moans against my lips and rolls on top of me, kissing me passionately. His weight settles me and makes me feel grounded to the earth. I wrap my legs around him, eager to feel his hard length inside me.

He sits back on his knees and stares down at my naked body on the bed. Holding his cock in his hand, he strokes it while biting his bottom lip, his eyes feasting on the sight of me.

"Look at you," he says with a low growl. "How can you say you're not perfect?"

"Jack," I whisper, reaching for him.

Leaning over me, he guides his cock between my legs and slowly eases himself inside. Our eyes bore into each other as he enters me. Being filled by him consumes me. Knowing how much he treasures me while using my body at the same time is like nothing else I've felt before.

He turns his gaze down to the spot where we are joined. I watch as his brow furrows with arousal.

"Look at how well you take me, little bird."

I let out a loud moan, pinching my own nipples as he moves in languid strokes, in and out. Something about the way he speaks to me during sex sends me over the edge.

"Turn over," he murmurs in a command.

Pulling out long enough to turn me onto my knees, he thrusts himself back in, this time with enough force to make me cry out.

He moves with purpose now, pounding in so hard I have to grip the sheets. I'm a whimpering, moaning mess with my cheek pressed against the mattress.

The cum from the sex we just had provides lubricant, making me so wet for him, and it all feels so filthy and so beautiful at the same time. Everything Jack and I share is made of pleasure. The way he talks to me, touches me, looks at me. It's nothing like the cruel man I once knew.

"I want to fill you up, little bird," he proclaims through grunts. "I want you full of my seed. Can I do that?"

I'm so close to the edge, and to my surprise, his words have me screaming with arousal so intense, I nearly come already. I know it's just dirty talk. It must be.

But the idea of being bred by him is suddenly so sexy I don't want it to stop.

"Yes," I scream into the mattress as he fucks me harder. "Keep going. More."

"You like that, don't you?" he asks with a punishing grip on my hips. "You like the idea of me fucking a baby into you."

"Yes!" I shout.

"The thought of your swollen belly makes me so fucking feral for you." Then he slams in again, hitting a spot inside me that has my toes curling and my body spasming. "You feel that, little bird? You feel how hard that makes me?"

"I'm coming," I cry out, shoving my hips back toward him as I reach down between my legs and pinch my clit to ride out the pleasure.

"I feel it," he groans. "Your pussy is so tight when you come."

My legs are trembling, and I can hardly breathe.

"I'm right behind you, baby." The next thing I know, he's shuddering and groaning so we're both filling the room with the sounds of our pleasure.

And then it's quiet. The only sound is our panting breaths.

All too soon, the fantasy is over, and I know he wants to return to reality—where Jack can't talk about us and our future and the possibility of a child.

As he eventually pulls out, the excess cum drips warmly down my thighs. I don't wipe it away or move to clean it up. I just collapse onto the mattress, and he moves to land beside me.

When he drags me onto his chest again, I listen to the cadence of his heartbeat and try to savor the perfection of this moment. And then my eyes open, and I stare at his left hand as it grips mine.

My heart soars as I realize he's no longer wearing his ring.

Rule #36: It could work.

Jack

I WALK HOME FROM THE CLUB AROUND 6:30, FEELING LIGHTER than I did when I went to work this morning. It's like that conversation with Camille today lifted something from my chest that I had been carrying for so long.

When was the last time I spoke about Em with anyone? What was I so afraid of? Talking about her gave me peace I didn't expect.

Talking about a future with Camille gave me even more.

The future has been this elusive harbinger of sorrow for so long. It's as bad as the past, really. Both hurt. The reminder of what I had lost and the idea of living longer without it both ache in ways I never understood.

But with Camille, for the first time, talking about the future didn't hurt or scare me. Camille and I could be happy together. I truly believe that. We could make this work.

But am I rushing into this? Am I running from Em's death directly into the arms of another woman? Is that fair to either of them?

As I reach the apartment, I hear music playing inside. With a smile, I unlock the door and walk in to find Camille and Bea dancing and singing in the kitchen again. There is something cooking in the oven—not burning, thank God—and my daughter is twirling around the room while Camille holds her hand to steady her.

When they see me, they don't freeze in terror like they had before. Instead, Bea grins wildly, running up to me and taking my hands.

"Dance, Papa!" she squeals.

It's a fast-paced French pop song. Gripping Bea's small hands in mine, I twirl her around the room. "Turn it up," I say to Camille, who's biting her bottom lip as she admires us.

Bea shrieks with laughter as I spin her. Her joy is infectious. It seeps into my pores like medicine, curing ailments I didn't even know I had. I just know I feel better when I hear it.

When the song ends, I hoist my daughter off the floor and hug her to me, kissing her on the cheek as she wraps her arms tightly around my neck.

A timer beeps, and Camille turns away to pull a casserole dish that smells and looks like lasagna out of the oven. As she places it on the trivet in the middle of the kitchen island, our eyes meet.

Everything we did and spoke about today hovers between us. My heart lurches in my chest, overwhelmed with this feeling I have for her. It's more powerful than I remember falling in love to feel like.

I want to be around her *all* the time. I want to own her while also being owned by her. I want her to exist in every future iteration of my life.

The thought of her pain or fear haunts me in ways that make me feel like a caveman, and the need to protect her takes over.

I'm sure this is love.

And if I'm doubting myself, it's only because this doesn't feel like it did with Em. But if it's not love, then what is it?

When I spot a familiar card on the counter, I carry Bea over and pick it up.

"Is this my mother's recipe? Where did you get it?" I ask.

Camille grins sheepishly. "I found it. I hope you don't mind. Bea told me it was your favorite."

"It is my favorite," I reply softly. The aroma of Jade's lasagna suddenly makes me homesick, which is lovely but also a cruel reminder that I'm supposed to be leaving soon. But how could I?

I haven't told Camille about my plans to move back to California, and I think in my heart, I set those plans aside when I met her.

This nostalgic reminder filling my kitchen is making me want to revisit that plan. I still want to go back to America. I want to take my daughter back so she can grow up around my family.

Would Camille go with us? Or am I putting an end to this before it's even started?

As we set the table together, it's as if I'm being ripped in two. Bea chatters on excitedly without leaving a moment for either Camille or me to talk. She tells me about her day at school and what she learned. When we finally sit down and start to dig in, I stare across the table at Camille. Each of us has a subtle smile on our face, and I wonder if she's thinking the same thing I am.

This could work.

"You mentioned your parents are still married then," she says when Bea finally stops talking long enough to eat.

I dab at my mouth with a napkin as I formulate my response. Speaking about my unique family is something I'm used to, but it still takes consideration.

"My parents are still married," I say with a nod. She keeps her eyes on me as she waits for me to elaborate. "My mom and my dad...and my other mom."

Bea kicks her feet under the table, smiling up at me. It's nothing out of the ordinary for her now.

As for Camille, she's frozen in place with her fork halfway to her mouth.

"Papa has two mommies and a daddy," Bea says sweetly.

"Oh," Camille replies. She puts the bite in her mouth and chews with a contemplative look on her face.

More than anything, she's probably shocked that a guy who grew up in a home that exemplified love and acceptance struggles with it so much. I'm sure in her imagination, I wasn't raised in a home with six people who loved each other unconditionally but rather molded in some emotionless factory where I was taught three expressions—brooding, grumpy, and annoyed.

I wouldn't blame her if she did.

As we eat, I share the story with Camille about how my single mother fell in love with not one but two people. How they made it work because they loved each other, even when the days were hard or my sisters and I faced mockery in school because our family looked different.

"That's really beautiful," she says softly while looking at me.

"It is."

Her immediate acceptance makes my heart hammer loudly in my chest as if it's demanding attention. It wants me to acknowledge how perfect she is, as if I don't already notice.

The three of us wash up the dishes after dinner together. The music is playing again, but not as loudly. Bea dries the utensils in her tiny hands as I dry the larger dishes.

It's a priceless moment, frozen in time, and everything feels perfect, *too* perfect. I remember the last time things felt this good. The first year of marriage with Em. She found out she was pregnant. We were over the moon. Everything was perfect, and nothing could bring us down.

Until a blood test came back with frightening results. A happy pregnancy turned into a terrifying one. Even after Bea was born and our world felt so much larger and more beautiful, my wife had to undergo harsh chemo treatments that never worked as hard as the cancer did.

Nothing felt perfect again.

"Papa, will you tuck me in tonight?" Bea asks as she clings to my leg, stealing me from the hurtful memories.

I glance up at Camille, who is still scrubbing the casserole dish. She freezes as she watches me, and I know that in her mind, she's silently praying that I say the right thing.

I love that my daughter is her first priority.

"Of course I will," I say, softly stroking my daughter's head. "I would love to."

Draping my towel on the counter, I glance back at Camille before taking Bea's hand and letting her guide me toward her bedroom.

Bea skips to the dresser against the wall, pulling open the top drawer and standing on her tiptoes to retrieve her pink satin pajamas. "Let me help," I say as I pull them out for her.

"Thanks, Papa," she says. Kneeling on the floor, I help her into her pajamas, marveling at the cute freckles on her cheeks as I button her shirt. She's being extra sweet to me tonight because having me in her room and helping her like a real parent is a novelty to her. And as much as I love that, I should be here for all the fits and tears too. I should be here for everything.

"Can we read Maman's book tonight?" she whispers once her pajamas are on.

"Of course," I reply without question, although I don't know which book she's referring to. "We can read whatever you'd like."

She hops excitedly into her bathroom, and I watch her brush her teeth, shaking her little hips as she moves the brush back and forth in her mouth. Once she's done, she runs back into her room and picks out the old French copy of *Madeline* that was once Em's as a child.

I swallow the pins and needles building in my throat and paste a smile on my face.

"Papa's not good at French," I say with an apologetic look.

"Yes, you are!" she squeals innocently.

These tiny moments feel enormous. Missing out on two years

of this is tragic. But as I take the book from my daughter's hand and settle into her tiny bed beside her, I remind myself that I don't have to miss them anymore.

Bea cuddles into my side, and I drape an arm over her pillow. My heart practically expands out of my chest as I press my lips to the top of her head.

Then I struggle through the book with my terrible French. When I mispronounce a word, she quickly corrects me. She giggles when I say a few words *very* wrong, but she never scolds me. It's adorably wholesome, and it reminds me so much of her mother. She is filled with so much kindness; it's written in her DNA.

While I read, I remember the day she was born. The way it felt the first time I saw her. Lying in her mother's arms, she stared up at Emmaline through squinting eyes. My heart became a stranger to me that day as it leapt out of my chest and attached itself to her.

Bea was a beacon of light in a dark storm. When everything felt weighed down by doom and fear, she brought hope and love into our lives.

And maybe that's why I kept my distance once Em died. I didn't want to dim Bea's light.

As the book comes to an end, I rest my chin on her head and hug her close. She makes me feel more alive, and for the first time in two years, I let myself revel in just how much I love her.

I am her father, and it's about time I start acting like it again. Before her life passes by and her childhood memories are full of a sadder version of me.

Bea is already asleep, snoring quietly, nestled into my side. I lie with her for a while before I notice Camille step into the doorframe. She watches us with affection as I quietly slide out from under Bea. I curl the blanket around her so she's cozy and warm, and then I tiptoe out of her room.

Meeting Camille in the hallway, I forget what roles we are

supposed to be playing. Is she my nanny? My sub? My girlfriend? Do these even matter?

Taking her face in my hands, I pull her lips to mine and kiss her softly. She leans into me, holding my arms for support.

"It could be like this," I mumble softly before I kiss her again. "This could work."

She hesitates.

"What's wrong?" I ask.

"Nothing," she lies. "I just...I want this just as much as you do, but I'm scared."

"What is there to be scared of?" My head tilts as I move my hands to hers. Tugging her with me up the stairs, I don't take her to the bondage room tonight. I want her in my bed instead.

She doesn't protest as I slip her shirt over her head and kiss a line down her jaw and the side of her neck.

I know what she's referring to, but I'm ignoring the warning signs. We're moving too fast. I'm still processing so much grief. My daughter and Camille's job are on the line.

Instead of facing those, I pull her into my bed and lie on the pillow with her straddling my hips. I stare into her eyes as she rides my cock, and I let this pleasure we both feel when we're together drown out the rest of the noise.

What I said earlier still rings with truth—this could work.

For now, I'll cling to that possibility. Everything else will be waiting for us tomorrow.

Rule #37: You are not a nobody.

Camille

My hands are shaking as I dab concealer on my face. Behind me, my dark green dress hangs on the back of the door. The babysitter we hired to watch Bea tonight should be here in about an hour. She's a friend of Elizabeth's who has known Bea since she was born, but I'm still a ball of anxiety over the thought of leaving her.

None of this feels right.

Jack is taking me to the grand reopening of his club tonight. Not as a nanny or as an employee but as his date. Or his sub. Or his…girlfriend? I'm not quite sure.

The past few weeks have been a dream. I sleep in his bed every night. We've had more sex in the past two weeks than I've had in my entire life. The connection between us feels larger than life, and I know deep in my heart that this is love.

I love him.

It surprised me so much that the man who was once cold and emotionless was hiding someone so warm and loving, but now that I have this glimpse of him, I don't think I could ever let him go.

But there's something nagging at me. I'm unable to surrender to this happiness with him, and I can't tell if I'm just being cautious or paranoid. Is it the letter hiding in my desk drawer? Is it the fear that Bea could be caught in the cross fire? Is it the fear that I'm merely a replacement for Emmaline?

Is it all these things?

I hear his footsteps down the hall as I try to put on my mascara. My shaky hands cause me to smear it all over my brow line. With a huff of frustration, I toss it down on the counter and reach for the tissues to clean it up.

He steps into the bathroom, looking far too handsome in his black pants and a tight black dress shirt. I love the way his broad shoulders fill out the shirt and how the dark colors in his clothes make the green in his eyes burn brighter.

"What's wrong?" he asks softly as he crowds me against the counter.

"Nothing," I mutter in frustration. "I'm just nervous, that's all."

"Nervous for what?" he asks, setting his hand gently on my shoulder.

I let my hands drop as I glare at him in the mirror, my head tilted to the side. "You have no idea how nerve-racking this is for me. I know it's your club opening, but you are the owner, and everyone will be looking at you. And you're bringing *me*. A nobody. A plain woman who works for you. An outsider."

Taking me by the shoulders, he spins me toward him. "Stop it."

"I'm serious, Jack," I cry.

"I can see that you're serious," he replies, taking the tissue from my hand. "Take a deep breath, little bird."

I force air into my lungs, but my chest feels tight, and my body won't relax.

Silently, he uses the tissue to carefully wipe my brow clean. I'm staring into his eyes as he works. There's something so delicate and hypnotic about it that my shoulders gently melt.

"You are not a nobody," he says quietly.

"Yes, I am, Jack," I reply.

He balls up the tissue and tosses it in the trash. Ignoring my argument, he picks up the mascara and unscrews the top.

"Hold still," he says. Then with steady hands and a relaxed expression, he applies the mascara to my right eye. I can hardly move. There's something so cool and confident about the way he does this, as if he owns me. As if I'm just a thing for him to dress up and play with.

And oddly…it calms me.

"Look up," he commands, and I obey.

Crowding so close to me that I can feel his breath on my face, he flicks the brush against my lashes. Then his eyes meet mine, and he seems so stern, almost like he's mad at me.

"You are not nobody," he says again, this time with more conviction. "You are Camille Aubert. You are the headstrong, brilliant, compassionate woman I hired. You are *mine*. Do you understand why?"

My head barely moves back and forth as I shake it. Before answering, he reaches down to the counter and picks up a dark shade of pink lipstick. He pulls off the cap and twists it. Then he takes my jaw in a firm grip, which I take to mean that he's serious.

I stare at his eyes with rapt attention as he leans in and draws the lipstick across my lower lip.

"I chose you because you are perfect in every way. You are perfect *to me*. You are everything I have ever wanted and will ever want, and I chose you as my date tonight because as long as you are in the room, I see no one else. Understand?"

I can hardly move. Tears prick behind my eyes, stinging as I fight off the urge to cry. I know he means this in the kinkiest way, but now I know he feels this way romantically too.

The idea that I mean this much to anyone is overwhelming. I want to mean the world to Jack. I want to mean what Emmaline meant to him, and I know that's wrong of me, but I do.

His grip tightens. "Tell me you understand."

I force myself to swallow. "I understand," I whisper.

"Good girl," he says, and the warmth of that phrase slides down my spine like honey.

He finishes my lipstick, applying it to the top lip. Once it's done, he stares down at my mouth with a mischievous look.

"I'd like to see this color smeared across my cock."

My belly ignites with heat at his filthy words. Rubbing my lips together, I fight a smirk as I reply, "I think that can be arranged."

With a dashing smile, he presses his lips to my neck, inhaling my scent. I expect him to pull away, but he doesn't. Instead, he softly states, "Tonight, I want to show you off."

"Well, it's a good thing you did my makeup then," I reply with a laugh.

He pulls away. "No, I mean on stage."

My eyes widen as every muscle in my body tenses. "What?"

"Just a simple suspension. You do it all the time."

I swallow. Sure, I've done a demonstration at the club, but never a suspension before. There's a difference. Suspensions require more focus and strength.

"If you don't want to, I understand." He leans and whispers in my ear. "But I think you owe it to yourself to prove that you're not a nobody."

As he pulls away, I narrow my eyes at him. "That wasn't fair."

He chuckles, leaving the bathroom. I fight back a smile at hearing his laughter as I quickly clean up my makeup, chucking the items in the makeup bag.

I know he's right. I belong in that club as much as the next person, and with as many suspension positions as we've been trying lately, I know we could do it. And honestly, why not?

* * *

"I'm excited for you to see it," Jack says from the back seat of the car. He squeezes my leg gently before intertwining our fingers and pulling me to him for a kiss.

"I have seen it," I reply.

"No, I mean...done. In action," he says. Tonight, he looks like a man on top of the world. In that black-on-black suit with a gold watch band on his wrist and expensive cuff links, he appears almost godly.

And he's mine.

Don't get ahead of yourself, Camille.

There are a lot of hurdles to jump before I can start saying things like that.

As we turn the corner onto the club's street, I notice the line of limos and black cars parked along the side. Attendants in white valet uniforms open the doors, and well-dressed men and women climb out of each car, walking up to the entrance of the club.

It's nothing like the mess of people I found out here the first time I came, partiers drunk in the street.

Jack eyes the building appraisingly as we pull up. Someone opens the door for Jack first, and he steps out before coming to my side and opening mine for me. I take his hand as he leads me onto the pavement as if I'm suddenly the celebrity here.

There are no cameras or crowds. It's all very discreet yet classy.

"Bonsoir, Monsieur St. Claire," the man says as he pulls open the door of the club for us.

"Bonsoir," he replies politely.

My arm is linked through Jack's, and before we go in, his eyes rake up and down my body. I wait for him to take the lead and walk through the doors, but he hesitates, staring at me instead.

"I forgot to tell you how beautiful you look in that dress," he says so kindly it takes my breath away.

"Thank you," I whisper, unable to move as the warmth of his compliment covers me like a cozy blanket. It's not just that he thinks I'm beautiful or wants me to know how much he admires me, it's that Jack truly sees me. He treasures me. With him, I no longer feel alone.

What has happened to the man I first met? Am I naive to

assume I've somehow changed him? Is it foolish of me to hope that he stays this way forever?

"Shall we?" he asks, and I silently nod.

Then he leads me inside.

Rule #38: It was never about sex.

Camille

THE CLUB IS NOTHING LIKE IT WAS BEFORE. THERE'S A HEAVY BEAT of music overhead that's slow and sultry, giving the place a sense of rich opulence.

As Jack moves through the club with me on his arm, I scan my surroundings, just trying to take it all in. It's odd how much it feels like I don't belong here, and yet the club feels like a warm hug.

The staff is kind, smiling at me as they welcome me in and hand me a glass of champagne. The scent in the room is floral, like fresh linens covered in roses. And there are no dark, ominous corners that would make someone feel vulnerable. Everything is open, giving this floor of the club a friendly vibe.

"What do you think?" he murmurs next to me.

I turn toward him with my lips pressed together in a tight smile. "Jack, it's perfect."

A gray-haired man approaches us with a beaming smile. "Jack!" he calls as he puts a hand out for him.

Jack releases my arm and shakes the man's hand with apprehension. "Matis," he replies nervously.

"You did it," the man celebrates. "Look at this place!"

"It's too soon to call it a success. Let's see how our first quarter numbers look," Jack answers with a wrinkle between his brows.

The man scoffs loudly before putting an arm around Jack's shoulders. "Stop worrying about the numbers and look around. People are here. They look happy and comfortable. That's all you need to worry about. Fuck the data, Jack. This is how you tell your club is a success."

Jack doesn't look convinced, but he tries to at least nod for the man.

Matis notices me standing at Jack's side. With a charming grin, he quickly releases him and puts out a hand for me to take.

"My goodness. Who is this angel?" he asks as he lifts my hand to his lips.

I can barely make out Jack's low, growling hum as he tugs me against his side. "Matis, this is Camille Aubert, my date."

Matis notices immediately, releasing my hand with a wolfish smile and a wink before stepping away. "Message received."

I can't help but smile because the man is just so dashing. I would guess he's in his mid-fifties, but I certainly wouldn't kick him out of bed. He's incredibly handsome with salt-and-pepper hair and wrinkles around his wide smile carved into his bronze skin.

"Camille, this is Matis Moreau. He owned this club for thirty years before passing it down to us," Jack says as he holds me with a possessive grip on my waist.

"I have known Jack since he was a boy," Matis says jovially as he shakes Jack's shoulder.

I glance up at Jack and notice the blush on his cheeks. "How are things downstairs?" he asks to change the subject.

"Go see for yourself," Matis replies, gesturing toward the elevator. "You might recognize a few special guests."

Jack narrows his eyes at the man before pulling me toward the elevators. We leave Matis behind as we make our way to the lower level. I can tell that Jack is nervous as the doors close, shutting us inside alone. As it moves, I turn toward him and stroke his cheek.

When our eyes meet, his features soften, and I notice him visibly relax. "I'm proud of you," I whisper, but the words are barely out of my mouth before he pulls me into his arms.

"Stop it," he says. Then he kisses me, holding me tightly against his body.

"Stop what?" I ask.

"Being so—"

The doors of the elevator open, and we both peer out into the sex club. The ambience down here is far more erotic. The soft, neon lights are dimmer, the music louder.

There are more people down here too, but the conversation is quiet. Jack takes my hand this time, intertwining our fingers as he pulls me through the club. The first familiar face I see is Elizabeth's. She's standing by the bar, and she is the picture of grace and beauty. Her dark brown hair cascades down her back, and she's wearing a black dress fitted to her body with a slit up the thigh that nearly reaches her hipbone.

She's the sexiest person I've ever laid eyes on, and it's alarming to see her in this light.

As she takes in the sight of Jack and me together, her gaze drifts down to our linked hands and then up to our faces. She doesn't say anything right away; she just waits for her brother to speak.

Across from her is a beautiful blond woman I haven't met yet, but she smiles brightly at me with piercing dimples in her cheeks and bright blue eyes.

"Hi, I'm Amelia," she says in a greeting, putting out her hand for me.

"It's nice to meet you," I reply, shaking it. "I'm Camille."

"What a pleasant surprise," Elizabeth says as she takes a sip of her champagne with a crooked smirk against the rim of her glass. "It's about time you listened to me, Jack."

"Elizabeth," Jack says in a warning.

I glance back and forth between the two, confused as to what they're referring to.

His sister replies with a sigh. "I have to go check on the dancers," she says before marching away.

None of us say anything as we're left in awkward silence. I stare at the stage to avoid anyone's eye contact. There's a single dancer performing on a hoop hanging from the ceiling. She's dressed in nothing but a glittery black thong. Her movements are graceful and sexy as she glides to the music.

"Everything is beautiful, Amelia," Jack says to the woman. "You should be very proud."

She shrugs with a bashful grin. "Thanks, Jack."

When he places a hand on her shoulder, he does it with brotherly affection, and I can see by the look in his eyes that he cares about her. In fact, I see now just how much Jack cares about all of them, except for Julian of course. But I see the way he greets them all as if they are his family. I wonder if he knows how lucky he is to have them all.

I spot a pair of mischievous eyes across the club, staring back at me, and I recognize them as Julian's. Clutching tighter to Jack's side, I stare back at the man as I take a sip of my bubbly. This only makes him laugh, but he's in the middle of a conversation with a couple, so he doesn't bother coming closer to us.

"Is that who I think it is?" Jack asks, nodding his head toward the couple Julian is speaking to.

Amelia turns and nods. "Yep. They've been looking for you."

This makes Jack tense. His spine straightens as he adjusts his tie.

"Believe it or not, but Julian has been on his best behavior all night," Amelia adds.

"I choose to believe not," Jack replies before polishing off his drink. "Where's Phoenix?"

"Running around and stressing about something, I'm sure,"

Amelia adds. "She wants the six of us to make a statement. Probably in about twenty minutes."

"So I should get this part over with then?" Jack asks, glancing in her direction.

"What are you so afraid of? Go talk to them. They'll be happy to see you," she replies, making me curious as to who the mystery couple talking to Julian could be.

Jack's hand touches the small of my back as he leads me by his side through the club. There are people mingling in couples and small groups all around us, and I understand that this is opening night so people are not behaving in here like they normally would.

For one, no one is having sex on the dance floor.

As we approach Julian and the couple, he gives me a quick wink before glaring at Jack, who holds me close to his side.

"Well, there's the man we've been looking for." An older man with graying hair and a handsome smile puts a hand on Jack's shoulder.

"Emerson," Jack says as he greets him. "I'm so honored that you came."

The woman puts her hands out to hug Jack. "We wouldn't miss it for the world." She's a stunning woman, I would guess in her mid-forties, with long, thick brown hair and a kind smile. Something about her looks down-to-earth and relatable, like she might feel as out of her element here as I do.

After the hug, Jack turns toward me. "Camille, this is Emerson and Charlotte Grant. They own the greatest kink club in the United States."

My jaw drops. I've listened to Jack talk about them and their famous club for weeks. While I don't know much about what they've done, I do know the impact they've had on him. This is the man Jack looks up to. The one he has tried to emulate.

"It's nice to meet you," I say to both of them.

I can't take my eyes off the man. He has an air of confidence about him that makes it hard to look away. And the woman stands at his side, looking up at him with adoration.

Immediately, I wonder if Jack and I will look like that someday. Is it silly to want that already? Probably, but I can't help it. I want to watch him age, growing more handsome with time like I assume this man has.

"Your mother sends her love," Emerson says to Jack.

"She didn't want to intrude on your big day," Charlotte adds with a soft smile.

"No one wants their mom at their sex club," Julian jokes as he takes a sip of wine.

I laugh, but Jack doesn't. He only glares sideways at his business partner.

"I'm glad you two are here," he says to the couple. "Truly, I'm honored. It means the world that you came all this way."

I can see how much he admires them and how nervous he is. I wish I could make him see how perfect this place is and how proud he should be.

"You two have done a phenomenal job here," Emerson says to Jack and Julian. "But your work has just begun. You took a hard year and you learned from it, but the learning curve isn't over yet. If you both decide to fully commit to this club, you'll learn a lot more over the years. Remember, you'll have to do more listening than talking. To each other and to your team. Owning a club isn't about sex. It never was. It's about people. Don't ever forget that."

"Thank you," Julian and Jack reply humbly, one after the other.

It's obvious how much they both look up to this man. Hell, even I'm feeling inspired, and I don't own a club at all.

After they say their goodbyes, Emerson and Charlotte leave our small group. I'm alone with Jack and Julian, and I can feel the tension between them like a thick fog.

"Phoenix wants us to make a speech," Jack says.

"You lead," Julian replies gruffly.

THE GOOD GIRL EFFECT 295

"It's up to both of us, Jules."

The other man glances up at Jack as if the use of his nickname triggered some emotional reaction. "Okay. I'll round everyone up then." With that, he leaves, weaving through the crowd.

Alone with Jack, I stroke a hand down his arm. His eyes meet mine, but I don't say anything to him. I don't have to. With just my eyes, I can convey enough, offering him comfort so at least he doesn't feel alone. And when I see the flicker of a smile on his lips, I know he can feel it.

As the rest of the owners are wrangled up to the front of the club, they take the stage together. I hang back and watch Jack so he can find me in the crowd when he needs me. Even before it starts, he does. It makes me feel useful, knowing I mean something to him. Knowing he feels what I feel, even when he's surrounded by hundreds of people.

Once everyone is quiet, Jack starts.

"We'd like to thank you all for coming to our grand reopening," he says proudly. Before continuing, he glances down at the other people standing on stage with him: Julian, Amelia, Phoenix, Weston, and Elizabeth. "I fear that when the six of us first opened this club, we did so by trying to recreate something that was already perfect. We tried to emulate something our parents created."

Julian's head turns, staring at Jack with something like affinity in his eyes.

"The club we created was great," Jack says, this time looking at the man beside him. "But it wasn't ours, not really." This time, as he looks at the crowd, he clears his throat. "And it's made me realize that maybe something can be perfect but not right. Maybe by trying to recreate something perfect for someone else, we made something wrong for us."

The people on stage with him nod, wearing expressions of confidence.

"But when I pulled these five people in and I encouraged them to really put their hearts into this club, what they created was…magic. Amelia, with this stunning design, brings something youthful and welcoming to the space. Weston, at the bar, has invented cocktail and mocktail creations like nothing you've ever tasted before. Phoenix, with her brilliant business mind, somehow figured out a way for us to even afford this massive overhaul."

The crowd laughs as Phoenix blushes.

"And Elizabeth…" Jack says, holding up his glass. Her throat moves as she swallows, hiding her emotions behind a strong facade. "Elizabeth has turned this stage into a home for real artistry and talent."

Elizabeth turns toward her brother, and I make out her lips silently mouthing the words *thank you* to him.

Last, Jack turns toward Julian. He pauses as they stare at each other, and it's almost hard to believe in this moment that they can't stand each other. In fact…I'm almost starting to believe they can. Jack claps a comforting hand on Julian's shoulder, bringing him close to his side.

"And of course, my partner, Julian Kade. It only took one bottle of whiskey and a stern lecture from Matis to make us understand what needed to be done. A man who doesn't have to work but chooses to work his ass off for what he believes in is a man of great character. And I'm lucky to have him as my partner."

The room is so quiet we could hear a pin drop, but no one can tear their eyes away from the team on the stage, specifically the two men staring at each other. It's hard to tell if they want to hug each other or punch each other, but it's clear there's a lot happening in that loaded gaze.

Finally, Jack turns toward the crowd, lifting his glass again.

"To Legacy," he calls out. The crowd echoes the toast loudly before breaking out in cheers.

"Now, let's party!" Weston bellows charismatically, riling up the people. Instantly, the music starts playing again, and the dance floor fills up.

There's a light in Jack's eyes as he finds me in the crowd.

I smile, knowing that once he finishes with the party, he'll have me in those ropes again. He can lose himself in the work of tying them, and I'll get lost in the nearness of him.

I'm hovering near the bar as Jack bounces from member to member, chatting with them and welcoming them to Legacy. Sipping my champagne, I watch him with pride.

He looks in his element, even if he doesn't believe it. The grumpy, elusive man I met who hated everyone turned out to be a people person after all.

"I'd call it a success, wouldn't you?"

I turn to see Julian standing nearby with a glass of something amber in his hands and mischief in his eyes. Turning away from him, I reply, "Yes, I would call it a success."

"I think you had a hand in it," he says, and I do everything I can not to spin back to face him again.

"Me? Why?"

"Well…someone had to be responsible for thawing that cold block of ice. Without you, he would have never walked into my office four weeks ago and proposed we make these changes." He sidles up beside me, but I still refuse to look him in the eye.

Julian has a manipulative side, and I don't trust him. After that day in the club where he got me in trouble by strapping me to that wall, I refuse to put an ounce of faith in this man.

"Jack is responsible for Jack's behavior," I say plainly.

"Ah yes," he murmurs close to my ear. "And who is responsible for Jack's good moods?"

I press my lips together to ignore him. But I can't help feeling an ounce of pride that it might have been me, or rather the relationship between *us*, that helped turn things around for Jack. He has changed a lot in the past six weeks. So maybe I did play a small part…

"It's a shame he's leaving."

Julian's words settle slowly in my ears before I process them. *It's a shame who's leaving?*

Eventually, I turn toward him. "What are you talking about?"

His brow furrows as he leans toward me with forced concern. "You didn't know?"

"Know what?"

"Jack has been telling us for the last year that he was only going to stay in Paris until the club reached its one-year anniversary, and then he's taking his daughter and moving back to California to be with his family. I thought you knew that."

I stare at Julian's face, watching it morph from a performance of pity to sly deceit. He's telling me this to taunt me, maybe even ruin our relationship. Why? I don't know. Jealousy, resentment, cruelty. After seeing him and Jack onstage, I thought they had mended things, but now I see that Julian likes to meddle and disrupt the peace just for the fun of it.

For these reasons, I try not to let it bother me. Jack would have told me this already. Our relationship hasn't been serious until recently. If he had plans to move to America, he would have shared them by now.

Wouldn't he?

I can't deny that it all makes sense. Jack's loyalty to this club has been half-hearted. I could always tell there was a sense of urgency in his behavior as if he just needed to get through the next month or week and then everything would be different.

But surely he can't be thinking about moving away *now*. Bea is so happy now.

Everyone is so happy now.

Just then, Jack looks up and finds me. I notice the hint of hesitation on his face, and I imagine him hiding something from me. Maybe Julian was right. Maybe Jack is still planning to leave, and he just needs to find a way to break it to me.

Rule #39: There must always be trust.

Jack

I CAN FEEL CAMILLE'S SKEPTICISM AS I FINISH OFF HER ARMS-forward harness. With her fists together under her chin, she's taken on that calm, serene expression she always does when I'm binding her.

Even so, I can tell she wants to say something. Likely, she wants to ask me how I'm feeling. Maybe I still seem tense. Fuck, I am still tense.

Tonight wasn't just about the club. I'm proud of how the grand reopening went. Even after everyone we knew left and the patrons began to play, I could feel a sense of pride for what we've created.

But it's about so much more than that. It's about tying up loose ends here in Paris.

Ironically, that's exactly what I'm doing now with Camille. Finding the friction center of her harness, I wind the long synthetic rope through and slip it through the hoop above her head.

As I make eye contact with her, I ask, "Are you ready?"

She nods confidently.

With that, I gently pull on the rope until she has to stand on the balls of her feet. I won't suspend her like this yet. I intend to have her hanging upside down in an inversion, but first, I need to finish the harness on her legs.

"Are you feeling okay?" I ask, brushing a strand of hair from her face.

"Yes," she replies. "Are you?"

I give her a look that's partially scolding. "This isn't about me," I whisper.

A small crowd of people have gathered around our station, watching us work, but neither of us pay them any mind. We've kept the back room mostly the same with some upgrades in decor, furniture, and security. But the main purpose of this room is for demonstrations and, well, showing off.

And right now, I'm showing off this beauty.

"It is about both of us," she whispers in return. "And tonight is very much about you."

I lean down to work on the dragon hip harness, wrapping the doubled rope around the soft flesh of her thigh, careful not to pinch her delicate skin.

"Tonight is not about me," I mutter as I work.

Emerson Grant didn't fly all the way from Briar Point, California, just to see me. These people didn't show up tonight to see me. They came to see the club.

And when I leave, which I someday will have to do, the club will be fine without me.

My hands halt as the thought paralyzes me. Leaving Camille feels impossible now, but it can't be. I've just thrown myself into this…relationship…too fast. Just like with Em, I fell too easily.

This isn't like Em, my relentless mind reminds me.

Camille sees into my soul. That's the only way to put it. She has a way of lifting the veil of my mind and crawling inside, but instead of running from the darkness she finds there, she wraps her loving arms around me and thaws everything that froze the day Em died.

In the past weeks, she's changed me.

She brought me back to life. How could I leave her after that?

I get lost inside my own mind as I finish the harness around her hip. Instead of standing up, I lean forward and press my forehead to her hip bone, inhaling her nearness.

"Jack," she whispers.

Snapping out of it, I stand up and walk away. Grabbing another rope from the rack, I do a quick single cuff around her other thigh, but I can feel her watching me with concern. Ignoring it, I loop the second rope through the suspension loop.

As I gently pull on it, her left leg raises so she's left standing on her right foot. She's not worried about her safety; that I can tell by the look on her face. She's concerned for *me*, which is ridiculous.

"I saw the look in that man's eyes," she says. "He was very proud of you, and I think you should be proud too."

Ignoring her, I lock off the rope on her left leg so she's secure. Then I double-check everything to be sure she's safe.

"Jack," she insists. "Look at me."

When my eyes find hers, she sees through everything. If she could move, I know what she'd do. She'd touch my face and pull my mouth to hers for a kiss. She'd burrow herself in my arms and warm the center of my chest like a glowing fire.

"Are you anxious about the club?" she asks. "Or are you anxious about me?"

What a time to have this conversation. There are people watching us just a few feet away. She's about to be hanging upside down, and now is really not the time to be having a relationship talk.

"Do you regret bringing me?" she asks.

At that, my brows fold inward. I take her face in my hands and softly kiss her forehead. "Not even a little bit."

"Then what is it?" she pleads.

Pressing our foreheads together, I stare into her eyes, and it becomes abundantly clear what all this is about—*trust*. Camille trusts that I won't hurt her or that I won't let her get hurt. And it's not just about ropes and knots and hitches.

"I have to tell you something," I say softly.

Her eyes grow soft as if she's preparing herself for the worst. And I know I should just come out with it. I owe her the truth. After all the trust she's put in me, the least I can do for her is give her everything she's given me—loyalty and faith.

But when I open my mouth, the most true and honest thing I have comes slipping out.

"I love you."

I feel like a coward as her eyes water, and she stares at me as if she's waiting for the real truth.

But that is the truth. I do love her. With my entire heart and probably for longer than I've been able to admit, I have loved her.

For her flaws and quirks and personality, I adore her so intensely it steals my breath and stops my heart. She walked into my life when I was at my worst and gave me everything I didn't deserve: patience and grace.

But I don't just love her for what she's given me; I love her for who she is. Willful and stubborn and funny and curious. From the first moment my ropes touched her skin, I knew I was in trouble.

"I love you too," she whispers. Our faces are so close I'm sure no one around us can see the monumental thing happening between us here, but they don't matter.

I take her mouth in a kiss as she's half-suspended with only one foot on the floor and her arms tied to her chest.

As I pull away, I'm still holding the rope to her right leg in my hands. With a smile, I ask, "Do you trust me?"

She grins in return. "Of course."

I toss the rope through the suspension loop a couple of times to give it strength and stability. Then, using the hoop as a lever, I tug on the rope until Camille's right foot leaves the floor.

Her head falls back as she hangs in a horizontal position. Locking the rope in place so her bent legs are off the floor, I hold a hand behind her neck for support.

"Are you okay?" I ask.

She smiles up at me. "Yes."

"Ready to go upside down?"

She nods.

Reaching up, I give the rope holding her chest harness some slack, and as I do, her upper half lowers until she's inverted. The people standing around us clap quietly, watching Camille with interest.

I double-check each lock-off knot to ensure its security. She can only stay in this position for a minute, so after checking in with her a couple more times, I give the loop a small spin.

Then I step back and admire her from this angle. She looks stunning like this. It's the trust she gives me and the way her body relaxes into the ropes that make her look almost angelic like this. With the single braid in her hair hanging below her head, she closes her eyes as she hovers, slowly rotating midair like the work of art she is. Her cheeks turn dark red as the blood flushes her skin.

I glance around at the people watching, admiring her the way I am. A couple nearby whisper to each other excitedly.

"Do you teach people how to do this?" the woman asks, and I nod.

"We'll offer workshops," I reply, and she grins excitedly, clinging to her partner's arm.

"It's like...art," the man adds as he turns his head sideways, appreciating how stunning she looks.

I nod, watching Camille as she slowly spins in her suspension.

And I realize this is what it's all about. We had it wrong all along. Before tonight, the club lacked a soul. I had no idea what went into bringing this place to life, even when I worked here for years before owning it. Maybe Matis and Ronan tried to explain it to me, but I wasn't listening. I just figured if we kept it open and made money, that was enough.

I assumed it was about sex, money, and pleasure. Even I exploited this club because I was in pain, but in doing so, I missed out on what it's really all about.

A place to belong.

A place to find yourself.

Like Emerson said, it was never about sex. It's about the people.

Camille is resting against my chest on the ride home. For the first time in a long time, I am at ease.

I can't help but wonder if I didn't tell Camille the truth about moving back home because maybe that isn't my truth anymore. I could stay for her. And for the club. That pull to get out of Paris is gone now.

Right now, I only want this.

When we get back to the apartment, I pay the babysitter and see her to the car so she gets home safely. Camille is already up in my room when I get back inside.

I do a quick check on Bea, watching her sleep peacefully in her bed before closing the door and walking upstairs.

Camille is lying on her side, fully naked, on top of my bed. I stand in the doorway and stare at her as I loosen my tie.

"I was looking forward to undressing you," I say as I tear my tie off.

The corner of her mouth lifts in a smirk. "I thought I would save you the trouble."

Rather than go to the bed, I drop into the chair in the corner of the room. Leaning back, my legs spread as I stare at her naked body draped across my bed. Sliding my tie through my fingers, my cock hardens in my slacks. Filthy ideas fill my mind as my arousal builds. Just the sight of her has me practically panting, and I know exactly what I'd like to see.

"Let me see how you touch yourself, little bird."

Her lips part at my command. Camille has such strong-willed confidence, but the moment it comes to sex, she turns bashful, and I find it so fucking adorable. Makes me want to dirty her up that much more.

Her hesitation is brief, and I take that as a testament to the trust we've built. She is safe and comfortable with me. Biting her bottom lip, she spreads her legs only halfway and slides her hand between her thighs. Through hooded lids, I watch her slip her finger through her folds and sink the middle one inside her, letting out a soft mewling sound as she does. It is as stunning as I imagined. She moves with delicate grace, slowly losing her composure as the pleasure takes over. Her fingers move faster, and her chest shudders with each shaking breath.

"Keep going," I say, my grip tightening on the black silk tie in my fingers.

I watch her play with her pretty pussy like she and I have all the time in the world. And maybe we do. It's such a foreign concept to me now, to have so much time with someone and no dark clouds waiting on the horizon.

With her back arched and her legs writhing on the mattress, she pumps her slick fingers in and out. I can both see and hear it, and it has me fidgeting in my seat. I'm imagining it's my cock sinking inside her, and it moistens at the tip at the mere thought.

"I'm ready for you, little bird," I command with a rasp in my tone. "Crawl to me."

As she pulls her hand from between her legs, I see the moisture on her digits.

"But first," I bark, watching her from across the room, "lick them clean."

With arousal in her eyes, she lifts her hand to her mouth and sticks out her tongue. With a moan, she sucks on her middle finger, and it takes everything in me not to march over there right now and fuck her like the animal I am. She does this to me. She makes me wild for her.

"Come here, *now*."

I'm gripping the edges of the chair as she climbs down from the bed. Once she gets to all fours, she keeps her eyes on me as she crawls slowly toward me. She's torturing me because she can.

When she finally meets my feet, I reach down and bury my hand in her hair. Dragging her face up to mine, I kiss her hard. I take ownership of her mouth, my tongue invading and licking every inch of her before biting on her bottom lip to hear her cry out.

"Mine," I growl, making her smile against my lips.

"Mine," she replies just as her hand squeezes my rigid length through my pants.

"It is yours," I say with a smirk. "So take it out and show me how you worship it."

My hand stays in her hair as she unclasps my buckle and pulls down the zipper of my pants. Her movements aren't rushed, but I can feel her excitement as she reaches in and encircles her fingers around my hard shaft.

Without wasting a second, she wraps her soft, wet lips around the head of my cock, kissing it gently. Then she slides the tip of her tongue along the slit at the end, and my hips levitate off the chair.

"Fuck, baby," I growl breathlessly. "Do that again."

Smiling, she lowers her head and kisses the tip again, slipping the tip of her tongue into the slit. My head hangs back as she kneels at the altar of my cock, proving her filthy devotion.

"Good girl," I mumble. "Good fucking girl." My words grow incoherent as she eases her lips down to the base of my cock or at least as far as she can go before she starts to gag. Each time, she works her mouth lower. Feeling the back of her throat, I grip the chair tightly to keep from coming.

My shaft is slick with her saliva as it pools at the base, but she doesn't let up, going lower and lower each time. And when she starts to fondle my sac, I nearly lose my mind.

With a muffled sound, I tear her off and watch as a drop of cum leaks from the tip of my dick.

"That was close," I say, panting.

Holding her arm, I drag her onto my lap until she's straddling me. With her perfect little breasts in my face, I take my time kissing each one. Biting the nipple makes her gasp and purr, so I tease her a while longer.

And when I finally dock myself at her entrance, her cunt and my cock are both soaked. With our eyes on each other, I ease inside her until she's seated as far as she can go.

My body is rigid and still as she steals my mouth with a kiss. Then, with our foreheads pressed together, I guide her hips up and down.

Between each thrust, I mumble incoherently. "So tight, little bird. So perfect."

She hums to keep from screaming, picking up speed to chase her own pleasure.

"We were made for each other, Camille."

Holding me tightly, she stares into my eyes as she moves, pounding her body on my lap harder and faster. I watch her expression change into ecstasy.

Reaching down, I press my thumb to her clit. Her eyes close, and her lips part. Before long, her pussy tightens around my cock.

"That's it," I murmur. "Good girl. Come on my cock."

Her spine curls and her legs squeeze around me as she rides out her orgasm, and I swear it's the most beautiful thing I've ever seen.

I fucking love watching her come.

And like the good girl she is, she keeps up her movement on my lap so that I can chase my own release after her. Watching and feeling her finish sends me over the edge. With a tight grip on her hips, I pound her down on my cock until my own climax takes hold.

Throwing my head back, I spill my cum inside her. Pleasure radiates down my spine, and for a long time, I can hardly breathe. I just feel her, smell her, taste her.

She makes everything better, even my fucking orgasms.

When we're both spent, we collapse together in the chair. She's resting against my chest, no doubt listening to my heart pound inside my rib cage.

For a moment, everything is perfect.

Rule #40: The truth always comes out.

Jack

CAMILLE IS SLEEPING PEACEFULLY ON MY CHEST WHEN I WAKE TO the sound of tiny feet pitter-pattering across the floor downstairs.

"Oh shit." I scramble out of bed and throw my sweats and a T-shirt on. Finger combing my hair to the side as I scurry down the steps, I find my daughter standing at the bottom in pink polka-dot pajamas with a wide-eyed expression on her face.

"Camille is missing!" she cries. Her hair is still tangled from sleep as if she just rolled out of bed and went to her nanny's room first.

I chuckle to myself as I reach the bottom floor. "She's not missing."

"She's not in her room!"

"I know she's not," I reply, ushering my daughter toward the kitchen so I can make her breakfast and me coffee. "She's...erm... upstairs."

"In your room?" Bea asks, looking perplexed.

"Yes. She was...helping me with something. She'll be down in a moment."

"What was she helping you with?" Bea asks as she climbs up on the stool in front of the counter.

I fight a smile as I start to make a pot of coffee, rinsing the carafe in the sink. "Um…" It feels wrong to lie, but it's not like I can tell my six-year-old the truth, especially without talking to Camille about it first.

"She was showing me how to iron my suit," I say.

"This early in the morning?" Bea asks.

As I put coffee beans in the machine, I change the subject so my daughter stops asking so many questions. "Did you have fun with Monique last night?"

"Yes," she replies excitedly. "We watched *A Little Princess* and made cookies and stayed up until ten!"

I smile as I turn toward her. Crossing my arms over my chest, I stare at her.

Today is the first day I can finally accept that this life is perfect just the way it is. Camille and I love each other. Who cares that she was my daughter's nanny? She won't be for long. Starting now, she'll be my girlfriend.

Am I a fool for thinking I can have it all? I know Bea would be ecstatic to have Camille as more than a nanny. And I know Camille is worried about the risks, but there would be risks no matter who I was dating.

And don't the benefits outweigh the risks?

I can see our future so plainly it feels unreal. Every morning, waking up next to her. Spending our weekends together as a family. Raising Bea…and maybe more children. Going to the club at night like we're living double lives.

It's all within reach.

As I make Bea breakfast, it's all I can think about. Camille sleeps peacefully upstairs as I sip my coffee, anxious to tell her how I feel. It's more than just *I love you.*

It's…*I want you forever.*

As Bea watches cartoons and eats her breakfast, I slip out of the room in search of some paper and a pen. It's been a while since Camille and I wrote each other a letter, and I'm desperate to express what I'm feeling in this moment.

Instead of waking Camille, I creep into her room. I want to do this while she's still sleeping. Last time, I found the pen and paper in her desk drawer, so I assume that's where she keeps it.

When I pull open the drawer, I smile down at the collection of letters I've written to her over the past few weeks. I pick them up and reminisce at how far we've come in such a short time. Or rather how far *I've* come.

The letters started filthy, then disciplined, then hopeful, and eventually downright romantic.

As I sift through them, I can hardly believe the transformation I've seen in myself. But then I come to one in the back that catches me by surprise.

It's not a letter I wrote to Camille. It's a letter I wrote to... Emmaline.

I'm frozen in place, staring down at the envelope, remembering the moment I addressed it and stamped it and placed it in a mailbox over seven years ago.

My skin grows hot and my heart hammers wildly in my chest as I reach into the envelope and pull out the letter. Between the folded pages is a photo.

I nearly gasp at the sight of it. Em and I huddled together in front of the Sacré-Cœur just a day before she left Paris. I sent it to her only a week later, begging her to come back, professing my love for her, asking her to marry me. And she said yes.

The love of my life.

I stare at the photo and suddenly feel sick. *What am I doing?*

How could I move on so easily and so soon? How could I do this to her?

My eyes sting as I stare at the photo. Then I flip open the letter as if the answers to my questions will be hiding inside.

But I can't even skim through the words I wrote because my

attention is stolen by a drawing at the bottom in black pen. A style of drawing I've seen over a hundred times in my home over the past two months.

My hands start to shake. Nothing makes sense.

"Jack?" Camille whispers from behind me.

I spin around, holding the letter, photo, and envelope. She glances down at it, and I see the moment fear registers in her expression.

"Where did you get this?" I ask.

Her chest is moving quickly as she stares at the things in my hands. She won't look me in the eye. *Why won't she look me in the eye?*

"I found it," she whispers.

"Found it where? When?" I ask, a familiar rage growing inside me.

Finally, she glances up at my face and into my eyes, but it's not the same. She can't see inside my soul like she normally can. Instead, she starts to cry.

"At a bookstore in Giverny. I was bringing them to you. I was returning them so you had this reminder of her, but…"

My brows furrow. None of this makes any sense. "But what?"

"But…Phoenix thought I was here to apply for the nanny position."

There is remorse in her tone, but it's foreign to me. I can't seem to hear it as I crumple the paper in my hand. She flinches, reaching for the letter like it's somehow more precious to her than it is to me.

"You mean…you *lied*. You took this position. You…took care of my *daughter*, and this whole time…"

She takes a step toward me, reaching for my hands, but I am too blindsided to make sense of any of it. How did I let this happen? I hired someone from off the street to be a nanny for my little girl. Someone who wasn't qualified at all…and for what?

"Were you stalking us?" I ask. When I look at Camille, it's like I don't even know her suddenly.

She drops her hands and straightens her spine. "Of course I was not stalking you," she argues. "It's not my fault you hired someone without any experience. It's true I didn't know I was coming here to apply for a job, but I applied for it anyway," she snaps. "It's not *my* fault you hired me!"

"You're a fraud!" I bellow.

"I never lied about anything!" she shouts.

My daughter appears behind Camille, clutching close to her side. "Stop yelling," Bea murmurs tearfully.

Camille shields her, and I want to reach for my daughter, but for what? To protect her from Camille? The woman who has cared for her and loved her like her own this entire time. It doesn't feel right. None of this feels right.

"Your papa and I are sorry," Camille mumbles, kneeling down to face Bea. "We won't yell anymore, but we need to have a grown-up conversation."

Camille looks over her shoulder at me, and I let out a heated sigh before turning away and running my hands through my hair.

"Now, go watch your cartoons."

"Okay," Bea murmurs sadly before shuffling out to the living room.

The moment she's gone, Camille closes the door so we're alone.

"I am not a fraud," she states quietly.

"You're fired," I grit through my teeth, and my heart bursts in my chest at the way she puts a brave face on. Without showing an ounce of weakness, she holds her chin high as it trembles. I wish I could say the same. Just uttering those words makes my legs shake and my heart shatter.

"Fine, but I am not a fraud. And I didn't lie."

"Why didn't you tell me?" I implore her.

"When could I have told you, Jack? You wouldn't let me speak! You silenced me every chance you had. And what about you?" she whisper-shouts.

"What about me?" I ask.

"When were *you* going to tell me that you're moving back to America? Was any of this real to you, or was I just something to fill a wife-size hole for you?"

I take an angry step toward her. "I changed my mind."

"What do you mean you changed your mind?"

She's standing toe-to-toe with me, shouting quietly in my face. "I'm not moving back to America. At least I wasn't. And how dare you say that to me? You were never a replacement."

"So you are moving back now?"

"Yes, maybe," I growl.

"Why?" she argues. "Because you found out I'm *not* perfect? You found out that I'm nothing like her? I won't live in her shadow, Jack. I refuse to."

"No," I reply, feeling flustered. Fighting with Camille makes me forget why I was angry. In fact, it only makes me want her more. "Fuck, I don't know." I turn my back on her, storming across the room to breathe. I pull at my hair, trying to make sense of my emotions.

"You know what I think?" she asks from behind me. "I think seeing that letter reminded you of what you had with her. Seeing that letter reminded you that I'm not her."

"You're not her," I grumble lowly to myself.

"And you're mad at me for that," she snaps, and I hear the tears in her voice. There is raw emotion and pain in her words, and it guts me. "You're mad at me because I'm not Emmaline."

Spinning toward her, it's like I'm coming undone. "No," I bark. Then I take her face in my hands, pulling her so close it hurts. "I'm not mad at you because you're not her," I mutter through my own tears. She's staring into my eyes with longing and agony. "I'm mad at you because you made me love you more."

When she blinks, more tears cascade over her cheeks, and I feel so inclined to kiss her it scares me. My body is drawn to hers like she owns me and is calling me home.

Instead, I release her jaw and step away.

Love has removed all the options and has given us only consequences.

She wipes at her face, sniffling to keep from crying more.

"Camille," Bea calls from the other side of the door.

Neither of us move.

Then Camille quietly says, "If I'm fired, I'll tell her. I'll say goodbye and pack my things."

Her voice shakes on every word, as if the idea of letting that little girl go would be her reckoning. I'd be a monster to do that to either of them.

"No," I grunt in surrender. "You're not fired."

She drags in a grateful breath and wipes her eyes. Then she turns her back on me and rushes toward the door. Opening it up, she fakes a smile and takes my daughter's hand.

"What's wrong?" Bea asks.

"Nothing is wrong," Camille lies. "Do you want to go to the park today?"

"Okay," Bea replies hesitantly.

The two of them disappear into Bea's room, and I drop onto Camille's bed. Burying my hands in my hair, I try to make sense of what just happened and how all my dreams for the future just fell to pieces.

Rule #41: Wine always pairs well with secrets.

Camille

JACK IS A GHOST AGAIN. WHEN HE COMES HOME FROM WORK, usually very, very late, he goes straight to his room upstairs, and he locks himself away most hours of the day.

There are no more shared dinners. No trips to Disneyland or walks in the parks nearby.

There is no more sex and no more bondage.

It might as well be the first day I started.

The moment I walked into my room that morning and found him holding that letter, I knew it was over. It was never about me lying or keeping something from Jack. It was about him still holding on to the past and never giving himself enough room to grieve.

In Jack's mind, Emmaline is still here, and he's being unfaithful to her. In his mind, he's a terrible man, a terrible father, and a terrible husband.

He refuses to let her go, to the point where he finds himself comparing her with me. His love for her and his love for me. Her place in Bea's life and mine.

I wanted to be touched when he admitted that he loved me more, but I wasn't. I was heartbroken because it meant that Jack was still holding on to the past. And I don't belong in the past. Not when I want his future.

I'm just relieved he allowed me to stay for Bea. I'm still shattered that he and I no longer have a life together, but at least for the time being, I can have my time with his daughter.

I don't know how long it will last or what will become of us, but I'm taking it day by day. Bea is my first priority, now and always.

Bundling my coat around me, I walk against the harsh wind after dropping Bea off at school. It's nearing winter, and the city has grown brisk in the mornings. Still, I'd rather busy myself with errands and tasks while I'm out than go back to the apartment when I know Jack could be there.

I can't face him. I don't know if I'll ever be able to again.

It's sad, really, having felt a love so real and then having to live with it just out of reach. Eventually, I assume I'll be able to see his face again without needing to leave the room and sob quietly into a towel or the sleeve of my shirt. Eventually, I hope the sound of his voice no longer pierces my heart like a knife.

And I refuse to hope that we will just get over this and find our way back to each other. Jack has serious work to do on himself before I'd let that happen. I refuse to live in his dead wife's shadow, even if he says his love for me is stronger.

There never should have been a comparison in the first place.

But I know in my heart that Jack won't heal the way he should because that would require him to face his pain and actually feel it rather than just run from it. Ironically, the man would rather lose the *two* loves of his life than work on healing and talk about his emotions.

When I arrive back at the apartment, my nose is so cold it burns, and my fingers are frozen as they clutch the bag of groceries to my chest.

After getting inside, I set the things on the counter and blow into my hands, trying to warm them.

"You need a pair of gloves."

I nearly scream as a woman's voice cuts in from out of nowhere. Elizabeth steps into the kitchen while my heart is still beating wildly from the terror.

I clutch my chest in fright. "Mon Dieu!"

"Pardon," she replies in a half-hearted apology. "I still have a key from when I lived here."

"What are you doing here?" I ask.

Elizabeth has such a stern expression that I remember how Jack once called her the meanest person he's ever met, and I assumed he meant that because she is his sister. Don't most siblings consider the other mean?

But in this case, I believe him. Elizabeth has claws, and she frightens me.

Crossing her arms over her chest, she wears a stoic look as she faces me. "What happened with you and my brother?"

I let out a sigh. "Nothing."

"Tu me prends pour une idiote?" she asks.

"No, I do not think you are an idiot," I reply in a huff, "and stop speaking French. It's throwing me off." Which is true. Her French is disarming, and I know she's doing it to prove her intelligence. And maybe even her dominance.

"Then stop lying," she replies flatly.

"Fine," I reply, placing my hands on my hips. "Your brother taught me rope bondage upstairs at night, and that's all."

"That's all?" One single brow rises on her face.

"It's none of your business," I argue.

"It's my business that Jack barely shows up to work anymore. He went from being finally happy again to being miserable and elusive again."

"Why do you even care?" I reply angrily. "I thought you hated him."

She reacts like I've slapped her. Her jaw drops as she glares at me. "You thought I hated my own brother?"

"You don't talk to him. How could you even tell if he's happy or not?" I snap in return.

"Do you even understand why I was so mad at Jack?"

I relax on an exhale, and although I know I don't need to be getting deeper into Jack's personal life, I am curious to hear this story.

When I don't reply, she walks into the kitchen and retrieves two wineglasses from the cabinet and a bottle of cabernet from the rack.

"It's ten in the morning," I say, but she ignores me as she pours.

"Sit," she commands.

I try to resist, but after a moment, I give in and take the stool next to her. Taking a sip, I listen as she tells the story.

"I told you how I was living with Jack and Emmaline when she passed away. She was like a sister to me. I held her hand as she passed."

"I'm sorry," I whisper. We both take a drink in the moment of silence.

"I was only twenty years old. In a foreign country, far from my parents and any family outside my brother. And when Em passed away, I needed him. The day she died, he disappeared. For a week, no one could find him. I was alone with Beatrice, who was only three at the time. I was grieving and alone, but he took all that grief for himself and gave me no room for my own."

My heart feels heavy as I stare at her, watching her eyes moisten.

"My parents flew out immediately to help with the funeral and with Bea, and eventually Jack came back, but he never *really* came back. He was present, but he wasn't really here. For nearly a year after she died, he couldn't look anyone in the eye. Not me. Not Phoenix. Not even his Bea.

"I know Jack was grieving the loss of his wife, but I was grieving the loss of my best friend *and* my brother."

"That must have been so hard," I mumble quietly.

"It was. I moved out," she says, staring down at her wineglass as she swirls it. "Bea went and stayed with Phoenix for a while. Shortly after that, I heard he planned to move home. He was just going to leave me here. As if none of our life here mattered. When Ronan Kade offered the club to us for a year, I only agreed to do it because I assumed it would change my brother's mind. I thought it would convince him to stay. It turns out I was wrong. *You* were the one who convinced him to stay."

My face falls in regret as I reach a hand out and place it on her arm. "You know that if he decides to go back, the life you built here still matters. You can do it without him."

"I know that," she replies with a tilt of her head. "But I don't want my brother to leave. Or my niece. I just want them to be happy, and for the past two months, they have been."

Her eyes bore into mine, and I understand what it is she's asking.

"So tell me," she adds. "What happened between you two?"

With a sigh, I take a long drink from the wineglass. Then I tell her everything. From the night he dragged me out of that club to the night he told me he loved me in the very same spot. I even tell her about the letter and the fight we had the morning he found it two weeks ago.

We polish off the entire bottle of wine before noon, and I should probably feel guilty for how drunk I am in the middle of the day. But with the month I've had, I deserve this.

"Okay," she says, not sounding near as slurry as I do. "Here's what we're going to do."

"Nothing," I argue, setting my wineglass down with a clumsy *thunk*. "That's what we're going to do."

"Listen…" she says, putting her hands out. She doesn't seem tipsy at all, but she does appear more relaxed, like she won't claw my face off or stab me in the throat. "My brother has some groveling to do."

"Groveling...no. Healing...yes," I say, pouring the last few drops from the bottle into my glass. "Elizabeth, the fact of the matter is...I did keep a secret from him. Sure, it was just a letter, but that letter served as a reminder that Jack and Emmaline had something I wanted."

"Okay, then just apologize to him," she says sternly.

"It's not that easy. He has to want me regardless of his wife or the letter. Not more or less than her. And to do that, he'll have to accept that she's really gone."

Elizabeth leans back in her chair, looking defeated.

"I know you're right," she mutters to herself.

"I want him to be happy too," I say softly.

"Well, for what it's worth," she replies, standing from the chair, "this was fun."

"It was?" I reply, sitting upright. It's not what I expected her to say, so it takes me by surprise. I haven't had a lot of female friendships in my life, so to feel as if I might be forming one with Jack's sister has me suddenly hopeful.

"Yes, it was. I like you."

She starts to walk away, and I follow. "Well, next time you want to scare me to death and share a bottle of wine, I'll be here."

"Good," she replies frankly. "And...don't give up on Jack just yet. He...might take some time to come around."

"Okay," I say noncommittally. I don't suspect he will this time, and I don't have the heart to hope for it either.

"Bye, Camille," she says before opening the front door. Then, a moment later, she disappears through it.

Rule #42: It's not that complicated.

Jack

MY HEAD IS POUNDING WHEN I PEEL MY EYES OPEN. I HEAR MY name being called, but I only groan and roll away from the sound.

"Jack, wake up," she calls again, this time more assertively. When Phoenix shoves me hard in the shoulder, I give in.

"What the fuck, Nix?" I bark, turning back toward her.

"Your phone has been ringing all morning," she says before tossing it on my bed.

Technically, it's not *my* bed. It's her guest room bed that she occasionally lets me crash in when I get too drunk at the club to go home. Which has been more frequent lately.

I sit upright in the bed, my back against the headboard. It doesn't matter that I'm in just a pair of boxer briefs. Phoenix and I have seen each other in our underwear since we were kids and never once felt anything more than friendship for each other. It was always more comfortable that way.

Picking up my phone, I see it's my dad's number in the caller ID, but it stops ringing before I can answer. Between him and my two moms, it's been nonstop from them. I know they're just concerned. And I assume it was my sister who clued them in on my recent…breakup? If that's what we're calling it.

A breakup before it even started.

Phoenix drops onto the bed and stares at me. "If I tell you that you can't crash here anymore, do you think you'd stop drinking so much?"

I tilt my head at her. "No."

She lets out a sigh. "Jack…"

"Don't start," I mutter as I rub my brows.

"It's been two weeks."

"I don't know what you're talking about," I argue. Technically, I haven't told anyone about Camille. Not the relationship. Not the breakup. None of it. But they always fucking find out.

To my surprise, she shoves me hard in the shoulder. "Don't lie to me, Jack St. Claire."

My eyes widen, seeing my normally docile friend so angry.

"I have been with you through everything. We've been friends since we were kids. When no one else understood what it was like to have a family like ours, you were there. You have *always* been there for me, and you know I would do anything for you. Which is why I'm going to kick you out of my house and tell you that it's time you get your life together."

My brow furrows as I stare at her. I want to yell at her and tell her she has no idea what it's like to go through what I went through, but I don't. Because she's right. As much as I hate it, I know she's right.

"I'm sorry," she whispers when she sees my anger. "But you can't keep living like this. I know you loved Em, but her death was not *your* death."

"I know that," I grumble without looking at her. "You don't get it, Nix. It wasn't just her death. It was like…I lost everything I had planned for my life."

"So plan something new," she urges. "Jesus, Jack. You still have that precious little girl. And a beautiful woman who loves you. Is getting drunk and crashing in my small apartment really better than that?"

I climb out of the bed and march across the room. "Of course not." Grabbing my slacks from last night draped over the chair, I tug them on impatiently. I'm slipping back into the state of anger and depression I was in before Camille came along. Back when my fuse was short and nothing felt fulfilling.

"Then what are you waiting for?" she asks, and something in me snaps.

"I'm fucked-up, Phoenix!" My voice booms, echoing against the walls of her petite guest room. "They don't want me. Not like this. They are better off without me, and you know it!"

"What are you talking about?" she replies with confusion.

"Think about it, Nix. I got Em pregnant, and that pregnancy killed her. If she had never married me...she could still be alive."

Phoenix's eyes go wide before glancing toward the door. When I turn to see what she's looking at, I spot my sister lurking in the hallway.

Fuck.

With a huff, I pull my plain white tee over my head. I need to get out of here.

But even as I move toward the door and Elizabeth blocks it with an emotionless expression, I know I can't get out of this so easily.

"Phoenix, can we have a minute?" she asks calmly.

My gaze meets my sister's. I spot a hint of pity there, and pity is the last thing I want.

"Of course," Nix replies before leaving the room and shutting the door behind her.

My sister crosses her arms, and we stare at each other in silence.

"Jack..." she says softly.

"Not you too," I groan as I run my fingers through my hair. "First our moms, then Phoenix, now you."

"You want me to throw you a pity party because you have so many women in your life who care about you? Get over it."

With a disgruntled sigh, I drop onto the chair and rub my hands over my face. Impending emotions rise to the surface, and to be honest, it frightens me. If I let them out, they could run me over like a stampede. I'm not sure I'd get back up from that.

Elizabeth sits on the bed across from me. "Cancer killed Emmaline, Jack. You know that."

I let out a heavy breath as I lift my head. "Of course I know that."

"Because it sounds like you're blaming yourself, and that's not true."

"I know," I mumble under my breath.

"I don't think you do."

Part of me realizes that I should be grateful that my sister is even talking to me. But the other part of me hates that it has to be under these circumstances.

"I'm fine," I lie. "I've just…had a bad month."

She stares back at me without responding, as if she's not buying it. And she shouldn't because it's utter bullshit. I haven't just had a bad month. I've had a bad few years. I've been running from my own pain for so long that I've conditioned myself to believe it's all I'm good at.

I didn't just break up with Camille. That fight about the fucking letter and Emmaline was resolvable, but I didn't give it a chance. What really happened is that I pushed her away because it was easier than facing the possibility that I could lose her the same way I lost Em.

As my sister stares at me, it's like I'm in a losing battle against the truth. There is no lying to myself or running away anymore.

There's just…feeling it.

Tears prick my eyes, and I grind my molars together to fight against them. But I'm so fucking tired of running and fighting that I start to let the pain win.

When the next three words leave my lips, it feels like tearing down the dam.

"I'm not fine."

And that's it. The painful prick of tears subsides when I finally let them fall.

I hold my hand over my brow to shield my face from her view. Each sob feels like being knocked over again and again. Everything hits me at once. Losing Emmaline, abandoning Bea, failing my sister, walking away from Camille. All of it.

When a soft hand lands on my shoulder, I look up to see Elizabeth crying too. Tears cascade across her cheeks, and I burst to my feet to pull her into a tight embrace. My tough-as-nails sister sobs into my T-shirt.

Holding each other, we both cry. And to my surprise, I'm not trampled by the emotion. In fact, once the tears subside, I find that I can finally take in a full breath. For the first time in years, I feel lighter.

I know it won't last forever, but the weight of all that grief I was carrying for so long is finally gone. It will be back. I'm not naive. But for now, I'm going to savor this calm.

"I'm so sorry, Elizabeth." I'm still holding her in a tight hug, and I don't want to let go.

"I know you are," she replies. "I'm sorry for being so hard on you. I know you were still grieving."

"But I shouldn't have left you alone."

When she pulls away, glancing up into my eyes, she gives a sad shrug. "I was never alone."

"Good," I reply.

We each take a moment to dry our tears and compose ourselves. Exhaustion rolls over me like a truck.

"If you give me a minute to take a shower, I'd like to take you out to lunch. Really get a chance to talk."

She looks up with a smile. "I'd like that."

As I get into the shower, I stand under the spray and think

about Camille. She's the first person I want to reach for. I want to tell her that I finally let go of everything I was holding on to. And it might not seem like much, but for me, it was huge. She would know that.

She'd be proud of me.

But I can't call her or speak to her. Not yet.

I'm still so angry at her for lying to me, but I'm more mad at myself for rushing into things before I was ready and possibly ruining something good. At least now I can admit that I have work to do before I get back into a relationship.

When I get out of the shower, I throw on some clean clothes that I keep at Phoenix's place in case of emergency—or times like these. I quickly get dressed and meet my sister and best friend in the living room.

They're sitting on the couch together, watching television while Phoenix works on her laptop. I stop at the table behind the couch, spotting a familiar photo in a frame, so I pick it up and I'm immediately hit with a wave of nostalgia. It's a group photo of all of us taken when we were still young, me in my twenties and them in their teens. Phoenix's twin sister, Austin, is there too, with her boyfriend, Liam.

Our parents raised us together. They tried to make us a family. I wish I knew when it all fell apart.

My wife died. Austin and Liam went off on their own. My sister and I stopped speaking. It was like adulthood severed our relationships, and the family we built as kids burned to ashes.

Ronan wants us to get that back, and I realize it's on me now. I wanted to leave Paris so badly to restore my family, but what about *this* family? If I can bring back what we had, isn't that worth staying for?

I can't leave.

"Ready?" Elizabeth asks.

I set the picture down and nod.

"Yeah. I'm ready."

My sister and I are sitting inside a café along rue des Trois-Frères. She's sipping her cappuccino and picking at a croissant as I watch the people walking by in their coats and scarves. So far, our conversation has been short, although there is a lot to talk about.

For now, I'm just enjoying the fact that she'll sit in comfortable silence with me. It's more than I had a year ago.

"I spoke to her, you know."

Her blunt admission catches me off guard. "Who? Camille?" I ask, sounding more desperate than I mean to.

"Yes."

"And what did she say?" I ask.

"She said she wants you to grovel on your knees and win her back."

I tilt my head and furrow my brows. "No, she didn't."

My sister laughs quietly to herself. "She didn't. She said she wants what all of us want, Jack."

"Which is…"

Then she turns and stares into my eyes. "For you to take care of yourself. To heal as much as you can. To come back to us."

Of course. But she makes it sound so simple.

Picking up my coffee, I stare out at the street, focusing on nothing at all. I try to imagine myself healing. I picture Camille and Bea with a better version of me. A version they deserve.

"She still wants me then?" I ask.

My sister twists her lips. "For some reason, she still wants you. But she doesn't want to live in your wife's shadow. She wants you to want her for *her*. Not because she resembles someone you once loved."

I set my coffee down too hard, and it clatters against the table. "Is that what she thinks?"

Elizabeth looks exasperated as she rolls her eyes again.

"Honestly, this is why I'll never fall in love. What a mess you two are. You both love each other, but you're too stubborn and proud to admit how you feel."

"All right, if you're so smart," I argue, "tell me what the fuck to do."

"First of all, take care of yourself. Get some support and allow yourself to grieve Emmaline finally. Then tell the woman you love how you feel." She lets out a huff and picks up her cup. "It's not that complicated."

I laugh as I lift my cup to my lips. "Someday, you'll understand."

"Never."

Rule #43: Emotions must be felt.

Jack
One month later

THERE'S A WHITE PLAQUE BENEATH A LARGE OAK TREE THAT overlooks a small park where children are playing.

In loving memory of Emmaline St. Claire, mother, daughter, wife.

In her honor, I make a donation to this park every year. Enough to keep it clean and maintained. Enough to keep her memory alive. It was her request that she have a garden planted here in her hometown.

In the spring, her mother and I have flowers planted—pink and white begonias, her favorite. They are beautiful and sweet, just like Em.

Sitting on the iron bench next to the tree, I watch the children play at the playground, including my daughter squealing in French with the other kids. In her small red peacoat and gray knit hat, she looks more like a dream than a reality.

I always wanted to be a father—more than anything. I wanted to give my kids what my parents gave me. Now that I have Bea, I realize nothing is as simple as I thought it would be.

The last few weeks have been hell, which says a lot, coming from me.

The only reason I can say this with full confidence is because I know what hell feels like. I watched my wife wither away over two years. I watched her suffer and die a slow, painful death while desperately clinging to life.

And while I felt all those awful, terrible moments in real time, I quickly shoved those emotions aside for the nearly three years since. I turned off my feelings. I dug a grave, and I buried myself in it.

In the past month, I had to reopen old wounds and feel them all over again.

So yes, it has been hell.

I don't feel like I'm healing. I feel like I'm just hurting, but Ronan says this is part of the process. He lost his first wife and child, so he's been down this road before. He was the one who tried to shove me toward counseling when Em passed, but I refused.

This time, I finally obliged.

I found a counselor I like, and I meet with him once a week. I hate every awful, miserable second of it, but at least I'm trying. If I'm honest, trying fucking sucks.

I'm not doing this for Camille, although she's the reason I keep going. My counselor asked me to identify my *why*. My reason for healing and living and surviving with all this grief living inside me.

I immediately thought of Bea. My daughter has lost enough already, and she deserves a father.

But I'm pretty sure it was a trick question, one that didn't take me long to figure out. The real *why* is me. Because I can't give Bea or Camille the version of me they deserve until I fix me.

And mostly because I owe it to myself to start living again. Would it be nice to finally have a second chance with her again? To envision that future that felt so crystal clear just a couple months ago? Yes, of course.

But even if that future never comes to fruition, I want to feel alive again.

A cold winter chill moves through the park, and I bundle my coat tighter around me. Christmas is only six days away, and I know I shouldn't rush these things, but I want to spend it with the people I love.

I want to spend it with *her*.

My counselor, Paul, keeps reminding me that there is no end goal or finish line with these things. When I feel ready to talk to her, I should. But I'm not sure I'll ever feel ready. The things I said to her were unfair. The way I treated her, as if she was in competition for my heart, was wrong.

I'm not the type of man to talk to a ghost or a placard in front of a park, so I definitely won't be doing that, but if I were to say something to Emmaline, this is the place I'd do it. And maybe I'm here just to feel her presence.

And maybe if I was going to speak to her, I'd tell her that...I miss her. I miss our inside jokes and the way she made a cup of tea every single night at exactly 7:30. I miss her socks on the floor next to our bed. I miss her shortbread cookies and her smile.

Hell, maybe I'd even tell her about Camille and how much I think she'd like her. If they were friends, I think Camille would be the bossy one who would cause a scene in restaurants if the waiters were rude to Emmaline. I think they'd talk about Monet and Coldplay and how bad my singing is.

I'd tell her that Camille loves Bea, and I think Em would be grateful for that.

Never the jealous type, I think she'd adore Camille. She would be disappointed in me for treating her like I did, but she wouldn't yell. That wasn't Em's style.

If Em were here and I could really talk to her, she'd tell me to stop focusing on the what-ifs and regrets. It doesn't matter that there would be no Camille if Em hadn't died. She'd tell me I worry too much or that I'm too sentimental.

I would tell her that I still love her. I think I always will because that's what happens when someone dies. My love for her froze in that state forever, and I'll never fall out of love with her because she was never around to let me.

But my heart isn't frozen. It's a living, beating organ with room for more.

I'd ask Em to wish me luck. Fuck, I might even ask her advice. How the hell am I going to make up six weeks of near silence to Camille?

She'd probably tell me to stop talking about it and go do it.

She would definitely wish me luck.

"Papa, my hands are cold!" Bea says as she comes running up to where I'm sitting alone. I take her tiny hands in mine and warm them by breathing on them.

"You have to keep your mittens on," I reply gently.

Holding my daughter's hands in mine, I stare down into her blue eyes, and for one beautiful moment, I see her mother. Not just in the shape and color but in the gentleness and warmth behind them.

A part of Em is still here.

Pulling my daughter toward me, I wrap her up in my arms and hug her tightly. Her tiny hands grip my coat as she burrows herself in my chest. For just a moment, I imagine I'm hugging Em.

"Papa," she whispers.

"Yes?"

"Can we get hot chocolate?"

I smile with my chin resting on her head. "Yes, of course we can."

Releasing her, I smile down at my daughter. But before standing, I reach into her pockets and slip her mittens on each of her cold hands.

"Keep these on, please."

"Yes, Papa."

"Did you like visiting your maman's park?" Emotion makes my voice raspy, and it nearly breaks mid-sentence.

Bea seems to notice immediately and leans closer as if she is the one comforting me. "Oui, Papa."

As we stand up, I take her hand, and we walk together toward the nearest café. Sometimes, it's hard to move on and leave the mistakes I've made in the past. I worry that Bea will remember the damage I've done and the years I was too absent to show her my love.

But I can't change the past. I can't bring Em back. I can't unsay the things I said to Camille. All I can do is learn from my mistakes and keep going, one step at a time.

"Merry Christmas."

I glance up from my desk, a half-written mess of a letter in my hands. Elizabeth is leaning against the doorframe with a small box in her hands.

"What is this?" I ask as she walks in and places it on the desk in front of me.

She shrugs. "Nothing. Don't make a big deal out of it."

Curious, I pick up the box. In the past month, since my sister and I have had a heart-to-heart and I've apologized for the way my behavior affected her after Em died, she's been slowly warming up to the idea of having a relationship with me again.

She comes over more often now and even hangs out with Camille on Camille's days off. It's a far cry from the woman who wouldn't even look in my direction four months ago.

"We can't exchange gifts yet. I'm giving you your present on Christmas," I say.

"Just open it," she says with an eye roll.

"Fine," I reply with a huff. Tearing open the package, I lift the lid of the box to find a snow globe filled with a glass palm tree, sand, and seashells. As I hold it, I glance up at her in confusion.

"Since you decided to stay in Paris for a while, I thought you might be homesick and could use a little something from California," she says sheepishly. "Mom helped me pick it out."

"Elizabeth…" I say, staring at the glass ornament. Flipping it over, I watch the sand fall back into place, and oddly enough, it does remind me of home. It creates a warm buzz in the center of my chest.

"If I could have had real American cheeseburgers delivered, I promise you I would have," she says with a smirk.

My mouth starts to water at the mention. "I'd do some shady stuff for a few In-N-Out burgers," I reply.

She nods her head emphatically. "Or that greasy place Dad used to take us by the harbor."

"Oh God, yes," I reply.

A moment later, we're both smiling, and I can't explain how amazing it is to reminisce with my sister again.

"Thank you for this," I reply, not entirely referring to the snow globe. "Really."

"You're welcome," she mutters without making eye contact. "And for what it's worth, I'm really glad you're staying."

"Well, you'd never forgive me if I left you alone with Julian."

She rolls her eyes. "You're right about that."

Just then, he passes by the office, sneering at both of us before lifting up his middle fingers on both hands. "I heard that. Fuck you both."

Elizabeth and I cackle.

It's dangerous to wish that everything could be falling into place, but with how well the club is doing and my sister talking to me again, I start to believe it just might be okay.

There's just one more thing I have to do, and everything is riding on it.

Rule #44: You won't know what's inside until you open it.

Camille

I haven't been sleeping well lately. I hear every sound, every creak in the floorboards and door closing somewhere in this large apartment.

More than once, I've gotten up in the middle of the night and opened my door in hopes of finding him standing in the hallway. But every time, the hallway is empty, and he's still so far away.

Today is Christmas Eve. I've never dreaded a holiday more in my life. I've booked myself a ticket to go home to Giverny for two days. Bea should spend the holiday with her family, and I know that if I'm around, it will make it all hurt that much more.

Marguerite has offered to let me stay with her. She's going to her granddaughter's house for Christmas, and she invited me to join, but I don't think I will. I intend to use the day to make a new plan for my life. I can't be a nanny forever. I have to move on eventually. But I'd like to stay in Paris, which won't be cheap or easy, so it better be a very good plan.

Before the sun rises, I climb out of bed. Walking out to the living room, I start a fire in the fireplace and brew myself a cup of coffee. Sitting on the couch, I listen to the crackle of the flames. The Christmas tree in the corner illuminates the room in a warm, white glow.

It's relaxing and quiet until I hear a creak on the stairs. Tensing, I wait.

Jack and I haven't been in a room alone together since the fight in October. He made it quite clear that things between us were over when he retreated to his room, cutting off all communication between us.

I should be glad he at least let me keep my job.

But in the moments we have seen each other, speaking only about Bea while in her company, I've noticed a change in him. There's something raw and sincere in his eyes now. I want to believe he's healing, but I don't make it a habit to hope for things anymore.

He walks into the living room, and I watch in my periphery as he sits on the other end of the couch. In a pair of black joggers and a plain white T-shirt, he looks so familiar to me it hurts.

Two months ago, I would have crawled into his lap. I would have pressed my face against the soft cotton of his shirt and felt his arms wrap protectively around me. He would have stroked my hair and kissed the top of my head.

Now, we sit in silence.

And when I can't stand another second of it, I speak. "I'll be on the ten o'clock train, and I'll be back in two days. I've prepared a soup. It's in the icebox. You'll have to warm it up—"

"Camille," he says, staring at me, but I won't turn toward him.

"I wrapped a few gifts for her. They're under the tree. And a couple for Elizabeth and Phoenix too."

"Don't go," he pleads, and it cuts deep in my heart.

I can't utter another word without the threat of tears, but I do eventually turn my head and look into his eyes, which is a mistake.

I forgot how comfortable his gaze is, how peaceful and warm it feels to stare into the abyss of those haunting green orbs. It makes my loneliness ache that much harder.

"Beatrice should spend the holiday with her family," I say with moisture in my eyes.

"You are her family," he replies, and I have to look away. It hurts too much.

"No, I'm not," I argue. "I'm her nanny." Standing from the couch, I try to walk to the kitchen, but Jack takes my hand to stop me.

"Camille, please."

Turning toward him, my anger boils. "Please what, Jack? We tried and it failed, just like we were afraid it would. Luckily, Bea wasn't hurt, and we can make this work. I'll keep my job for now, but I think we need to just accept that we can never go back down that road again."

I tear my hand from his grip and walk toward the kitchen. I hear him stand from the couch and follow me.

"Please don't say that," he begs.

"You called me a fraud," I argue, turning toward him.

"I was wrong," he says, taking another step toward me.

My back hits the kitchen counter, and a panic rises inside me. If he gets too close, I won't be able to resist. I'll fall right back into his arms and forgive everything without either of us learning or accepting a thing.

"It's too late, Jack," I say, hearing my voice crack.

As he takes the last step in my direction, standing so close his body is flush with mine, I let out a quiet sob.

"It's not too late," he begs.

But before he can utter another word, I press my hand over his mouth to stop him. "Please," I whisper. "Don't." The last thing I want in this moment is hope. Hope can be cruel. It can make you believe things that will never come true, torturously making you feel that loss all over again.

His eyes bore down on me, desperation and pain in them. I feel it too. But I see the moment he surrenders.

Taking a step back, he moves from my reach, and my hand falls back to my side. I wipe the tears falling across my cheeks as he stares sadly at me.

Finally, on an exhale, he turns and walks over to the Christmas tree. I watch in confusion as he leans down and picks up something from the pile.

With remorse on his face, he returns and hands it to me. "This is for you. Open it when you're alone."

Curiosity weighs heavily on me as I stare down at the rectangular box wrapped in red-and-white paper. He got me a gift?

This is all so strange and foreign. I have no idea how to behave, and I certainly didn't get him a gift.

"Thank you," I murmur.

With that, he turns away and walks up the stairs. I hug the box to my chest and squeeze my eyes closed to keep from sobbing right here in the kitchen.

⚬⚭⚬

Bea sobbed when I left this morning. I didn't know anything could be as hard as walking away from her as she cried. It's the first time we've been apart in nearly six months. And the moment I'm in the car on the way to the train station, it's like my heart is being pulled back to the apartment in Montmartre.

Jack stood by her side looking despondent as I carried my small weekender to the door. I could see so many things on his lips that he wanted to say but didn't.

During the entire ride, I'm filled with anxiety and indecision. Am I doing the right thing?

In my heart, I don't want to leave, not even for two days. But I can't keep doing this forever. I can't stay in that apartment and waste my life away on the memories of a short love affair that didn't work. I can't keep playing the part of Bea's mother forever.

So this is more than just a holiday away from them. It's a chance for me to rethink my life and where it's headed. It's time I do as my father said I should and spread my wings and fly.

Of course, the only place my wings want to take me is back home to them.

The driver drops me off at Gare Saint-Lazare, and I climb out with my bag slung across my shoulder.

"Joyeux Noël," I say to him before he closes my door. He returns the greeting with a polite smile.

Then I'm on my own. My train doesn't leave for another forty-five minutes, so I find a café at the station that is still open. I buy myself a latte and a pastry and sit at a small table with my bags at my side.

The gift from Jack is calling my name. I should have left it in my room at the apartment, but I couldn't resist. It's the only gift I've received this year, and I'm too curious about what is inside to ignore it.

Pushing my food and drink aside, I pull the box out and set it on the table.

Just open it, I tell myself.

What am I so afraid of? That whatever is inside will be too heartfelt and thoughtful to ignore? That once I see what he's bought for me, I'll be reminded of how in love with him I am and have no choice but to go home?

Or perhaps the opposite. Maybe the gift is too plain and means nothing. Maybe it's a candle or a pair of slippers and it only proves that I don't mean as much to Jack as I thought I did.

Somehow, I just know that's not the case. Curiosity is what got me into this mess. It's only appropriate that I let it take me the rest of the way.

Twisting my lips, I begin unwrapping. Immediately, I recognize the pink-painted wood and the floral design on the edges.

Confused, I stare down at my jewelry box.

Why would Jack give me my own jewelry box?

Then I remember the day I bought one for Bea at the theme park. I had told Jack how my father would put gifts in it every year on my birthday. Did he really remember that?

And if so, what is inside?

Biting my bottom lip, I slowly open the lid.

When I spot the familiar beige paper of his stationery, I slam the box closed again.

It's a letter.

Am I ready for this?

Maybe what is in this letter is what he tried telling me early this morning. He sounded as if he wanted to give us another shot, but I was too afraid. What if nothing has changed? I can't go through this again.

An elderly couple nearby glances my way as I stare down at the ominous jewelry box like I'm afraid it might detonate if I touch it. I smile up at them before picking up my latte and busying my hands while I deliberate what I'll do next.

I go through every single scenario of what could be in that letter. I'm fairly certain Jack didn't fire me via handwritten letter on Christmas, so that means that whatever is in there is meant to make me feel better. What am I waiting for?

My heart beats wildly in my chest, begging me to open it.

So, with shaking hands, I do.

The letter is in an envelope, much like the one he wrote Emmaline. But instead of her name, it's mine addressed across the front. Peeling back the paper, I pull out the letter.

While the train station speaker announces trains departing and arriving and Christmas music plays lightly overhead, I block it all out and read Jack's handwriting.

Dear Camille,

I can imagine it all very vividly in my mind now. I can see you finding that letter in the random book in your tiny used bookstore. I can see you scribbling animals on the inside cover. And I can imagine how strongly you connected to that photo and what I wrote to my soon-to-be wife inside.

I can see it all so well because I know you so well now. You don't do anything with half of your heart. You're used to giving more love than you receive. And when you look at someone, you truly see them.

These are all things that made me love you.

I know you brought that letter to my house that day to return it, but I'd like to believe you were brought here by something stronger. Maybe it was fate or divine intervention.

Or maybe you took one look at the photo and saw a man who needed you. And I did.

To be honest, I still do.

I need your stubborn will and fiery temper. I need your strength and your wisdom. I need the laughter and joy you bring to my life. Bea and I both do.

It was always more than bondage and ropes, and we both know it. What you gave me upstairs in that room is far more than I ever expected. You gave me your trust. Your heart. And confidence. You pushed me to be better not only for my daughter but for myself too.

But I know I can't ask you to fulfill my needs without fulfilling yours. And I think what you need right now is to know that I love you for you. You are not too much. You're not too loud or too curious. You are not filling a hole in my heart or replacing a person I've lost. That hole will always exist, much like the hole left in your heart the day your father passed. I've been to enough counseling in the past two months to understand that.

But our hearts and lives will grow around those holes, and I hope more than anything that we can do that together.

I love you so much it hurts, little bird. But I don't want to hold you down anymore.

When you do fly off, I hope you will take us with you. And if you can't, I understand.

At least I hope you can take our memories and this apology.

I'm sorry.

Joyeux Noël.

Yours,
Jack

Rule #45: If you're going to do it, do it right.

Jack

"Don't you want to decorate the cookies?" I ask, passing Bea a tray of sugar cookies. My kitchen counter is covered in sprinkles and icing.

With a despondent shrug, she takes the icing and unenthusiastically smears it across the white sugar cookie.

"When is Camille coming back?" she whines.

"In two days," I reply.

"I miss her already."

"She left an hour ago," I say. Placing my hands on the counter, I slump with a defeated sigh. This is all my fault. If I had just apologized weeks ago, then she might have stayed, but I wasn't ready. I was too afraid that if I tried, she wouldn't accept it and then really leave for good. And I didn't want to ruin Bea's Christmas like that.

"You miss her too," Bea says, noticing my glum demeanor.

"Of course I miss her too," I reply.

"Can you call her?" she asks. "Tell her she can sleep in your bed again, and maybe she'll come back."

My head snaps up, and I stare at her in shock. "Beatrice," I say in a scolding tone, without fully knowing what I'm supposed to be scolding her for.

"What?" she asks innocently. "When Camille slept in your bed, she was much happier."

"She never slept in my bed," I argue, which is a lie.

"Yes, she did. Sometimes, I would get up in the middle of the night, and she would be in your bed."

I'm appalled. My jaw hangs open as I stare at my daughter, suddenly humiliated that she found her *nanny* in my bed. I should be ashamed of myself.

"You shouldn't have seen that," I mutter quietly.

She only shrugs. "I love Camille. I think you should call her and tell her she can sleep in your bed again so she comes back."

"It's not that easy."

"Because Maman went to sleep?" Bea seems to get smaller as she says that. Playing with sprinkles between her fingers, she almost looks ashamed of even bringing up her mother. What a mess I am. I haven't even spoken with my own daughter about this.

Rounding the corner, I sit in the chair next to Bea and take her hands in mine so she can look into my eyes. "Beatrice, you know your maman didn't go to sleep, right? She got very sick and died."

"I know," she mumbles sweetly, scrunching her lips.

"You do?" I ask.

"Yeah. Tante Elizabeth told me. But I don't want to hurt you, Papa."

My chest cracks and shatters at hearing my daughter say that. Pressing my molars together, I lean forward and pull Bea to my chest, wrapping my arms around her. "You don't have to worry about that, sweetheart. You won't hurt me if you talk about your maman. In fact, you can talk about her as much as you want. And if you have any questions about her, you can always ask me. I promise it won't hurt me."

Her tiny arms squeeze around me as we hold each other.

"I love you very much. You know that, right?"

"I love you too, Papa."

I don't know what I was so afraid of. I was terrified that talking to Bea about Em would cause my daughter more trauma and pain, but I was so wrong. Asking about her mother isn't hurting her or me. Instead, she smiles against my shirt, letting out a delicate sigh.

"Is that why Camille can't sleep in your bed anymore?" she asks after we pull away from the hug. "Because Maman died?"

"No," I reply. "She wasn't supposed to sleep in my bed because she's your nanny."

Why am I even telling my six-year-old this?

"So she can stop being my nanny," Bea replies, moving her attention back to the icing and sprinkles. "Tante Elizabeth doesn't have a nanny, and she has ladies who sleep in her bed all the time."

"Beatrice!" I snap, staring at her in shock. "How do you even know that?"

"Because when I sleep over, they knock on her door, but she tells them they can't sleep over because I'm there."

Apparently, I'm going to have to have a serious talk with my sister. How many different women is she seeing?

Shaking away that thought, I focus on Camille instead. It's not as simple as Bea is suggesting, obviously. She still puts her shoes on backward, so what does she know?

But I can't stop thinking about my apology in that jewelry box. Was it enough? Should I have said those things to her face? I mean...she really didn't let me talk, so it's not like I had a choice. Ironically.

Am I really going to sit around here and waste away for the next two days when I could just tell her to her face how sorry I am and how much we love her? And maybe it would just be as simple as telling her that she can sleep in my bed again. And she can stop being a nanny.

I can prove that I've healed and grown in the last two months.

Feeling excited and a little wild, I glance down at my watch. Her train has already left.

But Giverny is only an hour away. Bea and I could be there this afternoon. I'll tell Camille everything in person that I said in that letter, and we'll beg her to come back, for real this time.

"Get your shoes on." I stand from the stool and rush toward the stairs to get my wallet.

"What?" Bea shrieks. "Where are we going?"

"To the train station. We have to bring her back," I call.

"Yay!" Bea cheers.

I hear sprinkles hit the wood floor, but I don't care. I'll clean it up later. Bea's tiny feet stomp through the house as she gathers her shoes and coat. I'm calling the car as I button up her coat and pull a hat over her head.

The car pulls up five minutes later, and I quickly usher my daughter inside. She's beaming with excitement, and I worry if I'm doing the right thing. Bringing Bea into this feels wrong, but she has as much fight in this game as I do. She loves Camille just as much, and she deserves a chance to chase after her too.

When we pull up to the station, we rush out of the car. Bea takes my hand as we run together toward the ticket booth.

She's laughing excitedly as we weave in and out of the crowd. It's infectious, so I find myself smiling along with her.

"Jack?"

When I hear my name, Bea and I come to a complete stop. Spinning around, I stare in shock at Camille standing near a bench. Her eyes are swollen and wet, and there are blotches of red splattered across her nose and cheeks.

"Camille!" Bea shouts excitedly. Sprinting toward her, she leaps into the woman's arms.

The look of relief and love on Camille's face as she gathers my daughter in a tight embrace is palpable. Camille closes her eyes, love etched into her features as she presses her cheek to my daughter's.

I take a step toward her, and I realize that if I'm going to do this, I'm going to do it right.

"Je suis désolé." I stammer my apology. My French is so rusty and was never very good to begin with, but I can do this for her.

She takes a step toward me.

"J'aurais dû...m'excuser plus tôt."

I should have apologized sooner.

She winces, which probably means I'm butchering this. But she lets me continue. And I don't know what else to say but the obvious.

"Je t'aime."

Her eyes moisten again. I haven't fucked it up yet, so I keep going.

"Je suis en thérapie. Et...j'essaie de m'améliorer."

Maybe the most challenging words to say in any language—I'm trying to get better.

"That's good," she mumbles softly. "I'm proud of you."

"Please come home," I plead.

Camille sets Bea down and takes her hand as she closes the space between us. Standing right in front of me, she stares into my eyes. "I missed my train."

"You did?" I ask with hope.

She nods. "I was so busy reading this letter." Reaching into her pocket, she pulls out the folded-up paper I put in her jewelry box.

I've never felt more on edge in my life. I keep staring at her face, reading her emotions, hoping everything I conveyed in that letter was enough to bring her back into my life.

Forcing myself to swallow, I ask, "And...what did you think about it?"

Tears fill her lashes again. "I love you so much it hurts too," she says with a sob. "And I don't want to fly off anymore. Not without you."

Relief floods through me as I gather her up in my arms. Pressing my face to her neck, I breathe her in as her arms go around my neck. Bea hugs my leg as the three of us stand together as one.

When Camille pulls away, her face is wet. Holding me by the cheeks, she stares into my eyes before dragging my mouth toward hers for a kiss. After two months without her lips on mine, this kiss feels like heaven.

I want to rediscover every inch of her like it's the first time.

"Papa, tell her!" Bea says, hopping up and down beside us.

"Tell her what?" I ask.

"That she's not my nanny anymore."

Camille's eyes widen with alarm.

I chuckle as I kiss her again. "Yeah, you're…sort of fired, I guess."

"Fired?"

"So you can sleep in Papa's bed again!"

Camille looks at me again with her brows raised and a hesitant smile.

"I'll explain when we get home. As long as you are coming home."

She nuzzles in closer. "I am coming home."

Beaming, I kiss her again. "Good. Je suis très excité."

Camille lets out a laugh as she covers her mouth.

"What?" I ask with a perplexed expression.

Leaning in, she whispers in my ear, "That means…I am very aroused."

"Oh fuck," I mutter, making my six-year-old giggle and cover her mouth. "I knew that."

"What does it mean?" Bea asks, hopping up and down.

Camille takes her hand as they walk ahead together. "Nothing."

Grinning to myself, I pick up Camille's bag and walk on the other side of her. Sliding a hand around her waist, I lean in until my mouth is next to her ear.

"Well, to be fair," I whisper, "I am a little of that too."

"Me too." She giggles as she looks up at me. "Let's go home."

Rule #46: There's only this moment.

Camille

I'M STANDING BY JACK'S SIDE AS HE RINGS THE DOORBELL. His hand winds around my waist, and I glance up at him with love in my eyes. This is really happening. We're actually doing this.

It's not quite the same as announcing our relationship at a sex club. This is showing his friends and family that we are a real couple, not a nanny or a sub or anything like that. I'm his girlfriend, and we are in love.

This isn't Legacy. This is Julian and Amelia's parents' home for the Christmas Eve party.

The door opens a moment later, and a beautiful blond woman who looks like the spitting image of Amelia opens the door. She has long, platinum hair and stunning blue eyes and doesn't look nearly old enough to have kids Julian and Amelia's age.

"It's Jack!" she calls, rushing toward him and pulling him into a tight hug.

After the hug, he places a comforting hand at the small of my back. "Daisy, this is my girlfriend, Camille."

"Of course!" she calls out excitedly. "I've heard so much about you."

"And what about me?" Bea asks from my side.

"Buzz, buzz, little Bea," Daisy says, kneeling down to tap her on the nose. "How could I forget you? Want to come inside and help me put up the Nativity?"

Bea nods excitedly. Daisy takes her hand, and they scurry off together, leaving Jack and I to walk into the party alone. There is already a crowd of people here, and I know just about everyone.

We're greeted by Phoenix, Amelia, Weston, and even the bartender, Geo, who owns the bar down the street from the club. Matis is standing near the fireplace with another older gentleman, who I assume is Julian and Amelia's much older father, Ronan.

When I hear a shrieking sound, I freeze in place. A moment later, Elizabeth nearly knocks me over as she tackles me with a hug.

Getting an abrasive hug from just anyone would be shocking, but to get one from Elizabeth is even more so.

"Relax, Lizzie," Jack says as he takes my hand.

She grabs my shoulders, and I can tell immediately that she's even tipsier than when we shared a bottle of wine.

"I knew he'd get his shit together," she says before punching her brother in the arm. Then she turns toward me and smiles. "I'm so glad you're here."

"Who let her near the eggnog?" Jack asks with a laugh.

"Don't judge me," she argues, trying to keep up her mean facade and failing. "I'm celebrating."

Phoenix approaches us and gives me a hug. "I'm glad you're here," she says.

"What happened to her?" Jack asks, glancing at his sister.

Phoenix only shrugs. "One thing about Elizabeth is she only lets loose around people she trusts, and I think she's just happy to have everyone together."

"Yeah, it is nice," Jack adds. "Too bad your sister couldn't make it."

"You have a sister?" I ask, glancing at the redhead.

She smirks. "Yeah, a twin sister, not identical."

Jack chuckles. "They couldn't be more different."

"She and her boyfriend, Liam, are backpacking through Europe somewhere. I was hoping they'd make it here by Christmas, but I guess not."

Elizabeth rejoins the conversation, handing me a glass of champagne. Glancing around the room, I realize how lucky these people are to have each other. I had only one person in my family, and when I lost him, I felt so alone in the world. I tried not to let it show, and I did my best to build armor around myself so I never had to feel that loneliness.

But now, they are pulling me in and making me one of them.

"Camille, look!" Bea calls from another room.

I follow the sound of her voice into a large formal living room where she and Daisy are setting up a small terra-cotta Nativity scene. My father and I had a similar one in our home.

"It's beautiful," I say.

Daisy strokes Bea's hair before kissing her on the cheek, and it warms my heart to see her so loved by so many.

"My kids haven't given me grandbabies yet," Daisy says. "So I'm very glad we have this little Bumblebee."

Bea giggles as Daisy pulls her into her lap and tickles her. I don't know much about Amelia yet since I haven't had the chance to get to know her, but I find it very unlikely that Daisy's son, Julian, will give her grandkids anytime soon.

Speak of the devil, he walks into the room and watches us with his arms crossed over his chest. "I've been sent in to let you both know that dinner is ready."

"Oh, perfect," Daisy says as she climbs off the floor. I watch as she wraps her arms around her son's shoulders and plants a kiss on his cheek. Biting back my smile, I can spot the moment his harsh demeanor fades and a hint of softness shines through.

The cruel prince isn't so cruel after all.

When Daisy leaves the room, I glance up at where Julian is still hovering nearby. He's scowling again. There are a lot of things I'd like to say to him about how he treated me before, but I don't want to start it now. I have a feeling with Julian, it wouldn't be a simple conversation.

Then, to my surprise, he quietly murmurs, "I'm sorry for sticking my nose where it didn't belong."

My head twists up toward him.

"I have a very bad habit of just being too..." When his words fade without finishing his sentence, I do it for him.

"Too much?"

His brows lift, the scowl disappearing. "Yeah."

A small huff escapes my lips as I reply, "Me too. It's okay. I forgive you."

His sigh is audible as his tension melts away. The scent of pine and spice fills the room, music playing in the distance as he relaxes.

"Look, Julian. I made the Nativity," Bea says.

With a smile, he leans down and ruffles her hair. "You did a great job, Bumblebee. Now, come eat. Both of you."

Then he disappears from the room. He'll probably never bring this up again, and that's fine. I have a feeling the rivalry between him and Jack isn't as fierce as it once was or as much as he'd like everyone to believe it is.

I see a warm side of him that he so desperately wants to hide.

Bea and I join the rest of the family in the enormous dining room. As Jack pulls out a seat for me, I sit down, and he takes the one by my side.

For the first time in my life, I am a part of something bigger than me: a bright future and a loving family.

Bea is cuddled between us in red satin pajamas. She's snoring quietly as Jack reads *The Night Before Christmas*. In the living room, there's a small plate of cookies next to a glass of milk. The Yule log burns in the fireplace, and three stockings hang from the mantel.

Noticing that his daughter is asleep, Jack sets the book down and glances up at me. We've hardly had a moment alone since the train station this morning. I'm eager to have him to myself.

After we both ease out from Bea's bed without waking her, we meet in the hallway. He quietly pulls her door closed before turning toward me.

Finally alone, his eyes find mine, and I know he's feeling the same thing I am.

Reaching for me, he takes my hand and pulls me toward him for a kiss. His arms wind around my waist, hoisting me off the floor.

Getting lost in the kiss, he murmurs against my lips, "I want you upstairs in the room waiting for me."

I pull away and stare up at him as I'm assaulted by a heated arousal low in my belly.

Holding my waist, he tugs me against him as he adds, "Naked."

"Yes, my love," I reply softly.

Pulling away from his arms, I walk up the stairs. There's a buzz of anticipation under my skin. It feels like ages since I've been bound up by him. I miss the calm connection between us. I miss feeling his fingers work and the control of his movements.

When I reach the room, I get to work removing my clothes and tossing them in a basket in the corner. Once I am completely naked, I kneel in the middle of the room and wait for him.

His footsteps on the stairs make me moist with excitement. My heart hammers faster in my chest, and it reminds me of the first night I met him up here. The way it felt to know we were crossing a line and indulging in things we shouldn't.

Now I'm free to have him as much as I want forever. It feels like a dream.

When the door opens, I turn my gaze down to the floor and

wait. He walks into the room steadily and stops behind me. As he braids my hair, I get lost in the movement.

Once he's done, he tugs on my braid, forcing my face up toward him. He smiles down at me, and I smile back.

It's just us.

"A simple bind tonight," he says as he strokes my head. "I just need to be inside you."

"I'm yours," I whisper in return.

I am his, and he is mine. This is our promise to each other.

It means that no matter what life throws at us or what we face, we will always have a safe space to return to. I will be his comfort and his home.

And he will be my family.

Jack slowly unbuttons his shirt and pulls it from his shoulders. He's building the suspense, making me wait, just like how our relationship started. The agony of wanting and waiting makes the payoff that much better.

I watch as he opens the door of the wardrobe and pulls out the rope. Kneeling in front of me, he binds my hands. Just feeling his deft movements as he loops, knots, and ties my wrists together feels like home. It's a loose bind around my wrists, like wearing a pair of handcuffs.

"Kiss me, please," I beg when he's done. One tug on my bound hands, and I'm jerked toward him. My lips land against his, and he kisses me with passion and desire.

"Take out my cock," he mutters against my mouth.

Reaching down, I work open the button of his pants. It's awkward with the ropes around my wrists, but I manage to get his trousers open enough to reach in and wrap my fingers around his stiff length.

He lets out a growl and kisses me harder.

"I can't wait any longer," he says, removing his pants in a rush. Then he moves to his back and pulls me on top of him. My legs straddle his hips as he aims his cock for my core. It's times like these, when Jack's passion takes over, that I realize how perfect we are for each other. He can be as impulsive and excitable as I am. At times, he can be *too much* too.

Staring into his eyes, I lower my hips a little slowly, swallowing his cock as I go. The pressure of his length filling me up is exquisite. Small moans and gasps escape my lips as my body is reacquainted with his. Once I'm seated on top of him, we stare into each other's eyes with love.

"I'm yours," he whispers.

We stay like this for a while. There are no words left to say. No wounds to mend or apologies to accept. I know where he stands, and he knows where I stand.

After a moment, I start to grind my hips, finding so much pleasure in the sensation. His hands rest softly on my thighs as I move, setting the pace and intensity. He looks like he's in heaven, watching me find my own climax with his body.

Moving my hands to my clit, I rub it fiercely as I chase my pleasure. Watching him lie on the floor of the room where we first fell in love feels like a full-circle moment.

He's mine. The man in the photo is forever mine.

I was never supposed to be here, and somehow, I've made it my home.

Hypnotized by the sensation and rapid movement of my hips, I nearly lose track of time and space. When my moans grow too loud, he clamps a hand over my mouth and stares up at me with fire in his eyes.

But I don't stop moving or rubbing at my clit. His other hand reaches up and squeezes the mound of my breast, pinching the nipple and making my body tight with arousal.

"That's my good girl," he praises quietly when he sees I'm about to come. "Let me feel it. Come on my cock, baby."

I'm so close. I can feel it. It's just on the horizon.

Then he utters those words that send me over the edge. "Good girl, little bird," he says. "Good fucking girl."

And just like that, my body detonates with his praise. My legs are shaking and seizing with pleasure. Light explodes behind my eyelids, and everything in me melts with the heat of this fire.

As I collapse against him, his cock twitches and shudders inside me.

His hands are tight around me as he fills me up.

Suddenly, I remember the first time he uttered those words and how it made me feel. And I realize that maybe that was the start of it all. Turning a cold, heartless man into one who could make me feel so warm and treasured was really where I began to fall in love.

Once we're both spent, I rise up and smile at him. He kisses me softly on the lips as he takes my wrists and loops them over his head, pulling me closer to him. My hands are resting at the back of his neck, so we are one. Bound to each other for now. Forever.

"My good girl," he mumbles against my mouth.

"My sir," I reply.

Even as he whispers those words again, giving me the security and comfort I need, I know that nothing will ever top the effect they have on me. He is mine, and I am his. It doesn't matter what came before or what comes after. All that matters is the moment we're in right now, and as long as we're in it together, I know everything will be okay.

Or rather, better than okay—it will be perfect.

Epilogue

Jack
Two years later

"I'M SO EXCITED," BEA SAYS, BOUNCING IN THE SEAT NEXT TO ME.

A smile stretches on my face as I reach across the back seat and take her hand in mine. She's beaming as she wiggles in her seat.

I still can't believe this is happening. Again.

I don't know what I did to deserve a life like this. I didn't know if I would ever find happiness like this again. I was consumed by grief for so long it felt like I was frozen in a block of ice for years. Camille came into my life and brought the warmth that thawed me.

When the car comes to a stop, Bea practically bursts out the door while it's still moving.

"Slow down, Bea," I say as I climb out after her. Chasing her up to the front door, I grab her hand and force her to walk slowly by my side.

"How do I look?" she asks with a giggle. She's in a crushed red velvet dress with a white collar and a black beret. She's been obsessing over today's outfit for months.

"He won't care how you look," I reply. "But for the record, you look beautiful."

"First impressions are important," she says, and it makes me laugh.

As we make our way down the long hall, my own heart picks up speed. After so long, this is finally happening. The moment we've been anticipating for nearly a year.

When we reach room number 17, I press the door open slowly to ensure Camille is ready. I notice my sister first with bloodshot eyes as if she's been crying. Then I nod at my dad, leaning against the wall, with my mother on one side and my youngest sister, Scarlett, on his other.

Then I find Camille. She and I make eye contact, and to my surprise, she looks nervous. My heart nearly explodes with love. To me, she's never looked more beautiful.

"We're ready," she says before biting her lip.

In the chair by the window, my mom is sitting with her phone aimed at the door, ready to catch Bea's reaction.

I push it open the rest of the way, and my daughter enters the room, cautiously looking around.

Then she spots the baby lying in his mother's arms, bundled in a soft white baby blanket and knit yellow hat on his head.

Bea presses her hands to her face as she approaches him.

"Ready to meet your little brother?" Camille asks with tears in her eyes.

Bea nods.

My wife scoots over to make room, and I lift Bea onto the mattress beside her. Everyone snaps pictures as Camille sets the newborn in his sister's arms. Bea smiles down at him like she's never been happier in her life.

Again, my eyes find Camille's. It's like looking into the sun. She is so stunning in this moment, I can hardly take it. My wife. The mother of my son. The stepmother of my daughter. The glue that holds this family together.

There are times when the fear that I'll lose her like I lost Em comes creeping back in. Thoughts that threaten to tear me away from this life, but I've grown stronger. I can handle whatever is thrown our way. I've crawled out of the darkness once. I can do it again.

But today is not that day. Today, there is nothing but light and love. My family is all in one room. My children are surrounded by love. What could be better than this?

Camille wraps an arm around Bea and snuggles her close to her side. Then she kisses the side of her head as Bea strokes her baby brother's cheek.

"He's so cute," she says. "Tristan Laurent St. Claire."

She's been practicing his full name for weeks.

Laurent, of course, after Camille's father.

"We're going to be best friends, Tristan," Bea whispers, making Camille blink tears down her cheeks.

When I hear a sniffle, I turn to find my own sister dabbing at her cheeks. "Don't get too sentimental on me," I say, but she simply rolls her eyes.

"Whatever. I am not," she replies with a tsk.

"What's wrong, Lizzie?" our dad asks. "You don't want kids someday?"

"God no," she replies before glancing back at Bea and the baby. "No offense."

"None taken," Bea replies, making everyone laugh.

Everyone snaps pictures and makes small talk for a while until Tristan starts to fuss. I take him from Bea's arms, and she pouts when she realizes she can't hold him anymore.

"We should get going," my mother says as she places a hand on my shoulder. "You four need some family time together." As she looks down at my son, she gently touches his brows with adoration in her eyes. "I remember the day you were born," she whispers. "It was just you and me in a hospital room like this one. I was scared out of my mind, but you turned out all right." With a smile, she ruffles my hair like I'm still a kid. Then she kisses my cheek. "Enjoy this moment because it goes by in a flash."

"I love you, Mom," I say.

"I love you too," she replies.

After saying goodbye, Scarlett, Elizabeth, and my parents leave the four of us alone. As soon as the door shuts, I glance over at the girls on the bed. They're cuddling and smiling at me.

"Scoot over," I say. They quickly make room as I take a seat next to them with Tristan in my arms. When he cries some more, I hand him to Camille so she can nurse him.

Bea nuzzles herself under my arm, and I kiss the top of her head. It feels like the entire world exists in this bed. Everything that matters in the world is right here.

To think none of this would have happened if Camille had never opened that book.

Keep reading for an excerpt
of *Keep Me*, the first book
Sara Cate's Sinful Manor series.

Killian Barclay is a grumpy Scottish billionaire
who hates me...and now I'm his wife.

Keep Me

SINFUL MANOR

USA TODAY BESTSELLING AUTHOR
SARA CATE

Chapter One

"You've arrived at your destination," the GPS announces.

"That's the one, on the left," Aaron says, looking up from the map on his phone to the large brick mansion on the hill.

"That?" I reply in shock.

"Barclay Manor. That's it," he says, staring out the window. Rain pelts against the windows of the car.

"Aaron, you said your family had a *house* in Scotland. *That* is a castle."

"Technically, it's a manor."

"Semantics," I reply, gaping through the windshield at the massive gray stone building. It looms over us like a bad omen. Aaron pulls off on the side of the road, and I turn toward him in confusion. "What are you doing? Drive up there."

"I can't," he argues. "That sign says *Private Property.*"

My jaw drops. "So what? It's not like people *actually* live here."

"That's exactly what *private residence* means, Sylvie."

"We came all this way."

"So? What would I tell them? They're not going to let me in just because my great-great-grandfather once visited here in the summer and wrote his book on the typewriter."

"That is *exactly* what you tell them. Based on these photos, we have proof that the typewriter is in there. We came all the way to fucking Scotland to see it. Now you're telling me you're going to just drive away because of a tiny little sign?"

He turns toward me and gives me a condescending glare. "Don't talk to me like that, Sylvie. I'm not afraid."

I roll my eyes. "So at least drive up there."

He lets out a huff. "Fine. You want to go to jail in a foreign country, let's drive up there."

He's so dramatic. I don't say a word as he pulls the car up the long gravel drive, through an open gate framed by two tall brick structures on either side. The one on the right displays the words Barclay Manor 1837, and the one on the left has the Private Property sign.

The driveway is long but secluded. There are dense trees on either side, and judging by the map on Aaron's phone, there's a body of water not far on the other side of the manor. As we travel up the hill toward the manor, the rain continues to pour. It's rained every damn day since we got here last week. New York isn't sunny, but at least it's better than this.

"See, there is no one up here," I say when we get closer to the house. Aaron slows the car, clearly nervous. "Go around back."

His head snaps in my direction. "What? Why?"

"Because it's probably easier to get in back there."

"Get in? No, no, no," he barks, quickly turning the car around like he's about to flip a bitch on this narrow drive.

"Aaron, will you just relax? No one lives here. There's not a car in sight. My friends and I used to sneak into our school all the time as kids, and that had much better security than this place has."

"You're going to just walk into this nearly two-hundred-year-old manor like you own the place? Are you out of your fucking mind, Sylvie?"

"If someone sees us, we pretend we don't speak English and act like tourists."

When it's clear he can't turn his car around on this road, he pulls up farther to where the road winds around the building. He goes to the back first, his knuckles white around the steering wheel.

"Look!" I say, pointing from the passenger side. "There's a door on the side."

"Yeah, and it's probably locked," he replies, coasting the car to a stop.

Just then, the door pops open. Aaron and I both gasp and duck at the same time as we watch a woman emerge. She's wearing a black miniskirt and a white shimmery blouse missing a few buttons in the front.

One step out the door, she suddenly realizes it's raining. Instead of pulling an umbrella out, she covers her head with a black jacket and gazes around the yard as if looking for something.

Then, she's jogging in the mud and rain with her shoes hanging from her fingers instead of on her feet. And she's running straight toward *us*.

"What the...?" Aaron murmurs.

She stops by his driver's window and waits as he slowly rolls it down a few inches.

"Are you my lift?" she asks with her thick Scottish accent. There is black makeup streaking down her face and her lipstick is smeared around her mouth.

If I didn't know any better, I'd assume this woman is doing the quote-unquote *walk of shame*.

"Uh...no," Aaron stammers.

Her head pops up as she stares down the drive we just came from. "Och!" she chirps, then takes off in a jog through the mud toward another car slowly crawling up toward the house.

Aaron rolls the window back up and turns toward me in astonishment.

"Can we get out of here now?"

"What?" I reply. "No. The door is totally unlocked!"

His eyes widen further. "It's someone's house, Sylvie! Did you not just see the woman walk out of there?"

"Even better," I reply as I unclip my seat belt. "I can claim I'm her friend if someone sees me. I came all this way, Aaron. I'm getting in that fucking house."

"You're unhinged," he mutters as he faces forward and stares in shock. "People tried to warn me that you're a loose cannon, but I figured that would mean you're fun and unpredictable. I didn't think they meant it in a criminal way."

"Wait, who said I was a loose cannon? Never mind. It doesn't matter."

It really doesn't matter. I can think of a handful of people off the bat who I know would say that to my boyfriend. People in our social circle define *fun and entertainment* as tearing down other people and talking shit as if they're so much better than anyone.

The only way I've figured out how to avoid that is to beat them at their own game.

They want to call me irrational, then I'll show them irrational.

With that, I smile at Aaron and snatch my phone off the center console, shoving it into my pocket before throwing the hood of my rain jacket over my head.

"Be right back," I say as I open the car door and jump into the downpour.

"Sylvie!" Aaron calls from the car, but I cut him off by slamming the door shut and sprinting toward the place we just watched the girl emerge from.

There's a moment somewhere between the car and the door when I realize that this is, in fact, a bad idea. I'm walking into someone else's home uninvited. I could just knock and ask nicely to see the library, but where's the fun in that?

This is the moment when the adrenaline kicks in. It's invigorating. Fear, anticipation, and excitement all blend into one as I reach for the door handle without a clue as to what's on the other side.

It's an antique brass doorknob on an old wooden door. The

forest-green paint is chipping away at the edges, and the knob squeaks as I turn it. As expected, it opens without an issue.

Once inside, I pull the door to just an inch from latching closed. It's my idea of a quick escape plan just in case these particular Scottish homeowners are the kind that like to pull an axe on their intruders or have large wolfhounds to protect the residence.

Shit, dogs. I didn't think about that.

The house is seemingly quiet from here. I'm standing in a large entryway, although, to be technical, this is the back of the house. So maybe it's called an exit way?

The floor is all hardwood, and the walls are painted. It looks as if it was recently renovated instead of featuring the stale, dated decor I was expecting. It smells nice, as if there's incense burning somewhere or men's cologne sprayed nearby.

In front of me is a long hallway, and I take each step slowly, listening for people or voices in the house. I pull my phone out of my back pocket and pull up the camera app to have it ready. When I get a picture of that typewriter, Aaron is going to eat his words. This will be nothing more than a funny story someday.

There are closed doors on either side of the long hallway, but none of them look like the kinds of doors that would lead to a large library like the one we saw in that photo of the typewriter. So, I keep walking slowly while listening.

At the end of the hall, I step into a giant entranceway with a grand staircase that leads to the second and third floors. The height of the ceiling in this part is massive, and I'm struck silent as I stare upward at it. This place is like nothing I've ever seen.

And if it wasn't for the warm smell of spice and musk, I wouldn't believe this is a residence.

My phone buzzes in my hand, drawing my attention from the ceiling and grand staircase.

I glance down to see a text from Aaron.

Get the fuck out of there. Now, Sylvie.

I roll my eyes and swipe the message closed. He's always so paranoid. Such a rule follower. He used to be fun, but the last year with him has been painfully boring. Every day is so predictable it makes me sick. I'm going to prove to him right now how fun and spontaneous I can be. I'll snap a picture of that old typewriter that his great-great-whatever wrote some dumb old classic novel on, and that'll show him.

When I glance up again, I spot an open door on the second floor. In the room, I spot a shelf of old books. *A library.*

Pocketing my phone, I carefully tiptoe up the stairs. I don't hear a single sound in the rest of the house. If anyone is here, they're probably sleeping or in the shower or something. They'll never know I was even here.

There is a single stair that creaks as I settle my weight on it. With a wince, I freeze and wait for the sound of footsteps, but there's nothing. Quickly, I finish my climb, reaching the top and slowly creeping into the large room. The ceilings in this room are far taller than I expected. Each wall has a tall ladder attached to a slider. For a moment, I can do nothing but stare at the massive space.

As my gaze casts downward, it catches on something on the other side of the room. Resting on a large ornate wooden table is a huge vase full of flowers next to a dusty old typewriter.

"Gotcha," I whisper as I quickly tiptoe through the room. The floor in here has a thick rug that muffles my footsteps.

I slip my phone from my back pocket and open the camera app. Aiming at the typewriter, I take a multitude of shots from various angles.

"Eat your words, Aaron," I whisper.

Then, while I'm at it, I take a few shots of the library too. It's so old-fashioned looking, like something out of a fairy tale. I don't know anyone who owns this many books, and if I did, they wouldn't store them in a room like this.

There's a creak in the house, and I quickly spin around, watching the door.

Fuck.

Time to go.

With my phone clutched in my hand, I make my way toward the door I came in through. There's no sign of anyone on the second floor, so I book it for the stairs. My heart is pounding, and adrenaline is coursing through my veins. The long hallway ahead leads to the exit. Just a few more feet and I'll be outside, sprinting toward Aaron's car in the rain, laughing about how wild this was.

Reaching the bottom step, I leap to the right.

An enormous hand wraps around my arm, hauling me to a stop before I can make my escape. I let out a scream, turning around to gape at the impossibly large man scowling down at me with my arm still gripped in his fist.

"Who the fuck are you?" the man bellows in a deep Scottish brogue.

I open my mouth to respond, but nothing comes out.

"What are you doing in my house?" he continues.

"I—I" I stammer.

Get it together, Sylvie. This was your idea. Don't let this giant oaf intimidate you.

Acknowledgments

Damn, it feels good to be home. Even when home is like a kinky Parisian sleepaway camp. It may not be the brick-and-mortar Salacious Players' Club, but it feels just as good.

I have to thank my incredible agent, Savannah Greenwell, for always having my back and working with me to make my career the best it can be.

Rachel Gilmer, my editor, and everyone else at Sourcebooks Casablanca for letting me just write and write and write.

My incredible beta and sensitivity readers—Jill, Becca, Claudia, and Amelie for toughing out some wild edits and big changes. And you know, helping with the French and rope bondage...I won't specify who did what. My dev editor, Becky, for helping to turn a pile of fancy French rubbish into something resembling a pretty decent book.

My cover artist, Cat with TRC Designs, for like all the random messages.

The goodest girls of all—my incredible team, Misty, Jill, Lori, and Nasha. You babes could rule the world; I'm convinced.

To my readers, whether you found me in the club, in the

church, or on the island, I'm so grateful that you keep encouraging this wild behavior. I appreciate every single one of you.

And last to my friends and family who deal with me in all my messy phases of book writing from the time I cried in a water park to the time I hopped on a flight and went to Paris for "research." It's still so absolutely bananas to me that my job is to write down the kinky stories in my head and you all just go along with it, supporting me in every endeavor. It's the world's biggest blessing to have you in my corner.

Pack your bags, Alley. Trip Daddy has five more books to write.

About the Author

Sara Cate is a *USA Today* bestselling romance author who weaves complex characters, heart-wrenching stories, and forbidden romance into every page of her spicy novels. Sara's writing is as hot as a desert summer, with twists and turns that will leave you breathless. Best known for the Salacious Players' Club series, Sara strives to take risks and provide her readers with an experience that is as arousing as it is empowering. When she's not penning steamy tales, she can be found soaking up the Arizona sun, jamming to Taylor Swift, and watching Marvel movies with her family.

Website: saracatebooks.com
Facebook: SaraCateBooks
Instagram: @saracatebooks
TikTok: @SaraCatebooks